LORD OF A SHATTERED LAND

The Chronicles of Hanuvar

BAEN BOOKS
by HOWARD ANDREW JONES

THE CHRONICLES OF HANUVAR
Lord of a Shattered Land
The City of Marble and Blood
Shadow of the Smoking Mountain (forthcoming)

LORD OF A SHATTERED LAND

The Chronicles of Hanuvar

Howard Andrew Jones

Copyright © 2023 by Howard Andrew Jones

Earlier versions of some portions of this book have appeared previously in the following:

"The Way of Serpents," was first published in the *Goodman Games Gen Con 2016 Program Guide* and reprinted in Issue 0 of *Tales From the Magician's Skull, 2018.*

"Crypt of Stars," *Tales From the Magician's Skull*, Issue 1, 2018.

"The Second Death of Hanuvar," in *Tales From the Magician's Skull*, Issue 3, 2019.

"Course of Blood," in the Zombies Need Brains anthology *Galactic Stew*.

"Shroud of Feathers," in issue 6 of *Tales From the Magician's Skull.*

"The Warrior's Way," in *Weird Tales* #366.

A Baen Books Original

Baen Publishing Enterprises
P.O. Box 1403
Riverdale, NY 10471
www.baen.com

ISBN: 978-1-9821-9347-8

Cover art by Dave Seeley
Map by Darian Jones

First printing, August 2023
First trade paperback printing, June 2024

Distributed by Simon & Schuster
1230 Avenue of the Americas
New York, NY 10020

Library of Congress Control Number: 2023011867

Printed in the United States of America

10 9 8 7 6 5 4 3 2 1

Dedication
For Harold Lamb,
who introduced me to both skilled serial storytelling
and to that greatest of generals, Hannibal.
His work continues to inspire me.

Contents

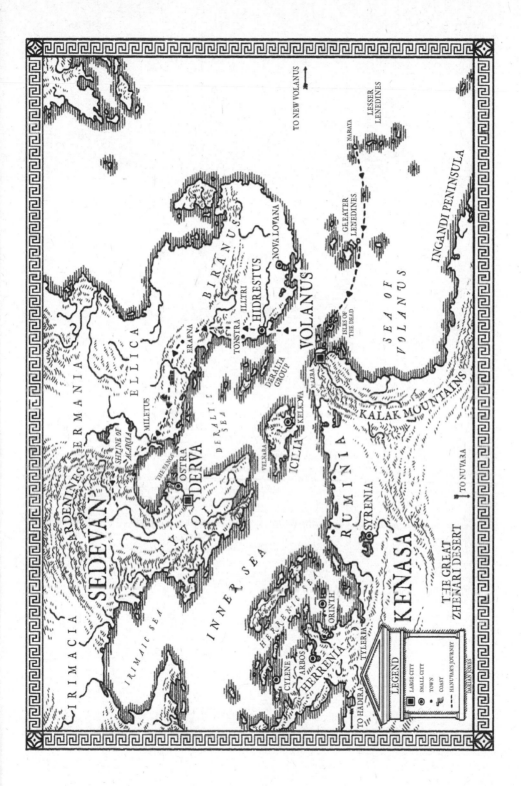

Book 1

Freely Adapted from
The Hanuvid of Antires Sosilos (the Elder),
with the commentary of Silenus

ANDRONIKOS SOSILOS (THE YOUNGER)

Preamble

When he was young, the Dervans say, Hanuvar swore an oath before his father and the gods. With one hand on an altar red with blood, he pledged to give no rest to Dervans, and to seek their end so long as he drew breath.

Hanuvar's enemies spread this fable to explain his matchless drive and, with the hubris of their kind, assumed themselves the center of his universe. Even those who know a greater measure of the truth repeat the lies so Hanuvar emerges as a figure ominous as a thunderhead.

Any who knew him tell a different tale, though few of them are left, and none who knew him half so well as I. While many have praised his guile and his skill, another gift too often goes unsung: He set fires in the hearts of those he met. If you marched with him for even a little while you came to share his dream, and would hazard blood and soul to see it through.

You ask what truly drove him on? The answer is a simple one: Love. He loved his daughter. He loved his people. He loved his city.

The silver towers of sea-girt Volanus perished with its walls, as did the shining winged serpents who had called the city home since its founding. The Dervan legions wrought this end. They threw down the city's idols and they melted down her altars and they carted off her treasures. They sowed her fields with salt. His daughter and his people, they led away in chains.

The Dervans dared this only after they had seen Hanuvar plummet to the cobalt waves. They jeered the name they once spoke with dread. Some few feared his death was false, that he had worked some strange new scheme, they were mocked. Once, he had brought the Dervan Empire to its knees. Now its legions had struck back and they proudly boasted they had slain him with his city.

3

You who read this know that they were wrong, but cannot guess the fuller tale, for I have never set it down. Long years have passed, and I pray I've time to tell it all and skill at last to render it in a way that might have pleased him.

And so, I sing of a man in the shadow of war. He crawled from the wine-dark sea onto an island at the world's edge. Only foes stepped forth to greet him. For any other that would have been the end. For Hanuvar, it was only a beginning.

—Antires Sosilos, *The Hanuvid*, Book One

Chapter 1:
The Way of Serpents

I

He had lived in darkness, among the unseen things that chittered in the walls. Now a shirtless, barefoot slave preceded him, the orange glare of his lantern dangling from an outthrust hand. Grim guards marched behind, identical in turquoise kilts. The tramp of their feet had such clockwork precision, Hanuvar left off numbering his own paces and counted theirs.

The procession wound past the cell doors standing silent and gray like so many tombstones and into a hall stacked with wooden barrels and chests. Beyond lay the stairs, which led to blessed sunlight and an unpleasant end. Twelve paces stretched between him and that firstmost step, then ten—and then the slave veered away, leading him under a stone archway to the right. Hanuvar counted these paces too. He would know the way even without a lantern.

A turn under an ancient archway brought them to a hall awash with such brilliance Hanuvar narrowed his eyes. Three days within the cell had left him challenged by the wall's torches.

The corridor held a mystery greater than the flood of illumination. Three men knelt beside a pile of stone bricks and a bucket of mortar. They shaped a low wall across the bottom of an open doorway. On the other side of the growing barrier, a shelf of jeweled goblets twinkled brilliantly, next to a small basket of pearls. Did the islanders mean to wall him in with the treasures? That made

5

no sense. The ruler would earn a kingly fee for turning him over to the Dervan Empire. Hanuvar had known his fate the moment they'd found him half drowned on their beach.

The slave set his lantern on the floor and genuflected at the stout man in ochre silks who stepped out over the growing wall.

"On your knees." One of the guards prodded Hanuvar with the butt of his staff.

Hanuvar knelt. The stone was cold against his legs.

"I do not like your look." So saying, Narata's king stepped in front of him. Hanuvar had not only an excellent vantage point from which to observe the ruler's sandals, speckled with polished jade and onyx, but to obtain his hostage. They'd obligingly granted him a tarnished spoon, the handle of which he'd sharpened into a point and tucked into his belt.

Yet he did not act. This meeting felt less like a prelude to Dervan arrest and more like an interview. He would bide his time.

"You may rise," the king said, as though permitting a grand luxury.

"Slow," one of the guards cautioned. Hanuvar obeyed, his eyes fixed upon the king's.

Like Hanuvar himself, the king neared his fiftieth year, but aside from their dark, olive-toned skin, Hanuvar found nothing similar in their appearance. The king's balding head was crowned with a diamond-studded headband, and his clean-shaven chin and cheeks were padded with fat. Hanuvar stood a full head taller, his shoulders broad, his scarred arms and legs corded with muscle. His dark hair, peppered with gray, was thick and full. He wore a dirty white knee-length tunic, belted at the waist. His gray and dark brown beard was more than a week overdue for trimming.

"I have treated you well, General," the king said. "I hope you will remember that."

Hanuvar remembered the dark cell with the meager food, the pillowless stone shelf, and the doom he knew they'd summoned. He kept his expression bland. "I will remember all you've done for me."

Like many tyrants, the king seemed to lack the capacity to perceive irony, although it might have been that he heard it too rarely for apperception. He nodded once, as though he'd received the praise he was due, then continued: "Circumstances being what they are, I'm willing to offer you an alternative to imprisonment and death at the hands of the empire."

Hanuvar said nothing.

"Are you not curious?"

He awaited details. "Speak on, O king."

"They say you know the ways of the great serpents."

Whatever the king meant by that, he clearly hoped for an answer in the affirmative, so Hanuvar gave him one. "I do."

The king motioned Hanuvar's guards back. Only a few moments ago Hanuvar would have sprung forward to press his sharpened handle to the king's throat. Now he grasped another option. It would be far better to walk free after striking a bargain than to flee with a hostage.

The king explained. "This morning, a kekainen bird brought a message from the outer isles. The southerners have swept forth in a great raid. Their ships fill the ocean. They have burned and looted throughout the Lenidines, and they are on their way toward Narata."

That explained only a little. Did the king truly hope to hide his wealth from the merciless southerners behind a false dungeon wall?

"Have you nothing to say?" the king snapped.

"Do you have a question?"

The king scowled. "Can you or can you not summon serpents?"

No man alive knew how to call the great winged asalda. Those who'd never worked with them misunderstood the nature of their relationships with humans. "I know their ways," Hanuvar said.

"And can you master them?"

Now he lied outright. "Yes."

The king nodded. "In the center of my island lives a great winged serpent. My grandfather's father made a pact with the creature, so it would protect our island if we kept her from harm. I'm sending a priestess to remind the beast of her duty. And I am sending you to command her should she break her oath."

"And I'm to go free afterward?"

"Of course."

A lie, clearly, but Hanuvar bowed his head as though he believed. "I'll require the flask I carried."

"My wizard tells me it's full only of ashes. Is it some magic unknown to him?"

"How do you think I control the serpents?"

"Ah. I see."

"I'll want a sword," Hanuvar continued.

"When your task is through."

"And a ship." The king would never grant him that, but it was crucial the monarch think Hanuvar believed him.

"Certainly," the king pledged breezily. "Now you must hurry. The messenger bird arrived hours ago. My priestess tells me that means the southerners will arrive near dawn. These two will lead you where you need to go."

"I need food." The lunch hour had come and gone without a meal. "And a bath and shave."

"Fine. Eat quickly."

The king half turned, waving a hand, then halted in midmotion. "Hold." He considered Hanuvar once more. "You know siege craft, don't you?"

"Somewhat."

The irony of asking this of the general who'd brought the Dervan Empire to its knees escaped the king. "This stone work—will it hold? Given time to dry?"

"Yes. But if you want to fool the southerners, you have to do a better job disguising your entryway."

The king's jowls trembled in agitation. "What do you mean?"

Hanuvar advanced to the doorway, seeing a couch, wine jars, and a food-laden table set before gold statues and a basket of sapphires and rubies. "The southerners are old hands at sniffing out treasure. They'll see the outline of where a doorway used to be. If you want to conceal yourself, you need to rip out the doorway's frame to blend the stone with the existing wall."

The king blinked at him and turned his head to consider the masonry. Two of the workmen looked up while the other troweled mortar. "Idiots," the king said finally, "why didn't YOU point that out? Rip this down and start over! Immediately!"

They blinked in surprise, then hurriedly began to remove the stones they'd just laid. Hanuvar expected they'd be killed the moment they finished their work so none could reveal the king's hiding place. He couldn't help wondering what measures the king had taken to ensure a way out should his loyal retainers be slain—or neglect to open the vault for a few weeks.

But that was the king's concern.

II

The cliff's edge loomed just past his outstretched fingers. Hanuvar shifted his left foot, then froze as a trail of dirt crumbled beneath his sandal. It spilled onto the upturned face of one of the twin guards—Meshtar, he thought—then rattled down the rock face to the distant jungle.

Meshtar shook his head like an angry dog. Hanuvar secured his footing, and with a little more leverage, gripped the edge of a sturdy rock and hauled himself up, dislodging an even larger stream of dirt onto the twin. In another moment he had gained the plateau. Bright blue flowers blossomed on green stalks, waving in the warm air.

Hanuvar lay on his stomach in the tough grasses and offered his hands to Meshtar. The guard grunted his thanks as he reached the top, then flopped down beside him to assist the others. Hanuvar climbed to his feet, wiping sweat from his newly shorn cheeks, and watched.

Next up was dark-haired Rudra, General of Narata, though general was a grand term for the commander of an island force numbering less than a hundred warriors. Rudra styled his hair elaborately, so it rose in a black wave. Hanging from his belt, opposite the garish sword sheath, was Hanuvar's flask, the size of a small water jug. The general had insisted on carrying it himself until they reached the serpent, saying he didn't trust Hanuvar not to work sorceries against them.

Following him was the young sea priestess, Lalaca. The azure pendant of her office hung to her azure bodice. Her matching flowered skirt swirled about her calves as they raised her. She stepped away to brush dirt from her hands.

Finally came Meshtar's brother, Beshkar, his small eyes set and determined. Hanuvar had already decided the general was a soldier only in title. Strong, able, silent, these two were the real threat.

Hanuvar unstopped his wineskin and drank.

They had advanced past huddled refugees into the jungle's depths hours before. The island's only large settlement was a two-hour hike behind them, lost beyond the waving greenery.

"How much farther?" Rudra asked.

Lalasa answered, her voice high and clear. "We look for a bridge now, to Mount Danar." The sea priestess shook out her hair, gathered it together and tied it more tightly behind her head. She ignored the frank appraisal from the twins. That a woman in her middle twenties was the lead priestess in the island nation had surprised Hanuvar, but he had not yet asked for an explanation, and no one had offered one.

"Let's keep moving," Rudra ordered.

Lalasa pointed left. This time Rudra led.

There were no man-made trails, but they came to an animal track, and walked it, veering left. Hanuvar pushed past a brown vine big as his arm and stepped over a fallen tree bole thick with yellow ants. A rich, floral scent perfumed the air.

They reached a clearing. A single goat cropped at the thick green grass that lay between the jungle and the cliff edge thirty paces on. A dilapidated wooden suspension bridge stretched from it to another cliffside.

Rudra stepped into the clearing without hesitation.

Something crashed violently through the bushes on their right, alarming the goat, which fled into the brush. A leathery, skeletal thing erupted from the jungle, leapt in front of the bridge, and opened its beak with a hiss.

Rudra froze, but the twins drew steel. Lalasa touched her pendant.

The creature was half again the height of a man. Leathery skin flaps stretched between its long bony arms and its waist. It shook its blue-feathered head and clacked its beak. "If you would pass, you would pay!" it rasped.

"What would you have us pay?" Hanuvar asked.

It tilted its head and stabbed the sea priestess with sharp eyes. "Give me the soft one!"

"We have fine wine with us," Lalasa countered.

The thing cocked its head, swift and birdlike.

"Yes," she said. "Fine and sweet."

"Give me the drink!"

Lalasa looked to Rudra, who stared back blankly until she pointed at his wineskin and motioned toward the monster.

Rudra fumbled to untie the skin from his belt. He threw it at the creature's clawed feet.

It bent, snatched up the skin, and fumbled with the stopper before losing patience and biting it off. It upended the container into its beak and guzzled greedily. Dark red wine trickled down either side of its face.

Meshtar swore in disgust.

"More!" The thing shook the empty skin at them.

"We will give you more after we pass," Hanuvar said.

The bird-thing's gaze shifted between them. "You will each give me the sweet."

"We'll give you one more," the sea priestess promised. "We'll leave it for you on the bridge's far side."

"All!" It flapped its wings rapidly.

"One," the priestess said. "Or we will go back into the jungle."

The bird-thing hopped once, then scurried to one side. "I will watch. If you trick me, I eat you."

"Try and we'll kill you," Rudra growled.

Hanuvar led the way onto the bridge.

The bird thing obviously hadn't spent its spare time in maintenance of its ambush point. Some of the ancient planks pointed skyward, as though heavy weights had been dropped on their far ends. Hanuvar and the others stepped carefully over the gaps, through which they glimpsed a gurgling jungle stream a hundred feet down.

They soon stood on the other side. Lalasa lifted her wineskin high so the monster would see it, then bent to place it on the bridge. The creature was already scampering to retrieve it as Lalasa guided them into the jungle.

Hanuvar listened for sounds of pursuit, but heard nothing.

When the sun lowered over the palms circling a little clearing, Lalasa called a halt. "We'll rest until the moon is high."

"We should keep moving," Rudra said.

"And how will we see, with the dark jungle on every side?" Lalasa asked. "Now's the time to rest and eat. We'll move when moonlight marks the way."

Rudra grumbled to the twins, who gathered wood for a small cook fire while he hunkered down on a nearby boulder and slapped at insects.

Hanuvar stepped to the clearing's edge and bent down to touch his toes. More and more each year he felt the aches and pains of age.

"You care for every weapon after use," his father had told him when he was young. "So too should you care for your body." And so Hanuvar had learned to ease strain from his muscles and joints, moving carefully through martial forms with his father each morning and night.

He had turned his attention to his calf muscles when Lalasa joined him. There in the shadow of the trees she was little more than a silhouette exuding the mixed scent of fragrant soaps and healthy sweat. She brushed off a nearby log, sat down, and watched him. For a time there was no sound other than the calls of night animals, one of which let out a repetitious shrieking whoop.

"You are really a master of serpents?" the priestess asked.

"I know their ways." Hanuvar climbed to his feet, widened his stance, and slowly rotated his arms.

"You speak the truth," she said. "There's sadness in your mind when you think of the golden serpent in the water."

Hanuvar paused, staring at her dark form, and strove to blank his mind. He'd underestimated her. "You're a mind reader."

"Not one of any great skill. But I sense the feelings of others and sometimes glimpse portions of their thoughts. It's like pressing up against a thin curtain. I can see what lies on the other side if the 'light' is right."

"And what do you read from those three?" Hanuvar asked quietly. His head turned toward the twins, one of whom was adjusting the fire tinder while the other dug through his supply pack. Rudra drank from Hanuvar's wineskin, which he'd appropriated shortly after they left the creature.

"From the general? Little," she whispered. "Nervousness. Irritation. The other pair . . . there's darkness there, and I don't want to venture close."

"They're soldiers."

"They're killers."

"So am I," Hanuvar said.

The priestess grew silent. Hanuvar bent his head toward his knee.

She shook her head. "It's not the same. There was a boatman in the village where I received my training, renowned far and wide for his skill. Men said he had been blessed by the gods, so wondrous was his talent. His mind felt something like yours."

He laughed lightly. "I'm not blessed."

She spoke swiftly, with great feeling. "I'm sorry they imprisoned you. They had no right. The Dervans are no allies of Narata. You should have been sent on your way."

She was young, but surely she knew the appeal of gold. He wasn't surprised so much that they'd imprisoned him, but that anyone so far from the mainland had recognized him from his belt crest and signet ring.

Hanuvar sat beside her, his mind returning to those impossibly long weeks on the deserted islet building rafts. Neither had been truly seaworthy. The second had delivered him within sight of Narata's coast before sinking. It had been a long swim, and not his first.

The priestess had called him blessed, but a blessed man could have convinced more of his people to heed his calls to arms. A blessed man would not have lost his army, his people, his family. His city. His friend, Eledeva, the golden serpent.

After the Dervan catapult stone had struck her from the sky, Eledeva had been too injured to fly, but she had carried him through rough waves for most of a day. And then she too had perished, and his only hope had been that tiny islet upon the horizon.

The priestess interrupted his musing. "Was Volanus truly as lovely as they say?" Her voice was kind. Had she glimpsed the last view of his city etched in his mind, as tendrils of smoke stretched skyward above the burning temples and the red-tiled houses? Could she hear the screams of his people?

"It was like any city," Hanuvar answered flatly. "There were criminals and priests, beggars and rich men, performers and warriors and bakers and cobblers. More often than not those who ruled had more money than wisdom."

"You're lying," she said after a moment.

He met her eyes. Here at close range their whites glimmered with a red pinpoint from the cook fire. "Her beauty was peerless," he admitted. "But her silver towers lie shattered by the sea and the blood of her people has run into the water. Derva crouches like a fat toad amongst the ashes."

Lalasa said nothing, but he felt her recoil. Doubtless now she sensed the truth.

"I too am a killer, Priestess," he said. "I can recite poetry and the works of Aedara, frame witty quips, trade pleasantries with ladies of the court. But the Dervans fear me with reason."

"You will help us, won't you?"

Hanuvar studied her. "Why do you aid a tyrant?"

"I seek the asalda to help the king help his people." She paused. "At the very least, the southerners will burn the city. But you know as well as I that they make a sport of hunting islanders. Sometimes they leave the women after they rape them, but sometimes they take them, or kill them."

"So do the strong among the weak."

"Is that what you did, among the weak?"

"I sought to crush the empire before it destroyed us."

"You're a man of oaths, and principles," she stated, almost as if to remind him of the fact.

"Your king will turn me over to the Dervans when we return."

"Help me complete my task," Lalasa said with quiet urgently, "and I'll aid you—" She broke off as Rudra drew close. The small fire backlit the general.

"What are you two whispering about?"

"Serpents," Hanuvar answered.

"Are you? I'm watching you, old man. Don't trust him, Priestess. They say he's the father of lies."

Lalasa didn't reply, and Rudra shifted under their scrutiny. "How close are we?"

She answered. "When we see a narrow outcropping at the top of a steep slope, we'll know we're close."

"But how close are we to that? Is the serpent even there?"

Lalasa breathed heavily. She raised one hand to her blue pendant, which glowed gently, suffusing her fingers and the revealed curve of her breasts. "I will see." She drew a deep breath and closed her eyes.

She was thoughtful, poised. It might be her religious order had chosen her for leadership simply because of her empathy and capability. She was just a little older than Hanuvar's daughter had been when she'd been awarded an officer's post in the Eltyr.

At the thought of Narisia's likely fate, his jaw clenched.

Lalasa shook violently and her head flung back. Her eyes opened and she fell limp.

Hanuvar grabbed her shoulders before she hit her head on the log. He called her name to rouse her.

The priestess moaned, blinked, but it was a moment before she focused on Hanuvar.

"Is she all right?" Rudra demanded.

Lalasa stared past Hanuvar's eyes. "We are half a night's journey away still." She grasped the log with her hands. Hanuvar released her and she righted herself.

"You found the serpent?" Rudra demanded.

"She's there. Her mind brushed mine . . ." Lalasa shuddered.

"Eat," Hanuvar said. Sorcerers were always weak after working magics, and he smelled the enticing aroma of crisping pork from the cook fire. "It will restore your strength. Come." She took his hand as he stood and helped her rise, then released it and walked with him toward the fire.

III

The moon rose at last, bathing the jungle in silver light. The island creatures croaked and gibbered to it as Hanuvar and the others advanced through thick foliage. Rudra and the twins wielded manakas, wide, single-edged blades, to chop the clutching leaves.

Hanuvar walked at the rear. He might have disappeared into the jungle, and the others, desperate to find their asalda, wouldn't have time to follow. Yet if he fled he'd have no way off the island. He had no weapon apart from a spoon with a sharpened handle, and, most importantly, the general still carried his rounded flask.

Better opportunities surely lay ahead.

"Halt," Lalasa called, and Hanuvar found himself confronting a large, dark wall of rock.

A steep cliff shot free of the jungle plants and climbed vertically two hundred feet. At its height the moon shone on a pitted black projection shaped like a finger, pointing northwest.

The smooth, ancient stone showed few handholds. There was no climbing that way. Hanuvar's eyes searched the cliffside.

"Here," said Lalasa. She had wandered to the right. The others followed.

Thick, hairy vines clung to the black stone at the point beside the priestess and stretched to the limit of their sight. Whether or not they rose to the cliff's height Hanuvar could not determine, for detail was lost in the dark.

"You first, old man," Rudra told him.

Hanuvar smiled thinly. He wrapped his hands around one of the vines and pulled, found them rooted securely to the stone. He looked up at the challenge ahead, then began his ascent.

He moved slowly, hand over hand, finding sure purchase among the thick plant fibers, working to the height.

Grunting with the final pull to the top, Hanuvar arrived at a circular lake fenced by wide-leafed trees, waving now in a cool wind that rippled the dark waters. Beyond the lake stood the final crest of the mountain.

He stepped back to the cliff to watch the progress of his companions. He heard the slightest noise, as of a tent-flap in the wind, and wheeled into a fighter's crouch, the spoon's sharpened handle in his fist. It was the bird-thing, on wing and bearing down with outstretched talons.

Hanuvar dropped too late. A clawed hand clipped him in the head. He lay stunned as it circled.

In one thing he was fortunate. The creature was a glider, and thus it struggled to gain height for its return. Hanuvar was up by the time it neared again.

The creature hissed and bore down toward him, its speed rising.

Hanuvar leapt as it closed. The bird-thing let out a raspy scream of surprise and pain, for Hanuvar's aim and its own momentum had driven his makeshift knife into its chest. They fell in a jumble of limbs.

The monster clawed at his shoulder and Hanuvar gasped in pain. He bashed the clacking beak aside and thrust his weapon deep in the creature's throat before rolling away.

He climbed to his feet as the thing thrashed out its life. By the time the others reached the cliff top he had washed out the long slash in his shoulder and rigged a bandage from his tattered tunic edge. The twins walked over to prod at the bird-beast while Lalasa examined Hanuvar's injury.

Rudra seemed more concerned with Hanuvar himself. "How did you kill it?" Somehow his voice betrayed suspicion, fear, and awe all at the same time.

"I've been a warrior for more than twice your lifetime," Hanuvar answered.

"But it was stabbed. And you had no sword."

"True. I had no sword."

"I think you'll heal fine," Lalasa said behind him, "so long as you keep the wound clean and change the dressing. The cut is fairly light." She tightened the bandage as she spoke.

Rudra frowned. "Where do we go now?"

Lalasa stepped out from behind Hanuvar. "There."

Rudra walked closer to the water and peered in. "What do you mean, 'there'?"

"We swim." Lalasa pointed to the lake's north end. "There's an underwater tunnel that leads to the asalda's lair."

Rudra's teeth showed. "How are we supposed to do that? We can't breathe underwater!"

"The scrolls tell of the old king's journey, General. There's air in the asalda's cave, but you'll have to hold your breath for a long while to reach it."

Rudra frowned at the water's edge. Meshtar and Beshkar stepped up beside him.

Meshtar's blade flashed as he tore it from his sheath. He caught the general's chin in one hand, slashed the blade across his neck with the other. Blood spattered, and Rudra collapsed, flailing.

"What have you done!?" Lalasa cried.

"We have two things the Dervan pay well for," Meshtar said with a self-satisfied grin. "We know the dwelling place of a mighty serpent. One they will gladly capture or butcher for their sorceries.[1]

---

[1] The animosity between humans and the winged serpents, or asalda, stems in part from the eagerness of sorcerers to harvest their organs for their rites and of hunters to demonstrate their skill and ferocity in the slaying of such cunning animals. While most readers are likely familiar with (probably exaggerated or invented) tales of individual asalda allying with or even befriending humans, the relationship forged between the two asalda of Volanus and the people of the city is unique to the historical record. Only in Volanus were the creatures comfortable enough with the presence of humanity to freely choose living for generations among them.

In almost all other recorded interactions, the best that relations between asalda and humanity could be described as is neutral. More often the two species are deadly adversaries, though asalda do not seem especially fond of human flesh. —*Silenus*

And we have their greatest foe. Alive. Although if he proves troublesome, there'll still be some money for his carcass."

"You killed General Rudra!" Lalasa's voice shook with rage. "What about the island? Your people?"

"What about you?" Beshkar said. Meshtar laughed as Beshkar advanced on her. "I've wanted a taste of you since you showed up last year."

"Save some for me," Meshtar came forward, Rudra's blood dark on his weapon.

Lalasa fumbled for the knife on her belt, her movements growing frantic as they touched its empty sheath.

Hanuvar inched forward, head bowed. "Don't slay me."

"I'm not interested in you right now," Beshkar said, stepping past. "Just stay out of the way."

Hanuvar had held Lalasa's knife against his arm. He flicked it up, drove it into Meshtar's throat. While the dying man reached for his neck, gurgling, Hanuvar grabbed his sword and drew. He kicked hard at Meshtar's knee and toppled him.

Beshkar screamed in rage and slashed high at Hanuvar's head.

The blow rang off his brother's sword, held stiffly in Hanuvar's hand.

Hanuvar's sword arm was numb from the terrific strike, but he kept it steady and circled right.

Meshtar lay twitching, bloody fingers pressed to his ruined throat.

His brother snarled. "You'll die for that!"

Hanuvar smashed his sword into Beshkar's before it completed its downward arc. The younger man grunted, his eyes following the blade as it swung wide. Hanuvar then drove his blade through Beshkar's chest. Curious horror registered on Beshkar's face as he realized the extent of his injury, then he folded to the ground. Hanuvar yanked the sword free and slashed through Beshkar's neck. He stepped back, glanced at the dead Meshtar, and knelt to wipe the blade on the grass. He hadn't expected that particular development, but things had resolved well.

"Adras and Sussura, but you're fast," Lalasa breathed. She gave the dying men a wide berth and walked with Hanuvar to Rudra. While she bent to inspect the general's wound, Hanuvar sank to one knee beside him.

"He's already dead," she said.

Of course he was. "It was a professional stroke." Hanuvar rolled Rudra over to better undo his belt.

"What are you doing?"

"Taking back my flask."

Lalasa said nothing while Hanuvar shifted the dead general's belt to his own waist and compared swords, in the end choosing the less decorative but better-balanced blade he'd taken from Meshtar. He replaced the general's sheath with Meshtar's, but kept Rudra's knife. He wiped Lalasa's blade in the grass and set it aside for her, then moved on to their packs, consolidating the small amount of food and cooking supplies into one.

Lalasa watched silently until he'd finished transferring the money in their coin purses as well. "You don't mean to go on."

"No."

A chill wind blew as they faced each other. Hanuvar didn't usually justify his decisions, but her earlier kindness prompted explanation. "Dealing with an asalda isn't the simple matter your fool king thinks."

"At least give me some of your sorcerous powder," Lalasa said.

Hanuvar touched the cap of the flask at his belt. "I have no sorcery, Lalasa. These are my little brother's ashes. I must bear them to the Isles of the Dead."

He could see little more of her but outline, yet he felt her gaze.

"I felt the truth of your words before." She sounded hurt, confused. Betrayed.

"Eledeva was my friend—an ally of my city from its founding days. I have no magic other than experience and the loyalty of allies and family. And most of those are dead."

"So is your duty to the dead, or the living? Can't you help me? People will die if we don't gain the asalda's aid. Women and children."

"This is a wild asalda. It will want a promise to bind our word. A blood sacrifice."

She breathed deeply and he knew then that she understood.

"Your king was an idiot to think otherwise."

"But what about the serpent's agreement with the old king?"

"An unlikely story. I doubt any agreement will be honored with a representative who doesn't smell of his bloodline. One or both of us would perish." He spoke on, though he knew she wouldn't accept his offer. "It was a fool's errand. You couldn't know. Come with me and live."

Her eyes blazed in indignation. "I thought you were the man who spun victories from defeats, who mastered armies three times larger than his own. Who devoted his life to the protection of his city and his people. Surely you know some—"

"There are things I must live to do."

Silence fell over them. Her mouth thinned and she turned her back. "Leave me."

He did not, though. A moment later she slid free of her sandals and shimmied out of her skirt, her slim figure clothed only in a close-fitting tunic.

She stepped gracefully into the water without looking back and dropped forward with a splash. The moonlight flashed against the water kicked up by the pale soles of her feet.

Hanuvar watched from the shore, his world suddenly further diminished, companioned now only by the dead. Sometimes it seemed they were all he had left. The woman too would die if he did nothing. Yet what was her fate compared to that of the remnants of his people, who could have little hope without him? He must live.

He wrestled with his conscience, for she, too, risked her life to save her people. Somehow he could not find it in himself to let her die.

Hanuvar cursed, tore off belt and gear and clothes, and dove in after her.

IV

The cold plunge lent new energy to Hanuvar's tired body, and he swam vigorously to the north side of the lake, where Lalasa waited, treading water.

"I thought you said that this was a fool's errand."

"I am a fool," Hanuvar said.

She smiled. "Take a deep breath. According to legend, it's a long swim."

"I hope you know the way."

"Everything I've read so far has proven correct. Breathe deep and follow."

A difficult thing, Hanuvar thought, beneath the waters in the dark, but then Lalasa closed her eyes and the pendant hanging about her neck glowed blue once more, lighting the water and outlining her wet clothing and her small chin.

The priestess sucked in a deep gulp of air, then dove, the dark hair tied behind her flowing like a black ribbon. Hanuvar swam after, and on toward a large cleft in the rock wall. A wide tunnel stretched beyond. How great was its extent, and might they be able to escape it if they ran low on air?

But Lalasa swam upward before his own lungs grew terribly strained. Beyond her the tunnel roof rose into a larger chamber. He followed, and then he breached the water, sucking in air tainted with the smell of damp earth—and something else, the faint odor of a den, and scorched stone.

Lalasa struck out for a rocky shoreline. Something nearby struck the water with an immense splash and sent it surging. To the left, Hanuvar glimpsed a long serpentlike coil spiral into the water and disappear.

There was no talking to a serpent that had already begun its attack.

Lalasa pulled up on a rocky ledge and turned, her mouth open in astonishment. Water surged below him.

He did not know if he was panting from exhaustion or fear, but he reached the slippery rock and threw himself over the rim. The injured muscle in his shoulder protested as she grasped his hands and helped him upright.

The pendant bouncing on her chest glowed fiercely. From the water a thing of nightmares loomed, supported by a glistening silver neck wide around as two barrels.

The serpent's skull was the size of a six-man rowboat, and her flaring nostrils wider than dinner plates. Further back, two immense slitted eyes glowed like emerald suns. The head rose steadily until it hung at least two body lengths above.

"Name yourselves, intruders!" The asalda's voice echoed from the cave walls like the ringing of great gongs, and teeth the length of sabers flashed wetly in her mouth. As he had scarce dared to hope, she had granted them the opportunity for conversation. He meant to make the most of it.

"I am Hanuvar, son of Himli, of House Cabera, friend of the asalda known in my tongue as Eledeva. We come in peace."

The serpent head swayed closer. "You are not welcome!" The nostrils widened. "You bear the memory of asalda upon you, but that does not grant you entry."

"We have come at the behest of the king of Narata, great one," Lalasa said, her head bowed.

"Why does Nara not come himself?"

The priestess hesitated. "Nara is long dead, great one, and his great grandson rules the island."

"Has it been so long?" The asalda did not wait for an answer, commenting as if to herself: "You humans live such meager lives."

"Our lives are all too brief," Hanuvar agreed. "And many of them are threatened even now. The people of Narata seek your aid. A great fleet of raiders nears their shore, and their defense is poor."

"The king would invoke the pact made with you by his grandfather's father," Lalasa said.

"The pact?" The serpent sounded almost amused. "You seek my aid, you, who clearly have no knowledge even of my name?"

"It . . . it was not known by the chronicler. I must ask your forgiveness—"

"You ask much, unnamed woman."

"I mean no disrespect," the priestess said, stepping forward. She raised her head with regal grace. "I am Lalasa, a daughter of the sea. And these folk of Narata are simple and forgetful and do not know the proper words or honors. But they mean you no harm, and their word is good. They still protect you, as you protect them, and they seek to invoke the pact they made with you ages past."

"Protect me?" The asalda's voice rang from the stone, rising shrilly in disbelief. "Do they think I need protection?"

Neither Lalasa nor Hanuvar dared answer.

"It is clear you have forgotten much!" The serpent's head lowered until it was almost level with their bodies. "The pact was simple. I would leave you humans be if you would leave me to my doings and stay clear of my mountain. These simple things you have done. Until now. Your people have mostly kept your word, a rare thing in the history of your kind."

"She would make a new pact with you," Hanuvar said.

"Would she? Where is her tribute? I do not trust the word of humans who bear nothing to seal their promise."

So it was with asalda. The taking of oaths was a weighty matter to them, and they did not trust save when humans had proven faith by sacrifice or harmless predictable presence.

"I am your tribute." Lalasa started forward.

The serpent's head rose.

Hanuvar barred Lalasa's way with an arm and pushed her back.

"Not you—" the priestess cried.

"She means that she brings word of tribute," Hanuvar said. "The king is weak and dared not come himself, but he waits for you."

"You would have me go elsewhere for tribute?" The serpent's teeth shown.

Hanuvar bowed. "The king realizes it's much to ask, and so he has made great tribute for you. He has given himself to you with baskets of jewelry and gold. They lie hidden from prying eyes three hundred man paces east from the central tower of the palace, in a chamber just beneath the courtyard."

"How do you—" Lalasa asked, but Hanuvar shot up a finger in warning without looking back at her.

"This is unorthodox," said the serpent. "Yet I see the picture of this place within your mind. Why are the treasures hidden?"

"To keep it safe from the raiders. If you stop them, it is yours."

"I shall take your tribute." The serpent's head rose. "And the raiders shall perish utterly. Now leave me."

Hanuvar bowed from the waist, and the priestess echoed his gesture.

"Go!" The great creature roared. "I tire of your intrusion!"

Hanuvar dropped into the water, motioning Lalasa ahead of him. They kicked hard for the tunnel, the priestess's pendant silvering the water beneath her. Hanuvar didn't look behind him, though he felt the great eyes of the serpent burning into the back of his head. He tried not to think of it swimming after, its vast mouth opening wide. He didn't think it would, yet the minds of the asalda were never fully knowable. Who was to say that it might not take them in tribute as well?

The water beyond the tunnel seemed lighter. When they broke the surface, a red glow hung in the tree limbs along the shore. Dawn had come. As the two of them swam, a long rippling form with immense black wings exploded from the water and soared effortlessly into the sky.

They treaded water and watched the serpent's sinuous form glide up and eastward, beating its wings almost as an afterthought.

Once they reached the shore, Lalasa paused only to grab her clothes. She hurried through a stand of trees. Hanuvar followed to the cliff's edge. The whole of the island lay spread before them, and they looked down across miles of jungle canopy. Hanuvar saw the bridge they had crossed. The high, brown stone tower of the palace rose far to the left, near the shimmering blue waters. The serpent dropped beside it and disappeared from view.

"You've slain the king," Lalasa said, voice quiet with awe.

"Far better him than you. Any good leader should be willing to sacrifice himself to protect his people."

"He has no heirs—"

"Good."

Lalasa stared at him. The dawn's light glistened on the water drops beading her forehead. She shivered in the morning chill. "How did you know the king's hiding place so precisely?"

"I counted my steps."

From her expression he saw she didn't understand, but she didn't press further. "What will you do now?"

"I will inter my brother's ashes upon the Isles of the Dead. Then—" Hanuvar's voice dropped. "Then I have a long journey before me."

"You could rule Narata," Lalasa said, stepping close. She stood but hand spans from him. Her eyes were great dark wells. "You are very wise. You could take on a different identity—"

He shook his head no. "If I stayed, the Dervans would find me, and any who shelter me. Your people should appoint some other worthy person to lead. A wise young woman, perhaps."

A light kindled in her eyes.

"Come. I'll build you a fire. And then we'll leave this mountain." He turned, and she followed him from the ledge.

❊ ❊ ❊

Within days the first of the blackened ship timbers reached the shores of Narata. They continued to sweep into the eastern beach for weeks after, sometimes in the company of burned body parts, bits of cloth, and occasional articles of clothing. By then Lalasa had used her new status to set a triumvirate in the king's place.

And Hanuvar had sailed west, toward the land of his enemies.

Lalasa had gifted him with a small sailboat. Though supplied with ample stores, there were not enough to see him safely to his distant destination, and by and by he had to stop among the Lesser Lenidines for water and food and a few moments upon dry land. There he was to find an unforeseen challenge, and an unexpected ally.

—Sosilos, Book One

Chapter 2:
The Warrior's Way

I

Hanuvar crouched at the trailhead, gripping his blood-tipped spear. The monster's comings and goings had beaten a path through the jungle down to the rocky defile and into the yawning black cave where it laired. Its recent passage had silenced the closest birds and animals in the canopy; they watched and listened like he did. Out of sight the monster surely did the same, all while flexing its great clawed hands and wondering if the human who'd wounded it would follow.

Only a madman would confront the thing in the cramped darkness of its retreat. Hanuvar weighed another option. He had spotted a ledge to the cave's side. He could leap diagonally to it from the descending trail without crossing in front of the cave mouth. From there he could lie waiting for the beast's next emergence.

He was a study in quiet strength, a fit older man of broad shoulders, his short dark hair and beard stubble peppered with gray. A sailor's tan darkened his olive skin, apart from old scars that showed lighter on his muscular limbs. His frayed, knee-length tunic was as washed out as his eyes, beige where they were gray, but his strapped brown sandals were in excellent repair, as was his belt and the two dark flasks, short sword, and dagger that depended from it. The haft of a broad-bladed manaka sword, for slicing tropical foliage, thrust up over one shoulder.

Hanuvar's gaze shifted to the sinking red smear of the sun, half hidden by the dense tree line on the hill behind. The birds resumed their clamor, but it would not be long before their sounds were replaced by those of the island's night denizens. Much as he hated the thought of bedding down while this hungry beast ran loose, he could not afford to hold vigil outside its lair all night, nor to labor long hours smoking it out. He must depart in the morning, rested and resupplied for the next leg of his journey.

Reluctantly, he retreated.

By the time he'd returned to the boar carcass, rodents were into it. They fled at his approach, and he considered the ant-swarmed remains. He'd set a snare for the beast, but its squealing had lured the ancient bipedal monster from the jungle depths. It was the lizard, not himself, who had delivered the animal's death blow.

While he had seen depictions of tarifen[2] and read accounts of their savage predations, he had never seen a live one, nor had any reputable person of his acquaintance, for the green-scaled, man-sized predators had been exterminated from the lands of his people centuries before. Sailors from Volanus had revictualed in the Lenidine islands for uncounted years and had never reported tarifen here.

But then he had deliberately made landfall on one of the most remote islands in the chain, hoping to avoid both locals and Dervan naval patrols. While he supposed it possible the beast had swum here, more likely he hadn't encountered an immigrant, but a lone survivor. In some ways, it was not unlike himself. Until that realization, he'd felt no affinity for the beast. But then it would have been strange to have experienced a sense of kindred when it had risen from the boar carcass, hissing from its dagger-fanged maw.

The scent of the raw meat and the musky odor of the boar's hair and skin was strong contrast to the island's abundant floral scent,

---

[2] While a Volani word, tarifen is originally of Ruminian extraction, and can be loosely translated as "blood-claw." Once indigenous to the continent of Kenasa and some of its outlying islands, today the tarifen survive only in history and myth, for they have been hunted to extermination, although (almost certainly apocryphal) reports of individuals and small hunting packs in remote lands persist. A bipedal lizard ranging from four to eight feet in height, the tarifen were voracious and as likely to stalk humans as other game. Unlike other large carnivores, they possessed no fear of man. I have personally viewed a collection of dried tarifen parts in a Nuvaran palace, reportedly preserved from a great hunt two hundred years previous. Even dead the large fanged mouths and terrible claws are striking. —*Silenus*

baking greenery, and the underlying notes of rotting vegetation. Though the boar was hardly enticing now, Hanuvar's mouth almost watered at the thought of smelling its cooking flesh. He had just decided he could smoke the ants away and recover a fair portion of the meat when the surrounding birdcalls dulled. The unmistakable sound of human laughter rose faintly over the ordinary cacophony of the jungle.

He stepped into the heavy, draping leaves and turned, seeking the direction of the sound. It lay to the west, the chatter of several men, a few voices raised in song, and a high-pitched piping instrument.

Deciding the novel noises were no threat, the birds resumed their raucous cries and drowned out the men before Hanuvar identified their language.

Working quickly, he hung the boar from a limb, cut its throat, and gutted it. There it would have to remain, for he dared no further preparations until he assessed the threat of the strangers. He cleaned his weapons by driving them into the ground, then resignedly abandoned the carcass and headed toward the intruders.

II

The isle stretched a little over three miles in length and was no more than a mile at its widest, a warped crescent with a bulge near its southern tip, where the monster laired. If the land had a name, Hanuvar did not know it.

He had dragged his sailing skiff onto on the rocky western shore, concealing it under bushes he felled. A better beach lay along the inward curving eastern side, where white sand sloped gently from the clear blue waters to meet the wall of jungle. A small freshwater lagoon lay within easy walking distance of the shore, and so did the low line of hills curved along the island's spine.

Hanuvar had avoided the fine stretch of sand to escape detection. The strangers apparently were less concerned with discovery, and as he neared them he wondered if he would find Lenidine natives, a Dervan patrol, a far-ranging trade ship from a nation of the Inner Sea, or something else entirely.

The rumble of human speech grew more distinct as he passed

through the hills. He crawled into the shadow of a silver leaf palm and looked down onto the inviting stretch of sand, brown now as the sun dipped below the tree line behind him.

A sleek ship with a high prow and a single oar bank rode at anchor only a hundred yards out, its lone mast starkly outlined against the evening sky and the endless swath of water. Two crewmen sorted gear on its deck. The rest of the sailors, over two dozen, took their ease on the beach around a blazing fire. A few turned boars on spits while others lined up, laughing, to dip mismatched mugs and goblets into a large wooden barrel.

This was no Dervan patrol ship, and Hanuvar doubted these were merchants. Judging from the gold anklets on dirty limbs and the bright belts on worn tunics, these were mercenaries at best, and more than likely pirates, resting a half day's journey from the better trafficked sea lane and its protectors.

Two thirds of the sailors were men, and nearly everyone shared the dark hair and complexion common to the people of the Inner Sea, although there were some coil-haired Herrenes, two ruddy blonds, and even a wiry, mahogany-toned Nuvaran, sitting with his back to the others while he faced the sea and played a somber melody on his reed flute.

Most interesting of all was the large, handsome woman in the brimmed, silver-banded hat. As she walked among them, one hand resting comfortably on the pommel of her sword, the other gripping a goblet, Hanuvar understood she was checking with the scattered groups. She consulted with the cooks, joked with a trio cleaning some blades in the sand, and moments later pushed others away from the liquor barrel. Apparently she didn't want her crew drinking themselves insensible.

Female captains had been far more common among his own people than those of other lands, and for a brief moment his heart climbed at the thought he'd found a fellow Volani still alive and independent.

But then he saw the slaves and knew she could not be one of his own.

The three young native men sat under the guard of a surly, spear-bearing sentinel between the surf and the fire. Their wrists were bound behind their backs. They wore only loin clouts. Probably they'd once possessed the shell necklaces and bracelets traditional to their people, but those had been appropriated by their captors, only the first of the indignities that would be pressed upon them until they were sold to a Dervan flesh market.

Hanuvar's lips turned down. He had witnessed uncounted preludes to violence in his time, but was far from inured to them, especially since the unpleasant fate in store for these young men was similar to that faced by the survivors from his own city.

His initial impulse was to work out a means to free them. Then he reminded himself this was not his fight, and that if he were to fail in this venture, he would be of no use to his people. As his father had taught him, he would pick his battles.

An unseasoned man might not have heard the faint whisking noise to his rear, or would have discounted it as wind. Hanuvar rolled immediately to his side, just before a spear drove into the ground he'd quitted.

He sprang to his feet, sword in hand, thinking to face a pirate scout.

What he saw instead was a wiry native girl, no older than fourteen or fifteen, her teeth showing white in a hateful grimace. She snatched her spear and thrust again at him. Hanuvar swept the jab aside with his forearm, grabbed the spear shaft back of the point, and advanced with a sliding step that forced her backward. She tripped over a tree root and hit the brush behind her with a leafy crash. That in itself might not have alerted the pirates, but the family of long-tailed parrots that rose screeching from a nearby branch surely did.

Hanuvar slapped the side of her head with the spear haft as she pushed to her feet. The girl dropped, moaning, one hand to her temple.

He grabbed her spear and his own, pivoting to scan the camp site. The captain was pointing in their general direction, and a trio of men plodded toward their hill.

As he stepped back he found the girl struggling to stand. He hoisted her by the elbow and addressed her in her language. "Run, foolish child. Pirates come."

He sent her stumbling and she regained coordination as she got under way. He left her, jogging deeper into the brush.

He retreated from his original camp to a wood-topped hillock closer to where he'd hidden his skiff. He had long since learned to adjust to setbacks, and so didn't brood upon the lost meal and the delays this day had brought, or curse at the chill night that awaited him—for surely he could make no fire now. He had known true cold, and this would be but an inconvenience.

Darkness fell, the temperature dropped, and the wind rose. He didn't expect the pirates to spend a long time searching, but he sat quietly, alert for them. He heard only the night calls of the jungle's animals, and the lap of the ocean. He wondered if he would recognize the call of a tarifen, or if it made one.

He heard nothing more of the pirates until, finally, the distant sound of the flute cut the darkness. Still he waited.

When a nearby footfall sounded, it was the girl, climbing her way up the hillock toward him. She paused to examine a limb he must have brushed against and then continued upward.

He stood and lowered his spear.

She stopped just beyond the weapon's thrusting range and boldly raised her head. "I want my spear back," she said.

He liked that. She said other things, but his Lenidine vocabulary wasn't large. "Slow down," he said. "Speak again."

"Give me back my spear," she repeated gruffly.

"You tried to kill me with it."

"I thought you were one of them."

"Then why did you think I was spying on them?"

"Pirates fight each other all the time. You look like them," she added defensively.

His words sounded stilted even to him as he explained himself in her language. "You made things difficult for both of us because you did not think the situation through. Now the pirates know we're here. They surely found our prints."

She stared at him, then nodded once. "You are right," she said, adding: "You sound like the war chiefs." She pointed to the spear he held. "I can make another spear, but you already have yours, and I am running out of time."

Time was his own adversary. He was curious to hear what challenge it presented her. "Time for what?"

"The pirates will probably leave in the morning. I need to free my brother and the other boys before then."

He should have guessed that. "The odds are poor for you." He bent to retrieve her spear, then lobbed it so it landed a few steps to her right. He tightened his grip on his own weapon but did not level it at her. "This isn't a job for a single warrior. Where are the rest of your people?"

"This is the testing isle," she said. "We're here for the rite of the warrior's way."

In the Lenidines, custom sent young males to live for a week on a remote island. Often they were to return with a special feather or rock only found at the location, and that, in addition to living in the wild, confirmed their transition to manhood.

"Why are you here?" he asked.

She'd been waiting for that question, or one like it, for she took immediate umbrage. "I knew I could pass it, and better than they. I am the swifter runner, the better caster!"

"You came after them, on your own. Without the knowledge of your people."

He knew he had guessed right when her anger rose. "You think a woman isn't good enough to be a warrior?"

"My daughter is a warrior," Hanuvar said. "So are many of her friends." And most of them, probably all of them, were dead, but he did not say that.

The girl's manner shifted to one of tremendous curiosity. "Where are you from?"

"Volanus."

"You are really from there?" Her interest shone keen and bright, like the moon exposed by a cloud break. "They say that land has many chiefs and war chiefs who are women."

His people had titled them counselors and generals, but the girl's information was essentially correct. "Yes."

She bubbled on with childlike fascination. "They say Volanus is so vast it takes more than a day to walk from one side to the other. Are there really great silver towers that almost touch the stars?"

He could not put from his mind the vision of the easternmost tower's side being smashed in by a Dervan catapult stone, or of smoke rising from the roofs scattered over the temple islands.

"Yes," he said flatly. "It's a large city. There are silver towers, but they don't come close to the moon. Don't believe everything you hear."

The native girl had crept closer and the moonlight shone on her wide eyes. She opened her mouth, almost surely to ask more of Volanus' lost glories. "Enough," Hanuvar said. "What is your plan to free these boys?"

"It has several steps. It will be hard to explain."

"Draw it for me."

She nodded as though this were wise, and retreated to brush broad leaves aside, exposing a swath of dirt, just visible in the moonlight. She drew with the point of her knife: the curve of the beach, the bonfire. The log where the boys sat. The greater wall of trees, the encroach of the jungle from the south and west.

He watched her work. "How long have you been on the island?" he asked.

"Three days. The pirates captured the boys when the sun was highest. I saw you sail in this morning, while my idiot brother and his friends were dreaming on the beach. I think one of them might have seen you."

"If you saw me on the beach, you must have known I wasn't a pirate."

"I didn't want an enemy at my back." She looked up at him, her voice challenging, "You do not dress like a great warrior's father."

"My belongings were lost in a battle and long journey."

Immediately she eyed him with more respect. A warrior returning to his home was very different from an outcast or criminal.

"I see your map," Hanuvar said. "What is your plan?"

"I have water jugs. Clay. This afternoon I gathered snakes. I put them in the jugs, and stoppered them. I will throw the jars into the middle of the pirates. They will break, and snakes will crawl everywhere. The pirates will run and cry like babies."

Hanuvar smiled wryly. "They'll certainly be surprised."

"While the pirates are distracted, I will sneak close and cut the boys free. The pirates will chase us, but I will set stakes before I throw the jars, and the pirates will trip over them in the dark. That will slow them down. We will reach the boat, and paddle from the island."

"The best plans are simple ones," he said approvingly. "And the gods love daring. What is your name?"

"I am Takava. Who are you?"

He bore one of the most famous names in the world, one likely to be recognized even here, by a young woman impossibly removed from the Dervan Empire and the ruined city of his people. Speaking the truth would only complicate matters. "Call me Melgar," he said, taking the name of his youngest brother, whose ashes he bore in one of the flasks at his belt. "Your plan has fine features but you've missed some of the challenges."

She squared her shoulders and lifted her chin defiantly. "You know better because you are a man?"

"I know better because I have led more battles. Do your warriors challenge chiefs when they offer counsel?"

"No," she said grudgingly. "What have I done wrong?"

"The limbs of the boys will be hard to move after you free them." He struggled to explain what he meant with his limited vocabulary. "Their arms and legs will be stiff. They will not move fast."

Her smooth forehead furrowed.

"Your diversion is clever," he assured her. "But it may focus too much attention on a single place, from where you throw the snakes."

Her little shoulders slumped, and she no longer resembled a budding war hero, but a discouraged adolescent. "What am I to do?"

"Allow me to make a few suggestions."

III

Some had once thought to control Trisira through force of strength, but she knew true power lay not just in a slash with a sword arm, but a few drops of the right substance stirred into a goblet, or bright coins crossing the right palm.

True leadership was about wits, and required constant alertness. And so she never drank as deeply as her comrades, always kept her temper, and wakened at the change of every watch. Thus, from old habit, she roused at two bells to check on the crew.

The fire still blazed on the soft beach, and the men and women lay circled in the sand, in their bushy hair and mismatched clothes looking much like flotsam washed from the ocean depths. At the thought that their still forms resembled corpses she swore and made the sign against the evil eye, hoping she wasn't conjuring a dark future.

She saw the cook's broad chest rising and falling. As though the visual cue weren't clear enough, many of her crew snored. Reassured, Trisira pushed to her feet, and Golius, sitting watch with his back to the fire and the waves, nodded to her.

She walked about the camp, stopping to look at the three sleeping boys, still bound, their lead ropes tied to a stone anchor her men had dragged ashore. Finding them this afternoon had been a lucky break. They'd fetch a fair price at the right market, and the short, handsome one might sell high.

Light sparked on the edge of her vision, and she turned to spot the flarc of a campfire, a quarter mile away on the low hills west of their position. That evening the parrots had been startled from the brush beyond the beach, and her men had found two sets of tracks, though it had been too dangerous to follow far in the twilight. The boys claimed that the only other person on the island was an old man who'd beached his boat earlier in the day, and knowing that they were on their traditional manhood rite and the isle was routinely unoccupied, she doubted they lied. They were supposed to be alone. The old man might have had a passenger the boys hadn't seen. But why would he have lit a fire?

Trisira found the sentry at the far end of their camp nodding off and cuffed him awake. She showed him the distant blaze with a jab of her finger. Quietly she wakened her first mate, Olocano, and sent the Nuvaran to investigate with four men. As they headed out she woke two more sailors to stand watch.

Might some native have set a beacon to warn other islanders someone had interfered with the manhood rites? The Lenidine natives could have a man watching out for the boys. But if so, it didn't make sense for their guardian to light a fire to the south, for the populated islands lay northward. The more Trisira pondered the situation the more confused she became. It might just be possible the Dervans kept some lone scout on the island, who meant to alert a patrol vessel to her pirates. But the Dervans beached at night, and she happened to know that the fleet was spread thin owing to the worries of war in the west. Might there really be ships beached nearby to observe that beacon? She doubted that.

She paced the camp edge, eyes turned from the fire. As she studied the dark wall of jungle something directly west made an alarmingly loud cawing noise, like a hybrid of bird and human. At almost the same moment, an object hurtled from a group of boulders on her right. Time slowed as she spun to eye it, and she could have sworn it was a clay water jug, a red spot of flame reflecting on its rounded side.

It crashed into pieces against a rock near the fire, flinging broken clay and writhing serpentine forms.

One of her men woke, screaming at the dark shape wriggling over his naked chest.

"Snake!"

Even the drunkest of her sailors wakened, cursing and shouting and screaming, as the snakes raced through the camp site and over them. In their alarm, the frightened reptiles sometimes clamped on exposed legs and arms, or reared up to hiss warning.

Trisira tried to scan the darkness for attackers, but she'd ruined her night vision when she'd turned to watch her people fight the snakes near the fire. Out there in the darkness someone shrieked insults at them. She shouted at her second mate to take men and kill their taunter, then hurried into the midst of her sailors, ordering them to stop panicking, but she might as well have tried to order wild piglets. Only after she'd pulled a venomless tree snake from the hysterical cook did she spot four figures darting toward the jungle, the tallest in the lead. The three who followed were smaller, their stride wobbly. Her slaves.

"The slaves are escaping!" she shouted. "After them, you dogs!"

Two of her men grabbed spears and bolted in pursuit. Trisira followed, hand to sword hilt. The four figures reached the beach edge then disappeared into the dark curtain of trees.

Ulren, her second mate, was only a few steps behind. He was a middling sailor but a cunning swordsman and swift runner. Eager for the fight, he shouted at the boys, promising vengeance.

And then he tripped headlong in the sand. He let out a long scream the moment he landed, stopping only to draw a shuddering breath.

His companion, the big Ceori tribesman Hovan, slid to a stop, staring down at his friend working feebly to rise. A moment later Trisira halted beside them. Ulren had tripped over a staggered line of tree limbs to land belly first in a field of sharpened wooden points.

The swordsman screamed the louder as he pushed up on one trembling limb.

The stink of offal hit her. Trisira had smelled enough comrades or foes take stomach wounds, or defecate in battle, to know one or both had happened to Ulren, and the high-pitched screaming was an irritant. She looked up at the swaying line of fronds through which the slaves had fled, and pointed Hovan through it.

The northman shook his head. "The tall one was no normal," he said in his barbarous accent. "Silent like a forest ghost." His gaze shifted back to his friend, now sitting upright and moaning.

"Help me, Captain!" Ulren begged, then fell into a shuddering cry again.

A dark wet hole showed through his cheek, and a snakelike thing hung down from his belly. Part of an intestine had been torn free, along with a chunk of muscles and flap of skin. The biceps of his sword arm trailed from a few strands of fiber alongside his elbow. Seeing this, he cried out once more.

Trisira's first slice hit, but Ulren didn't stop shouting until the blade buried deep in his chest and found his heart.

IV

Hanuvar knelt with the boys only a few feet from the jungle's edge, watching the captain peer in their direction while the big Ceori looked down at the dead man. Four more pirates had run up behind her, asking for orders, but she continued to stare into the darkness. He doubted she could see them.

Finally, she backed away, snapping orders Hanuvar couldn't make out. She was the most dangerous. If he'd had one more soldier in his force he would have arranged for a spear or arrow to bring her down in the initial onslaught. Leaderless, the pirates would be far less likely to cause additional trouble.

But he had only himself and the girl, and Takava had set the fire and performed the bird calls beautifully from the other end of the camp, then shouted insults until some of the pirates had pursued her into the jungle.

The boys had remained quiet throughout the rescue and the

flight. Finally, as the captain retreated with the others, one of them whispered at Hanuvar's back. "Who are you?"

"A friend of Takava's."

The shortest of the three spoke in wonder. "Takava is here?"

"She planned your rescue," Hanuvar answered. "If not for her, you'd be heading out to sea at dawn, to be the playthings of old women, or men."

"That pirate captain said I was pretty," the short one said, oddly defensive, "and promised to take care of me."

"Then go back to her, fool," one of his companions said derisively. "If she liked you, would she put you in ropes?"

The third boy spoke directly to Hanuvar. His voice had a deeper, rasping quality the others lacked. "Will they come into the jungle after us?"

"It's unlikely, but not impossible. Let's find Takava."

They retreated. In the dark, he had little sense of the boys save that one was shorter, and one had a distinctive voice. The shorter one continued to bicker with the one who'd mocked him, and Hanuvar admonished them to silence. After, not a word was spoken. He stopped now and again to listen for pursuit. Finally, they climbed the hillock where he and Takava had made their plans.

She hadn't returned. Hanuvar bid the boys to sit, then searched the surrounding brush. He found no signs of recent passage. "Did you learn anything about the pirates?" he asked them. "Was the pipe player a capable warrior?" Hanuvar had seen him leading the party the captain dispatched toward Takava's fire. A second group had hesitated to go deep, but the pipe player had slipped into the foliage.

The raspy voiced one answered. "He's the crafty one. The captain calls him Olocano. He is the subchief. He speaks our language, better than you. He seemed to know jungle ways better than the others."

That wasn't the kind of news Hanuvar had hoped to hear. Either Takava was hiding from pursuit, or she had been found, meaning capture, injury, or death. And unfortunately there weren't just human adversaries to contend with. There were savage-tempered boars, and, even worse, a wounded tarifen, likely hungry and angry both. Since he had seen it in the daytime, it probably wasn't a nocturnal hunter, but he wouldn't have bet his life on that, much less hers.

He explained to the boys about the tarifen, asking if they'd seen it.

"We saw its tracks," the smaller one said. "We thought it was a spirit."

"It's not a spirit. It's a hungry animal." Hanuvar unsheathed his manaka blade, and his knife, telling them to make spears to defend themselves with, and to use these weapons in the meantime if needed.

"Where are you going?" asked the raspy-voiced one.

"To find Takava."

"I am her brother," the boy said. "It is my duty to go."

He shook his head. "Stay. Three of you together are a bigger threat to the tarifen, if it comes. If you hear the pirates closing in on you, head to your boat and get away."

He didn't wait for their response.

While Hanuvar was an experienced woodsman, this jungle was different from the lands he had most frequently traveled. His step was neither as light nor as sure as it would have been in a temperate woodland, and the darkness was an impediment no matter the climate.

He picked his way forward, and as he turned south he heard men shouting that one of the slaves had gone this way. Neither he nor the boys had left tracks in this direction, so the pirates had to have stumbled across Takava's prints.

Before much longer, bright points of light winked in and out as lanterns passed among trees. Pirates were beating their way forward through the jungle in two groups. They would only be pressing forward if they were certain of their quarry. And there were only two reasons Takava had not already shaken them. Either she was slowed by a wound or, knowing her pursuers were tracking her steps, she was deliberately keeping them from the half of the island where the rest of them had retreated.

This latter option was most likely, and Hanuvar's respect for her climbed higher still. A leader needed to put her charges before herself.

The slap of feet on leaves rose behind him. Hanuvar crouched, wheeling, just as a small form hurtled from the brush and lantern light spilled onto him from only a few paces out.

His spear was up but he recognized Takava rushing him and turned the point. She grabbed his arm and tugged him to one side, calling him to drop. He did, even as something alternately black and gleaming struck her side. She gasped as she fell.

One of their pursuers let out a savage, exultant cry.

Hanuvar scrambled to his feet, helping her rise, shifting as he did so. A second knife blade soared a foot past his shoulder.

He understood then that the louder pirates were putting on a show, and that someone even more clever and capable was following on the flank.

Takava was having trouble rising. Hanuvar lifted her in his arms, the spear borne beneath her. She was lighter than he'd guessed.

Head low, he turned south. His hands were soon wet from her blood-soaked tunic. Despite the shout of pursuers and the bright spot of a distant lantern, he paused to shift her in his arms. She was pressing her hand to the wound. "How bad is it?" he asked.

"It doesn't feel good." Her laconic aplomb, more to be expected from a veteran warrior than a youngster, impressed and alarmed him.

"Did you get the boys free?" she asked.

"Yes. They're fine."

He found his way uphill and down and finally emerged into familiar territory. There, in the moonlight, was the little clearing with the trail that led into the rocky defile. The glow of the pirates' lanterns was only a hundred yards or so behind.

He searched vainly for new tracks made by the tarifen, but the moon's light was little aid for fine details when he was moving at a jog.

There was nothing for it but to take the chance. He raced halfway down the rocky slope and then sprang—not toward the cave, diagonally to his left, but toward the rocky ledge he'd spotted earlier, diagonally to the right, sloping back from the trail.

He landed on its edge, teetering for a moment, then leaned forward. Aided by the overhang's rearward slope, he caught himself, crouched, and pushed into the greenery.

Some small thing scurried from their path and into the protective cover of a nearby shrub, partly overhanging the back of the ledge. Whatever it was seemed frightened of them, which was probably a good sign. Gently he laid Takava down.

"Lie still," he whispered.

"I will."

He freed his sword and cut off a swath from his tunic, then pressed it to her injury. He felt a deep gash in her side. He worried the knife had penetrated an organ.

He lay next to her, told her to keep her eyes down. She lowered her head and both hid under the drooping fronds of a fern.

Only a moment later the captain arrived with a band of panting men, dark figures at first, then briefly outlined as a lantern bearer came up behind them. The Nuvaran Hanuvar now knew as Olocano squatted by the trail head, then pointed down slope.

Five more pirates turned up. There were ten total, talking quietly among themselves, all but the first mate looking grim and sour. They might not be voicing their feelings, but their stances revealed them. They didn't want to be here. Hanuvar hardly blamed them. He wouldn't want to be tearing through the jungle searching for a fugitive in the middle of the night either.

The hard-eyed captain pointed down slope. "You can stop your bellyaching," she said. "Olocano says one of them's wounded now, and they've retreated to that cave." She pointed downslope. "They've nowhere to go."

"We know how to get people out of caves," the Nuvaran said calmly.

"Indeed we do," the captain agreed. "You three, trim some of those limbs down."

The thought of the chase being over seemed to invigorate the pirates, for they turned immediately to work, hewing through the bushes with their wide-bladed weapons.

The captain came halfway down the slope, obliterating any sign of Hanuvar's own passage. Their first fortunate break in some time.

She peered at the cave, lifted a hand to one side of her face, then shouted: "We know you're in there! And we know one of you is bleeding. If you come out now, we can treat you. You don't have to die."

As the light played across the ground near the cave Hanuvar slitted his eyes. He wondered what it would take to anger the tarifen or draw its interest.

It might be that he'd wounded the beast more severely than he'd thought, and that the thing was dead or dying inside its lair. It might be that it was out hunting this very moment.

The captain stepped out of the way as two of her men dragged bundles of branches heavy with broad, thick leaves up to the cave maw. A scrawny pirate used lantern doors to fix the light on the ground in front of them.

Hanuvar wished that they'd be quicker about it because Takava's injury needed tending. He had left off praying weeks ago, and could not imagine why the gods would save an injured girl who wasn't from their own land when they hadn't shown any interest in preserving their own people.

The first two pirates started back up the trail with the captain, and another one started down, bearing more leaf-heavy branches.

"It's going to grow really unpleasant in there," the captain shouted from the trail head. "Fast. And once I get this smoke going it may be hard to stop. I can't guarantee that we can get you out alive even if we want to."

The pirate reached the pile of tree limbs and dropped his bundle on it. "I can hear one of them moving around in there," he called up to the captain.

"Come on out!" she called.

When the tarifen burst from the cave, its scales shown in the lantern light, a dozen different shades of brilliant green. Its wicked sharklike teeth glinted yellow-white as it roared.

The pirate with the lantern screamed. He shook as he swung the light into its face. The beast slitted its great eyes and pounced off powerful black legs.

Too late the pirate dropped the lantern and reached for his weapon. The light wobbled madly as the tarifen's curved talons shredded flesh and muscle and fabric, and the shadows of the struggle were painted on the nearby foliage. The monster closed its crocodile maw on his neck and silenced his screams. Blood spurted and the beast shook him like a dog with a duck, then released his body and looked up slope.

The captain had been shouting for her men to ready spears, but the pirates were already in retreat. As the tarifen bounded up slope, the captain and her mate bolted after them. Hanuvar heard a scream, and the monster's roar, and a death rattle and the sound of tearing flesh. Then the beast growled and padded in pursuit of the others.

"It doesn't feel as bad now," Takava said weakly.

Even in the lantern's ruddy glow she was pale. The rock was heavy with her blood. The girl saw the direction of his gaze, considered the blood, then faced him. She looked more tired than alarmed. "Your city," she said. "Is it really as beautiful as they say?"

Not for all the treasures of the world would he have told her what it looked like now. Instead, he spoke of the Volanus of his memory. "It is. In the morning, the priestesses of the sea temple sound the horns to greet the sun's emergence from the waves. The light gleams on the spires of the silver towers, so bright they seem aflame. The buildings climb steeply along the shore, gilt with bright tiles of blue and red and gold. The water of the fountains rises along the wide avenues. People from all corners of the world walk her streets, bringing their wares to sell and trade. At night there is music, and folk gather at the stages to hear the stories of our people."

"Women really can be warriors there?" she asked.

"Yes. But only the brave and clever ones. Like you."

"Why are you crying?" Her weakening voice sounded critical. "Warriors don't cry."

"They do when a hero dies," he said.

She must have liked that, because her last expression, before it blanked in death, was a smile of approval.

V

At dawn they buried her near the shore. While the boys held graveside vigil, Hanuvar returned to the white beach to find the pirates vanished, leaving only their dead behind. Among them was the captain, though she had not perished from the bite of the monster. A sword stroke had cloven her from behind. It might be that the first mate had decided on a promotion, or that some lower hand had taken out his frustration. Her killer might have been the Ceori whom the sea birds were nibbling, further down shore.

He saw no tarifen tracks on the beach, nor did he seek them or their maker, for he kept to the island's north. The boys helped him hunt, cook, and smoke a boar that day, and he sat with them over an evening meal near Takava's grave. He had already told them he would leave in the morning.

"How much longer will you stay?" he asked.

"Until the trial is over," the short one answered, "and we are warriors."

Hanuvar studied the indecision on their somber faces for a long moment before speaking. "I think your grandfathers would say you have passed your trial."

"Melgar is right," said Batera, Takava's brother, he of the raspy voice.

"You have a story to tell your elders," Hanuvar said.

"It is a story of our defeat," the short one said dispiritedly.

"Maybe you can have your own story some day. This is the tale of a beast, the last of its kind, who hunted your enemies for you, and an island that should be its sacred ground. But most of all it is the tale of a brave warrior who would have been a war chief."

"You mean Takava?" the short boy asked. "Women cannot be war chiefs." He opened his mouth as if to say more, but fell silent at Hanuvar's dour look.

"If your people had made no place for her at their fires, I would have made a place for her at mine."

Batera eyed him curiously. "In your city?"

"In the battles that lie ahead. I would have been glad for a keen-eyed warrior of good sense. Tell your chiefs that a general of Volanus said this."

"I will," Batera vowed, and the others nodded.

He left the next morning at sunrise. His last look back showed the boys readying their own gear for their hike to their boat. His eyes shifted to the palm waving over the deep grave where they'd buried the girl, then he turned his attention to the current, and the wind, and the long journey that lay before him.

❋ ❋ ❋

History tells us that every last Volani fell by their sword or was carted off to slavery, but that isn't entirely accurate. At this late day many of you likely know that in the years before the city's destruction, Hanuvar had led thousands away to found a hidden colony, and had in fact returned to Volanus to seek additional colonists, arriving just before Derva delivered his city's death blow.

But there were other survivors even than these. Hundreds of traders and sailors were absent during their city's conquest because they were travelling the Inner Sea. Hundreds more had grown wary about rumors of a renewed war with Derva and had already fled to other lands.

Lastly there were a handful, driven by personal ambition, cowardice, greed, or some combination thereof, who had thrown in their lot with the winning side.   —Sosilos, Book One

Chapter 3:
The Crypt of Stars

I

When the screaming stopped, Indar stepped to the long shadow of the outbuilding and expectantly watched its door. But no one exited, and as a low masculine moan from within the structure climbed into a panting wail, Indar retreated in discomfort.

His meeting with the general had been scheduled to start almost a half hour ago. Frowning, Indar considered the ocean, pale blue beyond the reefs and dark upon the horizon. The morning sun cast a shimmering pillar of bronze across the water.

He looked out from a low hill near the ancient Volani garrison. The red soil and palm trees presented a certain stark beauty, but the Isles of the Dead were no tropical paradise. Little fresh water fell upon the mazelike island group, and few edible plants rooted among the sun-blasted rocks. The soldiers formerly stationed to patrol the islands had always bemoaned duty at the garrison, and now the hundred-odd survivors of the Dervan invasion had even greater cause for complaint, for the enemy empire had them digging into the very graves they had sworn to protect. Indar heard the clink of their shovels and picks below the hill, along with the curses of overseers. They were worked long hours for the baubles concealed in minor graves, claiming that entrances to the tombs of the powerful Volani families scattered among the islets were hidden even from them. Indar had told the general that was almost certainly true.

There was some hope that the officers recently shipped from Volanus itself might be better informed.

Indar winced as the screaming rose to a crescendo, then abruptly ceased. Whether it was because the officer had finally decided to share the location of a tomb, or because he had passed out or died, Indar couldn't know. He hoped for the first, because that would put Mitrius in a much better mood.

A short while later the outbuilding door swung open and General Mitrius stepped blinking into the sunlight. Unaware of scrutiny, he pushed a hand up his high forehead and through his dark, receding hair.

Indar made his presence known by walking closer, then offered a formal bow and hand flourish.

Mitrius responded with a brief nod. Dark circles showed prominently under his eyes. His breastplate shone and the general held himself straight as a spear . . . yet his face had grown haggard in the week since Indar's arrival.

Mitrius closed the door behind him. He offered no apology for the delay as they trudged the long distance across the square toward the Volani officer quarters, now occupied by the general. The dry sand crunched beneath their sandals.

"A nasty business," the general confided. "Are you certain none of your contacts know anything? We would naturally reward them for information that produced results."

"What sort of rewards?"

The general looked at him sidelong. "Do you know something?"

Indar hadn't meant to imply knowledge he didn't possess. How could he so quickly forget the covetous Dervan interest in treasure? "I know the location of my own family's tombs, of course. But—"

Mitrius cut off this line of conversation with a decisive slice of his hand. "As I've said, they're inviolate. I have appreciated your counsel on Volani matters, but I think it's time to make better use of you. I want you to speak to the prisoners this evening before they eat. Offer any one of them their freedom if they reveal the location of a tomb."

"Me?" Indar could scarce believe the suggestion.

"They'll trust your word more than ours. Even if they don't like your politics, they must respect you."

Indar fought a laugh. While he knew he was no traitor, other Volani had been less charitable, and he thought these captured soldiers—likely every one of them an adherent of the Cabera family—would as soon kill him as look at him.

The general reached the door to his quarters, acknowledged the sentry's stiff salute with a nod, and placed his hand on the latch. "I'm prepared to offer concessions to any who step forward. If they see you, whose family prospers while they sit in chains, I think it might be considerable inducement."

The general opened the door and Indar followed into the reception area, bustling with well-manicured slaves in bright tunics. One of them closed the door, shutting out the blazing sun and the distant crack of whips.

II

Hanuvar had observed the garrison from the height of a craggy cliff for the last three days. Careful scrutiny had provided him with the numbers, habits, and patterns of the Dervans. There were less than a hundred of them. Likely more had been used in the assault against the garrison—for over three hundred Volani troops had been permanently stationed on the isles—but the bulk of the invading force must already have sailed back to the empire.

The Dervans prided themselves on their soldierly precision, and Hanuvar was grateful to them for it. He now knew the quarter hour when the sentries changed, the hour when the prisoners were fed, even the time when the Dervan general took his dinner.

He would have preferred to learn the names and habits of the enemy officers, but that would have required taking a prisoner, and the enemy would scurry like bugs if one of them went missing. Their schedule would change. He couldn't have that.

Hanuvar climbed carefully down from the cliff and picked his way along the rough shoreline hidden from above by a rocky overhang. It was early morning, and the sun was just cresting over the rust-colored cliffs, brightening the blood-red water of a narrow, shallow course to pink. Legend had it that Lord Vazhan begged the Lady Neer each day to release those souls given over to her shadowy realm. His greedy wife never relented, and thus he sorrowed, staining the water of the inner channels with tears of blood.

Hanuvar had seen the isles lashed with winds and rain on visits escorting honored dead. When the water cascaded down the cliffs, the rock and soil turned it red. And so he knew that even if the lord of the underworld wept somewhere, it was the isles themselves that painted the waters their sinister color.

Only his errand coaxed him into open ground. He had to obtain the gatzi[3] when they were at their most vulnerable. He moved swiftly between dusky purple shrubs that clung tenaciously to life on the rounded rocks. Yellow seabirds hung high overhead, almost motionless in the air currents.

As he climbed the slope a shadow set in the cliff resolved itself into the deeper darkness of a jagged cave mouth. It was from here the gatzi flew forth each evening. Their meals of choice were the scuttlers that scavenged over the outer beaches. Habitually the shelled creatures crawled up from the sea at night, and habitually the gatzi descended with their talons and razor jaws to devour them. Given the right stimulation, though, gatzi would attack nearly anything, and those unfortunate enough to stumble into a nest of the things seldom lived to tell of it.

The only folk Hanuvar knew who deliberately set out to find gatzi were suicides, sorcerers, or the occasional party sent to destroy them. Hunters were inevitably well armed with torches, spears, and protective gear, and even those brave souls never walked into a gatzi cave alone.

Hanuvar had no choice. He had fashioned thick gauntlets for his hands from canvas sacks that had once carried his supplies. Only two of those sacks remained, and these he bore over his shoulder, one sewn into the other. At his side hung a sword he'd brought from the distant isle of Narata. A fair blade, if not a fine one.

The stench of the cave hit him some twenty feet out. The gatzi

---

[3] These terrible nocturnal avian predators are almost never encountered beyond the continent of Kenasa and its close isles. While a variety of crabs form their primary diet, they easily frenzy over competition with their preferred prey, and have been known to attack and kill small bands of men and women who wander into their hunting grounds. As a result, they are hunted to extermination in all civilized lands. Volani legends state that a vengeful Nuvaran sorcerer king unleashed them against northern Kenasa when his legions refused to cross the deserts to subjugate the peoples there. Nuvaran scholars write instead that Volani sorcery created the beasts as a barrier to Nuvaran expansion and further claim this is why a vast multitude of gatzi reside to this day in the desolate Ingandi peninsula that extends eastward from Kenasa. While the truth may never be known, the wise reader should question whether any sorcerer has the power to fashion such a plague. —*Silenus*

den reeked of the dead things the ocean coughs up, fouler than the breath of a man dying from corruption.

As he trudged closer the odor grew stronger and somehow even more foul, and he paused to tie a cloth over his mouth and nose. It was neither as pretty as the painted masks the gatzi hunters wore, nor as thick. Its elegance did not matter to him; he only hoped he would be shielded enough from the fumes that he would not succumb.

He paused upon the threshold of the cave, staring into the darkness until his eyes adjusted. The floor was sticky with chalky, lumpy gatzi droppings. Here and there it moved, for it was home to tiny worms who thought the leavings the finest form of sustenance, and larger insects that preyed upon them. They grew, ate, bred, and died all in another creature's filth.

The cave was narrow and high. The gatzi would roost deep within, far from the hated sunlight.

Hanuvar advanced into the darkness, walking cautiously through the crunchy, writhing floor until the light behind was but a distant porthole. He breathed through his mouth, and even then the vapor was so pungent his eyes watered.

He almost missed the gatzi. Their front rank huddled on an outcropping just below eye level; Hanuvar could not count their numbers, but he sensed the shelf stretching back into a vast space. Those gatzi nearest the rim resembled a rock formation, and it was the sharp regularity of their outlines that drew his attention. They were identical lumpy bundles of feathers, each roughly the length of his arm and spaced two hand spans apart, arranged so precisely it looked like Dervan legion work. Every one of them had tucked its head under its right forewing.

Hanuvar had never thought to stand so close beside a single gatzi, let alone hundreds.

He unslung the sack from his shoulder, his heart quickening, and reached with one gloved hand to grasp the nearest at the base of its neck. It was surprisingly bony, and light. The gatzi stirred only a little at first, but it hissed after Hanuvar dropped it in the sack. By the time he had slid a second through the opening, the objection from the bag had grown louder.

Hanuvar snatched three more in swift succession and dropped

them in the bag. He hoped for nearly a dozen, but as he reached for another its head rose and he found himself mere inches from the open, stinking maw with its double rows of triangular teeth. He pulled back just as the beak snapped shut.

The monster that was the gatzi flock filled the chamber with echoing croaks, stirring the air with wings.

He thrust one last groggy one into his sack, then turned and ran for the light, the bumping, writhing, cawing bag held at arm's length from his body. Behind him came a whispering thunder of wings, the hiss from a hundred throats rivaling that of an asalda.

The cave mouth was so far away.

On he ran, splattering cave muck with every stride. At any moment he expected to feel the talons rend his arm, the awful, diseased maws shredding the back of his neck like saw-toothed daggers. Something brushed the back of his shoulder, his hair—

And then he was in the light, blinded with its brilliance, kissed by the heat. He lost his footing on the rocks and swept out his arms as he fell. He dropped the bag. He landed with a thump, slamming his palms into the stone to take most of the impact, just managing to keep his head from striking a rock.

He slitted his eyelids against the burning sun. A few black spots that were gatzi flapped out, circled dizzily, then fled back into the cavern. Hanuvar lay staring at a fluffy cloud, then chuckled. What would the Dervans have thought of their hated enemy if they could have seen him then? He was nothing but a frightened, clumsy old man. In a better world his roaming days would be through. A man his age should be soaking up the morning sun, swapping stories with old friends, and watching his family grow to dare adventures of their own.

But that would never be.

Hanuvar climbed to his feet. His left knee was sore again, as it so often was these days. The gatzi within the bag rustled feebly. He tied their prison shut and lifted it. The sun visible through the cloth would leave them stupefied.

He started for his overhang. Once, he'd been better at waiting, but now, whenever he was not active, his mind returned to his burning city and to its butchered people, and his daughter, and his brothers. Once there had been four. Now there was only himself, and the ashes of his baby brother. Melgar would be the last of them ever interred within the family crypt.

III

The Volani had simmered with anger the moment Indar entered their midst, a fury so pronounced he sensed they might attack him even though spear-bearing legionaries ringed them. Had they greater savvy, they would have bowed their heads to him and begged forgiveness. They remained under the sway of the Cabera family, no matter the doom that allegiance had brought them.

The evening wind sapped the sun of its burning power, though its warmth was still heavy in the air. An image of Volanus rose unbidden to the forefront of his memory, with its cool evening breezes rustling leaves on the boulevards beneath the silver towers. He knew a sudden pang of loss.

One of the two soldiers flanking him cleared his throat.

Drilled in oration since his youth, it still took Indar a moment to gather his thoughts. He had practiced his speech for an hour, and now gave his audience the sympathetic frown he thought provided his best opening. "I've watched you for days, wondering what I could do for you. You're victims. You were tricked, led down a path that your leaders could have seen, if they'd any kind of forethought. It isn't your fault. You were told to trust them. And now you're here."

"Traitor!" one of them shouted, and grumbles of assent rose from the throng.

The soldiers at Indar's side tensed, but he raised a hand. "I know you're angry! You were soldiers, serving our city. And you didn't ask for this! But I swear I am not your enemy! Who really brought you to this point? Where is your council? Where's Hanuvar? They're the ones who told you the Dervans could be bested. Had they listened to my father, you would not now sit here as prisoners."

Someone yelled something foul about his father and one of the legionaries beside him grumbled. Indar had been impressed by the number of Dervan soldiers posted here who understood Volani and supposed it had been someone's clever choice. He motioned the man to stand easy.

"My family urged peaceful surrender!" Indar said. "We knew the might of Derva! Had the Seven possessed even a modicum of the vaunted wisdom they claimed, they would have seen what we saw. But because of them, you sit in bondage. Where are the shofets and the hallowed Seven? Most cowered in the temples." Repetition of the Dervan lie would only bolster their sense of unjust suffering. While it was true Belevar had hidden in a temple and sobbed for mercy, five had died by their swords or on them, even ancient Mevlia.

He managed greater conviction as he spoke on, for he knew, just as his father had long warned, that the Cabera family had guided Volanus to ruin. "And what of your great protector, Hanuvar? He didn't even turn up until the city was aflame! Dervan power flung him into the sea."

He paused to look over the weary faces of the hundred who watched. "The Cabera family brought you no lasting victories," he continued. "They doomed our city with their deliberate provocations. But you need not be doomed. Life need not be such a trial. If any one of you aids the empire, he could live as free as I. Derva rewards its allies. Think of it. You'd have comforts like wine, and fine food, and regular baths. And you wouldn't have to spend the rest of your life in the baking sun digging up old bones. I ask you only to *consider* my offer this night. If any of you knows the location of an important tomb, you will be rewarded the moment you step forward." Indar held up his hands. "Now this is a weighty thing, and I want no hasty decisions. Think on it for the night. Remember that the dead are dead. It is time now to think of the welfare of the living."

The faces that stared back at him were drawn and somber. He couldn't guess their thoughts, but he pressed on, hoping he'd led them to consider a changed perspective and witness a spark of hope. He wagered these qualities might weigh against stubborn Volani pride. "I'll speak with you tomorrow after the morning meal. For now, I bid you a good night."

A few cursed at him as he turned away. He didn't respond. Some would step forth in the morning, if protection were offered. He'd have to make sure they were immediately whisked away from the others.

The general's priest had watched from beside the ring of soldiers, and the little scarlet-robed man joined Indar as he left the prisoners.

"I think that was well said," the priest declared, his diction precise, his tone faintly nasal, as though distorted by traveling the length of his long straight nose. "You have a wise way for such a young man."

"Thank you." Indar didn't feel that twenty-six years was especially young. He had already been married and divorced, and supervised the family holdings during the long months of his father's absences. But that was nothing to the Dervans, who seemed only to value men with gray at their temples.

The priest's robes swished against his thighs as he walked. His placid face turned to Indar's. "You may well inspire a change in attitude."

"One of them is bound to be smart enough, or miserable enough, to speak out."

"I prayed at length this afternoon," the priest continued. They strode on across open, rocky ground for the living quarters. "And I spread the sacred bones. A momentous change is on the wind. I'm not sure what it entails for you."

The priest's smile was still affable, but his eyes were cold. What was he after?

"I am a friend to Derva," Indar said. "I desire only peace between our peoples."

"Oh, of that I am certain."

Indar feigned politeness. "What did you learn from the bones?" He knew the priest wished him to ask.

"They spoke of conflict, and a dead man. He is a man of some importance. I trust for your sake that the bones mean you will lead us to a dead man. I would hate to think that you would meet with any sort of unfortunate incident."

"That's very considerate of you."

"Your father would certainly be disappointed. I know he has high hopes for you at the court." The odious little man cleared his throat. "Darkness comes. I have duties. You should report to the general. Good evening. May the Night Wise guard your steps."

"And may their blessings guide you." Indar pressed hands to forehead and bowed. He watched the priest leave, wondering if he hurried off to care for the mewling thing he kept in the wicker basket beside his window. Indar had no desire to find out.

IV

Once the gatzi smelled the planks where Hanuvar smeared broken crabs, they sped into the night like arrows. The poor sentry didn't have a chance. He'd knelt to examine the carcasses piled upon his patrol route, which ensured he was not only closer to the scent but that he smelled more strongly of it. One moment he was a dark form hunched on the dock, the next he was a screaming and writhing mass collapsing under the devouring assault.

Hanuvar no longer knew the number of men he'd slain, but he'd seldom been responsible for so gruesome an end. He preferred quick deaths for his enemies, as he'd delivered to the other Dervan sentry whose scarlet tunic, cuirass, dangling baltea, and helm he now wore. The helmet was a bit loose, but Hanuvar didn't expect anyone to notice at night.

He heard the rest of the Dervan watch before he saw them, shouting from the wall above. Then came footsteps on the stone, cries to aid a downed man, and the postern gate was thrown open. Four soldiers rushed onto the docks.

Hanuvar slipped into the garrison.

He kept to the shadows as shouts rang out, walking swiftly for the old stone mess hall. All Volani captives were housed there, for the garrison had no prison, and the mess was the only room large enough to contain them under a minimal guard.

The Dervans had set thick metal loops on either side of the hall doors, which were locked by placement of an iron bar. Hanuvar carefully supported the bar so it wouldn't clang against the loops as he slid it free. Once it was clear, he set it in the shadows and swiftly stepped inside, closing the door behind him.

"Olmar," he said softly.

The room's only light slipped through high windows, recently bricked by the Dervans so that they were too small to accommodate escape. By it he saw those within the dark chamber had not even the luxury of blankets. They slept curled on the bare floor, their arms or bunched-up shirts for pillows. A few sat up at Hanuvar's call. They smelled of sweat and blood and hopelessness. Some few among them, he knew, were women, not just Eltyr, but the wives of soldiers.

He pulled off the helmet. "Olmar," he said again, and stepped deeper into the room.

"Hanuvar—" said a voice, and then the silent forms were sitting or climbing to their feet. His name leapt from mouth to mouth, like fire spreading among the grain fields. Some cried that it could not be, others that he was a ghost. One laughed, madly, saying that he was there to rescue them, and even though Hanuvar was certain the Dervans were distracted, he worried the noise would bring them running.

"Silence!" he ordered. "Keep from the door!"

The captives ceased their gabbling, and those inching toward the portal halted their progress. They strained for better view of the figure before them.

"General?" One of the men limped forward. Hanuvar knew the low-pitched voice, but not the limp. That was new.

"Commander Olmar." He'd recognized him during the long days of watching, one of his brother Adruvar's best officers.

The figure halted a few paces off. "It *is* you—but you're dead . . ." There was a frightened quaver in the man's voice. "You fell into the sea."

Hanuvar spoke quickly. "I am no spirit. I am a man, and I have come to save you."

They began to chatter again, in joyous disbelief, but Hanuvar threw up his hands. "Quiet! We've little time. Listen to me, and you will soon sail free. Olmar. Come here."

Olmar walked forward, favoring his right leg, a thickly built man with a wild mane of hair. "General?"

"They want our tombs. I want you to give them one. My wife's family's." He could only hope, when he saw her in the afterlife, that Imilce and her forebearers would understand.

Olmar gasped in astonishment.

"I will tell you where to find it, and a handful of other tombs. We must be prepared to make this sacrifice." Hanuvar turned his back to the others and whispered its location to Olmar, confiding to him the placement of several more. The officer nodded, replying in the affirmative when Hanuvar asked him if he understood.

"There's much I would know," Hanuvar said, "but we'll talk after." He turned to address the throng. Even though he could not see their eyes, he felt their attention fixed upon his every move.

"How many of you are fluent in Dervan?"

Nine raised their hands, and when he asked how many spoke it with little to no accent, only three arms remained. "Make sure you accompany Olmar tomorrow. Claim they have some special knowledge," he told the officer.

Olmar nodded sharply. "Yes, General."

Hanuvar could almost sense the sand grains falling in the hourglass. If some alert sentry were to wander by and seal the mess hall, everything he'd worked for would be lost. Yet he could not depart until he'd given them tangible hope. He addressed them once more. "In the morning, Olmar will guide some of the Dervans to a tomb. Do your best to loot it dry, so the Dervans will grow eager, and Olmar will tell them where others are. Once they transport you there to begin work, await my word. Then we'll strike. And then you'll be free."

Hanuvar smote the Dervan breastplate, then turned for the door. He left without a backward glance.

Outside the air was clean and cool. No one seemed to have observed his exit. He sealed his people in their prison, stepped clear of the building . . . and saw the postern gate was shut. A half dozen soldiers clustered beside it. A man with a centurion's lateral crested helmet cursed them. Had they noticed a missing man yet? Had they already carried in the gatzi victim?

The Dervans had moved even faster than he'd feared. He would have to rely on his backup exit. Without hesitation Hanuvar walked for a set of stone stairs to the upper level. A soldier was walking the crenelated wall above. "Is he going to make it?" the fellow called down.

"I don't know," Hanuvar answered in accentless Dervan. "He wasn't moving."

As he climbed he saw the shutters opening in a window built into the wall below the stairs. Was someone looking out at him? He glanced back, knew a chill when light reflected off eyes too round to be human. No time to worry about that—he headed into the gloom.

The wall looked very different from this side, but he had measured carefully. On his left was the flat, dark expanse of the garrison compound, on his right the merlons of the outer wall. Beyond that lay a drop to the sloping shore, save for a narrow stretch...there. He checked both ways once more, stepped quickly to the battlement and hung by his hands. The sea lapped the wall below.

The soldier Hanuvar had spoken with heard a splash and strode over to investigate, calling out to the man he'd seen. But Hanuvar, pulling off armor beneath the waves, didn't hear. It would have been ideal to swim with both the helm and the breastplate, but that was one miracle too many for him to work in a single night. They would have to remain on the seabed.

V

"I felt certain one of them would come forward," Indar said. "But I didn't expect it would be Olmar."

A half-eaten biscuit sat in a saucer on the general's desk, next to a few white dunaline rinds and some empty eggshells. Indar had not been asked to breakfast with the general this morning. He had begun to suspect Mitrius didn't like him, perhaps because of their age difference, or Indar's friendship with the emperor's favorite nephew. Or it might be the general had realized Indar's star was rising, while his own was surely waning. Else why would he have been given so miserable a post?

"You told me you had good news," the general said.

"He'll give us the location of a large crypt. And," Indar could not help pausing for effect, "it's the tomb of the Idresta family."

The general's eyebrows rose precipitously. "The family of Hanuvar's wife?"

"Yes, General. Olmar had attended a family burial. One of Hanuvar's brothers by marriage. And Olmar's brother was one of the Vazhan priests, those sworn to oversee the sacred isles. He showed Olmar the locations of some of the other noble tombs as well."

The general frowned. Indar wondered if anything made him smile.

"He knew all that, and confessed nothing under torture?"

"I..." Indar couldn't dredge up any sort of clever answer.

The general sighed. "It makes one wonder as to the efficacy of our methods."

Indar had no doubt as to the effectiveness of Dervan torture. He was certain he would have happily told them whatever they wished if he'd even been shown the instruments, much less endured their attentions. He flushed, feeling vulnerable and foolish.

General Mitrius, he realized, was talking. ". . . wishes his own freedom for this information?"

"He asks for comforts for all his men."

The general's frown deepened and he sat back in his chair. "What specifically did he ask for?"

"Actual beds, with mattresses. More substantial meals. More breaks. No whips for men he swears will labor honestly."

"It's not so much," the general said. "He knew we couldn't grant all of them freedom, and so rather than asking solely for himself, he asked only for those under him to be treated like men. I wonder, Indar, if I would have done the same in his place?"

Indar hesitated, unsure how to answer. "You would not have allowed yourself to be in such a situation, General. Your intelligence—"

"There will always be a victor and a vanquished, young man. Only the gods know which one will win out. I will meet their demands, but they must first show me proof. Let us take two dozen of them to one of these burial sites and see if anything is there."

"Yes, General."

"And if there is, then maybe you, at least, can return to Derva and leave these accursed islands."

Indar heard bitterness there, and sought to mollify the general's feelings. "I'm sure you will be able to return soon yourself."

Mitrius' frown deepened. "I don't know if you heard last night, but we lost two men. Gatzi killed one near the docks. He seems to have stumbled on them while they were eating. A gruesome death. We think another might have been attacked by some on the battlement and fallen into the water, but we've found no sign of his body."

"I'm sorry to hear that." Indar hoped that it wasn't a swarming year. If it was, there would be much worse in the days ahead.

"We shouldn't be here, pecking at the ground like chickens," Mitrius continued sourly. "This place is for the dead, not the living."

"That may be so," Indar conceded with a forced smile, "but the emperor will surely be pleased with a new source of wealth for Derva's coffers."

The general's tone changed abruptly, like the shutting of a door. "Go speak to Olmar. Tell him I accept his offer, provided I receive proof today. Have Olmar pick his twenty best men. Remind them the faster they work, the faster we can all depart these wretched islands."

"Yes, General." Indar bowed and left, thankful the sinister priest was nowhere in evidence. He'd begun to suspect the man was spying on him.

By midday a cadre of wretched prisoners was boarding one of the captured Volani ships. The general left more than half his contingent at the old garrison, assured he had men aplenty to shepherd the remaining Volani.

Indar watched the great red cliffs as they sailed south through the labyrinth of tiny islands. How many of his ancestors were interred within? What did they think when they looked down on him? Did they, too, think him a traitor?

He had turned his back on the fools who drove Volanus to death, and his father had seen to it the family would live on as valued servants to the Dervan Empire, but this was different. He revered his ancestors and their accomplishments. Was that why he still felt so troubled?

Then again, his unease might be because whenever he turned he found the priest's eyes upon him. He was seated further back along the deck. The fellow would smile, nod pleasantly, and look away— and then stare at him once more. What did he want? What was he watching for?

Worse was the wicker basket beside the priest. A scent of dirty feathers drifted from it. Occasionally it rocked a little and the priest hushed it tenderly.

Indar was glad he had a knife at his belt. He might not be able to take down one of these soldiers, but if he had to, he was certain he could kill the priest.

VI

The Dervans had been thrilled with the riches in the tomb and, just as Hanuvar had supposed, quickly erected a temporary camp closer to the wealth and relocated their prisoners there. It wasn't just that the Dervans were eager for the treasures. They wanted to complete their mission so they could put these desolate islands behind them.

He moved against the new camp in the deep night after the prisoners had been transferred. One by one he struck down the three sentries. Before too long the Volani most fluent in Dervan were in legionary armor and pretending to guard their fellow prisoners. Olmar and ten other Volani followed Hanuvar over the rocky ground, shovels and picks in hand.

After an hour's walk, they set to work on an unassuming block of stone around the cliffside from the camp. Hanuvar spoke only to guide their efforts.

They had but two lanterns, shutters directing ghostly beams upon the scarlet-striated rocks. Olmar kept watch. The soldier did not speak of what the Dervans had done to him, but he often grimaced as he moved. He had insisted upon accompanying them, and Hanuvar had not gainsaid him.

It took nearly an hour to clear the dried, baked soil from the stone slab, another quarter hour and the combined efforts of nine strong men to leverage it from the square of darkness it concealed.

They worked wordlessly, out of both respect for the dead and the desire to avoid detection. Aside from his own instruction and the occasional grunt or low oath, the only noise was the clink of spade or pick and the rising wind, moaning through the canyons. Dark clouds drifted overhead, blanketing all but a narrow strip of sky through which a sliver of the moon shone whitely down.

When at last they had dragged the protesting rock clear of the hole, Hanuvar called for Olmar, replaced him with a dour younger man, and descended the dark stairs with a lantern. All but the sentry came with him.

It was cool down there in the old stone. A short walk brought them to a round chamber with a black marble table built around an empty urn. Here had offerings been made to the dead of his family.

A stark relief of Vazhan wept on the wall, leaning over the table, his colors long since faded. Hanuvar recalled his appearance from his last visit, noting then that someone should see to repainting his tears. His cousin had promised to do so.

"Olmar," Hanuvar said without looking from the relief, "do you know anything of my cousins' fates?"

"Not with certainty, General." Olmar's voice was grim.

"They are dead," Hanuvar said.

"That is what we've heard. But I know no details."

Hanuvar asked the question for which he dreaded the answer. "And my daughter?"

"They say she was taken. Her husband died in the street, fighting."

So Narisia lived. But what kind of life might that be? And how long would it last? He followed that painful question with another. "When I left, she thought she might be pregnant. Did she have children?"

"She had two. I do not know their fates."

He steadied himself against this wrenching news by looking only at the weeping relief. "How many of our people did the Dervans take alive, Olmar?"

The commander was slow in answering. When he did so, his voice was weak. "Less than a thousand."

Hanuvar stared at the man in disbelief, for a vast multitude had called Volanus home [4]

"We fought them," Olmar said, his voice thin. "Block by block. House by house. Until there was no place left to retreat. The temple to Vazhan and Lady Neer was aflame, and some fell back to die within its walls."

Knowing that the death count would be terrible, he had still not guessed it would be so high, and he struggled to comprehend the staggering enormity of the loss. He failed.

"After that, when they had us in chains, there was a fire in the larger prisoner enclosure. I could hear them screaming that night..." Olmar's voice trailed off, and then he found the strength to continue. "It wasn't a war. It was an extermination."

Hanuvar forced calm upon himself, and focused upon the present. "There are weapons here," he said. "We will need them in the coming hour. And hereafter."

---

[4] The emperor's census of Derva at the time calculated that there were well over 750,000 citizens and slaves residing in the empire's capital. Estimates are that Volanus housed less than a third that number, but even still, that means some 250,000 souls called Volanus and its suburbs home at the time of the city's destruction. Disregarding a few thousand who fled as the invading army closed in, it is difficult even now to contemplate the vast numbers who fell, for according to records, only a little over 1,200 people survived to be taken into slavery. Several long months were to pass before Hanuvar himself gained access to these more accurate numbers. —*Silenus*

He had never heard the voices of the gods as the priests did, but for the first time in weeks he had prayed to them that morning, wondering all the while why they should aid him now when they had allowed the empire to destroy Volanus. Hearing Olmar's grim tidings he was sure they were deaf, or dead, or only a dream.

"General?" Olmar prompted.

Hanuvar turned and faced them, the lantern deepening the hollows in his face. "This is the tomb of my family, down from the days of founding, and I bear with me the ashes of my brother, Melgar. He's the last of us who shall ever be interred within. And we are the last who shall ever pay homage here."

They waited for him to speak on, and he wished he knew all their names. There wasn't time.

"Since the founding, only those of our bloodline have passed through this portal. Yet you may cross it with me this day. There are so few of us left. We are all one now." He turned to the relief and pressed in upon the eyes, hard. The ancient magics worked a final time, and an eerie whistle rose from deep within the stone. The hairs along his arm and back of his neck stood quivering.

The old stone image sank slowly down. Before them loomed what at first seemed an underground lake, for the lantern beams that played over the space reflected off a liquid surface. And then those with him beheld what only the family of Cabera had looked upon for generations, a stone walkway built across an ocean of quicksilver, forever lapping the shores of the miniature inner and outer seas spread to either side of the path. Hanuvar heard the men talking in wonder as they walked on, pointing to the isles, the carved peaks and hills that rose from the ancient map. Someone noticed that diamonds were worked into the ceiling, arranged in the constellations, shining forever above the changeless sea. There too was a great emerald, along the shore. Eternal Volanus. Here in the tomb it still shone in all its beauty. And here in the tomb did his city belong.

A metal door set with gold waited at the path's end, his family's crest of a swift ship with a soaring bird above carved into its surface. Hanuvar pulled upon the handle and the heavy portal swung easily outward.

Beyond, the bodies and urns of the centuries of Cabera dead lay in ranks of stone niches, stretching into the darkness. And here, too, to either side of the door, his lantern gleamed upon a martial display of swords and shields.

"They're treated with draden oil," Hanuvar said, "by the young men of our family each time someone is interred within. All but the oldest of these should be free of rust."

"You didn't say there would be armor too," one man said in nearly breathless awe.

"They're beautiful," said another, stepping forward to tentatively caress a hilt.

The arms and armaments had once been meant to honor the spirits of the men who had worn them. Now, though, the living needed them far more. "Dress in the armor. Carry as many weapons as you can. And then we return to camp. We must capture and crew the ship before dawn."

"But where do we go?"

"I'll tell you after our victory." They could not know— yet. What if the attack failed? "Ready yourselves. I have a duty to perform." Only then did he lift the flask from his belt. It was a poor container compared to those upon the biers glittering with gold and jewels, carved with swordsmen and ships. "It's time to carry out the last wishes of my brother." He took one of the lanterns and left with it for the tomb's recesses, leaving the men among the shining weapons.

His sandals slapped over the cold, dark stone, his lantern's light flickering over the dusty bones, and his thoughts sped down through the years. Here was his grandfather's skull, and he recalled kissing that forehead a final time as they laid him there. Here were the bones of his aunt, and his baby sister.

Here was his father's niche, empty for want of a body slain by Dervans and left for carrion. Hanuvar caressed the carven letters of his name. What would his father say to him now? Memories crowded for place like little children vying for attention. How young *had* he been on that first campaign with Father? He didn't know, could scarce recall a time when an army camp had not been his home. He had wanted nothing more than to stand worthy in that man's eyes and to emulate all that he was. Later he realized that glory had been thrust upon his sire, that his father stood the line because there was none better. Given a softer world, Himli Cabera would gladly have been a gardener.

Hanuvar no longer wondered what he might have been, only what he might have said had he been granted more days with those he loved. This night, so close to the bed that should have been his father's last, he longed again to hear that calm, commanding voice. What would his father have done in his place? What counsel would he offer now?

He would urge him to waste no time.

Hanuvar stepped away. From far off, he heard his companions carefully donning armor.

Fabric yet clung to Adruvar's frame, the mighty hands withered and still across his powerful chest. There lay Harnil, his crooked smile dust; death had reduced his handsome features to a grinning mockery and robbed him of distinctive identity.

He set Melgar's ashes in an unmarked niche. The youngest of the four, he'd been the brashest of them all. A brilliant swordsman, and brave to a fault. After he'd survived that chest wound, the slash that cost him his left arm and the illness that followed, Hanuvar had thought Melgar unkillable. But he'd sickened in the new colony, and on his deathbed asked only that Hanuvar bear him to the family tomb. Legends said that those close to death often saw the future, but Melgar must surely not have done so, or he would have foreseen that when Hanuvar's ship neared Volanus the Dervans would be at the city's neck.

Hanuvar knelt by his brothers one last time, his eyes straying to the stone bed that would surely have been his own, someday, had there been anyone to carry him here after his death. He would die in some far-off, lonely land, and his bones would spend eternity in a Dervan trophy case.

This moment, though, was for his brother. He bowed his head and began to pray.

VII

Indar awoke to horror, and knew a pressure against his chest. It was the quiet of the deep night, yet there was light in his tent, and by it he saw a black, skull-like face looming over him. He failed to scream only because he choked on an air bubble as he sucked in a breath.

The stinking black-feathered creature with scalloped wings

chattered angrily at him, and he felt its claws through the blankets as it shifted its catlike weight. The priest looked down at him on one side, a soldier with a lantern on the other.

"You sleep deeply," the priest said.

"What is this?" Indar demanded more shrilly than he planned.

"You are coming with us."

"Why?" Indar's voice broke in fear.

"Because I have found you out, Indar."

The creature hopped off his chest and watched unblinking from the edge of the bedroll.

Indar sat up quickly so it would not return. "What are you talking about?"

"You pretend it well. But my little servant has seen your friends."

"I have no idea what you're talking about." Indar was surprised to hear annoyance in his voice. He would have assumed he'd project only his gripping terror.

"We will see. Dress and come."

The priest left the tent, thankfully taking the hideous creature with him. The legionary remained, scowling.

Indar threw on his clothing. Outside he found a dozen unhappy soldiers, as well as General Mitrius. Upon Indar's emergence they set out at a brisk walk into the night, the priest leading, and Indar soon saw that they were leaving the camp. "Where are we going?"

"To meet your smuggler friends," the priest answered.

Indar fell in step beside him. A thin sliver of moon painted everything in whites and blacks.

"I don't know any smug—"

"You make things worse for yourself, Indar," Mitrius said wearily.

"Palhecoc saw them at work on a tomb," the priest said. "And told me of it." He rubbed a finger under the chin of the thing on his shoulder.

"It was not our men," Mitrius said. "Our sentries and guards are in place and report all prisoners accounted for. Therefore they must be yours. For who else might have alerted them?"

Indar struggled for inspiration. How was he going to convince the general he hadn't been involved in whatever was underway?

"I swear by my grandfather's name that I know nothing of this," he said finally.

"Oh, don't play innocent." The priest sounded pleased. "You must have a ship waiting nearby. You sent word to them once you finally knew the location of a tomb. Weren't the riches the emperor had already given your family enough to satisfy you?"

"That's ridiculous!" Indar could hear the conviction in his own voice. Surely the priest did as well. "General, I'm a man of my word, you know it!"

"I know that you work against your own people," the officer replied stiffly.

"You're wrong," Indar snapped, wondering why he felt rage at the same time he knew numbing fear. "You will see I have nothing to do with any nonsanctioned operation and—" Indar's voice trailed off. He'd been contemplating a threat, and remembered he was surrounded by men who'd kill him at a word.

It was a long, grim walk, and his heart sped the entire way. The general commanded his soldiers to quiet. The only conversation was that whispered back and forth between the eldritch creature and the priest. Indar was mostly thankful he did not understand them.

He guessed it was some three quarters of an hour into the journey when the priest sent his winged horror flying ahead. He'd had the men shutter the lanterns before they rounded a corner of a cliff. A channel of water no larger than a stream stretched along their right, and a jagged rock wall stood upon their left, heavy with shadows and shallow caves.

There was no sign of any ships—which presumably one would see if there were smugglers or thieves about—but Indar said nothing. Better if he remain completely silent, so as to give no cause for censure from the priest.

A dark shape winged out of the night and settled with a flap of wings on the ground before the priest. Indar gave an involuntary shudder. The thing bowed, then chattered at its master.

"It has slain one of them," the priest relayed after a moment. "A sentry, I think."

"Let us see," said Mitrius.

The creature bounded ahead, flapping its wings determinedly until it had lift. It settled down beside a body, then tore at its neck with the claws spurred along the back of its long fingers.

"You, look ahead," Mitrius commanded, pointing two men forward. "Here is your man, Indar."

"That's not—" Indar stared. "That's one of the prisoners, General. Olmar's friend with the missing fingers." While the bulging, staring eyes distorted the young man's visage, there was no mistaking the scraggly beard, the thick eyebrows, or the digits absent from the left hand.

Mitrius peered down at the body. "He's right."

"There's an opening here, with stairs going down," the centurion called to them.

"Someone's found and opened a tomb," the priest said to Mitrius.

The general frowned.

"As I said," Indar declared with stiff dignity, "I had no knowledge of this."

The general paid him no heed. Indar wondered, as the general's gaze turned on him, if he would apologize. But Mitrius faced his soldiers. "This prisoner had a weapon. There are surely more, and they're likely armed. Some of our workers must have gotten free. Stay alert."

"What would prisoners want with a tomb?" Indar asked, glad to be so obviously innocent. "Wouldn't they just escape?"

"Riches, of course," the priest answered without looking at him. He scooped up his beast. "We will stop them."

General Mitrius called for lights once they arrived at the stairs. They descended the flight in twos, Mitrius and the centurion first, followed by the priest and Indar, then the rest of them. In moments they had reached an antechamber, and Indar scanned the walls. So too did the priest, and the two of them spoke breathlessly, almost as one as they recognized the Volani lettering. "The tomb of Cabera."

"This is Hanuvar's family," Indar said.

The priest chuckled. "Well, these slaves have done us a favor! The emperor himself will hear about this find!"

The legionaries marveled at the quicksilver lake beyond, and goggled at the immense map, taking in its beauty even before they noticed the riches set into the stone of the landmasses, a jewel sparkling at the site of every city. "Hands away," the priest said. "My pet is watching. This is all for the emperor!"

Mitrius took the whole thing in, looking troubled. Indar understood his thinking. What could the prisoners possibly want with the tomb of their dead hero's family? Of all sacred ground, surely this was the last they would ever have wished to disturb.

The general led them across a stone walkway that bisected the map and started across the gem-studded expanse of continent. He had almost arrived at the steps to a gilded door when it opened before him. He backed away, grasping his hilt.

In the open door, backlit by a blinding radiance, stood a man in armor. He was lean, powerful, with high, broad shoulders. There was no mistaking that proud hooked nose, the silver-flecked hair, the slate-gray eyes. In the shining armor he looked for all the world like some war god descended to mortal realms.

Indar's blood chilled, and he stammered out what he knew, what many of the Dervans doubtless knew: "It's Hanuvar!" He didn't say that he'd returned from the dead, that he'd risen from his own tomb. Indar knew it, just as every man there knew it. Even General Mitrius froze.

The dead man leapt with a savage war cry. Too late did Mitrius throw up his parry. Hanuvar's sword cleft bone and brain and dropped him. Hanuvar ducked a swing from the centurion and plunged his red blade into the armpit gap of his cuirass. The officer screamed and fell backward into a carved mountain range.

Behind Indar the legionaries cried out to their gods. Ahead, framed in the doorway, came more dead of the Cabera clan, each clad in shining armor.

The priest urged his pet forward but Hanuvar cut it down in midflight. The priest was still gaping stupidly as the sword sliced off his head.

"Spare me!" Indar cried. "I'm Volani!" And he threw himself flat.

Hanuvar's ghost leapt over him, swinging at another legionary.

The Dervan soldiers screamed and ran.

"Chase them down!" Hanuvar roared, and his men raced after, splashing through the cold, silver fluid.

Indar was hefted into the air by the scruff of his tunic. The blazing eyes of the vengeful wraith stared into his own.

"You've soiled yourself," Hanuvar said.

"Spare me—"

"Will you offer me riches?" The ghost's voice dripped contempt. "What will you give me? My cousins' lives? My daughter's?" His voice shook. "My city?" He pointed the sword at the younger man's throat.

"I followed my father!" he said.

And for some reason that gave the spirit pause, for the sword thrust did not come. Instead the ghost bore him backward and slammed him hard into the wall. Indar gasped in pain, felt something give behind him. A lever, he realized with a sickening lurch. Many Volani tombs had them, and at their trigger the tombs would be sealed by falling rock. He cried out in fear at the sound of a great rumble from the doorway where Hanuvar had come, but the roof held steady. A dense cloud of dust wafted out from the entry to the crypt.

Hanuvar dropped him.

Indar, crouching in the quicksilver beside the path, trembled under the dead general's gaze.

"Live long, boy," the spirit said. It walked toward the distant clash of steel. "Squeeze every moment from it that you can, for you bought it dearly. If our gods yet live, they will not be kind to you in the hereafter."

And then he was swallowed by the darkness.

Indar found that he was sobbing with dread. Even if he had desired to retreat deeper into the tomb he could not, for he was certain nothing lay beyond the doorway but crumbled stone. And he dared not follow the spirits, so he sat in misery beside the bodies of the Dervans, under a thousand diamond stars.

VIII

In a little over an hour they had surprised and overpowered the rest of the Dervan legionaries. By the next evening, the surviving enemy soldiers had finished loading supplies aboard a captured patrol ship. Hanuvar left them alive on the shore and bade Olmar guide the craft along the eastern rim of the isles. Only then, at the prow, did he speak to Olmar of their destination. "Our colony lies in the far southeast. Two weeks beyond the mountains of fire and the isles where the leopards run. Steer toward the top star in Sedrasta's horn." He presented him with a handful of gemstones culled from the tombs they'd plundered thoroughly. "Revictual at the isle of Narata in the eastern Lenidines. You know it?"

Olmar nodded slowly. Once, he had captained a ship in the fleet. "I do. It's tiny and remote."

"A priestess advises the rulers there. See that no one learns your final destination. It must be secret. Our people must remain safe."

"This is all true?" Olmar asked. There was a tremor in his voice. "There is a new Volanus?"

"It's but a few thousand folk." When Hanuvar had returned to Volanus, he'd hoped to lure a few thousand more to join him there. It was best not to dwell on what might have happened if he'd arrived even two months earlier. "Now. You need to stop at this island." Hanuvar pointed. "I left my skiff on its far side."

Something in his tone alerted Olmar. "You're not coming?"

"There is more that I must do."

"Hanuvar—"

"There are other survivors, aren't there?" Hanuvar asked him. "Scattered through the empire?"

"Of course. But not all of them will be close to ships. They will be slaves, trapped deep in Dervan lands. They may be too weak to travel. It's impossible. There's no hope for them. Come with us and live."

"Was there hope for you?" Hanuvar demanded.

Olmar fell silent in surprise.

Hanuvar had not meant to sound so caustic. His voice was softer as he turned. "I will find a way, or I will make one."

The men and women scarcely knew what to say as they neared the beach and Hanuvar took the rowboat to shore. They called to him, blessed him, thanked him, watched him stride into the darkness. They did not expect to see him again.

▨ ▨ ▨

Elsewhere, though, were others who felt sure he would be seen, for word spread quickly, borne first by official Dervan reports and then by rumors that grew in the telling. Hanuvar had risen from the tomb of his ancestors to wreak vengeance upon the Dervan Empire, a legion of undead warriors at his call, and he would not lie down again until his people were avenged and the emperor himself perished screaming on the altar to his dark gods.

Thus did Hanuvar free the first of his people, in the weeks before I met him in Hidrestus. There, in the largest Dervan city upon the empire's eastern rim, he found more, slated for battle in the local arena. And while their liberation seemed a relatively simple matter, other minds had planned darker schemes. In truth, it was a wonder any of us escaped alive.   —Sosilos, Book One

Chapter 4:
The Second Death of Hanuvar

I

The clack of dulled swords receded as the overseer led Jerissa from the practice arena. Outside, in the larger compound, likewise walled in gray stone, all was quiet apart from the endless, dispirited patter of rain against the sated earth and the decrepit roof tiles. The muted light of the gray skies did no favors to the sagging mess hall and the rest of the buildings. Three barracks stood empty, their doorways open only to darkness. Jerissa guessed the old gladiator school must once have housed three to four times as many fighters. Now it was home only to Jerissa's women and their minders.

"Up the stairs, Eltyr," the overseer said gruffly.

She knew his name was Kerthik, although she'd never called him that, just as he'd never used her real name. At first the generic "woman" was the least offensive appellation he'd employed, but after the initial week the insults had halted altogether, and he had referred to her simply by the name of her sacred corps. Whenever he addressed Jerissa now, it was as "Eltyr."

She'd never taken the stairs, which led to the wall's height. Earlier today she'd looked up from the practice yard to see the school's owner watching from a jutting balcony with a uniformed centurion and a well-dressed brown man. Presumably Lurcan wanted a word with her, although she couldn't imagine why. She was training her charges the best she was able, and their improvement had been remarkable.

No one logical could complain. But then it was foolish to look for logic from Dervans, or perhaps, from the world in general.

The stairs creaked under her tread and she noted the red paint on the finely carven balustrade was chipped and fading. As a native of Volanus, she had little experience with Dervan gladiator schools, but she assumed they were usually maintained more scrupulously than this.

Inside the walls of the training arena she heard her sergeant shouting at someone to block with the flat, not the edge, and shook her head.

"They're shaping up," Kerthik said behind her. That had sounded almost complimentary. Surprised, she glanced back, but found little to read, for the brute's dark eyes were flat, expressionless. So, too, was his face, except that an old scar pulled down the left side of his mouth. Though his belly had gone to fat, his entire demeanor suggested power coiled for instant release. She had seen how quick his corded hands were to grasp the whip at his belt. In middle age or near it, he took pride in his appearance. His dusty blond hair was always well groomed, and his simple tunics clean and well mended.

They reached the walkway atop the wall. No one now reclined upon the balcony's couch under the old canvas awning, nor did anyone sit on the bench that crowded close to the sturdy rail.

Again she checked with Kerthik, who pointed her forward. The walkway branched off into the second floor of the stone villa attached to the school. This, she knew, was where the guards lived, and she suspected Lurcan made his home somewhere within.

She looked down at her charges as she walked, wondering if gladiators here had ever dared rebel, and if guards had fended them off from this very wall.

Her women, each dressed like her in a scratchy, sleeveless gray tunic that hung to their knees, had laid down their swords, and were now flat on the wet soil, stretching in unison. Sergeant Ceera stalked through the drizzle among them, correcting even this activity. A Dervan physician had carefully tended the sergeant's battlefield injury, but she limped still, and likely would to her dying day.

Within the practice field's perimeter, a half dozen guards leaned on spears, loafing or leering at women they were forbidden to touch.

The arena battle lay less than a week away, and Lurcan wanted all his women in peak condition.

Jerissa arrived at last at a cedar door banded with dark iron, tucked beneath a slanted wooden overhang.

She stopped, thinking Kerthik expected her to open the door, but knowing better than to assume when in the presence of a superior officer. And for her own peace of mind she'd reluctantly granted him that designation, for she refused still to think of herself as anything other than a soldier.

The overseer ignored her unvoiced query and motioned her to one of the two sturdy timbers supporting the door's awning. Here, she swiftly calculated, they were out of sight of the guards. She eyed Kerthik warily.

He glanced over his shoulder, then spoke with quiet, pressured speed. "The master's visitors want to speak with you. They were sent by a senator. They want to know if you're really from the Eltyr Corps."

Why such secrecy discussing something so obvious? "You know I am."

"Yes. But they don't have to know it."

She didn't understand what he was driving at.

He seized her arm and she immediately pulled back, discovered his grip unyielding as iron forceps. She held off her natural instinct to kick the side of his knee.

"Listen. If you fight well, they'll spare you." He loosed his hold, quickly peered again over his shoulder, then stepped to the side. In a flash of insight she realized that would block sight of her should anyone come up the stairs.

He continued in little more than a whisper, his voice hoarse. "You've got the skill. You could be a money earner for Lurcan. Serve him well for a few years, then you can buy your freedom." His finger rose in admonishment. "But if you tell that soldier who you really are, you won't be going any place with hope. You need to tell him you and your sergeant are just slaves, like the rest. That you're pretending to be Eltyr. For the games."

After her capture she'd divorced herself from most of her emotions, lest she be driven mad, and it took a moment to understand that Kerthik's words were offered as a sort of kindness.

She could not have been more surprised if he'd sprouted feathers and laid an egg. Only a few weeks ago he'd taken a whip to her.

He looked awkwardly down past his big belly to his sandals, as if troubled by what he found in her eyes.

She shook her head, slowly. He had a dream for her, but it was a small and stunted thing. "Don't you see, Kerthik?"

He started a little at her use of his name.

She tapped her chest. "They might as well have thrown me on the pyre with my sisters when Volanus fell. I'm already dead. I'm just a walking ghost."

His brow furrowed, but he had no reply. She turned from him and opened the door.

A cool, wide room lay before her, thick with cushioned couches and chairs that must have looked expensive ten or fifteen years prior. Lurcan, the corpulent owner, sprawled in one corner across from the brown-skinned man she'd seen earlier. Nearby, a table had been set with jugs of wine, goblets, and various delicacies. A pale slave boy stood beside it, ready to serve and equally ready to consume, judging by the way his eyes roved over the sesame seed rolls.

Lurcan looked up through lidded eyes, his ample cheeks flushed with good humor. "Ah! There you are, Eltyr." He gestured to the guest across from him. "You see, Antires, she's fit and trim."

"I see!" The visitor smiled and raised a goblet full of red wine. He was handsome, with short curling hair, almost certainly a native of the Herrenic peninsula, judging not just from his name, but from his russet-brown skin and the swirling decorative flourishes on the edge of his fine red tunic. There was no sign of the soldier who'd accompanied him.

Kerthik bade her stop before the master, but she was already doing so.

"She's taken over the instruction," Lurcan continued to Antires, which was mostly true, though Kerthik still demonstrated tactics favored by gladiators. "She trained many of the Eltyr soldiers, so she knows all of their strange and fabulous techniques."

"She sounds marvelous." Antires sipped his wine.

Lurcan beamed, then nodded to Kerthik. "Take her to see the centurion. He's in the old office."

"Yes, Master," Kerthik answered. "Move on, you."

As they walked past the refreshments she suddenly craved them even more than freedom. Gods, what it would be like to taste fine wine again! But Lurcan would no more have offered a drink to her than he would a horse.

Kerthik motioned her ahead so that he'd never show his back to her. He might accord her respect, but trust was foolish.

She turned the latch and pushed open the door into a small room with a dusty desk and a pair of stools. Apart from the furniture, there was only a stack of chipped urns in the far corner, and a man in uniform.

He stood with his back to the door, facing a small window. He was, unmistakably, a soldier, one of those who would be obvious as such even if he weren't clothed in regulation gear, from the scarlet cloak over his broad shoulders to the segmented cuirass, and the strapped hobnailed sandals. A short sword and knife were belted to either side of his waist. While in good repair, every inch of equipment had seen use. This was no barracks-room veteran. He was obviously a line officer, and one grown gray in service.

"Centurion, I have the woman," Kerthik said.

The officer replied curtly, without turning. "Leave us."

Kerthik hesitated, and the man at the window put his hand to the pommel of his gladius, perhaps out of habit.

Shooting her a final warning look, the overseer backed from the room and closed the door behind him.

Jerissa studied the soldier's stiff back and the nearby urns. It would be the work of a moment to heft one and crack his skull. The empire would be out a seasoned officer.

But then she'd be dead, and her charges would be that much closer to their doom.

She listened to Kerthik's retreating footsteps, thinking about how her future, and that of all the women with her, was already damned. If she killed this man there might at least be a few moments of justice. She could take up his sword and slay Lurcan and his minions. If they escaped, there would be pursuit and bloodshed and failure in the end, but wouldn't it have been worth it, to die free?

The next thing she knew she was starting forward.

And then the soldier turned and she saw his cool gray eyes and proud hooked nose, and the strong, square jaw. There was an instant of startled recognition, confusion that the man looked so much like someone he couldn't be, then the incredulous realization that this was not mere resemblance. Yes, he had neither beard nor mustache. His hair was silvered. He wore the uniform of the enemy.

"Hanuvar," she whispered, and backed away, her blood speeding in fear. She had seen him die.

His voice was soft, his eyes showing a brief flash of regret, or even pain. "I am no spirit."

His presence here was so unexpected, so startling, that she had trouble processing it, and continued to stare. It was him. Hanuvar, who had conjured victories against such impossible odds the Dervans had named him sorcerer. Hanuvar, who for more than a decade had held the implacable Dervan legions at bay in their own lands. Hanuvar, who had vanished for years, only to return to die with the city he had shielded for so long. She herself had witnessed his plummet into the cobalt waves as the walls began to crumble. She had thought it fitting he die with Volanus. For so long as he had lived, there had been hope in the city of silver towers.

His voice was low, commanding. "Jerissa. Speak to me." He stepped around the desk and stopped before her. "I mean to buy your freedom. Lurcan claims you're all Eltyr. But I don't recognize most of you. How many are truly women of the corps?"

This was actually happening. She sucked in a breath, met his eyes, and decided to address him as though this impossible vision really were a superior officer and not some ghost, or delusion. "Two, counting me," she said, and then at his nod, her mind awoke at last.

If this was real, he meant only to free the women who'd served in the famed elite female corps that had guarded the sea gate of Volanus since time immemorial. "But most of these others are women from Volanus."

At this news he frowned.

"They're not soldiers. They're bakers, shoemakers, even a bookseller and a midwife. I've been working night and day to train them to defend themselves . . ." she faltered, lest she break down. His appearance had opened the door to a host of emotions she'd thought buried.

She cleared her throat and pulled herself together. "We're all going to be costumed as Eltyer and sent to battle against gladiators dressed as Dervan legionaries. If Ceera and I aren't there, they'll still send the other women. They'll be slaughtered."

He answered without hesitation. "We'll take them with us."

"But where can we go?" Their homeland lay in ruins. The Volani colonies were Dervan outposts now. What destination could there be?

He offered a brief smile. "I dare not say, until you're free, and on your way."

"But how can you even . . . how can you afford—"

"I've raided the tombs of our dead. They can purchase freedom for the living."

She sensed there was much more to it than this. That he could walk the streets of a Dervan port town unrecognized was not so strange, given that few Dervans were likely to recognize the great general, and that most from the Inner Sea shared a similar complexion. And it was not so strange that he spoke Dervan with no accent, for many in the Inner Sea were fluent in more than a single tongue. What she really wanted to know was how he had survived, and how he came to be here, when he should be rotting on the ocean floor.

"How are you here?" she asked.

"That's a long story." He did not say they lacked time for it, or that it had scarred him. That was manifest in his eyes.

She had thought herself abandoned by the gods. But right before her was proof that they had heard her entreaties. "Each night since our arrival here I broke the bread and prayed to the blessed five, though I had no wine, nor candles," she told him. "I asked for help for the women under my command. And here you are."

She did not understand why her words made him uncomfortable. He changed the subject. "I'll make arrangements with Lurcan. Tell no one of my true identity. One wrong word will jeopardize it all."

"Yes, of course, General."

"How many Eltyr truly survived?"

She shook her head. "There couldn't have been more than two dozen of us. Maybe less. And most were wounded. I'm not sure where they ended up. The Dervans made careful note of it all, though." Her mouth twisted in scorn. "I'm sure they have records." The methodical Dervans always had records.

His voice was tentative. "Was my daughter among them?"

"She was charged with Praelyff Meruvar's safety, General. I didn't see her after the assault began."

"And did you hear of her after?"

Jerissa shook her head no. But then as she had been marched in chains from the smoldering ruins of the city by the sea, she had passed so many broken bodies. She'd given up looking at their faces.

Hanuvar nodded once, as if to mark the end of a subject. He began another. "Stand ready, Eltyr. I must arrange larger transport, so relief may take another day."

She nodded. And then, without thinking, she blurted: "Thank you, General."

"Thank me when we've cleared the obstacles. I may yet need your sword arm."

II

Garbed in a blue robe, his feet in the finest leather sandals, Theris sat in contemplation of his goddess, round, smooth-skinned face bathed in the perfumed incense he himself had blessed. He was content.

Fate had decreed he be reigning high priest in the year of Ariteen's ascendancy. After millennia, her most propitious hour was almost at hand. In but two days all would know her not as some obscure incarnation of the upstart Serima, but as supreme deity, and the empire would transform from one enslaved to greed and bloodshed to one alive with love.

Gradually he grew conscious of a steady knocking. "Enter," he said, opened his eyes, and smiled at the sturdy young man lingering in the threshold. "Yes, Ortix?"

"There is a visitor, Blessed One." Ortix pressed open palms to his heart and bowed. "He comes from the School of Lurcan. Where the female gladiators are housed."

"Curious." Theris put hands to the black-cushioned arms of his chair, and pushed himself upright. "What does he want?"

"He does not say, Blessed One. But he appears troubled."

"Let us see if we can ease his pain."

Theris ducked his head to pass beneath a stone lintel and into a wide, cool chamber beyond, its low ceiling stained from ancient smoke. Ariteen's sacred breath perfumed the vast underground room and roiled like fog through the dim recesses.

The revelry for the most devout and select of his flock had ended for the day. Some on the worn gray flagstones lay entwined and some lay apart, but a rapturous smile stood out upon every upturned face.

Theris and Ortix threaded their way through the recumbent men and women and the mist and the rough-hewn pillars. As they neared the exit, they passed three bodies shackled to the floor, and Theris' expression fell. A necessary sacrifice. But these had been loved while they died, and their paramours lay insensate across them, uncaring that their skin and clothes were soaked with blood. The deaths would not be in vain, for soon now all would know the love of Ariteen.

Ortix preceded him up the stairs, the smoky glass dulling the red orb of the lantern he carried. Being a goddess of both love and protection, Ariteen preferred the shielding cloak of night, and her worshippers honored her temples with minimal illumination.

They arrived at the ground floor, and the central hall with its soaring arches and great open spaces. He preferred the under chambers, carved from old silver mines in centuries past, but many expected their temples to appear more traditional.

The visitor waited inside the antechamber, eying a colorful mosaic of Ariteen in her aspect as lover. Many young men had found the image of great interest, for her assets were rendered with loving detail as she leaned down to bestow a rapturous youth with a kiss.

The visitor turned, and Theris saw his face was misshapen by a scar that pulled down one side of his mouth. His clean, well-tended tunic was tight over a muscular upper chest and large belly.

"Blessed One." The man gave a brief head bob. His voice was low, gruff, but there was no missing a hint of nervousness.

"This is Kertha," Ortix informed him.

"Kertha, welcome." Theris glided forward.

"It's Kerthik, Blessed One," the man corrected.

Theris spread his hands. "Whatever name, all are welcome in this chamber, which celebrates our goddess and her many aspects. What has brought you here?" He felt his fine mood ebbing while the man stared and stared, apparently struggling with whatever it was he'd come to say.

"You have a message?" Theris prompted.

"The women," Kerthik managed at last. And once he began he spoke hurriedly. "It's to be a true contest, isn't it? So that those who fight well are spared? It's not to be one of those set pieces where everyone on one side dies, is it?"

Theris spread slim arms in his wide blue sleeves. "What curious questions. Your master is being well compensated so that it shouldn't matter what happens." He eyed the man. "But you haven't come upon your master's behalf, have you, Kerthik?"

He saw the light of fear in the man's eyes and put a hand to his shoulder, guiding him to the mosaic of Ariteen as the loving mother. Here she was fully clothed and her eyes were not so lascivious, though under her curling gray-blue locks she was just as lovely. "Our goddess is a protector, and so are we, her speakers. What is it that troubles you, Kerthik?"

"I worry for them. The servant of a senator has come, and he means to buy them."

"What?" Theris heard the snap in his voice and quickly strove to right his anger.

"Senator Marcius means to buy them and carry them away. For questioning, I think."

Theris' calm vanished utterly, and his heart thrummed with nervous energy. While Caiax had delivered Volanus' death blow, it was Senator Catius Marcius who had pushed the Dervans on to the final war. It was common knowledge he had been wroth that even a few Volani survived to be enslaved. Probably he meant the Eltyr for some other, less useful fate, which would jeopardize all that Theris and his followers had worked for. Ariteen needed the blood of both men and women for the ritual. "Is the senator in the city?"

Kerthik shook his ugly head. "Only his man. A centurion."

"I see." Theris cleared his throat and tried not to show his obvious relief. "Your master has been well paid for his portion of the festival, and our expenditure to the amphitheater has been astronomical."

"This centurion is willing to pay more. Vastly more."

"We had an agreement," Ortix cut in.

Theris shot his young assistant a warning glance, both for speaking out of turn and for showing inappropriate emotion.

"I will have to speak to this man," Theris said, his voice calming.

"The combat is intended to honor our goddess in her protective aspect. Were the ceremony to be altered in any way, it would be of great insult."

"So they're to be spared then? The brave ones?"

Theris favored him with his most melting smile. "But of course, good Kerthik. Don't fear. We'll find this centurion and straighten things out."

After that assurance, and a few awkward pleasantries, the man excused himself. Theris stood staring after him long after the temple door swung shut.

"You lied to that man," Ortix said. He crossed his arms over his lighter blue acolyte's tunic.

"My son, the signs foretold that there would be a final obstacle in our path, and that great fortitude would be required to overcome it. Our goddess would advise us to be wily."

"What do you plan to do?"

Theris stroked his beardless chin with a beringed finger. "First, I will have you deliver a message to the governor. He'll be displeased to hear anyone's interfering. Then I'm going to have you find out where this centurion is staying."

"What do you want me to do after that?"

"The governor will follow my lead," Theris said. The old man was wrapped about his finger tightly now. He might not be party to the changes that would soon overtake the world, beginning in the provincial capital he ruled, but the governor recognized the wisdom of Ariteen's practices. "A squad of legionaries ought to be enough to silence one lone centurion, don't you think?"

"What about the senator?"

Theris laughed. "By the time the senator hears anything, Ariteen will be walking again among us. What will one missing centurion matter then? To the senator, or anyone?"

III

Hanuvar had selected lodgings on the second floor above the chandler's shop because of its small windows, single entrance, and solid door. Antires, the actor he'd hired as his go-between, had initially complained that it was dark and reeked of perfumed wax. But the young man didn't find the place so onerous when he was offered free food.

That evening Antires joined Hanuvar in the room for a meal of baked fish rubbed with lemon and pepper and garum, a fresh-baked loaf of dark bread, some fried chartish greens, and even some fruit pastries for dessert. Being a Herrene he'd selected a wine seasoned with citrus. Probably he expected Hanuvar to complain about that, so he didn't.

They ate in companionable silence at the little table, the stools creaking as they reached for various portions. Most of Hanuvar's disguise sat neatly upon another table, though he still wore his scarlet uniform tunic and soldier's sandals.

"Centurion," the Herrene said, finally, addressing Hanuvar by his assumed Dervan officer title, "the ship you've picked is nice, but I don't understand your crew. Why are you selecting sailors like them?"

He pretended ignorance. "Like what?"

"Old men. Slaves." The Herrene paused only for a breath. "Is it because they're Volani? Why so much interest in them?"

The young man was closer to the mark than Hanuvar liked. "I'm not paying you to ask questions," he replied. "I'm paying you because I need someone smart and courteous."

Antires gave a little bow. "I suppose that if I asked questions every time Dervans did something mad, I should never fall silent."

"And I have acted mad?"

"First you wish me to play your servant and entertain fat Lurcan. Then you decide to buy a ship. Then you go out of your way to crew it with reprobates and slaves."

"I make do, Antires. You must use the tools at hand."

"Your navigator's hands seem to have palsy," Antires pointed out.

"His mind is sharp."

More importantly, the old navigator was Volani, a slave from the first war, only recently freed as he'd grown feeble. Many of the other sailors were political prisoners and most were slaves, seven from the galleys, and five of those were in such sad shape Antires had thought Hanuvar stripped of his senses when he bought them. But those five had been sold into slavery from the sack of Volanus.

The actor took a swig from a tin mug he'd brought with the food. "Why didn't the senator send you with more men?"

"The senator is frugal," Hanuvar replied.

Antires smirked. "That's a nice way to say that. What I can't figure is what the senator wants with these Eltyr. I mean, if there were any questions that needed asking, wouldn't Consul Caiax have done that when he captured them?" He snapped his fingers. "But Senator Marcius hates the Volani, doesn't he? Is it true he ended every speech for the last eight years the same way, no matter the subject? That Volanus must be destroyed?"

"I didn't hear all of his speeches," Hanuvar said curtly. "It's not my job to ask Senator Marcius what he wants. Or yours." He wanted to end the questioning without completely alienating the actor, who might still prove useful.

"It just doesn't make sense. I mean, Volanus' fields have been sown with salt. You can't get much more vanquished than that. It's not like the Eltyr can tell the senator secrets useful to defeat Volanus anymore."

"Different people know different sorts of secrets," Hanuvar remarked.

"Like those galley slaves? Or have you confused lice with secrets?"

Hanuvar paused in rubbing the bread heel through the sauce left beneath the fish and shrewdly eyed his companion. "What is it you Herrenes say about curiosity?"

"What is it you Dervans say about practicality? I don't know what your scheme is, but it's not practical."

Antires was right. Hanuvar fervently hoped no one else was paying as close attention. "Assuming I even knew what the senator wanted, and I told you, what would you do with the truth?"

Antires blinked in surprise. "Why, nothing."

"Nothing?"

"Well, not until you'd paid me. But if there's some kind of behind-the-scenes investigation going on, surely you need someone to write up the story once it's time to spread the word. I'm your man for that."

"Yes. I saw the sign in your window. Writer for hire. Right next to the lettering that proclaimed you an actor, translator, and negotiator."

"I am many things," the actor declared with a flourish of his hand. "So must all successful men be."

The younger man gave up trying to tease the truth from his elder, then proved so restless after dinner Hanuvar suggested he act a few scenes from his favorite plays. He'd rather Antires not wander out drinking to spread gossip about their activities.

The Herrene brightened at the invitation. "Most Dervans don't seem to like anything but broad comedy."

"I've traveled."

Antires spent an hour populating the little room with doomed lovers, brave generals, dying kings, and sword-wielding heroes. Hanuvar appreciated the distraction, for in quiet moments he thought too readily of the city he'd last seen burning, and his daughter's sea-gray eyes. The actor banished these recollections to the shadows. The words were alternately eloquent and overly formal, often laboring a little too hard to tweak the heart strings, but some of those speeches, like the aging tyrant begging forgiveness of his dying son, awoke his sympathy, and Hanuvar was moved to melancholy even after laughing aloud at comically brave Dorik readying for battle.

In the end he clapped roundly and praised Antires, who bowed, and gratefully accepted the full goblet Hanuvar passed him. They were on their second bottle, and it was far from the actor's first drink, although apart from a flushed face his imbibing had left his performances unmarred.

"I see I touched the heart of a stony soldier with the words of Herrenic playwrights."

"Answer me this, Antires. Why do playwrights always tell of kings and generals? Why not ordinary people?"

"They write about those with the power to do things."

"The world would be better off if we exalted kings and generals less."

"Few living kings and generals seem worth the trouble to write about," Antires agreed. "Except maybe one," he added with a sidelong look. "You Dervans all claimed Hanuvar fled Volanus because he was a coward. But he returned in the end, to die with his city. Even when all hope was lost. How many other kings would do that?"

He was young, flushed with pride in the heritage of his own people, and a little drunk. Old resentments of a people dominated by the Dervans for less than a generation were easy to rekindle. He probably thought himself daring to praise Derva's greatest enemy before an officer of the legion.

"Volanus had no king. Hanuvar was a general."

"I know that," Antires said truculently. "I'm just saying, he at least was worthy of a play, though he'll probably never get one."

Hanuvar hid his wry amusement with a disinterested answer. "Maybe you should write one."

"And where, in all the world, would it be staged?"

Hanuvar was saved from having to find a reply when a loud knock sounded upon the door. His hand immediately went to the sheathed sword on the table beside him, a movement noted by Antires.

"What are you on the alert for?" the Herrene asked.

"Centurion?" A young boy's voice was dulled by the heavy door. "Are you in there?"

He rose, sword still sheathed, but supported in his left hand while his right wrapped the hilt. "I am. Who sent you?"

"Master Lurcan, Centurion. He needs to speak with you privately, this evening."

"Very well. Give me a moment."

Hanuvar sorted his thoughts as he reattached the Dervan sheath to his weapons belt. Almost surely Lurcan sought to raise prices.

Antires gauged him with rising curiosity. If this meeting proved to be about haggling, Hanuvar didn't need the Herrene. And if it was something more dire, he needed Antires free.

Hanuvar addressed him, his voice pitched low. "How drunk are you?"

"Only a little."

"Then listen well. If something goes amiss, make sure the ship is readied. Do you understand?"

"Aye—"

Hanuvar cut off whatever question was dawning on the actor's lips. "It's paramount those gladiators get on that ship." He placed three thumb-sized rubies in the hands of his companion, rendered silent by stunned regard. "This is to smooth any difficulties. There will be more like that for you, if you follow through. Do you understand?"

"Yes," Antires stammered.

"Be on guard until my return." He left his helm and cuirass, but threw his cloak over his shoulders and cast open the door.

The boy on the wooden landing was no more than ten, barefoot and scrawny, with a shock of dark hair. He was different from the one Hanuvar had seen at Lurcan's school that morning. He bobbed his head. "This way, sir."

Hanuvar followed him down the stairs and into the street, past a tavern alive with light and the laughter of late evening revelers. The sun was down, and the stormy skies were closed over the stars like a tomb door. The rain dribbled down in a fine mist, coating his skin in a sheen of moisture.

In many Dervan cities, walking without escort was dangerous at night, because the unlit avenues were the haunt of footpads and criminals. Hidrestus was better lit than average, reminding Hanuvar in a pale, shadowy way of Volanus itself, though the flames in the lanterns hung every block were distorted by their glass so that they shone like rheumy gold eyes. They did not compare favorably to the bright lights of his vanished home. Rock oil was reportedly obtained from caverns only a few miles to the north of Hidrestus, and to save expense, some magistrate had switched the lanterns over from olive oil during a regional blight years before; it didn't smell as good but at least the lights were maintained. The streets too were cleaner than other Dervan cities, but whether this was due to better sanitation standards or the frequent rain he did not know.

After three blocks the boy diverted into a dark lane and Hanuvar grabbed his shoulder. The boy started.

"Where are you leading me?"

"The backside of Tretak's tavern," the boy answered.

"Why there?"

"I don't know," the boy admitted. "But it's supposed to be a secret meeting."

Hanuvar released him and bade him on, his hand staying on his sword hilt. He watched for pursuit.

The boy headed into the lane, helpfully pointing out a pile of wooden boxes half hidden in the shadows. After twenty feet the lane opened into a wide clearing, a courtyard surrounded by the dark shapes of two-story buildings. Suddenly the boy dashed ahead, and a light flared on the left.

In a single heartbeat Hanuvar understood the lay of the situation. Four legionaries were ranged before him, and a fifth scuffed the soil behind. A deliberate warning, he thought, to alert him to the man's presence so he wouldn't attempt to flee the others.

The one on the right held a lantern, and stood beside a gaping rectangular pit. Beside it lay a wide, heavy wooden panel large enough to cover it, along with thick metal crossbars.

To his left stood another legionary, a pock-marked, scowling man. A younger soldier with an optio's[5] white pteruges, clear brown eyes, and a strong cleft chin stood only a few paces ahead, and behind him was the youngest of the lot, a man with a little Herrenic blood, judging from his darker complexion and coiled hair.

The boy hesitated beside the foremost legionary, who barked at him to go. The soldier eyed Hanuvar as the youth jogged into the darkness then smote his fist to his breastplate in salute. "Hail, Centurion."

"To what do I owe this pleasure, Optio?" Hanuvar asked.

The cleft-chinned leader shook his head. "It's no pleasure on my part. But I'm a soldier with orders. And my orders mean that you're going to end up in that old mine shaft."

"It seems a dishonorable end."

The officer nodded with some sympathy. "Especially for a veteran. This end is beneath you, and beneath me."

"Soon he'll be beneath us all," the legionary holding the lantern said. The soldier a few paces behind Hanuvar laughed.

"Shut up, Surin." The leader's lips curled in disgust as his eyes flicked to the lantern holder. They went back to Hanuvar. "I can offer you only one thing."

"Which is?"

He showed his open palm in a conciliatory gesture. "The means to your end. I've a jug of wine here with a quick-acting poison. It'll be a little unpleasant, but much better than the alternative."

"A stab in the gut?" Hanuvar suggested.

"If you wish. I was thinking a crack over the head. We might be able to finish you in one blow, which could be easier than poison.

---

[5] An optio is the lowest-ranking officer in a legion, although seniority is as important among optios as it is among centurions, meaning that seasoned ones are accorded greater respect both from their peers and superiors.   —*Silenus*

But if the attack doesn't end well, it could take several blows. You probably know how these things go."

Hanuvar heard the creak of sandals from the man to his rear, knowing he was poised to rush. He calculated the steps between them all, their likely reach, their states of readiness, their probable skill. Only the man behind was an unknown, but the optio was no fool; he would have placed someone both fast and strong there.

"Was the poison your employer's order?" Hanuvar asked.

"My orders were to make you disappear. Completely. There are still a few openings to the old mines. A veteran deserves an honored burial."

Hanuvar nodded once. "So there are men of honor in the legion, still. I'll take your offer, then, with three questions."

The optio motioned to the younger man behind him, who raised a small clay flask and took a step up beside his leader.

"Ask," the optio said.

"Why does your master need these women so much that he would kill to keep them? I would have expected a bribe first."

"The governor's cousin is Consul Caiax, and he's been promised women gladiators when the consul shows up to watch the games. The governor can't have the consul disappointed."

Hanuvar had learned Caiax himself would be in attendance, but he'd pushed thoughts of vengeance from his mind. He meant to draw as little attention as possible. "What's your name?"

"I am Septim Masir, First Optio. Why do you ask, Centurion?"

"I would remember the name of an honorable man."

The optio seemed to like the compliment, but his brow furrowed in puzzlement. "That's a curious thing to say."

Hanuvar shrugged. "I'll take the poison now."

"I thought you had three questions."

"You've told me all I needed."

"Very well." The optio nodded to the man with the flask. "Kibrin?"

Hanuvar extended his hand as Kibrin advanced, presenting the wine container. Then the general exploded forward, snared Kibrin's wrist, and dragged him over his extended foot. Kibrin plunged screaming headfirst into the pit.

Having wrested the flask, Hanuvar sent it hurtling at the lantern holder.

The flask shattered against the lantern, spraying its bearer with glass, oil, and flame. In a heartbeat the frightened legionary's arm was completely engulfed in fire that blazed greedily into his red cloak. He cried out piteously for help.

Before the flask had even shattered Hanuvar spun to face the foe charging from behind. The grizzled veteran was almost on him, his sword tucked close by his waist for swift thrusting.

Hanuvar threw himself at the man's ankles and the soldier fell over him. Rolling to his feet, Hanuvar pivoted with sword in one hand and knife in the other. While the angry optio shouted at his remaining soldier, Hanuvar rushed the legionary he'd tripped, who was climbing to his knees. He kicked the man in the shoulder and sent him sliding into the pit, where he vanished with a shout. A moment later the man who'd carried the lantern, frantically beating his fire engulfed cloak, was sent stumbling after him, shrieking the entire way down.

They were a noisy bunch, he thought, for the scarred soldier cursed as he raced at Hanuvar. A wiser man might have waited to flank with the optio, but this soldier was enraged.

He also was clearly accustomed, like many a legionary, to fighting with a shield on his left arm. His sword form was perfect, but his left arm hung useless. Hanuvar beat a savage thrust aside and drove his knife into the man's neck. He leapt back to defeat a mad series of slashes launched before the soldier's body registered it was dying.

The soldier staggered to the side and dropped to one knee, feeling for the wound as he set his sword down. Hanuvar turned to sidestep the optio's cloak, thrown in an attempt to blind, then the officer twisted to follow him.

"Who *are* you?" the optio demanded.

Unless it could be used to some advantage, only fools wasted energy talking in a fight. Hanuvar stayed silent.

They exchanged thrust and counterthrust, with only the dim flare of a flaming dead man in the pit below to light their way. The optio strove to stay turned to offer a smaller target.

Hanuvar knew the younger man could outlast him, and so he pressed for advantage, slashing and driving the officer toward the pit.

And then something seized Hanuvar's ankle. The dying man had grabbed him. The optio attacked with a savage cry of satisfaction.

Hanuvar twisted, parried a blow that would have caved in his skull, and lost his balance. He freed his left foot as the optio closed in. Hanuvar saw the pit yawning, and the flame more than twenty feet below. A weathered wooden ladder hung along the crumbling side. He sprang off his right foot, hoping to clear the pit. He just missed the far edge, losing both blades as he snatched at the ladder. The knife smacked into his cloaked shoulder as it dropped away. The wood was worn smooth by countless hands, slowing his descent, but his grip was uncertain and his feet never found a rung.

When he dropped at last it was from somewhere between ten and twelve feet. He winced as he landed, for his left knee reminded him of its old injury with the subtlety of a dagger thrust. He staggered and fell beside the body of Kibrin, lying with his head and leg twisted unnaturally. He saw the dead man's mouth parted in a scream of terror by the horrible light of the flaming Surin and the body of the other legionary, across whom he lay.

The smell of burning flesh polluted the air.

Something shone close by on his right, and he turned his head to discover his sword lying nearly upright against a mound of dirt only a hair's breadth from his chin. A little further over and it would have been driven through his head.

"I'd meant to honor you," the optio shouted from above. "To ease your way!"

Hanuvar saw the outline of the legionary looming in a lighter square of darkness above. The optio continued petulantly: "Now you can starve to death!" And so saying, he disappeared. Hanuvar smiled ruefully that he had thought well of Septim Masir, First Optio. Far easier to be gracious in victory than defeat, though admittedly some didn't manage even that. The Dervans were so certain of their superiority they thought any victor must surely have cheated them. Clearly the optio believed it unfair of Hanuvar to fight so hard to survive.

As he climbed warily to his feet, he kept his eyes fastened above, so that he saw the moment when the thick board was dragged across the opening. He heard the crossbars dropped into place a moment later. No doubt they would shortly be locked tight.

He turned to contemplate his options, alone now but for the dead.

IV

Hanuvar didn't return the next morning, or afternoon. At dawn the day after, Jerissa and her soldiers were led into the main building, where they were treated to hot and cool baths in a lower level. Masseuses worked over each of them.

This afternoon, their gladiatorial games would commence. Might these be preparations for that, or might Lurcan be pampering them before he released them to the man he thought their new owner?

She thought the latter unlikely. Something had gone wrong.

After she'd exited the masseuse's talented ministrations and donned clean clothing, Kerthik bade her follow with a crooked finger. This time he led her to a dark corner away from the others. With his broad back blocking the view, none of the other guards, or women, might see his expression, or hers. And in the hall echoing with the low chatter of the women, he might be expected to be unheard by others as well.

The overseer looked as though he meant to speak, for his mien was grimmer than ever. Yet he met her eyes and looked away.

"Out with it, man," she said, 'an officer's snap in her delivery.

He didn't take offense; her urging seemed to be the impetus he needed. "I want you to know the truth," he said haltingly. "I didn't know. I didn't mean to lead you on."

"Lead me on?" Could he possibly think that she had room in her heart to consider romance with one of her captors? Even Dervan servants were mad, and sick.

"To give you hope." She saw his sorrow, and knew it was honest. He continued. "I truly believed those who fought well stood a chance. But they're going to kill you. All of you. That's how the governor wants it, to symbolize the fall of Volanus. Lurcan's even sorry about it, the old bastard, but the governor doesn't want Consul Caiax to be disappointed, so he's pushing hard—"

"Caiax? Caiax is going to be here?"

He nodded slowly, and must have seen the fire that flared within her. He had guessed the course of her thoughts, for he shook his head. "You won't be able to get anywhere near him."

She thought of the tall, hunched man she'd seen striding through the ruins, directing columns of soldiers. Caiax had plundered the harbor's island temples and crucified the priests and priestesses before the whole of the city. He'd faithlessly promised peace only if the people marched away weaponless to abandon Volanus forever, but peace was never an option, only subjugation. The Volani generally had chosen to perish with their city, though that had been denied to those carted away in chains.

Caiax was calculating, methodical, and merciless, the Dervan ideal. That he was also a liar, butcher, and exterminator of a people seemed to be cause for celebration among the Dervans, who looked upon the aging soldier with the reverence some bestowed upon the gods. For destroying Derva's ancient rival, Volanus, he had reportedly been accorded more honors and accolades even than Ciprion, who'd fought Hanuvar's army to stalemate years before, even though Caiax had bested a city with merely a shadow of its former power.

Her intent must have been easy to read. "Don't think you're the first who believed they could throw a spear into the stands," Kerthik said. "Before you can even aim, the guards will have you pincushioned with arrows."

She licked her lips, realized she still held his arm, and released it. "Has there been any word from the centurion who visited?"

"He hasn't been back."

Small wonder. If Caiax was in the city, there was a fair chance Hanuvar might have been recognized by him or his soldiers. For his own safety, the general might have had to abandon his plans.

"I'm sorry," Kerthik repeated. "I know you would have triumphed in the ring in a fair fight. These rich bastards don't honor skill anymore. They just want blood."

He was so full of woe he seemed almost sadder than she did. No, he *was* sadder, she realized. She looked down at her hands, clenching and unclenching them. She would show the blood-mad Dervans that these final Eltyr would stand and fall with honor.

"Lurcan had been planning to host a big feast for you, but since none of you are going to survive, he doesn't want to spend the money." His mouth twisted bitterly. It seemed the smaller injustices rankled him most.

She clapped his shoulder, squeezed it. "It's all right, Kerthik. I was a soldier. I expected to die with my weapon in my hand. Among friends. I'll still get that chance."

His answering nod was tight. "I know you will fight bravely," he said. "I should have liked to have known you as a friend."

He meant more than that, of course, but it still touched her. He, alone among all of these, recognized her not as a commodity, but a human being not unlike himself. She offered her arm, and after a moment, he clasped it.

"Why did you tell that centurion who you really were?" he asked as he loosened his grip. "Is it because you didn't think it would matter?"

"He promised he would take us away from here."

"To live?"

She nodded.

"You believe him?"

"I do. But something went wrong."

"I'll find him," Kerthik pledged.

"It's too late." She shook her head.

"No, I'll find him. If there's a way, I'll do it." He nodded once to her, and strode quickly off. "Drebal, you're in charge! I've got an errand to run." He headed for the exit.

Ceera, toweling herself off, limped over to her. "I had my eye on him the whole time. I thought you were going to take him down. What was that all about?"

"You can make friends at odd times."

"Him?"

"He's just a man with a dream," Jerissa said. "You'd think he'd know better, in a place like this."

V

His first step was to secure supplies. After he fashioned an improvised torch from articles of legionary clothing and the haft of a spear, he beat out the fire on the roasting corpses, liberated wine flasks, a little food, and even some oil from the dead. Some business above had used this area as a store room once, but all that remained were dilapidated shelving and some broken clay shards.

He discarded the notion of attempting an exit through the entrance the optio had blocked off. The Dervans would surely be watching it even if he could somehow lift the bars. If there was a way out, it lay in the mine shafts. According to the locals, they were supposed to honeycomb much of the land beneath the city. The mine had apparently played out centuries ago, and the deepest portions had been sealed.

He then turned to consider the walled-off entry to the mine shafts. It might once have been secure, but the mortar was old, and a few judicious blows loosened the top rows of bricks on the right. With only a little more effort, he opened the way. He gathered his supplies, broken portions of the ladder and other dried wood, and moved away from the terrible stench.

He well knew the tale of Peliar and his descent into the underworld, but there were no spirits to converse with here. There was only the long corridor, wide enough for a man pushing a cart, perhaps, but either the men from bygone days had been shorter, or they'd always walked with a hunch, for the ceiling was so low he had to keep his head bent. Joists were fashioned of wood, reinforced sometimes with stone, and most looked solid still, though a few had begun to bow, and he would not have cared to push very hard against the fragile-looking wood.

The place was alive with cobwebs and millipedes and rats, but none were of gargantuan size, and none looked likely to gather in great masses and pursue him, as they had Peliar. The webs he swept away with a spear, and the black-eyed rodents fled at sight of him.

Eventually he arrived at an intersection. It proved easy enough to mark upon the walls with bits of rock, harder to etch into them, should he have to retrace steps once his light faded. But etch he did, ever choosing the corridors that sloped upward, or at least stayed level. Those that stretched steeply down he avoided.

Hanuvar was well used to gauging time, feeling its relentless pulse almost like the regimental drummers who kept men marching at a constant pace. He reckoned that for the first while, at least, his time estimates would be reasonably accurate, but with no light to judge but that from his torch, his estimates of the length of his stay would eventually grow flawed.

Halfway through his second hour he found his first cave-in, and doubled back. Late into the fourth hour, he discovered a sealed door at the top of a ramp, and a trio of men that had, some dark day decades past, laid down to die. They hadn't given up without a struggle, for he saw that they'd assaulted the rusted metal door and its hinges with rocks, seriously denting the surface. They'd even managed to pry one of the pins out of a hinge. Little good it had done them. Probably a great mass of dirt or debris lay on the other side of the wall blocking their egress, for Hanuvar sensed he was not yet at ground level.

Who they were or how they had gotten here would remain a tragedy he had no time to mourn; of more immediate concern was avoiding a similar fate.

His own fatigue had mounted. He would need his strength to continue this journey, and his full wits, and decided that he would sleep, though he resolved not to do so among the dead. He retraced his steps to a closed-off passage he'd earlier cleared of cobwebs. The joists there seemed especially sturdy. He set tools aside and performed a solemn and lengthy series of stretches before pillowing one cloak he'd recovered from the dead Dervan legionaries, deploying his own for a blanket. He set flint and steel to hand, unsheathed his sword, and blew out the light. As he drifted off, his mind turned briefly to tales of the Vanished Ones, which had haunted him when he was a child. Their empty cities still lay intact in remote corners of the world. Some said that they had retreated to the depths of the earth, others that the subterranean entrances found near their dwellings were not mines, but the places where demons had emerged to drag all of them away.

But he had seen enough of men's evils that he worried less about those that were likely imagined.

His dreams were shoddy things, beginning with promise but dying in nonsense. He imagined his brothers back to life, but they wanted nothing more than to complain about how many miles they'd had to run. His wife wasn't glad to see him because she worried her dress was the wrong shade of blue. Eledeva darted through the water beneath the ship, her gold scales shining, but refused to resurface, no matter how desperately he shouted. And then his soldiers called to him, asking where he'd gone. Their voices rose through the air, his name a mighty three-syllable chant. He emerged from the tunnels to stand before the victorious throngs. But then he realized what he'd taken for his army was nothing but a forest of stunted trees that disintegrated into dust as the wind blew up.

He woke to darkness, lit the stub of his torch, and readied another while he wolfed down some blueberries and stale bread. As bad as the dreams had been, he felt a little refreshed. A few moments of stretches cleared the kinks from his muscles, and then he resumed his search.

He knew he wasn't yet in danger of running out of light. His food supplies were low, but that didn't worry him, either, not yet. His driving concern was the fate of the Eltyr. He hadn't been looking for them, but then he'd hardly have expected them here, on the empire's edge. He'd thought only to pass through the port city, but there'd been no missing the announcements lettered in the forum, advertising the great games and the presence of genuine Eltyr.

Now, as he searched through the endless tunnels, his frustration grew. All might come to naught—their lives, his life, the lives of so many others he meant to help.

Hour after hour he explored the tunnels. His neck and shoulders ached from being hunched for so long. He was on his third torch for the day, and running low on oil. Time sped on, and after he stopped for another meal he began to think that a second night might already have fallen.

Giving up on the higher tunnels, he ventured deeper, pushing through fatigue and finally reaching one that stretched on and on. It sagged under ancient beams, the titanic weight of the earth pressing relentlessly down. Long had the supports lasted, and it might be they could hold for decades more, or mere moments. He slid past a place where the cave wall was half sunken and took a left fork, finally glimpsing the end of a shaft in a pale strand of sunbeam shining down from on high.

Hanuvar advanced to the tunnel's end and a tiny squared-off chamber. A pile of dirt and rocks rested against the wall. He swiped his spear to clear a mass of cobwebs.

The shaft stretched fifty or more feet straight up, to where a beam of light slipped down through a narrow gap in wood. Hanuvar thrust the torch haft into the dirt pile and paused to straighten his weary back, to shake out his arms, to shift his neck. Until his confinement here, he'd taken the pleasure of standing upright for granted.

He scanned the walls. While this shaft, too, might have housed a ladder long ago, it held none now. At its narrowest point, it stretched five feet side to side. Once, he might have prayed to the gods of his people before attempting such a venture. Now he sneered at the thought, readied his flint and steel for easy access in his belt pouch, and snuffed the torch in the dirt.

Coughing in the darkness and the smoke, he wrapped the torch's warm end in fresh rags he soaked with the tiny remnant of his oil. Then he shoved it in his belt, braced hands on one side of the wall and feet on the other, and started the long, painstaking four-limbed walk up the side. Hand, foot, hand, foot, progressing by inches.

Twenty feet up, the space widened by a half foot, which at least allowed him to stretch out the cramp in his right leg. Ten more feet, and he felt his arms trembling. In twenty more feet, his other leg cramped.

But he pressed on, and as he drew closer to the light he tried not to think about the deadly fall that lay below, twisting instead to look above, confirming that the shaft was sealed with wood.

He bore on, stopping just a few inches below the barrier. Though his muscles burned, he caught his breath while suspended against the cool earth of the walls. After a brief moment, he began the next phase. He jammed his right elbow against the wall, supporting himself by that point and his quivering legs. He set the torch haft in his teeth, and then, with steel in the hand of the arm he'd braced and flint in the other, he struck again and again until sparks flew and took hold of the stinking, oil-soaked fabric.

The resulting light blinded, and the heat against his face alarmed him. He only just kept his teeth gripped about the haft as he struggled to maneuver so he could safely grasp the torch with his hand.

He despised acting with haste, but he knew his strength could not long hold. Releasing flint and steel to drop into darkness, he thrust his left hand to the wall to steady himself, then stretched the torch against the wood, and held it.

This flame was his friend. In less than a heartbeat, it took hold, and the wooden barrier blazed up.

Too quickly, he thought. He released the torch, saw it tumbling down even as the fire ate greedily in a rectangle overhead, growing brighter and brighter still. The torch lay a vast distance below, a flickering warning of just how far there was to fall.

And he knew the threat above. He started the long way down as the fire crackled and roared. Flaming timber had nowhere to go but down, upon him.

He hurried, foot, hand, foot, hand, as each of his limbs shook with fatigue and the inferno roared above. He slammed knuckles into a patch of rock, drawing blood. He gritted teeth as he teetered there, cursing his gods. "Kill me then," he said. They must want all his people dead, he thought, feeling small even as the thoughts crossed his mind. For it was petty to hate the gods, who were disinterested at best.

Finally, only a few feet from the bottom, he could hold himself no more, and dropped. He hit first with his feet but lost balance and caught himself in the rough soil with his palms.

And then from above he heard a terrific crack of timber, and a rumble.

He pushed himself up, took a step, and dived into the tunnel.

A boulder slammed into the shaft only a heartbeat later, spraying out a plume of dirt and sparks. It must have been secured against the entryway, to seal it from trespassers.

Hanuvar knelt, breathing heavily. It looked to him as though the light in the chamber had diminished. But he didn't act yet. He let his body calm, stretched arms and legs once more, flexed fingers, and returned.

At the shaft's bottom there was just room to crawl over the boulder and remnants of the wooden barrier that lay beneath it, still smoking. Corners of it were alive with flame. He worried that Dervans would have seen the fire, but he'd had no other choice.

Far above lay the gray sky, partly hidden by some other obstacle. Another boulder was wedged across two thirds of the opening.

He shook out his limbs, stretched his calves. It would be better to wait, catch his breath. But who could say exactly where this exit was? He guessed it was east of the city, but he could well have been turned around. Dervan soldiers might even now be rushing to investigate.

And so, for the second time, he started up the shaft. It was easier in one respect because he better knew what lay before him, but a greater challenge with wearied limbs. Still, he had conquered it once, and he knew he could not fail. Too many would have no chance if he failed.

His arms were burning with weariness as he neared the muted sunlight and the remaining boulder, precariously balanced. As he eyed it warily, a stream of dirt trickled down his forehead. He saw the rock shift, pulled his hand away and held himself as far to the right as he could.

The boulder plunged an arm's length into the shaft, spraying fragments as it gouged into the softer stone. He studied the dark rock, only finger spans away, as he would an enemy combatant. He pressed himself into the corner to avoid it but his arm brushed the rock as he climbed higher, and the thing shifted again, falling another hand span.

That was the last time it moved, and moments later he pulled himself past, over the verge and into the overcast sunlight. He gauged the time as early afternoon.

He crawled over a mound of debris and bramble, then considered the broken walls of an old cemetery and stunted windblown trees. He was east, as he'd guessed, on a scrubby height a quarter mile from the city's landside walls. He could look down across the whole of Hidrestus to the bay. There lay the little temple district on the highest hill near the water, and to the right of it the rectangular forum. The long straight lanes of the newer suburbs west of the city were interrupted only by the oval colossus of the amphitheater, stretching a couple of stories higher than everything else.

Two things troubled him on the instant. While he was gratified to see the large ship he'd purchased still rode anchor on the shifting gray water, he was none too pleased to observe a Dervan galley pulled up to a long stone quay. It flew no flag, but it was easy to guess that an imperial presence of importance had arrived. Caiax.

More troubling was the awning stretched above the arena. The practical Dervans wouldn't have bothered with a rain guard for the seats unless they expected spectators that day. So far as he knew, there were no other events scheduled until that featuring the Eltyr, and thus no other reason for the awning.

As he forced his way downslope through some bushes, he knew his first true stab of panic, for he heard the distant roar of thousands of voices raised as one. He had been trapped within the tunnels even longer than he realized. The games were under way.

The skies opened up into a spiritless drizzle and Hanuvar pushed his weary legs into motion. Though they protested, he headed for the city at a flat-out run.

VI

Theris settled into the black marble seat, well-padded with yellow cushions. Though he might have taken affront to being seated upon the governor's left in the dignitary box, he was glad not to have to listen to the old man's anile commentary, now being showered upon the lanky, hunch-shouldered visitor in a senator's toga seated on the governor's right. In a row of seats behind them was the young, bored, and beautiful wife of Caiax, looking as serene as a statue, and their two daughters, whose hushed chatter evinced eagerness for the struggle to begin. Judging by the intricate pile of dark hair crowning each, they'd been tended by an army of slaves for hours.

While the governor doted upon Caiax, Theris was less impressed. To his mind, the famed consul's eyes were beady and acquisitive, as if he measured the worth of everyone and everything he saw on some secret scale, and found all of it wanting. There was sharp intellect there, but it was reserved only for counting.

The goddess might find some souls more challenging to awaken with love, but her guidance would see true. Theris considered the walls, where blessed Ariteen's sacred symbols were painted. The arena itself had been sanctified. Owing to the weeks of rituals, the ground and air were saturated with moisture, and the skies were dark. The stars were right; the way was cleared for her arrival. Now only a little blood was needed.

His gaze swept overhead, to where the vast canvas awning had been drawn over the arena. This left the illumination further muted, which was ideal, though in some places it was brightened by torches, or, in the box where he sat now with honored guests, by elegant lanterns. That light glared on the well-shined shoulder plates of the governor's honor guard, and two grim legionaries from Caiax's army, whose resplendent red capes were trimmed in gold.

Once, when he'd been quite young, Theris had journeyed to Derva itself and attended a celebration in its amphitheater. The city of Hidrestus' stadium wasn't on quite as grand a scale, but as the provincial capital was yet an imposing structure, a large oval seating thousands upon tiered stone benches. Its architect had designed it so audiences might quickly and easily be funneled to and from their seats. At least they could be, normally. Soon, of course, his followers would see to the closing and locking of the exit doors.

Theris had toured the underground sections of the arena, where a complex system of pulleys and gears could raise and lower key portions of its floor to permit reinforcements and sudden surprises.

Today a circular stone wall rose about the arena's center, a miniature fortress complete with battlements and metal gates. Directly across from the dignitary box the sea-green flag of Volanus hung limply from the fortress's largest tower, and at that tower's base a pool of water sparkled.

"That's nothing like the real wall of Volanus," Caiax told the governor. "It was ten spear lengths high in many places, and its battlement wide enough for two chariots to drive side by side."

His cousin nodded patiently. "Well, it *is* theatre. We are expected to imagine."

As Caiax grunted his disapproval there was a fanfare from the musicians in the stands below. An expectant hush fell over the crowd as the trumpeters were joined by a drum roll. Upon a raised platform across from the dignitary box, a mellifluous spokesman addressed the crowd through a speaking trumpet, providing a brief but salutary introduction of the governor, Caiax, and Theris himself. Each stood in turn, and then Theris introduced the games in honor of sacred Ariteen.

As the crowd clapped and whistled and stomped feet, Theris resumed his chair. Almost immediately came a new fanfare, another drumroll, and then an armored figure appeared upon the stage battlement in the arena's center. He was a big, bearded man with a green-plumed helm and gleaming armor. A shield hung on his arm, and he clutched a spear in one fist. The shirt beneath his breastplate was sea-green.

"Is that supposed to be Hanuvar?" Caiax asked skeptically.

He may have doubted, but judging from their catcalls the crowd knew who the figure represented. The actor milked the moment, marching back and forth in what Theris suspected was supposed to be martial confidence, though it seemed almost a skipping prance. The armor-clad figure stopped and shouted, gesturing dramatically with a sweep of his spear as his deep voice carried out over the crowd.

"Do the Dervans think they can take my city? I was only ever beaten once, and I tricked the coward Ciprion into letting me go!"

Theris saw the governor grin and glance at his cousin, knowing that the line had been inserted to please the consul. But Caiax showed no reaction to having his old rival insulted.

The false Hanuvar cried out once more: "These walls will hold against all comers! The Dervans will fall! They are no match for me and my beautiful but deadly Eltyr!"

This speech was met with more boos. Some even lobbed fruit rinds and other trash, though little cleared the stands. The actor shouted some more, then a new fanfare sounded and gladiators dressed as legionaries charged into the arena. The fortress gates disgorged additional men dressed in sea-green, and as the crowd cheered, the groups broke into tight knots to battle before the fortress wall.

The Hanuvar actor raced back and forth on the miniature fortification above them, shouting encouragement and insults as weapons clanged into shields and helms. Limbs were hacked and men fell to bloody ruin. Sometimes the actor hopped up and down with rage, waving his spear. The crowd shouted with rising excitement as the blood spilled, Caiax's daughters among them.

Determined to be master of the obvious, Consul Caiax leaned toward his cousin, saying huffily: "That's not how it happened at all."

"No?" the governor asked politely.

Caiax's bony finger pointed toward the arena floor. "That man's playing Hanuvar like a fool. He was the most dangerous man the empire ever faced."

"Oh, the crowd loves it," the governor said with a laugh.

"They wouldn't have loved facing his armies," Caiax groused.

Theris leaned just a bit, forcing cheer into his voice. "Well, his armies are dead, and so is his city, thanks to your bravery."

"Yes, quite," the governor agreed. "Your ballistae drove him into the sea, and your commands shattered the walls of his backstabbing, mongrel race."

Caiax scowled like a man with constipation. Theris looked away, studying the arena. Ariteen would shy from even the wan sunlight pouring through the center of the awning, for she was a goddess of darkness. But there, in the gloomy pockets on the arena edge, he saw what he was after, and smiled. The mist had begun to gather. All she would need was a little more sacrifice.

"Pardon me, Blessed One," a voice at his elbow said, and Theris looked up to find young Ortix beside him. "You wished to speak to the Eltyr before they left for the arena floor. They're nearly ready."

VII

Jerissa and her warriors waited beneath the amphitheater beside one of the elevator platforms. A group of muscular slaves huddled to one side. Around them were the ever-present guards, hard-eyed men in armor, warily watching the thirty well-armed women. Voices carried from outside. Occasionally it was a cry of pain, such as Jerissa had heard in the midst of battle. More often, though, it was the shout of the crowd. Their stamps and claps rang off stone walls and set them vibrating.

She couldn't help wishing she'd never heard from Hanuvar to start with, for that brief hope had made this final disappointment that much more painful. Lurcan was walking up and down in front of them, telling them to be good girls, and that those who fought well would be spared.

Jerissa ground her teeth until she had heard enough. "Don't lie to them," she said.

Lurcan scowled. "Watch your tongue, woman."

She shrugged. What could he do now?

He raised his hand as though to hit her, but stopped as his guards made way for a tall man in a fine blue robe with flowery edge embroidery. He bestowed a regal nod upon frowning Lurcan, then halted before her, opened his arms, and smiled. Strange, that the Dervans would send a priest to bless them. But then he looked an odd priest, for his eyes were glazed like those of a lotus eater.

"Noble ladies," he said, his voice that of a practiced orator, "you do not know it, but you go forth with great purpose this day. You battle not just for your honor, but for the honor of Blessed Ariteen, a protector who surely smiled down upon your own doings, for she, too, is a guardian." His gaze met Jerissa's and she saw that behind that peculiar glint he actually meant what he was saying, though the sorrow in his eyes was of shallow depth. "I am sorry that you have come here, to this place. But your brave actions here, this day, will have repercussions you could never imagine. And because you go forth to risk your lives on behalf of a goddess I cannot expect you to know, I will share with you a secret none but the most devout have heard. Ariteen arrives, this day. It may even be that some of you will see her as your deity, and it might be that some of you will be chosen for her sacred embrace."

He brought his hands together with a fluttering motion, then mumbled strange words over them. Jerissa stared uncomfortably, wondering what she was expected to do. She had heard the prattle of priests before, but this one disquieted her. As he continued speaking she felt strangely exposed, as though some unseen audience observed her.

Finally the priest finished waving his hands over them, nodded a final time as if in approval, and departed. A puzzled-looking Lurcan left with him. The guards, though, remained.

Jerissa turned to her Eltyr.

Each carried a sword and shield and spear. Their armor was of fair make and approximated the traditional Eltyr breastplates, and their tunics of sea-green with gold banding were a close match to the real thing. Her eyes roved over their faces. Some looked numb, others fearful, but more looked angry.

She raised her voice to them. "We go today to face men ordered to slay us. So it was at the sea gate only a few months ago. And while it fell, we took a toll so high that the whole of the wharf and the waters beyond were stained with Dervan blood!" She saw their eyes light at that, and remembered the bodies strewn along the dockside, the foaming seawater turned crimson.

"You didn't ask to join our band, but you have worked hard, and studied well. You came to me as bakers and millers, waitresses and wet nurses. But when we go forth this day, it will be as Eltyr!" She raised her fist and let forth the ululating call of her order.

Ceera lifted her own fist and repeated it, then the women under her command raised their own voices in a cry that set Jerissa's ears ringing.

They hadn't much longer to wait. The arena manager received a signal from a runner, and then informed them it was time to file onto the lift. Jerissa led the way. Slaves stood ready at each corner, four of them to a rope, readying for the command to lift the platform while others worked the pulleys that winched an opening aside through which the lift would rise.

As the arena manager motioned the slaves to the elevator platform, Jerissa turned to her charges, snarling at them. "Make me proud. Show these bloodthirsty cowards the strength of Volani women!"

As they let out the cry of the Eltyr, they rose toward the open square through which light poured. The thin clack of metal on metal, the screams of the dying, and the roar of the crowd echoed in her ears.

Her hand tightened around her spear haft. This, she would hold back, until she had shepherded her warriors through to nearly the end. Then the Dervans would see if their archers could stop her. Caiax had a date with her spear point. The gods owed her that.

VIII

When the centurion presented himself at the ship, he left little time for inquiry. He was bruised and dirty and streaked with soot and even more closemouthed than before. Several days of beard growth stubbled his chin and upper lip. As soon as he confirmed that the slaves were not aboard the ship, he commandeered a supply wagon. Curious, Antires rode with him as the officer recklessly urged the wagon on through the city streets. During the centurion's long absence, Antires had tried his best, but no amount of bribery had opened Lurcan's doors to him again. There'd been better luck with Kerthik, who'd told Antires only an hour before to present himself at the amphitheater's service gate if he found the centurion.

Once they reached that gate, it took Kerthik a considerable time to arrive at the door when Antires pounded upon it.

The scar-faced overseer opened the door at last and eyed them, crestfallen.

"They've already gone up," he said. Then, accusatorily, he eyed the centurion. "Where have you been?"

"Take me there," the centurion ordered.

"It will do you no good. They just went up—"

"Take me there," the centurion repeated harshly.

And so they jogged through the underground tunnels, passing barred rooms that reeked of animals and dung and fear, sloping down and further down and past guttering torches in a vast labyrinth of walls and pillars. The crowd roared, a great, hungry beast.

A group of guards eyed them curiously, and Antires heard them hoping that they'd still manage some good seats as they headed up and out to the arena. He and Kerthik and the centurion stopped at last near a backstage manager. The agitated younger man was in close conversation with a single guard, who held a manacled bearded fellow dressed in a Volani helm and armor. Standing beside him, done up in identical sea-green garb, was a stagey Dervan actor known less for his acumen than his loud voice. The actor was trying to pass over his shield to the slave, but the manacled man was refusing to take it.

The centurion glanced at them, and the group of slaves ready at the pulleys that would winch up a small elevator platform. The square through which the elevator would rise cast an almost blinding light into the dark space.

"You've gotten him too drunk," the manager was shouting at the guard.

"He's not too drunk to drown, is he?" the guard replied.

"How long have the Eltyr been up?" the centurion asked.

"A few minutes," the manager answered distractedly. He jabbed a finger at the guard. "Get him up there and push him into the water. Now."

The centurion drew his sword and pointed it at the manager. "You and the guard. Into the cell."

The manager blinked, not in bravery, but in stunned wonder. Antires understood his confusion.

"Now," the centurion said. "Or I'll kill you."

"Wait a moment," the guard said, but the centurion had gone entirely mad, for he slammed the man in the temple with the flat of his blade and the guard's knees went loose. He sagged.

Suddenly Kerthik was on the manager, knife to him. He, too, must have lost his mind.

The centurion was instantly in charge. "Throw these three in that cell."

"Hey," the Hanuvar actor objected.

Kerthik's grin had no humor in it. "Get in there. You heard him." Bewildered, the manager, Hanuvar actor, and dazed guard stepped into the indicated cell.

"I'll take that shield," the centurion said, then snatched the spear the guard had leaned against the nearby wall. "Your helm," he said after a brief hesitation. The drunken slave removed it with surprising speed, despite his manacles.

The centurion had always possessed the manner of a soldier, but something in his appearance altered the moment he donned the helmet with winged-serpent emblem beneath its green horsehair plume. It was only then Antires paid any attention to the centurion's beard and mustache growth, and the sharp gray eyes. He might not even have noticed them if the man hadn't suddenly hefted the shield with the winged-serpent crest of Volanus upon it.

"Hold this place until I get them out," the centurion said, even as Antires stared, his mind struggling to keep up with what his eyes had discovered. The soldier pointed with the spear to where a ladder stretched along a pillar nearby, up toward a sealed exit. "Get that door open."

It was only when the centurion stepped to the elevator platform, illumined by a shaft of sunlight, that Antires fully admitted to himself who he faced. It was less like meeting a ghost than suddenly beholding Acon, god of war.

Antires paled. He had so many questions, and so much defied his understanding. He was chilled, as though he'd walked through a graveyard at twilight. Most pressing, though, was what this man expected to do if he rode the elevator into the arena. "You can't expect—how are you—why—" He couldn't even mouth a full sentence.

"Because no one gets left behind," Hanuvar said. "Hold the way, Herrene, and emulate the brave men you so admire! Let none keep you back! I'm bringing all of them out, or dying at their side." He gestured to the slaves, who looked uncertain.

"You heard him!" Antires shouted. "Raise it! Hurry!"

And at his command, the slaves bent to his wishes, and the scourge of the Dervan legions rose to meet his fate in the arena.

IX

The Eltyr line held their formation as the legionaries crashed against them. Shields dented and splintered and blades fell and rose again, dripping red with blood. The male gladiators shouted their war cries, but rising above it all was the chilling, ululating call of the Eltyr.

Caiax murmured appreciatively that the women were giving it a good show. Two dropped back, bleeding, but the shield line closed, and withstood all attempts at flanking.

The crowd was riveted.

As the actor playing Hanuvar disappeared, Theris noted that the mist stirring in the dark recesses of the amphitheater had thickened. He searched the nearby faces, but to a one they were centered upon the clash of arms as the gladiators dressed in legionary armor pushed into the solid line of Eltyr.

Suddenly the arena announcer shouted through his speaking trumpet. "And now Hanuvar himself returns!"

A man dressed in sea-green armor had been raised on an elevator through a hole in the top of the stage battlement. He was clearly different from the previous actor. But there was no "retainer" behind him that would have pushed him into the artificial "sea," the pit of water that sloshed at the foot of the fortress wall, placed so Hanuvar's death by drowning would be reenacted before the cheering throngs. This new Hanuvar brandished his spear and tossed it over the merlon. It flew with unerring accuracy into the side of the foremost legionary. The line of gladiators in Dervan garb stumbled and the Eltyr moved quickly to seize the moment. Caiax's daughters cried out that it hadn't been fair.

The governor leaned toward Theris. "That doesn't seem sporting, does it? Isn't this the part where he's supposed to drown?"

Theris only nodded distractedly and watched the mist.

"That's a different fellow," Caiax remarked. Then added: "He's a much better likeness."

Then the Hanuvar actor lifted his voice, shouting words Theris didn't understand, though he recognized the ringing, bell-like sounds of Volani. Distracted as he was, these commands somehow sounded far more martial, and he clearly heard the word "Eltyr."

Caiax straightened in his seat, then stood, blood rising in his face. "That's him. That's Hanuvar!"

His wife spoke at last. "Don't be absurd, dear."

"It's him!" The consul pointed a stiffened arm, as though it were somehow unclear who he meant. "He's ordering them to fall back!"

And they were. The Eltyr performed an awkward retreat with their shield wall toward the sealed doors of their imitation fortress even as Hanuvar disappeared from view down an inner stair.

Curious as that development was, Theris' attention was pulled away by sudden screams on the darker, south side of the arena, furthest from the booth of the dignitaries. The mist itself had risen, towering six or seven times the height of a man. Fog streamed away from what resembled a figure draped in a flowing garment.

"Ariteen." Theris reverently pronounced the name of his goddess. Why the people screamed he couldn't imagine, unless it was with surprise. Already the great mother extended strangely fluid limbs and mist to bless those nearest in the stands. They appeared stricken with joy as she embraced them. Some even stood and shook with strange, spontaneous spasms of delight. The arena's archers, perhaps confused, loosed arrows at her. But what good were weapons against a deity? She forgave them with caresses of coiling mist and they shuddered in ardor and collapsed. She glided on, blessing all she neared, and the screams spread.

The governor seemed to have noted the confusion on the other side of the arena. "What's going on there?" His voice, normally imperious, quailed a little. "What is that?"

Theris rose and spread his arms, beaming beatifically. "That, Governor, is my goddess, come at last to bring love to all the world."

X

At the bottom of the stairs to the stage fortress, Hanuvar found another manager, screaming at his guard to force "Hanuvar" into submission. They assumed he was the prisoner intended for drowning. He caught the guard's blow on his shield then smashed his skull with an overhand sword strike, splattering the manager with blood and brains. He finished the gaping manager with a quick thrust then stepped over the bodies and threw off the bar closing the heavy wooden doors. It creaked as he forced it open, and immediately a bloody woman dressed in Eltyr garments staggered into his arms. He steadied her, ignored her gaping astonishment, and pointed behind him. Antires had emerged from a small square panel in the floor ten paces back and waved her toward him.

"Hurry!" Hanuvar urged.

After she staggered off, Hanuvar watched through the fortress doorway as the mass of some forty gladiators strove to break through a shield wall formed by nearly three dozen women warriors.

The door was too narrow for more than four of the Eltyr to retreat at once—instead, per his orders, the front rank had formed a solid screen, shields up and spears bristling, while women slipped back. He stepped through, snagged a spear from a gasping young woman with a broken nose and bruised face, then sent it sailing over the heads of the Eltyr and into the mouth of a shouting gladiator.

The crowd caught sight of him once more and booed, thinking he played a role.

The line faltered as the warriors pressed on. Jerissa, in the lead, was bowled over by a sudden assault from a tall, powerful opponent.

Hanuvar elbowed past a swearing woman, all the time shouting for them to fall back. He arrived in time to plant his shield against a strike that would have driven a sword through Jerissa's neck.

He'd faced countless Dervan legionaries, but few so muscular as the gladiator before him. The blow he caught set his shield ringing.

He bashed his shield rim into the fellow's hand. This sent the gladiator off balance and Hanuvar plunged his sword deep through the man's cuirass. He spun to the left, dropping with raised shield, and blocked a blow from another gladiator.

Jerissa scrambled to her feet and joined him, her eyes wide in wonder. "You came," she said.

"Yes." The two fell back as the gladiator legionaries pressed in.

"But you'll be killed," she said.

There were more vital matters to attend to than conversation. For some reason, the assault had lessened in intensity. Those to the rear of their foes seemed distracted, and the screams of the crowd had risen in pitch. Did they finally understand he was no actor? Were the gladiators holding back because Dervan guards were readying a flight of arrows?

A spear splintered on his shield, and he lopped a thrusting arm off at the wrist. As the gladiator dropped screaming, all opposition ebbed.

Panting for breath, dripping sword still at the ready, Hanuvar looked past a wary gladiator and into the stands, where mist rolled across the gloomy benches and aisles. Something moved within, a form Hanuvar took at first for a gigantic woman in a gauzy dress shaped from vapor.

But as the thing swung wide to avoid a burning lantern, he saw the monstrous image wasn't any kind of woman. It had no true visage, merely a gray faceless orb with black blotches, like the top of a rotting mushroom. Hairlike translucent tentacles swayed from the orb, whipping now and then to touch those nearest. It left its victims dead or senseless in its wake.

It must have been wandering among the stands for a good while, for vast numbers lay motionless, or gravely wounded, judging from their twitching forms. Dozens ran within the stands, screaming in fear, among them the arena bowmen.

The male gladiator nearest Hanuvar cursed in horror. He glanced at the Eltyr, then shouted at his men to retreat. What began as an orderly withdrawal erupted into chaos as they reached the exit gate. They shouted in panic and banged on the door to be opened.

Hanuvar's senses rebelled at the sight of that thing gliding through the stands; he bared his teeth in silent struggle with the atavistic urge to run from the presence of the supernatural. Old training kept him still, verifying the terrain, his placement, the exits, the position of his allies and enemies. A glance over his shoulder showed him all but Jerissa had vanished through the doorway of the false fortress and, hopefully, to the open hatch beyond. Antires, though, stood staring raptly in the doorway and shouted for Hanuvar to look out even as Jerissa cried the same warning.

A sharp blow snapped into Hanuvar and drove him back. An arrow stood out from his armored shoulder. He felt the sting of its edge in his flesh. Instantly his shield went up, and he winced at the pain as the muscle obeyed his will. He saw now what Jerissa had observed, a man with a bow advanced to the edge of the dignitary box, even now ripping a toga from his shoulders. He was flanked by two soldiers casting anxious glances at the monstrous mist thing approaching on their left.

Caiax. His followers might be concerned with the monster, but he had eyes only for the arena floor. He was a tall man, and with his lean, hunched shoulders and prominent nose he resembled a vulture, though one dressed in borrowed plumage, for his tunic was resplendent with gold thread. He'd probably grabbed his weapon from one of the arena guards. Normally archers would have been posted along the walls at numerous points, but they were in flight.

To the right of the box, the monstrous, impossible being swept slowly back and forth through the stands, chasing down all who lived. Some of its quarry thrust themselves into the hallways that should have emptied from the amphitheater, but found no exit, and their massed bodies provided easy fare. Others scrambled up and around the dignitary box, where they huddled with the remaining crowd, for a time beyond the creature's reach. A few hardy souls had retreated high into the stands where the canvas awning stretched taut over all but the dead center of the arena, and some desperate men climbed into the rigging.

Hanuvar tore the arrow from his shoulder with a curse and cast it aside, studying the situation. Above him, black eyes glinting, Caiax put a second arrow to bow and let fly.

XI

Theris had stepped to the edge of the dignitary box, and gradually his beaming smile had worn away to slack-jawed horror. He watched his goddess roll on like some contemplated the steady progress of the tide. Mist from Ariteen's greater mass coiled snakelike around the men and women she passed, growing opaque and solidifying as it thrust into mouth, nose, and ears of the fleeing mob. She left her victims dead and still, though they moved in a fashion, for those in her wake erupted with mold and mushrooms.

She drew ever closer, now gliding higher into the stands, now lower.

His heart thrummed in his chest and his pulse all but burst with the desire to leave. Yet he could not find the will to act. It was as though he watched it all from some far remove, the terrified cries of the crowd, running this way and that, the twitching corpses, the drifting menace, the sickly sweet smell of corrupting fungus. It was no easy thing to acknowledge error, much less understand that your entire life, and those of thousands of your predecessors, had been founded upon such profound misunderstandings of a god's true nature.

Ariteen had come at last, as long foretold. She made all equal in death. She shared her love with all as she met them, leaving life to erupt in their jerking corpses.

Caiax remained, down at the very edge of the box, oblivious to the menace and firing into the arena itself. His wife and daughters had already fled.

The goddess's attention was diverted when the general's guards gave up at last and sprinted frantically for the top rows. As she climbed after them, stretching with her transparent limbs, Theris finally found his resolve, and turned to flee toward the other side of the box, thinking to leap the barrier.

But his sudden movement drew her regard. She lashed out with one long tentacle. It reached his waist and solidified and Theris let out a horrified gasp.

Her touch was tender, and as he was lifted into the air, he realized he had been wrong to doubt her. Surely he was meant for greater things.

Then a dozen other appendages drove into him, lashed up through each of his orifices. He screamed in fear and pain, and then a tentacle pushed into his mouth. His failing body erupted with new life, hungry and eager for him, and he was laid down with infinite care upon a bench beside a purple and white blotchy thing his dying eyes recognized for the governor, blooming with all manner of mushrooms.

XII

Hanuvar caught the arrow on his shield. "Fool!" he shouted. "That beast's killing your people!"

The mist thing drew ever closer, but Caiax, teeth gritted, fitted another arrow to his bow. Before he nocked it, Jerissa let fly. At the last moment the consul saw the spear from the side of his eye. It drove into his belly and he sagged, both hands around the haft. He dropped below the stone balcony.

Jerissa's lips parted in a savage smile, and she looked to Hanuvar, who seemed a little stunned.

Jerissa backed toward the gate. "Hurry," she cried.

But Hanuvar advanced toward the arena wall. A hesitant Jerissa came after.

"Grab that torch!" he cried. "Set it to the rope!"

He pointed at the railing ten feet above, and she understood his meaning. He signed her to climb to his shoulders and he grunted as she set a foot on his injured side. From there she leapt for the railing, caught it, held with one hand near one of the sturdy ratlines that hooked the canvas awning in place.

On her right, the monstrous mist thing drifted past the dignitary box. To her left, only a few hand spans off, the lantern projected from a pillar demarcating the end of a row. Arms leaden with fatigue, she pulled herself to the rim. She felt the eyes of the crowd upon her, hundreds of them, withdrawn to the last untouched corner of the arena.

When she turned to the terrifying thing she saw it lay only a bowshot away.

With a bloody hand she grabbed at the torch, found it hammered in place. Desperate strength tore it free, breaking it along half its length, and she put the flame to the rope. Tough fibers resisted the flame long moments as the terrible entity rolled ever nearer and a forest of tentacles quested toward her ... but then the rope caught with red and she sent the torch sailing into the monster. The fire swept up along the ratline and climbed toward the awning.

The mist monster retreated from the sudden flare, and Jerissa retreated to the area railing. It seemed a longer drop than would be comfortable, but she let go and hit the sand with a stumble.

Hanuvar had made a speaking trumpet of his hands and shouted to the crowd. "Get to the arena floor! Hurry! It fears the light!"

That done, Jerissa and Hanuvar ran at last for the exit, sidestepping the corpses of gladiators and fallen women alike. She stared at her dead warriors as she passed, committing them to memory. Above, the fire reached the point where the ratline met the canvas. It hesitated almost like a cautious living thing upon the edge, then suddenly spread out and up and the awning blazed a vibrant red.

Jerissa risked a last glance through the gate of the false fortress before running for a ladder visible through the opening in the arena floor. She saw the terrible monster writhing in upon itself, withdrawing and shrinking toward whatever shadows it could find. Frantic survivors had taken Hanuvar's advice and now dropped toward the arena floor, away from the flames. The gladiators milled forward with them. Apparently no one on the other side of their exit door had ever heard their pleas.

The Herrene who'd come with Hanuvar to Lurcan's school waited beside an opening, torch in one hand. He'd gathered cast-off cloaks and spears and wooden scraps and encircled their exit with it. "Start on down," he said. "I'll set fire and follow."

It hadn't occurred to Jerissa that the mist thing might pursue them into the darkness, and she appreciated his foresight.

In a few moments she and Hanuvar were below, and the Herrene scrambled after.

Kerthik was waiting, his scarred face lit in a grim smile. "I sent your sergeant and the others out, though she didn't want to go," he told Jerissa, then turned to Hanuvar. "I hope you've room for one more, wherever you're going."

The Dervans would certainly have no place for him, now, Jerissa thought, but looked to Hanuvar.

"We can always accommodate a friend." Hanuvar nodded to the wobbly, drunken slave still dressed in the Volani colors. "Take him too."

Kerthik looked confused at the order, but threw an arm over the fellow's shoulder, and together the five of them hurried through the labyrinth and out through the back gate.

Ceera had somehow acquired a couple of wagons that the women warriors had piled into.

The slave laborers who'd operated the lifts had come out with them and now watched nervously beside the carts.

"Come with us," Hanuvar said. "Be free!"

And with that invitation, they clambered into the overflowing vehicles. Hanuvar himself jumped aboard, and in moments, under the cracking whips of Ceera and the Herrene, the vehicles were rattling over the paved streets. Behind them the canvas ceiling of the amphitheater sent flame and smoke licking toward the clouds.

They passed small knots of men and women staring in horror at the crown of flame visible above the buildings.

"I saw that . . . mist thing," Antires said to Hanuvar, who held tight to the seat as the cart careened on the uneven track. "Do you think you killed it?"

"It doesn't like anything bright, and it's surrounded by the light." Hanuvar's eyes sought the fire and smoke pluming into the sky. "It would be hard to survive that."

XIII

Only a few people were on hand to stare at them as they piled out of the wagons near the dock. Most were either at the amphitheater or standing in the street watching the smoke.

Their ship crew stood ready, no matter the lashing wind and foam-capped waves, and they received their passengers with mounting surprise. Hanuvar had carefully picked the crew. Many were not Volani, but were, like them, homeless, and friendless. In a way, they were all his people, for they were downtrodden victims of the Dervans. He had already spoken to the sailors obliquely of freedom, but he hadn't revealed his identity. He wished that he'd thought to procure a healer, too, but he hadn't had the time. Likely some of the women warriors helped aboard by their companions wouldn't survive their injuries.

Would that so many things had gone differently, all along.

Jerissa, finished with her initial assessment of the wounded, joined them. He felt the heat of her eyes, though her voice was soft. "Why didn't you come sooner?"

What she really wondered was why so many had perished that should have lived. It was the question he would have asked, in her place. "The Dervans had me, Jerissa. I came as quickly as I could. I wish I could have gotten all of you out alive."

She shook her head. "You've done more than I would have dreamed days ago."

"What's their condition?"

"We lost four. Three more may not make it. But if they die, they will die free. And none of us would be alive if not for you. Thank you."

He nodded soberly. Pointless to dwell on might-have-beens. There were so many of them.

He called for his people, these few, and Kerthik and Antires and the old white-haired navigator stood with them near the gangway.

"You're free now," he said. "Derva no longer holds your bonds. You journey to a land without kings, or slaves. It is but a small settlement, but the air is clean and fresh, the fruits are sweet, and the crops grow well. Work in defense of the land, and you'll be welcome."

"All of us?" Kerthik asked.

"My word carries weight," Hanuvar said. "If you don't intend to go, you'd best clear out, because the Dervans will come hunting soon. Though my guess is they'll be too busy trying to figure out what happened to launch any organized effort for a little while."

"I'm done with them," Kerthik said. "I'm for this new land."

Hanuvar turned to Jerissa. "You're in command. I've confided the secret of our course to this man, and he will guide you home." He nodded at the navigator.

Though momentarily confused, her expression cleared. "You're going to free some of the others, aren't you?"

He spoke with an intensity that startled even himself. "I'm going to free them all."

"You should take me."

He'd expected that, and shook his head. "No." Her accent, her very carriage, were too obvious. Besides, the ship needed a captain, and New Volanus needed Eltyr. "Shepherd them home. We will need you to guide our armies. We must be ready, should the Dervans ever learn our secret."

While she wrestled with accepting that order, he shifted his gaze to Antires. "New Volanus could stand some actors and playwrights," he said.

"Maybe they could. But I'm coming with you."

Hanuvar laughed. "I appreciate your quick thinking at the arena, but I travel alone." The last thing he needed was a civilian trailing him from place to place. Even one brave enough to have entered a Dervan gladiatorial arena of his own accord.

"Traveling alone almost got you killed," Antires countered. "I can help you. I can show you tricks of the trade. Makeup, accents, behaviors, all kinds of things. You can't always pretend to be a soldier."

While Hanuvar was certain his own deceptive skills were far superior to what the young man assumed, he understood that there was something to what the Herrene said. It wasn't just his assistance at the arena. Without Antires' efforts during Hanuvar's absence, freeing Jerissa and all the others would have been impossible. He had proven an able ally, and Hanuvar knew he was unlikely to find another like him. He also knew that Antires had little concept of the challenges ahead. Hanuvar would never be able to share his goals with the Herrene, for fear that if the younger man were captured the Dervans might learn too much. And his end, not just as an enemy of Derva but as an ally of Hanuvar, would not be pretty. "It could be a harder road than any you've known," he warned. "We may fall in battle, and if we're captured alive we face a grisly death."

"That doesn't frighten me," Antires said.

"It should."

"Well, perhaps it does, a little. But I must know what happens next. And someone has to write all of this down. Some day I'll make it a play that will grant me immortality to match your own."

Hanuvar chuckled and shook his head. He raised his hand to Jerissa and the others and wished them safe journeys, then clapped Antires on the shoulder and the two walked away as good wishes rang after.

Hanuvar looked back only once as the ship cast off and rolled out onto the heaving waves. Soon he was bandaged and divested of uniform, a nondescript cloaked figure riding into the rain with a companion upon one of the great roads, an artery that wound on toward the heart of the empire.

░ ░ ░

In mere days, new rumors were added to those already spreading, that Hanuvar had risen from his own tomb, accompanied by a legion of undead warriors. That he had hunted down the man who'd destroyed his city, Caiax, and mortally wounded him with a flaming spear. He was said to command ghastly sorceries that had conjured a soul-eating demon formed of mist, and to have magically sealed the gates of an amphitheater before setting its roof aflame.

None knew where he would next appear, but the emperor reportedly doubled his personal guard, summoned his priests and sorcerers, and dispatched the feared magic hunters known as revenants to track him down. But how could they find a ghost? And even if they could, how might they slay a spirit of vengeance?

. . . He had declared in my presence that he meant to free all of his people, but when I pressed him on the matter he shared almost nothing of his plans. When I pointed out that they had likely been sold to many owners scattered through many places, he but said he was conscious of the difficulties. He meant to sail to Derva from the nearest large port, and so we travelled the major northwest road for Tonsta, which lay only a week away.

I asked many questions of him while we rode and discovered that while history fascinated him, Hanuvar had little interest in discussing his own. In the ensuing years I spoke with many of the famous who practiced modestly, and most of them secretly longed to be better known for their triumphs, or to air long-held grievances. Hanuvar was not one of those, and weeks were to pass before he shared much of anything personal, and that only grudgingly.

He took to instruction about acting far more readily, however. Hanuvar possessed a gift for languages and with it an excellent ear, so that he could easily adopt an accent. These natural-born talents, in tandem with his astonishing memory and a fascination with human nature, meant he had a great affinity for the playing of parts. And that would prove useful to him.

I am not without a measure of pride, and I fully believe he found my instruction useful. Certainly he said that it was, and through the time we spent on theatre craft each evening I saw him begin to hone his instincts into a crucial survival skill.   —Sosilos, Book Two

Chapter 5:
Shroud of Feathers

I

Under the shade of a tall cypress, Antires knelt at the cook fire, stirring the sliced onions and cabbage as they sizzled on the black skillet. A woodlark, perched in the branches above, warbled cheerily. For all that it had been a long, warm day of travel, the young playwright looked content.

But Hanuvar glowered as he stomped up beside him.

"I don't believe it," Antires said, and with a wooden spoon almost as brown as the hand that gripped it, pushed a darkening slice of onion to the skillet's edge. He reached for the flask of olive oil.

His gray horse, picketed beside Hanuvar's bay roan, looked up from where he was busily nibbling grass and snorted, as if expressing his own disfavor.

"No?" Hanuvar straightened, casting off the illusion of anger and age like a cloak. "You asked me to look mad."

Antires finished dribbling in more oil, then set the flask down and stirred the vegetables. "You were carrying yourself like a weak man, but when I asked you to show anger, it was the rage of someone confident. When you play a character, you have to remember what their story is."

Hanuvar's own folly amused him. Always be ready to learn, his father had said, no matter your teacher. He had too quickly equated the playwright's youth with lack of knowledge.

Hanuvar sketched a bow. "Shape the clay, potter."

"Stick out your lip so you look like you're pouting. You're resentful, not ready to kill."

Hanuvar hunched his shoulders and imitated a lazy soldier turned out from bed for the watch.

"That's better. Maybe too much pouting, though. Don't aim for the back row. Small expressions. You don't want to be challenging in your anger. Oh, yes. That's—" Antires quieted as Hanuvar raised a palm.

The woodlark had gone silent and the horses lifted their heads and pricked their ears. Hanuvar turned, hand to the pommel of the gladius at his waist. He had rid himself of the Naratan blade, which was too distinctive. He heard the scuff of a sandal from the shaded dirt path to the road.

Hanuvar was waiting with bared sword when a trio of men advanced from the encircling trees. The two carrying hunting spears were stocky with middle age. The third was a lean youth with a bulbous nose, and he brandished a pitchfork.

Two more men crashed through the brush to the south, and three others stepped through a screen of cedars to the north.

Antires pulled his skillet off the coals and joined Hanuvar, blade unsheathed. He made a brave figure, and those approaching would be unlikely to guess he only mimicked a blademan's stance.

A bald man with thick black eyebrows came to the forefront of the intruding band, brandishing his sword as he spoke with a snarl. "Drop the swords if you know what's good for you."

Hanuvar answered without lowering his weapon. "If you want them, come and take them."

That didn't seem to be the answer the bald man expected. He shifted uncomfortably.

"What have you done with Tura?" the boy with the pitchfork demanded. His fingers tightened on the weapon's haft.

"We know nothing of a Tura," Hanuvar replied.

"You must have us confused with someone else," Antires suggested in a honeyed tone. "We're just passing through."

The strangers fidgeted and looked to the bald man. He scowled. "You're lying. She came this way. You've killed her, and kept the bird for yourself."

"We don't have any birds," Antires said. "Or women."

From further down the trail the jingle of reins and the stamp of hooves grew louder. The intruders relaxed visibly and Hanuvar guessed their real leader was almost here.

He found a measure of solace in what the men had said so far, for this confrontation apparently had nothing to do with his hidden identity. Rumors about his return to Dervan lands would inevitably spread, but so far he and Antires seemed to have outsped them.

That didn't mean there was no danger. The men who'd surrounded them had the wary, nervous manner of a potential lynch mob. One on one they were hesitant, even cowardly, but the right nudge might launch the group of them into murderous fury. Right now their intent wavered, and Hanuvar sensed their next action would be shaped by the approaching rider.

Only a few moments later a young soldier reined in a splendid gray at the clearing's edge. He wore legionary mail and tunic with the white pteruges of an optio. A sword was girded at his waist, and in amongst his saddlebags was a clutch of javelins.

Hanuvar felt the brush of the optio's eyes, steady and searching. They didn't light with any particular concern or recognition, further reassurance that this intrusion had nothing to do with him personally. The officer considered Antires before addressing the mob in a mild voice. "What are you doing, Cerka?"

The bald man pointed to them with his free hand. "We found these men here, right in the path. They have to know!"

The optio's mouth turned down in displeasure, and then he faced Hanuvar. "State your names, travelers. Tell me where you're from and where you're bound."

Hanuvar lowered his sword but didn't sheathe it. "I am Artus," he answered, "late of the Third Cohort of the Mighty Sixth."

The optio nodded as if Hanuvar's words had confirmed a suspicion. "What rank did you muster out from, Artus?"

"Centurion."

The optio nodded his head once, in respect. "I am Optio Lucian Silvi." He almost sounded apologetic as he continued: "Do you have your discharge papers?"

"In my pack. I'd share them, if these men weren't ready to skewer me when I lower my sword."

"There'll be no skewering. Your companion?"

Antires answered easily. "I'm Starik, his nephew. And we're bound for Tonsta. We come from Iltri. And we don't know anything about this Tura the boy was shouting about."

"They're lying!" the young man with the pitchfork cried.

One of the crowd muttered his agreement and Cerka began to talk. Their voices were drowned out by the optio. "They have horses," the young officer said curtly. "Did any of you happen to notice horse tracks before this?"

The men traded uncertain glances.

Cerka frowned, his heavy brows drooping. "They could be hiding her."

"Or," the optio said, "they were traveling the main road on their horses, and stopped off at a campsite to eat, at supper time. Like normal men who have nothing to do with Tura."

Hanuvar was privately impressed; Lucian Silvi had delivered just the right note of dry exasperation. Now the optio put a snap in his voice as he looked to the villagers. "Lower your weapons."

The crowd objected, the pitchfork-laden boy expostulating loudest.

"Now," Lucian said, steel in his voice.

When all eight of the men complied, the optio looked wordlessly to Hanuvar, who sheathed his own blade. Antires did the same.

The optio nudged his horse forward. "If you wouldn't mind, I'd like to see your papers."

Hanuvar stepped to his pack and pulled them from an inside pocket. If necessary, he could have produced different identity records, courtesy of stamps he'd liberated from the Dervan officer's compound on the Isles of the Dead, but these, complete with an appropriate imprint, showed that he'd mustered out three months before with the rank of centurion, after twenty-five years of service. Lucian scanned them, surely noting the detailed duty record, including two demerits and three commendations for valor.

He returned the papers. "Thank you, Centurion. I serve with the Indomitable Seventh, Fourth Cohort."

Much of the Seventh, Hanuvar knew, was scattered along the coast, its individual cohorts enforcing law in the smaller settlements. "Where's the rest of your unit?"

"My second's in town nursing a twisted ankle. The rest of my men are hunting sheep rustlers. I've had to lean on these men for aid. We're tracking a missing young woman and we're short on qualified help."

Hanuvar knew what that final statement meant. In moments, Lucian could order him and Antires to assist. But the legionary was being polite to someone he had accepted not only as a fellow soldier, but a seasoned veteran.

"We'll be glad to help, if you'll have us," Hanuvar said. Any other reply would have provoked suspicion. And no matter how much he chafed at delay, suspicion was something he could not afford.

"The legion thanks you for your aid," the optio said formally to them both. One of the members of the mob handed his spear to Cerka and wandered away into the brush beyond the campsite.

Antires watched the bearded man's departure, then spoke to the young soldier. "What's happened to the woman? And what's this about a bird?"

"She was abducted," the young man said bitterly. He leaned against his pitchfork, driven into the ground beside him. "And she had our lucky bird with her."

Hanuvar had never before heard of a village with a lucky bird but said nothing as Lucian explained further.

"That's what some of them think. But there's no sign of a struggle."

"She's lost her mind with grief so was an easy target," Cerka asserted, still scowling.

"What do you think, Optio?" Hanuvar asked.

The legionary hesitated before offering his own interpretation. "Her mother, the village priestess, died suddenly this morning and Tura didn't take it well."

The bearded man spoke to them from the campsite edge. "It looks as though she passed through here, but she pressed on south. Toward the fens."

The campsite was clearly a frequent stopover point for travelers, but Hanuvar had seen no recent footprints when they'd arrived a half hour ago. While he supposed it was just possible a skilled tracker could have seen something he'd missed, he was troubled by a significant look passed between the bearded man and Cerka because he couldn't tell what it meant.

The optio seemed oblivious to the interplay. His heavy lips turned down. "Surely she'd have the sense to keep away from there."

"Not if she's gone mad with grief," Cerka said.

"Let's pray she's not that mad." Lucian turned to Hanuvar with a rueful smile. "This may be soggy work, Centurion."

"I'm sure I've seen worse," Hanuvar answered. "Let's go find her."

II

As the dark of evening gathered in the trees, they advanced into the muddy fens, and at Hanuvar's suggestion, Antires returned with the horses, their own three and the optio's gray, to camp on firmer ground. Twilight was near, but neither the optio nor the men he led seemed inclined to abandon their quarry. The bearded Tibron advanced into the long grasses, the earth squishing beneath his sandaled feet. Beautiful violet flowers drooped on shoulder high stalks.

The fens were both lovely and deceptive, for solid ground was almost indistinguishable from deep sink holes, especially in the twilight. The grasses grew to the same height regardless of the earth's solidity. Biting insects swarmed and heavily thorned vegetation tore at exposed flesh. Fanged reptiles, disease-bearing rodents, and larger hunters likely frequented these environs. Hanuvar thought survival chances were thin for anyone unprepared to traverse such a place alone. They might find their quarry retreated to some dry piece of land to starve or collapse in fever, or she could be lost forever, drowned, or thoroughly consumed by the region's carnivores.

The optio ordered them to advance in two lines just in sight of each other. As the gloom deepened, they reached a region thick with bramble and cedar, rising above channels of knee-deep water. The optio, leading Hanuvar's group, carried a lantern, as did Cerka, behind Tibron, the tracker leading the other line. Their lights slashed through the building darkness and glittered on the dark water.

Tibron occasionally peered at the rare patch of muddy high ground or the way the marsh grass bent. More often he touched something hidden in the fold of his tunic. Once, Hanuvar heard a faint crackling as Tibron clasped his garment, the noise just audible above the incessant drone of the fen's countless, unseen amphibians. Twice he'd spotted small broken feathers left in the tracker's wake. He couldn't identify the kind of feather, or, more importantly, explain Tibron's actions, and he decided not to inquire. Not yet.

Hanuvar's doubt over the tracker's skill flowered fully when they crossed a spur of dry land and Tibron walked blindly past a distinctive mark. Hanuvar bent to confirm his suspicion, grimly noting the print of claws at the end of a heavy foot pressing down sodden leaves. Something had passed through the mud, dragging a long tail behind it.

The optio doubled back through the cool, calf-deep water to check on him. "What is it?" he asked. Lucian had shed his helmet, and without it his youth was more evident. Surely he wasn't much older than twenty-two.

"Saathra," Hanuvar answered. "And the marks are fresh." He stood. "If there are saathra here, it's suicide to continue. It's hard enough to spot them in daylight. Your Tura may already be done for."

The optio ran a hand through short, thick hair, his heavy chin outthrust. "She's a smart young woman. She'll keep to the high ground." He sounded as if he spoke more from hope than conviction.

"Then we seek her in the morning," Hanuvar suggested.

The tracker called back to them. "Hurry up! We're gaining on her!"

"Just a little longer," the optio said, almost as if begging permission.

"Have these men gone this deep into the fens before?" Hanuvar asked.

The optio's frown showed he thought he understood Hanuvar's concern. "We'll be careful," he promised.

They pressed on, and Hanuvar went unhappily with them. He instructed the villagers to watch for movement in the water, though in the failing light that would be a challenge.

As they splashed away from one small hillock and on for another, they startled a herd of long-legged deer, whose eyes glowed redly with reflected lantern light. The creatures took stock of the oncoming humans then fled, their hooves pulling up phosphorescent muck as they splashed off, so that a green trail pointed the way after them.

Hanuvar and the men advanced into waist-deep water. Something heavy slapped into his leg and only his training kept him from panic. A large animal surged past him and he called warning as he turned to seek it. A heartbeat later the boy with the pitchfork, struggling through the dark water, stiffened and screamed.

The water foamed as the youth tottered, and Hanuvar glimpsed a muscular blackish form writhing beneath the surface. The boy stabbed wildly with his pitchfork, and the weapon lodged in the muck, standing at a slant. He opened his mouth in another scream, then was jerked under.

One man struck the water with his sword. Heart racing, Hanuvar seized the pitchfork and searched the churning water, but could neither see nor feel a target. He stepped back, scanning for the boy and the saathra, and for others of its ilk.

The rest of the band scrambled up a muddy bank, save for the optio, wading forward with a spear.

The water behind the soldier erupted, and Hanuvar lunged past him to jam the pitchfork at a shovel-shaped reptilian head. The tines bit deep, and the water darkened. The wounded monster flailed in agony, tearing the weapon from Hanuvar's grasp.

"Go!" Hanuvar cried. For where there was one saathra, and blood, more were likely.

He and the optio lurched toward dry ground, and Hanuvar heard the splash of something following even as the figures on the bank pointed past them and shouted in alarm.

Neither he nor the young soldier turned to look. Three of the men leaned out from tree trunks along the slope, hands outthrust. Hanuvar floundered forward, certain now all his plans would come to naught and he'd be torn to pieces in the water. But somehow he scrambled up the muddy slope, over a tangling tree root and into the hands of Tibron, who helped him up the slope. The optio, panting, stood beside Hanuvar. They exchanged a glance, then looked down at the frothing water surging with serpentine forms.

Hanuvar pointed to a little rise at the center of the high ground. "That's where we'll make camp. Let's hope it stays dry, because we'll need a fire through the night. And watchmen who'll stay alert. Those things might crawl up for dessert."

III

Once the fire blazed, they shared a meal that was an odd mix of flattened, mushy meat and half-pulped fruit. The bread had to be discarded. The two men in charge of carrying supplies had stumbled, soaking and squashing the food.

The night was haunted with the calls of fen creatures. Not only did the men hear the whine of insects and the croak of frogs, there were stranger sounds, low and mournful, high and chittering, even one that sounded like a cross between a mad dog and a laughing child.

After sharing a few words about the dead young man, they had fallen silent, warming their feet and footgear at the fireside.

After a time, the optio spoke quietly to Hanuvar. "The Mighty Sixth. You must have seen action in the war against Hanuvar, then."

"I did," Hanuvar said, in a tone that he hoped would discourage further questions. He had chosen the sixth for his cover because he'd interacted so often with its men. Spies and informants and occasional parleys had given him a fair knowledge of the names and the behaviors, as well as the appearance, of many of its officers and most prominent soldiers.

"Hanuvar," Cerka repeated, and Hanuvar fought from starting at the sound of his own name. He slowly looked over to Cerka, noting a splatter of mud along his bald pate. "I guess he wasn't nearly as much of a tough bastard as they said, huh?" Cerka asked. "I hear he screamed like a little girl when they killed him."

That confirmed what he'd earlier guessed: these men knew only about his supposed death, not his survival. Good.

"Did you ever see him?" one of the other men asked.

"A few times," Hanuvar answered.

"What did he look like?" This question came from Tibron. The bearded tracker sat on a stone beside Cerka.

"He was tall with jet black hair and a beard." Hanuvar traced a finger along the side of his face. "He had a wicked scar down one cheek, and an eye patch. I knew the man that tossed the spear that did that to him."

Sooner or later word of his survival would reach every corner of the empire, and if he could sow confusion about his actual appearance, so much the better. But he wasn't interested in talking about either real or imagined versions of himself. "I think it's time you men were honest about how you're tracking Tura."

Cerka's eyes hardened. "What makes you think we're not being honest?"

Tibron tensed, and the rest of the villagers stilled, watching closely.

"Because he's not an idiot," the optio answered, then faced Hanuvar. "You've seen him breaking the feathers, haven't you?"

"Yes."

Cerka scowled. "He shouldn't be sticking his nose where it doesn't belong."

"The centurion's here of his own free will," the optio reminded them. "He's helping us find Tura, and he risked his life holding off the saathra while you heroes climbed to safety. So I think you owe him the truth."

Cerka's scowl deepened, but he fell silent. The other men looked shamefacedly away.

Tibron turned over a hand. "Life in our village has been tough for years. A lot of men died in the war, so we haven't had enough hands to work the farms."

A long-faced man nodded his agreement. "We got hit by a drought. All spring long. It would rain on villages a half day away, but not us. Things just kept getting worse as our priestess grew sicker and sicker. It felt like we were cursed."

The optio got to the point. "Cerka found a blue egret at the edge of the fens."

Hanuvar couldn't hold back his surprise. He'd heard legends of the azure birds and the mystical powers associated with their plumage, but he'd never seen one. "I thought those were a myth," he said.

"It was the real thing." For once, Cerka was animated and almost smiling. "I couldn't believe it. Its wing was injured, so I took it back to the village to get it healed. Things turned around on the instant. It started raining that afternoon. In two days our crops were growing."

"I swear, even the sheep grew fluffier coats." Tibron solemnly lifted his hand. "That's why some rustlers nabbed them. All it took was one week. Everything got better."

"Except for the priestess," the optio reminded them.

Tibron sagged. "It seemed like she was going to rally. She'd been sick for weeks."

"She died," Cerka said. "And when she did, her daughter ran off."

"I thought there were kidnappers," Hanuvar said.

"I saw some shifty strangers around the village last night," Cerka explained. "And I thought some might be after the egret."

Lucian turned to Hanuvar. "I told them from the start I thought she'd just run off. But your camp was in the way, and Cerka here was afraid someone wanted the egret for themselves."

"Not just me," Cerka objected.

Hanuvar cut him off. "Why would she run off?"

Tibron answered. "The egret wasn't getting better. It kept losing feathers. And that upset the priestess, who declared before her death it must be returned to the wild."

Cerka scoffed. "We were taking good care of it."

"Maybe you were and maybe you weren't," Lucian said. "Tura didn't think so. I'm pretty certain at this point she just decided to take the bird away herself."

"Why didn't you just use the magic feathers to heal the bird and the priestess?" Hanuvar asked.

Tibron opened his hands. "We tried that. The wishes aren't all powerful. It's as if you can only win one roll of the dice, not an entire game, if you know what I mean. I can tell which way Tura's going, but the feather doesn't keep leading me to her. I have to keep checking to find her."

"And you break them to make them work?"

"Yes. I kind of found that out by accident. I tripped and stepped on one when I made a wish." Tibron chuckled. Some of the others laughed.

"We're short on feathers," Cerka said. "But if we keep the egret, we'll still have general blessings. The rain, the sheep—that happened before we had to break any feathers. Just having it around makes things better. And we can collect any feathers it drops and keep them for emergencies."

"So are you here to bring back the woman, or the bird?" Hanuvar asked.

Scanning their faces, he thought he saw an obvious dividing line. Many, like Cerka, were desperate for the egret. Others, like Tibron, were concerned about both. Perhaps only Lucian was more worried for Tura.

After an uncomfortable silence, they spoke over one another about how much they loved the young lady, whom they'd known since she was an infant, but they knew their lie was exposed, and the conversation was forced and awkward until the optio assigned them shifts and ordered those not on sentry duty to grab sleep.

Late that night Hanuvar finished his watch and lay down, one of the men's spare shirts rolled under his head for a pillow. He'd wakened Lucian after him. By agreement they'd taken the watches in the night depths, trusting their abilities more than those of the other men.

The legionary walked the perimeter, then sat on a boulder near the camp's edge. The rest lay close to the low burning campfire, each stretched out in the sound sleep of the exhausted. A few of them snored. All was dark beyond them, the deep black of the hidden places of the world, where trees crowded heavily upon one another and lifted leaf- and vine-heavy limbs toward the heavens. The night creatures still chirruped. Moonlight streamed down through breaks in the canopy, silvering the odd branch.

"I can see the moonlight on your eye, Artus," Lucian said quietly to Hanuvar. "You're still awake."

"Yes," Hanuvar admitted. He turned his head to the dark figure seated near him.

"You're probably wondering why I didn't call out Cerka sooner," the optio said after a moment's hesitation. "I think he made up that story about kidnappers because he wanted more of us to go in with him. Maybe he's eager to hold onto that lucky bird, but a lot of us do care about Tura."

"I was thinking about my daughter," Hanuvar said, surprised by his own admission.

"Oh," Lucian remarked with a mixture of surprise and curiosity. "Where is she?"

Hanuvar didn't know what the Dervan legions had done with

Narisia, and whether she was alive or dead. He didn't say that, but he kept his answer truthful. "I'm on my way to find her. Really, I'm heading for a kind of reunion, and I hope she'll be there."

"I'm sure she'll be happy to see you."

"I'm not sure she's still alive," Hanuvar said. "My family's scattered. Because of the war."

"I'm sorry," the optio said with sincerity. "How old is she?"

"Twenty-seven."

"I'll pray you find her," the optio said.

Hanuvar wondered what the young man would say if he knew he would be offering prayers for one of the Cabera family, long feared by the empire's leaders. Regardless of who made religious appeals, they were probably in vain, for his family had almost certainly been exterminated with most of his people.

At the faint whisper of movement through the grass to the south, Hanuvar sat up, turning his head at the same time Lucian shifted.

A figure advanced from the gloom and on through the grass, uncannily passing without disrupting the din of the fen. She stopped just short of them, a thin barefoot woman. Her stola was hitched high, revealing muscular calves. She possessed a receding chin and a long, small-nostriled nose with an upward tilt. Her neck was long and graceful, her almond-shaped eyes luminous and large, her carriage self-assured. Hanuvar could not decide if she were homely or strangely beautiful. Perhaps she was somehow both, and as he witnessed the optio's silent regard, he understood that here was a face the right person might never tire of gazing upon.

"Don't wake the others," she said in a hushed voice.

"Thank the gods you're safe, Tura," the optio said, his sincerity suggesting a regard greater than any dutiful servant of the empire held for an ordinary citizen.

Hanuvar thought he detected an answering light in Tura's own eyes, but her expression grew somber. "You must lead them away," she said. "It won't be safe for them if they follow much longer."

"It's not safe out here for anyone, including you." Lucian started forward. He halted when the young woman immediately retreated.

"I'll come back," she promised, "but not until I've returned the egret to his home."

"Can't you just release him here and now?"

Her brow wrinkled in consternation. "I'm taking him to sacred land. He's in bad condition and I'm not sure even the spirit stone will save him. Cerka's been plucking him."

Lucian scowled. "I should have realized that."

"The egret's part of the spirit world," Tura said. "And if you abuse a spirit, you invoke nature's wrath. I'm returning him to his home since he cannot fly there himself. It's the right thing to do. And I'll pray the spirits will be merciful to our village."

"I've met my share of spirits," Hanuvar said. The two faced him in puzzlement, as if they'd forgotten he was standing to one side. "Do you know what you're walking into? They may demand a price."

"A wrong was done by my people," Tura stated with quiet dignity. "I am my mother's daughter, and she was their shepherd. First I shall return the egret. Then I will learn what the gods would have of me."

Cerka lunged up in a crouch from Tura's left, hands outstretched. A vine tripped him, and he landed flat on his stomach. His breath left him in an explosive grunt.

The woman gasped and back stepped.

"Stop her!" Cerka cried. "You can't let her take the bird back!" He struggled to rise.

Lucian reached out too late, for Tura was running at full speed and quickly vanished into the darkness. Hanuvar was reminded of the grace of the fen deer.

Cerka pushed to his feet. Others of their expedition rose groggily.

The bald leader shook his finger at the optio. "Why didn't you do something to stop her?"

Lucian glowered. "I'm trying to think of a good reason I shouldn't beat you to a pulp. And all I can come up with is I don't feel like getting my hands dirty."

"But she's going to take the beast back!" Cerka's outrage rose in a whine "You heard her! You're the village officer! It's your job to protect us!"

"That's what she's trying to do." Hanuvar stepped up beside the legionary. "How many feathers have you plucked?

Cerka looked startled. "The bird was losing feathers. We didn't pluck any."

"You're a bad liar, Cerka," Lucian told him. "Which did you want more—fame for being savior of the village, or the power the feathers give you?"

"Go easy on him," Tibron said. "You know how it was."

"I know how it is now," Lucian said. "Tura's off there alone in the darkness. The spirits are angry, and she may have to give herself up to save us. Even if they don't kill her, she's got to find her way back through the fens by herself. I'm going after her."

"We're coming with you," Cerka said.

"You're going back." Lucian drew his gladius.

Cerka puffed out his chest. "We'll report you to your general!"

"Go right ahead."

"I'm going with you," Hanuvar told Lucian.

"You've got your own woman to find."

"I'd rather walk the marsh with you than keep watch on them."

After only a brief hesitation, the optio agreed. "I'll be glad to have you."

While the villagers watched sullenly, Hanuvar and the optio grabbed their gear and headed forth. Tura's wake had dredged up the phosphorescent glow, leaving a faint trail stretching out through the water.

"It won't last long," Lucian said.

"Then we'll move fast." Hanuvar glanced over his shoulder. "They can follow us, though."

"They'll be fools if they do," the optio replied tightly.

IV

Tura's path stayed to shallow water and dry land. She proved easy to track, both by the glow left in her wake and the tread of her narrow feet over the muddy banks, almost visible even without the optio's lantern.

They struggled up and over a muddy rise and then confronted a wide gap of black water, a ribbon of fading green light showing the way across. The optio called to her. "Tura, it's me, Lucian. Just me and the centurion," he added, with a look to Hanuvar. "We don't want you to go on alone. We'll help you return the egret, and help you find your way back! You don't need to keep running!"

His shouted words stilled the call of the nearby night creatures, and both men strained to hear a reply. There was none. After only a moment, the cacophony resumed.

Lucian looked to Hanuvar, as if gauging his companion's interest in crossing the dark water, and then shapes rushed at them from the night. Hanuvar raised his sword as something splashed up glimmering foam that ultimately revealed them as fen deer, their upper bodies shrouded in darkness beyond the reach of their paltry lantern, apart from eyes reflecting the light, and the glistening gleam of wet antlers.

The deer stopped a javelin's throw out and then all fifteen stood in a long line, eerily still.

"I think we're supposed to go with them," Hanuvar said, and started forward through the cool water. Lucian joined him.

The deer turned, one by one, and plodded ahead, seven of them to the left, eight to the right.

Hanuvar had been a part of many processions in his time, but never one such as this, bounded on either side by animals that under normal circumstances would either have fled, or charged with lowered antlers. Never had he so closely observed deer, alive, and he studied the sleek muscles moving under their furred flanks, and the lift of their proud heads. He, who had seen so many marvels, marveled a little.

Guided by their stately escort, Hanuvar and Lucian sloshed as quietly as they could through shallow water and across little rises topped with gnarled trees and reaching scrub. If there were saathra near, they kept well away.

Finally, as the dark bulk of another hill rose in the gloom, the deer stopped and faced the center of their column. They lifted their heads high, as an honor guard might raise spears to a ruler. Hanuvar and Lucian passed through them and reached the foot of the hill. There they discovered the crumbled remnant of a stone pier, and moss-covered steps leading up from the water. Hanuvar turned and bowed formally to their escort. Lucian must have thought it a good idea, for he imitated the gesture.

The deer were already darting off, as if remembering they had some important engagement.

Turning, Hanuvar noted a faint green radiance upon the stairs that climbed from the ancient pier. Tura had been here before them.

As he and Lucian started up the crumbling stone, a cry of fear rose through the night somewhere behind, followed by frantic shouting.

The optio looked at him. "I guess Cerka and some of his friends were trying to follow."

"And the marsh spirits weren't as kind to them," Hanuvar said.

"They were warned."

"Some people won't act with good sense even when you order it."

Beyond the last stair they found a circle of grand cedars filling the air with their sharp, clean scent. They entered to find an inner ring of mossy, vine-wrapped standing stones. The moon shone into their center upon a sloped hillock rising a man's height above the clearing floor. It tapered to a narrower circle at its apex, wide enough to support a rough stone table and a few feet of ground around it. Upon the table sat a little bundle, and the woman knelt in supplication before it, head low.

Tura must have heard them as they drew close, but she did not turn. Neither spoke to her, for this seemed a place unused to men, and it felt sacrilege to introduce their voices without invitation.

As Hanuvar climbed the short steps built into the hillock's side, he spotted a little wooden cage beside the table, and then, drawing near the young woman, he saw the bundle on the table shift fitfully. The moonlight showed him the tips of feathers.

Hanuvar looked down at the little bird. He wasn't sure what he had expected, but it was a creature that looked little larger than a half-grown rooster. The bird resembled an ibis, though its beak was long and straight. It tipped its head to consider him with one dull eye. A ruff of feathers crowned it and spread down the back of its neck, lighter on the ends than the base. Probably it would have looked larger if it retained more feathers, but much of the little bird's skin was exposed, so that its back resembled that of the lowest hen in a flock's pecking order.

Tura roused and turned her head to speak to Lucian, who'd drawn up on her right. "I'm too late," she said, so softly that her voice barely reached Hanuvar. "It was weakening as we went. It can barely stand now. And my prayers have done nothing."

"Why didn't you say something sooner when you discovered the bird had been plucked?" Lucian asked.

The young woman climbed to her feet, back stiffening. "You blame me? I walked in to see Cerka lifting a pillow from my mother's face. He came after me! I was lucky to get away with my life, let alone the egret's!"

"That's a lie," said a voice behind them.

Hanuvar pivoted. Too late he saw that the villagers had crept up from below. He felt honest bewilderment that the untrained men could be so stealthy when they hadn't evidenced such capability earlier. Six remained, advancing in two arcs from left and right.

"How did they surprise us?" Hanuvar asked Lucian.

"The feathers," the priestess said softly. "I can feel the power on them."

"We don't want to hurt you," Tibron said. He was leading the group on the left. "We just want the bird."

"The egret's nearly dead." Tura threw back her shoulders. "You've done enough already, and the spirits of the fen will take their vengeance."

The men on the left paused. Cerka, though, pressed in from the right, daring to place a foot on the first stone step. "We've got to get the rest of its feathers while it's still alive," he said.

Hanuvar and Lucian drew their weapons at the same moment.

"Choose well," Hanuvar said. "You have magic, but we have the higher ground. And the training to counter your numbers."

"But you might lose your balance." Cerka pulled a small feather from his sleeve, and broke it.

Hanuvar's left foot slid out from beneath him. He thrust out a hand as he dropped, catching himself on his palm.

Once, he had been forced to keep a handful of sorcerers on his staff, to better guard against the magic of his enemies. Though dire spells had sometimes been used against him and his forces, he'd never faced such sudden disabling magic. Spells powerful enough to disrupt the natural order required days of preparation, and exhausting ritual. The sorcery's sudden effectiveness impressed and alarmed him.

He hadn't fully regained his feet when the first spearman charged. Against some other man, the advantage his opponent held might have been fatal.

Hanuvar knocked the spear haft out of line with his sword and rolled through a half somersault to close with his assailant and swing a fist into his groin. The younger man wailed and fell backward into one of the two coming up behind him. They tumbled into a heap at the foot of the mound.

On his feet now, Hanuvar leaned away from a vicious club blow to his head. He stepped sideways, then lashed out with his sword and cut deep through his attacker's neck. His blade was keenly sharp, and pierced skin, muscle, and larynx. The club wielder dropped like a stone, twitching and gurgling. Hanuvar pivoted. His only remaining opponent watched hesitantly from below.

He'd lost sight of Cerka.

"Drop your blade, Centurion," the leader called.

Hanuvar whirled. Lucian lay groaning beside the table. Cerka clasped Tura, sword blade pressed to her side.

"No one else has to die," he said. "The feathers can right any damage that's been done."

"You've assaulted an officer of the legion," Hanuvar said.

"Lucian? He'll be fine. He just hit his head on the table when he lost his balance. Now drop your sword."

Hanuvar had backed to the far side of the table, the better to see his opponents across it, and the assailants at the foot of the hill. The bearded tracker was there at the other end, eyeing Hanuvar, spear pointed loosely even as he reached with his free hand for the blue egret.

The bird's head moved only a little to observe the tracker's descending hand.

One moment there was a flutter of large wings behind Hanuvar. In the next a brilliant white light filled the little area. Hanuvar, facing away from the source of the glare, saw Tibron throw up his free arm to shield his eyes. Though alarmed by what was happening behind him, Hanuvar took advantage of his foe's distraction. He vaulted the table, grabbed Tibron's spear, and brought his sword into the side of the tracker's head. At the last moment he decided against a mortal wound and clouted him with the blade's flat.

Tibron moaned and doubled over, dropping the spear to put both hands to his head.

Only then did Hanuvar turn and see the mother of all birds.

It hung in the air, a great horse-sized avian of iridescent feathers.

Its wings beat far too slowly to suspend it so gracefully above the earth. A golden aura shone around it, seemingly generated by the stir of its wings, and its eyes burned with the brilliance of suns.

This creature was a strange and beautiful mix of eagle and peacock, with a long swan neck, and a body from which two black claws depended from powerful legs. Black, too, was its beak, and as it opened, a warm sound, like the dawn given voice, reached them, though the beak did not rise and fall in time with its speech.

"You have brought pain to my hatchling," the great beast announced. It was not an accusation, but a statement of fact devoid of anger.

Cerka's hand tightened around Tura. "You don't want me to harm her too. All we want is some of the magic you're hoarding."

The mother bird did not answer.

"You keep it for yourself," Cerka cried. "You could share it with any of us! Do you know how grateful we'd be? We would bring you anything you desired. We just want a little help now and then. A gift."

"Here is my gift to you," the avian spirit declared.

Cerka looked down at his arm. He laughed, happily, and loosed Tura to turn to the others in wonder. His entire body began to shimmer with white and gold.

"It's, it's amazing," he said with a gleeful smile. "I've never felt so glorious!" He was still smiling as he and his clothes and his weapon fell away into golden ashes that trailed down across the stone table before being swept into the night.

The priestess sank to one knee. Hanuvar scanned the faces of his enemies. Two genuflected. One at the base of the hill was already running for the stairs to the pier. Hanuvar knelt as well, but pressed his fingers to the neck of a prostrate Lucian before he saw the young man's blinking eyes. He helped the legionary sit, and the optio groaned as he put a hand to his head.

The mother bird warbled a hauntingly sweet string of notes and her child stood on wobbling legs. He spread his sparse wings, and then floated, to his mother's side. He perched upon her shoulder, and she leaned her head gently against his body.

Bathed now in his mother's glow, the glorious, vibrant colors of his own blue feathers were obvious, even if they were bedraggled. In five short breaths the rest of his feathers shimmered into existence and he was fully restored. His head turned to the mother and Hanuvar felt certain the egret's eye met his own while the bird twittered a sad little melody.

The mother's head turned to regard them again, staring with its pupilless, glowing eyes.

"The preservers may stay. The rest of you—begone!"

That was enough for Tibron, who rose, backed away, and then fled with his fellows for the stairs. They left their weapons, and the lone dead man, behind.

The younger bird sang to the mother, who swung her head from side to side. Finally, she let out a single clack, and the egret silenced.

"To you three I will grant blessings," she declared, her beak open and unmoving once more. "First, the priestess; to the gift of your wisdom and bravery I will add long health and vitality. You shall lead your people well, if they've the intelligence to heed you."

"Thank you," Tura said gravely, and bowed her head.

The bird's attention shifted. "To the young man, I grant restored health, and the right to safely walk my lands. Ward them and prosper." Finally her gaze settled upon Hanuvar, who met those eyes unflinching. "For the old soldier, a warning. Your enemies will find you on the sea road. Keep to your old trail, and by it you will find your people."

Hanuvar's brows rose at this information, but the great bird had yet more to say. "Lend aid to the priestess in Erapna. She will tell you what you most wish to know."

Hanuvar started and bowed his head. The spirit must be referring to his daughter's fate. Erapna lay further along the mainland to the northwest, toward the Ardenines.

He had planned to head west to the port town of Tonsta and sail for Derva itself. The changed route would add months to his journey. Each day's delay was one more his surviving people lived in slavery and privation, under threat of death. His hands tightened into fists even as he recognized he should feel only gratitude. For he would be no help to his people if he were caught and executed by Dervan authorities. While certain that would someday be his fate, he meant to free as many of the Volani survivors as possible before he died.

"Now go," the mother bird declared. "Give thanks to the bounties my land provides, on the high days of every year. Honor the old ways and take only what you need. Do not fail me." She finished with a rending shriek, then rose with a beating of great wings, her child still perched upon her shoulder, and she sped shining into the sky. They watched her climb until she was simply one more bright star in the firmament, rising toward the moon.

They slept under the cypress beside the temple, then, come morning, started back.

There was only a little talk during the long trip, but at some point, the priestess's hand found its way into the legionary's, and sometimes his hand slipped about her waist. They only relinquished their hold upon one another when they stepped into the clearing where Antires sat near the horses.

"What," Hanuvar said, "no breakfast?"

"And well met to you too," the playwright answered, rising with a glad smile. "I saved you some pan biscuits. I didn't know we'd be having guests."

"Break out the pan and let's make some more," Hanuvar said. "Tura here hasn't eaten for the last day."

Antires bowed to her. "I'm at your service then, young woman. I'll set straight to work. I don't suppose any of you are going to tell me what happened?"

"Maybe in a little while." Hanuvar accepted the wineskin offered by his friend then turned to offer it to Tura and Lucian, but they sat beside one another on a rock, facing away, her head against his shoulder.

"What did I miss?" Antires asked. "Tibron came past earlier but wouldn't talk much. He told me he'd seen a spirit in the fens. He refused, even at sword point, to lead me to you, and swore you'd be unharmed."

"We were."

"And there was a spirit?"

"Yes."

Antires sighed in frustration. "By the gods, man. Do I have to drag it out of you? Was this another monster tale?"

Hanuvar answered after a moment's thought. "The only real monsters were human ones."

⁑ ⁑ ⁑

I had spent long days with Hanuvar before I noted something that struck me as strange. Apart from his morning and evening stretches, his habits were those of a Dervan traveler, even to stopping at roadside shrines to pay respect. I was no great authority on Volani practices, but one sun-dappled afternoon on an empty stretch of road, with rolling grassland stretching before and behind us and the occasional grove of stone pines throwing shade, I asked if his people's traditions were so similar to those of the Dervans, or if he'd simply adopted them while campaigning in their territories.

He favored me with an amused, sidelong glance that was far warmer than you might expect from such a great warrior.

"So I've guessed wrong," I said to him. My horse snorted, as if he had found my words absurd.

"I must always play a part," he said, and while I guessed at his meaning, I was determined to better know the man, and so I sought clarity.

"No actor needs to play his part beyond the stage," I said.

He objected with a small shake of his head. "There are things I must not permit myself to do."

"Such as?"

"Take this moment as an example. It's a lovely day, under clear skies. An excellent traveling day. Were I not in disguise, I would break a meal cake and lift tribute to Hanis, father of wind and horses."

"And you can't do that?"

"I have no idea when I'll be watched. And what if I slip one day when I'm tired, and use a Volani phrase? I have broken myself of these habits so I don't make mistakes."

"That must be a challenge," I said, feeling empathy for his position. "I hadn't thought of that."

"Sometimes, small as those customs are, I miss them, very much."[6]

His words had inspired another line of thought, and I asked again for clarity. "I thought you didn't believe in your gods."

---

[6] The original text of Antires' history contains additional lines excised from the final. My ancestor Antires possessed a remarkable memory, and when coupled with his habit of keeping notes of his conversations with Hanuvar it seems likely that he accurately presented the general's words, even though he imagined the actions and dialogue of others with whom he never interacted. Why, then, would he record words in his original, then trim them for the version intended for publication, especially when they are revealing of his subject's character but do not malign him? It is difficult to know, but I think that since Hanuvar was so often direct in speech, Antires wished to maintain that tone, even though a reserved man may sometimes wax more eloquently.

I have preserved these words because I think that they provide a deeper look into Hanuvar's regrets. After saying that he missed these small customs very much, Antires originally had Hanuvar say: "For instance, on those rare occasions when we eat well, I long to raise a proper toast in the Volani style. And before I eat each evening, I would like to offer a little prayer to the gods of sea and air. And I would eat some kind of sauce that isn't a variation on the accursed garum with which the Dervans drench everything."   —Andronikos Sosilos

His look grew somber. *"I'm not sure they help me. But that's not what's important."*

"You're talking about small, personal things you miss, that your people do. Things that define you."

"They don't define me," he said, *"but they're familiar. And a source of comfort."*

There were few enough of those sources in the places we travelled. I thought another lay only a little further down the road, for my uncle and my cousin lived in one of the roadside towns, and I promised Hanuvar a cozy sleeping space and an exceptional meal, both of which had become rare, for we tried to avoid staying the night in villages over concern some veteran might think he looked familiar, even beardless and arrayed like a Dervan, complete to hair style.

We were to find instead that my uncle had died under strange circumstances, and that his friend and my cousin were certain the rich man who'd hired him, and a crew, to repair a section of sewer was behind his death. Naturally I was honor bound to look into the matter, and I was touched when Hanuvar said he would assist, even if it meant a journey into the dark beneath the town, in the dead of night.

—Sosilos, Book Two

Chapter 6:
The Eyes of the Reaper

I

Mortar and chipped brick erupted from the strike of Marcan's hammer, flying past the three men to rattle on the concrete walkway behind. The second blow smashed a head-sized hole in the wall, propelling shattered masonry into the darkness, where it clattered against unseen stones.

Light from Antires' lantern glistened off Marcan's sweat-slick bald spot as he lowered the hammer and peered through the opening.

Hanuvar turned to scan the darkness to left and right, alert for the glow of distant, lantern-bearing patrolmen, or the scuff of approaching feet. Chances that guards would venture into the sewers in the dead of night were fairly remote, but not to be completely disregarded.

The shuttered lantern showed brick walls sloping to arch overhead, a few feet of narrow walkway where he stood with Antires and Marcan, and the hint of ripples in the sewer channel a foot below the walkway's edge.

When this expedition had been proposed, Hanuvar had been prepared for a stinking journey through filthy waters. The Dervan Empire, though, even in this little river town, prided themselves on their engineering. It was possible to walk upright upon either side of the sewer, which was flushed regularly by overflow from the aqueduct that swept cold water down from nearby hills. While an unpleasant tang lingered in the air, he had walked down alleyways that smelled far worse.

He returned his attention to his companions just as Marcan hefted the sledge and smashed a third time. The impact echoed through the tunnel.

Antires shifted uncomfortably at the sound, searching the darkness for any who might have been alerted. Hanuvar understood his friend's concern but doubted the noise could be pinpointed from above, even if someone did hear it.

Like Hanuvar and Marcan, Antires wore a simple tunic and sandals. Should they be seen and questioned, each could claim to be maintenance workers. The Herrene bore himself without complaint, but there was no missing his nervousness. The defacement of state engineering projects would hardly be celebrated by the Dervan government, let alone if they were carried out in the company of Hanuvar Cabera, the empire's most hated enemy. Likely Marcan would not be breaking public works with such cavalier abandon if he knew the true identity of one of the men who'd descended with him.

Marcan remained certain that his best friend, Antires' late uncle, had been killed because of something he'd seen during the sewer repairs he and their fellow laborers had undertaken last month. With fearless, single-minded devotion, Marcan had led them through the darkened streets and into the labyrinth of tunnels to this place.

"Here," Marcan said, his voice rasping and gravelly even as he whispered. He pointed to the wide hole he'd opened in the wall amongst the small square of clean new bricks.

Hanuvar looked into the dark cavity, seeing a space that stretched into the gloom. Antires joined him.

"No one was aware there was anything back there," Marcan said. "Certainly not some closed-off tunnel. Plaunus found it, and when he did, he headed in with Aridian's big slave and a couple of others." He leaned his sledge against the wall, and continued grimly. "He never came out."

He was repeating himself a little, as men did when aggrieved, and he simmered still over the injustice of his friend's death. He had already explained that he thought Plaunus hadn't died because of falling masonry, but had been slain by the servants of the patrician who'd hired them. Aridian's slaves and servants had not permitted anyone into the hidden chamber afterward to see what had happened.

Marcan set his hands to the bricks on one side of the hole. "You can see just how badly they finished the repair job. They wouldn't let trained brick men back in to patch it. Look at that mortar work."

Antires politely pretended interest then answered briskly. "Well, let's see what they were hiding."

Marcan lifted the lantern in one beefy hand. Its doors squeaked as he forced them wide. He had the sturdy, broad build of a man who'd labored all his life. His belly was thick, but he didn't look soft. He stepped through the gap.

"It stretches back quite a ways," his voice rang hollowly from the other side.

Antires stepped through. After a final survey of their surroundings, Hanuvar followed.

"A hidden room," Antires said.

As Hanuvar joined them he discovered a rectangular side chamber longer than it was wide. The bricks in its walls were smaller than those of the sewer channel, and a dirty brown color. The floor was packed earth. The brick ceiling arched to a much less pronounced degree than the tunnel's, and one side sagged noticeably. Hanuvar was uncomfortably aware of the thirty or more feet of dirt above.

"This isn't part of the sewer, is it?" Antires asked. Even when speaking quietly he had the learned diction of an actor and orator. Hanuvar had seen him take on many roles, and knew he could easily duplicate Marcan's gruff vernacular if he wished.

"No part of the sewer at all," Marcan agreed. "I wonder how that patrician knew it was hidden here? I bet all the repairs he sponsored were really just an excuse to find this place." Marcan's shifting lantern light fell upon a bronze door, black with age, at the rear of the little chamber. As the three men stopped in front of it, Hanuvar saw four separate iron crossbars stretched horizontally across the bronze. Once, they had been set into the brick. Someone had torn them free, and recently, judging from the fresh scatter of brown brick dust at the door's base. Then, after being pulled out, the rusty bars had been restored.

"The bars are on the outside," Antires observed. The actor usually didn't make a habit of stating the obvious. "Anyone who wanted inside could simply have chipped these out of their housing."

"Yes," Hanuvar agreed. "Whoever built this meant to keep something from getting out."

The Herrene looked at him sidelong. "I knew that—but it's a cursed thing to say out loud in the underworld. Do you think that something inside there killed my uncle?"

"If some *thing* had killed him, I don't think even a rich man could have stopped the rumors," Hanuvar answered. "Your uncle may have been killed so he wouldn't tell anyone about what was found inside."

Marcan nodded stolidly. "That's the truth of it. There's no spirits in the sewers. As many times as Plaunus and I have been down here on projects, we'd have seen something if there were. What I don't see are any big chunks of rock lying around that could have smashed him flat, like Aridian's big slave told us."

Antires eyed the door doubtfully. "I suppose we'd better look inside."

Hanuvar's gaze shifted from the bars to the door itself and locked upon the two ovals on the bronze at head height. Some ancient hand had drawn them, and for a brief moment, staring at the faded gold circles with their black centers, Hanuvar imagined he was confronted by malignant eyes.

He was no more keen to open that door than he'd been to enter the sewer, but this was a family matter for Antires, and as the Herrene's friend he was honor bound to assist him.

Antires widened the lantern beam as far as he could. While Marcan tugged the bars free of their housing, Hanuvar shifted his attention from the opening they'd made over to the walls about them, and then to the ceiling and its low spot. He had long since removed the sheathed sword from the tool satchel he'd carried over one shoulder, and he now buckled it on. He fully expected anything left beyond that door would be unable to harm him, but he'd seen men die for trusting too strongly in their expectations.

Marcan grunted as he pushed the door open. Hanuvar thought it would creak—the metal hinges must have been untouched for centuries—but of course the Dervans who'd been here before them had oiled the hinges. They were practical in everything, from sewer repair to tomb robbery to genocide.

The door revealed a rectangular space alive with color. Antires stepped over the threshold, hand to his knife hilt. Marcan went after, and both men were soon inspecting the small chamber.

Hanuvar knew no reason all three of them should be on the far side of a door that could seal them within and so remained where he was. He could see all he needed from where he stood, in any case.

From the packed dirt floor to waist height the chamber's walls were red—not the red of a warm, comforting fire, but a rich crimson shade, like blood. Then there was a dividing line, a barrier of black stark and sudden as death. Above it the wall was whitewashed, and there Hanuvar saw a parade of bright, stiff figures and symbols. He could speak more than a dozen tongues, and knew the writing of them all, but these were letters in a language he did not understand.

There were figures as well, similar to those he'd seen in ancient tomb drawings: figures who genuflected to a large man in a chair, and others who presented him with goods. That same ruler stood facing an army of warriors in strange round helms, bearing only shields. One of his hands was open and upright. The front rank of soldiers bowed to him.

The eyes of the ruler in both images were lined in gold.

"An Ataran king," Antires said.

Hanuvar had guessed as much. Centuries ago, when Derva had still been a small city-state, the Atarans had risen to brief prominence along the shores of the Inner Sea before they were overcome both by invaders and troubles within.

"This must be the king's tomb," Marcan said.

"It's a small tomb for a king," Hanuvar pointed out. From his doorway vantage point he studied images along the rest of the wall, portraying more of the ruler's life. It was not so uncommon to see carvings of ancient rulers surrounded by bodies of the conquered, but the sheer number of corpses, as well as crudely suggested pools of blood, were oddly unsettling. And, different from all other ancient depictions he had ever seen, the record ended with the king's downfall. The monarch rested on his knees, surrounded by a wild-eyed mob with clubs. Three in that crowd supported barrels on their shoulders, tilted to pour grain, or sand, onto their fallen ruler. In the next image the mob lifted a head with dully glowing eyes while others beat at a blood-red thing that seemed to have dripped from the headless body. His soul, perhaps.

"The Atarans tired of kings," Antires said. "Everyone tires of kings," he continued after a brief pause. "But they keep finding their way to power anyway."

Hanuvar's view of the room's center had been obstructed by Marcan. When the laborer stepped aside, the general spied the stone sides of a rectangular enclosure, the size of a small sarcophagus. A stone lid lay smashed to one side.

"Whatever it was they carried out in those sacks must have come from in here," Marcan said.

Hanuvar thought that likely.

"That lid looks heavy," Antires said. "But surely that wouldn't have crushed uncle so flat they couldn't recover his body."

"No," Hanuvar agreed.

Marcan's lip curled. "They must have carried Plaunus out in one of those sacks. Bastards."

They left the chamber and Marcan shut the door behind them. As he replaced the bars, Hanuvar couldn't escape the gaze of those golden eyes, staring at him from the ancient, pitted door.

II

"I know your secret," Drusira announced flatly.

She stood beside her brother, who stirred in the wide bed. He lay on his back, lit by a stream of morning light broken by the brown latticed window. His mouth was agape, and the white bed sheets were twisted about his waist. Without his fine tunic he looked simply a lump of sagging flesh. It was true, she thought, that good cloth made a man. Not only did his clothes obscure the extent of Aridian's excess, they likewise hid the absurd amount of fine black hair coating most every inch of his skin except his head. Drusira's brother was nearly bald, apart from the sides of his skull, where he grew his hair long so he could paste it across the middle. This morning both sides hung nearly to his shoulders.

She poked him with one perfectly manicured finger. "Aridian. Wake up."

He groaned, and then a self-satisfied smile, repellant and catlike, blossomed on his wide lips. He looked to his right and let out a pleased little grunt, staring at the naked back of the lithe young woman lying at his side.

Drusira's patience had ebbed so far that a sharp tone entered her voice. "Aridian."

He turned toward her, his smile fading.

Drink and sleep had dulled his squarish features. If he were to lose a hundred pounds, Aridian might have been almost as handsome as their father had been. He had the long, hooked nose that looked good on the men of the line—something she was glad she herself had avoided, unlike her unfortunate cousin—and a strong chin. But two more chins wagged beneath it, and his eyes were set a little too far apart. He had always looked stouter than most of her relatives, but after their father died five years ago, Aridian's pronounced weight gain had done nothing to improve his appearance. Twenty-five, fat, and balding, he was an unattractive prospect when so many aristocratic families had more holdings, and an upward trajectory.

And yet there he lay with the willowy beauty and wife of a senator's son. That Aridian had long lusted after her was no great secret. Nor was the fact that she had held him in utter contempt. Until yesterday.

"It's the eye drops, isn't it," Drusira said. She saw the little jar beside him on the bedside table.

Aridian frowned at her, then sat up slowly, rubbing his forehead. Probably he was suffering from a hangover. An unstoppered amphora and two cups sat near the foot of the bed, though the stink of wine seemed not to rise from them, but the sheets themselves, as if they had sweated alcohol while they slept.

"An entire courtyard's closed down and under guard," Drusira said. "The slaves are talking about the thing inside. And don't try to look at me so! I won't let you work your spell on me."

Aridian grunted, then set wide, hairy feet on the bedroom floor. "It's been too long since I used the drops for the spell to work," he grumbled. He stared up at her and she fought the impulse to meet his eyes. Maybe he was right, and there was no effect, but he'd lied to her before. "Who told you?" he asked sharply. "Is that fat little maid of yours prying again?"

That he should call pretty Merfia fat when he was more pig than man irked her, but then he himself had never thought any but the most slender of women deserved his consideration.

"Leave her be. You've hardly been secretive. In the last three days there have been five separate women, none of whom would have looked twice at you before." He scowled at that, but she went on. "If that wasn't strange enough, you had the slaves performing acrobatics. All reported your weird ability to command them without speaking."

Aridian growled. "The tongue of a wagging slave can be cut."

"Oh hush. If you do obvious things in front of a slave, you deserve to have tales told. So all that pawing around in rotting texts finally brought you some measure of power. You can order people by looking at them, yet you only use such a gift to force women into your bed?"

"They're the kind of women I deserve," Aridian objected. "And I hardly force them. They come to me. Eagerly." He looked back to the insensate woman on the bed beside him.

Surely Aridian knew he lied to himself. Drusira's first instinct was to tell him they weren't coming of their free will, but she suspected that would lead her nowhere. "Is this all you intend to do with this magic?"

He pulled back his upper lip to expose his front teeth and briefly imitated a rabbity nibble to mock her overbite, something he'd been doing since they were children. Drusira's now ex-husband had quickly taken up the practice himself. "Ferreting out secrets again, are we, Drusira? Don't worry. I have more plans. I'll secure our fortunes soon."

It was so typical that he thought first of comforts, and not of their ultimate fates, nor that of the loyal slaves who'd have to be auctioned off. A series of his poor investments and extravagant purchases had pushed them very close to bankruptcy. She had to put him on a better track. "Whatever magic you've mastered must be handled delicately, to raise our standing not just in the city, but in the province. Maybe even the empire. But you can't make it so obvious."

"Clever Drusira." He pushed his hair over the bald patch and combed it with his fingers. "You're already angling to better your station. Just like a woman."

Once, she might already have been flustered by his mockery and jibe, but the last year with her sibling, not to mention the hate she'd endured from a husband who'd previously pledged eternal love, had steeled her. She ignored the pointless insult as she had so many others across the years. "Someone has to look after the family's future, don't they? Were you planning to use your sorcery on more hapless beauties at this evening's party?"

His answer was slow in coming. "Maybe."

He'd been acting like a greedy baby, but she smiled indulgently. "You were overdue for some kindnesses," she said. "But from here on we should do nothing overt. Nothing that other people can observe and be alarmed by."

"You're right," Aridian admitted grudgingly. "Maybe you're due for some kindness too, sister. I can share this power. I know you want it."

She gulped, wondering what it would be like to effortlessly command a man's attention the way Aridian's bedmate did. "It's like a belladonna treatment, isn't it? You place it in your eyes?"

"Yes," Aridian said. "Exactly."

"And it comes from whatever you keep in the courtyard?"

"Yes." Aridian rose, wrapping part of the linens around his loins. His conquest mumbled but did not wake.

Aridian threw on his tunic and slipped into sandals. Already he looked better, especially with his chins raised. There was a bleary look in his eyes, but something magnetic there as well, a bit of a brown-gold glow. She was careful not to examine them too closely.

"Where did it come from?"

"Originally?" He spoke with dramatic menace. "The old Atarans claimed they summoned it from the darkest hell." He waited a moment, then laughed. "But wizards always exaggerate. They're braggarts."

It hadn't occurred to Drusira to consider the truthfulness of wizards before, and she wasn't interested in doing so now. She just wanted an answer that troubled her less. "So it's not from one of the seven hells?"

He shrugged heavy shoulders. "It's not from around here, but it certainly hasn't told me where it's from. That's another thing the

Ataran chroniclers lied about—it doesn't talk at all. And they also went on and on about how dangerous it was, and how it had been the ruin of Ataran's enemies before it went for the throne itself. But you should see the thing. There's no way it could take a throne. It can't leave its blood bath, and even if it could, it's hideous. No man would follow it."

Drusira swallowed her fear. "What does it look like?"

"Come along. I'll show you."

Drusira followed him through the villa to the eastern courtyard. In summer the door to any of the courtyards would normally have been kept open at all times, even during rain.

But the portals were closed. And as Aridian pushed through them, his big manservant rose from where he'd been sitting in the shadow. The pale northerner towered over them both as they walked up to him.

"Is it well?" Aridian's voice betrayed a hint of his concern.

The slave bowed and spoke in his low, accented voice. "Yes, master. It was given the blood of four freshly slaughtered dogs this morning, and it lies sleeping within. It continues to grow."

Aridian nodded, his gaze already drifting to the ugly, high-walled rectangle of brick that had been erected to one side of the weed-choked center of the courtyard. Drusira followed as he walked past the dried-up pool, remembering when there had been fresh water and little golden fish swimming there. Something had gone wrong with the plumbing line, and repairs would have been exorbitant. So much had changed. Once, the planters that ringed the walls and the balcony above had been thick with flowers. Now those few that boasted any kind of plant growth held only rank brown volunteers.

There was no missing the reek of blood as they closed on the strange new structure. No attempt had been made to build it prettily. It looked as though someone had begun to erect a new brick oven. Flies swarmed thickly above it, and crawled along its rim.

Aridian halted a few steps beyond and laid a plump hand on the edge of his tunic. "Blood keeps it calm," he said. "When we first found it, I thought it was dead, but after a few hours soaking in the blood, it was restored."

"Does it eat the blood?" She knew a chill that alarmed and delighted her just a little.

"In a way. Come. I'll show it to you."

"I'm more interested in the drops than the thing itself—"

"It can't harm any of us so long as we keep it supplied with blood. It's like a drunkard. It just lies there and rolls around."

When she joined him at the enclosure's side the flies buzzed up, and she waved them from her face. Aridian nearly brushed the bricks with his shoulder as he peered inside. She stood on her toes to see over the rim.

She'd expected something horrifying, but the bottom of the stone enclosure presented only a pool of dark liquid and a slick crimson thing lying mostly submerged. She was looking at the creature's shrimp-like carapace, each flange of shell overlaid upon the one before it.

She guessed the beast wasn't much larger than a lapdog, and then it shifted and she realized it was curled in upon itself.

"It did get bigger," Aridian said in pleasure.

"Where do the droplets come from?" Drusira asked.

"They ooze from a gland under the plate just behind its head."

"Does it have a head?"

"It's there. Do you see? At that end." He raised a stick that was leaning against the side of the structure and reached inside to poke.

The creature writhed and spun in its odorous bath and then she witnessed both its incredible speed, and the grotesque tentacles twisting in front of its gaping mouth. She blanched in horror, then, as its multiple eyes turned in their stalks to observe her, she knew the brief slither of alien thoughts through her own. It was hungry. Ever so hungry, and it might never have enough blood to sate it. Then the contact broke and it rooted in the blood, and she turned away, stifling a scream.

Aridian laughed at her. "Don't worry, sister. It doesn't need you."

III

Antires' cousin Resephone had tried to wait up for them, but too many sleepless nights had caught up to her, and when Hanuvar and Antires had returned early that morning they'd found her stretched out on the couch in the receiving room. Antires had thrown a blanket over her, then he and Hanuvar had stumbled off to their beds. Marcan left for his apartment.

Now wakened, Resephone had demanded a recounting of the night's discoveries, so they had gathered to speak in the tiny inner courtyard of her small house. Since she remained standing, Hanuvar and Antires hadn't taken the bench she'd offered.

Even when angry, Resephone moved with grace. Though she was now a professional potter, she had been a dancer, and had the poetically lauded, if actually uncommon, build attributed to Herrenic women: high full breasts, wide hips, and a slim waist. Another woman might have flaunted such a figure, but her long stola draped her loosely from throat to calf, tight only at the waist courtesy of a simple belt. Her skin was a darker shade than her cousin Antires, more a rich ebon than his warm, reddish brown.

As Antires finished describing their expedition, Resephone's wide nostrils flared and her head rose determinedly. "You two must come with me to the office of the town vigils, and share what you found. Your testimony, and that of Marcan, will convince them of the truth."

At Antires' silence she frowned. "Why do you look at me like that?"

He offered empty palms and tried to explain. "We broke the law when we went into the sewers at night and smashed open the wall. What do you think the vigils will say to that?"

"I don't think they'll care. You've exposed a crime."

Hanuvar spoke calmly. "In my experience, rich men often own the men who enforce the laws. Are you friendly with any magistrates?"

"Do I look like a woman who has friends among the magistrates?"

Though far from the poorest of Dervans, Resephone's small home and simple dress made her plebian social status obvious even to the casual observer. And more, she was a woman, and of foreign ancestry. Hanuvar didn't answer her rhetorical question, saying instead: "There are few satisfying options here."

She spoke bitterly. "So you wish me to walk away with my father unavenged? He was murdered! Probably to conceal the discovery of this . . . tomb, so Aridian wouldn't have to share the riches he found!" She curled long fingers on her hips. "It can all be proved, down to Aridian firing the maintenance workers and having poorly trained slaves finish the repairs. But you think I should do nothing?" She jabbed a finger at Hanuvar. "Would you walk away when your blood cries for vengeance?"

Antires sucked a breath in through his teeth. "That's not really an appropriate question," he advised.

Her eyes narrowed. "What's that supposed to mean?"

"My father was slain too," Hanuvar confessed. "I avenged him by carrying on his work against his enemies."

Resephone frowned. "And what work was that?" She paused only briefly. "You won't tell me, will you." She threw up her hands. "My husband has left me. My father is dead. My cousin turns up for a surprise visit, but will he aid me? No, he's in a hurry to leave from the moment he got here, with a man he has known for—how long?" Resephone thrust a hand toward Hanuvar. "A month?" She fixed Hanuvar with her dark eyes. "Where is it you're taking him? It's no place good, is it?"

"It's not likely to be." Hanuvar nodded to Antires. "I've told him this."

Resephone's gaze swung back to her cousin, who stood hapless and uncharacteristically awkward. "You, my only relative in the provinces, will leave me, won't you? What's this old man's hold on you, Antires?"

"He's my lover."

Resephone rolled her eyes. "If you must lie, do better than that. I thought you were an actor! You think I don't know the look of a man in love?"

"I'm on a journey he wants to write about." Hanuvar thought even this was saying too much. While he doubted Resephone could guess his identity, any who spoke with her at a later date might be able to trace his movements through her.

"Of course. He's off after glory." She frowned at Hanuvar. "What are you, some famous criminal? No, don't say anything else. I'm tired of lies."

Antires' look to him was pleading.

Hanuvar searched for possible angles of attack. Reluctantly he considered the only other option. "You said the rich man sent you an invitation."

He'd thought her eyes flared dangerously before. "Yes. His message expressed regret that 'so beautiful a woman should suffer such tragedy,' and he hoped I would attend the banquet in my father's memory. He's an infamous lecher, and I don't want his eyes, much less his hands, on me."

"I still can't believe he's celebrating a sewer repair with a banquet," Antires said.

Hanuvar wasn't surprised. The Dervan aristocracy strained for any opportunity to distinguish themselves with public works. He looked at his friend, then at the woman who had opened her home to them both. "I'll help you," he said. "Because you gave us sanctuary, and because you are blood to my friend. But I can give you only one more night. We'll go with you to this banquet, as your entourage."

"You think you'll pass as a relative?" Her tone was skeptical.

"I can pass as many things," Hanuvar assured her. "A relative by marriage. Your godfather."

"And what do you mean to do, when you come to the banquet?"

"Find a way to learn the truth," Hanuvar said.

"How?" she demanded.

"He always finds a way," Antires said.

She studied them both, and her anger ebbed. "Are you going to kill Aridian?" she asked with muted curiosity.

"Would it bother you if I did?"

"I want justice. But I want to know what really happened to my father, and why."

"You'll know," Hanuvar said.

IV

Drusira had been on hand to greet all the guests that evening as they were ushered into the atrium, from the old magistrate and the young city treasurer to the parade of bored middle-aged patricians. The slaves had hung the most expensive tapestries, and colored paper lanterns dangled over the main courtyard. Dancers and jugglers from far lands entertained the crowd while pretty slave girls kept the libations pouring freely. Every last spare coin had been employed for this night, to suggest that wealth and abundance were commonplace. A sacrifice, she hoped, to bring greater fortune.

She stood listening on the edge of the dining hall while musicians played a skirling melody and guests clapped along amid bursts of laughter. Merfia begged her pardon and told her more guests had arrived. Drusira left to meet them.

Even if she hadn't already known which guests were the ones she herself had added to the list this morning, it would have been easy to guess, for most of her brother's involved a pretty woman, either on the arm of an elderly man, or accompanying a matron and her husband. The lovely Herrene who had just been ushered through the portico was certainly her brother's guest. Her dress was simple, but her fine dark skin, cascade of braided curling hair, and statuesque figure needed little adornment.

With her were two men. One was a young Herrene, lighter in skin though still dark, handsome and somehow sly. And there was an older man in a plain, trim white tunic, clean shaven and powerful, no matter his graying hair. His gaze was direct and bold. Drusira found something harsh, dangerous, and strangely engaging about him.

"Welcome," she said. "I am Drusira Melva. It's a pleasure to have you in our humble abode."

The woman bowed her head as to a better, though as a guest she should not have done so. "Thank you for inviting us," she said. "I am Resephone, and this is my cousin, Antires."

The male Herrene must have been more used to polite society, for he took her hand, kissing her fingertips.

"And how do you know Aridian?" Drusira asked.

The woman's full lips turned down in a frown, and she opened her mouth to speak. Before she could do so, Antires answered.

"Regrettably," he said, "my uncle, Resephone's father, perished at a work site sponsored by your family. He was the manager of the repairs. We're here in his stead."

"Oh, I'm sorry to hear that." Rather than prolonging the awkward moment, Drusira shifted her attention to the second man. "And who is this?"

"A family friend," Resephone said.

The older man stepped forward, an appreciative smile playing at his lips as he took her hand formally and kissed it. "This is more of a pleasure than I expected," he said. "I am Martial, godfather to Resephone. I came for her father's funeral. I must say, my lady, that your eyes are among the loveliest I've seen."

She was certain this compliment came in part because of the eye drops she'd applied. But as her eyes shifted to the stunning Resephone, her hand went to the necklace of pearls about her throat. She saw his gaze rest there.

In a way, his attention was as strangely exciting as that fear she'd felt when she'd approached her brother's monster. "How nice to meet you," she said. "Come. Tell me of yourself." She offered her arm, and he took it, and she led him away from the lovelier woman, though she spoke back to both. "Enjoy yourselves! I'll bring him back presently."

She hadn't really tried her power yet. But as they stepped from the atrium and diverted through the study into a side hall, she gave into temptation, flashing her eyes and putting her will into her voice, as Aridian had instructed her. "Tell me, Martial. Do you think me beautiful?"

"Yes," he answered without hesitation, and then frowned a little, as if confused.

She was surprised herself. She thought she had used her power upon him, and compelled him to speak the truth. She tried again. "You really think I'm beautiful? What of my teeth? Don't they mar my appearance?"

Little light reached the inner hall that evening, but his eyes seemed to have no trouble meeting hers.

"They make you distinctive," he said, and again looked puzzled. Perhaps he wasn't used to speaking so forthrightly.

She couldn't believe it. Here she was just wanting to play with her newfound magics a bit and command him, yet he already liked her! She laughed and patted his arm. "Come. We've a lovely collection of ancient swords. Perhaps you'd like to see them. The music's already begun to grate upon me."

"I would follow you anywhere, my lady."

"You carry yourself like a soldier," she said. "Surely you're some officer."

She thought to hear him admit he was simply a seasoned veteran, of no higher rank than optio.

"I am nothing, now," he said. "But once I was an officer."

She turned and looked up into his eyes. "What rank?"

"A general," he answered, then stared at her curiously.

"What happened? Why aren't you a general now?"

He looked reluctant to answer, but she could feel the magics compelling the truth from him. "I lost my army," he admitted.

"Gods." She patted his arm and led him further into the hall, past her brother's suite. She wasn't looking at him as she asked the next question. "And they stripped you of your rank?"

"You're a very compelling woman," Martial said, and something in his tone warned her he was on his guard.

Aridian had told her the secret was to talk about things that made your quarry comfortable. Things that they would want. If you discussed objects or people they might have dreamt of, you could more easily weave a spell.

She opened the door that led to her own suite and guided him to the sitting room, a wide chamber decorated with three couches centered about a table. A few candles guttered along her makeup desk. It would have been more proper to attend to her appearance in her bedroom, but the windows in the sitting room allowed ever so much more light.

"We can look at swords later," she said. She took his hands and tugged him toward the center couch, and he easily acquiesced and sat beside her. She felt his calluses as she looked deeply into his eyes. They were a stormy gray. "Tell me what it is you most desire."

"My daughter," he said.

She was struck with horror. She'd thought she had the attention of a handsome man of real character. But her power to coerce the truth had revealed that he, too, was twisted. Then she perceived the pain in his expression and wondered if she misunderstood. "Why do you want your daughter?"

"Because I fear for her," he said. "I can't find her. She's probably dead."

She put her hands to his face. He struggled to look away, then relaxed, at last.

"Oh, poor Martial. Who would have known I would find such a gentle soul in a soldier. Here. Look at me. I want to tell you of wonderful things. Tell me that you will listen."

"I will listen."

"Tell me that you will believe everything you hear."

"I will believe everything I hear."

She smiled and kissed him, but his return kiss was as passionless as his words. Aridian hadn't warned her about that. Well, she knew how to set things right. She would conjure him a vision that any soldier would wish.

"It is a beautiful day. The crowds have gathered along the Avenine Way for miles, and they watch as your chariot is pulled forward by six black stallions. Can you see them?"

"Yes."

"Do you hear the crowds? They chant your name. Again and again they call to you, for you have won a great victory for the empire."

His face twisted as though he'd been riven with pain. Drusira could only assume it was because he'd never thought he would be rewarded for his service. "Shh," she said, a hand to his cheek. "All is well. The people of Derva are grateful to you. Do you understand? They're grateful. Look. There's the triumphal arch, and your chariot passes beneath it. Behind you march thousands of prisoners, and tribute you won from your victories. Waiting up there on the dais, on the very temple to Divine Jovren, is the emperor himself! Do you see him? He calls your name, and bids you kneel before him as he lays a wreath upon your brow. You are a champion of the Dervan people!"

She thought, as she discussed more and more glories, that his pain would ease. But he bared his teeth and now his mouth opened in a silent scream. Finally, eyes closed, he gripped her upper arms and shook her.

"You're hurting me!" she cried.

His voice was a hoarse whisper. "Cease your magics!"

"Let go of me," she said, even though she felt a thrill to be clutched so tightly.

His head bowed, and he trembled, and she realized suddenly that he was racked with grief, though he made no sound.

A moment ago she'd known fright. Now she knew only compassion, leavened with guilt, for she had brought this upon him when she'd only meant to give him pleasure. She embraced him and dragged his head to her shoulder. She rocked him, patting his back and shushing him, as she had once done with her little niece when she'd scraped her knee. She had seen one of her slaves doing this with her child, and wondered, if her own son had lived, if she might have gentled him like this.

"I'm sorry," she said. "I didn't mean to hurt you."

He held her, tightly, as though he drowned. As though he hadn't held to anyone in a long, long while. As though his strength had ebbed and he had to borrow some of hers.

She stroked his hair the while, wondering how she had come to this place.

After a short time, his breath eased, and she heard his voice in her ear. "The world has puzzles for me yet. There is kindness in you, lady, even in your cruelties." He spoke on. "More fool I, who should know better than to judge the merits of a person by preconceptions."

"You're a strange man, Martial. But I am sorry."

He pulled away from her shoulder and without looking into her eyes, pressed lips to her forehead and kissed her. "I know. And I'm sorry too. Tell me how you came by the power you used on me."

"Oh, I can't."

"How long have you possessed it?"

"This was the first time I tried to use it," she said. "And I bungled it somehow. I thought if my brother could use it, it must be simple."

"How long has your brother had it?"

"Only a few days." She sighed. "He's seduced so many women."

"You needed no magic to seduce me."

Her heart fluttered like a bird. "I wasn't going to do *that*. I just wanted to see what it was like to know for sure if someone liked me."

"He acquired the magic from the sewers, didn't he? In the old tomb?"

That was strange. "How did you . . . how do you know about that?"

"Resephone's father was the foreman in charge of the repairs, and he died there. Your brother's servants said it was an accident. But there was no body. And you know how Herrenes are about funerals. They think the soul will wander the earth unless they can give him proper rites."

She tried to search his eyes, and then looked away, realizing she might unintentionally throw a spell on him again. And then another thought came to her, and her mouth opened.

"What?" he said.

She shook her head. "Oh no."

"What?"

Aridian had told her how he'd taken pains to make sure no one could pass on what had really been found, that only slaves had seen the place. That he had replaced all the workers.

But suppose that he'd lied? Suppose the foreman had seen something? "I think . . . I think maybe we should talk to my brother."

It was then they heard the tramp of feet down a distant corridor, and Drusira recalled there had been no music for the last few moments, apart from the steady beat of two drums, struck in unison like a mighty heart.

"That's strange," she said. "It sounds like the party's moving to the rear of the villa." And her brother wouldn't permit that, for that was the most deteriorated part of the building. As well as the creature's hiding place.

"They sound like an army on the march," Martial said grimly.

An idea struck her. She understood that if she were to join the others she would experience such joys as she had never dreamed. She shook her head, wondering where such a notion had come from, but she could not dismiss it, and she quickly wondered why she would wish to do so.

ν

The woman went rigid in Hanuvar's arms. He would have searched her face for signs of illness, but dared not risk meeting her eyes, for he still reeled from the powerful effect of her suggestions.

"We must go," she declared. Her voice lacked inflection of any kind, but delivered the full-throated power of her sorcery. It rattled through him; only the well of resistance he'd found when she suggested nightmares as great victories kept him safe, and even still he dared not meet her eyes.

"Fight it," he told her, and gripped her tightly.

"Come with me," she said, her head lolling. "Great things await." She struggled in his arms.

Sorcery had hold of her, and he could not break it. He rose with her; then, before whatever possessed her seemed certain of his actions, he guided her to a wardrobe. She turned to struggle only as he pushed her inside. He barred the door.

The sound of the drumbeat receded, but he heard it still, like the throb of some monster heart deep within the villa. Leaving her chamber, he found the swords Drusira had mentioned hanging on a central wall and quickly selected the finest. It might be that Antires and Resephone were unharmed by whatever enchantments were in play, but he did not mean to investigate without cold steel.

He'd have given a lot to hold a spear and shield as well.

It would be folly to advance boldly into unknown terrain against an unknown number of enemies. Had he an army, he would have deployed scouts; since he didn't, he stayed to the shadows as he prowled into the deeper recesses of the villa. He found the crowd formed about a central courtyard, tightly packed and swaying in unison.

He had no wish to confront those numbers directly.

He sought and found a servant's stair and threaded through the second-floor chambers until he looked down on the rectangular courtyard from a dark loggia with wide stone rails. For a brief moment he thought he'd spotted enemies in the darkness. Shoulder-high statues of dryads were placed every six paces, alternating between large urns filled with dead plants and bare dirt.

Torches flared in cressets set against pillars supporting the balcony. The partygoers, entertainers, and slaves, some sixty in all, formed a living wall around a central weedy pit in the center of the crumbling courtyard, and their bodies moved in time to the beat of two muscular drummers standing to one side. A small line of men and women queued up before a lidless rectangular structure, from which an object leaned.

Even seen while half obscured by shadow he felt something obviously, innately wrong with that object, and a chill coursed through Hanuvar as the thing shifted under its own power. He understood then that he looked upon a living creature. It had a glistening red carapace. Four long, waving tendrils projected from its head, and he was trying to decide whether they were arms or antennae when one of them slashed out at the obese man who was first in line.

Blood gushed from the man's stomach wound, and he cried out. "Please," he pleaded weakly. "I found you! I helped you!" Despite his protestations, he did not retreat. Instead, he drew closer still. "I'm not like the others!" the big man wailed. "I'm special!"

The creature drove all four of those projections into his body, and the man groaned as blood welled up and dripped down him to the tiles, but he did not withdraw, and he did not fall.

Though decades of warfare had inured him to all manner of injury, this grisly end repulsed Hanuvar. Searching for Resephone and Antires among the blank-eyed watchers, he discovered his friend was third in line, and his cousin stood directly behind him, smiling with anticipation, as though welcoming a gruesome death.

The man's body hit the old stones with a moist plop and the beast's four blood-slick tendrils commenced their waving. At the same time, a shrill voice rang within Hanuvar's head. "Look at me!"

Hanuvar turned his back to it and stepped into the shadows.

Despite facing away, he felt the might of that gaze.

The voice rose from within him. Cloying. Powerful. Strangely disjointed, as though it struggled to convey its dark feelings into words he would understand. "I felt you the moment you entered this structure. These others I shall feed upon. But I have another use for you!"

"Why me?" Hanuvar asked. He only half listened for the answer, racking his mind for the means to slay the monster. His first thought was fire, but the beast was surrounded by moisture as well as innocents who would be hurt by flame. And then there was the fact that the ancients had apparently closed the thing away rather than chopping it into tiny pieces. That led him to suspect it couldn't be killed by normal means.

The thing continued. "You are a hunter, a king, a killer, a force among these little entities. With you as my vessel, I will be ever so much greater."

Hanuvar heard noises below and peered from his hiding place. Two figures climbed an old trellis toward the balcony. He stepped toward them. "What are you?" he called.

The thing's plaintive cry echoed in his head. "Pity me, for I did not come to this land of my own will. I was summoned long ago to serve your kind. Now I am trapped, and struggle to survive."

Hanuvar had long found it strange those with great power so often thought themselves beset upon. "You're a victim, then."

"Yes. But not so helpless as the fool who found me thought. He believed he subdued me with blood. He but strengthened me so my powers could be restored!"

The first climber reached the gallery. Hanuvar drove his sword pommel into the man's knuckles. The climber released his hold, falling into the fellow below so that both crashed to the courtyard pavers. Others already scrambled to follow. Worse, he heard footfalls in the corridor. Figures were lumbering toward him. Hanuvar faced them, hand tightening on his sword hilt. And then, at sight of his assailants, he scowled and lowered the weapon.

One was a plump, older woman. With her came Resephone, her beauty dulled by her blank-eyed stare and her tottering gait, so different from her easy grace. They advanced with hands outstretched. Their jaws were slack. He felt an echo of the creature's power in their eyes, and so slitted his own. He turned, rather than raise arms against ensorcelled women, and almost walked into disaster.

A huge man dressed like a household slave had crept up from behind. Hanuvar raised a hand too late to block the incoming punch. His sidestep saved him from full impact, but even a partial blow from that great fist staggered him. He blinked stars out of his vision as the matron behind grasped his arm. Resephone gouged talonlike fingernails into his calf.

Hanuvar twisted away, swatting the older woman in the head with the flat of his blade. Resephone wrenched his ankle and he stumbled, catching sight of the large man lurching after.

He'd broken free, but his ankle pained and he didn't think he should put his full weight on it. He limped as he hurried along the railing, all his instincts urging him to flee. He could make his way down by the servant's stair, or even drop from a front window.

But that would mean abandoning his friends, and all these others. He rushed past a trellis, shaking under the weight of three new climbers. The thing called for him to look as he halted beside one of those large pots he'd spotted earlier. The big man followed only a few steps to his rear.

He grasped the urn under its swollen lip, and then, his ankle smarting, he hefted it a foot above the railing. It was lighter than he'd feared, owing to the desiccated soil within, but still a strain. He dared not look down, for fear that he would meet the monster's stare, yet he had to verify the angle of attack. That's when he saw the multifaceted eyes in that terrible face, with its clacking parrot's beak and writhing cilia, glistening with blood. He felt icy tendrils of foreign will reaching out from the foothold it already had within him—

He released the urn.

The creature must have sensed its fate, for its efforts to reach Hanuvar ceased even as the planter dropped toward it. There was a crash of clay on stone, followed almost immediately by the stench of blood.

The big man caught one of Hanuvar's arms and spun him around. He turned on his bad leg and would have driven a hand at the man's throat, but his opponent tucked in his chin.

The brawler cocked back a fist. Hanuvar flexed hands, conscious of the footfalls to his rear.

Then the big man stared, dumbfounded, and shook his head.

Hanuvar pried the man's fingers from his shirt. "Are you free of it?"

He seemed to be, but Hanuvar didn't waste more time watching his attacker. He turned to find the two women at his rear blinking stupidly. He wheeled to the railing, and was struggling to lift a larger planter when he felt the big man at his side. "This will hurt it?" the slave asked in a thick Ermanian accent.

"Cover the thing in dirt or sand," Hanuvar ordered. He hoped he had the truth of it, based solely on images glimpsed on that ancient subterranean wall.

Resephone appeared at his shoulder, her face stricken and confused. Nonetheless, as Hanuvar and the muscular slave bent to lift the larger pot, she grasped it with them and helped carry it to the edge. After they dropped it over side, Hanuvar looked down, noting that the second planter had not only cracked open the creature's brick container but that the dirt was soaking up the blood. The creature squirmed in the foul mud, stretching tendrils toward a stream of red muck.

The crowd backed away, muttering among themselves. Someone behind a nearby pillar sobbed uncontrollably. Hanuvar waved to Antires, but the actor didn't see him.

Hanuvar's new ally needed no urging, and the big man stepped to the nearest planter, his mouth twisted in hate. He lifted it on his own, and the third vessel exploded right upon the reaching tendrils, hurling bits of pottery and dirt in every direction. Hanuvar watched to see if the weight and velocity did anything whatsoever to the being itself, for a human would have been pulped by the three attacks.

"Is it dead?" Resephone asked, breathless.

"No." Whatever strange realm the creature had been conjured from birthed entities that lived by different rules. Despite a solid hit, the monster's carapace looked unbroken, and its tendrils still quivered, lusting desperately for someone's lifeblood. But it had shrunken in upon itself, diminishing by at least a quarter.

He hadn't forgotten the rest of the instructive pictograms upon that ancient mural. Even as his huge ally sent another planter plummeting over side Hanuvar pointed to the one beside it. "That next. I'm going downstairs to finish it." He spoke to Resephone. "Stay up here where it's safe."

"I'm coming with you!"

He didn't have time to argue. Hanuvar ran limping for the stairs. He stopped only to break the leg off an ornate side table, carrying it with him like a club.

By the time he had reached the courtyard, the mob of guests was in full stampede. No longer confused or subdued, but terrified, some cried out in anguish as they ran.

Hanuvar knew their departure meant troops would shortly be dispatched, and he had no inclination to be questioned by them.

Antires waited to one side of the courtyard doorway. Even in the gloom Hanuvar saw his friend's wide smile of relief. "Praise the Gods. You're both unharmed!"

"What about you?" Resephone asked, throwing her arms around her cousin.

"I'm fine." Antires clasped her close.

They celebrated too soon. "Find a crate or chest large enough to hold it," Hanuvar said. "And blankets. Hurry!" He started past them.

"What are you going to do?" Resephone asked.

He answered without looking back. "Break it."

He found the being surrounded by shattered pottery and scattered dirt. Its feelers and tentacles scrabbled at the pale body of the big man. His empty eyes glistened in the torchlight.

Hanuvar snatched up a discarded cloak, tossed it over the creature, and advanced with his wooden club. He brought it down on the beast's back, striking again and again. Each impact resulted in a satisfying crunch, and the diminishment of the writhing body beneath the blood-drenched cloth.

It spun beneath the blanket, scrabbling against the stone floor on dozens of segmented legs, and Hanuvar closed his eyes to its burning gaze he couldn't see, even as it stretched for his mind while those tendrils sought his flesh.

"You fool!" it cried. "You could unite with me, and I could grant you whatever you wish!"

"What I wish," he said, "you cannot grant me." He brought the cudgel across the squirming tentacles and it squealed in agony. He rained down blows upon it and ignored its rasping pleas for mercy.

What seemed an eternity later, Antires and Resephone arrived with a storage chest. Antires then pulled a thick wool blanket from it and tossed it across the writhing monster, now shriveled under the cloak to the size of a piglet. It squirmed feebly as Hanuvar lifted it in the fabric, and he felt the questing thrust of one of its terrible feelers against the cloth.

He threw it into the chest and slammed the lid closed. Only then did he scan their surroundings. The three of them were alone in the courtyard. Of the big slave who'd aided him, he saw no sign.

Resephone's eyes were huge. "What was that monster?"

"Something that doesn't belong here," Hanuvar answered. Antires passed over a second blanket and Hanuvar used it to wipe gore from his limbs. "How are you two?"

"Well enough, I think," Antires answered. "Once Aridian stood up and spoke to us all I could feel that thing in my mind, and it wouldn't—"

Hanuvar cut him off. "But you're fine now? We'll talk later. Go. I'll catch up to you. Ready our things. We're leaving tonight."

The creature thudded feebly against the side of the wooden chest and Hanuvar suppressed a grimace.

Weeks ago, Antires had stopped asking for details when Hanuvar gave orders, but Resephone didn't yet know that when he urged haste, it was necessary. She paused even as Antires moved off.

"Who are you, really?" she asked.

"I'm your cousin's friend."

Antires beckoned to her.

"That's not an answer," she said.

"It's the only one that counts." Hanuvar's eyes fell to the blood-soaked, mutilated corpse of Aridian. "Your father's avenged now. I'll find someone who can tell you where his body's buried. Now go. I'll meet you at your home."

He followed them out of the courtyard, but turned down a different hall.

When Hanuvar opened the wardrobe door Drusira was seated on its floor. She lifted a hand to shield her eyes from the influx of lantern light. "What happened?" she asked. "I heard screaming."

"The magic had you in its thrall." Hanuvar set down the lantern and helped her to her feet. "How are you now?"

"I'm fine. But what's happened?"

"The monster's captured, but I don't think it's dead. I'm not sure it can really be killed."

"Where's my brother?"

There was no easy way to blunt the information, so he didn't. "He was one of its victims."

She nodded quietly. "Because I had some of the monster's power, it tried to use me. But you saved me." Was that a hint of the creature's power still, in her gaze? Or was it Drusira's own?

He squeezed her hand and released it. "Now you have to save yourself, and your people. I've placed it in a chest. It must be hidden away, in the dark. Make no record of where it's kept, but leave pictograms to tell it must be kept from blood, and that its eyes are dangerous. Do you understand? Not writing, pictures, so that anyone who finds it can know. Make certain it's clear it can only be weakened by having the blood beaten out of it and soaked away with sand or dirt."

"Yes."

"Let it dry up and perhaps, someday, it will be nothing but dust."

"You can't see to it?"

"No. And you must ask your brother's slaves where Resephone's father was buried, so she can give him proper funeral rites."

"I will." She clutched at his hand. "But won't you stay?" She added with childlike vulnerability: "I need your strength."

He bent to kiss her. "There are things that I must do. Find your own strength, and look to no man to confirm your beauty."

As he released her he spotted a little stoppered pot on the side of her dressing table. Was he imagining its mystical pull? He lifted it. "Is this the creature's magic secretion?"

"Yes."

He weighed the stopper in his hand as he metaphorically weighed the possibility presented him. How much simpler the challenges before him would be if he could command men's unswerving obedience. No gates would be barred. All his people could be found and freed with but a few simple commands. Surely the creature could not affect him if it was locked far away, could it?

He hurled the jar to the floor tiles, where it smashed into tiny pieces. The shining liquid spread among its shattered fragments and dribbled away. He lifted a hand in farewell to Drusira, then limped out from the villa and into the night.

※ ※ ※

Once, one of my nephews asked if I thought I better understood how a slave must feel, to have surrendered my will to that malevolent blood thing. He was young. What slave marches joyfully forward at his master's every whim, even unto death? Resephone and I knew what we did, and we thrilled to it. Once it decided to expend its power, it leapt from one to the other of us in that small space, where we stood talking nose to nose and eye to eye, until we all were extensions of its will and thought ourselves happy to be so. The ease with which that being worked its power still brings me chills.

Resephone pleaded with us to stay the night after we returned to her home, feeling a natural indebtedness to us and a responsibility besides, since Hanuvar had been injured by her. We did not. Certain that authorities would be alerted, Hanuvar wished to be on his way, even though it meant travel through the darkness. We left her, then, and long years were to pass before I spoke with her once more.

Though she knew Hanuvar was no ordinary man, she did not then guess his identity. Over the coming months, when rumors spread that Hanuvar lived and had even passed through the provinces, she scoffed like any rational person who hears talk of conspiracies and rumors, though they be daily fare for so many. And then, one evening when she was washing her plate after dinner, she fell to wondering about me and my mysterious friend and she froze with the wet rag halfway to the plate. She managed not to drop it.

"It had not occurred to me that Hanuvar, the monster, might fight other monsters," she said when she told me of that moment.

Naturally I told her that he was not a monster, but she had so much sympathy for all those who had perished in the Second Volani War—

known by some, her among them, as the Hanuvaran War—that she was unable to see him in a different light. Even when I pointed out that he had been fighting, like the Herrenic city-states in Utria, to break the Dervan yoke, she could only say that there should have been a kinder way.

I think there might have been, but only if the gods made a kinder world.

That conversation transpired more than a decade after our adventure with Resephone. In the days immediately following our encounter with the monster, it seemed to me Hanuvar had grown a little more relaxed in my presence. One evening, as we were brushing down the horses, he asked a question I sensed he'd long been wondering. "What brought you to the fringes of the Dervan Empire?"

I answered readily enough. "My family were refugees from Arbos. My great uncle upset the city's tyrant with a few, shall we say, injudicious poems, and the whole family had to run for it. We ended up in southern Tyvol, and we spread out from there."

He paused in his brushing and looked up from his horse's chest. "But you, specifically?"

It pleased me that he was curious, but the real reason I remember smiling at that was because I was amused by my youthful wanderlust. "I wanted to go wandering and see the sights. A young man's fancy and all that. And I was smitten with another actor. I thought I'd follow him to the ends of the world. I did, but he turned out to be in love with his reflection. He left the troupe halfway along when some patrician fell over himself for him. Me, I kept going."

"And how did you like the world's end?" Hanuvar asked.

"It turned out there was more world to see. But I was low on funds, tired of bad food, and bored with the stuffy plays the troupe was putting on."

"So you left, and set up shop for yourself."

"Where I was making ends meet, barely, until a madman turned up riding the other direction."

He chuckled. Bit by bit I was to grow accustomed to that sound, and discover that it was not so rare as you might suppose. At least when Hanuvar was among friends. —Sosilos, Book Three

Chapter 7:
The Voice of the Forest God

I

Leaves threw shadows onto the old, tree-lined road. The afternoon sun was a comfortable hand on Hanuvar's back. Only a week ago he had planned to travel southwest, to the sea. Now, he still bore west, but he had angled north. He no longer caught the occasional hint of salt in the air. Instead there were only the deep, rich scents of the countryside, a heady mix of wildflowers and grasses, pine needles and warm earth. Birds sang to each other from the nearby branches, the fluting calls of dark thrushes dominant.

Antires rode quietly at his side, his eyelids heavy. Uncharacteristically, the Herrene's flow of questions had stopped. The afternoon felt a lazy one, inviting a halt against a hillside to consider cloud shapes and drowse for a few hours before sitting down with family at the evening meal.

In a different world, Hanuvar might have experienced that opportunity. In this one, he pressed on. Within the next hour, he expected to reach the village of Erapna, and there, he'd been promised, lived a priestess who could tell him his daughter's fate.

Hanuvar placed little faith in soothsayers and priests, but a powerful spirit had repaid his own kindness with the admonition to avoid the sea, telling him further that an Erapnan priestess would help him if he aided her in return. And so he rode, his thoughts upon the determined, black-haired girl he had met only at war's end. Long years of campaigning had kept them apart. He and his own brothers had been raised in armed encampments, and much as he loved his father, he had sworn that his own progeny would have childhoods further from war, never thinking that but one of them would survive infancy, or that he would see her so rarely.

But even growing up apart from him she had proven a warrior after his own heart: clever, swift, skilled with sword, wise with words, a natural leader, and officer of the famed Eltyr, the warrior guard of the Volanus sea gate. After the end of the second war, when he had been elected shofet, he had come to know her well, not just as a daughter, but as a friend.

He had assumed her lost with so many others. The thought that she might have survived the city's destruction was almost too overwhelming to contemplate.

His reveries were interrupted when a woman's frightened scream rang through the nearby hills. The thrushes fell silent. Antires let out a cry of surprise and straightened, asking what was happening even as hoofbeats drummed the earth beyond the next turn.

A fear-maddened white horse tore into sight, galloping across the fields toward their road, a dark-haired woman bent forward in her saddle, clinging for life to the reins. A quarter mile behind, a small band of armored men pursued, but Hanuvar was almost certain they were her guard, for they were shouting at her to hold tight.

The woman's efforts to stop her horse were ineffectual, and the guards lagged too far back to assist.

Hanuvar kicked his bay roan, and the gelding responded instantly, galloping forward in a spray of dirt. He called for Antires to ride up on the right as he rode up on the left, but the Herrene, no great horseman, was already trailing.

The mare turned onto the road as Hanuvar caught up. He had little sense of the woman other than a feminine figure in a light blue stola with a mass of brunette hair. Her dark eyes were almost as wide with panic as those of her frightened horse.

He scanned the road ahead, alert for ruts, spotted none, then leaned out from his saddle.

The woman's horse veered from his reach. Hanuvar's gelding matched speed, either sensing his intent or merely inspired to race, and Hanuvar snared one of the dangling reins. He immediately straightened and called for his horse to slow.

The mare fought him, with all the considerable weight of her body. But Hanuvar looped the rein about his arm, tugging hard as he slowed his roan, bracing his hand to his saddle lest he be torn from his seat.

He urged his gelding into a turn, and this ate into the frightened mare's speed. The rider still clutched at her saddle, the remaining rein held taut but ineffectual against the intense escape instinct driving the horse. A large dart stood out from the animal's rump, waggling with its every move. A stream of scarlet blood trickled from the injury down the mare's white shank.

He led the horse through enough small circles that it stopped at last, though it still stamped vexedly. He leaned toward the woman. "Come to me," he said.

Her guards had closed the distance and one shouted in alarm as he lifted her bodily from the saddle. She leaned into him. She smelled of flowers and sunny hair, and under her pleasant roundness she had firm muscles. He turned his own horse from the wounded mare and lowered the woman gently to the ground.

The horsemen trotted up, but he still paid them no heed. Hanuvar had leapt down and snagged both the mare's reins, holding them tight as he pulled out the dart. The mare didn't like that, either, and struggled to flee. He held her firm, and finally calmed her.

One of the guards leaned down at him, frowning. "Who are you?" he demanded. "You dare lay hands on a prefect's daughter?".

The woman turned, head raised, hand brushing back hair that trailed wildly into her face. "This man saved my life. Leave off the accusations."

She was not so young as Hanuvar had first thought, though that hardly diminished her appeal. There were lines of gray in her hair, and lines on her face, which was not the pale shade so typical of aristocratic Dervan women. She left off fussing with her hair and bestowed a fetching smile upon Hanuvar. "Forgive them, kind sir, and forgive me my appearance."

"There is nothing to forgive," Hanuvar said. "It's not every day a man meets a forest goddess."

She laughed. "You're too kind. But I thank you. And I thank you for your quick thinking."

The lead soldier, a craggy man with a scarred nose, dropped off his horse. "Pardon, milady, but he might well be one of the rebels."

She sighed as she looked at him. "I do wish you would think more before you spoke, Silus. The rebels were trying to kill me, or at least cause me bodily harm, and he risked life and limb to do the contrary. Did you manage to find them?"

"Four of the men are looking for them now. I'm sure they'll find the culprit. I did tell you that we were riding too far."

"I dearly wish that you had been wrong." The woman shifted her gaze to Hanuvar. "What is your name, kind sir?"

Hanuvar passed off the mare's reins to a scowling Silus and answered the woman.

"I am Entius. And that is my friend Stirses, on whom your men are holding spears."

She turned on the instant. "Leave him be as well! Gods." She scowled at her guards. "You didn't hurt him, did you?" She didn't wait for an answer, speaking directly to Antires as the disgruntled soldiers turned their weapons away. "Stirses, are you well?"

He bowed his handsome head to her. "I am, milady."

"They are overprotective," the woman said as she turned back to Hanuvar.

"They seem dutifully cautious," he replied. "What happened?"

"I was paying respect at a little woodland shrine to Diara. It's the strangest thing, but I've been riding this way for weeks, and never noticed the path before."

"The rebels probably made it more obvious to lure you, milady," Silus said gruffly.

"It felt more like I had been called there, until that dart hit my horse."

"Who threw it?" Hanuvar asked.

She waved a hand as if her brush with danger were a mere trifle. "I didn't happen to see them. But I'm not very popular in Erapna. I am Clodia Septima," she added. "I seem to have forgotten to introduce myself."

"Why would anyone wish to harm you?"

"My brother's trying to help the locals past some strange habits they've taken up in their worship. Are you new here yourself?"

Hanuvar's answer had long since been readied. "I'm on my way to the temple to pray for my daughter. She disappeared while I was in the service, and no one is sure where she's gone."

"That's terrible. I will pray for you."

"You are kind."

"It is the least I can do. My brother helps manage the temple now. I'm sure he will aid you any way that he can."

Hanuvar bowed his head. "I'd be grateful. I was told to seek a priestess."

"A priestess? I don't think that there are any left. But I'm sure he can help you. If it's not too forward of me to ask, what rank did you hold during your service?"

Hanuvar sensed the attention of the watching guardsmen, but had eyes only for Clodia. "I rose no higher than optio. I might have made centurion, but I was a little too fond of wine."

She eyed him keenly. "You don't strike me as a drunk."

"I've sworn off drink until I find my daughter."

"How very wise of you."

This woman charmed him. This was no pleasure trip, and he had no intention to stand out. But then he had already drawn attention and doubted a little more time in her company would jeopardize himself further. It could illuminate her troubling statement about the lack of priestesses and educate him about the local troubles. The Dervans had not long controlled large sections of the provinces, and resentment against the empire still simmered, though it manifested differently in different places. "Your own mount won't be sound to ride until she's properly tended. You may borrow mine until we reach the village."

Behind him the soldiers talked among themselves, and there was a warning note in their voices.

"He's a bit tall for me," Clodia said. "You'll have to help me up."

He cupped her sandaled foot, noting the slender ankle and well-defined calf, then passed the reins to her.

He spent the next half hour walking at her side. Two of the sullen guards ranged ahead. The others followed, along with Antires, leading their pack horse. A few minutes into their journey four more soldiers galloped up to join them, and Hanuvar overheard them reporting to Silus that they had scoured the brush and found tracks, but hadn't discovered the assailant.

It was a pleasure to talk with an articulate, pretty woman. He turned all questions about himself to questions about her, and she was happy enough to discuss her life. She claimed to be a country girl at heart. She'd married a senator's son but he'd been stodgy and demanding, and after ten years she had divorced him. She enjoyed long rides in the countryside, the playing of harps—which she said she did only inexpertly, despite years of practice—and the study of history.

Hanuvar ignored the obvious snare of mutual points of interest, for he, too, was a student of history. Even telling her that he had always enjoyed music but never had the time to practice was probably too much detail.

Their idyll was shattered as they approached the lands just southeast of the village, and beheld a line of ten poles against which desiccated figures hung. Clodia turned her head in distaste.

Hanuvar judged that the victims had been crucified at least two weeks prior. "Rebels?" he asked.

"The governor's troops thought this the best way to cow them," she said. "It's made my brother's job a lot harder."

"And the villagers angry enough to attack you?"

She smiled bravely. "I've managed fine so far."

"You spoke earlier about not being sure there was a priestess anymore. Did they attack her?"

"No. I believe the last priestess was sent away. But my brother and the other priests have the right training to solve most people's problems."

Hanuvar doubted that their guidance would be much use to him, unless they could direct him to the correct priestess.

They arrived at the village outskirts, at which Clodia halted, insisting on returning Hanuvar's horse. Her villa was on the far side of the settlement, and she refused to allow him to trouble himself further. He did not object, though he was honestly sorry to leave her.

"Do you know how long you will be staying in town, Entius?" She brushed hair from her dark eyes once more.

"It depends upon what I learn at the temple."

"It truly was a pleasure to meet you. I can't ever properly thank you."

"The pleasure was all mine," he assured her. He thought he might have to demur an invitation to hear her play the harp, or turn down an offer of dinner, and was amused by his own disappointment that she offered neither.

While one of her guards dismounted so that Clodia might ride his horse, Hanuvar and Antires rode their animals further into town.

The Herrene eyed him with a knowing smile. "She's an attractive woman," he said once they were out of hearing range.

"She may be the only person in the whole village kindly disposed toward us. Her guards hate that I did their job for them. And did you notice the glares everyone else is giving us?"

Antires apparently only then saw the suspicious look bestowed upon them by a man walking along the side of the street. He had missed the first few from merchants and customers peering out from the tailor and barber shops.

"What's that about?"

"That's about moral rectitude not always being welcomed with open arms."

Antires visibly tried to parse meaning from Hanuvar's answer. "Sometimes you confuse me."

"We're dressed like Dervans, and came in with a local patrician's sister. The Dervans are telling these people they're worshiping their gods wrong."

"Oh. That will make them popular."

"Yes. "

"In retrospect it probably wasn't a smart idea to ride in with a Dervan woman."

"Thanks for the pointer," Hanuvar said dryly.

II

The temple to Diara was a small building on a hill near the village center, tall and narrow, with a single pair of columns. Fairly certain he would not find what he sought within, Hanuvar nonetheless entered, paid a tithe and lit a candle. After a short while he was ushered into a small chamber rich with clove-scented incense and small candles.

A moment later he was joined by a smooth-skinned patrician in a costly white robe. Almost surely this was Clodia's brother Paulus, whom he had assumed would be overseeing the temple, not taking full charge of its duties. In the eyebrows and the shape of the nose,

Hanuvar saw a heavier, masculine version of the features that had pleased him earlier.

The man saw his searching look. "You seem troubled. How may I help you?"

"I was told to speak to a priestess," Hanuvar said.

The priest's brow furrowed. "Told by whom?"

"People on the road. They said she could advise me about my problems. Is she not here?"

"There is no longer a priestess of the temple."

"Where can she be found?"

"She was dismissed. But I can assist you with your problems. What are they?"

This entire encounter was going to be a waste of his time, but Hanuvar didn't wish to withdraw too quickly and arouse suspicion, nor did he think it wise to inquire too pointedly about the whereabouts of the priestess. And so he manufactured a reply, his voice low and his eyes downcast, as though he had grown embarrassed. "I'm low on money, and I'm far from home. I work hard, but I can never hold onto my earnings."

"I will happily advise you. Sit, my son." Paulus waved a hand to a cushioned bench. "I will breathe of the sacred vapors and tell you what I learn."

Hanuvar sat while the priest lowered himself onto a cushioned stool and moved his hand in a circle, the better to draw the incense to his nostrils. He closed his eyes and bowed his head.

Hanuvar watched him, trying not to fidget during the ill-spent time. Incense and candle smoke wafted toward the ceiling.

Finally, Paulus opened his eyes with a sad smile. "The gods have spoken to me."

"Have they?"

"Rest assured, they have. They say that the reason you are low on money is because you spend too much of it on low women and wine."

"They are right," Hanuvar admitted grudgingly.

"Ah, you know the truth already. Have you a wife?"

"No. She died."

"Find one. A woman will keep you busy, and happy, if you find the right one. And have more children. You are not so old yet to have some who can care for you as you age."

"Wisely said. Thank you."

"You need no other guidance?" Paulus sounded honestly surprised.

"I had seen the right path already. Sometimes you just need to hear someone else confirm the truth."

"Spoken like a man with some years behind him. Good luck, my son."

Hanuvar found Antires sitting on the bottom step outside the temple, one hand on the pack horse's lead line. He stood as Hanuvar started down. "That was fast. Good news?"

Hanuvar answered softly. "The priestess remains elusive. I received a morality lecture from a priest. And he channels the gods about as well as I do. We'll have to make inquiries. Let's head to that tavern."

"I thought you hated taverns."

Hanuvar preferred to buy food from farmers' stalls on the road so he was seen by fewer ex-soldiers. While retired soldiers were often discharged with plots of land, this deep into the provinces their numbers were few still, and he'd encountered more of them in taverns than in the fields. "We need information. And you don't have to worry. The chances I'll be recognized are relatively low in most places."

"How low?"

"My parleys were held with line officers. Any of their guards, or Dervan soldiers I spoke with over the years, saw me in uniform. I was younger, and bearded, and most of those encounters took place on Dervan lands proper, not in the provinces."

"But some scout or soldier might have retired here."

"They might have. But then I have no Volani accent. My hair's cut to the nape like an ordinary Dervan citizen, I wear a citizen's ring, and I'm clean-shaven."

"Just remember to move like an ordinary citizen. You still walk like a military man."

"Thank you, Mother. I've already told people here that I'm a soldier, remember?"

"Someday you're going to have to disguise yourself under some other identity. Always having the same kind of story is going to make you too easy to track."

He suspected Antires' criticism held more than a kernel of truth, but there were thousands of former soldiers in the empire of his approximate age. "Perhaps. For now, let's worry about finding something to eat."

The thatch-roofed tavern smelled of old wine and oak and overflowed with shadows. Seven locals were clustered in two groups about the long tables, and every one of them fell silent and stared as they approached the low counter. Antires' hand lifted in greeting was not reciprocated.

Hanuvar and Antires took their bowls and drinking jacks to an empty table and sat on benches across from each other. The jacks were clean, the wine gently watered, and the meat held a pleasant, smoky flavor. Hanuvar had started on his third bite when two of Clodia's guards pushed into the tavern, led by Silus, their scarred-nosed leader.

They were received more poorly than Hanuvar and Antires, for the villagers looked up from their meals to glare at their backs, and the bartender frowned as he took their money.

Without his helm, their leader looked younger. His brown hair was thick and curly. He scanned the tables for challenge and Hanuvar readied himself.

The village men found sudden interest in their food. Hanuvar met the guard captain's eyes.

Silus sneered. "If it isn't the hero." He pushed away from the bar and swaggered forward. His companions trailed after. He spoke as the old floorboards creaked beneath his tread. "You in league with this lot? Did you goad them to attack Lady Clodia's horse so you could get in good with her?" Silus stopped at their table.

"This isn't my fight," Hanuvar said.

"It isn't his fight," Silus repeated mockingly to the guard on his right. "Is that what you told your centurion? Is that why you cashed out as just a lowly optio after, what, twenty-five years of service? You a coward?"

Hanuvar knew the basics of the script they followed. Silus would either be expecting him to protest and endure more insults or rise to the bait so Silus could show his mastery. He met Silus' eyes. "They didn't promote me because I beat a cavalry officer nearly to death."

Antires' eyes widened in dumbfounded amazement. Hanuvar had

instructed him that they were always to seek a low profile, and here he was deliberately encouraging trouble. If the Herrene didn't understand, he'd have to learn later.

Hanuvar's reply wasn't the answer Silus appeared to have expected, but he took it as the continuation to a challenge. He laughed scoffingly. "I don't believe it. They would have crucified you for that."

"Well, he was a loud-mouthed braggart and needed a good ass-kicking, so everyone claimed they didn't see it. I'm not in the service now." Hanuvar rose. "I can kick a cavalryman's ass no matter who's watching."

The bartender's bark of laughter was the only sound in the room. Everyone else was silent and still. Behind Silus, his broad-shouldered companions traded troubled glances and looked to their leader.

Silus was a little taller than Hanuvar, but he wasn't so stupid that he could meet Hanuvar's eyes without sensing danger.

Belatedly, Silus found something to say. "Are you threatening me, old man?"

"I'm here for a meal. What are you here for?"

Silus didn't seem to know what to do.

One of his companions touched him on the elbow. "Come on. He isn't worth it. Let's get a cup."

Silus scowled at his companion, then turned it on Hanuvar. "Ah," he said after a moment, "I'll be watching you. You stay clear of Lady Clodia."

Hanuvar didn't dignify the warning with a response, and watched, stone-faced, as Silus strode back to the counter with his friends.

After a moment, Hanuvar took his seat and resumed his meal.

Antires was predictably irritated. "I thought you were the one who said we shouldn't ever draw attention." His voice was a whisper, but there was no missing his agitation. "What was that about?"

"I'm playing a hunch."

"It looked to me you were trying to start a fight."

"I would have, if needed."

"Why would it be needed?"

"We'll see."

Antires flung open his hands in annoyance. "Do you always have to be so secretive?"

"I'll explain, later."

Antires sighed and resumed his meal.

The guardsmen lingered at the bar for only a little while. Silus scanned the room again before departure, and Hanuvar made sure to be tipping up his drink while he was doing so. He'd achieved his goal and further confrontation wasn't needed.

After the door shut behind the last of them, he headed to the front of the bar with his empty drinking jack. He passed it to the barkeep. "I'd like another."

Wordless, the bartender filled it from a pitcher behind the counter. He was a heavy-set, dour man with a thick jaw. Hanuvar took a long sip and looked over the room once more. The five villagers still seated there watched with less hostility.

"How long have you known Silus?" the barkeep asked.

"Two hours, and too long," Hanuvar answered, which inspired a short laugh. "Is he always this friendly?"

The man nodded. "He and all of Clodia's bully boys like to throw their weight around. Every chance they get."

"Clodia's brother is the new priest, right?"

"That's right."

"What happened to the priestess? I came a long way to have her tell my fortune."

Hanuvar had thought he sounded casual enough, but the bartender's gaze hardened. "She's gone."

"You mean the priests took her?"

"They might have, if she'd stayed."

Hanuvar swore; only in his expression was he acting, for his frustration was real. "I need to see a priestess, not a priest. Who else do you people talk to around here?"

"You want to see her just for your fortune?" the barkeep asked skeptically.

Once more the door opened. Hanuvar turned, halfway expecting Silus again. This time, though, a well-dressed brown-haired youth pushed in, stopping just inside the door and blinking as his eyes adjusted to the gloom. He spoke with the casual confidence of a rich man's slave: "I'm looking for the man who saved the Lady Clodia this afternoon."

Hanuvar groaned inwardly but let no expression show.

No one in the tavern answered. The boy's expression shifted to Antires, who was the only obvious foreigner, but the Herrene looked back without answering. As the boy's eyes roved to Hanuvar, he reluctantly lifted his hand. Perhaps if he downplayed what he'd done this interaction wouldn't spoil the fragile rapport he'd been building with the villagers. "I helped her with her horse," Hanuvar said.

The youth walked toward him, taking in his simple tunic with an amused smile. "Milady wishes to invite you to dine with her this evening." He placed a slim leather pouch upon the counter with a faint jangle of coins and pushed it a foot toward Hanuvar before removing his fingers. "Here is a token of her appreciation."

He knew then that he'd lost any headway he'd made with the barkeep, though he strove to explain things in a reasonable way. "I can't accept this. I didn't know who she was," he added, with a glance to the grim-faced man behind the counter. "She was just having some trouble with her horse."

"She feels otherwise," the boy said blandly. "It's yourn, regardless if you attend. You might want to put this toward a soak and a shave, eh?" He smirked.

"Out," Hanuvar said.

The boy departed. He had the good sense to hold off any further sniggering until the door shut behind him.

When Hanuvar turned, he found the barkeep and any who met his eyes watching again with suspicion.

Antires walked up to join him.

Wordless, Hanuvar picked up the coin purse, feeling an ample weight. He paid for the second drink from his own purse, then pushed through the door, searched to either side, and stepped through. Antires came after.

The skies had grown overcast.

"I see now," Antires said. "You were trying to win over the villagers."

Hanuvar didn't bother with an answer. "This is taking too long. We could be on the road and make at least six more miles before sunset."

Antires put a hand to his arm. This in itself was out of the ordinary, but then so was the younger man's gentle, searching gaze. "If you were seeking someone other than your daughter, wouldn't you put in the time?"

He questioned his friend with a look.

Antires went on: "You feel like you're being self-indulgent because you're searching for someone you personally know. So look at it this way. If you didn't know her, but had a lead on someone you could help, you would, wouldn't you?"

"You're right," he conceded. "I'll give it tonight." Taking a few coins for himself, he passed the purse to Antires. "Find us a good room, then take your ease. If you can make any surreptitious inquiries, do so."

"Where are you going?"

"To get a good shave and a proper bath. The fates keep pointing me toward Lady Clodia. Maybe she knows something more about the woman her brother replaced."

"And maybe," Antires said, "you'll have a relaxing evening."

"That's not the point."

"It wouldn't hurt you to relax," Antires offered. "You can do that, can't you?"

"I think I relaxed, once or twice, in another life." Hanuvar turned away. "I'll see if I still have the knack."

III

On reaching the grounds of Clodia's estate, Hanuvar had expected to be challenged by Silus or one of his men, but he didn't recognize the guards on duty that evening, and they simply directed him to the lady's residence, a smaller building in back of the sprawling villa.

The boy messenger was on hand to take Hanuvar's horse as he dismounted. Hanuvar watched for a smirk at his fresh garments and newly trimmed hair, though he wasn't sure what he'd have done if he'd seen one.

Another slave opened the door for him, but Clodia greeted him as he was taking in the small but richly appointed atrium, and guided him from there into the home, explaining that it had once been a guest house on the grounds and that she had appropriated it for herself.

Clodia's slaves had curled her hair, framing her fine features in lustrous ringlets. Her gold-tinted stola, like her flesh, seemed warm under the candlelight.

They reclined on the couches in the triclinium as they ate, Dervan style, chatting about the weather and their favorite horses, and other light topics. After an initial course of hard-boiled eggs, the servants arrived with venison and bowls to wash their fingers in.

"I hope you don't mind me keeping the courses simple," Clodia said.

Hanuvar was glad that in this province the dinner guests were expected to wash their hands themselves. It was hard enough to act like it was normal to be waited on by slaves, let alone when they performed unnecessary personal tasks upon him. "I'm a simple man," he replied. "And it's the company that brought me, not the food, fine as it is."

She opened her mouth as if she had something to say, then fell silent as a pale slave girl refilled their wine. "That's all, dear."

The young woman bowed her head and departed.

Clodia waited to speak again until the sound of her footsteps had faded. "I wasn't sure you'd come."

"I almost didn't." Hanuvar indicated the walls, painted with vines and forests and deer. "I don't belong in this fine place, with such elevated company."

"You may come from humble origins, but it's obvious you're a man of good upbringing."

He laughed at that. He knew that he should have done a far better job of playing the part of a gruff soldier, but he had too much desire for the woman's good opinion to be coarse or awkward.

"Why do you laugh?"

"Because I'm a silly old man, trying too hard to impress someone he shouldn't."

She smiled. "You may be older, but you do not seem old, Entius. And your compliments are flattering and well turned. You do not have the manner either of a recovering drunkard or a soldier."

"Then wine and candlelight obscure your vision, milady, for I think most would know my true nature if they met my eyes."

"What an interesting expression. What is your true nature, if you don't mind me asking?"

"I am a well-trained killer."

She chewed on a small cube of venison. "Is it something you are, or something you do?"

"Isn't there a philosopher who asks that?"

"Phenaxes. And something tells me you know his work."

"You'd be surprised what philosophers soldiers can be, when they're not drinking or whoring."

She shook her head, bemused. "And now you seek to shock me. You are pulled by contrary impulses, as if on one hand you wish to impress and on the other to push me back." Her gaze was direct, her words consoling. "You need not fear the difference in our stations. Aren't we both, at heart, simply citizens of the empire, burdened by years that have also enlightened us?"

He bowed his head to her. "You're a wise woman, and were circumstances different, I would lose myself with you in talk, and speak with you of poems and songs and pleasant things."

She seemed to weigh his words.

He continued, gently: "But there are vast distances between us that I don't wish to speak about."

"You're haunted by the battlefield. Those days are over."

"I wish they were. Give up your secret seeking and I will cease playing a role so we may better enjoy our evening."

She laughed. "I will take that then. I feel as if I've won a great concession, and I don't fully understand it. Why don't you tell me more about your daughter."

"She's bold and clear-eyed and well-read, like you."

"What is her husband's profession?"

"Her husband was a soldier. But he died in the Volani war."

"That was a long time ago. She has not remarried?"

For Clodia, the war had finished sixteen years before. "Not the Second Volani War. The third one."

She put a hand to her throat in sympathy. "Oh. It's very recent for her, then, isn't it? I'm so sorry. We didn't hear much about the last war. That must still be very fresh for her, then."

"Yes," Hanuvar agreed.

"Do you know why she fled?"

She had been dragged away by the Dervan Empire, but he couldn't say that. "She probably felt she had no choice."

"And she left no word of where she was going?" Clodia's mouth turned down. "I hate to say this, but it may be that she doesn't want to be found. That she needs to be alone with her grief."

"I worry for her. I was told the priestess here in your village could tell me where she had gone."

"Oh my. You mean the priestess might actually have known where she was? I wish you'd made that clear earlier."

"I don't like to overburden people I've just met."

"I can't imagine Paulus was very useful to you then."

"Do you have any idea where the priestess has gone? The villagers wouldn't talk about it."

"These provincials are backward. They're set in their ways, and they resent ours."

"In their defense, they probably don't like someone telling them they've been practicing their religion wrong."

"I'm sure that's true, but our customs are much more civilized." She laughed at his doubtful expression. "Oh, come, surely you don't think it's a good idea for a woman to constantly trouble herself over public matters. She should be managing her family, and leave that nonsense to the men."

That an intelligent woman would hold such a viewpoint disappointed him. "The empire doesn't seem to want women to do much of anything. In republican days there were women healers and midwives, and scholars, and priestesses."

"You know as well as I that there are still priestesses."

"I know some are still tolerated," Hanuvar conceded. "But I also know healers and midwives are being encouraged to find new professions. And the revenants aren't particularly patient with transgressors."

"Let's not talk about them. Let me ask my maids about the priestess. Many of the villagers hate my brother, and me, as a result, but some of them are kind. I've heard the priestess went into hiding. That's what many of them do, the poor things. But without the right papers, they can get arrested for witchcraft."

"It seems like the people in this community want this woman to be their priestess. And she wants to be one."

"So the locals should decide? I should have known you for a republican."

He shook his head no. He must have had more wine than he'd realized, for the movement left him a little dizzy. He put his cup aside.

"You're a scion of the emperor? That surprises me even more."

"I've no love for him." Hanuvar answered with his passion well checked. "It's him and his cronies who're working so hard to keep women like my daughter hidden away."

"You wouldn't keep your daughter protected from the world's troubles?"

"I would have her help me build a better world."

"What would you do with me, were I your woman?" She blinked heavily.

For a brief moment he thought she, too, must have had too much to drink, but realized something else had happened when he rose in alarm and his legs would not support him. The room spun, and someone laughed, and then the world rolled like a storm-tossed deck and he passed into darkness.

IV

He woke in the night to shrill male laughter and a dull headache.

As he sat up, he knew dizziness, and while there was a light in his face, and laughter, he couldn't fasten upon anything but a muscular figure with an antlered head.

Someone tossed a bucket of water at his face and the shock of the cold steadied him.

The roar of the laughter shifted, he wiped water from his eyes, and the scene achieved greater focus.

He was ringed by men, and a fire burned close. The cool night air stroked his limbs and with effort he shrugged off the stupor that clouded his thoughts, gaining impressions of the people around him.

He had been drugged. Clodia could not have been the instigator, for she lay groaning at his feet. On his right lay another motionless figure, garbed only in a loincloth, and it took Hanuvar a moment to recognize the portly older man for Clodia's brother, Paulus. Without clothing, he looked fragile and faintly ridiculous.

On the priest's other side two more figures lay, bloodied and bruised but conscious and clothed; curly-headed Silus and one of his guards. Hatred shone in the guard captain's eyes. His companion, a young man whose thick black hair was matted with blood, took everything in with wide eyes. His mouth was an oval of fear.

Hanuvar smelled pine, and the deep scents of the wood. A thick darkness loomed beyond and he saw the bulk of tree branches in the gloom.

His gaze settled on the circle of watchers. Perhaps a dozen men and women ringed them, sandaled commoners reeking of wine. Three he recognized from the tavern, including the barkeep. What he'd earlier taken for a monster was a thin man with a yellow-toothed smile wearing a furred hood topped with an eyeless, antlered deer head. Antler head pointed and laughed at him, and as Hanuvar's head cleared, he grew conscious of taunting from the others, mocking the look of fright in the soldier and the paleness of Paulus.

Either the wine or the food had been drugged, probably by the smirking servant boy he saw on the right, whose eyes were upon the breasts of his mistress, whose stola gaped as she groggily sat up.

Hanuvar feigned greater trouble than he felt as he helped Clodia to stand. She mumbled in consternation. This, too, evoked laughter. Hanuvar wanted to ask what was happening, but meant to be ready for action first.

Paulus had wakened too. His question was meant to be commanding, but proved warbling instead. "What is the meaning of this?"

The crowd laughed at him.

Paulus turned to his guard captain. "Silus, arrest these men!"

The watchers jeered, even as Silus answered. "I already tried, Your Eminence."

"How did they beat you and your men?"

"We cozied up to them, like," a woman's voice said.

She stepped out from the darkness, a trim woman in knee length skirt and short, tight shirt. Her face was long and clear, and she would have been lovely if there wasn't staring madness in her doe-like eyes. Her waist was girded with a belt of black fur, and a circlet ornamented with the skulls of small animals crowned her auburn locks. Blue paint spiraled upon her cheeks.

"And then," she continued, "they were as putty. A chance to put their hands on a woman, and your guards lost all sense. We slit their throats to work the magic of the hunt."

"You." Paulus pointed with a shaking hand. "You're that girl priestess."

"A girl?" the antlered man asked. "Don't you know a woman when you see one? Venia is one with the moon, and the forest. She walks in silence like the wolf, and when she bares her teeth, it is time to run!" He threw back his head and howled.

The boy and the barkeep joined him, baying at the silvery disk half hidden by tree branches.

"That's her," Clodia whispered to Hanuvar's ear, her voice still fogged with the drug. "Your priestess."

The priestess turned her head and regarded them with blank eyes. The spirit had informed him he was supposed to help her, but it was she they needed assistance from. How, then, to find out about his daughter from her? He saw no way to inquire. He likewise wondered where Antires was, but dared not ask, for fear of drawing the mob's attention to his friend. It might be these people hadn't bothered with someone in the town, striking only those within the estate.

Paulus stood, rumpled and barefoot and baggy eyed, yet somehow managing dignity. He looked puzzled to find Hanuvar standing beside his sister, but addressed her. "Have they hurt you, Clodia?"

She shook her head no.

"Not yet," Venia answered.

Paulus faced her. "What is it you want?"

"Blood," the youth replied.

The crowd heard him and laughed as one animal, as though he had invented comedy. Once more the man in the antlered hood lifted his head and howled in the darkness, untroubled by the incongruence of wearing a deer's head while imitating a wolf.

Hanuvar thought that he and the warriors might be able to handle the crowd, with a little luck. But then, from somewhere nearby, an inhuman cry answered antler man's call. It wasn't a wolf, or a hound, but something large. Perhaps if a bear and a bird had mated it might have sounded similar.

The laughter of their captors died. Their smiles were fixed as they looked into the woods. Hanuvar sensed that they expected the noise but were still less than comfortable with it.

Only Venia and antler man seemed unfazed. The latter pointed at them. "We're going to teach you Dervans what happens when you try to change the old ways!"

Venia trotted on silent feet into the night, toward the noise.

"You think to fight the Dervan Empire?" Paulus scoffed. "The legions will crush you."

"This time we'll unleash the power of the forest," the antlered man said. "We will throw them back to the sea!"

"You're a fool," Hanuvar said coolly. His voice cut through the babble of the onlookers, and the rising retort of Paulus. The crowd's attention shifted fully to him. "You cannot hope to outmatch the empire. What do you have? Fifteen? They have tens of thousands of legionaries. Cease your game playing."

"My games are just starting, old man!" The antlered leader laughed at his own joke, and the young servant took it up.

Venia returned, beautiful and feral and mad, a thing the size of a large wolf padding at her side. Brown fur coated its body, and it had two shining eyes. But it reeked of musk, and it had not a hound's face, but a predatory bird's, feathered in white. Its powerful legs were those of a great cat. Its throat trembled and from its partly open beak came a chittering sound, like a ferret at play

Answering calls echoed from beyond the firelight. Hanuvar estimated their number and swung back to look at the one beside of the priestess.

"We spilled the blood and prayed, and the beasts have come," she said. "Descended from the god lands. They are ready for the hunt."

"By the gods," Silus' fellow soldier said, voice shaking. "I'm just a guardsman. I don't even care about politics. Don't you know me? You see me at the tavern. I'm just a regular guy. I—"

"Shut up," Silus ordered.

The priestess stroked the head of the beast beside her, somewhere on the neck where feathers gave way to fur. She looked at them, her smile enigmatic. "Kill that one." She pointed vaguely in their direction.

The beast bounded forward. Hanuvar pushed Clodia behind him, but the creature threw itself upon Paulus. It struck his shoulders with its front claws and brought him down.

Paulus screamed in pain and Clodia in horror, and the thing tore him apart with its beak and claws, glistening with the dying man's blood. Hanuvar saw no way to intervene and live.

Clodia clung shaking to Hanuvar. The two soldiers stood. The younger of the two quaked.

The beast took pleasure in ripping further pieces from Paulus, scattering a hand into fragments, then lifted its blood-tipped beak and let out a shriek of satisfaction.

It turned and ambled toward its mistress. Clodia, sobbing, threw herself on the ground next to the horror that had been her brother.

Hanuvar watched the animal. By the time it reached Venia it appeared to be molting, for clumps of fur and feathers dropped off and fell apart; before long nothing of the animal remained.

"Five Dervans, five beasts," the priestess purred. "One for each of you. They cannot smell, but they can sense your Dervan blood. And they cannot return to their land until they each find one Dervan and take that blood."

The younger soldier was muttering under his breath: "Praise Sira, praise Sira" over and over again. Silus again told him to shut up.

"Let the woman go," Hanuvar said. "She shaped none of the policies you hate."

Venia's gaze shifted to Hanuvar and she smiled brightly. "She's a tool of the empire. Just like those soldiers, and you, the retired legionary. Traveling our lands, drinking our wine, occupying our temples. No. She will die, and the land will drink her blood. Something good will come from her, in the end. And from you."

"But we're going to have some fun!" said antler man with a grin. "We'll give you a head start. Run. They'll still find you!"

He threw back his head with a whooping bark. And others about the circle joined him in howls. So too did two of those shrieking birdlike voices.

Hanuvar bent and pulled the sobbing Clodia away from her brother. He rose with her, one hand closed tight so none would see what he had grasped. "Courage," he said, his lips pressed to the hair hanging down about her ear. "I can see us through this."

"How?" Her voice broke in fear and sorrow.

"You Dervans ready to run?" the antler man asked. He didn't wait for an answer. "Here's one, here's two, here's get ready, here's three . . . and go!"

Hanuvar clasped Clodia's hand and pulled her left. The people in the circle parted before them, laughing. He saw the smile of the young servant boy, his eyes lit with a different kind of lust, and then they had torn past him and into the dark forest. Moonlight painted occasional leaves.

Clodia was no frail creature of the cities, and lifted her stola with one hand to keep up with him in long strides. The laughter behind them died away. Somewhere off to the right Silus shouted to scatter—he and his companion had chosen different directions. Hanuvar approved. He wanted their hunters following in smaller groups.

Now all he needed was distance, and a good tactical advantage.

Clodia shuddered as she ran, fighting to breathe despite her sobs. She clung tight to Hanuvar's hand.

He counted the paces as they went, dodging about a fallen tree bole and pulling her after. The moonlight showed the way through the old forest. Deeper they wound, and he still sought, and scanned, and from somewhere behind he heard the antlered man yelling: "Go!"

Clodia was panting hard but still running with Hanuvar when he came upon another fallen tree near a large maple. He stopped and stared up at its thick branches. Though not as tall as he would have liked, the maple would do. He turned to the woman. "Climb. I'll stay below."

She shook her head. "It's no hope, Entius. How can you stop those things? Did you see what they did to my brother?"

"I'll handle the beasts and the hunters." He lifted her by the waist and she reached for the branch.

"This isn't really going to stop them," she said as she pulled herself up. He saw her head turn, though her eyes were lost in the darkness. "Stay with me. We can die, together."

"We will live," Hanuvar said. "But you've got to get as high as you can."

He turned from her, placing the two fingers he'd recovered from her dead brother at either side of the maple, then hurried through a slurry of dried leaves. Somewhere far off he heard a hooting bark.

He tested a dark limb along the fallen tree, decided it was too solid, tried another. Behind him he heard Clodia scale higher into the tree.

Finally he found a thick dried branch that felt promising, put his weight to it, and broke it free. After a few moments tearing off twigs and stubs, he had a passable club.

Far away a man screamed in agony. His cry rose higher and higher and then abruptly stopped. Maniacal laughter followed.

Nearer still came a hooting bark, and the sound of footfalls through the leaves.

Clodia's voice was soft, but urgent. "Entius!"

He called up to her, voice pitched low. "Don't come down until I tell you. Be silent now."

He sympathized with her, sitting in the darkness, the image of her brother's gruesome death surely etched upon her heart. She was frightened and alone. More than anything right now she needed comfort. But he could not give her that.

He waited to one side, crouching in the darkness of the fallen tree.

One of the bird lions bounded out of the darkness, its beak open. Hanuvar fought against the skin-crawling horror of its wrongness and tightened his grip upon the club.

It trotted in a circle about the base of the maple. Hanuvar crouched, waiting, wondering just how much hyperbole the priestess had used. Were the beasts really keyed only on Dervan blood, or had that been shorthand for them seeking quarry that wasn't one of the cult members?

He would shortly know.

"The trees won't help," someone called in a singsong voice, winded but joyful. "The trees won't help, the trees won't help."

Three hunters grew visible only a hundred feet out, jogging in the trail of the beast. One bore a dim lantern, glowing redly, shaking with each footfall.

The beast rooted around the bottom of the tree, bent, then nipped at something. It tipped its head back and swallowed.

Hanuvar smiled. In a moment, the creature had vanished in a flutter of feathers.

Its minders neared, then stopped a little shy of Hanuvar's hiding place. He recognized the barkeep's voice, speaking gruffly to his companion, still singing about the trees: "Shut up for a minute. Do you see where it went?"

"No."

The lantern bearer cautiously played the lantern beam over the surrounding forest. Hanuvar waited until it had swung past him, then crept out, the sound of his advance masked by the shifting of the three cultists in the forest detritus.

Probably the barkeep heard the splat of the club against his companion's head. The singer dropped, stunned or dead, and Hanuvar took his spear as the lantern-bearer spun, just in time to spotlight Hanuvar burying the spear in his chest. It was a deep, sure blow, tucked under the rib cage. The man was dead before he fell.

The lantern landed at a tilt, sputtering. Hanuvar drove the spear into the back of the bartender as he turned to flee. The man managed a single cry of alarm before he dropped. As Hanuvar finished him he heard a distant scream and wondered whether it was Silus or his companion.

"Entius—are you down there?" Clodia called. "Are you all right?"

"I'm fine. Stay up there. Stay quiet." Hanuvar righted the lantern, retrieved the second severed finger, and slipped into concealment.

He didn't have long to wait. The cultists were calling the name "Stamos" and then shouting that they saw his lantern. He heard them laughing and jogging forward.

The antlered one was shouting: "Keep that one leashed! They kill 'em so fast we can't see the fun!"

Hanuvar slipped behind the bole of a thick oak.

The servant boy wandered past, alongside a skinny woman with a lantern.

"Stamos! Stamos is dead!" the boy exclaimed. He no longer sounded half amused. Now the lantern light played chaotically around the woods They searched the killing ground, then advanced further, wielding the lantern beam like proof against the night.

Antler-head came jogging up from the rear, and at least two more could be heard trailing behind him.

His opponents were spread out, and while the circumstance was far from ideal, it might not get better. Hanuvar dashed from the brush and slammed the antlered man's head with his spear haft. This knocked his foe's deer-hood askew and set him reeling drunkenly. Hanuvar closed and struck him across the throat with the heel of his hand.

Antler-head sank to his knees, gasping for breath.

Hanuvar grasped his cheeks, pushed the severed finger through his teeth, and clamped the man's jaw shut. "Swallow," he ordered into his ear, the spear blade against his neck.

The man's throat moved, he pushed at Hanuvar's arm with shaking fingers . . . then swallowed as the spear blade pricked him.

The lantern light hit them and the boy shouted in dismay. "One of them has a weapon!"

Hanuvar shoved antler-head and hurried away. The light followed him until he vanished behind trees.

"Release the creature!" the boy cried. "He's right over there! We can see the kill!"

Hanuvar had worked his way to the right and now peered out from behind a tree bole.

Antler-head was half bald beneath his lost hood. One hand braced against his sore throat, he had struggled back to his feet and frantically signaled with his other hand, croaking something unintelligible.

The priestess ran into sight just behind the bird hound as it bounded right for antler man. He threw up both hands in an ineffectual warding gesture, and then the thing leapt and brought him down with a caw of savage delight. Venia shouted in dismay.

The beast tore him open and he screamed.

Five of the cultists watched in shocked horror, well back from the conflict, hands protectively placed on their knife hilts.

That was still too many to leave to chance. Hanuvar jogged up from behind as the bird thing disappeared in a flutter of feathers. The priestess, shouting "No," hurried for the dead man. Two of the bar patrons stood together. They turned at Hanuvar's approach, but the first was unprepared for the spear point driven through his side.

Hanuvar tore the weapon free and hammered the other man in the face with the haft. Both men dropped, the wounded man screaming louder than the dying one.

The skinny lantern bearer charged from the right with a sword, moving so fast all Hanuvar had time to do was brace; the woman managed to impale herself. She took the spear with her, but Hanuvar snatched her gladius from limp fingers.

He came up, ducking the wild swing of an axe from another cultist, then slashed out his opponent's throat. As that man sank in death, Hanuvar pivoted to ensure he hadn't miscounted his enemies.

There was only the priestess, kneeling over antler man's corpse, and the young servant boy, watching with rounded eyes. He clutched his lantern in a shaking hand.

With a savage chop Hanuvar finished the keening of the man he'd hit with the spear haft, then advanced toward the remaining two.

The boy knelt. "Mercy," he cried.

Hanuvar considered him, then stepped to the side, so he could see the priestess, the boy, and the path toward them. Presumably the other beasts had disappeared upon killing Silus and his companion. Those who had followed them might rejoin their priestess.

Venia looked up. Grief and rage had warped her youthful beauty. Tears tracked down through the whorls in her face paint.

"I upheld the ancient ways," she said, though he had the sense she wasn't really talking to him, but to the skies. "Why did the gods betray me?"

As he loomed over her, he grew aware of a familiar ache in his left knee. He breathed heavily, though he did not pant. Once, a simple exercise like this wouldn't have winded him at all. And maybe, when he was very young, it might have bothered him in other ways.

"The gods don't care," Hanuvar said bluntly, and changed topics. "A forest spirit told me to find you. That you would tell me my daughter's fate."

She looked at him long and hard, and then her eyes narrowed. "Her fate's to die on the dung hill, like you, Dervan maggot, her legs raised and ready for a hundred soldiers—"

She might have said more, but Hanuvar drove his sword through her. She slumped dead beside her lover.

Hanuvar heard footsteps behind him and pivoted, ready to slay.

It was no enemy, but Clodia. She stopped before him, her expression locked on something far beyond this world. And when she spoke, her voice was disconnected and toneless.

"She was blind and led her flock to ruin. She dared to think she knew my mind."

Clodia turned her gaze full upon him, and for the first moment that night Hanuvar felt true fear. This was not the woman he had known, but the voice of the goddess Diara speaking through her. "Your daughter lives, and has freed herself from the yoke of her enslavers. Whether you will reach her, I cannot say." Her brow furrowed ever so slightly. "Curious. Your own thread is hard to trace. It is as though you have been taken from the weave without being sheared. It may be that your story shall trail away to nothing, or that you will once more wreak great changes upon the tapestry."

He threw down his crimson sword and bowed his head, grateful to learn that his daughter had won free.

"You have earned a boon," the goddess said to him through the woman. "Ask of me one question."

He might have asked why the gods had not come to aid his own people in their hour of need, or how best to help his daughter, or even if he would ever return to New Volanus. But there was only one right question. The one that would benefit the most. "What must I do to succeed in freeing my people?"

The woman who wasn't fully Clodia regarded him with unwinking eyes. "Your plans are sound. You must better guard your step, though, to reach old allies. Your enemies are on your trail and will find you unless you better mask your path. Two alone are too distinctive. Dark gods seek you, but friends await. It will be a close thing."

He hoped for more, but Diara/Clodia turned from him. "Boy," she said, "go out to those others and tell them how your goddess spoke through your new priestess. Prepare the way for her coming. Do not fail, or there shall be another reaping."

The boy bowed low, stammered something Hanuvar didn't hear, then bolted into the wood.

Clodia turned to him, her eyes fluttering, and when she stepped forward, she stumbled.

Hanuvar caught her.

"Entius?" she asked. "What happened?"

"The goddess spoke through you. Don't you remember it?"

She opened her mouth as if to say no, and then closed it. "I have a vague sense of calm. Of patience lying upon a deep well of savagery. I wonder if that's what the forest is."

"It might be."

She touched his face, then stared at the blood that had transferred to her fingertips when she pulled them back. "Are you wounded? What happened down here?"

"If you didn't see it, best to judge only by our survival."

She took in the grim carnage in the lantern light at last. She looked over the bodies nearby, twisted in death. "You managed all this? What about the beasts? I thought they couldn't be killed until they'd taken Dervan blood."

"I found a way." At her blank look he simply said: "You really don't want to know."

"Are you a mage?"

He laughed once. "No."

She looked back to the priestess lying prone with the others. "Oh no. The priestess—did she tell you how to find your daughter?"

"The goddess did. She spoke through you. Did you not hear?"

"Maybe, partly, I felt the truth of what she said? That your daughter lives and is very far away." Her grip tightened on his arm as she peered at him. "You are different; a power that once dominated the loom of fate and may yet again. Who are you, really?"

"What does a name matter?" Hanuvar asked. "I am your friend."

He stooped to lift one of the lanterns. As they walked from the bodies he thought to hear a gentle soul like herself object that the dead needed burial, but she said nothing, and he wondered if that was her own choice, or that of the goddess.

"It seems you're a priestess now," he told her. "I think the village will have you. But will you have them? And what will you tell the priests who worked under your brother?"

"I will lead these people because someone must. And I think the priests of Derva would do well to heed me."

"I think you're right." He laughed. "A spirit tasked me with finding a priestess in Erapna. It didn't occur to me she'd be the first woman I saw."

※ ※ ※

Hanuvar had told me pursuit was inevitable, and while I believed him, even I did not guess how quickly word had actually spread about his continued existence. That he was feared, I understood, though it was not until later I fully credited the depth of that fear. Reports sped back and forth through the empire and action was promised to its ruler.

If the Dervans had better understood their quarry they might have caught him. They assumed he was after vengeance, so most of their energies were spent protectively. The harbor towns in the Tyvolian peninsula flooded with spies, for they assumed he would hunt the emperor. Because they thought Hanuvar leagued with sorcerers, or was sorcerous himself, they wasted fortunes on magical defenses, the majority of which would have proved entirely useless even if their enemy had been set upon their blood.

Only as an afterthought did they attempt to trace his movement through the countryside, more a perfunctory effort to ensure that all contingencies, no matter how remote, were explored.

Of course, not all efforts to trace him were ordered by the emperor. Some of his pursuers were motivated less by loyalty than reasons of their own.   —Sosilos, Book Three

Chapter 8:
An Accident of Blood

I

Even from a hundred feet away, Rennius' arm hairs pricked. He couldn't perceive many details through the wispy blue fog. But he knew what lay in the pillared gazebo at its center, and fought against the impulse to turn and run back through the broken field to the villa.

Gone were the gardens, the slaves who'd worked them, and the masters who had idled here. His father had no need for flowers. In their place was only the field of dirt and weeds and struggling grass—and the open stone outbuilding where a nobleman might once have reclined with his guests in the evening surrounded by blooms and their scents. Its couches had vanished with the flowers.

The icy chill, which had settled on the place when the mist came, hit him forty paces out. Somehow he forced himself on. The round stone gazebo was home to five lanterns warring feebly against the gloom, the smell of incense, Rennius' father, the mist, and the chanting sorcerer. The dark brown Hadiran sat on a little mat, his bald, wrinkled pate painted with knotted circles. Bedecked with a bright red robe and beaded yellow necklace, he rocked back and forth as the incense billowed beneath the blurry man-shape hanging in the air before him. Possibly he was mumbling in his native tongue, and possibly he simply repeated nonsense syllables. Rennius didn't know how to tell, and he didn't know how his father could stand to watch the Hadiran, hour after hour.

But no one would ever claim that Senator Catius Marcius lacked patience. Age had shrunken him, but he stood spear straight no matter his sixty-five years. From Rennius' vantage approaching on the left, the old man looked almost normal, a patrician in a white tunic with wide purple edging befitting his rank. His gray hair had receded to a curve well back of his forehead, almost meeting his bald spot.

Looks deceived. When Catius turned at the sound of Rennius' footsteps, as well as those who came after, the semblance of normalcy vanished. The right side of his face was pulled back by the purple slash of a scar dealt to him in battle forty years before, and his withered right arm was supported in a metal frame. Some other man might have concealed the shrunken, almost skeletal limb, or applied makeup to lessen the impact of the scar. Not his father.

Rennius heard his brother in his wake. Even if he hadn't known Flaminian followed, he would have recognized him by his tread. Two others moved with him. Most of his older brother's troops walked with the same martial precision, but Flaminian's steps sounded a degree more arrogant, as if each heel-toe movement was meant to leave a mark upon the world. Their father had driven into them that they were to shape the world or he would see them as failures. Flaminian had no intention of being seen as a disappointment to his father. That was Rennius' role.

Rennius stepped into the cold place, and saw his breath hang in the air. He pretended he felt no discomfort, that he didn't have to gulp at proximity to the blurry thing suspended in the mist in front of the Hadiran. He bowed his head in greeting. "Father."

"Something to report?"

"I'm simply curious to see if there's been a change."

"The Hadiran mumbles more," Catius said crossly.

Rennius did not turn to mark his brother's arrival. Yesterday he'd learned the trick of looking at the fog sidelong, briefly glimpsing then a wide-shouldered soldier in an armored tunic and helmet. Today as he looked sideways, he thought he saw the man with lifted sword, and a cloak at his shoulder. After a moment the image smeared, as though Rennius was trying to focus after a night's drinking, and he couldn't be certain he'd seen anything at all. He might be imagining it, just as his sister had assured them.

Flaminian crossed under the roof, a smaller man in legionary armor, complete with scarlet cape. His hair, bottle black, had not yet receded as far as their father's. It would, though, and Rennius looked forward to seeing his older brother's reaction as one more thing slipped from his control.

Flaminian came to a parade rest and saluted his father. He then stepped aside and two soldiers marched forward, expressions grave. Each bore a large white bowl with a steaming black organ aswim in dark blood, the hearts from white stallions. At their proximity Rennius looked to both the ghostly fog and the little brown man for sign of change. He saw none.

"Where shall we deposit them, Father?" Flaminian asked dutifully. His voice was deep, befitting a much larger man.

"At the foot of the sorcerer," Catius replied, his querulous voice a bitter snap.

Flaminian bowed his head respectfully and pointed to the witch-man. The soldiers walked together, their steps carefully matched. They even timed their kneeling as they sank, setting the bowls gingerly down. They withdrew, and the only sign that either was human was the wary glance the one on the left briefly gave the spirit in the mist.

Flaminian ordered his men to depart, and they tramped off in unison like the marionettes he'd trained them to be, out across the ruin of the garden.

The sway of the Hadiran accelerated; his voice grew louder. He stretched both hands and waved them over the steaming hearts.

With some trepidation, Rennius looked up to the spirit, thinking he might finally glimpse something more finely drawn. Yet even after the witch-man spoke for long minutes, he saw only the fog and the vague suggestion of someone within, as though the ghost stood upon a distant hillside obscured by mist.

Flaminian shifted uncomfortably; Catius frowned at him. His brother enforced iron discipline in others but never truly managed it himself.

The Hadiran chanted. The spirit hung in the stinking air. The blood cooled.

Finally the Hadiran sat back on his haunches, head bowed, and wiped sweat from his forehead.

"Unless my sight has suddenly failed," Catius said waspishly, "the hearts of two expensive stallions have helped not a whit."

"He does not want to talk," the witch-man said, his words blended together by his rolling accent. "He resists me."

Flaminian sniffed. "You were not hired to fail. My father has paid you well. We have endured your stink and your heathen chanting, and—"

Catius lifted his good hand and his son stopped his speech in midsentence. In the ensuing silence Catius reached over to adjust the height on his arm brace, ratcheting the elbow dial so that the withered limb bent downward. He then passed the rod of his office across to it, and Rennius knew a different kind of chill, for he recognized what this meant. The hand at the end of that crippled arm still worked after that injury long years before, and it grasped the flail of command. His father always held it when he was readying a pronouncement. Seldom had Rennius heard a pleasant one. "I asked for a spirit of the Cabera family," Catius said sharply. "That could be any spirit."

The Hadiran pretended stoicism, but Rennius could have sworn he smelled fear upon him. "It is Adruvar Cabera," the mage said. "I, Lotartys, have caught him. Name some other mage who can do that. He is suspended by my sorceries and cannot return to the dark lands."

"So you have said," Catius snapped. "Yet he will not speak. And if he will not speak, he's useless to me. You said you required more power. I spent the money you said you needed for it. But nothing has changed. For all the good you have done me, you might as well have summoned a fart."

The mage's dark forehead beaded with sweat. "Senator, I told you that more power might not work. That a better option would be to acquire more things Adruvar had once wielded or owned. That would bring him into better focus." He waved a shaking hand toward the tarnished helmet half hidden in the darkness beyond the spirit.

Catius spoke with icy disdain. "And I have explained that is not a possibility."

"What about someone who knew him?" the mage suggested. There was no missing the desperation in his voice.

"Everyone who knew him is dead," Flaminian said primly.

With a start, Rennius saw a possible solution. One that might not just spare the witch-man, but score a point against his brother. "What about an elephant?"

His father turned to regard him through narrowed eyes.

Rennius explained. "A circus arrived in town two days ago. They claim they have an elephant owned by Adruvar himself, and Hanuvar before him."

Flaminian laughed. "They say that about any elephant, to draw in the country folk. There are so many elephants Hanuvar supposedly left behind you could march on Derva with them."

The witch-man seized upon the possibility. "An elephant would suit. Their memories are long. They are like dogs. They forge relations with men."

Catius' lip curled. Rennius braced himself for the tongue lashing, or the passing of the rod, probably to himself, to beat the witch-man. Rods, after all, had to be wielded from the dominant hand, thus had Catius placed it in what had once been his own.

But his father turned to his elder son. "Find the elephant. Buy it. Bring it here. And then, Hadiran, you'd best make your spell work, or this garden shall host a second tongueless dead man."

II

Hanuvar, riding at Antires' side, looked little different from any middle-aged man traveling the roads of a Dervan province. He sat a good horse and his equipment was in fine order, but his clothes were travel worn. His saddlebags did not bulge. He led a pack horse weighted down with shovels and other gear, but a beast of burden shared between two travelers was not so strange a sight, and no one could guess that a warrior's armor was stowed within the canvas bags. Even that could be explained, though, for Hanuvar carried forged papers declaring him an honorably discharged veteran of the Mighty Sixth legion.

Over the weeks of their acquaintance, Antires had seen Hanuvar don several guises, and he had glimpsed small changes in the way each was approached, which he hoped owed something to his tutelage.

Yet none of those identities had affected as great a change on the general as that after his single night in Erapna. Antires had wheedled much of the tale from Hanuvar and inferred the rest. A more jaundiced man would have thought Hanuvar's improved mood had to do with the company of a lovely Dervan patrician. But while an amorous dalliance could brighten the affect of most men, Antires knew the change to be the result of Hanuvar learning his daughter truly lived . . . and lived free. His manner had grown noticeably lighter.

They'd wakened before dawn, as was always Hanuvar's habit. Now, with a half hour's travel behind them, the sun was up, Antires was fully awake, and he found himself wondering if he dared broach one of the many subjects Hanuvar had declared off limits. After Hanuvar had told him they would not be travelling by sea, he had begun to suspect Hanuvar sought to cross the Ardenine mountain range, many weeks ahead of them, and longed to ask whether this were true.

"Something's on your mind," Hanuvar said. "Out with it."

The man seemed to notice everything. Antires decided to try an oblique approach. "I can't help wondering. I know you mean to save all your people, but . . . is this how you're going to do it? Wandering from town to town in the empire?"

"That would take a lifetime. No." Hanuvar paused as his gelding snorted. "And you know why I can't share more."

"Because if I'm caught, I might not be able to resist Dervan torture."

"The fate of my people is at stake. I can't chance their lives. I'd prefer that you simply not get caught. For your own sake."

Antires' patience, so long held in check, vanished in a finger snap. "Will you share nothing?" The sharpness in his voice surprised even him, but he plunged on. "If I'm to write this account, or a set of plays—"

"A *set* of plays?" Hanuvar asked in wonder.

"Yes. To chronicle what you do. I can't manage anything if I never get to know you."

"You know me."

"Only what you show me. If you can't talk about your future, can you at least talk about your past?"

Sensing Hanuvar's thoughtful frown signaled an opening, Antires continued. He wanted most to hear about the general's daughter, clearly in the forefront of his thoughts yet rarely discussed. But he worried so tender a subject might terminate the discussion before it began. Hanuvar seemed to grow exceptionally distant on the few instances when Antires had broached the subject of his wife. He still knew nothing more about Imilce than that the marriage had survived despite a long separation forced by the war, and that both she and their son had died during a difficult labor. But there was another topic that might be a little less painful. "What about your brothers? The lion's brood. You never talk about them."

The older man looked down the road, curving through the farm fields ahead. "It's not because I never think about them," he said. He had the air of a man who meant to say more, but he fell silent.

After a time, Antires prodded him, gently. "They say Harnil was a shrewd planner." What the Dervans truly said was that he had been a treacherous cheat, but Antires guessed the truth was different.

For once, Hanuvar spoke easily. "The Dervans malign what they cannot best. Harnil was wily. People were drawn to him. He could win nearly anyone to his side. He might have made a fine general, but he was such an excellent go-between and scout..." His voice trailed off. Antires wondered if Hanuvar was thinking of the Dervan poisoner who had brought Harnil down in the final days of the second war, but when he continued, it was with a wistful smile. "No one could make me laugh more. He once made Melgar laugh so hard while he was drinking that wine came out his nose." Hanuvar chuckled.

"What kind of jokes?"

"Anything. He was quick with a quip, or a dry aside, or even a long story with a sting. You would have liked him best, Antires. He was a storyteller. Maybe he could have been a playwright."

Antires would never have guessed that. "I thought Melgar was the dramatic one."

"Well, he was the youngest, and he had a lot of big brothers to live up to. He was all for making the biggest splash. But he was probably the kindest, up until the last few years."

"What happened in the last few years?"

Hanuvar's gaze suggested he thought Antires had spoken without thinking, and Antires felt his cheeks flush. "The war."

"Yes."

"What about Adruvar?"

Hanuvar's expression tightened. "He was bold. And born with a bull's strength. His word was his bond. All of us were raised that way, but Adruvar—if he pledged something, he meant it from deep within. You'd have never won a firmer friend."

"You tensed when I brought him up."

"War is a foul business. Adruvar was surely too dead to care what was done with him."[7]

Antires thought then that the grim past had once more silenced the present, but Hanuvar proved more talkative than usual.

"Before the battle, one of Catius' sons intercepted Adruvar's courier. Double marching his legion to sneak up on my brother was the one clever thing Flaminian Marcius ever did. But as with his father, honor is only something you are accorded, not a character trait you practice."

"Subtle as a sledge," Antires said, repeating a well-known aphorism about Flaminian's father, Catius Marcius, the man who'd ended every speech before the senate with identical words, regardless of subject, from the end of the Second Volani War until the start of the third that delivered the shining city's destruction. Always he had concluded with a single, dire phrase, exhorting the extermination of a people . . . *"and further, I say that Volanus must be destroyed."*

Antires did not say the phrase to his friend, though it seemed to hang in the air between them.

Hanuvar had retreated once more into somber silence, and once again, Antires wondered how one man could live with so much loss. His land. His troops. His city and all its people. Father. Wife. Son. Brothers. Daughter—not dead but missing. Everything. He had to be the loneliest man in the world.

Antires would dearly have loved to ask more—the details of Melgar's daring raid behind enemy lines to recover the rest of Adruvar's body, or the truth about the peculiar friendship Hanuvar

---

[7] After having been slain in a battle with the army of Flaminian Marcius, Adruvar's head was cut from his body and borne overnight by a hard-riding Dervan cavalryman so that it could be tossed into Hanuvar's camp. In this manner the general learned his next oldest brother had died, and his army of reinforcements had been destroyed. While war is never the glamorous business poets pretend, this particular act stood in stark contrast to the way honored dead had been treated by both sides during the Second Volani War.   *—Silenus*

was rumored to have struck with Ciprion, the Dervan general who'd finally defeated him.

But before he could decide whether to chance more questions, they rounded a bend in the road, and saw the circus. Though he had seen many a circus, Antires had never fully lost his sense of delight in them.

A fair-sized entourage of more than two dozen gaily painted wagons sat in the meadow beyond the village outskirts, and if not the very largest he had seen, it held a prosperous air evident not so much from the equipment but the spirited manner of the people and the behavior of the animals. As the band readied for departure, the horses stood alert in their traces, their coats shining. The twin leopards in one of the cages were well fed and bright eyed. A few children from the nearby village, likely skipping their morning chores, stood watching the animals from a respectful distance. There was a cage of monkeys, too, grooming each other with brushes in an unsettlingly human fashion, not to mention some pretty young women, one of whom returned Antires' smile with one of her own as she bore an armful of fabric—probably a collapsed tent side—to one of the rear wagons.

An elephant stood off the side of the road, lifting hay into its mouth with its trunk. Only a slim rope secured its massive leg to a nearby wooden peg. Antires had seen the great beasts smash wooden barriers in bloody arena spectacles and had no doubt the animal could break that line any time it wished. He watched the rope with some concern as the beast turned to regard them, chewing.

It froze, trunk half stretched toward the hay. It flapped its ears. Its trunk rose and it trumpeted in excitement.

Neither Hanuvar's horse nor Antires' cared for the smell or sight of the strange moving hulk, much less the sound. Both shied. The pack horse pulled on the lead line tied to the rear of Antires' saddle, further troubling the playwright's mount. By the time he had gotten both animals under control, he had to take the general's as well, for Hanuvar had dismounted and now stood beside the elephant, patting the side of the beast's head while the creature's flexible limb felt about his shoulders and arms.

Hanuvar's face was creased with a wide smile, a unique moment in Antires' experience. It wasn't that he had never seen Hanuvar happy. He'd just never seen him truly delighted, as if for a brief moment he'd forgotten his cares. He was talking to the beast in a low voice, chuckling as he did so.

Hanuvar's proximity to the elephant had not gone unnoticed. A woman had turned away from one of the carts and now strode purposefully toward him. Small and slim, she had a long broad nose and olive-skinned complexion typical of the folk of the Inner Sea.

Antires called to an older boy among those watching the leopard cage, promising him a coin to hold their mounts and pack horse, suggesting further that they move the animals to the far side of the road. He then hurried to join his friend.

By the time he arrived, the attitude of the woman, now standing at Hanuvar's side, had grown bemused.

"She must know you from somewhere," the circus woman was saying. "They have fantastic memories." Her gaze flicked to Antires, who briefly studied her, finding a plain woman in her midtwenties. Her dark eyes were accentuated by kohl, and a necklace hung with spiritual sigils draped her neck. From this last he guessed she must be the circus's resident fortune teller and magic worker.

Hanuvar continued stroking the creature's jaw and murmuring to it. Antires was frankly surprised. Even supposing that this elephant were some former possession of Hanuvar's army, he'd have never guessed that the general would have personal knowledge of it. Surely the beast would have been handled by men far beneath him.

"Please step away from my elephant, you ignorant man," said another woman's voice, and Antires turned as a tall, athletic lady, skin dark as night, drew up beside the other. Her coiled hair was pulled tightly backward so it swayed to her shoulders. A Ruminian, the famed horse riders of the Kenasa coast. Her full lips pulled back to show clenched white teeth.

The Ruminian planted hands on her hips, not too far from where both a whip and a knife with a worn handle stuck up from her belt.

Hanuvar turned to her, his hand still upon the beast.

The Ruminian's eyes widened, her expression flowing from anger to wonder, and then to dread. She stepped quickly back, speaking to him rapidly in rhythmic, flowing Ruminian, her left hand shaping a sign in the air, as if to ward off evil spirits.

Hanuvar responded in that same language, and there followed a long interchange.

The fortune teller appeared just as puzzled as Antires, and finally looked over at him. "Do you know what they're saying?"

Antires recognized the sound of the language but knew only a few words of Ruminian. He shook his head. "I'm afraid I don't." He kept his guess to himself. This woman recognized Hanuvar, and her first instinct had been that he was a spirit. He was explaining that he was not, and maybe even telling her something of how he came to be here, depending upon her identity.

"Andros," Hanuvar said, addressing Antires by the name he'd adopted for this leg of their trip, "this is Shenassa, a daughter of an old friend of mine. And I am Helsa," Hanuvar said to the other woman.

"Are you an animal trainer?" the first woman asked dubiously.

"No, I'm a soldier. I helped in the mop-up operations with the Volani supply line." At the woman's blank look, Hanuvar continued: "There were units left behind when Adruvar Cabera and his army followed his brother over the Ardenines, including some elephants. I stopped some legionaries from abusing Kordcka. She must be going on thirty-five at this point."

"Helsa," the Ruminian woman said, unintentionally putting emphasis on the name, as if to confirm that she said it properly, "this is my friend Nyria. She is the circus mage and is second-in-command to the owner. Ah, speak of the cat and up she jumps."

A stout, bright-eyed woman with a wealth of black hair drew near, walking vigorously, planting the metal end of her staff with every stride of her left leg. A bundle of colorful feathers swayed from the snarling cat head of the staff as she moved, revealing then concealing the multitude of additional faces carved along its length.

She stopped and boldly surveyed them, as though she readied herself for a grand speech. "Good day to you, sirs," she said. "I thought that there might be a problem, but I see now I have interrupted a reunion."

"An old friend recognized me." Hanuvar patted the elephant. "It was only proper to pay my respects."

A warm smile touched the owner's lips. "Old friends are a treasure beyond measure."

Shenassa hurried to make introductions. "Mellika, this is Helsa, an old friend of my family." This time, the name came easily to her.

"A pleasure," Mellika said. "So you were a prior owner? I bought her from the legion some years ago."

"I saw to her briefly when the legion took possession of her."

"Ah. And you were kind to her. Animals know, and remember, even the ones you think wouldn't care. We practice kindness in our circus; it's why our animals and trainers are the best known in the province."

"I can see Kordeka's been well managed."

"Shenassa has cared for her most of her life."

A clop of hooves and jangle of reins from the south drew Antires' attention. A band of mounted soldiers rode from the little river town. These weren't ordinary cavalrymen, dusty and casual after a long patrol route. They wore parade helmets, each with a horsehair crest, and their armor shone brilliantly as the sun burnished its image on the muscles shaped in bronze. The second rider even carried a banner, that of a clenched hand holding a flail.

The entire entourage struck Antires as somehow absurd, down to the small man leading it, as though all of them were bad actors in a drama they took entirely too seriously. His first thought was that they meant to pass, but the attention of the small man in front was clearly turned toward them.

Hanuvar's perceptivity never failed to impress Antires; just as the playwright turned to check his friend's reaction he discovered him vanished. A moment's search showed that his sandaled feet were visible on the elephant's far side. Rather than following and drawing attention to Hanuvar, Antires shifted with his back to the nearby cart, watching. Mellika turned to face the riders, offering a broad smile as the officer reined in and looked haughtily down. He removed his helm. The Dervan's receding hair was ridiculously black for his middle years. He apparently had the money for hair dyes but no expertise in their application.

"Welcome, officer," Mellika said. "Today certainly is a fine day for visitors."

Neither the officer nor any of his men seemed to have taken notice of Hanuvar and appeared incurious about the meaning of the greeting. The officer had eyes only for the elephant. He stared at her as she flapped her ears and returned his scrutiny.

"I am the general Flaminian Marcius," he said with ringing, stentorian tones. His voice was deep.

The slayer of Adruvar's army. Antires looked for Hanuvar and still did not see him, hoping he was well hidden. He then fell to staring at the son of the bitter senator who'd spent most of his career pressing for Volani genocide. He couldn't help wondering if his talk of the man had somehow summoned him.

Flaminian's attention shifted to the owner. "Are you Mellika, the circus woman?"

"I am," Mellika said with a bow, one hand wrapped to the staff. "How may I—"

Flaminian didn't let her finish. "Did this elephant truly once march in the army of Adruvar Cabera? Tell truth. I've no time for games."

Mellika bowed once more. "My mother bought this elephant from the legion, along with an old Ruminian, whom she later freed. This is his daughter." Mellika gestured to Shenassa. "Her father was once an elephant tender both for Hanuvar and his brother."

"And now you will tell me this elephant somehow served with both brothers," Flaminian said sharply. "Did it then cross back and forth over the Ardenines?"

"No. She was a young elephant traveling with her mother when Hanuvar neared the mountains, and the trainers didn't think she would survive the trip, so she was sent back with some small divisions left behind. When Adruvar passed through with his own army, he took Kordeka and other elephants with him, but . . . Kordeka was not a war beast. She was too skittish. And so she was left behind, and when the legions reconquered the provinces, they took possession of Kordeka. I've a fellow here who could—"

Shenassa stepped forward. "It is all true, General. I am the daughter of the drover. He was old, and was left behind to care for Kordeka and other animals, in one of the supply camps."

Antires had seen the quickening of interest in Flaminian's eyes, something akin to a bloodhound catching scent of its prey.

"But she is no war elephant," Shenassa said. "She is too gentle. I hope you do not think she could be used in—"

Flaminian chopped his hand through the air. "Your thoughts are not of interest to me. It is enough that you speak true." He clapped his hands and on the instant, the soldier riding behind the banner man rode forward, stopping half a horse length behind Flaminian, who turned his head to speak to him. "Take the elephant. Leave them a thousand denarii."

"That is less than the elephant is worth," Mellika objected. "And she is not—"

"Buy another beast for your men to fight," Flaminian said coldly.

Mellika stiffened. "My men do not fight my beasts. They train them to do tricks, and that requires years of effort."

Flaminian's eyes narrowed. "I will give you fifteen hundred, because you spoke truth, and I think you speak it now."

"That is a fair price for a new elephant," Mellika said, "but she is not for sale. It would take years to train another, and her temperament cannot be—"

The general urged his horse closer and leaned forward, glaring imperiously. "I have the power to take this elephant without compensation. If I thought you were trying to bargain, that is precisely what I would do. Is that clear?"

"Your words are clear," Mellika said, stifling her anger, "but not your legal right."

"Do you know who my father is?"

Mellika did not answer, but she finally looked away, her knuckles white on her staff.

"You cannot do this, Mellika," Shenassa said. "Tell them—this is not a legal thing. They cannot do this!"

"This is the son of Senator Catius Marcius," Mellika said stonily, her mouth a grim line. "If I were to take this to the local magistrate, what do you think he would say to me?"

"But you can't—"

"Woman, your mistress has the right of it." Flaminian turned his head without taking his eyes from them, addressing the man to his right. "Pay the woman her fifteen hundred. You others, collect the elephant."

"But what are you going to do with her?" Shenassa protested.

The two bags the soldier lobbed landed with a weighty jingle at Mellika's feet. Flaminian turned his horse smartly and cantered back the direction he had come, his banner man riding behind. The others dismounted.

Antires found himself troubled over the elephant's fate to an extent that surprised him, given that he'd only met her. But that paled in comparison to his concern for Hanuvar. Where was he, and what might he be doing? When Shenassa crowded forward Antires used her as a screen to retreat. Hanuvar he found scratching his forehead and effectively blocking the side of his face as he moved behind the next wagon.

There were more shouts from Shenassa, a trumpeting from the elephant, and then the unmistakable crack of a whip used on flesh.

Still Hanuvar kept walking away. Stepping between two carts, Hanuvar retreated across the road and back to where the children held their horses. The soldiers were leading the elephant off, one guiding her by the lead rope around her neck. The animal obediently went with them, although Antires would have sworn she looked confused. Mellika still stood beside the unopened coin bags, scowling. Nyria knelt beside Shenassa, who wept on her knees in the dust of the road. A livid red welt stood out along the dark skin of the trainer's left arm.

Antires paid off the children, who were far more interested in the commotion than the money. Hanuvar was looking down the road toward the town and the vanished elephant and soldiers. Usually the older man's emotions were tightly lidded. Today, though, his anger was close to the surface. His mouth was tight, his nostrils dilated, and his eyes burned with an almost incandescent inner light. Antires realized what should have been obvious to him—only a man with a death wish would go out of his way to make an enemy of Hanuvar Cabera.

Shenassa pushed to her feet and slapped one of Nyria's reaching hands away. She strode determinedly toward Hanuvar, wiping her eyes as she went.

The pain was writ plainly across the Ruminian's features as she halted before Hanuvar, ignoring Antires. She spoke again in Ruminian, rattling the words off so quickly Antires had a hard time believing Hanuvar could follow them, much less respond.

Nyria had come up behind her. Mellika, now cradling one of the unopened coin sacks, talked with a knot of other circus folk, but she kept looking across at them.

The mage's kohl-lined eyes were wide in sympathy. She put a hand to Shenassa's arm. "He's just an old soldier," she said. "That was a general. Helsa can't help."

"You do not know him," Shenassa said angrily in Dervan, and once more shook off the other woman's hand. "You have no idea the kinds of things that he can do."

"Why didn't Mellika lie?" Antires asked. "The Dervans wouldn't have taken your elephant then."

"Mellika is a good woman, Herrene," Shenassa said, naming Antires' homeland bitterly, for there was little love between his people and hers. "She answered true to that warmonger. She told them truth of my Kordeka." She wiped at her eyes and once more faced Hanuvar. "Tell me, great one. There must be something to be done."

"Our options are limited," Hanuvar said. "It is difficult to hide an elephant, even if we can liberate her. And I lack troops to take her by force."

Shenassa's voice trembled, a mix of pain and despair and rage. "You mean to say that there is nothing to be done?"

Hanuvar replied, "Sometimes the way through is not clear until the terrain is scouted. I can promise nothing except that I will look into matters."

Nyria had been looking more and more curiously between the woman and the man. "Who is he, really?" she asked.

"I'm just a family friend," Hanuvar said.

"They will kill her," Shenassa said. "The townspeople gossip that the senator has summoned a ghost, and that it needs blood. They must want my Kordeka's blood. Please. You must help her."

"I need a moment." Motioning to Antires, Hanuvar stepped away.

Antires followed, wondering what the general could possibly be planning. Usually he handed out orders on the instant, so Hanuvar's hesitation was all the more remarkable.

Antires looked down the road where the dust of the Dervan cavalrymen hung in the air, and over to the crowd milling about the circus, broken now into small groups and talking among themselves. Hanuvar's brow was furrowed.

"Please tell me we're not going to start rescuing elephants now," Antires said.

"Kordeka was a mascot, really," Hanuvar said. "She shouldn't even have come along on the journey, but the men liked her, and morale is important. I didn't want them to see her die on the passage over. It was going to be bad enough on the big elephants."

"I didn't realize you'd left any men behind. Let alone elephants."

Hanuvar looked at him as though he were foolish. "I had to have a supply line," he said. "Tenuous as it was."

"Of course." He'd forgotten that the Volani, for almost a decade, had controlled much of the hinterland and part of the coasts. "And you'll have to forgive me—how long after did your brother follow you over the Ardenines?"

"Six years." Hanuvar had grown stern, closed, as he usually did when he mentioned his brothers. "In the last few dispatches he wrote, Adruvar sent word about Kordeka. She helped them haul and even erect barricades. Once she picked up a spear and chased some thieves away, waving it in her trunk, like she had seen the soldiers doing." Hanuvar looked away from the past and met Antires' eyes. "I thought myself beyond sentiment."

"No good man is. And it can be a redemptive quality in the worst of them."

Hanuvar let out a tense sigh. "I cannot help directly. Catius would recognize me."

He had known the request was coming. "Do you want me to scout things out?"

"I do and I don't, my friend. I would like to help Kordeka, but the danger for you is great. And I doubt that there's anything we can do even if we learn what they plan."

"I can concoct a reason for a visit to the senator's villa," Antires suggested. "I could pose as a buyer for the Coliseum."

Hanuvar's gaze was piercing. "I do not ask this of you. Your life is more valuable than the elephant's."

"I'm volunteering," Antires said. He didn't add that knowing the enemies of Hanuvar's people would improve his storytelling, for he knew that might change the general's mind. "I'm an actor," he reminded him. "A good one. I can do this."

Finally Hanuvar nodded a single time. "Kordeka is a forest elephant of the Ulivian bloodline. You can tell by the angle of the tusks. The Ulivians are famed as quick learners, and fighters. She is too old to fight in the arena, but could birth future champions who could be marketed as children of an elephant who served the Volani."

Antires had thought of a wrinkle. "Flaminian saw me."

"Probably he paid you no notice. But if he did, you explain

yourself as readying to bargain for the elephant yourself. You can show up dressed in finery. You were in your traveling clothes."

Seemingly on the moment Hanuvar had concocted an entire plan of approach. Antires grinned in admiration. "The Marcius family is rich. I know you can easily counter with the supply of gems you have, but will they need the money?"

"Catius is a miser. He'll take every sesterce you offer. If he doesn't have some greater profit in mind."

"What do you think he wants?"

Hanuvar shook his head. "That's what I don't understand. You'll have to play your role carefully."

"I always play my roles carefully."

"This is no joke. He may present like a narrow-minded fool. But he sees more than you may think."

"Is your father really the man who crippled him?"

"That's what Catius always said. If father fought him in the first war he was just one more soldier."

"He never mentioned it?"

"My father fought many men, and he was dead before Catius became famous. Now we will talk with the circus owner, and Shenassa. I'm sure the performers gave one or two shows here before packing up, and they would have relaxed in the taverns and soaked up some local gossip. Maybe they can tell us more about Catius' activities." While he sounded as though he were ready to move, he did not yet do so, and his eyes fastened once again upon Antires. "This may be the riskiest thing you've ever done. We'll get what information we can before you make your approach. You're just a scout, not a warrior. Make sure you understand and remember the difference."

III

The villa lay on the far side of the town, nestled in a narrow valley between high, tree-lined hills. As idyllic as the setting was, the grounds resembled an armed camp, for a small cavalry troop had set their tents and picketed their horses on the wide front lawn, and chopped down all but the ornamental pines lining the roadway.

Antires didn't think the destruction was carelessness so much as a statement of disdain over appearances, as though Catius thumbed his nose at things he considered decadent, like beauty and comfort.

A stern legionary on the property's edge eyed Antires' fine green tunic and sandals, listened to his story, then escorted him to the front door.

A meek slave allowed him entry into the clean but austere interior and was almost immediately pushed aside by a pale skinned noblewoman, who had popped out of a bedroom on the left of the atrium.

"Oh, praise the gods," she said. "It's someone interesting. You *are* someone interesting, aren't you?"

Antires knew he had a good smile, and he favored her with it. She was likely in her midforties, and her maid had obviously taken pains with her appearance, for her dark hair was piled high yet cascaded down to gentle the harsh planes of her face. A proper stola did not quite hide her robust figure, nor did her perfume quite mask the scent of wine. She had been drinking, and if not clear from the fragrant fumes, it would have been obvious from her eyes, not bleary, but glassy.

"Almost certainly, milady," Antires said.

"This is Stirses, a field agent from the Coliseum, Lady Lydia," the slave said with a bow of his head to her.

"How exciting," Lydia said to him. "Are you here to bring more elephants?"

"I have a few right here in my tunic," he said. It was a feeble enough joke, but she laughed, and brushed his arm with cool fingertips, holding contact there a little longer than strictly necessary.

"What are all those troops doing here?" he asked.

"Those are my brother Flaminian's. They're some sort of important cavalry. I feel sorry for those poor bastards, let me tell you. Oh, forgive me my language. One grows so tired of living in the provinces. Come, join me. We so rarely have visitors."

"I would be delighted."

"Would you like some wine?"

She appeared to have already had enough for both of them, but he said that he did, and this got her loudly demanding refreshments from the house slave, who hurried off.

She then took his arm and guided him through the entryway and out into a courtyard. Here there was a pool framed by stone benches. The greenery was well tended and included some shade trees.

"I would have thought most Coliseum agents were grubby little men who looked like they'd been kicked by a mule," she said.

"Some of us have to talk to important people, so it's good to employ those able to clean up nicely."

"And you certainly have." She seated herself on a sun-worn cushion atop a bench and patted the space beside her. "I do so miss our family estates north of Derva, but we make do."

"Your courtyard is lovely," he said as he took the seat.

"It is passable, and you are too kind. Father has treated these grounds terribly. They were so beautiful when we arrived."

"What brought you here?"

"You really don't know?" Her blink was a moment delayed by the wine in her system, though neither her words nor her diction were labored. "You must be one of those rare people who don't follow politics."

In Antires' experience, most ordinary people didn't pay much attention to politics, but Catius' daughter likely didn't interact with many of them. He smiled by way of answer.

"Well, once Father got the emperor to *finally* act against those nasty Volani, his block in the senate splintered. One of the emperor's little favorites betrayed him, started a campaign to promote proper Dervan Family Virtues—he even stole father's slogans—and the next thing you knew, that weasel was the new darling of the party. Father was sick of the senate anyway. Because they had turned their back on him, he turned his back on them and bought some old property in the provinces."

"Politics," Antires said with a sympathetic head shake. He wanted to steer the conversation's course onto more useful ground, but recognized his host was one of those who had to repeat certain stories before she could talk about anything else.

"Father really does have the best interests of Derva at heart. He may come across as harsh, but someone has to remind the people about what made us great. All those Volani and Herrenic ideas about mob rule are a plague." She touched his arm again, her cold fingers lingering. "I don't mean to equate your people with those money-grubbing Volani, but you must know that many of your customs are a little soft."

At the sound of approaching footsteps on the courtyard pave, Antires looked up, expecting the slave, but found a slim, tall man in a well-made green tunic. He resembled Flaminian, though he was taller and his hair had not receded as far, and its shade of black appeared to be natural. His face was creased with bitter lines, as of long suffering or self-pity.

Lydia addressed him sharply. "Leave us be, Rennius. I'm entertaining a guest."

Rennius did not withdraw, coming instead to a stop before them. "So I see. What does he want?"

"Do you know, I'm not entirely sure." She glanced blandly at Antires, patting his arm. "Stirses and I have just been chatting."

"I'm from the Coliseum," Antires said, rising with a bow. "Your brother purchased an elephant I was hoping to buy. I hadn't finished my examination when he rode away with her."

Rennius' expression cleared. "Oh. I'm afraid that elephant's spoken for."

"Is she?" Antires said, aware of Lydia's impatience. "What are you intending her for? Perhaps I could buy her after you're done."

"She may not be alive after they're done with her."

He didn't even have to pretend horror. "May not? Gods, man, that's a valuable elephant. Is your family going to kill her?"

Catius' son didn't answer.

Antires spoke quickly. "I would like to finish my examination. I'd be willing to pay a substantial amount of money if she really is a healthy Ulivian."

Rennius' eyes fastened on him. "How much money?"

"Three thousand denarii."

At that sum, Rennius struggled to look unimpressed and failed. "You have that on you?"

"I don't wander around with that many coins, no, but I have gemstones easily worth that amount."

Rennius nodded as though some test had been passed. "Well then. Maybe that can talk some sense into my father and brother. Come along with me, circus man. Apologies, Lydia."

"A pleasure, my lady," Antires told her, noting she held her tongue but did little else to disguise her disappointment, and then followed on Rennius' heel. They passed into a back hall, and after Rennius asked for and received Antires' full assumed name, the patrician addressed him with a knowing look.

"So my sister was venting about her exile, the purity of our family, and batting her eyes at you, I suppose?"

"I'm not sure about the latter."

"Then you're either dumber than you look or mistake me for someone who cares." Rennius opened a back door onto the grounds behind the villa.

"She's your sister," Antires said.

Rennius held the door for him, and they stepped through into a farm plot being worked over by slaves in sun hats. "An accident of blood. She probably told you that Father isn't really all that bad, and that all of his actions are for the good of the people."

Rennius started around the garden bed for a red brick path.

"She did," Antires answered, following.

"She's constantly trying to convince herself of that. Everything Father does, he does for himself. He talks about virtues, but it's all about vengeance. He's hated the Caberas ever since he was crippled in the First Volani War, and he transferred that hatred to an entire people."

"He should be happy then, because his vengeance was secured."

Rennius laughed shortly. "Happy? Father thought Caiax weak for letting any survivors live, even as slaves, because they can still whisper their corrupting philosophies to today's weak-willed youth."

Antires wondered if he might have found an ally. "It doesn't sound as if you like him very much."

"Liking one's father," Rennius repeated, as if testing the sound of the idea. "I've known people who claimed to do so. He might be more palatable if he didn't hold a death grip on our futures. Property, money, slaves, it's all in his name until he dies. And he just won't die."

"You don't need gold or property to be happy," Antires said, regretting his words the moment he spoke them. He'd broken character, something he had coached Hanuvar never to do.

"Says the pampered agent of the great circus!" Rennius countered. "You sound more like a poet."

Antires shrugged as if he were not alarmed by how close to the mark the older man had hit. "When you wander the road long enough, you end up with so much time to think I suppose one ends up sounding like a philosopher."

Rennius snorted. "So are you trying to lead me to inner contemplation?" Rennius' question sounded more self-mocking than accusatorial. They left the fields at last and started up another path toward a hedge wall the height of a man, and an arched trellis that gave passage through it. "I know what I am. Maybe alone among my family. Lydia's bitter and deluded and desperate for approval. She'd love to have been part of a family respected for its status rather than feared for its power. You should have seen how fast Father's faction turned on him once Volanus fell. Even they couldn't stomach Father's call to butcher prisoners."

"And Flaminian?"

They had drawn close to the trellis. "Flaminian lives in the shadow of a dead man, our eldest brother, slain in the Second Volani War. One of thousands Hanuvar's army blindsided at the battle of Acanar. That's where Lydia's husband died too. Every moment Flaminian fights to prove he's worthy of the mantle he can never—" Rennius fell silent the moment he passed through the trellis. Walking after, Antires saw the reason, for they had come upon Flaminian, burning incense before a vine-wrapped outdoor shrine supporting a faded white bust to the Dervan goddess of nature, Diara.

Flaminian had disposed of breastplate and helmet but wore his red uniform tunic still. He had turned and now considered his taller brother with wrathful eyes. "Who is this, Rennius?"

Antires had already forgotten how incongruously deep Flaminian's voice was.

"An agent of the Coliseum, Flaminian."

"A stranger. To whom you speak of the family."

Rennius' tone grew slyly scornful. "I was just getting around to telling him how brave and bold you are, and how Father never notices."

"And were you going to tell him you're a snide coward who imagines he's worldly?"

Rennius gestured to his brother. "You see, he's actually quick witted, but he has to pretend to be the marble statue of a soldier. It doesn't matter, Flaminian. Father has the heart of a stone."

Flaminian's frown deepened, but he looked away from his brother to Antires. "What do you want?"

Rennius answered. "He's here to see the elephant. He wants to buy it for the Coliseum. Have you already killed it?"

"The Hadiran is going to look at it after he rests."

"Father's letting him rest?"

"The witch-man was up chanting for almost twenty-four hours. This is his last chance. He might as well be ready for it."

"And Father's probably taking his midmorning nap," Rennius guessed. "So he doesn't know about you being sparing. Dreadful of you, showing mercy like that."

Antires didn't conceal his puzzlement, for he could imagine a true agent of the Coliseum would look curious. Gossip had it that Catius had brought a sorcerer to summon a ghost. What that had to do with an elephant remained unclear, and felt like a natural question to ask in character. "Your pardon, General, but what is the elephant to be used for?"

"That's not your business." Flaminian stared at him. "You were there this morning."

"Indeed. I was bargaining with the circus owner when you rode up."

"Unfortunate for you, then."

"He'll give us three thousand denarii for the elephant," Rennius said. "Do you think Father might like the sound of that? I seem to recall he didn't look happy you'd paid so much for the beast in the first place."

Flaminian's gaze burned hate at his brother, then shifted once more to Antires. "The beast doesn't look remarkable to me."

"It's not that she's remarkable—I'm told she's too domesticated for the arena. But she's a forest elephant of the Ulivian bloodline. As you no doubt noticed, their tusks have more of a downward trajectory than your standard elephant. They're hard to lay hold of these days because their numbers have been depleted. It's not just that they're smart and easy to train, they tend to be more fierce when they're young. They're excellent for a number of purposes."

Flaminian grunted, as if to suggest he knew all this. Antires continued, surprising even himself with the conviction of his seeming expertise. "I have access to a male Ulivian. With him, and her, the Coliseum could birth a line of future champions."

"It sounds as though she might be of some value to you," Flaminian observed.

Antires took that as a good sign. "You're absolutely correct. I can well justify more than what you paid for her, but I'd need to verify her age and general health before making any offer."

"You were not able to do so before?"

"I had not even begun my examination," Antires answered. "I'm afraid that you arrived only moments after I had my initial conversation with the quaint travelling circus owner."

Flaminian's expression remained unchanged. After a moment, though, he nodded once. "Come along, agent."

Beyond the little shrine lay what must once been a rose garden, vast and walled by the high hedges. Antires could not help but mourn a little for its lost beauty when he beheld a field of empty dirt with sad clumps of weed and the occasional forlorn thorny tendril— a few inches of rose stalk that had survived Catius' will.

"Cultivating the previous owner's flowers was a waste of manpower," Rennius remarked acerbically.

Midway between the outer hedge and a rectangular stone gazebo stood a line of thick oaks, and the elephant was chained to the largest of them, near a trio of soldiers who seemed as ill at ease as the beast. The elephant's trunk was raised and she had stretched the chain as far from the gazebo as she could manage. A tub of water and a pile of hay sat nearby, but the elephant appeared disinterested in either. Antires could not help staring at the gazebo, which for some reason filled him with foreboding. He sensed rather than felt that the place was cold, and saw tendrils of bluish mist drifting about its edges. This, then, was the summoning point. He only briefly wondered if he felt disquiet because he expected to.

"There's nothing to see there," Flaminian said gruffly, stepping to block Antires' view. The general's brow furrowed suspiciously.

"You think he can't tell there's something wrong there?" Rennius mocked. "Even the elephant senses it."

"I would thank you to still your tongue," Flaminian responded shortly.

"Then you must think this man is a spy?" Rennius laughed. "What dire secrets do you think I'll reveal to him? That Father is pouring money away to talk to a Volani ghost?"

"Shut up," Flaminian snapped.

Volani? None of the gossip had mentioned Volani spirits. Concerned now that the younger brother had just taken a step too far with the older and endangered Antires' life, he was surprised to hear Rennius laugh again.

"You don't think your soldiers are gossiping about this shit show with the town harlots?" Rennius asked.

"I haven't spent much time in the town," Antires said, then lied: "And I don't care what you're doing. I'm just here for the elephant." He made a great pretense of inspecting the beast, walking around her, having her pick up her feet, tickling her chin to get her to open her mouth, as he'd been taught, and even peering under her tail. The elephant was preoccupied with watching the misty area but cooperative enough. Antires stepped back to the men. "Good news, gentleman. She looks young enough to sire several calves, and her health is very good. By Jovren, look at those tusks! And those eyes! She is a beautiful specimen."

Antires couldn't read Flaminian's expression, and so added, "I can certainly offer you twice what you paid for her; three thousand denarii. As I mentioned."

"It's a lot of money," Rennius said to Antires. "Father will have to be consulted. Of course, he may just want to have the elephant gutted anyway."

Antires didn't have to strive very hard to put desperation into his voice. "Surely there are some other animals you can sacrifice to appease the gods. If you need bulls or something—"

"It has to be an elephant," Flaminian said. "But the witch-man said if it's the right one, its blood might not even have to be spilled."

"How will you know if it's the right one?" Antires asked, wondering how close he was to learning what these insane Dervans really planned.

"Only the Hadiran witch-man can tell us that," Flaminian answered.

Antires bowed his head, sighing. He gathered his thoughts, then spoke formally. "General, let me speak bluntly. Many sorcerers and priests are showmen as much as the entertainers I deal with. They're after spectacle, so that the people paying them feel like they got their money's worth."

He sensed that Flaminian understood the veracity of his argument. Rennius, too, listened with obvious interest. Antires continued: "I'm sure it would be quite a show to slay this poor animal, but I assure you that there is nothing magical about her. It would be a pity for us all to lose this animal's value to a charlatan's game."

"Your words have the ring of truth," Flaminian said, as though he thought it something serious people said when they agreed with you. He seemed oblivious to Rennius' resulting eye roll. Antires bowed his head at the compliment.

"Father will waken soon, and I will speak with him. Rennius, see that this man is given refreshments while he waits. Not here," Flaminian added.

"Of course."

Rennius motioned Antires to retreat with him. Once they were walking for the villa, Antires dared a question. "What is this business with a ghost? If you don't mind me asking?"

"You really haven't heard?" Rennius sounded surprised.

"No. I have only just arrived this day and went straight to my business."

"Huh. Well. I assume you've heard the rumors of Hanuvar's return?"

"Gossip. People will believe anything."

"That's certainly true. But there may be something to it. There was some sort of riot in Hidrestus and the governor himself was killed. Over a hundred people claim to have actually seen Hanuvar alive. And there's a report that he visited some islands off the coast of Volanus."

"So you believe these rumors?" Antires asked. He had, of course, witnessed the former, and dragged a few details about the latter from Hanuvar himself.

"I've seen legion dispatches," Rennius said. "Some of the testimony is quite compelling. Father means to learn if the accounts are true, and if so, where Hanuvar is."

"By talking to a ghost?" Antires asked.

Rennius lowered his voice. "By talking to the ghost of one of Hanuvar's brothers."

"By the Gods," Antires made no effort to hide his horror.

"The sorcerer claims to have caught Adruvar Cabera. I've seen a spirit that looks like a man in armor. The old Hadiran says he can't compel the ghost to speak unless he has something that the man actually owned, or that he valued."

"So you got an elephant?" Antires said, though he already knew the creature's connection to Hanuvar's brother.

"My brother kept Adruvar's helmet. And the sorcerer reported that item worked for trapping the ghost. But the witch-man says something living is better. And if the circus people are telling the truth, and the elephant knew Adruvar, well . . ."

"Even if the elephant can help, what can a dead man say about the living?" Antires asked.

"Firstly, whether or not Hanuvar is on the other side. But also, who better to guess what Hanuvar might be planning but his own brother, and second best Volani general?"

Antires fought down a growing sense of dread. Could this scheme actually work? If so, Hanuvar was in real danger. He nodded, and used his own worries to fuel what he thought an appropriate look at mention of spirits. "I suppose that would make sense, if such a thing were possible," he said.

He now had all that he required. Hanuvar had warned him not to overstay his welcome, and to avoid any unnecessary interaction with Catius himself. Yet moment by moment he was gaining more information, and the family had accepted his identity without question. The fact that he actually carried valuable gemstones upon him felt a shield of sorts, a final proof of his intent. Besides which, Rennius and Flaminian were both turning out to be reasonable men, and Rennius himself was helpful. Perhaps he really could persuade them to let him leave with the elephant.

Antires made his choice. "I wonder if you would mind me drafting a note to my traveling group, to let them know I may be running late."

"If you wish," Rennius said. "I'll have one of the slaves run the message to whomever you like."

Hanuvar had devised a simple code, should Antires have to send a message. The rest of the way back to the villa Antires agonized about how to convey his information covertly, worried the slave would read the note and relay it to his masters.

In the end, Antires kept things simple. First he wrote: "I have confirmed that the elephant is in good condition, and she has the kind of tusks we were hoping for." By arrangement, mention of the tusks was confirmation of the supernatural gossip. The trick was conveying the information about Hanuvar's brother, and Antires thought he'd come up with something clever, writing: "Please apologize to your brother—I won't be there to greet him when he turns up. But I know he will be as happy with the handsome head on this animal as I was. I hope to finish the arrangements soon."

"I hope you're not conveying any family secrets," Rennius said with a half smile. Antires sat back from the letter he was writing in the courtyard, at a portable desk a slave had brought for him.

"Not at all—you can see it if you want."

Rennius waved a hand negligently, called for a slave, and bade him deliver it to Antires' friend Helsa at the inn. Antires didn't think he'd ever seen a house slave move quite so fast as the one sent from the home of Marcius.

For the next quarter hour Antires carefully fished for more details, learning little more than Rennius' seething resentment about his father and his ill luck for being born into this family. The man's tone began to grate, and Antires was happy at first when Rennius fell silent and climbed to his feet.

The playwright rose and turned.

He had been told Catius was hideous, but as the old man strode into the sunlit courtyard he saw the word hadn't really done the man's appearance justice.

A web of white scars crept out from a purple slash pulling down the corner of Catius' right eye and lifting up one side of his slit of a mouth. An open metal frame supported his withered right arm. The liver-spotted fist at its end retained near normal proportions, as though an adult hand had been grafted onto to a child's wrist.

Rennius hurried to his father's side, speaking quickly to his ear, any suggestion of his pronounced dislike for the elder completely absent in his fawning manner.

The old man paid close heed to what he was being told, asking one or two syllable questions and eying Antires coolly. Then, his expression changing not in the slightest, he called for another house slave. A dark-haired man sprinted up, bowing his head respectfully, and Catius spoke quietly to him. The slave bowed once more and ran off. Antires couldn't hear what the old man had said but didn't like the concerned look that had flitted over Rennius' features.

Catius started forward. His stride was vigorous, determined.

The son followed the father, stopping on his left side. Catius fixed his watering red eyes upon Antires and addressed him without preamble. "A Herrene," he said with distaste. "So you offer money for my elephant."

"A generous offer. The Coliseum can use her for breeding a new generation of performers."

Catius grunted. He was silent for a time. "How long have you been in the field, looking for elephants?"

"About five weeks. I'm not just looking for elephants."

"I see." Catius seemed to take a long time to mull that information over. "What else are you looking for?"

"Lions are always popular, Senator."

"Your superiors must be idiots," Catius said. "Or you are a liar."

"I don't think he's a liar, Father," Rennius said. "Flaminian said he was there at the circus when he came to buy the elephant."

Catius turned his terrible face toward his son, eying him as though he were the idiot.

Someone was running down the back hallway—several someones, clattering in their hobnailed sandals. Antires turned to find three legionaries hurrying toward them, and felt his stomach lurch. What mistake had he made?

"This man is no Coliseum agent," Catius said to his son. "He wants the elephant for his own reason. Soldiers, arrest this man."

"What?" Antires stood straight. "I am a citizen of the Dervan Empire, on legitimate business. I have committed no crime!"

"Truly? Have you given your real name? Can you put me in contact with your superiors? What are their names, and where are they based? Where are your assistants, to transport the animals?"

"I resent all of these accusations. And I do not recognize your authority to arrest me."

"I recognize it. You may take it up with a quaestor when we're done talking with you."

"You will regret this," Antires said, speaking over his fear, as though he were the son of princes and a very kingdom might rise in anger at news of his mistreatment.

"I have only ever regretted failing to act," Catius said. "Flaminian?"

The elder brother had appeared behind the soldiers. He came to attention. "Yes, Father. What do you want me to do with this man?"

"Give him a little while to contemplate his situation. He should know that further lies will only make his situation worse. I honor truth."

"Who do you think he's working for?" Rennius asked wearily.

"Ciprion. Aminius. One of my enemies prying into my affairs." Catius scowled. "His appearance at this moment is entirely too coincidental. I will find the truth."

IV

In the cool of the evening Lydia returned to the courtyard, where Rennius had been pacing along the well-trimmed shrubs. Her handmaid must have gossiped about the Coliscum man's fate, for Lydia lamented to him, sipping wine while a pale, muscular Ceori fanned her. "He seemed like a nice man," she said. "I would have never thought him for a spy."

Rennius held off commenting that she rarely thought about much of anything but wine and handsome men. "If he's really a spy, he had peculiar goals."

"I hear that he didn't have papers on him," Lydia said.

"A lot of people don't have papers on them," Rennius countered. "And he was clearly thinking about the elephant like a Coliseum man would— not just about its profit, but its care."

"So he's a fine liar. Spies have to be, you know."

Rennius shook his head. "There's something odd about him, but he didn't seem to really know much about us. I think he really is interested in the elephant."

Lydia sipped. "How typical. You'll whine about seeing something no one else noticed but won't do anything about it. That's your story, isn't it? Clever Rennius, sneering at the rest of us, the smartest of us all."

"I don't see you doing anything but drinking."

"It's the one vice Father doesn't notice."

"He notices," Rennius said. "He just doesn't care what you do so long as you don't make a spectacle of it. Like sleeping with a Herrene."

Lydia smiled slyly. "Oh, that would really have riled him up, wouldn't it? I wonder what he would have done?"

"He would have arrested him on a pretext, executed him, and returned to ignoring you."

"He doesn't care about you, either, you know," Lydia said spitefully. "Nor does he care about Flaminian."

"Yet here we still are, one big, happy family."

"Going off somewhere to sulk?"

"I'm going to see what Flaminian's doing." He walked away.

"Going to go watch the torture, are you?" she called after him. "But you won't do anything. You never do anything."

She was right. He never did. But he still made his way beyond the villa toward the slave quarters. Dusk had come, and the cicadas whirred in the trees while a scops owl repeatedly shrilled its single, piercing note.

Nearer at hand, two of Flaminian's soldiers were marching the bare-chested Herrene to a tilted wooden plank from which manacles dangled. Stirses made an effort to hold his head high and maintain his dignity, no matter that he wore only sandals and a loin cloth. As yet, there was no mark upon him, but he walked with some obvious discomfort. Sweat drenched him.

Flaminian stood at their father's side, watching his soldiers force the purported Coliseum buyer to lie on his back, head lower than his feet. They fastened manacles to the Herrene's wrists, so that they were beside his shoulders, then secured his neck and locked wooden blocks to either side of his head so that he could not shift it from side to side. They wrapped his waist and ankles with additional binding.

"Has he said anything?" Rennius asked.

"He still lies," Catius answered.

The soldiers stepped back and looked to Catius for the order to commence. A slave stood at the nearby pump, filling the second of three wooden buckets. One of the soldiers brought the first bucket forward and dipped a cloth into it.

Rennius spoke, hating the deference in his voice. "Did he have the money he said he'd have on him?"

"He had gems," Catius said.

"Enough to purchase the elephant?"

"A little more, I think. The beast may somehow be important to his masters."

"It wouldn't be important to a spy," Rennius pointed out, and swallowed as his father's eyes narrowed. He dared to continue. "What have you done to him so far? An innocent man, or his family, could take us to court. But if you haven't drawn blood . . ."

"He's been in the coffin box."

"All afternoon?" The coffin box was used only for the rudest and laziest of slaves. Closed inside with your legs doubled up, it grew incredibly uncomfortable, very fast, especially since the box stood in the sun, and its front face was metal.

No wonder the Herrene was wobbling on his feet, stinking and wet with sweat. Rennius swallowed.

"You are weak, boy," Catius said. "You refuse to see what your eyes have told you." He nodded at Stirses. "There is a liar. I will break him."

"Because he wants to buy an elephant?" Rennius objected.

His father's mouth twitched. His voice lowered. "You challenge me in front of those not of the family?"

He knew what he should have said. That his father was cruel, and hateful, and that the Herrene should be released at once. But he heard his answer even as he despised himself for saying it. "I am sorry, Father."

"You will learn your place." Catius raised his voice. "Herrene! I ask you now. For whom do you truly work?"

The answer came as a weary gasp. "I am contracted to Titor Mennius out of Syrenia, who sells animals to the games."

"If you expect me to show you mercy, you look to the wrong man." Catius stepped forward, adjusting the winch on his terrible arm so that his rod of command rose once more. Rennius listened to the rasping click of it and looked desperately to Flaminian, who contemptuously ignored him.

"You think I will hesitate to kill an elephant, much less a lying Herrene? When I was fourteen, I beat a slave to death because he had stolen a single cake from my mother's ovens. I do not tolerate deception!"

"You're a murderer," the Herrene whispered. "Thousands of times over. Your city hates you. Your soldiers hate you. Even your children hate you. They're just too frightened to say it to your face."

"Will the Herrene prate to me about love?" Catius remarked. "There is only one thing true men respect. Fear is the secret to our empire. We will triumph, we will endure, because we are strong, and because our enemies know to fear us. As you should know to fear me. We shall see how defiant your eyes look after you have lain on the drowning table."

Catius stepped back. "Begin."

ν

The soldier lay the wet cloth across his nose and mouth with care that seemed almost tender, and a confused Antires thought at first that it was a kindness, for his lips were parched, his throat dry.

Then they poured the water over his face.

The liquid crashed down and filled his nose and mouth, and he sputtered and gagged and wondered why he hadn't thought to hold his breath.

There was a brief reprieve, and then a second torrent washed over him. He fought to turn his head, to lift away, but the bindings were too certain. He knew that he would drown.

Hanuvar had given him many warnings about Dervan torture, and Antires had always thought himself too clever to be caught. He also believed himself too honorable to betray a friend. The former had proven false, but he vowed he would say nothing about Hanuvar, no matter what was done to him, even as stark, panicked fear swept through him. He honestly did not know if he could endure this. Every portion of his being screamed out for him to beg them to make this stop.

But an important quality of bravery, Hanuvar had once told him, didn't mean that you had no fears, simply that you were more afraid for others than you were for yourself. Antires didn't know if that was true for him, but he wanted it to be.

After the third bucket the cloth was removed. Antires lay gasping, heart beating a sprinter's pace, his head pounding, for he had struggled mightily against his bonds and bruised his skin.

He grew conscious that the senator was speaking with a soldier who'd run up to him. Antires couldn't make out all of what was being said, partly because the soldier spoke in such a low voice and partly because it was hard to hear over his own gasping. By straining, he could just see the brothers. Flaminian listened attentively to the soldier. Rennius caught his eyes and looked away, shamefaced.

Antires had mistakenly thought Lydia was just a lonely, spoiled noble woman. That Flaminian was, at his heart, reasonable. That Rennius might even be a kindred spirit. But each was in thrall to their monstrous father.

The horrific patriarch turned on his heel and pointed to Antires with the rod clasped in his crippled arm's hand. "Unchain him."

As the soldiers stepped up to Antires, Catius sneered. "This is but a temporary reprieve, Herrene. Do you know what has happened?"

Antires didn't answer; he had no idea.

"Adruvar Cabera has suddenly grown more distinct. It happened almost on the instant your drowning began. Are you going to tell me why?"

Antires weakly shook his head, just freed of the blocks. "I never met Adruvar Cabera."

"I think you lie. I think you're a Volani agent. I think your blood might make the ghost talk even faster. Unless you can tell me where Hanuvar is and what he's planning."

"I don't know anything of that," Antires said tiredly. He coughed as the soldiers sat him up, and water dribbled from his mouth.

Catius laughed without humor. "I brought the ruin of the Volani towers. Breaking you will be as nothing. Bring him."

The soldiers grabbed his arms.

Volanus, Antires thought dully. He had never seen those silver towers, though he had heard the poets sing of them. It was said there had been hundreds of thousands living behind the city's walls when the Dervans besieged it during the third and final war. And barely a thousand had been led away in chains. Much of that dreadful toll could be laid at the feet of Catius Marcius. Oh, other generals had led the army, but it was he who had stoked the fire, not just through his exhortations at the end of every speech, but through long diatribes given over to nothing but warnings about the treacherous, subhuman Volani, who should not be suffered to live.

The soldiers force-marched Antires after Catius, striding vigorously through the twilight in front of his sons and on through a gap in the hedge toward the row of trees with the elephant. Kordeka trumpeted in alarm, still straining to pull from the tree. Antires understood her fear better now. A cruel fate, to be helpless in the hands of madmen.

His eyes shifted to the blue light glowing within the gazebo's mist. It burned brighter; it chilled the soul.

He couldn't reason it. Antires was no magician, but he understood that even sorcery obeyed rules. Rennius had told him that they were trying to call up a Cabera, and that to do so they needed something he had known. Something, or someone, that had been important to him. Adruvar Cabera had been dead for at least thirteen years. Even if Antires had known him, he would only have been seven or eight at the time of Adruvar's death. Antires supposed he might look older than he truly was, which had conceivably deceived the senator, but that didn't explain how his own presence could have any effect upon the spirit. There must be some other explanation. Maybe the elephant's proximity was making a difference.

Antires would gladly have been almost anywhere else other than that dreadful place. He thought Catius' sons hesitated before following their father under the gazebo's tiled roof. One of the soldiers holding Antires cursed as they brought him over the threshold, either because of the ghastly atmosphere or because of the sudden drop in temperature. It felt like entering an ice cave. Sodden as he was, Antires wondered if he'd freeze to death.

The candles stuck in four nearby lanterns flickered redly, their flames twitching widdershins at the same instant. Smokey incense rose from a diminutive fire and up through the eerie azure fog. At its dead center the ghostly image of an armored man floated above the floor.

The family resemblance to Hanuvar was striking. He was far younger than the general, broader, with a thicker chin and a nose that had been broken. He was all in grayish blue, so it was impossible to know the color of his hair. His face was twisted in discomfort, as if he fought against spectral pain. His eyes were closed.

An old bald man with a painted head mumbled at his feet.

"Well?" Catius snapped.

Voice low, the bald man continued his chant.

Antires looked at the spirit, awed and frightened. Could it really be made to tell something useful about Hanuvar?

"Answer me, mage," Catius demanded. "Why does he not speak?"

The Hadiran halted and slowly turned his head. He spoke, tired but triumphant. "You have asked him no question."

Catius grunted. "Very well. You there, spirit. Who are you?"

The voice answered in Volani and was the whisper of moth wings, and the patter of soft rain. Antires could just understand it. Only a generation before, Volani had been one of the most important tongues along the Inner Sea, for the city's merchants had traded far and wide. He had learned it to better soak up the sophisticated work of the great Volani playwrights. He'd never thought to hear it pulled through insubstantial teeth.

"Speak up!" Catius commanded, addressing the spirit forcefully if haltingly in its own tongue. "Who are you?"

This time the sound was more clear. "Brother, be careful."

"He's not answering me," Catius said.

"Do not relent," the Hadiran advised.

Catius growled, then resumed his questioning. "Who are you? Are you Adruvar?"

"...Adruvar..." The figure shifted in the gloom and his head turned. It had no eyes, only empty holes, and as that gaze fell upon Antires it was as though icicles pierced his skin. Already shivering he trembled more violently, whether from cold or fear he could not tell. The soldier on Antires' left whispered a prayer to Arepon the sun god.

"Well done, ghost," Catius said. "Answer my questions, and I will release you to your eternal rest."

The cry of another voice rose, a wail as of someone in terrible anguish. It did not seem to originate from Adruvar, though the noise emanated from the blue mist. The moan was joined by another, rising and falling. Every instinct in Antires' body urged him to flee. Though sore, exhausted, frozen, and parched, he might even have managed it, but the two soldiers held him tight. The fog thickened.

Once more Adruvar spoke. His voice this time was more clear, more focused, louder. "Do not come near. Do not attempt this."

"Mage," Catius said, "what is this nonsense? What is he talking about?"

"He is frightened," the sorcerer answered. "Don't you feel it?"

"He fears you, Father," Flaminian said, exultant.

More disembodied voices joined the wailing.

"Sir!" another voice called from behind them. A soldier stood just outside the gazebo, at rough attention, his features indistinct in the darkness. He saluted as Flaminian turned, then reported: "Someone's set fire to the outbuildings!"

"Well, put it out and kill them!" Flaminian said.

"Yes, sir. We are. But there's a lot of them! We need help!"

"Rennius," Flaminian said, "guard the prisoner. You two, go lend a hand. Go!"

Antires felt himself released, even as his stunned senses put everything together. The panicked-sounding soldier in the darkness was Hanuvar. And he must have been somewhere close all this time, which is why Adruvar had addressed his brother.

As Rennius laid hold of his arm Antires knew a greater fear than he had yet experienced, not for himself, but his friend.

Catius had barely glanced at the pretend messenger. He resumed his harangue of the ghost as Hanuvar and the two soldiers raced away. "Does Hanuvar live?" Catius asked "Where is he?"

Adruvar writhed, his teeth gritted.

"Make him answer me, mage!"

The sorcerer threw more incense into the fire at his feet, which flared up with a poof. "I am compelling him, but his strength . . . it grows."

So too did the mist, thickening in the gazebo. "Adruvar! Tell me where Hanuvar is, or you will be destroyed! Do you hear me?"

"There . . . there . . . there. . . ." the spirit said, as though the words were being forcefully pulled from him.

"What do you mean?" Catius asked. "Answer me! Where is he?"

"Here . . . here . . . here."

"You mean he's dead, with you?" Catius' voice rose in frustration.

Behind the spirit the mournful voices rose in a chorus. And in the eerie light Antires saw other figures beyond Adruvar's shoulder. Rennius swallowed and backed away minutely, still holding Antires' arm.

"Answer me!" Catius demanded. "I can destroy you, eternally, as I destroyed your people. Do you know who I am?"

"Murderer." Though Adruvar's voice was a whisper, it carried through the gazebo.

The voices repeated the word. "Murderer," another said, and another, and then it was picked up and carried from dozens of voices beyond the spirit in the blue gloom, passing on to more and more until Antires realized that hundreds lay just beyond the opening between this world and the next.

"Father," Rennius said, "I don't like this."

"Shut up," Flaminian told him.

But it did not stop, and the voices began to overlap each other so that men, women, and children spoke the same word at the same time. Hundreds upon hundreds of them.

Catius leaned down and slapped the sorcerer.

"Command him to obey me!" Catius cried.

Something fell out of the darkness—a round shape that smashed beside them with a fragile tinkling of fine glass. Immediately the scent of vinegar and sage and another, subtle floral scent rose in the air.

The Hadiran cried out in abject fear, throwing up his hands and shouting incantations. Flaminian searched the darkness, commanding that whomever had thrown the glass reveal himself.

Then the candles died, along with the fire. All was dark but the flare of the spirit light, and the rolling mist.

"What's happening, mage?" Catius demanded.

"They broke the magics," the Hadiran said. "Asphodel and sage and vinegar—I can't restrain him here. He'll be pulled back—"

But it seemed that the spirit was no longer restrained in any way, for Adruvar stepped free, a transparent man-shape outlined in cool blue, like a fine artist's preliminary sketch, only the most important angles of face and limb and armor well defined. A moment after, two more grew further detailed, one shorter, a cloak belled behind him, the other taller, leaner. They resembled one another, and Adruvar, and Hanuvar. Melgar and Harnil Cabera.

Rennius let out a quavering cry and his hand released Antires' arm.

Still the voices of a dead people multiplied, a call of thousands separated by a vast and impossible gap. The Hadiran writhed upon the floor and then stilled.

The trio of spirits drew curving gray-blue swords. Behind them, in a growing fog, moved other figures. The night flooded with shapes half hidden by the mist that rolled with them toward the villa. The spirits flowed out in a rolling cascade.

Catius shook his good arm in defiance. "You can't hurt me! You are but spirits! Cowardly spirits!"

Someone grabbed Antires and pulled him back. He stumbled, weak and stiff in fear. He found himself clutched by Hanuvar, disguised in Dervan military garb.

Catius saw the general too. And this, more than the presence of an army of ghosts, set him gaping. "You!" he cried, his voice choking.

"You," Hanuvar repeated.

"Kill him!" With a shaking hand Catius pointed to Hanuvar. "Flaminian, Rennius, kill him! It's him, Hanuvar!"

The elder son, backed to the gazebo's edge by the oncoming ghosts, turned with lifted sword. But he drew no closer to Hanuvar, for Adruvar himself hacked his chest with his transparent blade. The sword rent no flesh, but Flaminian fell dead.

"No!" Rennius cried. "I'm not like them!" But Melgar, teeth showing in a wicked sneer, slashed him in the throat and the younger brother dropped like the first.

Antires thought for certain that Harnil would then turn to Catius. The old man had drawn a knife and held it in his good hand. Somehow he had found the time to ratchet his withered arm up, the rod of command lifted high. His eyes showed white with fear.

But the brothers withdrew to stand with Hanuvar. Antires was but a hand span from Melgar's transparent cape.

A host of spirits half hidden by mist crowded upon Catius, latching hold of him even as his knife flailed uselessly through their semblance of bodies.

Vanished at last was Catius' composure. The spirits dragged him shuddering toward the glowing blue center of the mist. He gabbled in fear. Antires glimpsed the thousands awaiting him there, in the beyond. Obscured by mist, Catius continued his protests, his voice finally rising into a quivering scream of terror.

One by one, the ghostly brothers stepped to Hanuvar, and one by one he met their cold embrace, flinching not at all. Each stood with him for a long moment, saying nothing. They then stepped apart, their hands raised in farewell.

Hanuvar, solemnly, lifted his own, and then the spirits turned and stepped into the mist and the brilliant azure light. The fog dissipated swiftly as the illumination dulled. The sounds from beyond lingered for a moment: the chants of murderer, and the distant screams of a mortal driven mad with fear, and then that too was gone, leaving only the wind, a dead sorcerer, two dead brothers, and an old helmet.

VI

The next morning Antires woke in a wagon, where he lay in a huddle of blankets. Momentarily confused as to his whereabouts, he sat up, and then groaned. Nearly every muscle in his body throbbed.

Hanuvar walked at the wagon's side. The morning sun was bright, and Antires raised his hand to shade his eyes. "What happened?"

"You passed out. You'd endured a lot."

"I should say so. But how did you get free of all those soldiers?"

"The soldiers are dead. Only the slaves escaped alive."

"What killed the soldiers?"

"The ghosts, I expect," Hanuvar answered. "There wasn't a mark upon their bodies."

"And the elephant?"

"Marching in the column with us."

He was glad of that. Antires had been worried for her, but most of all for his friend. "You risked your life to free me," he said. "You shouldn't have done that."

"And I shouldn't have allowed you to risk your own life to gather information. But it's done."

Antires shaded his eyes and looked at his friend. "I didn't tell them anything."

Hanuvar's frown suggested that was the least of his worries. "I'm sorry they hurt you. None of the damage seems permanent, though, and the circus healers say you'll be all right in a few days. For best results, you're going to need to rest."

Despite his pain, Antires grew conscious of a more troubling worry. "Do we have time for that? Won't someone come after us?"

"There's no one left to come after us. Catius kept his doings secret.

Someone will investigate how thirty cavalrymen died, but there won't be any good answers."

Antires stated his fear more clearly. "You're not leaving me here with the circus, are you?"

Hanuvar smiled faintly. "I would be a poor friend if I did that. The circus will provide us with a good cover while we travel, at least until we draw closer to the Ardenines." He paused, his voice lowering. "Once we cross them, I will tell you what I plan. And I will want your help after, if you still wish to give it. I can't succeed by myself."

"I will help you," Antires vowed.

"You should wait until you hear what I mean to do."

"I know you well enough to promise it now."

Hanuvar patted the wagon's side. "What is it that alerted Catius?"

"Maybe my story wasn't as clever as I thought. But I think the senator was just paranoid. It was you who threw that glass in the fire, wasn't it? What was that?"

"Thanks to your clever note, Nyria, the circus' magician, cooked up ingredients she said would sever a spirit's hold on the real world. I thought it would simply send Adruvar back. But it also sheered the sorcerer's control over the spirits."

"So you didn't mean for any of that to happen?"

"No. I was just trying to free my brother. I should have known he'd do his best to free me as well."

Antires quietly absorbed that thought. "What was it like, to hold them, one last time?"

Hanuvar didn't answer.

"It's all right if you don't want to say."

"No, I think I owe you my honesty. I just don't want to insult you."

"How would you insult me?"

"I value your friendship, Antires. But it is not the same as the company of one's family."

"I don't suppose it would be. Although it would depend upon the family."

"True enough."

A long silence followed, over which Antires heard only the roll of the wagon wheels and the jangle of reins. "So," he prompted, "what was it like?"

It was a long while before Hanuvar answered, his voice remote and fragile. "For a brief moment, I was no longer alone."

　　　　　※ ※ ※

From that day forward Hanuvar grew more open with me, against his natural inclination, for he was a private man. Sometimes his struggle to speak against his better judgment was visible upon his face.

During the next few days he provided a more detailed accounting of the events he'd undergone between the fall of Volanus and our first meeting, and he supplied numerous smaller details I had not yet heard about incidents we had experienced on the road, alone or apart. He told me once that I had long since earned his loyalty, but that he realized after my encounter with the Marcius family that he could better return it.

Over the course of the following weeks our travel grew easier, relaxed even. The circus welcomed us and, even unwittingly, provided camouflage, as well as better travel fare, security, and, before too long, companionship. I know Hanuvar chafed at the delay, but I saw also that he enjoyed the company. In some ways, those days were among the most pleasant we ever spent together.   —Sosilos, Book Three

Chapter 9:
The Autumn Horse

I

Aleria had seen the oaken horsehead only once, but its ruby eyes shone in her memory like those of heroes in romantic poems. She thought of their luster that evening as she lit the twin ceiling lanterns, laid out her map, and readied for her visitors.

She wished she could obtain the gems without assistance. For the sake of the rubies, Bellarix and his cadre could be endured. In ideal circumstances, she'd have sailed back to Derva and assembled a top-shelf crew. But that would mean delaying another year, and she just wasn't that patient. Besides, she'd worked out a way to explain her plans so that even the most stupid of men would understand them.

As fate had it, the thickest of Bellarix's band turned up first, a filthy brown wineskin drooping from one meaty hand. Aleria welcomed him inside and Dolgrin ducked under the low lintel.

"Good evening to you, Aleria." He politely bowed his head, then lifted the wineskin to his lips and tipped it high. He wiped his mouth with the back of his hand, then stared dully at her before thrusting the wineskin forward. "Would you like some?"

Not only was the wineskin filthy, it reeked. "No," she said, and added: "Thank you."

"You're welcome." Dolgrin was huge and dim and perpetually sunburned. He was also oddly sweet, the only one of the band for whom she held any genuine affection. In his limited way, Dolgrin was reliable.

"What is that stench?" a male voice exclaimed. Valentius strode in without so much as a knock, his lean face pinched into a look of sour disapproval.

"It might be this." Dolgrin raised the offending wineskin. "I didn't think it was that bad."

"Not that bad? It smells like a drunk peed on a dead dog. Where did you get it?"

"It was lying along the road. Someone threw it out, and it was half full of wine." Dolgrin shook his large, well-cropped head in astonishment.

"Get rid of it," Valentius ordered. "It stinks up the whole place."

Dolgrin's brow furrowed. After a moment he turned to Aleria. "Does it really smell that bad?"

"I'm afraid it does," she said. "I have more wine, if you like."

"Oh, that would be fine, then," Dolgrin said agreeably. "I'll just pitch it out back."

"Throw it far." Valentius walked over to the table she'd pushed to the center of the room and sneered at the map. He was making doubtful noises as Bellarix arrived at last, trailed by the final two members of his band.

Their leader claimed his grandsire had been a Ceori chieftain and wore a thick blond mustache with long dangling ends as if to emphasize the relation. Like the others, he was dressed as a plebian laborer, with a belted, knee-length tunic, and strap sandals. He wore his hair short.

She greeted him, handsome, dead-eyed Felix, and his shock-haired brother, Minos, and reminded them she had wine just as Dolgrin re-entered. Somehow the stench still clung to him.

Valentius, bent over the map, made a pronouncement behind her. "This looks like it's going to be pretty involved."

"There are a lot of steps," she conceded, "but they're simple ones."

"Let's hear her out," Bellarix said. He had a habit of sounding reasonable, but she had never truly trusted his perpetually bland expression.

"I still don't see why we can't just rob the temple," Valentius said. "We can get through the locks and a few guards."

Aleria responded respectfully. There was no need to encourage the man's vindictive streak. "That might be true. But this means much less risk, and also gives us the cash box from the festival."

Valentius scoffed. "That's small change compared to what the rubies on that horse head statue are worth."

"We'll need the 'small change' to keep us going until we find a buyer for the rubies. And that box will contain hundreds of sesterces. It's worth our time."

Bellarix pulled on the absurd pointed end of his mustache. "She's right."

Dolgrin poured out wine cups for everyone. She'd dipped into her own reserves to provide her cover as a wine merchant, and she was into the last of the stock.

"Well, let's hear it then," Valentius said, and took Dolgrin's cup.

Aleria had sketched the street and the new grain depot, along with the dirt track to the east, where the race would be held. There were the bleachers on the village side of the track, the road behind it, and the squares and rectangles representing businesses and homes on the main street. She'd even carefully drawn the imagery shown on inn placards so the men could orient themselves. As maps went, she thought it a fine one.

She pointed to the left, where she had depicted a square fronted with pillars beneath a triangular pediment. "On the day of the festival, just after dawn, the escort will place the trophy horse head on a wagon, held upright on a pedestal so it can be seen up and down the street." It would be surrounded by garlands, and hung in green, in honor of the Greens'[8] victory last year.

Aleria checked her audience. Valentius listened while frowning, and Felix was cleaning his nails, but so far she had their attention.

---

[8] In the province of Ellica in the final years of the Emperor Gaius Cornelius, three racing factions were most prominent: the Greens, Blues, and Reds, with the Whites a distant fourth. The Black and Gold teams attracted few enough followers in much of the east that they usually allied with the Whites.

Just as within Derva itself, each racing color's most ardent followers were fanatical to a point very much like that of most devout religious adherents, but rather than memorizing sacred texts and knowing the steps of even the most minor of holy days by rote, fans of the horse or chariot teams could name all the greatest riders or charioteers, the races they'd won and where, and against what opponents, not to mention the most splendid of the animals that they had commanded.

As is still the case, who backed what team had very little to do with rigid distinctions. Where once the Reds had been plebians and the Blues patricians, and the Greens wealthy freedmen, after generations and intermarriage, loyalties were an unpredictable mess. Occasionally rival politicians would back one team or another and then new divisions might assert themselves for several years, though not in the latter days of Emperor Gaius Cornelius, who openly discouraged this kind of division because he wished no mobs beholden to anyone but himself.   —*Silenus*

"The magistrate and the city elders will march it to the field, where the local priests of Eperon honor the Autumn Horse, and after the priest stops chanting the horse head will be mounted here"—she stopped to tap the front center of her depiction of the stands—"on a marble post. Once the opening ceremonies are complete, the circus will begin its performance. It's to last almost three hours. The entire time, the crowd will be filing in, paying their fees for the privilege of the view from the bleachers. And every one of the coins goes straight into the lockbox."

She paused again to make sure they understood this point. "They'll keep taking money for admission straight up through the end of the circus performance. Then the lock box goes over here, on this wagon, where it will be kept under guard." She tapped her finger on the wagon image at one end of the track. "You'd think it would be trundled immediately away for safe keeping, but it's not."

"Why not?" Dolgrin asked, his voice mild. Though not a bright man, he was a curious one.

"Because the guards want to see the race, too. Everyone, and I do mean everyone, is going to be on that field or near it."

They all nodded at that, because they'd be there themselves if they weren't planning a robbery.

"After the circus, anyone who couldn't afford the fee is allowed in to see the race of the Autumn Horse." Aleria was readying to describe the next step when Bellarix interrupted.

"Is that supposed to be some of us?" He pointed to a pair of stick figures she'd drawn beside the wagon.

"Yes."

"Which one is me?" Dolgrin asked. "Is it the taller one?"

She hadn't meant to suggest that level of detail, but was willing to humor him. "Yes."

"I'm not bald," Dolgrin objected.

She took up the stylus and dashed a few lines suggestive of hair.

Dolgrin nodded in approval. "Which one is Bellarix? Shouldn't he have a mustache?"

Aleria expected Bellarix to stop this nonsense, but he instead shot her an inquiring look. He hated to have time wasted on the nonessentials, as he put it, but when it came to his mustache, he was extraordinarily sensitive.

And so she drew one upon the oval face of the tiny figure beside Dolgrin. She thought that would be the end of it, but she'd finally drawn the full interest of Felix.

"Where are we?" he asked.

"Yes," his brother Minos added, with a dejected air, as though he fully expected not to be included. "Where are we, then?"

She recognized she'd be unable to get any further until she addressed this sudden fascination with art. She applied her stylus to the inkwell and the map and very soon two additional figures stood upon the far side of the grain depot, complete with hair. She set down the stylus, sure she could finally return to more germane matters.

Minos frowned. "One of them has girl hair."

"That must be you," Valentius said with a sly smile.

"It is not!" Minos objected. "It must be Felix."

"I'm not a girl," Felix said.

Gritting her teeth behind smiling lips, Aleria sketched in a third figure, working to ensure his hair was as short as the first. "There."

"Who's the girl?" Dolgrin asked.

"Yes." Minos pointed at the middle figure with longer hair. "Who's she? Is that you?"

"No. She's just passing through," Aleria said, "and isn't important."

"Maybe she's my girlfriend," Minos said hopefully.

Valentius sneered. "You don't have one."

"But I could!" Minos objected.

Felix smiled confidently. "It's probably *my* girlfriend."

"Maybe I'll find one in the depot," Minos asserted.

"Boys!" Bellarix held up his hands. "We've lost the trail. How she draws us isn't important."

So long as you have a mustache, Aleria thought.

He continued: "The money and the rubies are important. Let's get back to those." He cleared his throat, then faced Aleria. "You were telling us that the money goes on the wagon. What about the horse head?"

She halfway expected Valentius to ask where he was, but he didn't interrupt, so she answered Bellarix. "The villagers believe the sacred rubies impart fortune to the team that won it last year, while it can see them on the field. And the other teams think that's an unfair advantage. So the priests have another ceremony, then the head is placed in a wooden container and formal representatives of the last year's team carry it to a nearby shrine, where it waits in its case until after the ceremony. Because I'm with the Greens, I'm part of that handoff. The rest of the Greens will want to see the race. They'll leave. But I'll chat up the priest; he's already kindly disposed toward me." She nodded to Valentius. "And your build is about the same as the Greens' leader, so the priest won't know you're not him when you pretend you've come back down to get me, not until you're close. I'm sure the two of us can handle him."

"And we'll just sneak out then, from the shrine, with the horse head?" Valentius asked skeptically.

"We might be able to manage that," Aleria said. "Everyone will be watching the track, and most of them will be drinking. But. There will also be an even bigger distraction."

"What are we doing?" Dolgrin asked.

She pressed a finger to the wagon she'd drawn. "I'm getting to that. What's supposed to happen is that the riders do some tricks, then the race starts. But that's not what's going to happen this year. Round about the time that the trick riding competition is going on, you two"—she pointed at Felix and his brother—"are going to be setting the rubbish pile behind the new grain depot on fire. It needs to be smoldering obviously."

Minos studied the side of the depot intently, as though he were willing the figure of the woman to life.

"We know how to set a fire," Felix said.

"Oh, I'm sure you do, but this one will take a little finesse. It has to be large enough that the smoke will be seen, but not so large it's already out of control and can't be stopped. The people have to feel they've got a chance to put it out."

"She's right," Bellarix said. "It has to be done properly."

"Aren't they going to be distracted enough by the competition?" Valentius asked.

"Yes," Aleria conceded. "But the cart with the money is at this end." She tapped the map's far side. "The fire will be on that end."

"Oh, that's clever," Dolgrin said with genuine appreciation.

"Thank you. So while everyone's distracted, that's when Valentius and I come out of the shrine, and head for our wagon. Which Bellarix and Dolgrin will have driven up near the money wagon. The moment

Bellarix sees the smoke he's going to run over and start shouting to the guards and make sure they see it. While they're distracted, Dolgrin will lean in and get the chest, and pop it into our wagon."

"And no one will see this?" Valentius asked skeptically.

"Remember that there will be a whole lot of distractions at this point," Aleria said. "I have it on good authority that the two old soldiers in charge of the coin chest are thoroughly smashed every year by the time the race starts. They should be easy to distract. If not, well, Dolgrin may have to bash a head or two."

"I'm good at bashing," Dolgrin volunteered.

"Valentius and I will put the horse head in our wagon, and then the four of us ride out of town. We meet up with Minos and Felix at that old villa four miles west, beyond the bridge."

"Is that where we split the money?" Felix asked.

Bellarix answered. "We split some of it, yes. But we need money to travel until we find a buyer. And to recover our outlay for our pretend wine merchant here." He looked to Aleria.

Most of the investment had been hers, but she didn't correct him. "I know a man in Derva who ought to pay a fine price for the rubies. It shouldn't be hard to buy passage this time of year. And we can travel in style, if you like."

"It seems a good plan." Bellarix put his hands down on the table and stared down at the map, as if looking more closely would reveal some heretofore unnoticed problem. He tapped the little image of a Dervan military helmet she'd drawn at either end of the field. "And the guards will be the first heading down to organize the buckets when the fire starts."

"This little town is so proud of its new grain depot most of the crowd will be rushing down to help put out the fire," Aleria said. "And a fair number of them will be drunk."

"Chaos." Bellarix straightened, smiling.

"I'm surprised no one else has tried it," Valentius continued. "Because it seems obvious, now that you've explained it."

Of course he would work to be insulting. Aleria blanked her expression. Also, most people would be troubled by the sacrilege, but she didn't point that out. "The best plans are always the simple ones."

"I like it," Bellarix said with finality. "What do you say, boys?"

The others all voiced their assent.

Bellarix twiddled his mustache. "What do we need to do in the meantime?"

Aleria allowed herself only a slim smile of satisfaction, and then explained, slowly, what kind of wagon they ought to procure, and how it needed to be painted.

II

In the early morning, Hanuvar followed the messenger boy out to what the village titled its Grand Racing Course, although it was really only a long row of wooden stands facing a dirt track. Despite the fact the race still lay three days out, a number of idlers lounged in the stands, their attention centered upon Septimus the horseman, wincing in the grass as one of the circus healers kneaded his calf. A band of village aristocrats huddled with concerned looks near the circus owner, Mellika, who had planted her decorative staff like a flag. She conversed most intently with a haughty woman of middle age whose height was further emphasized by an immense cone of curling hair.

Mellika saw Hanuvar and smiled in a mix of good fellowship and relief. She had a friendly, appealing face. Between her easy air of authority, suggestive of age, and her boundless energy and smooth skin, Hanuvar hadn't been able to decide if she was a well-preserved woman of middle years or a relative youngster.

With her free hand she beckoned Hanuvar to join their group. "Ah, Helsa." She used the name Hanuvar had assumed when he joined the circus. "You're just the man I wanted to see."

Mellika introduced him with a bow and a hand flourish. "May I present Helsa, our master of horses." Hanuvar accepted this sudden promotion without comment. As befitted his position as a circus stable hand, he had been polishing the metalwork on the horse bridles when the messenger boy found him.

"Helsa, these are the Blues who've sponsored our circus." Mellika then rattled off their long Dervan names, which Hanuvar memorized with little interest.

"This man hardly seems of the same class as Septimus," said Olivia, she of the majestic hair.

"He is not a trick rider, it's true," Mellika conceded. "But it may be that Septimus was too eager to impress. Helsa will take a more measured approach."

He found himself under Olivia's intense scrutiny. Judging by the twitching of her nostrils she had detected the scent of horse manure upon him.

She was almost surely an eques's wife or widow, for the three men beside her wore gold eques's rings on their left hands. The modern equites were almost as important as patricians, and many were far more wealthy than their social betters, for the Dervan ruling class found it beneath their dignity to put money into anything but property.

All of late middle age, the men beside Olivia wore finely tailored tunics, and one had even donned the lightweight toga praetexta.[9] Their receding hairlines were well barbered and dyed and their faces were plump and jowly. Their eyes were dark beads that would have been at home upon an abacus, so clearly were they calculating his worth to them.

"Well, what can you do?" Olivia asked.

The cluster of equites studied him, braced for disappointment.

Hanuvar had known far better horsemen than himself, but war from the saddle had honed a number of skills he could repurpose as a less sanguinary exercise. "I know a number of mounting and riding maneuvers. I'm fair with a javelin from the saddle, and am better with the sword, if targets could be set up."

Mellika flashed her brilliant smile. "Helsa has all the skill that you will need, my lady, providing that your nephew is an apt pupil."

Olivia looked off to the left as though she had just taken an especially large bite of herring that had gone wrong. "Apt," she repeated doubtfully.

Hanuvar followed her gaze toward a group gathered about a slim, pop-eyed youth of around twenty, topped with a shock of red hair. He had seen ostriches once, during a Ruminian festival, and the young man's blank, protuberant-eyed stare was not entirely dissimilar.

"I'm sure Helsa will be up to the task," Mellika said.

---

[9] Heavier, more traditional togas had long been out of fashion in Derva itself except for the most formal of occasions, but style changes more slowly in the provinces.　　　—*Silenus*

Olivia nodded decisively. "Good. Tell this fellow to begin the training at once. Rufus!"

The youth smiled, patted the arm of the busty young woman beside him, and hurried forward.

Mellika gestured to Rufus as though she were presenting a magnificent treasure. "Septimus was instructing this young man when he had his accident. The rider the Blues had intended was injured only a week ago, and young Rufus volunteered as his replacement." She turned to Olivia and spread her hands. "Let me consult briefly with Helsa, and then he will begin." She pulled Hanuvar aside.

Mellika's expression was apologetic as she spoke, low-voiced. "I'm sorry about this, but I couldn't think of another option. Septimus has a bad ankle now and knocked himself silly. These Blues haven't just sponsored the show, they're paying a considerable sum to help tutor this young man. Shenassa told me you are a fine horseman. Can you help?"

Hanuvar glanced at Rufus, tripping over his own foot as he returned to the woman and a little group of pampered youngsters. "How long do I have?"

"Three days." Mellika sounded even more apologetic.

"That's not a long time."

"The locals have a yearly ceremony and all the local factions are involved. Red, Blue, Green, and White."

"The Blues can't hire a seasoned rider?"

"Their rider has to be a member of the local organization, or they'd all hire ringers each year."

"I see. And there's a kind of exhibit before the actual race? Where they show their prowess?"

"Exactly. Nothing extravagant, but tricks to win over the crowd. Whoever gets the best reaction gets the best placing on the track. That's what they want you to help him with."

"I understand."

Mellika led the way to Rufus and his circle of peers.

Of all the tasks Hanuvar had performed while making his way toward Derva, this seemed likely to be the strangest. Had it not been for the warning he'd received that his travels with Antires were too distinctive, he would already be several days further along his route, but working with the circus provided necessary anonymity. Even as a new "master of horses," he thought the provincials would take little note of him, one more plebian amongst a performing troop.

"Ah, hello there," Rufus said in a cheerful, piping voice. "Helsa is it? I'm Rufus. Are you a slave, or a freedman?"

"A freedman, sir," Hanuvar answered.

"I thought as much. You do retain a bit of a servile air."

"You're an observant young man," Hanuvar replied.

"Well, let's get on with it. Show me some tricks."

"I think, first, I'd best see how well you ride."

The young man's eyes widened as though he had received deathly insult. He silently consulted a shorter youth with a wild tangle of straw-colored hair, and that worthy let out a low murmur of disapproval.

"Helsa means no offense, young sir," Mellika said hastily. "But he probably wants to see what you know before he knows what to teach."

Rufus replied stiffly. "I assure you that I will certainly be capable of learning anything you show me." The young people with him looked to each other with slight smiles.

Hanuvar spoke patiently. "A craftsman might explain it thus, young sir. I can't very well tell you how I'm going to paint the bricks until I actually see what the bricks look like."

"Well." The young man's brow wrinkled and he fell silent. He appeared to consider Hanuvar's statement with gravity, and finally conceded with a nod. "That's cleverly said, actually, Helsa."

"Thank you, sir."

Hanuvar asked Mellika to have his horse saddled and brought over.

A little blond slave hurried across the sward to Rufus, leading a handsome gray stallion with white points and a narrow head. Mellika and the healer walked off with the limping Septimus, who was supported by the circus strong man. The equites departed the field, although the gaggle of young men who'd stood with Rufus remained, as did the idlers, two of whom were watching him with considerable interest: an especially large brute of a man, and the busty brunette who'd been at Rufus' side. He recognized neither. The brute was too young to have served against him.

Rufus hauled himself into the saddle of his stallion with fair agility, turned the animal with his legs, then sent him riding down the track toward the newly built granary, a large, freshly whitewashed rectangular building standing two stories high. Prominent signs had been erected around the structure declaring no one was to climb to its roof, which would afford an excellent view of the race.

As he rode, Rufus kept a good seat, demonstrating far more athleticism than Hanuvar had expected. The young man took the animal twice around and circled Hanuvar once, smiling as if he had already won the competition.

By then Hanuvar had seen the circus messenger boy approaching with his roan, and he whistled. Immediately the animal trotted toward him, the boy hurrying to keep up. The gelding stopped with a snort at Hanuvar's side. Rufus' eyebrows lifted in astonishment. Hanuvar set one hand on the saddle and vaulted into place while the animal held still, head high.

"Oh, very good," Rufus said.

Hanuvar tipped his head in acknowledgment. "If I'm to demonstrate some tricks to you, sir, it might best be done away from the eyes of others."

Rufus took a moment to digest this, then his expression brightened.

"Oh, I see. You think there might be spies from the Greens out there. Oh, wisely reasoned, Helsa. We might manage on my private fields. Come, then. Percius, you don't have to race us, boy. He'll exhaust himself trying to keep up," he said confidentially to Hanuvar. "Loyal but not especially clever, you know."

"Loyalty can be harder to find than cleverness, sir," Hanuvar said.

"Oh, astutely said." Apparently wisdom was so absent from his everyday life that nuggets of it gleamed like gold. "I think that we shall work well together, Helsa."

III

That same evening, the leaders of the Greens gathered in a private back room of the Gray Duck tavern. Aleria quietly nibbled a greasy sausage, listening as the men groused about their chances in the upcoming race. She wasn't the only woman in the room, for serving girls periodically arrived with pitchers and platters. But only she and young Sonia were formal Greens.

By the simple expedient of keeping the Greens supplied with inexpensive wine, Aleria had made herself indispensable to the local leaders. They had won the race of the Autumn Horse for the last two years running, and through cultivation of their company she had not just been granted close access to the horse head, but learned about the elaborate arrangements involved in its protection and display.

She'd long since learned all she could from them and now joined them chiefly to ensure they dared nothing further to jeopardize her plans. If the Greens were caught interfering, they would be expelled from the race. More importantly to her, disgrace of the previous year's winning team could alter certain ceremonies involving the horse head, ruining her carefully laid plans. Last week one of them had been so worried about the original rider from the Blues that he'd arranged an accident that broke the man's leg. Fortunately, when Otho had tossed a branch into the horse's way he'd somehow managed to avoid being seen.

Now Otho was loudly expressing his concern over the Blues' new trainer, pounding his ham-hock fist into the table with such emphasis that those seated near him snatched their sloshing cups from the wooden surface. Pullio, the lean leader of the Greens, brushed wine droplets from his tunic with a hairy hand and glared across the table at pot-bellied Otho. "We don't have anything to worry about with Rufus. That idiot has no imagination. And he's clumsy besides."

Sonia smiled mockingly. "His friends have a pool running with good odds he'll trip and injure himself before the race." The men laughed and shifted their attention to her. Sonia patted the front of her dress, as though brushing dust from it, but more likely intended to draw male eyes to her shapely figure. "Yet I'm not sure you're entirely right, cousin," Sonia said to Pullio, her voice sweet and high. "He thinks this new trainer is talented, and he's learning a whole bevy of skills. Rufus has been sworn to secrecy about them." Sonia had easily found her way into Rufus' circle with a few wiggles and enraptured stares while the young twit talked of horses. "I managed to watch a little, before this new trainer of his insisted I had to go, and some of the moves looked impressive."

Pullio lowered his cup. "Who is this circus man?"

"Just a freedman," Sonia answered. "An older fellow. I hear he used to be some big horse trainer for the Circus Maximus."

Those, at least, were the rumors.

Pullio frowned, then came to a decision. "We need to stop worrying and sit tight. Albanus has this in the bag. His horse can outrun the Whites and the Reds, and he's far more clever than Rufus."

"Do you mean Albanus is, or the horse?" Sonia asked, and everyone but Otho laughed.

The big man grunted skeptically and waited to speak until the chuckling stopped. He interjected, truculently, "Rufus has a good horse. We'd be safer if we broke his leg too."

"Otho!" Sonia said sharply. "That's awful. You can't hurt the poor horse!"

"I mean Rufus," Otho said.

Sonia looked relieved. "Oh, that's fine then."

"No, Otho," Pullio said. "If you get caught, we're out of the race!" He added in a hissed whisper, "We're lucky that didn't happen with your first stunt."

Otho mulled that over. "What if I break the new trainer's leg?"

"That's just as suspicious," Pullio said. "No more leg breaking. Am I clear?"

"What about bribing this circus trainer?" Sonia suggested. She looked over at Pullio, then shifted her gaze to pale Oscar, then to Otho, and, finally, to Aleria.

"To do what?" Aleria asked.

"To stop training him quite so well, of course. Or to give Rufus some bad advice."

Pullio mulled that over. "We'd have to be careful. Attempted bribery could be reported."

Aleria decided it was time to take matters into her own hands. "I can feel him out, and get his measure."

She tried to gauge Pullio's thoughts as he considered her offer and fixed her face with a confident half smile.

Otho growled. "I don't like it."

"Afraid Aleria will fall for an old circus trainer?" Sonia asked sweetly. Otho only growled again and shot Aleria a look. It was no secret he favored her, though she'd done nothing to encourage or sustain his affection.

After only a little more thought, Pullio assented to her proposal, urging her to reveal nothing more than necessary to the trainer.

Oscar and Sonia agreed as well. Otho was the only dissenter. Soon, armed with information that the circus folks had been dining at the lower-class Red Boar, she set out in search of her prey.

She sipped watered wine in the corner of the dim old building, watching the evening crowd for a good quarter hour before Helsa finally turned up. There were far more interesting-looking circus folk to see: the grinning strong man, the dark Ruminian woman, and the acrobats, smooth and graceful in their movement even when seated at the low bar tables. Compared to them the trainer known as Helsa was positively drab, from the collar of his plain, soiled tunic to the bottom of his dusty sandals. He certainly didn't dress like a successful man. And that might make him far more open to outside sources of remuneration.

She watched him, gauging his nature and appetites. Wine passed freely among the rest of the tavern goers, but Helsa drank sparingly, talking in a low voice with the handsome Herrene seated across from him.

Helsa continually surveyed the room, not as a nervous man, but as one cognizant of his surroundings, reminding Aleria of herself. A good thief had to know the entrances and exits and have a sense as well of the people to every side. Why a horse trainer should practice the same habits she could not guess.

He caught her looking over at him, and he didn't take the chance eye contact as an invitation. He merely stared back before resuming his scan.

An intriguing fellow, older, but fine featured, she decided, and in good shape. The more she watched him, the more she wondered who he really was, and if he, too, was here in the village for reasons other than the ostensible ones.

His eyes caught her own again, and she felt the impact of their scrutiny. Here was not a man hunting a pretty face. Behind that regard was a man sizing up a threat.

She rose from her stool, side-stepping a table over which some Reds were dicing with circus folk while a man she recognized as a White promoter looked on.

She smiled when she came close. She glanced at the Herrene, watching with an amused expression, then addressed Helsa. "They say you're the gifted new trainer."

"What do they say about you?" he asked.

She had thought to place him from his accent, but he had a provincial drawl. She appreciated his redirection, for many men would immediately have sought to impress her with exaggerated tales of prowess. "It depends on who's talking. Why don't you buy me a drink and judge for yourself?"

His gaze seemed to weigh her, though she could not guess what his determination was, for his expression remained neutral.

"All right," he said.

"I was leaving anyway. I'll bring you back a pitcher." The Herrene clapped Helsa on the shoulder. A few grilled sausages and onions remained on the tray between them and Helsa offered them to her, but she demurred. She'd eaten her fill at the Gray Duck.

"I'm Aleria," she said.

"And I'm Helsa. What brings you to my table tonight, Aleria?"

"You intrigue me."

He might have returned the compliment, but he again surprised her with a blunt rejoinder. "And why's that?"

"You don't belong here. I mean generally. Either at the tavern, or with the circus folk."

The Herrene returned with a small amphora, checked with Helsa as if to be assured all was well, then departed.

Helsa poured out a cup for her and sat back, hand to his own half-full cup, though he did not drink. "Where is it you think that I belong?"

"I haven't figured that out yet."

"You seem out of place yourself. What are you doing in this village?"

"Selling wine. I'm a wine merchant, recently relocated."

"Are you with one of these factions?"

"The Greens."

"The Greens," he repeated. "Now that's the plebians, isn't it?" He sounded as though he wasn't sure, but Aleria guessed he was asking the question more to hear how she answered.

"Not exclusively. That's how it started, of course, but the loyalties get sort of mixed up over the years. Landowners free some of their slaves, and then the freedmen have to be loyal to their former family's team, and then that becomes tradition. You know how it is."

"Are you as devoted a fan as the rest of them here?"

"I like the races," she said, then, because she wished to stay on his good side and he seemed skeptical, she continued, "but I don't let it run my life."

"It seems to me that if everyone weren't trying to pull each other's levers, they could have a nice little place here."

"I hear it's not usually this tense. The race allows people to take out their frustrations in healthier ways. They can shout and roar and drink and most times they won't get their knives involved. You let people do that a few times a year and they'll get along the rest of the time."

"That may be true," he said, and sipped.

He was difficult to read. She decided to try prying him open by leaning forward on one hand and smiling in an inviting way, but at the last moment the smile shifted from that of a coquette to one honestly inquisitive. The phrase she used was a stock one, but this time she actually meant it. "You're an interesting man, Helsa."

"I try not to be. What is it you want with me?"

She let her smile broaden ever so slightly. "What do you want with me?"

For a brief moment she thought he was reaching for her hand, then saw him lift one of the onion chunks. "What I want is a night without complications." He popped it into his mouth and chewed.

"And you think I come with complications?"

He swallowed and reached for his cup. "A beautiful woman doesn't approach a middle-aged horse trainer to offer anything but. I'm just glad the Greens didn't send that woman who's after Rufus."

She dismissed the idea of pleading ignorance, and couldn't help laughing. "Gods, she's so obvious, isn't she?"

"She only uses three different poses."

Aleria affected Sonia's favorite stance, thrusting out her chest and biting her lower lip, her eyes blank.

Helsa laughed and she fell to laughing with him, and she suddenly realized her own guard was down at the same time he must have realized his was. He broke off. "What is it she's after? He's too zealous to throw the race."

"Are you worried about him?"

"I feel responsible for him."

"I think you like him!"

"He's not a bad sort," Helsa said casually. "He's kind to his slaves and his horse. And he's absurdly earnest."

"That sounds refreshing."

"Were you hoping to bribe me?"

"Oh, the Greens think they're great schemers. When I heard them worried about you, I promised to talk to you myself so they wouldn't do something incredibly conspicuous, or stupid. Or both."

"What are you going to tell them?"

"That you're onto us and that we'd better lay low."

"Do you think the rest of them will?"

Before Aleria could respond, his eyes tracked past her shoulder and he climbed to his feet with the smooth alacrity of a younger man.

She turned as Otho stopped at the side of their table. His thick belly heaved in a deep breath, as though gathering air for a dive or a battle cry.

"Otho," she started, but the big man cut her off and shook a meaty finger at Helsa.

She could smell the alcohol on his breath as his voice rose above the conversational murmurs filling the low-ceilinged room. "You stay away from my girl."

"I'm not yours," Aleria said with a growl. "And I'm not a girl." Helsa would think she had set him up for this. Worse, if Otho *did* injure Helsa, the trainer could tell everyone the Greens were deliberately interfering with the Blues. She climbed to her feet. "Leave us alone, Otho. Don't be an idiot! We're just talking."

Otho ignored her and pushed at Helsa's shoulder. The horseman swung away from the hand, and Otho stumbled off balance into the table. The amphora wobbled and she grabbed it before it crashed to the floor.

Nearby patrons quieted and turned. One of the servers was looking their way, but they hadn't grown loud enough yet to attract the barkeep.

Aleria addressed Otho sharply and put both hands to one heavy bicep. "Get away!"

The big man shook a fist at Helsa. "You even look at her again, I'm going to break your"—Otho's expression clouded, possibly because he suddenly remembered he had been told not to be involved in any more leg breaking—"sandals," he finished awkwardly.

Helsa tried bravely not to look amused, which set Otho snarling. "Think that was funny, do you?"

The horse trainer watched with cool alertness. Aleria wasn't entirely sure what it was in his stance or his gaze, but it was as if a mask had slipped. Here was a man familiar with killing another.

Helsa stepped nimbly outside Otho's blow, slapping the arm aside with one hand as he pushed it with the other, driving Otho into the brick wall. The larger man struck with enough force to drive out his breath, and then stumbled to his right, into a nearby patron and his table. Wine mugs twirled into the air and one of them smashed into Otho's forehead.

Helsa slid into the aisle, avoiding a mug that hit a table and sprayed another patron's chest with wine.

The tavern erupted with curses, and shouting men rose with clenched fists.

Aleria was already on her way to the street. She was surprised to find Helsa there a moment after, even as bedlam erupted behind them. Many men looked for any occasion to let steam off with a good fight. Helsa apparently was not among them. He headed away, sparing her a glance as he did so.

"Complications," he said.

She chuckled.

He paused. "Was there something more you wanted, Aleria?"

"I assure you I didn't want *that*."

"It was a pleasure to meet you. Good night." He turned and strode into the darkness, even as the whistle of the city guard patrol sounded and a quartet of soldiers jogged down the main street.

Aleria faded into the shadows and started back toward her lodgings. She sensed that Helsa was running some kind of gambit of his own, though she didn't think he was after the same goal. Still, he would bear watching.

IV

Rufus was a late riser, as Hanuvar could have predicted, but once he was in the saddle the young man was game for any challenge. The redhead threw himself into the practice of a running dismount. And if he spent almost as much time falling onto the grass as he did landing on the saddle, Hanuvar might question his coordination but never his optimistic spirit.

Sonia called on him midmorning, appearing to have worn the dress of a much smaller woman. When Rufus requested a break to speak with her, Hanuvar reminded him not to discuss any particular drill.

He gave the two of them time to chat and down some fruit juice, and for her to fan herself and thrust out her chest some more, then he politely suggested Rufus resume training.

Even after they'd walked off Sonia didn't leave.

The slave boy was offering the reins to his master when Hanuvar nodded back at her.

"She's still there."

"Oh, she just wants to watch a bit."

"I don't think that's wise, sir."

"She's a staunch Blue, Helsa."

"I just mean that she's clearly a distraction. An athlete such as yourself, working under time pressure, can only be focused upon two things." He realized then he'd unintentionally suggested the assets of which Sonia seemed proudest, and continued: "Himself, and his horse."

Rufus nodded with the solemnity of a junior officer being told he had to lead a scouting foray deep into enemy territory. "You're right, Helsa. I'll go tell her. It's hard to disappoint a lady so attentive."

He dashed back to order her gone. By the way she clung to his arms she was clearly pleading her case, but eventually she swayed off, followed by her own attendant, and a blushing Rufus rejoined Hanuvar. Once again Percius, the slave boy, presented the reins and this time Rufus took them.

"I hope you remained circumspect with her, sir," Hanuvar said.

"Circum what?"

"That you shared nothing of your training."

Rufus' expression cleared. "Ah, of that you may rest assured, Helsa. Well, let's be on with it, shall we?"

Once again, he applied himself to Hanuvar's instruction, and by midday Rufus' running saddle dismount no longer mimicked the grace of a flour sack tossed from a window.

Hanuvar permitted a second break just after stern aunt Olivia stopped in to assess her nephew's progress. Her expression showed no particular joy, but when she didn't seek Hanuvar out to complain, he judged her pleased. She sat and spoke with Rufus at length under a stone portico while the young man looked longingly at the food his slaves had brought.

By prearrangement, Antires turned up, and Hanuvar joined him in the shade of the overgrown mulberry bushes at one end of the track. The house slaves presented him with some simple fare, which he shared with his friend.

Antires watched the distant Percius brush down Rufus' stallion, waiting until the slaves had withdrawn before he said anything beyond pleasantries. "I think that animals get better treatment than a lot of the slaves around here."

That was always the way, and Hanuvar didn't bother responding. "What did you see?"

"There are people watching from the estate edges, like you expected. The guards drove them off, but the watchers got at least a little sense of what you were doing. How's the young lord coming along?"

"For someone with only a little aptitude, he's not doing badly."

"And what does his aunt say?"

"She hasn't said anything to me, and I mark that a good sign. So long as Mellika is happy, I'm happy."

"How's your accent holding up?"

"Just fine. It's good practice. Is the circus' little acting troupe warming to you?"

"Bit by bit. Mellika's holding a big party at the Red Boar this evening. We're on orders to turn up and take some toasts, but not to drink too hard."

"You're warning me not to drink?" He would've thought Antires knew his habits well enough by now.

"Sorry, no, that's just the way she said it. I'm warning you she wants you to turn up. Seems like the leaders of the Blues want you to give a speech."

"Lovely."

"I'd figure that you'd have plenty of experience giving speeches."

"It doesn't mean I like them."

The aunt departed at last, striding back to the villa like a warrior queen marching to battle. Rufus set to his meal. He only took a few more bites before a young lady with dark hair walked out from the villa, shadowed by an older matron. Rufus rose quickly and gestured to the repast.

"Is that our young gentleman's paramour?" Antires asked. He sounded confused.

"That's a different one."

He nodded. "She's a little stiff."

"The other one is considerably less so."

Antires smirked. "She's the one who nearly broke Septimus' head when she bent over to retrieve a hat, isn't she? I guess he was so busy looking at her he didn't notice he'd told the horse to jump."

"That's what I hear. And that's how I got this work."

"And that bean pole there has both women interested?" Antires shook his head in disbelief. "It's difficult to imagine anyone heartsick over him."

"These people set a lot of stock by these yearly races. He's a celebrity now."

"And everyone knows celebrities are better in bed," Antires remarked drolly.

"They just have a better class of bed."

Rufus' interview with the second young woman appeared far more formal than the one he'd held with Sonia. Its duration proved shorter as well. The young woman and her chaperone left without difficulty, and then Rufus walked back over to the track. Hanuvar dusted himself off. "Time to get back to instruction."

"I'll make myself scarce. See you this evening."

Hanuvar bade farewell to his friend and rejoined Rufus at the horses.

"Ah, did you enjoy your meal then, Helsa? A handsome bloke, that. Were you meeting your own love?"

"Ah, no, sir. He's a friend from the circus."

"So you're a man for the fairer sex then, like me."

"I suppose so, sir."

"Oh, come now, Helsa. Don't be modest." Rufus grinned and rocked back on his heels. "A handsome fellow like you. I bet you've roisted a few beauties in your time."

"That's not how I'd put it," Hanuvar demurred.

Rufus elbowed him. "Two good-looking fellows like us, we know the score, don't we? There's nothing women like more than a winner. And while I bet you've never won anything as important as I will, I'd just about wager you've managed some sort of prize over the years."

"I suppose I've had some successes," Hanuvar admitted.

"Well. Shall we be on with it, then?"

"Very good, sir." Hanuvar gestured to the man's stallion. "Let's run through the dismount again, then be on to one or two more tricks. Tomorrow's the big day."

"Goodness. It really is tomorrow, isn't it?" Rufus suddenly stilled.

"Is there something wrong, sir?"

"Believe it or not, I had lost track."

"You've a fine horse," Hanuvar reassured him. "And you're learning much faster than I expected."

"Thank you!" The youngster's beaming smile was without pretense. "Well, then. Let's be on with it."

V

While he had pretended to be reassured by Helsa, worry plagued Rufus for the rest of the day. He managed, just barely, to learn the trick of standing upon the saddle after the freedman had anchored some cunningly placed leather loops to it. The maneuver was a little dangerous, but the boys and both of the ladies he courted would surely be impressed.

Though sorely bruised, Rufus would have felt pleased and even proud with his progress if he hadn't been nagged by the thought of an uncomfortable decision he would soon have to make.

When his three closest friends took him out that evening for a celebratory tipple at the Gray Duck, he managed conviviality for a while, especially with Linus fronting the drinks. But Rufus grew more and more troubled while Linus bantered back and forth with Tully about the quality of the various horses. Gordius, of course, was more than halfway inebriated before they even arrived, and got most of the rest of the way there by consuming his supper in liquid form.

Finally, Linus noticed his friend's reticence. He flipped back his wave of hair, shiny as a horse mane, and looked across the bar table at his friend. "What's got your goat, Rufus?"

"I'm fine," he said, and smiled.

"He looks like he's seen a ghost," Tully said. "What a ghastly smile."

"Pressure getting to you?" Linus suggested. "I thought you were all keen over your new trainer."

"I am keen," Rufus asserted. "You're not betting against me, are you?"

"Me? How could you say that?" Linus' wounded air seemed somehow less genuine when he flipped his hair back again.

"Never," Tully assented. His thin-lipped mouth, ever ready with a laugh, drew into a solemn line.

Gordius drank.

"But confess to your friends, eh?" Linus leaned across the table. "We won't tell a soul."

Normally Rufus would have trusted these men with his life—they were his best friends, after all—but something in their eagerness made him just the slightest bit cautious.

"Have you been bungling the training?" Tully asked, his freckled forehead wrinkling. "You look a little worse for wear."

"I'm doing fine," Rufus assured them. "This Helsa fellow is the tops. A skilled trainer. He knows his business."

Linus looked skeptical. "Then why the miseries?"

Rufus leaned across the table and whispered. "I don't think you realize the other pressure I'm under tomorrow."

Linus exchanged a glance with Tully. "Not if you don't tell us."

Gordius smiled blandly.

"We're not good guessers, though we could have a go at it," Tully suggested.

"Oh, I like guessing games," Gordius declared. "Eleven."

"Shut up, Gordius," Linus said. "Go on then, Rufus. Quit with the drama and slice the cake, as they say."

It proved an embarrassing matter to explain, so Rufus hesitated before blurting his answer. "It's just that riders usually choose a lady's colors to wear on their sleeve. And that means I'll have to commit to one of the two I'm courting."

"More like they're courting you," Tully said. "From what I've seen."

"Yes, well, I had been looking forward to tomorrow but now I wish it would never come. You see, I'll have to choose between them and they're both such sweet girls. By committing to one I'll dash the other's heart."

"Oho!" Linus said. "So marital wreaths are in your future then?"

"Or at least serious talk of betrothals," Tully guessed.

Rufus supposed that was true, and, realizing it, took a deep drink.

"I don't see what the problem is." Linus waved dismissively. "Choose the one you like best."

"I like them both," Rufus protested.

Tully offered his solution. "Marry one, take the other as your mistress."

"Brilliant." Linus clinked his cup against that of his freckled friend's.

Rufus was irritated. "I can't do that."

"Wear a favor from each on a different arm," Gordius suggested.

Linus spared Gordius a brief look. "Either drink less so you're more useful, or drink more so you'll pass out. Well, Rufus, which one do you think would be better in bed?"

While he could not help wondering about such things, he would never have spoken about them in public. "That's rather crude, don't you think?" Rufus asked. He was starting to wish he hadn't mentioned any of this to them.

"Crude but important," Tully said.

"Hey. You! Rufus. Where's that trainer of yours?"

At that gruff-voiced query, Rufus looked up to discover a large, pot-bellied man waiting in the aisle beside their table. One side of his face was purpled and swollen, and his forehead was covered with scratches. He looked slightly familiar, but Rufus couldn't remember ever being introduced. "He, uh, I'm not entirely sure. Why do you wish to know?"

The man smashed his fist into his palm. "He's got a date with my fist!"

Tully's eyes lit mischievously. "Is he already acquainted with your fist, or is this a first-time matchup?"

Linus chuckled.

The bruised man gesticulated fiercely as if to demonstrate the force he intended to place behind a punch. "It'll be the first time," he said, "but it's going to get intimate!"

Linus hooted with laughter, and Tully joined in.

Rufus didn't follow, but the big man's expression darkened. He loomed over the table. "That's not what I meant. I oughta pound you!"

"At least bring me flowers first," Linus said. And even under that threat he, Tully, and Gordius exploded with laughter.

The big man snarled, clenching and unclenching his fists, then made a dismissive gesture. "Keep laughing. You won't be laughing much longer."

He turned and stomped off.

"That's where he's wrong," Linus said, and the three of them sniggered again.

"I don't see why you're laughing," Rufus said, frowning.

"Poor Rufus," Tully said. "We'll explain when you're older."

Rufus stood.

"Don't take offense." Tully patted the table in front of him. "We can explain if you'd really like."

Rufus shook his head. "It's not that. I've got to go warn Helsa that man is after him."

"You'd best hurry, if you want to beat him there," Linus said, and then he and the other two dissolved once more in laughter.

Rufus headed toward the track and the circus tents arrayed behind it.

A cordon of folk sat at a bonfire, obviously a kind of loose guard, but they proved friendly once he told them Helsa was training him for the races and that he needed to consult with him. They pointed Rufus to where the trainer pitched his tent, and he made his way there.

Helsa's lodging proved a small affair, a tent barely man-high, an old, stained cloth thing held upright in the four corners and peaked in the middle. He called out to Helsa from outside, and then, hearing no answer, peered inside. It was empty apart from a cot with a sleeping pallet, a pair of saddlebags, and a trestle table and stool.

Rufus couldn't decide whether he felt more uncomfortable waiting outside or invading the man's space. He didn't want to look foolish sitting in the dirt, and moved inside, only discovering that once the flap fell shut it was easier to find a stool with one's shins than one's hands, and tripped head long.

He had just managed to right himself and take his seat when the flap opened upon a figure holding a lamp.

Rufus shielded his eyes from the glare and then recognized the broad-shouldered figure in the doorway.

"Ah, Helsa," he said. "I'm glad you're here."

His mentor sounded slightly less welcoming than he had anticipated. "You're in my tent."

"I've come to warn you about a large, angry man. I think he means to challenge you to fisticuffs."

Rather than looking alarmed, Helsa fought down a smile. Typical of the man, to metaphorically laugh in the face of danger.

"I'll be alert for him," Helsa promised.

"And there's something else."

Helsa ducked to pass through the entry then hung the lamp from a hook thrust out from the central pole. He considered his employer sternly.

"I need your counsel," Rufus said.

"You've had too much to drink, and the night grows late."

"Yes, but it's the strangest thing. I feel as if I can see more clearly tonight than ever. Be honest with me, Helsa. Have you ever wakened to the fact you're surrounded by idiots?"

"It has occasionally been apparent." Helsa took a seat on his cot. "Is it just that you've taken up philosophy, sir, or has something in particular happened?"

"Philosophy? No. I have realized my friends may not have my best interests in mind. Certainly they are no good at advising me on affairs of the heart. I face a difficult choice, Helsa, and I am dispirited."

"What's happened?"

"Tomorrow, I will have to take a lady's colors and wear them about my arm as I ride. I will have to choose between two beautiful women. One of them will be terribly crushed."

"I see."

"You've seen them. They're both quite charming. My aunt approves of neither."

"Perhaps you should choose neither, then, sir."

What a terrible idea that sounded! "And have both girls mad at me?"

Helsa exhaled slowly. "Putting aside your aunt's wants, you should ask the woman you like best. Which one do you enjoy being around most?" At seeing Rufus' puzzlement, he continued. "Perhaps if you thought about their characteristics, in a list. Is one better to talk with, or a fan of poetry you enjoy, that sort of thing."

Rufus smiled in understanding. "One has lips as red as strawberries and the most delightful complexion. And, I blush to say, she is rather well endowed. The other is equally fetching in a long-limbed way." He sighed. "I've no idea which to choose."

Helsa cleared his throat. "It strikes me that you are listing only their physical characteristics, sir."

"Well, I'm not really interested in talking to them. Gads, what a bore that would be. Lots of nonsense about flowers and babies and moving furniture about to find the most pleasing arrangement, and long dull debates about when to change the seasonal hangings."

Helsa proved he was a man of discernment, for he nodded. "That does sound a trial."

"I knew you would understand. Have you ever known marital bliss?"

"Occasionally."

"But no more? That's the spirit. You may be surprised to learn this, Helsa, but I envy you. You can romance a new woman in every village, if you like, or stay well clear if you don't want the drama."

"You've guessed my life path well, sir."

"You're lucky to have such a rootless, carefree existence. Me, I am beset by obligations." He put his head in his hands. "Gods, what am I to do?"

"Here's a thought," Helsa said. "Choose the kindest."

He looked up. "How do you mean?"

"The one who seems kindest to her slaves and animals. That makes it more likely she'll be patient with children and husbands."

"I don't suppose that's terrible advice."

"Here's more advice. Get back to your home and get some sleep. Drink no more this night."

"Yes. Yes, of course you're right."

"Did you come here alone?"

"I did."

Helsa must have been suffering from a headache, because he briefly put his hand to his forehead and massaged it. He spoke as if in pain. "You do realize, sir, that any number of people would be very happy if you turned up injured or worse tomorrow morning?"

"Do you really think so?" He saw from Helsa's level gaze that he must.

"Come along." Helsa rose and took the lantern. "I'll walk you home."

"You're very good to me, Helsa."

"I know, sir."

VI

Aleria was no stranger to patient waiting, and had done so in worse company than with Dolgrin and Bellarix. Valentius was a different matter. The morning of the race she sat near the three in an alley northwest of the track, beside their wagon. Dolgrin leaned pensively against the wall in the shadows, drinking down a wine skin. Valentius had teased him about finding another discard, but had grown tired of the game and begun to fiddle with conveyance components. He finished checking each of the wagon spindles, then he paced the length of the wagon on both sides, as though it were a boat and he searched for leaks.

At least he wasn't pestering her, though he kept looking over at her, as if wondering something. She didn't ask what.

The appreciative roars of the crowd only a few blocks away filled her with curiosity, and it was easy to imagine the circus folks leading animals in tricks. It was hard to picture Helsa in a garish performance costume. Was he really a circus man?

Valentius drew a circle in the dirt beside the wall of the boarding house opposite, then chucked clods of dirt toward it.

After the hundredth or so plop of dirt into the circle, Aleria decided for his own good she had to leave. Otherwise she was going to brain him.

She dusted off her legs as she rose.

"Where are you going?" Valentius said. "I thought your plan said not to leave for a little longer."

"It's woman's business."

Valentius fixed her with a lizard-eyed stare, then returned to his game.

She headed onto the street, brushing dirt from the bottom of her dress. She hadn't taken more than a dozen steps when she recognized Sonia swaying toward the grounds of the track, followed by her maid. Before Aleria could duck out of the way, the slave called her mistress's attention and Sonia turned to wave, waiting for Aleria to draw even.

Today the younger woman must have had her slaves work over her appearance for long hours. Her hair hung in enchanting ringlets. Her cheeks had been expertly rouged and her eyes done in kohl so they appeared miles wide. Rather than looking as though she'd been sewn into her dress, today her stola was tight only at bodice and waist, as though she were modest and it was an accident that her low neckline revealed so much flesh.

"Why, Aleria," Sonia said. "I thought you would already be watching the circus. I imagine most of the good seats are taken."

"Why aren't you there?"

"Beauty takes time."

"Planning to break more hearts today?"

"I'm always ready for that." She smiled. Her lips had been smeared with henna. "I'm going to talk with Rufus before he rides." She lifted a little flask she'd brought. "And tell him this is for luck."

"Oh, Sonia, you're not going to drug him, are you?"

"You yourself said that trainer of his knows his business."

Aleria started to object by saying drugging Rufus might get him hurt or killed, and then realized she had no business caring what happened to him. The schedule was unlikely to be changed at this point no matter what Sonia did.

The other woman must have seen the emotions flitting over Aleria's face. "What's wrong? You don't approve?"

"You should be worried that he'll realize what you've done, or that someone else will, after the effect."

"Afterward, I'll be long gone, and my cousin will send me out to Derva with a nice little bag of coins." Sonia beamed.

"Good luck with that, then."

"Thank you. Aren't you coming in to the stands?"

"No, I have some errands to run."

"Well, don't delay too long." After a final searching look, Sonia departed.

It annoyed Aleria that such a blunt, rank amateur was having any measure of success.

When she finished her freshening up and returned to the wagon, Bellarix was pacing while pulling on the left end of his mustache. He visibly calmed upon her return, then motioned her into the alley, quickly, as if he were worried about discovery.

"Hardly anyone's on the street," she said.

"You were gone a long time," Bellarix objected.

Dolgrin met her eyes and then looked away, as if he were sad or embarrassed.

"What's wrong?" she demanded of Bellarix.

He motioned her forward. "It's the wagon. Look!" He pointed to the bed.

She guessed they'd somehow ended up with warped wagon boards or a wonky axle, and it wasn't until she leaned over the side and heard a footfall behind that she realized how foolish she'd been. She had just started to turn when something crashed against the side of her head.

Though stunned and in pain, it was the betrayal that hurt most, and she tried to prop herself against the cart as she turned, though her feet didn't want to support her and the world spun. She saw Valentius first, looming in the background like a bird of prey. Closer was big Dolgrin, face downcast, though he held the ball of fabric stuffed with sand that had been used to hit her.

She saw him mouth the word "sorry" even as Bellarix pulled the greased end of his stupid mustache. "It's a good plan," he said. "But we don't need you."

And then Dolgrin hefted the sap. She tried to twist away but tripped over her own sandal. She felt a jolt at the base of her skull and slipped into cool darkness.

VII

It thrilled Rufus to lead his own horse down the boulevard, right behind the dignitaries. By ancient tradition he would not ride the animal until after he arrived at the grounds.

He was disappointed that he'd have to miss the circus. He had heard they had acrobats and magic tricks, combats from very polished gladiators—though never to the death—scenes from great plays, and a variety of animal shows. He always liked the animals.

When they reached the grounds, it looked as though an invading army had camped out, for the bleachers were stuffed to the brim, and with the horse race just getting ready, men, women, and children were spreading blankets along the grass to either side of the stands. None were allowed near the circus equipment and stages set up in the track's center. These last were empty now, and the entertainers with their animals removed so that their sounds and smells would not distract the race horses.

The circus banners still hung above the stand facing the bleachers, and slaves of the race officials were replacing them with festive flower arrangements as a venerable priest, waving a yellow cloth, droned on in front of the four racehorses. Rufus couldn't understand a word of the ancient language the priest muttered, but reckoned it would sound more impressive if the man wasn't slurring in a senile drone.

Finally, that ordeal was complete and he turned his horse over to Percius. He stepped away from the other riders to join his friends and well-wishers. They were numerous, and their advice ranged from a stern admonition from his aunt not to ruin everything to a friendly arm clasp from Gordius. Helsa was there, too, urging him to trust his instincts and attempt only what he felt comfortable doing. He looked as though he meant to say more, but Helsa was ambushed by Rufus' aunt and harangued at length about her hopes for her nephew and dire threats should he prove a disappointment.

Rufus had made it a habit to avoid his aunt during her monologues, and thus pretended profound interest in the magistrate's speech and eased away. The magistrate's pronouncements, though, proved a crashing bore. Rufus anticipated that five or six more politicians waiting nearby would have something to say, at length, and then there would be another blessing or two.

He searched the crowd for Maria, and didn't see her. Sonia, though, had found her way through to his elbow, and proved more comely than he had ever seen.

"Rufus, oh, I'm so glad I was able to see you," she said. "There's something very important I have to say."

"Ah. Yes. It is always a pleasure to see you, too, Sonia. But there's something important I must tell you." He cleared his throat and was readying to give her the bad news, but then she took him by the arm and dragged him on. Her grip was surprisingly strong

"Come along. We must speak in private. Absolute secrecy."

"The ceremony's going to start soon," he objected.

"Nonsense. They'll prattle on for a good long while." She smiled encouragement, and led him through the cordon of nearby Blues and assorted onlookers. At first he thought she might mean just to get behind one of the supply wagons, but then he saw she was leading him on for the grain depot itself. He had thought it was closed, but a side door stood open, and she led him within, stopping just on the other side.

Outside all was bright and warm. Within, the warehouse space was cool and dark. It was to be consecrated in the next week; currently it was being used to house the more exotic circus animals. A row of lanterns hung along distant pylons, and by their receding yellow eyes he saw rows of wagons set up with cages, as well as the distant bulk of an elephant, eating from a mound of hay.

"You should look at me, Rufus," Sonia said. "Goodness. Alone in the dark with a woman and all you can think about are those animals over there."

"Yes, ah. Yes. You are quite beautiful, Sonia. But—"

She pressed something into his hands, and he looked down to discover he now clutched a small brown flask. She passed along its stopper.

"I didn't want anyone else to see this," she said. "It's been blessed. This will surely bring you luck if you drink it."

"Ah. Yes. Sonia, I think you should know. It's only fair." He was starting to say that he wasn't going to wear her colors, but she interrupted him once more.

"It doesn't smell like very much, but it doesn't really smell bad, does it?"

Politely he brought it up to his nostrils. He sniffed dramatically.

"You see? Go ahead. Drink it down."

In sniffing, Rufus had caught wind of another scent, and he stepped away from her.

"Rufus," she said, sounding frustrated, but he was walking away from the animals and into the darker recesses of the building.

"Rufus! Where are you going?"

"I smell smoke," he said, and continued his advance, corking the flask as he went.

The inside of the grain depot was divided into a series of large open rooms separated by high stone walls, and the structure itself was elevated several feet above the ground. He supposed that the areas were intended for different sorts of grains, or grains for different buyers. He wasn't really certain and didn't actually care, but he shared the same concern for fire in public buildings felt by every respectable Dervan. He saw a spark off to the left, and stepped around a corner to investigate. A pair of men stood beside a stack of wood alive with flickering lines of flame. The red and orange fire cast their shadows against the whitewashed wall.

"Throw some more oil on it," ordered the one further out, and the other lifted an amphora and sloshed some liquid onto the wall. Rufus was incidentally aware that he was often the last man on the uptake, but this time matters appeared astonishingly obvious. These men were deliberately setting fire to the new granary.

"You there," Rufus cried, pointing accusatorially. "Stop that immediately!"

Both men turned and looked at him, and he realized then and there he had made a dreadful mistake.

They topped him by half a head, and moved with the manner of gladiators, constructed of solid muscles from heel to head. The first came at him and a knife appeared in his hand as if by magic.

Rufus only became aware of the presence of Sonia behind him when he heard her scream. "Rufus! Get back!"

"What have we got here?" the knife man asked. Behind him the fire was licking up the walls.

"It's my girl," the other man cried. "From Aleria's picture!"

Sonia screamed and fled. The second man, laughing, tore after her.

The knife man advanced on Rufus. Normally he carried a knife on his person as well, but Rufus had divested himself of it, in the thought he would ride faster the less he weighed. Now it occurred to him he might not be riding anywhere, ever again, and it was a mite sobering.

He continued to back away, knowing that if he were to turn and run, this man would be on his back in an instant. Surely there had to be some circus folks tending their animals back here.

VIII

Olivia was promising she would write ruinous letters to her friends and relations in the provinces if her nephew should happen to lose the upcoming race on account of any of Hanuvar's instruction, but he had stopped paying attention. During an earlier portion of her extended harangue, he had noticed Sonia dragging a blank-eyed Rufus off, and while this worried him, he decided to do nothing until she led him into the grain depot.

He would not normally have interfered with a lover's rendezvous, but Rufus remained blithely unaware that the woman posed any danger. Probably she just sought to delay his start to the race. But then she might be seeking to have Rufus waylaid by thugs from the Greens.

And so Hanuvar raised a finger while the aunt was in midword, said "Pardon me," and broke away at a jog. He heard her exclaim, "Well, how very rude!"

It seemed as though various men, women, and children were deliberately setting themselves in his way as Hanuvar hurried toward the granary. Even as he fought forward, he questioned why he was striving so hard to look after the young man. In part that was because his aunt might very well cause difficulties for Mellika and her circus if Rufus failed to make good account of himself. Given that Mellika was providing a comfortable home and means of disguise for him, Hanuvar felt duty bound to protect her interests. But he knew there was something more to his actions even than this.

Once he stepped into the granary he moved to one side and waited for his eyes to adjust to the gloom. Off to his right many of the circus animals were caged or stabled, which still astonished him. Apparently the locals weren't worried about contamination. To his left, though, he heard voices, and saw a flicker of orange flame. Something was burning.

He started forward, then heard a woman scream, and broke into a run.

He arrived in time to see a man racing away with a woman over his shoulder. Sonia. Rufus was backstepping from a knife wielder. At sight of Hanuvar, the knifeman turned and bolted after the other.

Hanuvar stopped briefly beside Rufus, even as he heard shouts behind him of fire. "Are you unharmed?" he asked.

In the dark recesses of the grain depot where the figures had run, a rectangle of daylight appeared. Someone was opening a door, and Sonia was still screaming.

"Yes, yes, I'm fine. They've got Sonia!" Rufus cried. "I've got to save her!"

"I suppose someone will have to," Hanuvar said. Rufus started for the distant door, then stopped short as Hanuvar laid hand to his shoulder. "Two men, armed. You don't have a sword. Get help; I'll go after them."

"But you haven't a sword either!"

"I'll manage. Hurry!"

Hanuvar sprinted off. The fire was licking up one side of the wall. Behind him he heard the excited clamor of the crowd. The circus people should be able to get their animals out, but whether or not a water brigade could be organized to save the granary was another matter.

Hanuvar's way was lit by the glow of fire, but it took a moment to locate the actual exit. He stepped over the cast-off crossbar, then pushed open the door. He paused for only a moment, listening, then stepped outside.

The afternoon sun was just past its midday high and illuminated the green field on the far side of the granary, as well as a rubbish pile, and the wagon pulled up along the roadside, into which one thug was dropping a limp Sonia while the other hurried to catch up. Three other figures were already seated on the conveyance and one with a flamboyant Ceori mustache was demanding to know what they were doing with a woman.

He looked up as the gaunt man in the driver's seat beside the Ceori shouted and pointed to Hanuvar, then the Ceori whipped the horses into motion.

Hanuvar arrived at the roadway just as the wagon's two-horse team streamed off into a full gallop.

He was able to see into the back, where the two thugs sat with a larger fellow, all three wrestling a struggling Sonia. With them were two wooden chests, one of which was decorated in silver filigree. He decided against chasing, and doubled back to get a horse and guards. The irony that he, Hanuvar, was running to ask assistance from legionaries was not lost upon him.

The race crowd was in motion towards the grain depot, where a centurion had organized a water brigade. The circus folk raced headlong into the blazing structure, emerging with panicky beasts or wheeled cages of the others, but everyone else was either carrying buckets or watching in amazement as the fire blazed up along one wall.

Hanuvar kept to the crowd's fringes, searching for guards or a horse. Finally he saw Rufus and Percius leading two animals.

Hanuvar shouted and made for him, and that was when a large figure blocked his way.

At first he didn't recognize the pot-bellied man with the bruised face, and then he placed him as Otho, who'd accosted him the other evening while he'd sat with Aleria.

The man struck one fist into a palm. "There you are. I've been looking for you. You broke one of my teeth. Prepare for a pounding!" Otho's eyes widened, as if he had suddenly become keenly embarrassed. "What I mean is, you're going to be pretty sore when I'm done with you . . . Gods damn it!" Otho froze and his mouth worked without making noise, as if by motion he could generate the words he wanted.

Hanuvar had neither the time nor the inclination to let him find the preferred phrasing for his challenge. "Get out of my way."

"No, you've got this coming. We're going to settle this right now!" Otho furiously pumped his arms and shuffled forward and back, as if daring Hanuvar to advance.

Hanuvar faked a strike with his left, and when the big man shifted he drove in with all his speed and strength and struck the end of Otho's chin. The man's head tipped up. His eyes rolled back and then he sank with the coordination of a bean sack. Hanuvar sidestepped his collapse and darted toward Rufus.

"They put her in a wagon," Hanuvar shouted, pointing down the street.

"I saw! I got us horses! Are you game for a chase?" Rufus didn't wait for an answer. He leapt into the saddle—one of the maneuvers he'd been practicing—then bolted down the road.

The little slave boy gravely handed the reins of the other animal to Hanuvar. "Don't let my master get hurt," he said. Hanuvar, touched by the boy's loyalty, squeezed his shoulder.

He flung himself into the saddle. This animal was not a fine racer like Rufus', but the white gelding loped forward. Hanuvar wondered if Rufus had found time to ask for help of legionaries or if they would have assisted. All the ones he'd seen were in the fire brigade.

Beyond the grain depot lay nothing but farm fields. The wagon driver was far along, but Rufus' gray stallion was already near. As Hanuvar fought to close the distance, Rufus reached the wagon's side.

One of the thugs leaned out from the wagon's side rail and lashed at him with a whip. Rufus veered. The thug readied to whip again and then the cart hit a huge rut that set him stumbling toward the wagon's center. There he tripped backward over Sonia, missed the outstretched hands of one of his comrades, and fell off the wagon side. He was fortunate to tumble into the grass.

Still pacing the wagon at a gallop, Rufus climbed into his saddle and stood. Hanuvar sucked in a breath, as if readying for a blow.

Yet Rufus leapt with astonishing dexterity into the cart.

Hanuvar was impressed for only a moment, because while Rufus landed on both feet, he promptly fell into the wagon bed. He didn't rise.

Hanuvar maneuvered his horse past the groaning figure by the road side, mentally urging Rufus to rise before the others killed him. The smaller of the men in back was already crawling forward, his progress impaired by the wagon's jolting.

The driver's lanky companion kept looking over his shoulder at Hanuvar.

Ahead lay a small stone bridge erected over the glistening blue ribbon of a country stream.

Hanuvar was closing on the wagon's rear when swift hoof beats sounded behind. Another rider galloped past: Aleria, on a beautiful black mare, her disheveled hair streaming behind. Her mouth was twisted in fury.

Odd, Hanuvar thought, that of anyone who might ride to assist, it was her. A quick glance back showed him the village a good half mile to their rear, occluded by smoke and road dust.

Aleria rode in upon the left flank so Hanuvar came in on the right, drawing parallel with the wagon bench. The gaunt, sneering man beside the driver leaned out and slashed with a short sword. Hanuvar swerved, then tossed his knife underhand. The gaunt man twisted and Hanuvar's weapon drove into the shoulder of the mustached man at the reins. The driver shouted, and gave what must have been an involuntary jerk. The horses veered left, away from the bridge and down the gentle, grassy slope toward the stream.

Aleria took advantage of the commotion and leapt nimbly from her horse into the back of the wagon, cushioning her own blow by landing on the smaller of the men in back.

As Hanuvar closed on the side of the wagon once more, the gaunt man slashed and missed, then was jostled when a wagon wheel hit a low spot in the grass. His hands flew up and his blade just missed jabbing the driver's head. Something yellow and fuzzy flipped through the air.

Even over the rattle of the wagon Hanuvar heard the driver's wail of despair. "My mustache!"

The gaunt man lost his balance as a front wagon wheel struck a rock. He tumbled from the craft and landed senseless in the grass. Hanuvar's horse leapt over his rolling body.

The driver had lost control and the frenzied horses tried to veer from the burbling stream, now no more than a child's spear toss ahead. The water course looked an image from a rustic fable, complete with a span of rounded, mossy boulders rising from its center.

The smaller man Aleria had landed on lay limp beside Sonia, now pulling herself up. The larger man was lifting his fist for a blow when Rufus stirred and threw himself at the fellow's enormous fist, holding it back before it could connect against Aleria.

It was at that moment the horses turned too sharply and the wagon tilted.

Everything inside the bed was flung into the water: the smaller man, the big man, Sonia, the two chests, Rufus, and Aleria herself. The driver somehow sailed further, landing belly first on a flat boulder and then sliding off to drift downstream, struggling feebly.

Hanuvar slid off his horse and waded in. He first encountered the smaller of the assailants, lying face down in the water, and Hanuvar felt obliged to drag him to shore before he drowned.

Rufus, meanwhile, had pulled Sonia to the shore. Her arms had fastened upon Rufus, and she bestowed an odd sort of evaluating look very different from her mooning-calf gaze.

The big man surfaced on the far side of the stream beside a little flask. He considered his surroundings, frowned, then spotted the container. He tore the cork from its top. He sniffed it once, then quaffed the contents as he advanced for the shore and Hanuvar. A peculiar expression crossed his face as he reached waist deep water, as if he had suddenly remembered it might be time for a nap. By the time he arrived on shore his steps were uncertain. He plopped down on the shore, blinking heavily.

Hanuvar spared him only a moment's consideration before wading after Aleria, who had dived into the stream's center. One of the chests had smashed open and broken wood was floating downstream after the driver.

Aleria resurfaced, met Hanuvar's eyes, then dove again. The horses had trotted only a little further along the river bank and now stood, bewildered, fastened still to the wreck of the wagon.

"Rufus," Hanuvar called, "you should send Sonia for help. If she's up for riding."

The young man considered that advice, looked down at the woman, and nodded in affirmation. "An excellent suggestion, Helsa."

"And I think the leader is drifting down stream," Hanuvar continued. "You should chase him on your own horse. But be careful. He's likely to have a knife."

"You're so brave," Sonia said to Rufus, clutching him by the waist as he guided her up the bank. Somewhere out in the grass one of the other bandits groaned feebly.

Scanning his environment, Hanuvar found no enemies but the man weakly coughing up water on the shore near the larger fellow who had lain down in the grass. Spotting silver-filigreed wood upstream, he splashed onward and discovered the more decorative of the two chests wedged against a craggy boulder.

The chest was a smashed ruin, but the crudely carved horse head with the immense ruby eyes inside proved undamaged. By the time he lifted it clear, Aleria was pushing through the waist-high stream toward him, joining Hanuvar closer to the far shore, where the water was only calf deep.

She halted in front of him, eyes narrowed dangerously.

He looked up, saw Sonia riding at a slow, awkward canter toward the village on Hanuvar's borrowed horse. Rufus climbed into the saddle of his loyal stallion. Hanuvar watched the young man gallop off, then brandished the horse head before Aleria. "This is what you were really about, isn't it? You don't care about the race any more than I do."

"That's right."

"What's your connection with these kidnappers?"

"They're bandits, not kidnappers."

"Then why did those men take Sonia?"

"The short answer is that they're idiots. They're all idiots." She sighed in disgust. "And I was an idiot for working with them."

"Was it you who planned to set the grain depot on fire?"

"I planned everything, but they were supposed to set fire to the refuse pile behind it. This is what I get for putting my faith in men."

"I think it's more the quality of your help than the gender." He passed over the horse head.

Aleria's eyes widened and she looked down at the rubies, then back up to him, suspicious once more. "I suppose you want a cut."

"Where are you planning to sell the stones?"

"I've a buyer in Derva."

"Staying there long?"

She eyed him shrewdly. "You don't seem stupid enough to believe I'd leave money for you there."

"This winter or spring I might have a job in Derva I'll need help with."

She continued to weigh him with her eyes, then seemed to come to a decision. "All right, mystery man. I'll give you ten percent for helping me out of this mess. Ask for me at the Muse's Grace near the fountain of Thorius. If I'm nearby, maybe we can work together."

"I'll look you up."

"I'd best get moving. Villagers might turn up any moment."

He gestured for her to proceed, and she moved ashore, then paused to address him over her shoulder. "Is Helsa your real name?"

"For now."

She laughed. "See you around, Helsa."

She used a small, sharp blade she pulled from her hair to free the gems, hid them in an inner dress pocket, then tossed the sculpture of the Autumn Horse into the water and vanished through the brush. Hanuvar watched the wooden head drift downstream as he wrung out his tunic.

He was freeing the horses from the wagon's wreck when Rufus cantered back a short while later.

"He got away," the young man announced, dispiritedly. "Do you know what this was all about?"

Hanuvar eased the halter off the second horse, which high-stepped away to join his companion in cropping grass further upslope. He turned to Rufus and pointed to the men lying along shore. "I believe these bandits stole the head of the Autumn Horse and some coins, most of which are on the river bed. I saw the horse head drifting south."

The redhead's mouth fell open. "Gods. That's terrible! I wonder what kind of omen that is?"

"The omen is that you saved the young lady and foiled the robbers."

Rufus considered that and still found an objection. "But the horse head is lost! What a misfortune."

Hanuvar sheathed his knife. "The head may still turn up. And you emerged a hero. With a little luck, that fire will have been put out before much damage got done, thanks to you."

"Thanks to me?" Rufus asked doubtfully.

"You were on the scene in a timely way," Hanuvar pointed out.

Rufus climbed out of the saddle, his forehead creased with worry. He distractedly patted the side of his horse's head. "Well, it wasn't really that I was on the scene, Helsa. I was, eh, charmed there."

"You keep surprising me. A lesser man would step right up to take the credit."

"Would he?"

Hanuvar hesitated against what his instincts told him to say, then decided to speak from the heart. "Here's a final piece of advice, Rufus. Trust yourself a little more. Your instincts about who to take counsel from are sound. Be leery of Sonia. She's secretly a scion of the Greens and I don't think she originally meant you well."

"She is?" Rufus' mouth opened in surprise. "How do you know?"

"I have it from a convincing source. I don't think she charmed you into the granary to help you."

"That was a little peculiar," he admitted. "She did kiss me a bit when I sent her on her way, and said she was sorry. I wasn't sure what she meant."

Hanuvar chuckled. "People are capable of change, though I'd be careful with that one. If you mean to pursue her, you should see if she admits what her plans were."

Rufus inclined his head formally. "You've been very good to me, Helsa. From the start. And I thank you for riding after to aid me. I dare say I would have been overmatched without your help and that of the woman. Where did she go?"

"Back home, I think."

"My friends couldn't be bothered, even though I shouted at them to follow. But you were right there like a champion."

Behind him, the big man snored. The smaller one coughed up more water. Rufus glanced their way, then returned his attention to Hanuvar. "What I mean to say, Helsa, is thank you. And I wonder... if you are not set upon the circus, I should like to employ you in a permanent capacity."

Hanuvar smiled, saying nothing.

"Not as a horse trainer so much as a sort of permanent advisor."

Hanuvar shook his head. "That I cannot do."

"I see. Rootless, carefree existence and all that? In love with the road?"

"Something like that."

"I suppose I can be a bit of a trial."

Helsa offered his hand. Surprised, Rufus took it, and they clasped formally.

"I've the sense you don't do that often, Helsa," Rufus said as he released his hold. "I shan't forget you. I daresay you've probably never had so much impact upon so many lives before."

"I do what I can, sir."

⁂

While we travelled with the circus, we kept our ears alert for rumors about a host of subjects—news of Hanuvar, of course, particularly any pursuit of him, but also any information about the Volani. Most, we assumed, would remain in the Tyvolian peninsula, for the slaves had been auctioned off in Derva.

One day, though, we heard that a dangerous Volani wizard had been purchased by a crazy rich man named Decius Bavonus, just up the road. Gossip even provided the name of the Volani, Senidar, whom, it had turned out, was a scholar known slightly by Hanuvar himself.

"He's no wizard," Hanuvar told me. He was sitting down at the trestle table in his tent, pen poised over some parchment. "He's more of a librarian."

"That doesn't sound nearly as interesting to a gossip," I said. "So they improved the story a bit. Why would some Dervan aristocrat want a librarian?"

"He was well versed in rare manuscripts and magical lore," Hanuvar explained. "So it could be that our Dervan has dark interests. Or he might just want an intelligent tutor." He tipped his stylus into the ink.

"What are you going to do?" I asked.

"I'm going to send Decius Bavonus a generous offer to buy his slave. We'll be here for a few days; maybe we can arrange for the purchase before the circus draws anywhere close."

I thought that optimistic of him, but then he was a kind of wizard himself, so often achieving the impossible, so I didn't express my doubts. As it happened, the villa of Decius Bavonus lay outside a village small enough that Mellika's circus wouldn't be stopping there.

Hanuvar was surprised a return message reached him with great speed: Yes, Bavonus would be interested in selling his slave. How soon would his new purchaser be able to arrive to finalize arrangements?

Hanuvar was suspicious, of course, but was always ready to hazard his own safety for that of his people. Which is why he donned the garb of an eques late one evening, including a gold citizen's ring. I dressed as his retainer, and then the two of us rode off into the night. We expected to rejoin the circus in another day or two, and with luck, Senidar would be with us.

Events were to transpire somewhat differently than what we hoped.
                                                        —Sosilos, Book Four

Chapter 10:
The Missing Man

I

The dark youth bowed his head when he opened the villa door and greeted Hanuvar, who had announced himself with a lie.

"My master awaits within," the young man said, and stepped aside with a broad sweep of his arm. "Come."

Hanuvar scanned the dim interior of the empty entry chamber, though he had not left off examining the house slave, who waited with a curious wide-eyed blankness. Well groomed, he wore a plain beige calf-length tunic with simple belt and sandals. His owners surely intended he blend unobtrusively into the background, yet his disquietingly fluid movements promoted the opposite effect. He fairly vibrated with urgency.

Hanuvar wore an expensive white tunic, fine sandals, and a gold citizen's ring. Any astute observer would know him for an eques, minor nobility descended from those once wealthy enough to supply horse troops for Derva.

He spoke of his own misgivings with the arrogant, dissatisfied air expected of his assumed role. "I understood that I alone was to meet with your master. Yet I see there are a number of servants waiting outside among their masters' horses."

"Yes, sir. Many have been summoned this day."

"Competition to bid on the slave I am here for?" Hanuvar asked with a sniff.

"I could not say, sir."

As befitted his station, Hanuvar grunted disapprovingly, wondering why he hadn't been told others were interested in purchasing the Volani scholar. But then much about the current circumstance had struck him as odd, particularly the state of the exterior, which troubled him even more than the youth's odd manner. "Where are the slaves to take the horses? To work your yard and fields?"

Following up on his successful inquiry via messenger, he and Antires had ridden ahead of the circus through the night, arriving in the late morning to discover a host of other people's attendants resting in the shade of regal pine trees planted sequentially along the dirt road leading to the villa's central door. No servants had escorted their mounts to stables, and the animals cropped grass beside the waiting men. With an estate like this, a small army of slaves should have immediately greeted them, led the horses off, and treated the visiting servants to food and drink, but those resting outside complained that nothing of the kind had happened, as though that were not already obvious.

Hanuvar had left Antires with their horses and advanced to the villa, where he'd met the strange house-slave.

The youth didn't answer either of his questions. "All will be made clear, sir. If you will come with me?"

Remaining in character, Hanuvar scowled. "It had best be made clear quickly. I am on a schedule."

Hooves clattered on the road behind him. Hanuvar turned to see a rider on a dark horse rein in near Antires.

The new arrival arrogantly took in those around him before dropping from the horse and handing the reins to another man's retainer. He paused to adjust his dark cloak and brush road dust from his black tunic. Tall, broad, and tanned by long hours in the sun, he was crowned by well-trimmed ebon hair. Even from a distance, Hanuvar spotted the silver skull medallions holding the man's cloak to his shoulders, and understood why all those near the stranger watched with trepidation. One of the notorious revenants had arrived in their midst.

The officer adjusted his sword belt, then walked toward the villa with supreme confidence. Hanuvar hid his rising worry with aristocratic hauteur. This meeting grew more surprising and dangerous by the moment.

He showed no concern when the revenant's dark eyes caught his own, for the official he pretended to be would not be cowed by a centurion of the Order of the Revenants.[10]

The youthful slave performed his loose-limbed bow again, as though he were a puppet guided by unseen strings. "Our final guest," he said.

The revenant eyed him dispassionately, then turned his head to Hanuvar. His voice was smooth and coolly cordial. "I am Centurion Caius Murias Vace, of the fourth quarter of the Revenant Order."

Hanuvar inclined his head ever so slightly and continued to speak in the Dervan accent of a city native. "I am Kelenian Fenn, assistant to procurator Aurelian Troculus."

Vace's eyebrow ticked up, clearly recognizing the name of the famed landholder. "How interesting."

Hanuvar dismissed the idea that his presence was interesting by means of a negligent wave. "I thought revenants always travelled in threes."

"My colleagues seek a fugitive. Why did Decius Bavonus contact the procurator?"

"Contact?" Hanuvar inquired politely.

Vace frowned. "I assumed you were here for the same reason I am. Perhaps I am in error."

"I'm here to purchase a slave."

"How curious. I'm here to see what a slave has wrought for his

---

[10] The Order of the Revenants was founded by the emperor's decree a scant fifteen years before Hanuvar's journeys with Antires, near the tail end of the Second Volani War. The original intent of their order was to hunt down Volani spies, sympathizers, and collaborators. As is the way with powerful organizations, they quickly found new duties with which to occupy themselves. After Hanuvar's withdrawal from the Tyvolian peninsula, they continued their hunt for former collaborators and spies, but broadened their areas of interest to the persecution of magicians, social deviants, and priests working in unsanctioned ways. They employed what was thought to be a vast army of informants, though even at the height of their power a careful review of their documents reveals they were never so widely rooted as was believed.

For almost ten years they were a terror in Tyvol and especially in the western provinces, leading hundreds away for questioning and execution.

Their growing power was eventually reined in when Emperor Gaius Cornelius had the revenant legate quietly murdered and replaced with someone both less ambitious and less eager to drain the treasury on private crusades.

At the time of Hanuvar's travels, revenants were no longer so widely spread as they had been during the previous decade, but they remained an elite secret police force answerable only to the emperor himself, ever alert for intrigue and challenges to the empire.   —*Silenus* master." Vace appeared to be telling the truth, which likely meant he himself wasn't hunting for Hanuvar, although his two colleagues might be. "I assume he's the same slave you're after, a Volani scholar?"

"Quite probably, unless our host Decius Bavonus owns two Volani scholars."

"I suppose it's possible, though how many of them can there be left?" Vace grinned at his own joke. Hanuvar laughed politely at the reference to the genocide of his people, inclining his head while the revenant continued: "I hope he doesn't mean to have our two offices bid against one another. Mine can simply requisition the man."

"So can mine. But we need not be at odds."

"At least not until we see what the man intends to show us, yes?" The revenant turned to the slave, watching expressionlessly. "Are you going to lead us to your master, or not?"

"This way, please." The slave turned with his peculiar grace and eased into the home. Hanuvar resisted the impulse to signal Antires he was well. The person he pretended to be certainly wouldn't bother communicating with some distant slave or secretary.

The house slave closed the door behind them. With the sun but newly risen, little internal light reached through the villa's northern windows. The slave didn't bother retrieving a lantern as he headed into the dim interior, walking with little sound.

"There's something odd about that slave," the revenant muttered to Hanuvar.

"I've noticed," Hanuvar whispered back. His senses were taut, and his imagination rich with improbable scenarios, but before it peopled the room ahead with blood-smeared corpses, he heard a subdued chatter of voices.

They arrived at a pleasant atrium, illuminated by an open courtyard through nearby arches. Much like the fields outside, the bushes, trees, and flowers were circled by weeds and several weeks overdue a trim. Four people waited around a table with meager refreshments. The muscular, grim one standing with folded arms near a pillar was obviously someone's bodyguard. Another was a patrician woman with a broad chin and a pronounced scowl. Seated upon one of the nearby couches, was a younger woman, clearly a close relative, lacking the tight and predatory features of the older. Leaning toward her was a portly, balding man with a prominent hook in his nose. He wore a light toga praetexta.

The young slave cleared his throat. "The master has awaited your arrival, gentle ladies and sirs, and with everyone now here, I would like to take you to him."

"I think introductions are in order first," said the balding man. His voice was brash and certain, even friendly, though his bonhomie was absent from his eyes. He extended his arm toward Hanuvar, who took it. "I am Melius Tentor, Senator Aminius' first adjutant." Hanuvar didn't have time to reply before Tentor continued: "This is Arcella Sulena, the wife to this province's esteemed governor. And her charming daughter, Julia." He stepped to Vace.

"An honor," the revenant said, proceeding to introduce himself and then Hanuvar. No one bothered to introduce the bodyguard.

"What are all of you here for?" Vace asked.

It was Arcella who answered curtly. "Bavonus promised us a demonstration that would change the course of the empire. Something to do with a Volani slave."

"And he invited all of you?" Vace asked with obvious disappointment. He did not wait for a response. "And why are you here, milady, rather than the governor, or one of his men?"

Her answer was stern and sharp. "Because my husband trusts my judgment. And it's high time my daughter learned how to cut her own way through a man's world."

Hanuvar thought this speech was meant to intimidate or challenge the revenant, but Vace's eyes flashed in amusement. "What an interesting expression," he said.

"If it's a matter for the empire, all of our superiors need to be informed," Tentor said.

"That depends upon how important this matter turns out to be." Vace's gaze shifted to the house slave.

Once more the slave cleared his throat. "I do apologize for keeping you waiting. But the master is ready for you now."

"And he will not come here, to welcome us?" Tentor asked, with the air of someone repeating a query.

The slave bowed. "Master Bavonus begs that you be patient and realizes that his requests may strike you as strange. He asked me to assure you that all shall be explained to your satisfaction once the demonstration begins."

Hanuvar lifted his nose. "I am not here for a demonstration."

"I understand, sir. These matters are related directly to the slave, and his future. Please, come with me." With a beckoning gesture, the house boy backed toward a side hall.

Vace gave Hanuvar a curious glance, as if to gauge his thoughts, then they followed in a group.

"Bavonus is proving himself an eccentric," Tentor said, addressing them at large. "I hope he hasn't wasted my time."

"He dares not waste the time of revenants," Vace said with a cool smile, "or, indeed, a servant of the procurator, the advisor to a governor, and the adjutant to one of the most powerful senators in Derva."

One of Tentor's thick eyebrows arched up. "You seem amused."

"You'd be surprised how little in my job brings actual pleasure. This, at least, is diverting. My patience, however, is not eternal." He looked sidelong to Hanuvar. "You seem irritated, Fenn."

"I was dispatched to oversee a transaction," Hanuvar explained. "I've no interest in demonstrations or gatherings."

Arcella spoke to Hanuvar for the first time. "Don't you want to see just how valuable this slave might be?"

"He doesn't want to pay top money for him," the revenant said.

The slave turned into a side corridor that led to a stairwell and descended into the gloom without comment. At the bottom he lifted a lantern, briefly fussed with lighting it, then rehung it and opened a thick door wrapped in dark brass.

"Your master's on the other side of that?" Tentor asked gruffly.

"What he's created must be kept from prying eyes, sir." The slave opened the door on soundless hinges and revealed another stairway, this of pitted stone extending into absolute darkness. The slave used his lantern to light a second, smaller one hung on a peg just inside the door, offered the first to the bodyguard, who didn't take it, then to Tentor, who did. With a muttered "Please follow me," the youth started down, Tentor's lantern painting his huge shadow upon the wall.

The revenant took the lead. Hanuvar followed, with the two women after, Tentor and the bodyguard bringing up the rear. Apart from their own footfalls there was no sound; around them was the cool, still quiet of a tomb, though the place was free of cobwebs and vermin.

The stairwell stretched on long as two ordinary flights, and terminated in a long subterranean stone hallway only a little wider than the stairwell, with room for three people to walk abreast. A half dozen recessed doorways showed along both sides, made visible by a light shining through a doorway further down the hall. The corridor continued into the darkness beyond.

"What is this place?" Tentor demanded.

The slave answered without hesitation or hint of apology. "Our destination." He started forward, his lantern light playing upon the old stone and doorways. The slave made for the one where the light already shone, then stopped outside, and with another of his sweeping motions, encouraged their entry. Hanuvar hesitated while the others stepped past into a small sitting room with cushioned couches and walls painted with the depiction of a sedate dinner party. A jar of wine and set of goblets stood on a low table.

"Please, make yourselves comfortable. I will inform my master of your arrival and you will shortly be entertained by him."

Tentor headed straight for the goblets, holding one up in the light of three flickering oil lanterns and smiling a little at the emerald worked into its side. The governor's wife lifted another. "What do you suppose this is about?"

Hanuvar suspected it was about a diversion, and noted the revenant watching the slave walk into the darkness.

The bodyguard stepped close to Arcella. He, too, warily surveyed his environment.

"On your guard, Fenn?" the revenant asked.

Hanuvar knew then that the persona he'd crafted had slipped, though he tried to hide the change in his character with flinty arrogance. "Still amused, Vace?"

"Barely. Someone's putting on a show for us, and I'm wanting it to get to the main act." With a last glance toward the darkened hall, he stepped into the room.

Hanuvar followed. "Would you rather be hunting for the fugitive your colleagues are after?"

"My colleagues are seeking signs of Hanuvar."

Hanuvar managed a skeptical look. "I've heard the rumors, but they hardly seem credible."

"You haven't seen the reports, then. Consul Caiax himself swears he looked upon the real man."

Hanuvar's surprise shown honestly, not because of the report, but that Caiax had survived to relay one. The last Hanuvar had seen of the general he'd had a spear protruding from his chest.

"Other survivors of a garrison Hanuvar attacked have likewise testified," Vace continued.

He had wondered how long it would be before a new supply ship would reach the Isles of the Dead and return with Dervan survivors of the battle there.

The young woman, Julia, had been watching Tentor and her mother eye the goblets. She took a step closer to Vace and Hanuvar. "I heard he's a ghost," she said.

Hanuvar snorted at that.

"If he's a ghost," Vace said, "he's a very strange one, for he appears in daylight and carries a sword. Some claim he's a magic worker, for there are reports he's been conjuring monsters, and that he can change his appearance at will." The revenant offered a mocking smile, suggesting he found the account amusing without criticizing it outright.

"I'll believe that when I see it," Hanuvar said.

"If he could change shape, he might be anyone," Julia said to Vace. "Like you. Or the senator's aide. Or me, I suppose."

Hanuvar had noted that she spoke with a curious stiffness of her lower lip and glimpsed the reason in her last few words—her left lower incisor was missing. She must labor hard to conceal what some would view as an unflattering blemish.

Perceiving a new light shining in the hall, he stepped to the doorway and discovered a lantern sitting at the bottom of the stairs. Though this was odd given no one stood near the lantern, he was more troubled that the faint light streaming through the door at the stair head had vanished.

"What is it?" Vace asked.

"The door's closed." Hanuvar listened, looked both ways, then advanced toward the light, the revenant following. His left hand grasped the hilt of his knife.

As he neared the lantern an object lying nearby resolved itself into an adult body, dried, and apparently skinless. Hanuvar recoiled but shifted his attention, knowing a horrid distraction could be setting its discoverers for ambush.

The revenant almost sounded calm. "This man has been flayed," he said. "And it looks like someone has taken a few of his organs."

Hanuvar started up the stairs, watching the walls and steps. But there were no further surprises, other than that the door had been scored. Someone had tried to open it before. That it was locked was no surprise at all.

"It's locked, isn't it," the revenant called to him.

Hanuvar started down. "Yes. And the hinges are on the outside. Someone's playing a game with us. We walked right into it."

Vace looked back at the stiff corpse. "Placing the body could have been a trap to put us off guard."

"It's not. This is to alarm us." Hanuvar picked up the lantern. "Or to separate us."

"Wisely reasoned, Ferin."

Naturally a well-trained revenant would be alert, and while it was somewhat reassuring to have a perceptive warrior at his side, Hanuvar hardly felt at ease. The revenants were ever suspicious, and ever vigilant. And now he had let his mask slip, though he had retained his upper class accent the while. He hoped his pretend position as a trusted representative would shield his actions. Surely the wealthy patrician he pretended to serve might employ someone quick thinking and perceptive to act in his stead.

Hanuvar took the extra lantern with them when they returned to the reception room.

There Vace addressed the other four. "Friends, all is not as it seems. Our slave guide has disappeared. The door to the outside is locked, and a body was left for us to view."

Tentor lowered his wine goblet. "This sounds like the kind of games revenants play."

"I assure you that I am playing no game. And this is nothing like anything my people would do."

"What are you saying?" Arcella asked. "Was the body that of our host, or the slave?"

"It was too dried out to have been the slave," Hanuvar said. "I've never met Bavonus."

"We may all have been lured here under false pretenses," Vace said.

"But why?" Tentor asked, his voice rising in concern.

Arcella knew the answer. "One of our enemies wants to kill us."

The silent bodyguard put hand to his sword.

"But who wants to kill all of us?" Tentor asked. "And Fenn here wasn't even on the original invitation."

"It's not who we are," Vace said, "but what. We are Dervan officials with rank. That's enough to invite hatred from some."

"It's Hanuvar," the girl said in the resulting silence, then turned to Vace. "It must be him. You said your men were hunting him, and this slave is Volani, isn't he? The one who's so important? He must be working with Hanuvar."

Vace answered. "The Volani slave is likely a sorcerer who worked in high levels of the Volani government. We should be alert to the potential dangers this presents."

The girl's eyes widened and she spoke in dread. "You think there's a witch-man after us? That we're trapped here? What does he want with us?"

"Be calm, daughter," Arcella snapped. "We are more clever than a slave."

"Maybe there's some reasonable explanation for all of this," Tentor said nervously. "We should keep calm and explore the rest of these halls."

"Well, come along, then." Arcella frowned and pointed toward the doorway. "Let's get a sense of this place and see if there's another exit."

While Hanuvar agreed, he couldn't help thinking this was exactly what their unseen captor wanted.

II

Hanuvar kept his own counsel as they advanced into the hall. He didn't object that Tentor and Arcella had snatched the lanterns; he wanted his hands free.

Whoever was behind this had distracted them with the slave's departure while another associate left the body near the stairs. Their opponent was confident, well prepared, and dangerous, motivated not just by hatred, but by the desire to spread fear.

Could it be the master of the house, bent on vengeance against his fellow aristocrats? If so, would he have found a willing conspirator in Senidar? Though Hanuvar had known him only slightly, by reputation the scholar had been quiet and charitable, charged with overseeing the city-state's collection of sorcerous manuscripts, most of which even he was widely skeptical about. It was hard to imagine that his character would have changed so much that he would countenance these acts. But then it was difficult to know how a man could change when he witnessed the annihilation of his people. Madness might take many forms. Hanuvar knew traipsing through enemy lands to rescue any who had once shared his homeland was not the most rational means of addressing his pain, especially since it would almost certainly lead to his death.

But now was not the time for self-reflection. He couldn't be certain who was behind this elaborate trap, and their identity wasn't currently important. For the sake of the unknowing thousand he hoped to save, he had to focus fully on the present, and his survival.

He and the others cautiously explored their surroundings. Six chambers opened onto the hall. One was stacked with old furniture, another with empty amphora of various sizes, yet a third with what at first blush appeared to be kitchen implements, complete with cutting boards and jars filled with dried leaves and spices. Vace explained it was a spellcaster's laboratory. Hanuvar had guessed as much but kept silent.

The tunnel swept on, and beyond two more doorways lay an intersection with a hallway running transverse to their own. While Hanuvar was still debating which way to explore, the contents of the next chamber arrested the attention of Arcella and Tentor. It held a wealth of garments and additional chests, and the two patricians were further entranced by a small selection of rings, necklaces, bracelets, and earrings resting upon a wooden table. The precious stones upon them glittered in the light.

"We're not the first people who have been trapped like this," Vace said to Hanuvar.

"Likely not," he agreed. "Our captor could not have been doing this long without stoking some kind of suspicion, could he?"

"You would think not. It's astonishing what careless people can get away with, though. Sooner or later their mistakes catch up to them."

Tentor had opened one of the chests to uncover a supply of shining silver coins, plentiful enough to draw even the emperor's attention.

The bodyguard spoke at last. "That's a lot of money." His voice was dry and coarse, and Arcella looked sidelong at him. Until that moment Hanuvar had assumed their relationship was employer and employee, but the brief, knowing exchange suggested a greater intimacy. Scanning the faces of the others, he thought only the girl, Julia, had noted it. Everyone else, including Vace, was distracted by the treasure.

From outside came the faint creak of a hinge. Hanuvar immediately slid to the doorway and peered into the gloom. The sound had originated further down the corridor.

He pressed to the wall. The revenant stepped out in front of him, lantern carried in his off hand, and motioned him to follow. Vace drew his sword, a dark blade glistening with some liquid. Poison, probably, stored in his sheath.

Hanuvar heard a whispered exchange behind him. Vace hissed for silence. From up ahead came another footfall.

Vace advanced, searching the ground for trip wires, and came finally to the intersection. Their own hall terminated, but another stretched to their left and right. The revenant crouched, peering. Hanuvar drew up beside him, sensing something in the space in the corridor to the left, upon the floor. The distinct acrid smell of a body long preserved in resin reached him. Lantern in hand, a nervous Tentor passed Hanuvar and rounded the corner. He halted after only a few paces, calling out to the gods in horror.

Vace whipped around the corner after him. Expecting this to be another distraction, Hanuvar immediately looked the opposite way, seeing only darkness and what looked like a stack of broken crates. Julia crept up to his side, shivering.

"Watch that way," Hanuvar told her. "Our lives may depend on it."

She nodded, her eyes wide with fear. Hanuvar didn't see the others behind her.

Still moving with care, he advanced past the goggle-eyed Tentor, rigid as a target dead center in the hall. Vace crouched beside two bodies without touching either.

Both were blackened and skinless, their bellies scooped clear of organs.

"Where are the others?" Hanuvar asked.

Vace answered disapprovingly. "With the gold, I presume."

"I think I'm going to be sick," Julia said behind them.

"Watch our backs," Hanuvar told her.

Tentor's hand shook, and the light wobbled with him. "What mind would conceive of doing this to people like us?"

"Adjust the light," Hanuvar said, pointing. But Tentor didn't understand the instruction, so Hanuvar pried the lantern from him and advanced beyond the bodies, feeling the wall.

"We're being toyed with," Vace said.

Assuredly. They had been deliberately drawn here so they would be further alarmed. He searched the wall and floor for sign of any track, or the telltale floor scrape of a hidden panel. Nothing. Probably the bodies had been lying here from the start. But a sound had been made so they would be seen.

The corridor reached an end some six paces on, with no door. Hanuvar swept his hand along the wall and then, finally, felt a current of air. Bringing the light closer set the lantern flame wavering. He eyed the mortar in the bricks.

"It feels like someone's watching us," Julia said in a stricken whisper.

A man's shout and a woman's scream echoed behind them.

Hanuvar's instinct was to race back, but he let Vace precede him, alert still that someone might have placed a trip wire or other hazard.

They met nothing in the hall, though, and when they stepped into the treasure room, the bodyguard was gone.

Arcella lay there, at least what was left of her. Her dress had been rent down the front, and her skinless, hairless body lay wet and glistening, the lidless eyes rendered enormous. Unlike the other bodies, her internal organs still lay in their places. The reek was overwhelming.

Even Hanuvar was stunned by the scene, for he could think of no ordinary means by which the woman could have screamed and then been rendered skinless in the scant moment since they had raced to find her.

The girl breathed with a rapid wheeze, mumbling in fear and horror.

"It's magic," Tentor cried. "It's got to be some kind of magic! There's no other explanation, is there? They could come for any of us, any time. I don't understand. Her guard had a sword! How did this happen?"

"Her guard was probably looking at the gold," Julia said in disgust.

"But that doesn't explain how quickly they skinned the woman, does it?" the revenant asked.

"No," Hanuvar agreed. The daughter had drawn close to him and stared down at the unrecognizable thing that had been her mother. She gagged and wobbled, and Hanuvar clasped her shoulder to steady her. "There must be another exit from this room," he said to Vace, "or we'd have passed whatever it was."

"Unless it was a ghost," Tentor said.

"A ghost couldn't cart off the guard, could it?" Vace asked.

"I don't know!" Tentor's gaze swung wildly around the room, loose and unfocused, as if he expected to see a horror lurking in a corner he had somehow missed. "How do we know what they're doing or planning? They could do anything!"

"I don't think so," Hanuvar said. "There are other exits, and other doors. I'm sure I was close to finding a passage when we were lured back here."

Tentor stared at him, wide-eyed, more fearful than the girl who had just discovered her mother's mutilated corpse. Vace faced him as Hanuvar continued: "Whatever is killing us isn't all-powerful. They need us here. And they need us separated."

"An astute observation." Vace had not yet raised his blade, and Hanuvar was aware that it was ready at his side, still slick with poison. "Your procurator chose his servant well. If that is, indeed, who you truly work for."

"You doubt me?" Hanuvar asked.

"You're too good, Fenn. If that's your true name. You're no aristocrat's servant. Not even one who served a year or two campaigning. You're not just used to giving orders, you move like someone who's been in the front. You're as observant as I am, and you're not afraid of me. The others all are, even if they wouldn't admit it. But not you. I can tell. So you're either dumber than you seem, incredibly cocky, or you're something else entirely."

Hanuvar considered possible responses, including indignation, or insistence that the procurator's office had hired him for his expertise. He improvised a different answer instead. "You're right, Vace. There's no point in dissembling. I rank as a centurion in the Praetorian Guard, though I answer directly to Minister Sarnax. I've been sent to investigate the disappearance of one of our men."

Vace's expression cleared. The explanation made complete sense, as Hanuvar had known it would. Then the revenant's veil of suspicion returned. "Have you any proof?"

"I don't carry it, no. Not while I'm in disguise."

Vace grunted. "I wouldn't expect you to. But that does make trusting you more challenging."

"He could be part of this terrible game," Tentor said. He pointed his shaking finger at Hanuvar. "He could be Hanuvar."

"No," Vace said slowly, "he's as confused by this as we all are. Many of his guesses have been shrewd, and his observations sound. He's not in league with our enemies." The revenant sheathed his weapon with great care. "So, Praetorian, what should we call you?"

"Kelenian's my true name. Keeps things simple."

"All right then," Vace said amiably. "What does a praetorian centurion suggest we do?"

"Return to the hallway. I think we were close. And I think there are sealed doors near many of these rooms, for our enemies to come and go."

Julia spoke again. "What kind of thing can possibly hunt and flay so swiftly?"

"Something inhuman," Tentor said.

"Humans are capable of all sorts of surprising practices," Vace commented.

"Are they capable of this?" Tentor's voice quaked.

Vace answered. "It might be that the governor's wife is still alive, and that this grisly corpse was exchanged for her. I find that much more believable. Once men and women are frightened, it's easy for them to believe the impossible."

Despite himself, Hanuvar was impressed by the revenant's

reasoning, though he knew his conclusion was in error, for the corpse's size and eye color were those of Arcella. Vace considered the walls once more. "Bavonus has gone mad. Likely he's watching us, even now."

Julia pointed a trembling hand toward the thing on the floor. "You're saying this is not my mother?"

"It may not be," Vace said.

"I hope you're right," Hanuvar said. "Vace, can we cast your cloak over the body? Whomever it is, wouldn't it be suitable to cover her face?"

"I might need my cloak. We can use those clothes on the racks."

Hanuvar took up two of the coins and laid them across the ghastly staring eyes.

Julia suppressed a sob. Hanuvar climbed to his feet and tightly clutched her shoulder. The next moment she was crying against him, and he was patting her, though he searched the wall for places where they might be watched from.

Between sobs she said, breathlessly, with many pauses, "She deserved better than this."

Most people do, he thought, though he did not say it.

III

Dervans had little difficulty killing, but even Vace was squeamish about touching dead bodies that had not been ritually cleaned by the priests of Luptar, lord of the underworld. Hanuvar pretended he felt much the same and covered both bodies in spare cloth before dragging each of them to the treasury room where Julia's mother already lay concealed. Both times he was accompanied by the surviving members of their group, for he had suggested they separate no longer.

"It's curious, isn't it, how we work with care when we knew a person, but dead bodies are otherwise an inconvenience," Vace mused. "So much trash, and flotsam."

Hanuvar didn't acknowledge that. He asked Tentor to guess about the amount of oil they had, and the nobleman reported. "Maybe two hours' worth."

"That may not be enough," Hanuvar said. "If we have to, we can smash these shelves and some of this other furniture and use it for kindling."

"You're a practical man, Praetorian," Vace said. "None of the shelving looks especially sturdy. It should be easily destroyed."

"I saw a man!" Julia cried out. She pointed one slim hand where the wall met the ceiling. "Watching us! That stone just slid back into place!"

Hanuvar had unsheathed his knife and now advanced on the indicated opening.

"Was he Volani?" Tentor asked.

If Julia was surprised by the narrow focus of the question, it wasn't obvious, for she was alarmed enough by the sighting. "I don't know! He was right there!"

Hanuvar felt carefully. He detected a crack in the mortar, but could not move the stone.

"You were right, Praetorian," Vace said. "They *are* watching us. We can choose whether to stay here and pry at that, or go back to the hall."

"The hall," Tentor said without hesitation. His eyes had swung back to the ghastly corpses and the lumpy stinking thing lying beneath the spare clothes, now moist with blood and other fluids.

"The hall," Hanuvar agreed. "We know there's a door there."

"And you don't think it will be sealed off?" Vace asked.

"There may be another solution."

"Which you don't wish to explain, because we're being observed," Vace said. "Very well, the hall it is. It will certainly smell more pleasant. We can smash up some of this for kindling and come back as necessary."

Soon they had returned to the hall and Hanuvar chose a stone beside the hidden gap he'd discovered. He had recovered a sturdy knife from Arcella's body, and chipped with this, hammering the hilt with a sturdy shelf support beam and driving the point into the mortar.

Vace set Julia and Tentor to watching both directions.

"We will switch off," Vace said, "so that we don't let our attention lapse when we weary. And so that the man hammering doesn't grow overtired. I expect you to monitor the level of oils," he told Julia.

"Suppose there's another hidden door elsewhere," Tentor said nervously. "They could sneak up on us. Or suppose they drop poison on us from another hidden eye panel. Or fire."

"Stop suggesting things," Vace said with cold venom, and Tentor gulped, so swift was the changed nature in the revenant. Vace returned to his odd conviviality. "I thought you were the one worried about skin-flaying ghosts. Watch the hall. You can look for panels there if you wish."

"What will you be watching?" Tentor asked sullenly.

"Everything else."

In an hour's time Hanuvar had chipped the mortar free from the brick in the top corner of what he assumed was a door. It proved impossible to leverage out, so he started on the one beside it, reasoning that the more of them he weakened, the better their chances for pulling them loose.

He felt the revenant's eyes upon him, but said nothing. Finally, Vace spoke. "What do you think they'll do next?"

Hanuvar answered without stopping. "Two options are most likely."

"Which are?"

"I'm not sure I should suggest them, in case they haven't thought of them."

Vace laughed. "I like you, Praetorian. Will any of your men start to get suspicious, and come in to help?"

"I work alone. What about yours?"

"Not for some time. They're several days southeast of here."

Hanuvar couldn't help wondering which leads the revenants were following, and whether any clues could point to the circus.

"Maybe we should go work the lock," Tentor said nervously. "There's no telling if this will even amount to anything, and they could be planning any kind of response."

"There's no point with the outer door," Hanuvar said as he hammered. "It's scored already from some prior visitor's efforts. There's a bar on the other side."

"What if there's some kind of obstruction on the other side of *this* panel?" Tentor asked.

Hanuvar didn't point out that one of the reasons they were chipping stones was to make a bar pointless, although Tentor had noted their enemies could very well be planning a counterstroke.

"We'll deal with each problem as it arises." Vace mimed hammering to Hanuvar, who passed him the tools. They traded positions and Vace took up work where Hanuvar had left off.

"This whole thing stinks of Volani trickery," Tentor said. "Don't you think? It has to be them. Hanuvar never faced his enemies fairly. He always had some trick. I'm not surprised one of them is lairing in the dark." His voice rose and he lifted his balding head: "But we Dervans can find vermin in the dark, and crush them under our heels!"

"Do you really think it's Volani doing this to us?" Julia asked, suddenly plaintive. "Mother always said some people would blame bad weather on Volani if they could."

"We've been aware of the Bavonus family interests for some time." Vace spoke over the sound of his hammering. "They've accumulated a small library of sorcerous texts over several generations. But until now they have been loyal adherents."

"Until they got the Volani slave?" Tentor suggested.

"The timing is curious, isn't it?"

Julia sidled a little closer to Hanuvar and addressed him with quiet intensity. "Do you really think we can get out of here alive?"

"I do. But we have to stay vigilant."

"It can sneak up on us," Julia said. "And it must move fast."

"You yourself said that guard was probably distracted by the gold."

"Yes. Or my mother. He wasn't just her guard."

"I see."

"I'm not sure you do." The girl crossed her arms and raised her shoulders, as though they were walls she might shelter behind. "I can't believe she brought me along to this stupid place. I didn't want to go."

"Why did she bring you?"

"She wanted me to be more like her. To take charge. She keeps—kept—trying to show me things. And the stupid cow was rarely right about any of it." She wiped her eyes.

"Parents aren't perfect. If she was trying to look out for your future, then she was better than a fair share of them."

"You needn't worry," Tentor said with an oily smile. "Pretty soon your husband can take care of you. How old are you, anyway? If you don't mind me asking?"

"Shut up, Tentor," Vace said, without breaking from his work. Hanuvar approved. Tentor frowned, but did as ordered.

"I don't want to be married yet," Julia said, with the hint of a child's whine. "And I don't want to be here. And I don't have anything against Volani, so I don't know why they'd be angry at me. I certainly wasn't involved in that stupid war."

"If you're seeking to sway our watcher to sympathy, it can't be done." Vace paused only briefly to address her, then turned back to his work. "You could never reason with Volani. Even when they were beaten."

"They were always scheming," Tentor said.

The words of neither man reassured the young woman, who turned her gaze to Hanuvar.

"We're working to get you out of here," he said. He hoped they would succeed.

After a quarter hour Vace loosened enough mortar that they were able to pry the topmost stone completely free. They set it on the ground and shone the lantern into a dark space revealed beyond. Nothing looked back.

"That's one," Vace said. "Maybe four more before one of us can squeeze through."

"Assuming no one's on the other side waiting to poke us," Tentor said.

"Which is why one of us should be standing by with a sword, ready to poke them."

"I'll stand guard." Hanuvar could have suggested Tentor keep his fears to himself, but then waiting to attack was surely an obvious option their foes had already considered.

Vace handed him the sword with only a moment's hesitation. "Be careful you don't nick yourself with it."

"Poison?"

"The debilitating rather than the deadly kind, more's the pity." Vace turned and started to work upon the wall with the steady clink of the board against the pommel, and the ongoing spray of grit.

"So tell me, Praetorian," Vace said. "What kind of assignments are you usually deployed upon? Are you always a troubleshooter?"

Hanuvar had been fabricating his background over the last while, and the answer came easily. "I was guarding the emperor. Then I got assigned to watch over his nephew, but Enarius said I was too old to look at every day. So then they started sending me into the field. What's your background?"

"I missed all of the best actions," Vace said, something only the stupid, the young, or the madly fervent would proclaim about avoiding battle. "I was posted in the west during most of the Second Volani War, putting down all the little in-bred clan fighting and would-be Hanuvars in the western provinces. That Volani madman inspired a lot of maladroits to fight who wouldn't otherwise have dared. All those battles didn't amount to much. They certainly didn't help me get promoted."

Hanuvar feigned a sympathetic nod. "How did you end up in the revenants?"

Vace peered through the hole before resuming work, his voice conversational above the steady tink of his hammer. "My command stumbled upon a coven of witches advising the king of Faedahn. That was a bloody mess. I got us out of that alive and hanged all the women."

"I bet that impressed the revenants," Tentor said.

"It did," Vace confirmed. "The witches tried to use their wiles on me. To turn me to their ways." He looked over his shoulder at Tentor.

"Some of those Faedahn ladies are ripe," the aristocrat said. "That must have been tempting. How many did you hang?"

"Three hundred," Vace said.

Julia gasped. No matter the horrors she had already seen this day, apparently she could still feel shock. "They were all witches?"

Vace turned back to his work. "I wanted to be thorough."

Tentor licked his lips. "Did you question them first? To find out?"

"Some of them."

"Some of the pretty ones, I bet," Tentor guessed.

Vace's voice was thick with contempt. He faced Tentor, eyes bright with righteous zeal. "I was protecting my nation. Do you know what's wrong with Derva these days? People take advantage of their position instead of doing their jobs. It's bad enough that men like you sleep with slaves. You've too little interest in keeping our own bloodlines pure, and the women can't even be bothered to raise a brood of children. It's weakened us."

"I don't like your tone, Centurion," Tentor said.

"Do you wish to report me?" Vace asked icily.

Tentor gulped.

Vace thrust the knife at him, then turned it so the hilt was offered first. "Your turn."

Tentor pretended courage and offered an objection. "You haven't worked half as long as Kelenian, or whatever his name is."

"I'll resume after you work a bit. I think you need to spend less time talking."

Tentor scowled. "Senator Aminius can make trouble for you, when we get out of here."

"Can he? I think I can make trouble for you. And who says you'll get out of here? The only ones I'm really counting on making it out alive are me and the praetorian."

Tentor's frown deepened, but he took the knife. "What if whoever's back there sticks me with a sword while I'm working?"

"That's why the praetorian's going to watch the hole. I'm going to watch the hall, and the girl's going to watch the back wall. Now get to work."

Tentor glared at Vace after he turned away, then looked at Hanuvar, who affected disinterest. Finally, he set to work.

Over the next hour the senator's adjutant complained first about his wrist, then his arm, then about being hungry, but he continued hammering and every now and then pried weakly to see if the next block was loose.

Vace took his sword back and switched positions with Hanuvar, who sat watching the wall while Julia studied the hallway. Her expression was strained and she sometimes wiped her eyes, but her attention did not wander.

The lantern oil was running low when Hanuvar caught a brown flutter on his left. A tiny slip of paper drifted down, and above it a small gap in the stone closed without a sound.

Hanuvar shot to his feet, his movement stirring the air so the paper struck Tentor's wrist. The Dervan jolted back as if he'd been bitten by a spider.

Hanuvar advanced on the gap he'd seen close, and felt the mortar with his knife point. There was no obvious break.

Julia scooped up the paper and opened it. "There's writing on it," she said.

"What does it say?" Tentor asked.

Vace was peering through the hole in the bricks, now two spans wide.

"I don't know this language," Julia said.

Hanuvar turned, extending a hand, troubled about what he might see.

It was written hurriedly in slanted Volani. It read: "I didn't know it was you. Don't worry, I can get you out alive."

"What does it say?" Vace asked.

Hanuvar debated telling him, then handed it over, watching to see how Vace reacted. If he didn't read Volani, it would be easy to deceive him.

But Vace's eyes roved over it with the air of a man who understood what he was looking at before swinging up to look to Tentor, then Hanuvar.

"Girl," he said, "was it aimed for the praetorian, or Tentor?"

"I don't know. I didn't see it right away."

"And I was watching the hole. One of them is Volani. Or works with them." Vace faced them both, sword ready.

Tentor raised palms defensively. "I'm no Volani! Maybe it's the girl!"

"She's the governor's daughter," Vace reminded him with contempt, then looked at Hanuvar. "You could read this."

"So could you," Hanuvar pointed out.

"I can. But I know who I am, and I don't know who you really are."

"He can't be in league with them," Julia protested.

"He's not," Vace said. "But one of these two has been recognized. And I don't think Tentor here is a good enough actor. The praetorian, though . . . what a fine disguise his identity would make for a clever fugitive."

"I could say the same thing about a revenant," Hanuvar said reasonably, fully aware of the man's sword and the syrupy goo upon the blade. "But I don't think that's true. I think our enemy is trying to divide us further."

"He's right," Julia said quickly. "You said so earlier—Kelenian is with us. Whoever's behind this is trying to set us against each other."

"Do you think?" Vace asked. "I would be more inclined to believe that if I wasn't wondering how the note writer knew one of us could speak Volani."

"Well, if they're listening, then they know you're both investigators, and they might have guessed," Julia suggested.

Tentor sidled to one side, away from Vace, hand still raised. Vace's eyes narrowed to slits.

"Where do you think you're going?" Vace asked.

"Come on, girl." Tentor extended his hand. His eyes flicked up to Vace's. "I know she and I aren't working with any madmen. But I don't know about either of you. You're the asshole. The praetorian's been trying to keep us going. But the note landed next to him. And he's already lied to us once."

"It landed on you," Hanuvar said. "They're trying to set us against each other."

"Can you prove you're who you say you are?" Julia asked Hanuvar. "I believe you," she added. "But is there something you can say to them?"

"You're about Hanuvar's age," Vace said. "And you move like a soldier."

"There are a lot of men my age who are soldiers."

"Are those eyes gray, or blue?"

"What does that matter?"

"It matters a great deal," Vace said. He frowned at Tentor, still sidling toward the end of the hallway, then looked to Hanuvar.

"I think you need to settle down," Julia suggested.

"Think, girl," Vace said arrogantly. "Pretend you're some mad Volani wizard. You set a trap for a bunch of important Dervans. Only, a little way in you realize one of them isn't really Dervan. He's actually Hanuvar. Even a mongrel Volani has some sense of loyalty. And so he writes a note, and tries to send it to Hanuvar. But he messes it up. He was too stupid to write it in code, or didn't know one, or didn't think I would be able to read it."

"But why would Hanuvar be here?" Hanuvar asked.

"To find his sorcerer, of course. But lines of communication were crossed."

Vace's guess wasn't too far from the truth, but Hanuvar sighed in disappointment. "It sounds like you've decided I'm guilty. Our enemies could guess highly placed officers might know Volani. They might even have researched you before they invited you. And they've had hours to find a new way to unnerve us. I'd say they found one."

Vace's mouth ticked up. "That's plausible. But that's the problem with you. You're altogether too plausible. You think too swiftly."

Hanuvar sensed the coming lunge and slammed Vace's arm aside, then leapt back from the vicious back slice.

Tentor dragged Julia out of the way. She screamed in protest.

When the point swung clear of him Hanuvar punched the revenant in the throat and would have driven his knife into his side, but Vace threw himself back.

Hanuvar tossed the mortar dust into his opponent's eyes. Vace blinked out the grit, slashing wildly, and struck Hanuvar along the flank.

Hanuvar didn't have time to worry over the wound; Vace was off balance, so he grabbed him by the other shoulder and smashed him into the wall.

As Vace fought to push away, Hanuvar tripped him to the floor. The revenant landed on his back.

Hanuvar kicked Vace between his legs, kicked the hand still clutching the bloody sword so the weapon popped free, then dropped, thrust his knife into Vace's throat, and tore through him. He climbed to his feet.

Vace stared back in stunned disbelief while he bled out.

"Thanks for the acting lessons," Hanuvar said, his voice low. "I'll remember them when I'm hunting other revenants."

Vace's face froze in a look of dismay when he died.

Hanuvar wasn't upset he'd had to kill a revenant, but that he'd had to do so when the man's sword arm could still have been useful. He wasn't sure what the note really meant, or if whoever was behind this was really a friend.

His gaze flicked up to the hole they'd made and then to the spot where he'd detected the eye slot. Nothing. Finally, he examined the wound slashed through his tunic and discovered a light gash in the muscle above his hip bone. It bled freely, but no organs had been struck.

He felt dizzy, though. If Vace had told the truth about the poison, the liquid on the sword had been a mild paralytic or some sort of soporific, and he'd taken a dose into his bloodstream. If Vace had been lying, then he would shortly be dead. Of course, in this circumstance, even a sedative might lead to his death.

He heard Tentor's cry in alarm, then his scream, and Julia's echo of it.

Hanuvar pressed the bloody tunic to his wound, snatched up the sword, and headed into the corridor.

The lantern sat in the hallway's midst only twenty paces on, near the opening to the treasury room, and Julia knelt beside it, struggling to close the front of her dress. A pair of skinless red corpses lay behind her, glistening wetly.

She looked up at him.

"What happened?" He searched the darkness even as she stood.

"It came out of the darkness," she said. "And it moved so fast—and then . . ."

Hanuvar kept his sword loosely pointed toward her. She stood, and as she took a single step forward he took a single step back. All of the girl's teeth were in place now.

"What's wrong?" the thing who wasn't Julia asked in her voice.

"You've killed her," Hanuvar said.

It stopped its advance. In an eye blink a hundred small, feathery limbs whipped up from behind Julia and pulled back what at first seemed a pink blanket when Julia's dress fell away.

But it hadn't been a blanket, it had been skin, and without it, the creature was revealed for a generally manlike being, toasted brown in color, with two huge eyes. Its frame was a structural mating of a skeleton and insect, with spiny protuberances and internal support bones. Those horrible limbs rose from behind it with incredible speed, bearing another pink burden. The limbs pulled back and they stretched a new skin over the creature. In a moment Hanuvar was staring at Arcella's bodyguard. The skin hung loosely at first, but then the creature stretched with a faint creaking noise, elongating its neck and legs.

Hanuvar struggled with what he saw before him, wondering how he might strike something that moved with such speed. His dizziness did not help.

Those impossible limbs flailed again, withdrew the skin, and brought forth another. This was the sagging, naked flesh of the governor's wife. Again the body beneath adjusted, spread with faint creaking noises.

"You need not fear me," the monster said. It spoke with Arcella's voice. "I can take many forms. Whichever is more comfortable for you."

"That form isn't comfortable," Hanuvar said.

The skin slipped away in an eye blink and another was brought forth. Soon Hanuvar looked on the shape of the youth who had greeted them, though it was bereft of clothes. "Do not worry," it said. "I have orders not to harm you."

"Orders from whom?" Hanuvar asked.

A footfall came from the treasury room and a figure glided into sight. "From me."

He beheld Senidar, an ordinary man of middle age, dressed in a Dervan tunic with blocky blue decorative borders, belted at the waist. It was splotched with old, dark stains that probably weren't wine. He must have raided the wardrobe of his master. His skin was pale, his hairline receding.

Senidar lifted open hands in a welcoming gesture. "I didn't recognize you at first, General, probably because I didn't expect to see you. How could I? It was unexpected. Unanticipated." He laughed, then his eyes tracked to the bloody fabric Hanuvar held to his side. His expression fell. "How bad is your wound?"

"The wound's a graze." He did not share further information about his condition with these two.

"You can lower the sword. The creature's under my control. What are you doing here?"

"I was trying to free a Volani slave."

Senidar laughed and spread his arms. The creature, still wearing the naked skin of the house slave, bent over one of the bodies behind it. There was a fluid, ripping noise, and then it lifted something dark toward its lips.

"I freed myself!" Senidar cried. "That idiot Bavonus gave me all the tools I needed. He thought I could build a weapon for the empire! But I brought a weapon for me. For us!"

"How many has the thing killed?"

"Those you see here. Some of the district leaders. My 'owner,' and his family. Some of the key slaves. I had the taver wear the skin of the owner and free the rest of them."

"So every man and woman in the household," Hanuvar said. "And those with me. And the young lady."

Senidar's brow furrowed. "Why should that bother you? After what the Dervans did to our people?"

"Julia, the young woman it just murdered, was innocent."

Senidar shook his head in disbelief. "I would have thought you could see the truth. Our people were nothing to them but marks on a ledger sheet. They would kill us again, if they could. The entire society didn't care; their entire society profited from us. They are all guilty."

Hanuvar didn't remind him that these people hadn't designed their society, much less engineered the invasion of Volanus. But something in his look informed Senidar's reaction. "If you think I feel remorse, it has been burned away. Like ashes. Like Volanus."

There would be no advancing down that particular line of attack. Hanuvar gestured with his sword at the thing. "Where does this creature come from?"

"From the land nearby," Senidar said, then explained further: "The one you sometimes glimpse from the corner of your eye, where cats and madmen stare."

There was more in that statement than Hanuvar understood, but he was uninterested in further details. "And how do you control it?"

"With the sigil." Senidar lifted his hand. A twisted dark clay circlet rested in his palm, and strings tied through it encircled his wrist. "You have to know spells, as well, to control it. But it likes to obey, because I give it what it craves."

Hanuvar nodded as though he were having an ordinary talk with a sane man. "Can we travel with it?"

"It can assume any shape it has taken. You've seen it, and how fine a mimic it can be! The skins can last a good long while, and it passes well for human. Don't you think?"

"Fairly well."

"It can even mimic the voice of those it killed. I'm sure you noticed how good it is at that."

"Yes." Hanuvar smiled. He was taking on another role, today, that of a man welcoming madness. Antires would have been disappointed by his earlier performance. This one had to be better assayed. He spoke with the subdued pressure of a fellow conspirator. "We must travel in disguise, and you can't constantly have the creature leaving a trail of bodies. That will make us much easier to find. The revenants are already tracking me."

Senidar wasn't so mad he didn't understand that line of reasoning. "Where are you going, and what are your plans?"

"I'll take you into my confidence. Answer me this, though. If you send this creature back, can you call it forward again?"

"Oh, do not send me back," the taver said.

Senidar ignored its pleading. "I could," he said thoughtfully. "It would take more blood, to get it back to us but..." He paused, carelessly adding: "I mean to spill all the Dervan blood I can, anyway. As I'm sure you do."

"I've some experience with it," Hanuvar admitted, and Senidar laughed.

"So, what are your steps? I had thought to work my way to Derva, and the emperor."

"I will go to Derva," Hanuvar acknowledged. "But it must be done stealthily, and not in company of your creature. Send it away. We'll call it back later."

Senidar looked at the taver, finishing its work on a lung. Its eyes looked back at him, its facial expression unreadable.

The wizard touched the sigil resting in his hand, whispering a phrase, and tore a wound through the world's skin. A shuddering gap opened in the darkness to the right of the creature, a wheezing hole into a reeking twilight landscape of sinking suns and a huge blue moon and a sandy ground littered with craters.

Senidar breathed heavily and paled to a corpse-like hue. The sorcery must be taxing, but then it was also disorienting; Hanuvar, growing nauseous, braced himself against the wall with the hand he'd held to his side, for the world spun.

Senidar whispered more words in a sweet, flowing language Hanuvar never wished to learn, and the sigil in his hand glowed redly the while. The creature stared at him and opened its mouth. Little filaments stretched out from between its human teeth and wiggled, like an ant's antenna, and then it turned and considered the portal.

A scent of rent flesh and steaming blood wafted from within, worsening Hanuvar's discomfort.

The creature, though clearly drawn to the gaping opening, did not yet advance through it. It faced Senidar, its brows drawn together in exaggerated consternation. "Please, master," it said. "The prey here is so much more delicious, and simple."

"I will find you, and bring you back, and you will feast on many things."

It stared hard at Hanuvar, then stepped through the aperture. Its master whispered again to the sigil and the portal's edges blurred, faded. Reality was restored and somehow reassuring even with two bodies lying near the lantern, one of them mutilated.

The wizard turned to Hanuvar with a triumphant look. "You see? I have mastered it utterly."

"I see."

"Am I the first man you came to free?"

Hanuvar shook his head no.

Senidar beamed, even as he wiped sweat from his pale forehead. "There are other survivors who are no longer enslaved? I could teach the cleverest among them to do what I have done. Think of the vengeance we could take with an army of those things behind us!"

"I've already thought of that." Hanuvar lowered the sword and considered his wound. It seeped blood but did not leak prodigiously. He needed to get it sewn and bandaged.

"Of course you have," Senidar said with a shake of his head. "They always said you were ten steps ahead of normal men."

"Gather all you need," Hanuvar told him. "Your notes. Your tools. We should take the gems with us."

"Only the gems?"

"We can take some of the denarii, but gems are much easier to travel with. And then please get us out of this place. This basement smells like a charnel house."

"Yes. Yes, of course. With my doings, I have become accustomed to it." Senidar started to turn away, adding. "I would think that you, a general and soldier, would be immune to carnage."

"I've no liking for enclosed spaces. I've spent too much time outdoors."

Senidar believed that. "Ah, of course!"

They returned briefly to the treasury and took a bag of coins along with the gemstones, placed in a smaller cask. Then Senidar pressed against a stone in the wall. A section of it swung open into a dark passage. Cool, clean air wafted down. "This path leads behind all the rooms and up into the master's study. Master," Senidar repeated with a laugh.

"What was this place?" Hanuvar asked. They started inside. Senidar's lantern threw their lurching shadows on the wall.

"Decius Bavonus and his father fancied themselves students of the arcane arts, but they were dabblers. My notes are above. It's an interesting little library, even though they have dozens of useless scrolls mixed in with anything useful."

They arrived at narrow stone stairs, and Senidar glanced back at him solicitously. They started up.

"Don't you need to get that bandaged? How bad is it?"

Hanuvar steadied himself against the wall as he followed up the steps. "I just want to get into the sunlight."

They turned at a landing and arrived at what appeared a dead end until Senidar pushed and they moved out from behind a shelf unit, emerging in a small study with a wooden writing desk and a cushioned stool, overlooking a flowered courtyard going to seed. Hanuvar took all of it in, especially the exit routes, and turned his attention to Senidar. "Gather your notes. We have to hurry. The revenant said he had come alone, but revenants constantly lie. I'm worried you've been a little too overt with your movements."

"If you had let me keep the taver, we would have no need to worry, but I take your point. I keep everything right here."

While he bent to gather scrolls and rooted through the desk, Hanuvar tore a decorative cloth lying across a table supporting some family busts. He used it to wrap his torso. It would hold until he had time for sewing. In the meantime, Senidar finished placing a small pile of scrolls on the desktop.

"I'll need something to carry them in."

"I've a spare saddlebag. Are you sure that's all of it?"

"This is everything important. A lot of it is up here." He tapped his head, smiling. "I have clothes, of course."

"Don't worry about that now." Hanuvar still felt woozy, and blinked, trying to decide how much movement he could dare.

"I hope you don't think this too strange," Senidar said with a sigh. For the first time he sounded embarrassed. "I never meant to study this sort of thing, you know. I merely wanted to see what lay beyond. But once I saw what the Dervans had done . . . I had to do it. You see that, don't you?"

"I see it, and I understand," Hanuvar said gently. "Really, I don't blame you. I blame the Dervans for doing this to you."

"Blame me?"

"I will always wonder what you might have been."

The wizard's eyes widened. Hanuvar swung the pommel of his knife into Senidar's temple. The scholar sagged, and Hanuvar grabbed his head in both hands and twisted powerfully. He heard a snap, then eased the wizard's body to the floor.

"I am sorry," he said with honest regret.

The poison still had its claws in him, and the burst of energy left him shaking. He steadied himself against the desk, gathering his breath, then cut the sigil from Senidar's wrist.

He ground the clay sigil under his heel and tossed all the scrolls into the fireplace. He did not leave until every scrap had burned to ashes.

The afternoon had died and evening was settling in by the time Hanuvar emerged. He carried only a messenger's satchel, filled with scroll tubes. Each held gemstones or denarii mixed in with bits of cloth to keep them from rattling. His wound stung, and he fought fatigue, though dizziness no longer troubled him. Antires loitered close to the exit and his features settled into relief at sight of Hanuvar, though he then eyed him with unvoiced questions.

The other slaves and underlings still took their ease under the nearby trees. Many of them stood as Hanuvar walked clear, Antires following, and he felt their scrutiny. He had long since decided what he would tell them.

"What's taking so long in there, sir?" an officious looking younger man asked. "We were told the negotiations might take a while, but—"

"It wasn't negotiations." Hanuvar halted, speaking both to his questioner and the other onlookers. "It was a trap. There was a madman in there who was drugging people, then skinning them. I barely got out alive. I've recovered his papers and am taking them to the legion, but I need to see a physician. You'll find the bodies of everyone but the wizard in the rooms below, but you'll have a hard time identifying most of them."

They were asking more questions, but Hanuvar took a few steps, wobbling, and Antires made noises about getting him to a healer. The others fell back.

They left the people talking confusedly among themselves and nervously eyeing the dark villa. Hanuvar cantered off and Antires came after. Neither slowed until they'd left the place a good mile behind and ridden past another hillock. Somewhere ahead the circus would be making camp for the evening, and Hanuvar longed for the homely comfort of its tent and the companionship of its people more than he would have expected.

Antires looked at him searchingly. "How much of that explanation was true?"

"They're all dead," Hanuvar answered. "All of them."

"What killed them?"

"A thing from nightmares."

"That's not very specific."

"I'll get into the details later. Although you won't like them."

Antires eyed him doubtfully but didn't pry. "What about the Volani slave? Was he there?"

"He was there," Hanuvar replied. "But I couldn't save him."

※ ※ ※

Hanuvar shared this tale with me only reluctantly, telling me that I might do with it what I willed, though he hoped I would never have it staged. I think he worried it could deepen the fear and loathing of the Volani people felt by so many Dervans.

I long thought that I would honor his wish, but I am older now. This dark episode shows how war and hate and loss can warp even the best of men, and how evil begets evil. And so I have relayed it almost word for word as he narrated it to me.

After that grim day we were happy to rejoin the circus troupe, which by contrast seemed fashioned of light, so that even its most grating members appeared mild irritants at best. Hanuvar's wound healed relatively fast. As we drew ever northwest, we saw the snow-capped bulk of the Ardenines towering in the distance. Before too long we would have to separate, for the circus would return south on the coastal road while Hanuvar and I headed toward the mountains.

We planned only a few more stops together, one at the river town of Miletus, the closest settled point between the Tyvolian mainland and the eastern provinces. With the long Dervan summer nearing its final, most sweltering days, many of the wealthy escaped for more comfortable climes. One of these was Miletus which, if not exactly famed, at least boasted some spas and coastal winds. Thus was it home to a small, wealthy enclave that swelled at this point in the year, which was one of the reasons Mellika always scheduled the circus to pass through, for wealthy viewers often meant extravagant tips.

Among the patricians living there was the son-in-law of none other than Ciprion, the only general to have ever defeated Hanuvar in pitched battle. We did not know that, nor could we guess who it was who had recently departed Derva for reasons of his own.[11]

—Sosilos, Book Four

---

[11] Antires here alludes to what was once an event of common knowledge. A historian, of course, can never assume that his or her audience will understand every inference. One can never be fully certain of what subjects future readers will be cognizant. For example, how much familiarity shall we assume they will have with matters we take utterly for granted, such as women's hair styles or other articles of fashion? ... Only a few weeks prior, Ciprion, accused by his enemies of bribery and graft, appeared upon the floor of the senate not with a defense, but an attack. He brandished his accounts, asking his accusers to search there for the source of the thousands of gold talents his victories had delivered to Dervan coffers. He then tore them in half and threw them contemptuously at the feet of his fellow senators. He announced his resignation from the senate, saying that he was leaving Dervan lands forever, to reside within the provinces, and that he had further willed he be buried there.

This unexpected line of response ended the careers of all but his most clever attackers, but it also weakened many of his adherents, and caused all manner of consternation for them, especially ambitious younger members of his family, who feared their own political futures had been ruined. —*Silenus*

Chapter 11:
Shadow Play

I

Ciprion watched the waters break on the prow as the tubby ship rolled on toward the hazy line where sea met shore. Seagulls coasted in the clear blue sky over a trio of fishing boats anchored closer to land, their masts outlined starkly against the morning sky.

He shaded his eyes from the glare of the sun, rising almost in his face, wondering again what he would say to his daughter. Disappointment and anxiety would light in equal measure, if they had not already blazed, for she and her husband might already have received news of his speech on the senate floor and the sale of his properties in Derva. Neither action was likely to have benefitted her husband's political ambitions and neither he nor Cornelia were unlikely to understand. Even his old friend Laelius had thought him mad.

Only one person had remained steadfast, and he heard her sandals on the deck, drawing near. The sailors knew to keep clear of him in the mornings, and he had made that simpler by selecting the same out-of-the-way span of rail, absent barrels or bales or anything that looked vital.

He turned to show his wife his profile and to acknowledge her without really taking her in and wondered what she saw as she came forward. A man of middle age, his eyebrows too thick, and dark, like his unruly hair. Probably she would be looking for his eyes. Amelia had always liked his eyes.

But then he had always liked hers, right from the start, arranged marriage or no.

"You look as though you're brooding again." Amelia put her hands on the rail beside him. Her voice had retained some roughness since she'd dealt with that cough in the autumn last year. She had recovered, but her voice hadn't.

"I'm just enjoying the air," Ciprion said.

"You're a terrible liar."

He gave her his best smile, which had once charmed foreign princes and the occasional princess. Her long black hair was pinned so that it crowned her in a braid and fell only to her shoulders. Threaded with gray, it was still shining and lustrous. Her dress was a pleasant blue with a conservative patrician neckline, and the amber at her throat brought out a sympathetic hue in her light brown eyes. Over the long years he'd known her, Amelia's waist had broadened and her arms and neck had thickened, but no one could have convinced him she was no longer comely, for his tastes had changed and his love had rooted deeply. "You are as insightful as you are charming," he said.

Over the sound of her gentle laughter and the rush of waves and wind in the rigging, he heard another set of footsteps drawing close. He didn't turn, for fear he might make eye contact with someone he'd rather discourage from joining them. "Can you report good news?" he asked quietly of Amelia.

She replied in a mock military whisper: "I regret, General, that the enemy advances." And then she added: "Do be kind. He's mostly harmless."

Torvus stopped beside him, bestowing upon them the greeting beloved of acquaintances everywhere. "Good morning to you, Senator, and lady. What fine weather."

"Yes," Amelia said. "Good morning."

Ciprion nodded to him. Torvus was tall, with a square jaw and curling brown hair touched with gray. While grooming this morning he had missed a few spots on his chin, but then shaving on a rocking deck was a challenge.

"It shouldn't be so long until we see the shore now, should it?" Torvus asked.

"Indeed not," Ciprion replied pleasantly, then returned to

consideration of the ever-shifting whitecaps and the blurry green mainland.

Another man would have heeded this invitation to depart, but Torvus pretended not to have noticed. "I wonder if you had heard the news transmitted from the sun telegraph this morning?"

Ciprion's father would have corrected the man's semantics, for one did not hear anything from a sun telegraph. Via a series of towers settled on the islets known as the Fangs, it was possible to flash messages from the Tyvolian peninsula over to the eastern provinces, and because their vessel was on a course parallel to that of the towers, the flashes could be noted from the deck.

"I did not," Ciprion answered.

"Ah. Well, my friend the first mate—I believe I mentioned him yesterday—my friend actually reads the signals."

"How ingenious of him," Amelia said. "I saw those flashes, but how someone can make sense of them defies my understanding." She smiled blandly.

Amelia played the part of a dutiful, simple-minded wife, and the fool would never know. Had she wished, she could easily have learned to deduce the signal sequence.

"It's a complex business, my lady," Torvus said, "but my friend is very clever."

"So it seems," Amelia replied. "But is it wise of him to be spreading news of a military nature?"

"He told only me. And I thought it would be good of me to relay the information to your husband." Torvus held off saying more, as if he were a third rate tragedian waiting for a fellow actor to finish a forgotten line before he dared say his own. He even drew the moment out longer, as though trying to prompt a bit of dialogue. "Because I think it might concern him, gravely."

Ciprion tilted his head, pretending casual interest rather than displaying his irritation.

"Do tell," Amelia said.

That prompt was all Torvus had required. He said, with affected solemnity, "The immediate family of Senator Marcius has been murdered."

The amused twinkle vanished from Amelia's eyes. "By the Gods."

"Every last one of his children is dead," Torvus continued, "along with an entire cavalry troop. No one's sure how because there were no wounds and no sign of poison."

"And Catius?" Ciprion asked.

"Vanished." Torvus tried to look grim, and failed, betraying a hint of gleeful triumph at finally engaging Ciprion's attention.

"And there is no explanation?" Amelia asked. "No one saw anything?"

Torvus shook his head. "Messages through the sun telegraph are short and . . . bereft of details."

Amelia did not say the word sorcery, but it was surely on her mind, and she gave her husband a warning look.

"The family of Senator Marcius lived not so far from our destination. I would surely hate to think you were sailing near to anything dangerous, General. You or your charming wife."

"I am no longer a general," Ciprion reminded him.

"I mean merely to honor your service." Torvus stepped closer. "What would you say if I were to tell you I had more precise information?"

"I would be curious."

"Of course, of course." Torvus glanced sidelong at Amelia. "Forgive me, my lady, but I'm not sure the words I have are for your ears."

"Amelia provides my finest counsel," Ciprion said. "While she might be disappointed by foul language or actions, I don't think you will shock her."

"It's not foul language I mean to share, but foul plans."

"And you wish a fee." Amelia had warned Ciprion to be patient, so it was odd to hear a sharper note in her voice than Ciprion himself had used.

"By way of gratitude. That is all," Torvus said hastily. "After all, the news comes with some risk to me."

"It's risky to repeat words that someone told you in a sun telegraph?" Amelia asked, as though the matter remained unclear to her.

Torvus shook his head. "I knew this information before that. Sheer chance brought us together upon this ship. Suppose I was to tell you that someone is stalking your husband?"

"Hanuvar, I suppose?" Ciprion suggested. "Risen from the dead?"

Torvus actually looked taken aback. Not as though he was disappointed his secret had been guessed, but because Ciprion wasn't taking him seriously.

"Be off," Ciprion said. "No one is after me."

"I'm not selling you ghost stories," Torvus pressed. "This is real."

"I thank you for your consideration. Now, I have other matters to attend. Good day, sir."

"Is it the fee at which you balk?" His voice grew wheedling. "A sense of security is priceless, isn't it?"

"My husband has spoken," Amelia said. "Please do not end our association rudely."

Torvus bowed his head to her. "For your sake, my lady, I am almost tempted to reveal what I know for free. But a man cannot fill his stomach with thanks. Perhaps you will change your mind before disembarkation."

He bowed his head to Ciprion, too, then retreated toward the deck house.

Ciprion waited for his steps to recede before he addressed his wife. "Do you still think him harmless?"

"He just wants money."

"So do we all. Our funds aren't what they were, are they?"

"But what if he really is telling the truth?"

"He has been trying to touch me since he first saw me aboard, and the sun telegraph inspired a story from him."

"I should think what he said would inspire some curiosity from you. First Caiax is nearly killed, and now Catius' entire family is murdered."

"You think this has a connection to me?"

Her gaze sharpened. "You know the rumors about what happened to Caiax."

"Yes, it's entirely credible Hanuvar rose from a tomb he wasn't buried in, then hunted Caiax down with some kind of fog demon." He delivered his response in an amused, exasperated tone, hoping she would see the humor of the situation and laugh.

She did not. "The specifics may be wrong, but what about the truth of the matter? Who would Hanuvar most blame for what the empire did to his people?" Amelia paused, then answered her own question. "Caiax and Catius. And Ciprion."

"It is unlikely he lives. And it is even less likely he would come after me."

"If you hadn't beaten him, he might have won the second war. Or at least come out with a stalemate. And then the empire couldn't have moved against Volanus in the third war. He has no reason to love you."

"I've met the man."

Her voice rose in indignation. "Just because you were gentlemanly to one another, you think you *know* him? Have you conversed with him after our empire sacked and burned his city? Don't you think that might change him? Wouldn't it change you, if you had lost everything?"

His answer was slow in coming. "If I survived and the senate burned, I should be pleased, for the place is a cesspool. But if the people, and you, and our family had been wiped away..." Ciprion's voice fell. "If he does live, I can't imagine how he must feel."

Amelia did not lack empathy. She looked morose for a moment, but her brief sympathy for an enemy general vanished in a flush of concern for her husband. "He might be mad with vengeance. Oh, don't shake your head at me. I know you're fond of him, though you will not say it. But if there is one thing that could break a man like you—and you seem to think he is like you—it would be what Hanuvar has endured."

His reply was bitter. "If he lives, then Derva may deserve what he will hand her."

She put two fingers to her heart. "Do I deserve a dead or missing husband?"

This shamed him, and he spoke gently. "You deserve only the best things life may give."

"Then will you please take Torvus more seriously? It has been long years since you had a sorcerer on your staff to protect you."

"I shall take the matter under advisement. For you, wisest of counselors."

"Do not think on it too long, for we'll reach land soon." She fell silent briefly. "Pull your thoughts together. I'm going to make sure the slaves have our things properly sorted."

Of course the house slaves would have their things properly sorted—they had been with the family for decades and knew their business better than Amelia herself. He squeezed her hand as she left, acknowledging that she meant to give him space.

He could not imagine a future encounter with Hanuvar; the idea was ludicrous. Instead, unbidden, his thoughts returned to their first meeting.

After long years, Ciprion had brought the war to the fields near Volanus, and somehow—he had never learned how—Hanuvar had withdrawn his entire army from Utria. Ciprion and the great Volani general had dismounted in a wide space in the scrub land between their army camps.

Ciprion wasn't sure what the enemy general hoped to achieve, but he had accepted Hanuvar's invitation so he might meet the enemy he had so long respected, a man whose stunning victories had taught him much about winning his own.

That day, less than twenty years previous, Ciprion had worn his legionary breastplate and helm, with no sign of his office but the fine gold detailing on his helm. His translator, like Hanuvar's, waited two steps behind.

Hanuvar's garb was even simpler than Ciprion's own—a well-maintained but worn breastplate, a helm tucked under one arm. His beard was dark and well trimmed, his hair showing a few strands of silver. His weathered face was handsome and creased with lines that spoke of both humor and sorrow, and his blue-gray eyes burned with fierce intelligence. They fastened on Ciprion as Hanuvar raised his hand in greeting.

Ciprion returned the gesture, wishing he had removed his helmet. To do so now seemed an imitation, and so he left it in place.

"We may speak Dervan," Hanuvar said smoothly in Ciprion's native tongue, then switched to another: "Or we can converse in Herrenic, if you prefer. I know you enjoy the work of their scholars."

Ciprion inclined his head in acknowledgment. Hanuvar was known to have excellent intelligence sources. "An interest I hear you share. Dervan is fine. I assume you wished the translators here only to bear witness."

"Yes."

"You invited me," Ciprion said formally. "And so I have come."

"I'm pleased you accepted my invitation. I wanted to meet the consul who had taken Nova Lovana and won Biranus for his people."

"I confess that I wished to meet you as well. Your own achievements are hardly unknown to me."

Hanuvar chuckled.

He was more amiable than Ciprion had expected, and it awakened an answering spirit in him. "I have seen you before, you know," he said.

"So I'm told. Did you really pull your father to safety during that skirmish on the Icanus?"

"I did, though the storytellers have the details wrong. I didn't see you there. I glimpsed you, from a great distance, at the battle of Acanar."

"From which you led a small band of soldiers free."

"You know my history."

"I study all my opponents. Especially those whom I respect."

Ciprion accepted that with a formal nod. Almost he returned the compliment, and would wish, in later days, that he had.

With a subtle shift in his stance, Hanuvar suggested the time for informalities had ended; he turned to the point of their meeting. "You've been successful, Consul. And fortunate. But you know as well as I that fortune takes sudden turns. Success can elude even the most talented of men. Do you think Derva can gain more than she's already won if we continue this war? You're far from your lands, and will find no safe harbor should your forces be scattered in defeat."

Ciprion studied him, wondering what he might be prepared to offer.

"I know your record," Hanuvar continued, "and I think you and I may be the only commanders in this conflict who see war not as a means of acquisition or gratification, but as a road to greater peace."

"War is no poet's song," Ciprion answered. "It should be the last resort of honorable men."

Hanuvar looked pleased. "I would not have proposed this meeting if I didn't think it would benefit us both."

"Do you mean to propose terms different from the ones I offered?"

"We will relinquish all the islands, including the Deralta group. We will leave Biranus to you."

Ciprion did not immediately reply; he was waiting to see if Hanuvar would offer more. When he did not, he shook his head ever so slightly. "You offer an armistice without the surrender of your war vessels or the return of Tyvolian deserters and fugitives in your army." Ciprion raised a hand before Hanuvar could respond. "I know they compose the greater number of your veterans, and that you would no more betray them than I would my own troops. But I cannot accept less than the terms already agreed upon in Derva."

Hanuvar studied him, then bowed his head. "I didn't hold much hope for an accord between us, but I wished to meet you, and I do not regret it. We've no choice but to work to destroy the other's army."

"Duty gives us no other option."

They raised hands in salute, then parted. And soon thereafter, they sounded the trumpets and sent their lines into battle. And after that long, terrible day, Ciprion emerged triumphant.

But it had been a close thing. If Hanuvar's cavalry reinforcements had arrived in time, things would have gone very differently. Ciprion had never failed to reflect upon that, even in the midst of the triumph the emperor held for him. If luck had swung just a little differently, it might have been he who'd fled the field.

II

Help was always needed with the animals, for the circus required care not just for those who performed, but for the small army of horses, oxen, and mules that pulled their wagons.

Antires had suggested he join the small team of gladiators in their mock battles, disguising himself in a helmet with a face shield. But Hanuvar had no inclination to risk injury even in the carefully choreographed battles, nor did he want rumors of his martial prowess spreading among the circus members. And so he spent the majority of his time brushing fur, forking hay, or shoveling manure.

Work with the animals kept him busy, which was good, for it was harder to brood while he labored. Every hour he was conscious that not moving toward Derva must mean the death of more of his people. While he knew he would do them no good if he was identified, the slow progress tore at him.

They had arrived at the settlement of Miletus the previous evening. Now the early afternoon had come and only a few hours remained before the night's show. Hanuvar worked the corral where the horses were loosely tied, plying a rusty pitchfork to flip clumps of manure into a small four-wheeled cart. The sky was bright above, laced with clouds, and the sun was warm on his back. Flies buzzed, and horses stamped their hooves and flicked their tails to ward them off. The animals stood in a line in front of their fodder. Antires thought himself clever to remark that Hanuvar first tended what went in the front end, and then took care of what came out the back. Apparently he was unaware that it was a very old joke.

When Hanuvar was most of the way down the line of animals, Antires wandered up to watch. He was dressed in a red tunic and sandals, his hair and new beard neatly combed. Hanuvar guessed he had just finished running lines for some of the scenes the circus performed each evening. Shortly the actor would don his bright, showy performance clothes.

Antires said nothing, though his nose wrinkled at the concentrated scent of warm horse, and dried grass, and droppings.

"You could stop staring, and grab a pitchfork," Hanuvar suggested.

"And then I might be as fragrant as you are."

Hanuvar plopped another scoop of moist manure onto the cart. "Who is more fragrant? The man shoveling, or the man he tripped into the manure?"

"The answer to that riddle's best learned at a distance. I should finish getting ready." Antires said this but did not leave.

"And yet you stand and stare."

"At you, shoveling horse shit."

It amused him that Antires assumed such work beneath him. "I was a statesman for years. This is cleaner work."

Antires' eyes flashed in good humor, but he still looked doubtful. "I know you want to work behind the scenes, but you could at least help with some other duty. You could manage logistics, say."

"The circus has managers. I work with horses. I shovel shit. Horse, donkey, ox, leopard, or elephant. Aren't you the one who told me to own the role?"

So saying, he hefted the pitchfork, lifted the cart handle, and dragged it behind him as he walked the short distance from the horse corral to where the lone elephant was picketed. He scratched the side of Kordeka's great gray head and she touched his shoulder lightly with her trunk, flapping her ears, then resumed transferring hay from the large pile before her into her mouth.

Hanuvar dragged the cart to her back end, Antires shadowing.

Elephant manure was more odiferous than horse manure, wetter, and, naturally, larger. He decided he should probably dump what he'd accumulated, and was getting ready to drag the cart away when he heard a young, cultured Dervan voice near Kordeka's head.

"It's a female elephant," said a girl's voice.

A small boy querulously objected. "Well it's big enough to be a war elephant. Did you ever fight an elephant, Grandfather?"

"Of course he fought elephants, silly," the girl answered. "He fought masses of them."

Hanuvar started around the side to ensure the children were keeping an appropriate distance.

"Will there be any elephant fights at the circus, Grandfather?" the boy asked.

Hanuvar recognized the older voice that answered within the first few words, simple as they were: "It's not that sort of circus." But he'd already stepped into sight, and discovered Ciprion, who casually glanced up while answering the boy and girl. "It takes far more skill to train an elephant to do tricks than to . . . lead one into battle."

Both men ceased movement altogether; Hanuvar was not even aware that he breathed. For once his keen reflexes deserted him entirely, and his intellect was a barren desert.

He had at least eight years on Ciprion, and yet the Dervan looked older, his face weathered by disappointment. His dark brown eyes remained keen, however, and bright with surprise, then wary caution, in swift succession. The tunic Ciprion wore should have borne a broad purple stripe, as befitted a senator, but there was only a well-tailored brown border, suggestive of leaves.

The length of their stare might have lasted but a few heartbeats, or might have dragged a quarter hour, so slowed was time, so absent was Hanuvar from contemplation. He was just starting to raise his hand in greeting when Ciprion's eyes slid past his own and he turned back to the children. "We should go," he said.

"To the leopards?" the little boy asked.

Ciprion put his hand to the boy's back, moving him along. "Maybe later."

"But I do wish to see the leopards," the boy objected with a politeness beyond his years.

"Not now."

Hanuvar watched Ciprion guide them away, out beyond the empty wagons. The Dervan general neared a pair of soldiers idly walking along the circus edges. Hanuvar partly expected him to wave them close, to point them toward his old adversary.

But Ciprion passed the legionaries without comment, and he and his grandchildren walked out of sight behind a wagon.

Antires joined Hanuvar, staring off toward where Ciprion had disappeared. "What was that about?" the actor asked. "Did you know that man?"

"It's Ciprion." Hanuvar sounded as surprised as he felt.

"Ciprion?" Antires repeated, then demanded: "*The* Ciprion?"

Hanuvar didn't bother responding, and Antires swore. "Did he recognize you?"

"Yes."

"But he didn't even say hello," Antires said. "He could have said something to those soldiers. But he didn't. What do you think he's going to do?"

"Avoid the messy consequences." Hanuvar finally turned away.

"Why?"

"I'm inconvenient."

Antires puzzled over that. "I thought you were, well . . . friends."

"I wouldn't put it like that."

"Wouldn't you?" Antires asked. "He refused to make your personal surrender part of the peace terms. And he told the senate it wasn't Derva's business to interfere in the affairs of Volanus."

"He is an honorable man."

"Do you think he's hunting you?"

Hanuvar shook his head. "He was showing the circus to his grandchildren."

Antires looked doubtful. "What are you going to do?"

"I'm going to do my job." Hanuvar started back toward the cart. "Don't you have lines to practice?"

Antires sighed, lifted both arms to the sky as though demonstrating his frustration to an invisible audience, then walked off.

While Hanuvar rolled the cart away, he tried to reconcile the appearance of the man he'd just seen with the one he'd last encountered in Volanus.

On that occasion, almost four years ago, Ciprion had been wearing not just a senator's purple bordered tunic, but a full toga. He had arrived in Volanus with the official delegation to accept the final installment of the indemnity the people of Volanus had been paying to their victors every six months since the conclusion of the second war.

Hanuvar had been on hand to receive Ciprion formally, in the vast, vaulted Hall of the People, where he had presided as one of the two shofets welcoming the Dervan visitors. But it wasn't until a private dinner that evening that he'd had the opportunity to speak with his former foe.

Ciprion had arrived with his long-time friend and lieutenant Laelius, who had watched Hanuvar just as suspiciously as Hanuvar's brother Melgar stared at the Dervans throughout the meal.

While Hanuvar's one-armed brother and the scarred Laelius smoldered at one another across the rectangular table, Ciprion had remarked how impressed he was to see the prosperity of Volanus. They were dining Volani style, sitting upright in high-backed chairs in an upper floor of Hanuvar's villa. The Dervans wore fine white tunics with an eques's and a senator's colors, respectively, and he and Melgar had donned simple light blue tunics, short sleeved. He had given his guests the view overlooking the vast harbor, alive with lantern lights as the sun sank, a small mirror to the glory of the stars shining over the sea. The steeples of the great temples on the harbor islands were dark outlines against the night and the water.

Laelius, a broad man of middle years, shifted his toga and frowned at Ciprion's comment, adding: "Volanus prospers while Derva toils. It's a strange state of affairs for the victor and the vanquished."

Hanuvar responded without rancor. "We are allies now, and no longer at war."

That might have been the end of it, but Melgar had to interrupt. Age had sharpened his boyish looks so his features remained striking, despite a bright scar above his beard line. But the spark that had always burned in his eyes suggested fury now, not mischief.

"Whereas," Melgar said, wine drawling his Dervan accent, "Derva wars with both the Arbateans and the Cerdians. Your new emperor may be spreading himself thin."

Laelius' frown deepened.

Hanuvar knew neither Ciprion nor his friend cared for expansionist polices that the new emperor was so keen upon, for they drained imperial resources. But Ciprion had more or less removed himself from politics whereas Laelius had to remain involved or cease to be relevant.

"Are you waiting for the empire to spread itself thin?" Laelius asked Melgar.

"What is it you're waiting for? The emperor's table scraps?" Melgar looked meaningfully at Ciprion. "Or are Ciprion's good enough for you?"

Laelius' lip curled.

Hanuvar spoke shortly, and deliberately in Dervan. "Melgar, these are guests in my house."

Melgar's smile faded. He met his brother's eyes and a measure of shame actually reached him. "Yes. Forgive me." He bowed his head infinitesimally toward the Dervans. "I'm afraid I have a sour stomach. I'm sure it has nothing to do with present company." He bowed his head to his brother, rose, and left.

Hanuvar fought down an urge to ask him to stay, knowing his brother would return, but that his presence would in no way improve the tension. He'd have to handle this alone.

He looked across the table at Laelius. "I must apologize for my brother's conduct."

"We understand," Ciprion said.

Laelius bowed his head, though he still frowned. "There are men like him in Derva too. Veterans who remember the pains of the war too well."

"Are many of your people as angry as he?" Ciprion asked.

"I could not hope to count them," Hanuvar admitted. "But then the Dervan wounded are more numerous, for the war was on your lands until you brought your army here." He paused, then addressed their concerns directly. "I wish you to understand something. I know it would be folly to war with you. We were outnumbered by you even before we surrendered our ships and weapons after the armistice. It is my hope we will be allies, although it may be a generation before Dervans realize our sincerity."

"I'm glad you see it that way," Laelius said stiffly.

Silence fell across the table, and just as Hanuvar was regretting sending the harpist away earlier, Ciprion quietly addressed his friend. "Laelius, I wonder if you would give us a moment alone. Perhaps you could seek Melgar and try a more amicable line of conversation."

"Maybe I'll just get a drink." Laelius looked hesitantly at his friend, as if he were uncertain whether he really ought to leave, then, at a reassuring nod, departed the chamber and could be heard taking the stairs down to the courtyard, where the harpist played among the flowers.

"I wish my brother hadn't made that table scraps comment," Hanuvar said.

"Laelius shouldn't have pushed him."

"It was a small push. Melgar would have planted himself on a hill at Mazra and fought until his death if I'd let him. He's been aching to fight every Dervan he meets ever since. As if he's angry he didn't get to die battling."

Ciprion lifted a spoon, lowered it, sighed. "I'm afraid our people are doomed to this. Even the good-hearted ones. Laelius, your brother—they want peace, and they're still at each other's throats. Sometimes..." His voice trailed off.

"What?"

Ciprion hesitated a moment longer, then swept up his hand in an elegant gesture, indicating Hanuvar. "What you said, at Mazra, was right. You and I may be the only ones who see war as an unpleasant necessity to get us peace."

Hanuvar lifted his goblet. "Here's to peace."

Ciprion raised his own in salute, and they drank.

With infinite care, Ciprion returned the goblet to the table. He did not speak, but Hanuvar sensed him gathering his words, and left him the silence to find them. "Hanuvar," he said at last, "what you've accomplished here in five years is amazing. The senate thought it would take twenty-five years to pay off the indemnity."

"You have to know where to find the money."

"You made enemies looking."

He now knew the topic Ciprion was moving toward. "Enemies who've gone to Derva."

The senator's thick brows climbed his forehead. "Your intelligence agents are still in place, then?"

"My adversaries aren't half so clever as they think."

"How much do you know?" Ciprion asked.

"I know some of my political enemies are telling your senate I'm in negotiations with the king of Cerdia. Among other things."

"Are you?"

Hanuvar shook his head. "If Volanus is to thrive, all its people must prosper. None will prosper if we ally with Cerdia. But you already know it."

He had hoped Ciprion knew it and was gratified when the man nodded. "I wanted to watch you say it. I believe you. But my opinion doesn't count as much as it should." His voice grew grave. "They will come for you."

This was new information, and Hanuvar watched, waiting to hear what Ciprion meant.

It seemed at first the Dervan was changing the subject, for he next asked: "Do you know what our noble families have in common with yours?"

The answer was simple. "They hate losing money."

"And they are allied against you," Ciprion said. "Your aristocrats want you out because you raised their taxes. Our patricians want you out because you're too damned effective. They've drawn up plans to frame and arrest you and cart you back to Derva. I could never have predicted such an alliance...but I see from your expression you must have anticipated it anyway."

"I have contingency plans," Hanuvar admitted.

"So you know how to stop them?"

"Stop them?" He wished he might manage that. "No. Merely how to exit. I'd hoped I was overestimating the strength of their greed."

"Never underestimate a rich man's thirst for money."

"Of course. How long do I have?"

"A month. Maybe a little more. They expect my inspection tour to lull you into security, and then they'll visit. Charges and false documents will be handed over. Your senate will be shocked, horrified even, to learn how you've jeopardized the state security by leaguing against your loyal ally Derva." He smiled sadly. "You know Etipholes has King Tauric say to his ungrateful people: 'I was a fool to trust the faith of men.'"

"So said the tyrant. But it's not the people who've turned against me. It's those who feign to lead them." Hanuvar spoke sharply. "They're parasites. Every step of the way their short-sighted policies crippled us. If they'd fully backed me in the war, even you could not have beaten us."

"I know that."

Already Hanuvar regretted his outburst. "Forgive my bitterness."

"Because you learned you must leave your home?" Ciprion sighed. "You spoke with brief anger and didn't even curse. I would not have done so well." He looked as though he meant to say more, then changed the subject. "I had hoped you might have some clever countermeasure."

"I have many strategies to halt my own malcontents, but none to stop Dervan politicians. Not anymore."

"You told me once that fortune can take unexpected turns."

"Sometimes fortune turns on the forge of honor. I am grateful to you for your warning, Ciprion."

The Dervan bowed his head with great dignity. "Were our circumstances reversed, you would have done the same for me."

III

If things had gone better with Ciprion, Torvus might already be on his way southeast. But the old general was a miser, or he himself had been too obvious in his eagerness. You had to play with the dice on the table, and so Torvus had resigned himself to his course, however unpleasant it was. As he passed among the circus tents he neared a pretty younger woman who stopped and asked if he needed help. At one time she might have returned his own smile in a more interested way, which reminded him, again, of how old he was getting. He didn't think his disappointment showed in any obvious way. "I'm looking for Mellika," he said. "I haven't visited with her in many a year." He pointed to Mellika's wagon. Almost he told the woman who he really was, but he hadn't wanted to alert anyone to his presence, which is why he'd bypassed the Ruminian when he'd spotted her painting the toenails of her elephant.

The young woman let him walk through. He felt her watching him surreptitiously as he knocked on the wagon door.

His daughter bade him enter: "Come in."

He took the three steps up, opened the door, and stepped through into a small chamber rich with dark paneled wood. His daughter sat at a fold-up desk near an open window. She glanced up, then did a double take. He would have liked to have seen a smile, but her expression was neutral at best.

Torvus closed the door behind him.

Mellika had grown thick, like her mother after the first few years. She had her pretty long-lashed eyes, and his chin. She was swathed in a dress with a colorful cape and adorned with multiple bangles and bits of jewelry. The most important of it was the silver chain about her neck, the same one her mother had once worn. The amulet it bore was hidden beneath her high collar, which was threaded in red with the outlines of circus animals.

"You look well," Torvus said, and lifted his hand to show the small amphora he'd carried with him all the way from Utria. "I brought you some Fadurian wine."

"Father." She said nothing more.

"Aren't you going to offer me a cup? This is your favorite. I brought it to split with you."

Wordless, Mellika reached to her left, opened a panel from a space he knew well, and withdrew two goblets. She pushed the second toward him.

He wondered why she said nothing, not even a comment about his arrival or an accusation about his trying to bribe her with a drink. But that didn't matter, as long as she consumed it.

Torvus uncorked the flask, poured a generous amount into her goblet, and then a little into his own, and sat it on the table beside her.

"To your mother," he said, and lifted the drink.

"To mother." Mellika saluted the air and drank while Torvus pretended to do so. After, she smacked her lips appreciatively. Fadurian wine was expensive for good reason: the mountain vintage was one of the best in all Tyvol.

She looked as though she was readying to say something, so he spoke first: "I know I've done little enough to win your love. But you are my blood."

"That's what you gave me," she said coolly. "That, and an introduction to your favorite wines."

"I gave you life," he pointed out.

If there had been any warmth in those pretty eyes, it was vanished now. "You had less to do with my life than a rutting goat has with its kids." She set down the goblet. "You came here for a favor. State it."

"You're not going to ask what I'm doing here, rather than in Derva?"

"That would imply I cared, Torvus. My show's going on in less than an hour, so let's keep this brief."

He willed her to drink more while he acted as though he felt uncertain. "Things are bad for me, daughter. Worse than you can know."

She frowned. "And you need money."

He shook his head. He pretended to drink more, hoping that would encourage her, but she just watched, stony eyed. "A man always needs money. But this is different. I've gotten myself in debt."

She shook her head slowly from side to side. "I have people depending on me, and money's tight in an outfit like this. You know that."

"It's not money I need. I'm in debt to a sorcerer. He's a bad man."

"How did you—" She cut herself off and sighed. "Never mind. You think I'd have learned by now."

She hadn't learned enough by half. He just had to keep her talking long enough for the drug—if she'd imbibed enough of it—to take effect. He supposed there was always a faint chance she'd be convinced by what he said, but she was no easy mark.

"It started out small, like these things usually do. I owed him some money and thought I could sell him my services. But he got word that I used to own something he thinks is important. And he's told me he'll let me go free if I get it for him."

"Mother's amulet?"

The speed of her deduction surprised him, and he stared in appreciation. It was the equivalent of being caught flat-footed in the arena, and it left him open for further probing.

"By Arepon, I suppose you're going to tell me now it wasn't you who told him about it. 'Got word,'" she repeated with a contemptuous snort. "How else would he hear about it?"

"I was desperate." He tried not to stare at the goblet, or the little amphora.

She glared at him. "It was hers. Not yours."

"He'll kill me," he said. "I need that amulet."

"The circus needs this amulet. Without its blessing, how do you think my animals will manage the tricks they're known for?"

"You put too much stock in it. Your trainers are excellent."

"They are. But the amulet makes a difference, and you know it. Are you trying to tell me the sorcerer wants an amulet that doesn't work? Do you realize how stupid *that* argument sounds?"

She was working herself up, and he realized it might be mere moments before she simply threw him out.

He held up his hands. "Look, it's different than you think."

"Oh? Is it? Right now I think you promised a wizard something that isn't yours, and you're not going to get it. Is there something else?"

"What I'm trying to tell you is that it doesn't matter what you want. It doesn't even matter what I want. He got out of me that it's here, and he means to have it. I begged him to let me talk to you first. You may not believe this, but I don't want any harm to come to you. And harm *will* come to you."

Her lips twisted into a scowl. "Get out."

"You need to listen to me. He will kill. That's what he does."

He reached to the pouch at his waist. He had meant to leave this with her when he departed, but he had it now, and it might work the trick. He took a single step forward and set it on the desk, where it struck with a weighty jingle.

"Lead and a few coins?"

"All coins. It's not much. But it's all I've saved. It's for you. For the amulet. Take it, and you need never see me again. And you won't see him. Or, more likely, one of his creatures."

"Where did you get it?" Mellika sighed and, finally, reached again for the goblet. She took a long drink, set the goblet down, then touched the side of the bag. She didn't open it. Her eyes flicked up to him and they looked a little bit less harsh. "I don't truly know if the amulet works," she admitted.

"All the more reason to give it to me then. The wizard thinks it does."

"Mother always thought it did."

"But she was gifted at training. And so are you. Some people have a knack, and then they look to the gods or amulets or potions for explanation. You know as well as I how a con can be run."

"Probably not as well as you." Her hand touched the amulet under her collar. "What if you're wrong, and I give it to you, and the wizard discovers it doesn't work? Won't you be in danger?" She stared for a second and then put a hand to the desk. She swayed, blinked long and hard. "What..."

Torvus winced. He hadn't guessed he could really convince her. "I'm sorry, girl. You can keep the money. It's more than you may think. The effect should wear off by midnight."

She fought its effects and stood, hand protectively on the necklace. She glared hatred at him.

And then she sagged. He caught her before she struck her head, and manhandled her around the desk, gently as he could. He managed to get her onto the cot built into the carriage side beyond the desk. Once, some thirty years before, she'd been conceived on that very pull-down mattress. He laid her on her side, then, with great care, eased the amulet off her head. He considered it then, the old red stone with the claw mark and simple outline of a snarling cat, then ruffled her hair, eyed the sack of coins regretfully, and headed for the door.

He closed it very gently and was starting forward when a hand landed upon his shoulder.

He spun and immediately took a powerful blow to the chin. Torvus was no stranger to bar fights, but a rain of punches followed, each one landing in the place he wasn't blocking. A solid belt to the belly doubled him over and then somehow he was on the ground.

He blinked up at a muscular man with graying hair and a dangerous look in his eye. Only belatedly did he realize the stranger was already holding a delicate chain in his hand, and that it was the same one the amulet was attached to, cupped in the stranger's palm.

The pretty young woman he'd encountered earlier stood at his side, frowning, and on his other side was the Ruminian woman he knew must be little Shenassa, all grown up.

Probably one had been listening at the window for most of the conversation. Maybe the pretty one had recognized him by description and run off for help. It didn't matter. What mattered was the danger both he and his daughter were in.

"You don't understand," he explained. "I'm trying to save Mellika." He felt his jaw and winced. No teeth had been knocked out, praise the gods, but the stranger's attack was going to leave multiple bruises.

"Help her?" Shenassa asked. "By poisoning her? By taking her amulet?" She spat.

Torvus sat, but did not yet climb to his feet. "A bad man is after her. A powerful one. He'll send a beast to kill her."

"How much did you hear?" the stranger asked Shenassa.

"Enough."

"Who are you?" Torvus asked the man.

"A friend. You need to go."

"Listen to me." Torvus rose, and reading the stranger's wary gaze he showed empty palms. "I'm trying to help her. Kontar's a real wizard. He's sending a beast to kill a Dervan tonight. Everyone's going to be talking about it tomorrow. You'll believe me then, and it may not be too late to save her."

The man responded with whiplike sharpness. "What Dervan?"

"That general, Ciprion." At mention of the senator's name the stranger's grim features twisted into horrified shock, as if he personally knew the high-ranking Dervan. And then the look was gone and the lips were pulled back from the man's teeth. Torvus had thought he looked dangerous before.

"How soon?" the stranger demanded.

"I don't know how soon. Maybe now. I tried to warn him, but he was too stupid to pay me." Torvus had travelled ahead of Kontar after having successfully pleaded that he be allowed to have a few extra days to talk to his daughter, but this morning he'd discovered the wizard arrived only a day after himself.

The stranger's voice rose. "What's he sending against him?"

Torvus decided to speak the truth. "Red mokrels." At the man's blank look he explained quickly. "They're larger than regular monkeys. And he's taught them to strangle. But he has three men in his employ, too, to master them, and to navigate places the mokrels can't go unnoticed."

The pretty girl had vanished inside the wagon and returned, face taut with anger. "Mellika is alive but deeply sleeping."

"She'll wake around midnight," Torvus said. "I wouldn't hurt my own daughter. I left money for her," he added.

"Go," the man ordered with a snarl.

Torvus realized that he would have to. "You'll tell my daughter, won't you? You'll tell her what I said, and that the same or worse will happen to her that happened to Ciprion?"

But he was speaking to the empty air, for the man had tossed the amulet toward Shenassa and sprinted away, as if all the shades of the dead were on his heels.

IV

Ciprion had taken refuge in the little room at the far end of the suite in the eastern wing of his son-in-law's expansive estate. Amelia was still visiting with their daughter, but Ciprion had tired of Felix's veiled hostility. The young man still sulked that Ciprion had dared ruin Felix's political future.

He sat at a desk with a play by Etilus in the original Herrenic. It wasn't Etilus' best, but there were still fine turns of phrase, and it had been years since Ciprion had read *The Garden Plot*. Ostensibly he was working on his memoirs, but that parchment sat open and blank beside him for the second day running.

He wasn't sure what had caught his attention, but he felt a change in the air, and then a voice spoke behind him.

"Reading by candlelight is bad for the eyes."

It was Hanuvar. Gods. The Volani really was mad. "I hoped that you would not come," Ciprion said, though he did not fully turn. "This means the rumors are true."

"You can't believe everything you hear," said the man behind him. Hanuvar stepped to the side, probably planning to face him, so Ciprion turned toward the wall.

"Laelius read the reports from the arena in Hidrestus," Ciprion said, "as well as Caiax's eyewitness account. He wrote me about it, but I didn't believe you were really back. Until now."

"I was stunned when I learned Caiax survived. Did he happen to mention he could have helped me stop that thing in the arena? He chose to fight me instead."

"You've left a trail of bodies," Ciprion said grimly. It angered him that Hanuvar was trying to justify any of his recent actions.

"So have we both." His old enemy sounded surprisingly reasonable. "But it was Caiax's limited focus that got him wounded, and Catius' own sorcery killed him."

"You expect me to believe Catius practiced sorcery?" Ciprion said in disbelief.

Hanuvar explained calmly: "He hired a sorcerer to speak with the dead. To learn my whereabouts. It didn't go as planned."

The simple ring of truth was in his voice. "You're not lying."

"I have not come to lie to you. Why won't you face me?"

"If I survive our little talk, at some point I'm going to be asked whether or not I saw you. And I intend not to lie."

Hanuvar laughed. "You saw me at the circus."

"Did I? Who could be sure of that?"

"Aren't we too old for these kinds of games? Lie or not if you wish, to honorless men. You can't tell me you care what the senate thinks. Word is you left their number and sold your Dervan properties."

"That news traveled fast."

"I know also that you spent a fortune buying up Volani orphans."

Slowly, ever so slowly, Ciprion turned and met Hanuvar's eyes. The general stood tall and proud, his features thrown in stark relief by the light, so that his eyes seemed hooded and the flame light glistened in their depths. His was not the look of a madman. There was pain there, and wisdom, and, impossibly, kindness. Seeing that last was somehow worse than taking the blow he'd half expected. Before he knew it, he was saying more than he had planned. "It wasn't right, going after Volanus. You had no army or navy left. I did everything I could to fight it on the floor of the senate."

"I know," Hanuvar said quietly.

"It was beneath us. The men of sense are gone or put their convictions aside to score political points. In the end, all I could do was save a few children, and I couldn't even afford to save them all. I hadn't the wealth."

Hanuvar spoke with deep feeling. "It's a kindness I shall never forget."

"The gods shall curse our people, forever, for what we did to yours."

"You will keep the children safe?"

"They are safe. Some seventy of them, on a country estate where they're learning trade skills and are well fed. I will free them when they come of age, and it is written into my will."

"It means a great deal to me to know that they are in your hands," Hanuvar said. "Someone is trying to kill you, Ciprion. I left the bodies of two assassins beyond the potted plants south of the vegetable garden."

Ciprion fought down astonishment. "Then I owe you my thanks." He would have asked for more details, but he saw Hanuvar already planned to provide them.

"You are still in danger. They did not know who had hired them or their master. Who wants you dead?"

"Catius did. But since he's dead, I gather it can't be him. And assassination wasn't ever his style, anyway. One of the men who took over for the Dervan Values faction, perhaps."

A cloying, animal stench struck his nostrils just as a nightmare swung into their room. It was a dark, squat, red-furred shape, and it landed silently, then sprang forward, reaching for Ciprion with arms longer than a man's. Hanuvar interposed himself on the instant, striking with a short blade.

Ciprion threw himself back from the stool, his heart thrumming in astonishment and alarm from the sheer wrongness of the thing, a creature that moved like a man, but wasn't.

It swayed away from Hanuvar's strike, bared fangs, and ducked low, flinging itself at Ciprion.

He grabbed a knife from the table. The thing grabbed his tunic and yanked him forward.

Ciprion saw the spittle on its great fangs as it leaned for his throat.

Hanuvar's sword punched through its skull. Blood sprayed across the floor at Ciprion's feet and the creature dropped.

Ciprion steadied himself against the desk then backed off, for the beast kicked as it died, and its feet were clawed.

Hanuvar hurried to the window, peered out without exposing much of his head, then stepped back to wipe his sword on the stilled fur. "I learned mokrels would be employed. I thought killing their controllers would eliminate that threat."

"Apparently not."

A woman screamed, and both men started.

"Father!" There was no mistaking his daughter Cornelia's voice, and the sound of rapid footsteps. *Jovren, let my Amelia be well*, he thought, *let my grandchildren be unharmed*. He adjusted his grip on the knife and headed into the hall. He heard Hanuvar follow.

The household had risen, including drowsy slaves, and Felix, wearing a tunic he'd thrown on backward. Ciprion's granddaughter clung to wide-eyed Cornelia, who had halfway advanced into the wing from which they were emerging. Cornelia thrust a scrap of paper at him, and he tore his eyes from her grief-stricken face with difficulty. Oil lamps set in a nearby ledge gave him enough light to see the words scribbled on the parchment.

He read them, even as she gasped for him to do so. Written in loopy, scrawling Dervan letters, it said: "We have your grandson, senator. Present yourself to me at midnight under the grove of the second hill south of the village, or he will be torn to pieces. Come alone. Your time is over, but his need not be."

The vein at his temple throbbed. He looked up to find Amelia beside their daughter. Calvia had switched from Cornelia to her, and his wife was holding her grandchild close and stroking her hair. "How did this happen?" Ciprion demanded.

"Calvia says a hairy thing came in through the window," Cornelia said.

"It has huge teeth!" Calvia said, turning her white face to him. "And big scary arms!"[12]

He passed the note to Hanuvar. He saw in the other man's eyes that he too realized the first attack had been a jab, possibly

---

[12] While Antires' words are, as usual, accurate in the essentials, he suggests a greater degree of agitation in young Calvia than she herself reports. Other eyewitnesses assert that both grandchildren were remarkably self-possessed, conveying a sober dignity beyond their years as was their habit. Calvia is actually said to have reported the incident with astounding calm, though with obvious concern. This was also the first opportunity she had to observe Hanuvar. With the clarity typical of her, she later wrote, "As you may expect, the events of that night left an indelible impression upon me, images that stand clear and sharp even when entire months and even years are but blurs from which a handful of events emerge. I do not care to dwell on the mokrel's attributes, though they are well preserved in my nightmares. Rather shall I describe Hanuvar. He was dressed that night as a simple laborer, and there was nothing upon his tunic or sandals or accoutrements to suggest that he was anything else; it was only in the way my grandfather

anticipated to fail, while the more certain line of attack was sprung the instant the first morkrel died.

"Who is this man?" Felix pointed at Hanuvar. His voice was hoarse, and he cleared it.

"An old friend," Ciprion explained impatiently.

Calvia's eyes were huge with worry. "The thing carried the note," she said. "It dropped it on the floor."

"What friend is he?" Amelia inquired, her voice icy.

"Drusus," Hanuvar said.

"Of?" Amelia prompted.

"He was a cavalry decurion," Ciprion said. "That's not important." Amelia always knew when he was lying, but heeded his warning glance.

Hanuvar handed the note back. "My scout will know where your grandson is."

"Can you be sure?" Ciprion asked.

"We will know if we return to my place of business."

Cornelia was fighting hard to display the control of a proper Dervan mother, but her voice cracked. "Father, what are you going to do?"

---

gave such heed to his counsel that I realized he must be someone remarkable. That is not to say that grandfather was impolite to others; he carried himself with dignity before all. Rather, that to this man he accorded something more, not just in his words, but in the way he held himself beside him.

It is difficult for a child to guess the age of those far older, for to them even someone of nineteen seems of great maturity. Hanuvar was an older man, surely, for there was gray in his hair and his face was lined, but he looked to be younger than grandfather, though this was not the case. He stood a handspan taller than grandfather, which did not make him tall, though he was somewhat taller than the average. His body was muscular and I observed a short scar upon one calf and another near the sleeve of his right arm. His face was clean shaven and dark, perhaps somewhat darker than that of the typical Dervan, but not notably so. Having acquaintances who had been promised to much older men in marriage, I had grown used to evaluating the appearance and conduct of male visitors to the house. I judged this stranger handsome, in a rugged way, with a straight nose with a slight hook and small, flared nostrils and a mouth with lightly colored lips of moderately large size. His eyes were large, alert and keenly intelligent; on this first instance I thought them blue, but in a later meeting I judged them gray, and I think he was one of those people whose eye color was not constant, depending upon mood or lighting. His forehead was high and his hair was straight and parted to the right, though his bangs were straight, in the Dervan manner, and the length framed his ears and stopped before the nape of the neck. He carried himself with an easy self-assurance that reminded me of the way grandfather did. There is a difference between behaving as though you are used to being obeyed by inferiors because of your inborn status and being truly comfortable with yourself and your capabilities, used to commanding the attention of soldiers whose lives may hang upon your words to them. This attitude was present in his gaze, as well; it was not arrogance he projected but supreme confidence. That night his eyes were mostly focused upon grandfather, and one sensed his concern. Only once did his glance brush mine and it was as though I had encountered a willpower of titanic strength. I was later to learn that he could turn this magnetism on or off as he wished, which was well for him, for if he had constantly radiated such intensity he could not possibly have hidden himself during his travels."   —*Silenus*

"I should send for the guard," Felix said assertively.

Ciprion didn't have the patience for him. "Don't be an ass. If we send soldiers they'll kill Marcus immediately."

"I'll get the details," Hanuvar said. "Meet me as soon as you can." He nodded toward Amelia then turned and hurried back the way he'd come.

Ciprion started to say that he'd be right behind him, then realized, just as Hanuvar must have, that he had to put a few things in order. He took a few moments to reassure Cornelia, and to say to Amelia that he himself would be all right, with the help of Drusus. He saw he was having better luck convincing Cornelia and Felix than he was his wife, though she played along and instructed the rest of the family to let Ciprion handle it. She took his arm and pulled him aside.

Her look was haggard in the light, and it aged her. Never had her eyes been more piercing. "You trust this man, and his plans." It was more an accusation than a question.

"He killed my assassins on the grounds this evening."

"Maybe he's part of the trap. Can you trust him with your life, or that of our grandson?"

He answered without hesitation. "Yes."

She frowned. "Who is he, really?"

"I told you."

"I have seen you talk to a hundred former soldiers. And none of them but Laelius sound like that man does when he talks to you. Yet you've never mentioned him. He's no decurion. Who is he?"

Ciprion said nothing.

She spoke quietly, fiercely. "I can count on one hand the times you have lied to me about something important, husband. Why do it now?"

"To protect you." And to protect Hanuvar, he thought. "I have to go."

"Come back to me," she commanded. "With our grandson."

"I will," he vowed, and ran for the stables.

V

Clouds veiled the stars, and the branches obscured that veil so that Torvus walked through the woods in near darkness toward the little clearing where the wizard's wagons had been drawn up. A low campfire burned between them, painting the wooden panels with a warm red gold glow.

Torvus paid little attention to the fire or the young man sitting beside it. He scanned the tree where one of those hideous mokrels had lingered, the eyes of which he'd felt boring into his back when he'd last visited Kontar. He didn't see it now, but that didn't mean one of the things wasn't watching him still.

The young man at the fire certainly was. He was one of Kontar's two assistants. The mage named them students, though mostly they played the part of slaves, preparing his meals and driving his wagons. Now the two structures, not very different from his daughter's wagon, were shuttered and dark, save for the flicker of a small light from the wagon on the left.

Torvus stopped on the far side of the fire and the assistant stood up.

"Where's Kontar?" Torvus asked.

The young man's answer was careless, his look challenging. "The master is at work."

"I need to speak with him."

The assistant was readying to say that he'd have to wait, but Torvus wasn't subjected to that, because a huffing, panting noise sounded behind them.

Torvus knew a chill as it drew closer, for the source didn't quite sound human.

A squat, furred figure scampered out of the dark, its eyes shining in a human-shaped head, though it loped along on two legs and a single hand at the end of an arm longer than a man's.

A mokrel. And it carried a human child in one arm. Torvus stared in horror as the beast huffed to a stop near the far wagon, and it was only when the creature set down his burden that Torvus was certain the damned thing hadn't murdered the little boy. The child wore nothing but a sleeping shirt. He had chubby cheeks, and from his height was no older than five or six. His eyes were saucers still directed upon the beast that had carried him.

The mokrel shuffled to one side, still breathing heavily, then sat and scratched its back. The assistant stared for a moment, apparently unable to fake aplomb under such peculiar circumstances, but his sense of duty, or fear of shirking it, kicked in, and he said something about getting water for the beast before he headed to the front of the wagon.

Torvus pitied the frightened little boy. He didn't care if the wizard slew entire legions of men, but he couldn't stomach cruelty to a child. He walked the long way around the mokrel. He felt its eyes on him, but forced a smile for the boy and bent down beside him. "What's happened to you, little fellow?"

The boy looked well fed and cared for, and he smelled of expensive soap. He fixed Torvus with a dazed look and backed away. Torvus reached out to muss his hair. "Hey now, there's nothing to be afraid of from me. You need something to drink?" He patted his wine sac and untied it from his belt. "This is good sweet stuff, here." He'd kept just a little of the Fadurian for himself, undrugged, and much as he hated to share such a fine vintage, the boy looked like he could use a pick-me-up.

The door to the wagon opened and Kontar stepped out. He speared Torvus with a look, then pointed his beast to the front of the wagon, the route the assistant had taken. It ambled away.

Kontar flipped back his cape theatrically and stalked forward. He was not a large man, and perhaps he hoped to make up for that with his beard, which was long and straight cut across his chest. Tonight he'd pulled on a wig of thick, dark curling hair.

On the shoulder of his belted knee-length tunic perched a small green lizard with blue stripes and gem-bright eyes. Kontar had once proudly proclaimed it a blue fant, but Torvus knew one of the poisonous little things on sight. He'd once seen a man die from their bite after only a short while. That Kontar kept it always in his company, docile and compliant, was just one of many clues he hadn't noticed when he'd first met the wizard. He'd made the mistake of thinking him yet another con man.

Torvus knelt with the wine sac passed halfway to the boy, and was startled when he felt a tug. The child was finally taking the drink from him. He watched as the youth put it to his lips, and winced as some of the expensive vintage dripped down his chin. The child then handed the skin back with a polite thank you, and Torvus couldn't help admiring his courtesy even as the master drew up before him, frowning.

Kontar's deep voice sounded as though it might erupt with fury at any moment. "You look as though you have been beaten, Torvus," he snapped. "You shall spare me the details, and merely tell me whether you recovered the amulet."

Torvus had expected such a greeting, and had a response ready. "No, but I did something that may be of use in its recovery."

Kontar scratched the side of his nose with a beringed finger. "You said I didn't need to send the beasts. That you could manage it."

"I warned that the amulet might counter your own powers." Torvus smiled so his contradiction would hopefully be seen as a correction and not a challenge. "And I almost had it—but my daughter had a bodyguard I've never seen before. It's all right, though. I made clear that she must turn it over to me tomorrow after she learns of Ciprion's death"—at this information the little boy gasped, and Torvus shot him a quick look before continuing—"and saw just how serious it was to cross you."

"I see," Kontar said, his crooked teeth showing. "So you told your daughter I was planning to kill Ciprion?"

"For her to see how dangerous you are. To take my warning seriously."

Kontar advanced and slapped Torvus. The strike wasn't particularly painful, but Torvus still groaned. The child whimpered and slid behind him.

"I want that amulet." Kontar jabbed a finger at Torvus' chest. The lizard on his shoulder hissed.

"You'll have it," Torvus promised. "My daughter didn't believe how powerful you were. She'll learn, and then you won't have to risk anything else."

"I have been too patient with you. With its power I could have controlled both of the mokrels tonight myself at the same time, rather than having that idiot Vokius help me. I've no idea what happened to him or my guard, but I ended up having to switch my attention between the animals."

As lead student, Vokius had occasionally been trusted to control a mokrel, and Torvus could only suppose he had been dispatched with the guard to kill Ciprion this night.

From behind Torvus came the question from a small, brave voice: "Did you kill my grandfather?"

Kontar glared at Torvus, then shifted his gaze down near his waist, where the boy peered out from behind Torvus' leg. "If I had, you would not be here . But he proved resourceful, as I'd feared, and has thus cost me a great deal of money. You've no idea how hard a mokrel is to come by."

"You're keeping the boy as a hostage?" Torvus asked. "Is that really necessary?"

"You disapprove? How quaint. I find moderate need for your skills, Torvus, and none for your advice. Your connection to the amulet, while promising, has yielded me nothing."

"I've more skills than you've used."

"Master. I am your master, do you not recall? You've hardly earned your freedom, Torvus."

He bowed his head, hating that he had to do so. "I've more skills than you've used, master."

"That's better. Care for this brat then, until Ciprion comes."

"When will that be, master?"

"Soon, I think. Watch him well. I've had enough mistakes from you already." He called for the assistant, then turned with a dramatic swirl of his cape. At that very moment the boy darted off.

Torvus leapt and with two quick strides caught the boy's arms. The child squirmed, kicked him in the chest, and shouted to be let go as Torvus lifted him. He stood the child on the ground, facing the other direction as Kontar ran up.

The wizard bent down beside the boy, who stopped his struggling and stared wide-eyed at the lizard poised on Kontar's wrist.

The assistant arrived and stood watching from the side of the cart.

"Do you want to meet my lizard?" Kontar asked menacingly. The little thing tasted the air with its tongue and rocked back and forth along the knuckles of the wizard's hand. It was mere inches from the boy's face.

"Don't, master," Torvus pleaded. "He's just a boy."

But Kontar had eyes only for the youth. "Do you know what kind of lizard I command? He comes from the delta of Hadira. A single bite can kill in only a few moments. Oh, it's not painful. Just the tiniest little bite from his fangs. But the poison, ah, that's like slowly losing the ability to move your limbs, and the ability to breathe. Like drowning without being in the water. Would you like to feel what that's like?"

The boy looked up through big eyes. And once again he demonstrated great bravery when he spoke, for his voice, though that of a small child's, was level and direct. "Why do you want to kill my grandfather?"

For a brief moment a milder look replaced Kontar's customary arrogance. Perhaps the child's equanimity impressed him, for he answered in an almost pleasant way, with more detail than Torvus would have expected. "I have nothing against your grandfather. I'm a kind of problem solver, and someone else has paid me to solve some problem they have from him. I don't like working harder than the job demands."

The boy stared back. Kontar straightened, but the lizard still perched upon his hand. He turned to his assistant. "I hear Ciprion dotes upon his grandchildren." He stepped closer to the little boy and the blue faint hissed. "But I suppose we don't really need the child conscious to lure him further."

This last was too much. Torvus pushed the youngster away. "Run!" he shouted.

Torvus grabbed for his knife, but the little lizard leapt the gap – he hadn't realized they could jump so far. He swatted at it, grunting in fear, but the thing latched onto his hand and bit deep. It released, and hit the ground with a plop.

Torvus' gaze swung to the scowling Kontar. He took a step toward the wizard, for he knew he kept an antidote upon him. But then he staggered, and before he could think further what to do he was sinking to the ground. The assistant had caught up to grab the boy a short distance outside the camp cirle.

"I've come for my grandson!" a commanding voice called from down the trail.

VI

Hanuvar watched from the undergrowth as Ciprion advanced toward the clearing. Shenassa presumably followed on his right, though he could not see or hear her. Antires lingered further back, with a groggy Mellika, who had been roused by a healer. She had insisted on accompanying them.

"Do you hear me?" Ciprion called. "I see your campfire, but I will come no closer until I see my grandson!"

Hanuvar heard the faintest of rustling above, in the darkness of the trees overshadowing the trail. It might have been any nocturnal creature, but he knew it for the mokrel. He crept forward, spear at his side. At the campfire's edge, Hanuvar saw a small bearded man dramatically sweep one hand forward, palm up in the universal signal to halt.

"My beast sees your retainers, and I see what it does!" the wizard cried. "Ciprion, tell your followers that if they do not lay down their weapons and depart, your grandson will die. I've already had my lizard poison him. But I have an antidote. Come quick, while it's still possible to revive him."

Another voice, choked, weak, called out from near the clearing. "He hasn't been bitten yet!"

The wizard cursed and shouted something, and Hanuvar heard a little boy call to his grandfather.

Hanuvar charged. The mokrel dropped from the tree and ran on all four limbs toward him. But he ignored the rushing beast, throwing his spear not at the creature, but the wizard. He knew the cast was good the instant he hurled it, which was fortunate, because he had no attention to spare. The stinking manlike monster swiped at him with a thick arm.

He leapt back. The beast hooted, bared fangs, and advanced. But then Mellika was at his side, hand clasped to the ancient pendant at her throat. She thrust her other hand forward, and the beast halted, shaking its head as if confused.

Ciprion rushed, and Hanuvar saw the boy struggling fiercely in the arms of a young man.

The mokrel snarled, advanced, stopped, tilted its head.

"The wizard's got a strong hold on the beast," Mellika said, panting heavily.

The mokrel started to turn just as Hanuvar buried his sword in its neck. Much as he appreciated a gladius, it was a true pleasure to briefly wield a falcata, the long, curved blade of his people that Shenassa had lent him. With the weapon's greater reach he hadn't had to come in as close, nor take the full blood spray as the slice tore half through the animal. It slumped, dead, and Hanuvar raced past.

Shenassa was already there at the camp site, with Ciprion. The wizard's assistant knelt before Shenassa's spear and begged to be spared. Mellika's father lay moaning beside the wizard, who clutched the spear haft standing out from his supine body. Ciprion cradled the little boy in his arms.

His eyes were bleak. "The lizard bit his calf just as I reached him." The lizard lay in two pieces on the ground near Ciprion's sword.

Mellika's father pawed at the wizard. His eyes rolled and caught Hanuvar. He croaked a single word. "Antidote."

The wizard coughed. His wig lay just beyond his egglike pate, and blood poured from his mouth. Though he paled, his eyes brightened. He sneered and drove his elbow into a pouch at his side. Something inside crackled and smashed and the dying man laughed. "The boy's dead now," he wheezed.

Hanuvar yanked out the spear and drove it through the wizard's throat. He spun on the younger man kneeling before Shenassa, dripping spear in one hand, bloody falcata in the other. "Is there more antidote?"

"Yes," the man stammered.

"Bring it. Now." He thumbed Shenassa after him then walked over to Ciprion.

Mellika and Antires had joined them. The playwright's gaze shifted from the boy in the anguished Dervan's arms to the shuddering Torvus. Mellika crouched at her father's side.

"If there's an antidote," Mellika said to her father, "we can save you."

"I tried to stop him." Torvus' voice was labored. Hanuvar supposed he meant the wizard. "I didn't know he was going to take the boy. I swear. Tried to get him away."

"I believe you, Father," Mellika said.

Shenassa led out the nervous looking assistant, who held a small clay vial.

"That's the cure?" Hanuvar asked. "You're certain?"

"I'm certain," he said.

"Is there enough for both?" Mellika asked.

The assistant, gripped in one hand by a grim Ruminian and facing a man with two bloody weapons, clearly wanted to give the best answer. "The boy's small. I don't know. Maybe. But a man needs all of it . . . I couldn't find any more."

Groaning, Torvus pointed to the boy.

Hanuvar planted the spear blade first in the ground and snatched the little vessel from the wizard's assistant. He dropped the falcata and pulled free the vial's cork, then passed the precious flask on to Ciprion.

He saw Ciprion's eyes as he took the vial, and he wondered what he must be thinking. Probably he wondered if he was simply dumping more poison into the boy's body. The firelight glinted upon his sweaty forehead as he lifted the little vessel gently to the youngster's lips. The child drank it without spilling, staring at his grandfather the while.

Hanuvar turned back, finding Shenassa still poised with her weapon aimed at the apprentice. Mellika, brushing a tear from her broad face, knelt by her father and stroked his hair.

"I'm sorry, Mellika," he said, his voice failing.

Hanuvar returned to the wizard's assistant, who watched with frightened eyes.

"How long before the antidote works? The truth."

He spoke rapidly. "It shouldn't take long, if it's swallowed soon after the bite. And it was."

"Any lingering effects?" Hanuvar asked.

"He may be sleepy. Other than that, I don't know. Look, the lizard didn't bite too many people that the master wanted to live. It bit Vok . . . the other apprentice, once, and we had to give him the cure. He was weak for a few days, but was fine after."

"Who hired your master?" Hanuvar demanded.

The young man licked his lips, looking from the silent Ruminian to Hanuvar. "What are you going to do with me?"

"He's still thinking it over," Shenassa said. "I'm for gutting you and spitting on you while you die."

Hanuvar thought that threat finely played, for the assistant turned to him. "Aminius," he said. "The famous senator," he added, as if no one knew whom he meant. "And I don't know why. Only that the assassination had to happen outside of Derva, and that the master said we needed to lay low in the provinces for a while, but that the money was worth it."

"Go," Ciprion instructed. "Come near me or mine again and I will kill you on sight."

The assistant hesitated. "Now? I mean, can I get my cloth "

"Go!"

With that, the man rose, still careful of Shenassa's spear, then dashed into the darkness. They heard the pad of his feet fade into the distance.

Hanuvar wiped his weapons on the clothes of the dead wizard, said nothing to Mellika, sitting silently by the body of her father, and joined Ciprion. The boy was blinking sleepily and feeling his calf.

"It's just a little wound," Ciprion told the child. "You'll be fine. It's already stopped bleeding."

"I tried to be brave, like you," the boy said.

"You were very brave," Ciprion told him proudly.

The boy's little lips turned down into a frown. "I was scared."

"I was scared too," Ciprion admitted. "Brave men are scared, but they keep doing what is right anyway."

Ciprion looked up then, to Hanuvar, and Mellika, now rising from the body of her father, and Shenassa. Antires watched everything, doubtless taking it in so he could write down pretty metaphors about the night and the shadows and the hearts of men.

"I owe all of you a debt I can never repay," Ciprion said. "If there is ever anything I can do for you, you have but to ask."

Shenassa bowed her head respectfully. Mellika, though, shook her head in refusal. "It was my father who involved you," she said. "It was my duty to aid you, and I am only glad he did not hurt you through his schemes, and that the boy is well." She looked down at the still body of her father. She had rolled him over on his back, straightened his limbs, and closed his eyes.

"He was trying to warn us," Ciprion said. "He did not lack resourcefulness. I don't know if you saw, but he grasped the wizard's ankle when he tried to avoid your friend's spear cast." The general had wisely abstained from naming Hanuvar.

Antires invoked the words of one of the best known Herrenic playwrights. "The king at last has found the character he sought. It would have done him well to heed the siren call when he had pleaded deaf, but he gave good account with this, his final deed. Let no man speak him ill."

"Orestes," Ciprion said. "From *The Shadow King*, Act III."

Antires bowed his head, clearly pleased. "A talented playwright, who spun many a fine scene."

"I think I will take my grandson home now."

"What should we do with the belongings of these men?" Mellika asked.

Hanuvar saw Ciprion musing over an answer, and replied for him. "Search through their papers, learn if there's more that General Ciprion must be told. Look with care. Present the information to him tomorrow. I think, for your trouble, the belongings should be yours."

"My friend speaks true," Ciprion said. "Report to me in the morning. Be careful, though. Since the assassin kept a poisonous creature on hand, he might have other protections."

Hanuvar thought that wisely said. "I'll follow shortly. Let me have a quick word." At Ciprion's nod, he stepped to the side of Antires.

VII

Ciprion had only advanced a few hundred feet down the dark road before Hanuvar jogged up to join him. He no longer carried spear or falcata. He nodded at Marcus. "How is he?"

"I think he'll be fine. I still want a skilled healer to see him, but I was telling him that's more for his mother's sake than his. He understands."

"Mother worries too much," said the tiny, tired voice from the dark shape nestled in Ciprion's arms. "Grandfather, the man said that someone wanted to kill you. Why?"

He thought about the best way to explain something he'd thought never to have to say to a child, then found the words: "They didn't like something I said."

"What did you say?"

"All kinds of things," Ciprion said with a smile, thinking of the way Laelius had sometimes shaken his head at his outbursts. "Maybe too loudly sometimes."

"Calvia doesn't like it when I shout," Marcus observed.

"No one likes it when people shout. But that's not why they were mad."

"They're afraid of your grandfather," Hanuvar explained. "Cowards fear men of principle because they can't understand their actions, and they cannot buy them."

"Grandfather says men should choose their own leaders."

"I do," Ciprion agreed. "But you shouldn't say that too loudly, these days."

The boy shifted and seemed to settle.

"Do you really think Aminius was behind it?" Hanuvar asked softly.

"It may be. I'm not surprised. He hates that the emperor is still fond of me, publicly and privately."

The calm, quiet shape walking with him in the dark was the man once labeled the scourge of Derva. It was strange to think on that, and stranger still to hear that man ask, concern in his voice: "What are you going to do?"

"I have allies, and not all my connections are destroyed. I'm going to teach Aminius and his people a lesson. Tell me what you're going to do."

Hanuvar was a moment answering. "Would that I could."

Ciprion knew then that he shouldn't have pried. But he could guess one thing. "You're no more after vengeance than you were for territory, are you."

"I would drown in the blood I would spill if I were to slake my thirst . . ." he began, then fell silent. Ciprion felt his eyes on him as they passed another cluster of trees. "No. It's a simple thing. The Dervans took my people. I mean to take them back. However many remain."

"I know better than to ask how, and where you're going. But I will help you," he pledged.

"You need to guard your own blood first. But if you can aid me in two ways, I would be grateful."

Ciprion answered without hesitation. "Name them."

"There must be a master list of where and to whom my people were sold. I need to know where it is."

"Or to have a copy."

"I think the latter will be a challenge, even for you."

"Come now," he said with a smile. "You're not the only one who can accomplish the impossible."

"I don't want to see your family harmed while you take risks for me."

He shrugged. He thought he might manage it. "What is the second thing?"

"My daughter survived the assault. I've learned she may have escaped."

"I've heard nothing of this," Ciprion said with honest surprise. "But I can look into it. How will I find you?"

"I should reach the far side of the Ardenines in three months' time."

"Feeling nostalgic about your old journey?"

"Hardly. I've been warned against a water crossing. And I've been warned that I needed to better hide my steps. So I hid myself among my current company." Hanuvar looked off to the northwest. "I'll have to leave them in just a few days. I've hated the slowed travel but it has been good to be among so many friends."

"Who warned you?"

Hanuvar sounded embarrassed. "Spirits, believe it or not."

"Your gods warned you?" Ciprion said in disbelief.

"My gods have been silent," Hanuvar answered darkly.

"I've never heard from mine, either," Ciprion admitted. "You trust these sources?"

"Trust? I trust only the word of a handful of men and women, most of whom are dead. But these spirits returned favor for favor. And so I followed their counsel, crawling slowly down the road and stopping for days at a time when by any reckoning I should have raced across the face of the sea, for more of my people may be dying every single day. How long can they last?"

He asked a question for which he did not expect an answer, but Ciprion had one for him. In the face of such pain, he hoped it was true.

"Many of the survivors were specialists of one sort or another. I don't think large numbers were sent on to the galleys or the mines. But I know that must be small comfort."

Hanuvar nodded his thanks.

In the silence, suddenly bold, Ciprion recalled the question he had wondered for uncounted years, a thing he had never dared say aloud, much less to his Dervan friends. To give it voice seemed a kind of treason. Yet he could no longer keep back from it. "Have you ever wondered what it would have been like if we two had been on the same side?"

He saw Hanuvar nod, once, and then waited. After a short delay Hanuvar spoke with quiet dignity. "Had you and I been leagued together, no one could have stood against us."

A comfortable silence fell between them, broken finally by Ciprion as they neared the villa. "Probably we should not meet again, on this side of the mountains." They drew to a stop just beyond the road that let into the property.

Hanuvar agreed without hesitation. "Probably not. I'm sure my friend Antires would love to talk with you, though. He's the one who was quoting playwrights. He himself writes."

"'The Herrene,'" Ciprion remembered aloud. "Is he any good?"

"I've never read his work," Hanuvar admitted. "But he's a good actor and a fine friend. He has a mad idea he will write a play about me."

"That's not so mad."

Hanuvar laughed. "Maybe he'll write one about you. That one, at least, could be staged somewhere."

"Let him come. I'll gladly speak with him. And I shall find what I can for you. How shall I find you?"

Hanuvar told him then of a village and an inn well north of Derva, and Ciprion agreed he would leave word there, and suggested a phrase and counterphrase. Hanuvar approved.

There was much more he would have liked to have said, had they the time.

"I thank you," Hanuvar said "Be well. Guard yourself and your family."

"And I thank you. Watch your steps."

They clasped arms then, wordless, each lifted a hand in farewell.

Ciprion, bearing his grandson, watched the figure recede into the gloom, then turned and headed toward the villa. Very soon he had handed Marcus into the care of Cornelia, who had summoned a village healer and his attendants. Ciprion succinctly relayed what had happened. "He was bitten by a fant lizard, but he's had an antidote that seems to have worked." He passed over the bisected corpse of the little beast, in case it should somehow prove useful in identifying the poison.

The healer, a wild-haired Herrene, alarmed Cornelia when he declared there was no known antidote, but shortly confirmed that the boy seemed fine and that the wound itself wasn't necrotic. Probably, he speculated, it hadn't truly been a mature envenomator, as the kidnappers claimed.

Ciprion waved off the thanks of his daughter and son-in-law, told them that the instigators were dead, and said he'd tell them more in the morning. He then retreated into the eastern wing with his wife.

It proved far harder to throw Amelia from the trail, as he had anticipated.

"Where's your friend?" she asked once they had closed the door on their dimly lit bedchamber.

"Heading back to where he came from."

"And who hired the men behind this?"

"Aminius," he said, and saw her eyebrows rise before she scowled. He continued, "We may all be in danger, until I can demonstrate why an attack against our family is suicidal."

"Is that what Hanuvar advised you?"

He met her eyes. Of course she had deduced it. His wife was no fool.

"Are you sending him after Aminius?" she asked.

"No. Hanuvar has done enough to help us."

She exhaled in frustration. "And you think that erases all the misery he caused."

"I don't want to argue about this again." The harshness in his voice startled him, yet he could not restrain it. "He knew that unless he halted Derva, we would crush his city. And he was right. You have seen how right he was."

She met his eyes but did not shy from the anger there. "Maybe so. And what is his goal now?"

"Not vengeance."

"He promised you that?"

"He did."

"And you believe him. Why else would he be here? After what has been done to his country? After what you yourself know he has done in retribution?"

"It's not as you think. Those stories are lies."

She pursed her lips. "You want him to be good, because you admired him. You always were too ready to forgive him—"

"If I had seen what he has, do you think I could find the strength to practice mercy against my enemies—to lend them a hand even in their moment of greatest need? That I could manage kindness, even good humor?"

Amelia gave him a pitying look. "You torture yourself over things that have never happened. That could never happen."

"Without him, our grandson would have died this night. And you might well have lost me."

She studied him in silence, then let out a long sigh. "You mean to help him, don't you?"

"What would you do, in my place?"

"I know he has suffered. But he started a fourteen-year war. You're too forgiving."

"This is not about forgiveness."

"You're going to tell me it's about honor."

She was right, so he did not say it. "Perhaps it's not enough to ask you to trust him, not fully. I understand. The next time we meet, you can speak to him, and judge him for yourself."

"You think a single meeting would convince me?"

"I think you already have some sense of his character. After you actually speak with him, you would see him as I do."

She took a deep breath. "Very well. Your decisions have led to hardship for our family, but you have ever chosen the righteous path. Now what do you mean to do about the men who threatened my grandchild?"

He took her hand, and kissed it. "We are going to show them there are some lines that cannot be crossed."

"That does not sound like a man who has gone into retirement."

"I think my memoirs will have to wait. We'll be busy with more important things for a good long while."

※ ※ ※

Ciprion proved even more the gentleman than I had been led to believe and spoke openly to me for many hours that next day. I quickly saw how it was that he had charmed so many in his time. He was warm, gregarious, and well read. Those who thought him a mirror image of Hanuvar were wrong, though the men had similarities. Yes, Ciprion was brilliant and observant and possessed a measure of steel, but he longed for the simpler, comfortable things, and I think he better liked the company of his fellow men. But then maybe that's not fair to Hanuvar, who had little time to see to his own cares or wants. Or to build a family.

In any case, I came away from our conversation with a thorough appreciation of Hanuvar's so-called nemesis and hoped that we would meet again for future dialogues.

Shortly after that visit, Hanuvar and I took the road toward a final performance, then headed into the mountains. And we diverted none too soon, for it was there that a group of revenants finally caught up to us.

—Sosilos, Book Five

Chapter 12:
Snare of the Hunter

I

Outside the battered feast hall door, Myrikus checked to ensure the skull faced cloak tabs on his shoulder were upright, then pushed the garment back so its long black length was clear of his arms. A glance at his companions showed their own gear was in order, from ebon horsehair helmet crests to dark leggings. There was nothing to be done about their muddy boots, but Demian was scraping a few specks of mud from the musculature ingrained into the black lacquered chest armor of his uniform. He finished, then nodded his readiness.

Myrikus pushed the door open. As he entered, the scent of roast boar and wine overwhelmed the stench of the hot springs that had lingered over them since their arrival in the mountain town. The dull throb of voices they'd heard outside rose to a full-throated cacophony.

The feast of Acarcia was well into its second day, and it was likely many of the patrons crowded about the benches were on their third day of drink. They clapped and sang boisterously along with the trio of musicians on the cramped circular stage. Servers wove their way through the throng carrying platters of ham, bread, and cheese, and plentiful pitchers.

Myrikus left Demian at the door and advanced confidently toward the stage, Telian at his shoulder. He couldn't contain a smile as those nearest froze in a palpable dread, which spread before them as more and more were alerted to their presence. Some who goggled at them were sober, others well into inebriation, but their expressions were similar. It was right and proper that their elite order be regarded with such respect.

The music ground to a halt and the trio of drummer, piper, and vocalist backed warily to the little platform's back wall.

Myrikus glanced only briefly at them before climbing the stage's single step to face the crowd. Telian executed a pivot at exactly the same moment, just short of the dais, hand on the hilt of his gladius.

Apart from one drunk shouting about cider, silence reigned through the feast hall. Myrikus said nothing while the drunk's companions shushed her into silence. He savored the crowd's rapt attention and palpable anxiety. The servers retreated to the kitchen doorway.

Myrikus smote his breastplate. "Hail the emperor!"

Everyone fumbled to repeat the gesture then echoed the phrase.

He showed teeth in something like a smile, as though their sloppy movements had pleased him. "It is good to see so many giving reverence." Myrikus swept a hand toward the low bar, where two ashen-faced cooks watched. "I wish we had come solely to enjoy your festival. But we hunt a fugitive. Descriptions vary, but he's an able-bodied older man of my height with graying hair and a military bearing."

The patrons searched the benches to see if such a man were beside them. Those who loosely fit the description looked nervously among their fellows, to see if they were already under suspicion.

Myrikus doubted their quarry would be found so easily, but searched the throng, knowing keen-eyed Telian was doing the same. "He's a murderer, and a necromancer, and has sometimes claimed to be Hanuvar Cabera."

The name of the infamous Volani general set the room awash in whispered exclamations. There was perhaps no man more feared throughout the empire than the one who'd fought it to a standstill and once led an invading army within sight of Derva's gates. Hanuvar's city had been reduced to ashes and his people sold into slavery, but his name still evoked fear. Myrikus relished fear, but only when he commanded it, and he raised hands, speaking with a snap in his voice.

"Hanuvar himself is dead. This man is an impostor. We will capture him and punish him for his crimes." Myrikus paused for a moment. "You're going to help me. I'm going to sit right over there"— he pointed at an occupied table in a corner—"and my fellow soldiers and I are going to eat some of this fine food. Anyone with information can seek us out. Your lives can be easy. But, if I don't hear any useful information, matters might get a little more uncomfortable."

Myrikus didn't have to threaten explicitly; all the listeners knew the broad power that could be exercised by the Order of the Revenants, who could arrest anyone they cared to and subject them to extraordinarily persuasive procedures.

The festivalgoers at the table he'd indicated were scrambling to depart with their platters and bowls as the three revenants neared.

Myrikus sat, brushed crumbs from the table, undid his helmet, and placed it on the bench. While his companions joined him, a flushed serving woman arrived with slabs of meat, bread, mugs, and wine pitchers. Beefy Telian slapped her on the bottom as she scooted away, while Demian laughed in fellowship at her discomfiture.

Demian was some five years Telian's junior, and still in his midtwenties. The sandy-haired man was coolly proper as he used a knife to leverage a slab of meat onto his own plate. Telian simply used his hands.

Myrikus set to with his men, relishing the cool wine. It was good to have cooked food after the road rations they'd eaten most of the last week.

Telian wiped a spot of wine from his broad chin, glanced over the room, and quietly addressed Myrikus. "Why do you keep saying the man we're after is an imposter?"

"Because it can't be him. You still believe it? What do you think, Demian?"

"I think that's highly improbable."

"You heard him," Myrikus said. "High horse shit improbable, especially since Hanuvar's bones are resting on the ocean floor."

"But Vennian's pet witch said she was certain he was here," Telian objected.

Myrikus paused to finish chewing his first bite of ham, then swallowed and reached for his mug. "People say things all the time to get out of trouble. You know what we're going to get here? A free meal, gossip about some local problems, and a whole lot of nonsense from grudge holders. If we're lucky, we'll find a lead on some impenitent witches, or bandits. But we're not going to find Hanuvar, because he's dead."

Demian maneuvered another slab of meat onto his plate. "If Hanuvar came back from the dead, he'd be after vengeance. He'd go hunt the emperor, first thing."

"You afraid to touch your food with your hands?" Telian asked with a mocking smile.

"I'd be afraid to touch it with your hands."

"Well," Myrikus said, "I don't care what the tribune or his little 'reformed' witch said. Hanuvar's not going to be hiding at this little horse shit mountain festival. What's up here but meat and stink?"

"It has its attractions."

The brown-haired serving woman returned and nervously sat another pitcher on their table, although less than half of the first had been poured out yet.

She bent to wipe the table with a damp rag, and let slip a piece of paper. "I was asked to bring this to you," she said, and scooted away.

While Telian raptly watched her departure, Myrikus held the note open against the table without drawing attention to what he did. The message was short and blunt. *Meet me outside, in the alley back of the inn. I'm afraid he'll see me. Hanuvar is very dangerous, but I know where he is. Come alone so he won't be suspicious. I'm wearing a red scarf.*

Myrikus pushed the little paper across the table to his fellow soldiers.

"I didn't think it would be this simple," Demian said. "Do you think it's a trap?"

Myrikus chuckled. Who would dare attack revenants in the middle of an empire town?

"Whoever wrote that note seems pretty certain it's actually Hanuvar," Telian pointed out.

Myrikus sighed. "That's probably what the impostor's telling his associates. Telian, head out. You're searching for anyone watchful or sober who fits our description. Ask at the stables. Word's probably out we're here and our quarry may be making escape plans."

"You want me to report to the tribune?"

"No." That spoiled patrician would only get in the way. Besides, if there was glory to be gained here, it should go to this trio, not the tribune. "Demian, head to the far end of the alley. Find a good spot where you can watch and not be seen. I'll give you a few minutes to find your place, then I'll go to the meeting."

Both men saluted informally, donned their helms, and left the table. Telian doubled back for a final swig of wine, then followed his younger companion from the hall.

Myrikus forced calm as he finished his meal. The hall's numbers had more than halved while he was distracted, but he didn't want the remaining onlookers to think him excited. It would be wonderful to show that smug tribune that he and his boys knew how to run an investigation. Telian had been hunting witches with him for four years now, and they didn't need any patrician telling them how to root out a fugitive. Especially not a patrician with a pet witch of his own. Myrikus knew why the tribune really kept her around.

He downed a last swig of wine, pulled on his helmet, and stood, adjusting his cloak over his shoulder. Many pairs of eyes followed and murmurs blossomed in his wake.

The odor of the hot springs hit him as soon as he left the feast hall. His breath smoked in the evening air, and he was once more glad for the leggings and boots he'd donned before they started into the highlands. The skies were gray, for winter was much closer here than it was in the valleys below. Off to the left a scattering of dwellings sprawled over small hills. Open spaces between blazed with bonfires, around which crowds of celebrants drank and sang, no matter the chill. Directly ahead lay a screen of pine trees, and beyond them the road that led to the springs and temple to the old mountain god, along with a cluster of villas overlooking what was said to be a spectacular view of the Ardenine range.

He turned the corner of the hall and headed into the wide alley between the feast hall and a windowless wooden storage building. The deeper into the lane he walked, the more the side furthest from the feast hall sloped, until it was almost four feet lower than the half along which he strode. Barrels and crates had been wedged between the drop off and the storage building. Discarded tarps, broken wood, and detritus were piled against the higher structure's edge as well.

Alert for ambush, Myrikus put a hand to the hilt of his sword and stepped past a huge open barrel into which water dripped from the hall's two-story roof. And there, at the alley's end, a dark-skinned man waited, a red scarf at his throat. A curly-haired Herrene. According to some reports, the impostor had been seen with just such a man.

Myrikus didn't care much for anyone from the Herrenic coast, for they treasured mainly the past glories of their ancient culture, soft and feminine though it was. A lot of patrician decadence resulted from their adoption of Herrenic customs, like comic theatre and complicated singing.

As he drew close he looked past the informant to the cluster of small buildings beyond the alley's end. These were nothing but small homes and sheds, probably residences of the feast hall employees and slaves. He didn't see Demian, but then that meant the Herrene didn't see him either.

The dark man looked to be in his mid to late twenties. He shifted nervously as Myrikus strode up.

"You know where the man who calls himself Hanuvar is?" Myrikus demanded.

"I do." The answer was certain, and the Herrene's dark eyes were intent.

"Who are you?" Myrikus tried to look over the man's shoulder, to see what lay directly behind him, but the Herrene shifted, as though he sought to hide something.

"It doesn't matter, does it? Look, he's dangerous, and you've got to be quieter. If he finds out I'm talking to you—"

"He's not going to sneak up on us. I have people watching."

As the brown man shifted again, Myrikus' suspicions flared. "Step aside." He pushed him with his off hand and the Herrene slid away as if touched with a hot poker.

There was nothing behind him but an open barrel filled with rainwater, its bottom resting on the lower slope so that its top rose only a few finger spans above this half of the alley. But if the man had been trying to hide it, there might be something within. Or someone. With a final snarl at the Herrene to stay, Myrikus peered into the dark water.

The pole that slammed into his shins swept him sprawling in pain, belly down in the dirt, his helmeted head over the barrel. He was pushing himself up when something heavy slammed into his upper back and a hand drove his face into the water.

A second pressure landed on his legs and he knew then that two people sat on him. The Herrene, probably, and someone else. He pushed up with his arms, then found a dagger driven through one bicep. He instinctively opened his mouth to cry out, and sucked in the water.

As he struggled to break free and his lungs strove and failed to find air, he wondered where Demian had gone, but suddenly dying was much easier than he'd ever guessed.

II

Hanuvar levered the body the rest of the way into the rain barrel and pushed the revenant's booted feet down until the dead man was fully submerged. He looked up and down the alley, his gaze lingering only briefly at the dirty tarp under which he'd lain.

Antires, panting as though he'd run a long distance, eyed him accusingly.

"They're revenants, Antires. Their job is tracking down the emperor's enemies, midwives, the oddly gifted, and anyone else they don't like then hanging them, crucifying them, or burning them alive."

The Herrene nodded but his gaze was dark. "I still don't like killing a man."

"He'd have slain either of us, given the chance. And he'd have been much slower about it."

"He said he had someone watching."

"I left the other man's body in that storage shed." Hanuvar nodded toward the cluster of small buildings beyond the alley.

Antires' dark eyes widened. "How did you—"

Hanuvar shook his head. There wasn't time for detailed discussion. He had simply weaved drunkenly toward the other revenant. Often a direct approach worked best. A staggering drunkard, warned away, suddenly spinning to attack, had caught the revenant off guard. Success all came down to knowing the habits of your enemies and the ground you were to fight upon.

"What do we do now?" Antires asked.

"I need to know how they found us."

"You couldn't have talked to these?"

"No." There'd been no time to question the first, not when he'd been placed to watch for the leader's arrival. And Hanuvar had needed to dispatch the second quickly, in case the third came around.

"You can explain later. Shall I ready the horses?"

"I want you to look around. There may be more. They tend to travel in groups of three. Often multiples."

"So six."

"Or nine. Or twelve."

"Or three hundred," Antires said. "I get it. You sure we just shouldn't count ourselves lucky and leave?"

"No."

"Very well," his friend said reluctantly. "Where shall we meet?"

"Our room. If I'm not there by nine bells, start on your way."

Hanuvar heard the usual muttered protestations as he drew up the hood of his cloak. He stepped into the street and approached a bonfire where an impromptu dance was underway. Wisps of frosty air rose from the mouths of the crowd as they sang together. Somewhere outside he expected to find the third revenant.

III

Vennian enjoyed the warmth of the crackling hearth at his back, and fine wine in his goblet. The duck had been well seasoned with skin crisped to perfection. The reek of the mineral springs, though, marred everything, and he was astonished by the magistrate's claims that one grew inured to it. Even as he sipped the fragrant vintage, Vennian was aware of the omnipresent stench of spoiled eggs. It was enough to put a man off omelets for weeks.

Beyond the little cluster of couches where he lay with the village magistrate and his family, his two men had set aside helms and cloaks and mingled with the patricians gathered around the banquet tables. He hadn't known them long, for he had taken command of them after their predecessor had died under mysterious circumstances. But he had known their character from the first. They weren't the rough and tumble louts like Myrikus and his band, but proper revenants, raised in ancient homes and destined for high office.

The dozen-odd guests in the villa had initially been cautious of all three of them, until they'd realized that beyond their polished armor these revenants shared a similar background and reverence for the finer qualities of life.

Beyond them lay wide windows looking onto the springs, from which steam billowed. The villa had been built beside the best of them. The magistrate had told him that more dangerous springs lay to the east. The darkening sky touched distant snowcapped peaks with a dull blue, though enough light yet remained to conjure frosty sparkles.

Evara lay on the couch to Vennian's left, garbed in a finely tailored stola decorated with the black and gold of the Revenant Order. She looked deceptively at ease, a thin, well-groomed woman gracefully sliding toward middle age. The former witch had come a long way since he'd plucked her from that obscure backwater and set her on a righteous path. She picked at the duck leg on her plate with seeming concentration, but he knew the black eyes under her dark brow might be focused far beyond mortal affairs, giving him an advantage over other groups hunting enemies of the state. Or she might just be nursing resentments.

The magistrate finished his discussion with an older, dignified slave, who bowed politely before turning away. Some, Vennian had heard, believed all slaves were to be pitied, but those accorded status in a rich man's home lived better lives than many freeborn men.

The magistrate favored Vennian with an unctuous, gap-toothed smile. "My apologies. There was some confusion about the timing of tonight's sacrifice. Do you know that it was only a few generations ago they actually sacrificed a virgin during the festival? Ghastly waste of a good virgin!" He then laughed, and Vennian sensed this was a joke employed by the magistrate before. "Do you know, I'd think the gods would tire of virgins. More seasoned bed partners are far more interesting!"

"What do you sacrifice now?" Evara asked without looking up.

"A bullock on the first day, but every evening we prepare the finest of meals and send it into the abyss, the same way we used to hurl youngsters. Acarcia must like it, because all of the winters have been short since we took up that particular custom."

Vennian had little interest in the worship of the minor mountain god or his festival, and the magistrate must have sensed it, for he cleared his throat and changed topics. "You were telling me about this Hanuvar impostor of yours. What do you think he plans to do?"

Vennian's voice was thin, and sharp. In the field he used it to advantage, but its quality always troubled him in closer quarters. He spoke quietly, a habit he'd adopted to lessen his strident tone. "He will work mischief, wherever he goes. But he will not get far. We are very close on his heels."

"Destruction and death have followed him," Evara said without looking up. "From the fire at the amphitheater in Hidrestus to the death of Senator Marcius."

Vennian shot her a dark look she could pretend to have missed, staring as she was at her plate.

The magistrate's watery eyes widened. "He's an arsonist? You think he might burn down the villa?"

"With your guards and my men, inside and outside, I don't think there's any real danger," Vennian said. "In any case, we don't think this was his destination. We believe he's headed over the mountains and on toward Derva itself."

"Retracing his steps," the magistrate mused.

"Except that he's an impostor," Vennian swiftly reminded him.

"Maybe he thinks he really is Hanuvar. It's a wonder he hasn't tried to find some elephants."

Beside them, Evara's head whipped up as though she meant to violently rise. And then she might as well have been carved from stone, so still did she sit. Her eyes were closed, her expression remote and far away, just as it had been those nights Vennian had forced her. She was experiencing another episode.

He turned from the magistrate's confused questions and addressed her in a cutting whisper. "What's happening? What are you seeing?"

Her voice was low, though every vowel she spoke was stretched to twice its standard length.

"Hanuvar . . . He knows. He knows we're here."

"I thought you said it wasn't Hanuvar!" The magistrate's voice rose in alarm.

"Where is he?" Vennian demanded. He swung off his couch and stood over her.

"He's . . ." She shuddered. "He's killed them."

"Killed?" the magistrate asked. One of the nearby clusters of nobles looked up from their knot of conversation and stared in alarm. "Who has he killed? What's going on? Is she some kind of secress? Is it really Hanuvar?"

"No, no," Vennian said quickly over his shoulder, inwardly cursing Evara. Word had recently been passed along that they were never to reveal it was Hanuvar himself they pursued. Vennian gripped Evara's right arm. "Pull yourself together and report."

She remained entranced, even when he shook her. Her head lolled. "Dead, dead, all three are dead and he will not flee until he kills us all." She then opened her mouth and let out a strange, tittering laugh, her eyes rolling. Vennian slapped her.

She gasped, blinked, felt her reddened cheek, and color returned to her face.

Vennian's lip curled. "I've told you before that you must master your outbursts."

Fire blazed in her eyes for a moment before her inscrutable demeanor reasserted itself.

Vennian's rage boiled close to the surface. "What did you see?"

"A moment. Let me sort my thoughts."

"She is a seeress, isn't she?" The magistrate's voice climbed toward hysteria. "Have you brought a witch into my villa?"

Vennian had no patience for this nonsense. Teeth gritted, he looked over his shoulder at the aging magistrate, his sluggish wife, and their slack-jawed son. "She recanted and puts her powers to use for the emperor. Do you question the judgment of one of the emperor's officers?"

"No, I—"

The old slave ran in and bent at the magistrate's side, his calm shattered. It was no great trouble to hear what the man said.

"Master, there's a body near the sacrificial platform. A man in a uniform." He struggled not to look toward Vennian, but his eyes briefly flicked his direction. "A revenant."

While the magistrate asked for more details, Vennian snarled at Evara. "Do you have anything that's useful? At all?"

"If I can touch something Hanuvar's touched," Evara said tightly, "I might be able to find him."

Vennian brusquely bid farewell to the magistrate and gathered his two officers. Once more garbed with helms and swords, wrapped in heavy cloaks, he left with them and the witch and the alarmed old slave. Some of the magistrate's small guard force turned up, so unnerved by the presence of the revenants they looked uncertain whether they wanted to help or run. Vennian ordered them to keep the crowd back and look for suspicious people.

Little snowflakes swirled down through the dusky sky as the old slave led them. His dignified manner vanished, and he babbled now about how he'd been carrying the first platter when he spied the corpse.

Between the villa and the cliffside lay a grassy sward and dozens of smoking pools of water. Five hundred feet away, the cliff edge had been fenced with stone so drunken visitors wouldn't stumble off the mountain.

Pertian, the more seasoned of Vennian's two officers, spoke gruffly. "I still don't understand how he could sneak around without being seen. Until the guards ordered guests away, this place was crawling with people."

"Not so many," Vennian objected. "And most were well drunk and keeping to the mineral baths or the fire pits."

"There it is, officers." The old slave pointed to the cliff's edge.

Some enterprising soul had erected a trio of wooden decks that projected out from the cliff itself; Vennian supposed that they would afford an even better view of the drop or some distant mountain waterfall. He himself had never cared for heights and could scarce imagine walking to the fence near the cliff, let alone out onto one of the wooden observation points.

Yet that was where the headless body of one of his men was pointing, for it was stretched out on the ground with a hand aimed that direction. Sitting on that deck was a chair supporting what Vennian first took to be an empty helmet.

It wasn't empty, though, and the old slave knew it, for he bent over and began to retch.

Pertian considered the body with casual interest. "This is Telian. Look at those hairy knuckles."

Vennian squeezed Evara's shoulder. "You said you could gain information if you touched something the impostor had handled. He's clearly handled this body."

She shook her head. "I want that." She pointed to a placard now visible against the chair legs on the platform. "Touching the body might overwhelm me with the pain of Telian's last moments, and then I'd be useless for some time."

Vennian bit back a retort suggesting she was already useless. He barked for Garnan to retrieve the placard. The younger of the two officers grunted his assent, flexed hands in his fingerless gloves to improve circulation, and started forward, hand to hilt.

"Watch to the left," Vennian ordered Pertian. "I'll watch to the right. Let's follow on his heels in case the impostor's lying in wait. Old man, cease your vomiting and head in."

As he and Pertian and Evara followed Garnan toward the cliff side, Vennian was suddenly conscious of distant music and laughter rising from the main street.

Garnan stopped just beyond the projecting wooden deck and its chair, contemplating the bloodless, staring face framed by the helmet.

"What does the sign say?"

"I can't quite make it out." Garnan stepped onto the planks and bent to retrieve the placard.

Vennian heard an ominous creak, then the sound of splintering wood. Garnan started to turn, but the entire projection dropped out of sight, taking him with it. They heard Garnan's scream of terror receding for a long while as he plummeted down the cliff side.

Vennian spun on Evara, hand raised to slap her. "Why couldn't you see that coming?"

She cowered, lifted a hand to block, then lowered it, probably recalling resistance made him more angry. "My insights can't be controlled! You know that!"

"There's someone moving over there," Pertian cried. "You! Stop!"

Vennian looked away from Evara to spy a figure dashing into the mists to their left.

Pertian sprinted after, unsheathed gladius in hand. Vennian

lagged only a few paces behind, threading through drifting snowflakes and wafting smoke from the mineral pools. Pertian was still shouting for the figure to halt. Vennian had lost sight of their quarry, and simply followed his soldier.

Suddenly Pertian dropped with a cry. Vennian slowed, fearing for a moment there was a pit hidden amongst the grounds. But Pertian was still alive, and calling pitifully to him. Some unseen force pulled the officer backward on his stomach. He clawed for purchase in well-trimmed grass as he was hauled toward a smoking mineral pit.

Dashing after, Vennian perceived a rope wrapped about his companion's ankle. A snare. He also saw the wooden barricade emblazoned with skulls and a red warning sign lying face up as Pertian was dragged past it toward the steaming pool. The magistrate had told them a handful of the mineral pools were scalding hot, or worse, and used only for special sacrifices, being well marked and barricaded at all other times.

Vennian picked up his pace too late. He saw Pertian's eyes bulging in fear as the rope jerked him over the crusted ledge and into the wide circular pool. The soldier screamed as his legs hit, and then the whole of his body dropped in with a splash and a surprisingly small sizzle, and no sounds were left him.

Vennian couldn't even see the body cooking in the scalding water. Bile rising, he stepped back from the searing steam, searching the grounds. He started at a sound behind him, only to discover the witch coming from behind. She was panting from the run.

"Can you manage anything useful now?" Vennian demanded. "If you can't, you'll regret it for the rest of your limited days!"

"He's over there." Evara pointed toward a little shack on the edge of the mineral baths, near a smoldering fire pit. "On that roof."

"Go get the guards," Vennian snapped. He rushed forward, stopping at the fire pit to grab a torch. An arrow sped at him from the roof and narrowly missed his throat. He hurried forward, keeping on, teeth gritted. Two more arrows slashed down from the dark cloaked figure atop the shed, each drawing perilously close, but Vennian's luck held, and he reached the side of the building and dropped the torch at its base. He dove away as another arrow stood quivering in the ground at his feet.

The wood was old and dry and flared up on the instant. Red flame soared heavenward and a rush of heat spread out. Here, too, there was a single scream.

Vennian backed away, searching the darkness. If that had been the impostor, his fate had finally caught up to him. He'd seen no one leap clear, and nothing could have survived that blaze.

The witch drew up beside him once more. "I thought I told you to get the guards," he said, though he wasn't as angry as he might have been. He watched the flames.

He was a little startled when she put a hand to his shoulder. Her voice was kind. "I was worried about you," she said, which was a little surprising. So was the sword she drove into the back of his neck.

His arms flailed without his command, and his legs collapsed. He fell sideways and glared as he scrabbled for one of her booted feet. But she stepped out of range, her eyes shifting back and forth between him and the villa, obviously concerned about witnesses. As he died he saw the snarl of hatred on her lips, though he couldn't hear her words. He was dead by the time she drove one of the arrows into the wound where she'd stabbed him.

IV

The cave was very different from the soft beds Hanuvar and Antires had known last night, and from the cots they'd slept on during their weeks with the circus. For all that, the fire near the cave mouth was warm, and the supplies they'd brought from the feast were wonderfully fresh. They would enjoy them while they could, for they'd have to subsist on dry rations as they advanced into the mountain pass.

They had started their trip into the Ardenines with a few weeks to spare before winter would make the crossing impossible, and he hoped this storm was not a sign the season had begun early.

Hanuvar rarely second-guessed himself, but he often considered past events to better learn from them. It might be that the goddess Diara had been wrong, and that revenants and other foes could not have found him if he and Antires had pushed on—they would be well beyond this storm if they had. But Hanuvar had made the best decision possible based on the information before him. If he had sped on across the Ardenines, he would not have been able to aid Ciprion, or to stop the skin-shifting monster, or help poor Rufus.

Even as he worried that his crossing was imperiled, he missed the friends and allies he and Antires had made among the circus people. He had come to treasure not just their company, but their routines, from the dismantling of camp to their pre-performance energies to the songs they sang on the march. No more would he shovel hay before the friendly gray bulk of Kordeka, or watch Shenassa at target practice, or smile as the leopards bounded like kittens to Mellika's command. The road with them had not been without its toils, but it had been bright and full of laughter.

At least he was not fully alone.

Antires sat near the fire, busily jotting notes on a parchment in the code he'd devised. Hanuvar had discouraged him from committing anything to paper, worried their identities would be revealed if they were ever searched. But Antires insisted he had to record the most important details as they took place, to aid his memory. The cipher was their compromise.

Beyond him, their horses munched on hay flakes cast to the cave floor. They too were enjoying a last rich feast before the crossing, though they did not know it.

He heard the crush of snow under feet outside the cave. As Hanuvar put hand to a spear, a woman's voice called above the moan of the wind. "I know you're in there. I've come alone. To talk."

He stepped from the firelight. He'd never heard Evara's voice, but he guessed her identity on the instant. The revenant he'd questioned had said the witch was like a magical bloodhound.

"Come forward." He held the spear ready in both hands.

She stepped into the cave mouth, cloak-shrouded shoulders hunched to the cold. She was a small woman of early middle years, and the firelight harshened the lines of her face. She pulled a dark scarf from her chin and mouth. Her eyes held the weary, hunted look of someone worn down by combat or great stress. Hanuvar nodded Antires to the exit, and the writer threw on his cloak and stepped past her to peer outside.

The woman walked forward, and Hanuvar lowered the short spear. Her eyes met his, and their deep honey brown reflected the flickering scarlet flame. She started, and then she blinked in surprise. "I didn't . . ." Her voice trailed off.

Antires returned to report. "No one's out there. Not that I can see, at least."

Hanuvar considered the woman. "Are there others with you?"

"No. They think you were killed. Who really died in the blaze?"

"I left one of the revenant's bodies." He'd wanted one or two witnesses to think he had died, and had been much obliged when the revenant tribune had supplied the flame. "Why are you here?"

"I thought . . ." She shook her head.

She had expected something he couldn't identify, and its absence surprised her. Curious. He stepped back, gesturing to their little fire. "Come. You look cold."

She hesitated, then walked in and put her hands above the blaze, continuing to stare at him.

"I saw you kill the revenant," he said.

"Yes. I told the magistrate and his guards you'd been killed."

"Well, that's good," Antires said. He gave the woman a wide berth and joined Hanuvar's side of the fire.

Her gaze was solely upon Hanuvar. "I steered them toward you, you know. To make sure you got them. I don't know that Garnan would have advanced onto that outlook if I hadn't pretended I needed something you had touched. How did you manage to pull it down?"

"He climbed down the face," Antires explained, his pleasure in his friend's cleverness manifest. "He found some weak support beams. He tied a rope to the last one and looped it around a winch, then concealed himself and waited for their arrival." He then quoted Hanuvar: "Choose the ground where you mean to fight and lead your enemy to it."

"And you had a snare readied," she said to Hanuvar.

"You're staring at him," Antires said. "Is that because you just now decided he really is who they feared?"

"No." She spoke without hesitation. "I knew. Vennian knew."

"Then why do you keep staring?" Antires asked.

"Because . . ." Finally she looked to the Herrene and addressed him directly. "His aura's all wrong. The revenants—there was so much red, and swirling gray smoke. It's what I see now when I look in the mirror. But him." She pointed to Hanuvar. "Thousands, tens of thousands, died in your wars. And you murdered more men just today ... I don't understand."

"What does his aura look like?" Antires asked.

"It's almost completely pure," she said as if doubting her own words. "How can a murderer have a golden aura?"

"You're asking the wrong man," Hanuvar replied. "I'm a killer because I'm a soldier. And I became a soldier to protect my people. Why did you seek me out?"

"Are you going to kill more of them? More revenants?" Her eyes were searching, her speech pressured.

"Is that what you want me to do?"

Her answer was guttural and fierce. "Yes. They're holding dozens of your people, you know. One of your councilwomen. Your cousin. One of your dragon priestesses. The revenants dragged them all away to their secret tower. They won't come back. No one ever comes back."

He digested this news without response. He tried to tell himself this was no worse than he expected, but the specifics made that a lie. By dragon priestess Evara must mean one of those assigned as a special intermediary between the asalda and the people of Volanus. The Dervans, ever eager to impose their will upon others, still searched in vain for a way to master the will of asalda and use them as weapons of war. "Which of my cousins?" he asked. "Which of the councilwomen?"

"I do not know the name of your cousin. The councilwoman is Tanilia."

His nostrils flared. Tanilia, the mildest of all the vaunted seven, in the hands of the revenants? When last he'd interacted with her she had been dogmatically focused upon the creation and enforcement of regulations for balustrade heights, to protect small children living in apartments from falling. "Why her?"

"I don't know that." Evara's eyes shone with a kind of twisted hope. "They like to hurt people. They like to control them. They should be stopped."

"Yes." He understood her anger, but would not let his own change his chosen path. He explained with gentle clarity. "But I can't be an instrument of your vengeance."

"But are you the instrument of your own? We want similar things. And now that I see your aura, I think that maybe the gods want them too. Why else would they bless your actions?"

"I don't pretend to know the minds of gods, but whatever you see in my aura isn't thanks to my killing of Dervans."

She appeared to have trouble processing the statement. Her eyes shifted, revealing a soul unmoored and adrift.

He worked to bring her to shore. "There are better things to do than hunt revenants."

"Are there? You don't know the things they've done. The things I had to do." She flexed her fingers. "No, I didn't *have* to. I could have let them kill me, but it would have been a terrible death, and I was afraid." She continued bitterly. "I let them use me. I've revealed the hiding places of women who knew nothing of any kind of magic, just the aiding of childbirth, and a little herb lore. Of scholars studying the skies. Of truthtellers who embarrassed the better connected. They died horribly. All so I could keep on living." She looked up. "I killed Vennian, but his blood doesn't wash my hands clean."

"You're free now," Hanuvar said. "We mean to cross the Ardenines. You could come with us and begin anew in some little town. Practice your gifts as you will."

Her eyes were wary. "I'm not getting anywhere close to Derva. The revenants would find me."

"Something will find us all, in the end. We can make plans, but have to face each day's obstacle as it presents itself. And obstacles are more easily overcome in the presence of friends."

Her laugh was ill-humored and heavy with despair. "I am doomed. Don't you see that? Because of what I've done?"

"Then do better," Antires suggested.

She laughed again, at Antires, as though he had said something funny. It ended in a dry wheeze, and then her eyes burned as she set them upon Hanuvar. "Whatever you mean to do, the revenants will continue to hunt you."

"If they do, I will kill them."

"Then I will take solace from that. Right now you've confounded them. They're chasing a dozen different leads in a dozen different lands. Without me they'll lose your trail."

"That's good to hear."

"But there's something else following you. I've glimpsed it in my visions. It used to be a man, and now it's something more. It hungers for you."

"Where is it?" Antires asked. "What is it?"

"I'm not sure of the what. But it lies beyond the mountains, and it is gathering its power. You must remain alert."

"I will," Hanuvar assured her. Almost he extended his hand to her, but he guessed it would only make her shy away. "You do not need to go, Evara. At the least, share our fire tonight."

She shook her head as a dog shakes drops from its fur, then met his eyes a final time. "Farewell, Hanuvar." She turned and hurried from the cave.

Her tone suggested more than an ordinary goodbye, and he rushed after, only to meet a gust of icy snow. He stopped as a white swirl blinded him, for the trail's edge lay only a few feet out. When his vision cleared the woman was gone. All that remained was her scarf, blowing free down the mountain side.

Chapter 13:
The Light of the Lovely Ones

❖

I

The storm blew out after the first few days, leaving them to scramble through the high pass[13] and start the long way down through the scrubby highlands below the tree line. It seemed the blizzard at the start of their climb had been a singular event, and not winter's opening gambit. But Hanuvar left nothing to chance, and pushed them hard, so that they bedded down exhausted each evening.

On the fifteenth day, the two woke on the far side of the high peaks and had just fixed saddles to their animals when immense flakes of snow began to drift down out of the cloudy sky. It seemed little enough at first, but as the morning wore on, the rate of snowfall accelerated, and Hanuvar suspected rough times lay ahead. He had grown accustomed to privation after long years of campaigning, and his previous passage over the Ardenines. For all that Antires was in fair shape, he was no veteran, and was used to far warmer climes. By the late morning he was shivering regularly, and Hanuvar had to remind him to stop and stamp his feet and flex his fingers.

Antires might have done better if they'd been riding the horses and absorbing their warmth. Unfortunately the rocky ground was too uncertain for any extended time in the saddle, and the trail

---

[13] This was the Balevein Pass, rather than that used by Hanuvar's army during his invasion of Tyvol. For the first instance, and the later passage through the Ardenines by Adruvar and his army, Hanuvar employed the lower pass, known as the Cerendein.   *—Silenus*

frequently threaded through narrow drop-offs to tree-lined gorges hundreds of feet below.

By noon Antires had grown even worse, and followed Hanuvar's reminders sluggishly, all while insisting he be allowed to lie down and rest.

Hanuvar knew this for the embrace of death men craved in the very cold, high places. The chief of the physicians he'd traveled with had explained this could happen to even the brave, and those smart enough to know better, because their bodies were accustomed to warmer lands, where short term rest would repair, not kill.

He kept after the younger man to stay on his feet and encouraged him to sing. He talked with him about his favorite plays, favorite foods, songs from his childhood—anything at all to keep him alert.

Ideally it would have been best to stop and build a fire, but Hanuvar feared that the snow would keep coming and they'd be stranded in the highlands. As he forced them on, he decided to change their immediate objective.

Long years before, his scouts had brought word of a sanctuary on the Dervan side of this pass, a retreat for the sick and weary. Though he had crossed on a lower pass, wide enough to accommodate the troops and equipment they required, the sanctuary had sent him emissaries and pledges both of neutrality and offers to assist the sick and injured. He had never seen their settlement, but remembered the way told him by his scouts.

He had deliberately picked this pass because it was most direct— they were traveling too late in the season to risk a longer trek—and it happened to be near the primary route to the sanctuary. Even though only another few days of travelling would see them into warmer lands, it seemed they would have to stop. Antires just wouldn't make it without a reprieve.

And so Hanuvar diverted. After the first little while, Antires noticed the change in direction. The man's face was hidden by the hood of the thick furred robe he wore, and his voice rose weakly from within. "Why are we going upward?"

"You should know by now it's not always just one direction in the mountains."

Since that was true, Antires didn't question. Hanuvar didn't want his companion worrying, and so didn't explain further. He had enough apprehensions of his own and considered how best to address them as they pressed on through the cold lash of swirling winds. First, he worried that with a week's growth of beard he would be far more easily recognizable as the former leader of an invading army. Second, wounded combatants often lingered around places of healing, and Hanuvar dreaded some encounter with former friend or foe would find him out. And, if not that, suppose that the Dervans had destroyed the ancient place, or that it had been abandoned? His information was, after all, nearly a quarter century out of date.

Probably it still stood there though, as it had for hundreds of years previous, because people grew accustomed to shrines and temples and sacred places, and this sanctuary was said to be all of those.

As afternoon turned toward evening the snowfall eased, and Hanuvar spotted a light burning to the northwest. Before much longer the trail widened, leading past ancient steps cut into the stony slope that stretched up the mountain's face toward the light, and the craggy summit. Antires remarked upon the bright lantern and the stairs, but named it a star. His breathing was labored and his gait unsteady. The steps, even snow covered, were wide and deep enough for the horses, but Hanuvar didn't risk urging Antires to ride, for the snow hid patches of ice. He instead shouldered much of the younger man's weight as he guided him up each stair, the horses trailing behind.

A hundred feet straight up the stairwell rose, and then started into a switchback pattern before they neared a wide cave aglow with yellow lanterns. Figures in dark robes beckoned for them, and Antires woke to danger.

"It's all right," Hanuvar told him. "We're at a sanctuary." He projected confidence he did not feel, although when the robed folk arrived, they nodded pleasantly and aided their climb up the final steps.

Hanuvar politely held back from any offer of aid, hiding his face behind his scarf and hood, but letting the healers assist Antires and take the horses. He'd previously moved the most important of their gear to the battered pack now on his shoulder or hidden in the folds of his garments.

A smokeless fire crackled fifty feet back from the entrance, where Hanuvar spotted a row of empty cots and bedding. There was likewise a row of spears, stacked barrels, and shelves lined with tools and tinder. The cavern proved a long tunnel, part natural, part chiseled out, with a wider exit opposite and lower than where they entered.

One of the robed figures pushed back his hood, his smile kind, and offered Hanuvar a cup of steaming liquid. He accepted it with thanks. The moment the scent of the chicken broth reached his nostrils, his mouth watered. He ignored the impulse to drink and studied his surroundings. The robed folk were all in their late twenties to early thirties, too young to remember Hanuvar firsthand. Three were women and one a man, and none of them looked at him suspiciously. They had cast back their hoods and two of the women were already leading the three horses deeper into the cave. The third was steadying Antires beside the fire.

"This is terrible weather for travelling," the young woman beside Antires commented. She was broad faced, with a small mole beneath one of her dark eyes. "Was one of you injured?"

"Only from the cold," Hanuvar answered. "We're grateful to you for your hospitality."

"You are welcome. Everyone is afflicted with pains of some kind, and we will happily help you with yours." Again she smiled. It wasn't that her expression was false so much as unearned and a little lax, as though offered by someone deep in drink.

All four of these sentinels smiled too readily. After a few moments of study, Hanuvar decided that they were manifestly sober, and wondered if they had been selected for this welcoming quality, or trained to it, or if this was simply their custom.

This sanctuary was famed for its healers, and these clearly demonstrated some competence in their care for Antires, whom they soon had out of his outer robe and drinking the warm broth by the fireside. The woman with the mole suggested Antires ought to be looked over by a more experienced healer to be found in the hospital beyond, for she was concerned he might have frostbite. Hanuvar saw no evidence of damage to his friend's fingers or toes, but his color was certainly off and he shivered visibly; and so he bundled himself and Antires back up, helped his friend to his feet, and followed the woman down through the tunnel.

Beyond the cave exit they walked into a small bowl-shaped valley. The temperature was notably warmer, no doubt in part because the wind couldn't build much speed while sheltered in the peaks, but also because hot mist billowed up from fissures scattered through the valley. A sheltered corral lay on their left, where their three horses were helping themselves to hay. Directly ahead, three dozen small thatch-roofed buildings sat at the valley's center, beside a brook, bridged in four places by arches of wood. Snow-garlanded gardens and farmland rose in wide terraces to either hand. No one tended the stubbly fields, but well-bundled shepherds walked amongst small herds of sheep and goats browsing on crop leavings. A distant rooster crowed, exciting another to respond.

Antires, ever curious, had wakened further at sight of this. "What is this place?"

"Haven't you heard of us?" Rania, their escort, asked. Again she smiled.

When Antires didn't answer, she explained. "Our people are followers of the great physician, Entalus. For five centuries we have studied his teachings and provided succor to the wounded and broken."

"How many of you are here?" Antires asked.

"Enough to manage and tend those in need."

Hanuvar had the sense she wasn't being deliberately evasive, for her reply was breezy and cheerful. By his own estimates the valley might comfortably house two hundred, maybe a little more, but he had the sense there were no more than half that in residence.

They crunched through the snow-covered pathway that led to a huge central building. It alone was built of stone, and radiated stately antiquity, though the pillars themselves were bare of ornament, and no gods or maidens or monsters looked down from the pediment. Five chimneys climbed from its roof, each curling smoke heavenward.

"Who lives here?" Antires asked. "The healers?"

"Most of us study to become healers, and master the lessons of our teacher," Rania said. "The wounded and suffering live here as well."

"Are you a healer, then?"

"I'm studying. I came here four years ago." She continued as they neared the main building: "I had broken my arm. I was tending an olive tree and reached too far while my brother should have been holding the ladder. The arm never set right and always gave me pain. Until I came here."

"And you never left?"

"No. I can't fully move my arm"—she paused to show that she could not raise it past her shoulder—"but the pain has ebbed, and I've stayed on to help others. Some are in far more agony than me."

"It's said that you offer comfort to soldiers," Hanuvar said.

"We have some here. From many lands."

Hanuvar had briefly hoped she would say none were currently in place. "From which lands do these soldiers come?"

She climbed the three steps to the entry and smiled benignly at him. "Our guests renounce their homelands if they stay here, along with all their struggles and their hatreds. We do not discuss pasts, so that refuge might be provided to all."

"Of course," Hanuvar said, hiding his irresolution as he tucked his face more deeply in his winter wrappings. If there were any Volani veterans left here after the chaotic withdrawal from Dervan lands, he wasn't sure how he might be received. Even if they didn't blame their general for the injuries that bound them to this place, they might not welcome his intrusion into what remained of their lives. Would they castigate him? Pass word to the revenants of his passage? Or would they welcome an opportunity to reunite with their kin, or even be capable of aiding in their rescue, providing they were well enough to depart?

Inside, the main building reminded Hanuvar of a temple, with its long straight aisle terminating in a great apse, although it lacked a large statue to a god. Much of the interior was divided into little apartment blocks of roofless rooms of fabric framed by sturdy timber. The curtained doors were open to some of the living quarters, revealing that each had enough room only for a cot and a small table or standing shelves displaying a few scrolls or personal items. Rania told them that these were standard guest quarters, where they themselves would sleep this evening, then led the way to a half circle of couches and stools placed before a huge central hearth. Two other people took their ease there, one a young man with his leg missing below the knee, another a middle-aged woman who looked completely normal until she glanced up at their arrival. Her eyes were haunted with longing for something forever vanished.

They were dark wells, for drowning, and Hanuvar had to look away, wondering if his own face sometimes mirrored hers.

He stood to one side as Rania guided Antires to a couch near the flickering hearth and wrapped him in a blanket she picked from a fireside stand. As if by magic, more attendants in red tunics arrived with beverages, cheeses, and a bread loaf, which they deposited near Antires.

"What of you?" Rania asked Hanuvar. "Have you no hurts?"

"My needs are more basic. If you would show me to a washroom, I would be most grateful."

"But of course."

Hanuvar patted his friend's shoulder. The Herrene, slowly chewing some cheese, looked more content than he had in days. The shivering had stopped and his breathing seemed near normal. "I'll be back soon," Hanuvar said.

Antires returned a satisfied nod. "I'll be here."

"Your friend will be fine." Rania's friendly smile should have been reassuring.

Hanuvar followed her into the left wing, wondering if his sense of misgiving was in any way justified, and if he'd feel more at ease once he shaved.

Rania told him this section of the building was built over hot springs, which heated the many small pools bubbling in their stone foundations. Though tempted to soak, he finished his bath quickly, then shaved by aid of a small bronze mirror. He returned to the main chamber in less than a half hour, walking swiftly through the long rows of canvas cubicles, strangely certain Antires would be absent on his return.

But his friend still lay in front of the fire on one of the comfortable couches, struggling to keep his eyes open. Antires had finally grown comfortable enough that he had set the blanket aside, and his robe gaped at the collar. One half-full mug sat on a camp table beside him, but the tray of food had been removed. The dead-eyed woman did not look up; the injured man snored, curled into a protective ball on one side of his wide, cushioned chair.

Rather than approaching, Hanuvar watched, amused as his friend surrendered at last and closed his eyes. He enviously wondered what it must feel like to relax so completely.

At the sound of someone walking their direction from up the apse, he turned to find a woman, robed like the others in pinkish red, though her garment was more finely fashioned, into a proper Dervan stola. A pyramidal lantern of opaque glass, framed in brass, dangled in one hand, burning dimly from within.

She stopped a few paces out from Hanuvar. Her face was narrow, her chin pointed. She looked to be in her late thirties, though the years apparently did not weigh heavily, for she beamed like the others. If their expressions had been oddly pleasant, hers approached euphoria, as though she might erupt with spasms of joy at any moment. "I sense your pain," she said to Hanuvar, as though his discomfort were the most important thing in the world.

He indicated Antires. "It's my friend who's suffered. I've just come from a warm bath."

The woman walked closer and closer until Hanuvar understood she was intent on invading his personal space. She reached for his shoulder and grasped it. The scent of her hair ointment wafted over him, a mix of rose and some citrus fragrance.

He watched her face as her small, long-fingered hand tightened. Somehow he felt her touch as warm and soothing even through his clothing.

Her eyes had not left his own, and in their deeps he saw fascination and hunger. Intense physical interest from her would have been confusing enough, but this look was stranger still, and troubled him. But then so did the sense of warm contentment he felt at the woman's proximity. Contrary to his natural impulse, and all natural instinct, he felt the pull of a smile, and strove to keep his expression neutral.

"I sense the pain you carry within," she said.

"I am here only to see to my friend. He is the one who needs tending."

He put his hand to hers and gently withdrew it.

"Your concern for your friend is admirable. You're one of those who doesn't understand the weight of his own burden. You are lost, and seek a home, because you can no longer return to yours."

The accuracy of her words alarmed him. "Are you a mind reader, my lady?"

"No," she answered with a laugh. "I've learned to sense these kinds of things." Her smile was infectious. "Those who embrace the teachings of this valley find a land they can call home. Some suffer crippling physical injuries. Others have experienced privation, and misery, and loss. They have learned to laugh and smile again here. They are whole, no matter if they thought something missing before."

He bowed his head so he could shift his gaze from her own. "My friend and I cannot stay."

"I see I will make no progress with you until you are satisfied as to his safety." She glided past him and on toward the patients at the fire. The woman with the sad eyes transformed almost on the instant, her gaze no longer vacant. A smile touched her lips, and then she sighed in pleasure. The wounded man seated to her right slept on, but his brow smoothed, and he shifted into a comfortable sprawl.

Hanuvar followed, enjoying the sense of ease her company granted him. Stepping to Antires' head, he saw his friend grin in his sleep.

The woman set the lantern down upon the table and put a hand to its opaque side. Either she was inured to pain or the glass was strangely cool, for she did not flinch. She set her other hand to Antires' forehead.

She closed her eyes. After a ten count, they opened. Her smile remained kind, but her gaze was sharp and searching.

Hanuvar struggled to mask his own strange joy.

"Why do you hold on to your pain?" she asked him. "You're not one of those sort, are you?"

"I do not like to be changed against my will."

"I understand. But I ask you to think of this. Maybe your pain is what changed you against your will, and it is our healing that returns you to your natural state."

He allowed that was possible with a single nod, though he held off an impulse to praise her. "How is my friend?"

"I do not think there is lasting damage. He needs rest for another day or more. And I think we should watch his left foot to ensure that there is no frostbite."

"I didn't see you look at his foot."

"I can see the effluence of a patient's injuries without a mundane examination. For instance, I can see the places where you have old injuries by the way energy flows about your body. It is marred there near your knee, and along your arm, and in many other places, but most of all you have sustained injury to your very soul. There is such anguish there. What happened?"

"More than I care to say."

She lifted her lantern. Her smile dimmed, and he felt shame for that. "I have pried too far," she said. "I apologize."

"No, you are very kind, both to my friend and myself. It is I who must apologize. I am . . . a private person."

"As are so many who come here. Over time they know the power of our measures."

She passed on to the others, and Hanuvar watched her talking with the woman, whose eyes might still be ringed by dark circles but were no longer hollow. He defeated the impulse to remain close to that spiritual warmth. Instead, he stepped apart, wondering how far the effect spread, and whether it was the healer's power, or a property of her strange lantern.

From six paces out he still felt the effect. It didn't begin to lessen until he'd passed beyond ten paces, and he still experienced a measure of its power at twenty. At thirty paces he felt empty and apart, as though he were in the midst of the vast ocean, with nothing to see on any hand but rising waves and a pale sky.

That sense of loneliness was so ordinary for him he was shocked at how much he despised its reintroduction, and how difficult it was to defeat the impulse to return to the healer's comforting presence.

He knew he was not the kind who reveled in discomfort. Neither was he the kind who drowned his sorrow in wine; and the reeling ebullience of this experience was not so different from the artificial joy some were granted by an amphora.

The woman lingered over the two beside the fire, then passed slowly on along the hallway. Only once she was far along did Hanuvar return. Rania was gathering up Antires' half-empty mug, and a platter left beside the other patients. The crippled man still rested comfortably. The sad-eyed woman's thousand-yard stare had returned. And Antires shifted under his blanket, awake but sleepily eying his friend.

"This place is wonderful," he said. "Why don't we stop at more inns like this?"

Rania laughed and spoke to Hanuvar. "I saw Calisia tending you.

You should feel honored. She doesn't usually greet any but the most severely injured on their first day."

"There's nothing wrong with me," Hanuvar said.

Rania spoke with heartfelt sincerity. "She sees deeper than surface injury. Do you remember the tall man who helped with your horses? That's Decius. There's nothing physically wrong with him, but his son and daughter drowned and he couldn't save them. His agony is real. And she helped."

"I believe she could," Hanuvar said, then changed the path of the conversation. "You said earlier that no one likes to talk about their pasts, but what if I'm looking for friends? I'm wondering if veterans from the Second Volani War once took refuge here."

"They may have."

"And do you know if any of them remain?"

She eyed him for a long moment. "Sometimes men come here, seeking other men with prices on their heads. You can understand why we don't encourage this kind of inquiry."

"Of course."

"We would have to know and trust your motives first," Rania continued.

"I don't think we'll be around here long enough to get to know each other well."

"Don't be in too big a hurry. You should give your friend a few days to rest."

Hanuvar looked over at Antires, comfortably slumping on the couch. "Is that necessary? Another days' travel might see us out of the highlands."

"He's weak. Surely you can tell that."

"I suppose I can."

"I'll be back in just a little while to show you your chambers. Dinner will be served shortly." She turned away.

"Your pardon, miss," Hanuvar said, "but there's something I must know."

"Of course." Rania paused with platter in hand.

"How do you sustain yourself? We surely owe you a donation for your hospitality."

"We have little need for money."

Hanuvar thought that refreshing and a little strange, but then perhaps visitors brought them all they needed to trade for their healing skills. He bowed his head and the woman departed.

He knelt beside Antires, remarking casually: "We must be on our guard."

"For what?"

"There's something here I don't understand."

Antires rolled his eyes. "What you don't understand is a place where people are honestly trying to care for others." He spoke too loudly, and Hanuvar raised a finger to his lips. Antires continued in a whisper. "It's a rare thing, true. But instead of being suspicious, you should be grateful. Or at least you should savor it."

"How does this place survive?"

"They seem to have enough."

"What about Ceori tribes, and bandits?"

"Didn't you say your scouts had told you about it? What did they say?"

"That the Ceori considered it a holy site. But that wouldn't stop bandits. These people must have some kind of protectors."

"That doesn't matter to us, does it?"

"We have the lovely ones to protect us," the woman to their right said.

Hanuvar has assumed her lost in her own worries. He bobbed his head in greeting, then asked a question of her. "Who are they?"

"The protectors. Chosen from birth to guard the valley."

"What are they?"

"A warrior breed, selected for their grace, and power, and beauty. They're tall and strong and happy. It's said they can run further and faster than normal men, and throw twice as far. And in those rare instances when they must go into battle, they do so laughing, for they feel no pain."

"Do you believe that?" Hanuvar asked.

"I've seen them," she admitted. "And there are so many miracles in this place, why should I doubt stories about another one?"

"True enough." Hanuvar nodded his thanks, then returned Antires' amused smile, though he did not mean it. He wished to be gone from this place and its strange healers with their peculiar powers. Much as he craved company, he wished it to arise from the fellowship of men and women he knew and loved, not through some artifice.

One night, he thought. He would permit Antires to recover in safety, and take the opportunity to search for any of his surviving veterans.

II

Dinner was simple fare, eaten in a small room where less than a dozen people sat at long tables. There were hardboiled eggs, and soup, and dark bread. Hanuvar and Antires were seated in a room dedicated to the "newcomers," as one of their hosts told them, people who had happened by in only the last few weeks. Most were bandaged in some way. One of them was a pale, mustached man. Clothed as he was in checkered pants, his gold hair combed back, he was of obvious Ceori extraction, and Hanuvar knew from the yellow and green cloth pattern that he was a Cemoni tribesman. The man's right sleeve had been cut away and a bandage wrapped his lower arm and palm.

Hanuvar offered him his wineskin with the traditional greeting of the Cemoni tribe, whose language he spoke fluently, though he deliberately did so with a Dervan accent. The Ceori took the wine, offered a salute to his gift giver, then drank deep.

He lowered it with a smack of his lips. "You speak our language well, Dervan. How do you know it?"

"I've traded with people through the mountains many times." Hanuvar nodded at the bandage. "How did you come by that injury?"

"Battle," the warrior said with a dismissive shrug. "You should have seen the other five. Enurians," he added. His boasting was typical of his people. It wasn't enough that he probably had faced two or more enemy tribesmen, he had to add a few more, as if he were one of the deadliest men alive.

"How long have you been healing?" Hanuvar asked.

"About a week. The wound was infected when I got here and my uncle didn't think I would make it, but look." He flexed the fingers visible just below the clean white linen.

"Impressive," Hanuvar said honestly.

"It is." The Cemoni puffed out his chest. "Do you know, they didn't have to get me drunk to treat me!"

Hanuvar assumed he was boasting of his own manliness, but the tribesman clarified. "So fine is their medicine and the power of their magic I felt no pain! And there was blood, but they kept most of it in me."

"That's fine work," Hanuvar agreed. "Have you seen any old soldiers around? Some of the men from my brother's unit were said to have come here, and I know some patients stay on."

The warrior looked thoughtful, so Hanuvar passed his wine back, aware the while Antires watched curiously. The Herrene didn't know any of the Ceori languages.

The Cemoni took another swig, then passed the wine back. "Good vintage, that. Yes, I have seen some Dervans, but none your age."

Antires leaned toward him. "Are you asking him if there are any Volani?"

Hanuvar smiled and explained to the warrior, "My friend wants to know if there are any Volani."

"I understand Dervan," the Cemoni said, and thought for a moment. "I think I might have seen one limping around, an older fellow. But most of you dark foreigners look alike, unless you're as black as your friend there."

These lands had been passed back and forth among the Ceori tribes for centuries, and they still thought of their Dervan conquerors as interlopers rather than overlords, which is why so many had joined Hanuvar's forces.

The Cemoni's information left him troubled. He would almost have preferred a definitive no. He would have to continue his surreptitious investigation, which, given his assumed identity, would only be that much more challenging. No one would assume he sought Volani for a good reason.

After the meal, everyone was encouraged to visit the washrooms and then retire to their cubicles. Hanuvar dismissed the notion of exploring the valley at night. The dawn hours were a better bet, although he would have to look quickly.

Antires and he had been put into adjoining spaces, Hanuvar on a corner between two blocks of the fabric-walled rooms. Hanuvar sat on a stool and talked softly to his friend for a short while, but the playwright's lids were heavy and he soon nodded off.

Hanuvar managed his evening stretches within his curtained chamber then readied for bed. He laid his unsheathed gladius in reach, put his knife beneath his pillow, then lay back. Occasionally someone walked along either this aisle or one more distant, the tap of their feet beating a quiet pattern on the old stone.

Here in this templelike space he felt an impulse to speak to the gods of his people, as he had rarely done since he had departed for his fateful return voyage to Volanus. Only thrice, in the long days since, had he prayed, once before he attempted to rescue the captured Volani garrison, and again when he had placed Melgar's ashes upon his final resting place. But in truth those had both been formalistic rites rather than heartfelt expressions of devotion. His last true prayer had been offered the night he'd finally reached that sand spit of an island. And he had hardly managed that properly, being both exhausted and racked by grief for his people and the sacrifice of Eledeva.

It never helped to dwell upon the pain from the absence of those he'd lost, but sometimes he could not help thinking of them, and then he worked to recall their warmth and wisdom and company, to see their features before they lay bloody or broken. He didn't always succeed.

The ceiling was invisible, for the light of a few oil lamps scattered through the great building lacked the strength to illuminate the vast vault. Upon that dark canvas his memory conjured the glitter of the tawny gold scales of his friend and ancient protector of his city as a sunbeam broke through the clouds, bent through the water, and shone upon Eledeva as she sank. He tried to imagine her soaring, head raised in joy, but his mind returned him to her death.

He had known she'd succumbed to her mortal wound, and that his human strength could not possibly pull her to the surface, and yet he had reached for her, because an errant current swung up her head and for a scant moment he'd thought she'd found a final spark and would push with mighty wings for the surface.

Instead she dropped away into darkness, lost to him like all else.

She's gone, he told himself. She fought to her last so that you might live. Honor her, but move forward.

He had been a soldier all his life and learned the trick of grabbing sleep the moment it presented itself, but that evening he could not.

He pushed past the sorrow and reviewed his plans, still distracted by the surrounding atmosphere. This temple left him feeling open and exposed and on guard. He resolved to sleep only lightly, if at all.

And thus he awoke early at a scuffing sound beyond the curtain.

III

He did not recall the substance of his dreams, but at the last he had stood along the balcony, holding Imilce's hand while the sun rose beyond the sea. It was Ravella who'd liked to share his mornings, not Imilce, and their quarters in Utria had been far from his balcony in Volanus, but the illogic of the moment hadn't occurred to his dream self, and he woke smiling and content.

No matter his mood, he knew a sound had roused him, and so he flipped off the top cover and slid from the bed with knife in hand, moving at a crouch. He wore his leggings but was barefoot as he crouched by the canvas flap that was the opening. He breathed through his mouth, utterly still. Only after a moment did he realize that the old injury in his knee, always stiff in the mornings, did not trouble him. He started to grin at that realization, then gritted his teeth at the exaggerated reaction. Calisia or one of the others was into his emotions again.

Someone in the hall climbed to their feet with a creak of sandal and the crack of a ligament. They must have been sitting about four feet away and in the company of others, for he heard other sandals scuff the stone as the group receded. He let them pass then stealthily stepped from his resting place to peer into the corridor. He glimpsed one of the red-tunicked temple acolytes disappearing around the corner. None lingered.

His elevated mood eased at their departure and he savaged its afterglow with a snarl.

Were these healers truly so devoted to their craft that they would tend their unknowing charges while they slept?

Had they been seeing to him alone? If so, why?

He stopped to look in upon Antires, saw that he slept easily, and returned to his curtained chamber to dress. Though the temple remained dark, the feel in the air was of the hour before sunrise.

He reached another corner of the canvas apartments and

crouched. Seeing no one in motion, he found his way to a side door and slipped outside.

The sun had not yet broken through the dark height of the mountains, but the horizon had begun to brighten with predawn glow. A new film of snow had accumulated over the night, frosted and sparkling like star points. As Hanuvar moved into the chill air, his booted feet crunching through the crust, other cloaked figures left their own buildings. Many advanced into lean-tos to care for cows and donkeys and horses. Others walked toward the chicken coops. Yet more trudged their way out with buckets, off to gather water. The light climbed, and though the valley itself lay in shadows, the roosters crowed for the coming dawn.

Hanuvar passed among the edges of the little settlement, scanning the barns and outbuildings where the people worked.

He saw many men, and some women. Some had suffered physical injuries and disfigurements, and a few moved with difficulty, as though they struggled with something unseen, or some wound hidden by their garments. They were universally lean, their looks remote and inward turning. No one paid him any heed. He had the sense they would barely have taken note of him if he were to march by pounding a drumskin. Their hungry, fixed looks reminded him of old legionaries waiting for the tavern to open.

He glimpsed many Ceori, distinctive by garb and hairstyle, and Dervans, inevitably clean shaven, as well as an occasional Herrene, Cerdian, and even a lone little Ekamite. Nowhere, though, did he see anyone dressed like Volani, and he saw no one older than their middle thirties until he glimpsed a gray-mustached wood chopper.

Hanuvar saw him from the side, another Ceori in checked pants. Though his face was seamed and weathered, he stood tall and strong. His left arm was missing below his elbow, but muscle corded the other arm, bare to almost the bicep. With his hand he set a wood log upright, then lifted an axe and sundered it with a mighty blow before tossing each of the halves into a nearby wheelbarrow. He turned to pull another from the pile.

Hanuvar recognized something familiar in the man, and after a few moments of observation he saw past the wrinkles and the injury and knew that he looked upon Acunix, third son of an Isubre chieftain, a junior officer in Hanuvar's army, then a captain of infantry. Acunix had chosen to return to his people rather than journey with Hanuvar to stave off Ciprion's invasion. Once, he had valued the man's expertise, and listened to his counsel. He hoped that he still might.

By and by, Acunix grew conscious he was being watched, and he glanced at Hanuvar as he readied a third log and chopped it. His eyes were not only tired, they were defeated. Just as Acunix was readying to toss the halves into the wheelbarrow his head snapped again toward Hanuvar.

For a brief moment he simply stared. Then his eyes widened, alive at last. He dropped his axe and sank to his knees. His head bowed and he moaned, then mumbled in the language of his people.

"I knew you would come for me at last, Lord Arawen." His remaining hand shook.

"Rise, Acunix," Hanuvar said gently. "I am not the lord of the dead. It's merely me."

Slowly the Ceori dared to lift his eyes. "General?" he asked. The crush of Hanuvar's stride through the snow sounded enormously loud. He stopped before his former officer and offered his hand.

The callused, powerful fingers tentatively reached up, and Hanuvar pulled him to his feet.

Still the warrior stared. Hanuvar looked at Acunix's threadbare tunic and cloak, and the torc of twisted metal about his thinning throat.

"If you are man, and not a god, what are you doing here?" Acunix's voice held the embers of hope.

"I'm passing through. A friend was nearly overcome by the mountain journey. He seems fine now."

A troubled expression crossed the Ceori's face. "And they're going to let you pass through?"

"Is there a reason why they wouldn't?"

"So long as it's a minor injury, and they've got enough of us here they can feed on, they'll let you go. But if they've shown any interest in you or your friend, you'd best be careful."

Hanuvar didn't like the sound of that. "They've shown interest."

"How much?"

"A lot. In me," Hanuvar answered. "In my memories. A band of them were monitoring me early this morning. Giving me happy dreams."

"They weren't giving you happy dreams. That was just accident. They were eating your pain."

Hanuvar wanted to ask how he knew that, and how it was done, but those weren't the immediately important questions. "How much danger are we in? I told Calisia we were planning to leave."

"If she's really interested, she may not let you. Where's your friend?"

"Still sleeping."

Acunix's jaw opened slightly. Hanuvar had never before seen the Ceori look disappointed in him. "Why did you leave him behind?"

"I wanted to see if any of my veterans were hiding here."

Acunix shook his head. "I'm the only one left. You'd better go check on your friend."

"They were interested in me," Hanuvar reminded him.

"You don't realize what you've wandered into here. This is an ugly game board, and if they want you, they'll play him against you. Maybe they'll claim he's sicker than they first thought. Maybe they'll haul him off for surgery so he'll be a little longer recovering, so that they can get their hooks into you."

There was much more that Hanuvar wished to know, but he saw he had no time. "I would have your aid, if you will give it."

Acunix firmed his jaw, stilled for a moment, then bent down and snatched his axe. "I will follow where my general leads."

Hanuvar turned and strode quickly for the central building, the Ceori trotting at his side. "Why are you here? What happened to your arm?"

"They took it piece by piece." At Hanuvar's doubtful look, Acunix added: "You can't imagine, can you? The treatment feels good. So good, it's better than sex. It lingers with you."

Hanuvar found this difficult to credit. "That's why you stay?"

Acunix looked off toward the central building as he answered. "I tried to flee, once. The lovely ones brought me back."

There was that moniker again. Hanuvar would inquire more about them soon. For now, though, he saw Acunix meant to continue, and listened: "They only let you go if you don't know the truth—like those who've recovered from minor wounds. Or if you're going to bring back more people. Where's your beard?"

"I'm in disguise. Why did you come here? You were never badly wounded in the war."

"My people have a habit of fighting. You know that. I had most of a hand taken off addressing a matter of honor."

"Over what?"

"The taste of my brother's mead."

"Must have been some good mead."

Acunix smiled wryly. "Not really."

That was all the time they had for pleasantries. They neared the stairs of the main entrance. "Tell me about our opposition."

"This place only has a handful of warriors, but they're tough."

"You've fought tough men."

"These don't feel any pain. And there are a select few that have been changed."

"The lovely ones?" Hanuvar looked over to him.

"They've been selected from the start because they're well made men, but the dangerous thing is that they don't have ordinary limits. No pain doesn't just mean that they fight when they're wounded, it means they practice constantly. They don't do much more than eat and exercise. It's said they have their arms and legs broken again and again so their bones are longer and thicker than those of normal men."

Hanuvar looked over at the Isubre warrior to make sure he'd understood correctly. Acunix came from a culture that loved to boast and exaggerate, but all of those habits had been worked out of him as he learned how to deliver reports. Hanuvar judged that the Ceori spoke the truth, at least as he understood it.

They took the stairs under the pediment and Hanuvar pushed his way through the rightmost door. As before, the light shown dimly in the cavernous chamber, though this time sunbeams filtered into the space through high latticework windows. Acunix looked to left and right, as if he expected at any moment to be surprised by one of the lovely ones.

Hanuvar headed for the cubicle of Antires, imagining two possible outcomes. Either he would push the curtain aside and his friend would still be lying there, curious about the interruption, or he would push the curtain aside and find him gone.

Antires wasn't there.

"He might be at breakfast," Hanuvar said, gazing at the empty cot.

"The breakfast bell hasn't sounded yet. I suppose he might be in the privy."

"Or maybe we'll waste time looking there." He clenched his fists. "Where do they perform their surgeries?"

IV

Acunix said the easiest way to the healing rooms was through the kitchens, so he and Hanuvar joined the line of servants bearing the morning goods to the back entrance. Hanuvar assisted a man burdened with two containers of gourds and Acunix grabbed a bundle of wood and they queued up with the others. Hanuvar pretended he felt no concern, but seeing his impatience, Acunix told him the tenders would be working on a simpler course for the first half hour. While Hanuvar wasn't entirely certain what that meant, he inferred there might yet be time.

He surreptitiously watched the large man in dark furs guarding the door in the stone wall as they ambled close. The sentinel stood a full head taller and perhaps half again as broad through the shoulders as Hanuvar himself. If he carried weapons, they were hidden within his cloak, but Hanuvar briefly saw his wrists when he scratched at his face with a gloved hand, and they were almost as thick as Hanuvar's upper arm.

The guard's face was beardless, his eyes shining and large. Even at rest the corners of his mouth slanted upward, as though he was delighted by everything he saw.

Hanuvar looked down so he would not draw the man's regard. He walked slump shouldered, and with a slight limp. Before long he and Acunix had passed the guard's careless onceover to shuffle through a wide wooden doorway. Beyond lay a cluttered windowless backroom. A pair of attendants in red tunics and dark robes pointed those with supplies to shelves and empty spots on the long tables stretched down the center of the room. Flickering oil lamps dangled from ceiling chains.

Hanuvar contrived to stumble as he set his bundle down, knocking aside not just his own gourds but a basket of some gathered earlier. He apologized and bent to help, as slowly as possible. While he knelt, others placed their produce and left. Acunix bent to assist and managed to knock over a basket of tinder on a lower shelf, and then busied himself with cleanup duties. Before very long the two of them were the only servants in the room. One of the red-tunicked men told them to be quick about it, then closed the exit door and glared at them impatiently. The other departed through the curtain with two cages of chickens.

Hanuvar and Acunix made short work of their cleanup duties and hurried shamefacedly for the man at the exit door.

When they reached him, Acunix grabbed him by the throat while Hanuvar momentarily stunned him with the flat of his blade. They tied and gagged him in a corner and then Acunix slid the outer door's lock bar into place while Hanuvar moved to the curtain leading into the room beyond.

Hanuvar smelled blood as he neared it. He opened a small gap with two fingers and peered through.

The kitchen was a wide room lit by shafts of sunlight gleaming through windows set just below the ceiling. Stone ovens, blasting heat, stood open in the wall to the south, and the scent of baking bread wafted from some. The others must have been built to feed large groups.

A long aisle of heavy tables stretched along the kitchen's center. One was stacked with gourds, and a pile of winter greens. More sat empty.

A pair of goats lay beneath busy hands upon a cutting board midway along the room. While both still breathed, the fur and skin had been flayed away from the side of one of the creatures' faces, and an attendant was sawing the leg of another along the knee joint. Copious amounts of blood dripped down the stone floor, both from the ruined face and the half-dismembered leg, and yet neither goat behaved as though they were in distress.

Calisia watched with three men in red tunics, standing apart from the two involved in the surgery. She laughed silently while the others beamed. A pock-marked man waited beside her, his bright eyes glazed with delight. The breath of each came heavily, and drool dripped steadily from the lips of an attendant beside the goat, her visible hand shaking. Not just their faces but their stances betrayed a hungry yearning, as though they were eager for orgiastic pleasures painted upon tawdry tavern walls.

Though the sun and ovens supplied plentiful light, Calisia's lantern glowed more brightly than ever. It sat on the empty table before her, and she caressed its sloping sides with both hands.

Hanuvar quietly set the curtain back, examining his own reaction in disgust. The room of horrors troubled him only on an intellectual level, for the dark sorcery had reached him and left him invigorated and gleeful.

Acunix, at his shoulder, chuckled. "Do you feel that?"

"I do." Hanuvar's own voice was barely audible. "Is this where they'll bring my friend?"

"They work on men and women in the next room over. Calisia always starts her day here, though. Like a rich Dervan with a multicourse meal. She snacks a little first."

"What's in the lantern?"

Acunix shrugged. "Some say it's an emerald the size of a skull. Others say it's a withered human hand, or a small, hideous demon."

"No one knows, then," Hanuvar said. "But it's important to her. Do you think that light powers her magic?"

Acunix's face creased in thought. "It might. She always has it with her."

"I'm going to test a theory. Our three horses were left in the corral just outside the entrance cave. Can you ready them, and one for yourself?"

Acunix saw through his intent. "You're going up against them alone? Foes recover fast when they feel no pain."

"It's hard to be fast when your knee's taken out."

Acunix smiled thinly. "Don't you have anyone else?"

"In this valley I have you, and my Herrene friend. Will he be drugged?"

"Almost surely."

"So I'll need to carry him."

"Yes. You need me," Acunix said. "Don't worry. I only need one hand for an axe."

There was no more time to talk. Hanuvar peered back into the room. Both goats bled out while they were being carved, and both their butchers and the watchers shook in ecstasy.

"You go left." Hanuvar headed in.

No one noted him at first. As Acunix sprinted forward with his axe and drove it down through the surgeon's shoulder, Hanuvar tripped the first attendant against the stone table, sent the second spinning, and lifted the lantern.

The first man Acunix struck made no sound. Calisia's eyes rolled as though she were dizzy. She clutched vainly at the lantern's sides, but there was no purchase point and Hanuvar dragged it out of reach. He ducked a sweeping arm blow from the man to her left, sliced his leg above the knee, and slung the lantern into the nearest oven. It shattered with a satisfying crash. Something inside tumbled free, a bright shape caressed by flame.

His artificial joy vanished on the instant, replaced by the familiar adrenaline rush of battle, followed by a familiar sense of slowed time in combat. Screams erupted from a second man mortally wounded by Acunix. His opponent crumpled, wailing and clutching his injured leg.

"Why would you do that?" Calisia shouted hoarsely, even as one of the attendants thrust his hands into the fire toward the writhing thing and the shattered lantern. He joined the screaming.

Hanuvar leapt the lamed acolyte and threw open the door into the next room.

Other shouts of pain rang though the building ahead. In the next chamber red-tunicked attendants rose in alarm, then fled at the sight of Acunix's bloody axe. Three naked patients lay befuddled on stone tables before them. The youngest had a long series of scars up both sides of her chest and down her thigh. Another was the injured Ceori from the night before. The third was Antires. He smiled blearily at Hanuvar, who snatched a robe, wrapped him in it, and headed out the door with his friend over his shoulders.

"Darag's Balls," Acunix swore as Hanuvar raced into the main apse. "My bad arm feels like it's on fire!"

He and Acunix snatched up the belongings cached in the rooms Hanuvar and Antires had occupied and bore them along with the half-insensate Herrene into the frosty air.

Chased by nothing more than the cries of pain, they hurried for the corral. Antires roused as Hanuvar ran on, then loudly objected to being set in the snow. Hanuvar forced clothes on him while Acunix worked saddles onto their horses. As he finished, someone rang a bell from the sanctuary. Rania and another of the outer sentries wandered down from the tunnel to ask what they were doing. They weren't smiling anymore, and one of them carried a spear.

Hanuvar pleaded help with an injured man and stunned Rania when she bent to check Antires.

Acunix axed the other when she jabbed their spear at them. Hanuvar paused only to liberate a supply of spears, and then they were out and racing as fast as they dared down the long stairwell that led down the mountainside. A vast landscape of folded, pine-girt mountains stretched ahead.

Antires clung stubbornly to the saddle horn. His hat sat skewed to the left.

"Damn but my arm hurts," Acunix said as they reached the trail. They headed south. "The one I don't have anymore," he added. "Strange, isn't it? Do you have anything with a kick?"

Hanuvar handed him his wineskin, and the Isubre warrior had a long draught before he passed it back. "Dervan wine. It would take a lot of that to get to me. Damned magic. I had to present myself for treatment every other day or it would start aching like this." He looked back over his shoulder. "You think they're going to follow?"

"I don't imagine any of them will be in a forgiving mood."

The Ceori laughed gruffly. "Well, you threw their demon into a fire and broke their spell. Maybe that means they can't send the lovely ones after you."

"We can hope. Isubre lands are still about a day and a half out, unless your borders have shifted further than I know."

"Well, they're always shifting, but that's about right." They passed a huge lump of rock and lost sight of the stairs. "You never told me what you're doing in our lands again."

"Passing through."

"Only passing through?"

"For now."

Though Acunix was silent for a long moment, Hanuvar could sense he had more to say, and finally the veteran did. "You know some Isubre still think you're going to return and lead them against Derva."

"I have no army."

"I think they're hoping you'll build a Ceori army."

"The Dervans would eat them for breakfast."

"That would be a bloody breakfast."

Hanuvar told him what Acunix surely knew. "The Ceori are brave but don't have the numbers."

Acunix accepted the truth with a weary nod. "Why is the Herrene with you?"

"He wants to write a play about me."

Acunix gave that idea the resounding laugh Hanuvar thought it deserved. "I saw one of those when we were in Utria. So some actor in a mask will pretend to be you and moan to the gods, strut around with a sword, and talk about the battle he just had? That sounds *just* like you."

"It does, doesn't it?" Hanuvar agreed.

Acunix surveyed the dark-skinned younger man, barely holding himself upright and barely conscious of his surroundings. "Is he any good in a fight?"

"He's brave," Hanuvar said, "and he's been a loyal friend, when I've had few others."

"So he's sort of a mascot, then."

Hanuvar laughed. "Better than that."

The Isubre warrior didn't ask about much else. They weren't on a nature stroll, and had to devote most of their attention to navigating the often difficult terrain. After only a little longer the ground was even enough that all three were finally able to sit saddle for long stretches.

Hour by hour they passed on through the mountains, which rose above the forested paths. At midday they drew close to a large peak whose gentle, snowy slope climbed higher than its surrounding sisters. Contrary to popular belief, the Ceori didn't name every mountain, though this one was called Sarestix, a word that meant the Mother of Snows. Hanuvar would recognize the craggy bend at its height from nearly any angle of approach.

Antires had finally regained his senses and after complaining about how his tunic was on backward and adjusting other articles, he listened in astonishment as Hanuvar summarized what had happened. Once the Herrene had satisfied his curiosity, he all but pleaded with Acunix to speak about his war experiences with Hanuvar. Over drinks in a tavern the Isubre would have been expansive, but under pointed interrogation while negotiating deer trails in the high mountains he proved monosyllabic.

They had just veered slightly uphill, still under the crag of the

Snow Mother, when Acunix drew to a stop and held up his hand. Hanuvar halted on the instant. He heard only the call of birds and the whistling wind, but trusted the Ceori's instincts more than his own this close to the man's native lands.

Antires caught up to them and listened impatiently before breaking the silence. "What is it?"

"My arm stopped hurting," Acunix answered.

"What does that mean?" Antires asked. "I thought you killed their pain demon."

"I don't feel anything yet," Hanuvar said.

"The magic doesn't have its claws into you as deeply," Acunix said.

Hanuvar considered the surrounding terrain, then pointed up slope, to a narrow rocky promontory projecting from the mountainside a hundred feet above and to the left.

Acunix slipped from his saddle and strode swiftly uphill.

"What are we doing?" Antires asked.

"Choosing our ground." Hanuvar slid off his horse, taking the reins and those of the Isubre's mount. He started after his warrior friend. "Acunix, how far away can you feel that thing's influence?"

The warrior did not break stride, but answered with an over-the-shoulder glance. "No more than half a league."

Antires swore. He climbed out of the saddle and followed, pulling his mount and the pack horse as well. "He's a Ceori woodsman, though, isn't he? Can't we lose them?"

"Our tracks are easy to follow in the snow," Hanuvar answered. "And they may be sensing us through our injuries."

Hanuvar and Antires picketed two of the horses and trusted the others to stay close, then hurried up the steep grade. The outthrust cliff projected no more than twenty paces, and small trees at its edge leaned toward the drop. A selection of boulders large and small littered the flat, snowy ground before the edge. Acunix was already prying some of them up. Hanuvar ordered Antires to ready a stock of stone-laced snowballs.

"You expect to hurt them with these?" the playwright asked.

"We might get lucky," Hanuvar said.

Acunix, chopping ice from the bottom of boulders, addressed the Herrene's confusion: "If someone's throwing snowballs at your head, you might not see a spear someone else is lobbing."

As the Isubre said that, Hanuvar was arranging the spears he'd taken from the sentries.

Antires started patting snowballs together. "How many do you think they'll send after us?"

Acunix answered. "They only have a dozen real soldiers, and maybe ten of the lovely ones. They'll probably leave a few regular soldiers behind, but as to how many they send . . ." He paused in his ice chipping to favor Hanuvar with a half smile. "Well, the general threw their god in the oven. That probably doesn't sit well with the devoted."

"I should have killed Calisia," Hanuvar said. "The worst mistake I've made in months."

"You *did* think you'd destroyed her magic," Acunix pointed out. "And you never killed without reason."

While that was true, Hanuvar rarely assumed, and had done so when he thought their attack had worked. Pursuit might have been inevitable but would not have been as well coordinated without a leader. He frowned at himself. He labored with Acunix to prepare their battleground, alert for motion not just below, but the clear, gentle slope lying between their cliff and the forest edge above. If their opponents had any sense, it was from that direction that they would strike.

His vigilance was soon rewarded. Before much longer a red-robed man emerged from the forest higher on the mountain side. Another almost identical figure joined him. They stared for a long moment then returned to the cover of the tall old pines.

"They've no choice but a head-on assault," Hanuvar said, mostly for Antires' benefit.

"And we shouldn't worry about that?" Antires said.

"See that space that slopes down between the tree line and the start of our ledge?" Hanuvar pointed. "That leaves them wide open when they get close to us. So will a charge up either side toward us from below, although they're probably too smart for that." He put a hand to the boulders he and Acunix had arranged. "And we can duck behind these if they have spears or arrows. Though Acunix tells me they're unlikely to use them."

"They'll want to capture us alive," Acunix assured him.

Hanuvar slipped into his cuirass, waving away offers of help from Acunix and Antires. Before leaving the Isles of the Dead he'd selected the ideally sized armor from the Dervan supplies; from greaves to helm he was well fitted. There was nothing to offer either of his companions but the shield, useless to Acunix and unwanted by Antires, though the playwright placed it in the snow beside him while he manufactured snowballs. Antires was still making them when the first rank of attackers emerged from the trees on the slope above. Eight ordinary men dashed out in two lines of four, sword in hand. The shock troops, and the distraction. Far behind them strode two of the towering lovely ones, cloaked in blue and smiling brightly. Brass gauntlets gleamed on their massive forearms, and rippling biceps strained against their long red sleeves.

Hanuvar knew their intent—catch the three escapees fighting the front rankers so the more dangerous men could close and finish. Any veteran could have predicted that move, but it was an effective tactic. Hanuvar dropped one of the first four with a spear through the throat. Acunix's cast drove through the next man's chest. The injured soldier kept running; Hanuvar's next spear took him down.

The remaining skirmishers found themselves struggling through a field of well-placed boulders; one tripped and barely caught himself. The other was met by Acunix, who leapt their wall of cover with a savage cry, ducked a sword blow, and drove his axe through the warrior's face. As the dying man sank, Acunix howled in glee and yanked his weapon free.

Acunix climbed back to safety as the five remaining troops came on.

Antires laid into two men with a barrage of snowballs, having apparently grasped his goal was to distract and break the charge so the enemy's line was staggered. It was ever easier to meet a single man rather than a line of them.

Experienced warriors would have struggled to regroup. The warriors of the temple did not manage even that. While they might have faced bandits and hunted fugitives, they'd never matched weapons with true soldiers, and they paid for it with their lives.

The battle was far removed from the elaborate duels of Dervan gladiatorial combat. There was no patient circling, or thrust and counter thrust. The attackers charged in screaming, and soon it was a fury of swipe and thrust and kick and duck, the plunge of weapons into steaming flesh, and the spill of reeking entrails.

Though Hanuvar had battled in many strange circumstances, this one was distinct because his opponents did not immediately drop when given debilitating wounds. He slashed one man's arm nearly all the way through, but it was the momentum of Hanuvar's strike that stopped him from driving his own sword in. Hanuvar leapt back, and Antires pierced the man through the chest with a spear before sliding back. He'd been told to fill the gap, and did so bravely.

Another attacker dropped his sword after Hanuvar's preemptive blow cut through the fingers of his blade hand, but the man charged anyway, his other hand outstretched in a strangler's grasp. Hanuvar ran him through, but still had to pull the blade free and slash his neck before the body sank away. Only after his attacker fell did Hanuvar feel blood tracking down his neck, and a quick probe with his fingers found a superficial gash left by the man's nails.

Yet he felt no pain. Apparently the protective sorcery employed by their enemies was as indiscriminate as the joy.

The skirmishers were down, and before the lovely ones closed the gap Hanuvar had a brief moment to scan his men. Antires stood resolute, hood cast back, eyes glittering, his spearpoint trailing blood. Once he had said he was no warrior, but he could no longer claim that. Acunix was splattered with blood, and grinned madly through a mask of it. It was impossible to see at a glance if any was his.

The lovely ones trotted toward them, one ahead of the other. Each clutched a club with a flattened end. Nets hung limply from their off hands.

Hanuvar gave command. "Antires, snowballs on the last."

As the Herrene dropped his spear—he should have planted it so he wouldn't later have to scramble for it—Hanuvar shifted his sword to his left hand, unlimbered one of his two knives, took careful aim, and flung it at the first.

A meaty arm swept up as if to ward it away, and the blade drove deep into the back of the lovely one's hand. It didn't slow the big blond's progress in the slightest. Hanuvar took up one of the last of their spears, sword still gripped.

"He's mine," Acunix snarled, but Hanuvar motioned him back as a net with weighted ends sailed toward them. He plunged his spear into it and whirled it deftly overhead, then tossed it over his back, where it harmlessly draped a nearby boulder. The blond lovely one reached the wall and swiped with his club. Hanuvar ducked and drove the spear point into his opponent's face, resulting in an explosion of blood and teeth. The lovely one, now a mask of horror, was unfazed, even by Acunix slashing him in the side with an axe.

The second lovely one had slowed to shield his face from the Herrene's flurry of snowballs. Whether he felt pain or no, their foe couldn't fight the instinct to protect his eyes, and so he missed the approach of Hanuvar's spear until it was standing out through one of his overlong arms. As the mustached warrior grabbed the haft and yanked the point free with a sprinkle of blood, a third of the lovely ones raced at them, followed by three smaller figures on the tree line's edge, all robed. One was a slender, female form, a glowing triangular lamp held in one white-mittened hand. This last lovely one was the reserve, and by committing him the opponents revealed how desperate they had become.

Calisia pointed at Hanuvar, who would have given much for an archer or slingsman.

"They will smash your bones!" she cried. "But you will live on and on, broken and fertile with pain!"

The blond lovely one delivered a blow to Acunix's chest that sent the Ceori flying. The enemy warrior bled profusely from a deep wound along his neck, but moved as if unaware. Antires thrust a spear into his thigh, but the big man laughed. As he reached to pull it free, Hanuvar drove his sword into his nose and out the back of his head. The blond staggered and fell twitching.

Hanuvar shouted Antires down as another net whipped overhead. It wrapped around the Herrene's leg.

Hanuvar lifted the last spear and awaited the advance of the brown mustached lovely one, who cleared the boulders in an easy leap. Hanuvar drove a spear at his face then retreated, leading him back, knowing from the trail of marking stones he'd placed that he neared the drop off. Acunix rose and shook his head, blood flowing freely down one arm.

Their foe slung a wooden club at Hanuvar's head and he leaned away. Before he could recover another swipe came, and a third, and Hanuvar's spearpoint broke against the armor beneath his attacker's furred cloak. The lovely one's weird smile widened at sight of the broken weapon, then Hanuvar drove the broken point at his throat.

The warrior leaned away, lost his footing and stumbled, and Hanuvar dropped, slamming his side into the huge man's leg.

Hanuvar released his blade as he slid, his center of gravity keeping him from the edge. The warrior lost his footing and slipped off the cliff, landing head first close to where the horses were hobbled. One of them whinnied in alarm at his still, broken-necked body.

Hanuvar snatched up his sword and climbed to his feet. A garden of the slain lay on every side. Antires, spear in one hand, waited beside Acunix, sagging weakly. A terrible gash had opened the Isubre warrior's crippled arm. It wept blood.

The last of the lovely ones strode toward them, black haired and grinning. It might be that he was trying to rattle them with the spear he tossed, or he might simply have grown angry at the death of his fellows. His fixed expression gave little clue.

Hanuvar tried to sidestep the cast, and didn't pull back far enough. The spear was thrown with such strength that its edge cut through the sculpted muscles of his cuirass and sliced the front of his stomach. The impact upset his balance, but he felt no pain. The lovely one threw the net he carried in his other hand. The toss was well timed, and well aimed; Hanuvar threw himself forward and one of the weighted ends brushed his back. He shot to his feet, trying not to worry about how deadly his wound was.

The lovely one vaulted the boulders, batted aside a spear thrust from Antires, and smiled a terrible smile. "It won't be so bad," he said. "Calisia can save you, still."

The warrior didn't flinch as Hanuvar thrust at him with his sword. Hanuvar backstepped, aware there were only ten paces behind him. Antires yelled and jabbed. The lovely one grabbed the spear shaft, ripped the weapon from the Herrene's hand, then smacked him in the forehead with the haft.

As Antires sagged, Hanuvar charged.

He swayed away from one massive arm and drove his sword under the man's chin. The lovely one tucked in his face and turned so that the point lodged through one side, though it apparently didn't drive in through his brain case.

He only smiled the wider. "You can't really hurt me," he said.

"I just wanted your attention," Hanuvar said, because he'd seen Acunix limping from the side. The lovely one must have heard something, for he'd begun to turn when Acunix buried an axe in his skull.

That dropped him, and the lovely one lay shaking, trying to rise even as brains and blood leaked over his clothing.

Acunix, gasping, grinned at Hanuvar through his blood-streaked face, and delivered a blow that stilled the lovely one forever.

Hanuvar glanced at his armored front and the blood trickling down to his tunic, hoping the wound was just a slice through muscle. He yanked a spear sticking out of a corpse and dashed up the hillside.

Calisia and her attendants tried to run. He took her down with a spear cast. It didn't kill her, and she was fighting to rise when he drove his sword through her back. That would have stopped anyone else, but she felt no pain. Without being restricted by agony, she continued to struggle, which spoiled his aim. He had to stab too many times before he finished her. By then the other attendants had fled into the forest, and he couldn't be bothered to follow.

Once he was sure Calisia was dead, Hanuvar snatched up her lantern and marched back to his men, all too aware of the growing blood stain on his armor and down his tunic.

Antires was sitting up, conscious but wobbly. The Ceori had scrubbed his face with snow, but it had done little to aid his appearance, for he looked ghastly pale.

"Well, I've got a few broken ribs, and I've had a nice love tap."

"Looks like you've lost some blood," Hanuvar said.

"Looks like you're in the same fix." Acunix looked at the lantern. "I'd like to smash it, but maybe after we sew each other up?"

Hanuvar insisted on treating the Isubre first, though he cast off his helmet and cuirass and briefly lifted his tunic to expose the slash running diagonally along his muscular abdomen. Without any sense of pain it was hard to anticipate its severity until he probed it.

He cleaned up Acunix's deep, ugly wound along his bicep and then sewed it. The Isubre was paling, and watched Hanuvar's eyes while he worked, reading in them Hanuvar's concern.

"It's a bad one," Acunix said. "And maybe I've spilled too much blood, yes?"

"We'll find out."

"Let's get you treated before you're pale as me."

Hanuvar exposed his injury once more, gritting his teeth in anticipation as the Isubre slopped wine on the injury, then remembered he would feel no pain so long as the lantern glowed. Whatever was within shifted.

He would see to that later.

He washed his fingers in wine, then explored the wound while the Ceori and Herrene looked on.

"Just muscle?" Acunix asked.

He couldn't be sure. He thought he detected a whiff of internal juices. "It's deeper than I'd like. It might have nicked my intestines."

Acunix swore.

"Is that bad?" Antires asked.

The Isubre answered bluntly. "You get a wound in there, it's just about always fatal."

Hanuvar was touched that the younger man looked so distraught at this news. He motioned for the needle. It was pure silver, threaded with horse hair.

With Acunix helping hold the skin in place, Hanuvar carefully sewed himself closed, marveling a little at being able to do so without the slightest hint of discomfort. He wondered if he was going to bleed to death internally, or if the contents of his intestine would leak out to poison him.

Antires watched in concern, then, after a time, walked to the lantern and opened the panel closest to him. The Herrene arched his eyebrows and tilted his head. Whatever he saw, it must not have been hideous.

While Hanuvar finished tying off the threads sealing the wound, Acunix rose to join the Herrene, then swore under his breath. "You should see this," he said.

What sat within resembled nothing so much as a wingless butterfly the size of a hedgehog, with scalloped sides trimmed in gold and black, its cylindrical body spotted with blazing blues and reds that beat in time to the blood pumping at Hanuvar's temple.

Gazing upon it, a great sense of ease and comfort welled from within him, and Hanuvar understood that the citrus-like scent wafting from the being should be breathed in. Acunix pressed near to it, smiling.

Hanuvar leaned forward and pushed the panel closed.

Acunix spun, glaring.

Hanuvar met his burning gaze.

The Ceori scowled for a long time, and then his expression cleared and he flushed in shame. Apart from blood drops, it was the only color remaining on his face.

Hanuvar twisted his torso slowly, testing the wound. He should not have been able to stand that movement, but with the thing in the lantern so close, it didn't hurt.

"What do you think it is?" Antires asked. "And where did it come from? Do you think it's really evil?"

He couldn't know. And perhaps it didn't really matter. "Whatever it is, it feeds on pain, and rewards those who aid it with pleasure. It doesn't belong in the hands of humans. Fire didn't kill it."

"I say we hack it to pieces," Acunix suggested.

"We don't know if that would really finish it," Hanuvar pointed out. "It somehow managed to put itself together after immolation. Unless they have more than one." He looked to Acunix, hoping the Ceori would put his concern to rest.

"Calisia only ever had the one lantern. I think if there had been more some of the other healers would have been carrying lanterns around as well."

"Good. I want to take it to the heights and encase it in snow and ice."

Antires understood his thinking. "So even if it lives it can't get out."

"I'll do it," Acunix said.

Hanuvar's look suggested his opinion on what a terrible idea that was.

"It needs to be me," Acunix said. "Pain or no, you're going to have a fever soon, and your friend here might get you to Rudicia and Velix[14]

---

[14] Sosilos here fails to explain who these individuals are, probably assuming that Rudicia is well enough known by his readers that no explanation was necessary, although it may simply have been oversight. Rudicia was the chieftain of one of the most influential of the Isubre villages and nominal leader of the entire tribe. Velix, her husband, was a famed healer. The Isubre, of course, were one of the two Ceori tribes who had most heavily supported Hanuvar's ambitions during the Second Volani War, bolstering his invading army with thousands of warriors. Like many Ceori, the Isubre held a grudge against Derva, which had understandably resented their frequent raids.

Only a generation before, Derva had conquered the rich lowlands of Calenna, just south of the Ardenines, territory held for centuries by the Ceori. This created a buffer zone of protection between Derva and the aggressive tribes, one that enriched hundreds of already wealthy landholders, who flocked to purchase property in the new province. It also infuriated the Ceori, who looked down upon their former holdings from the mountain height where they had retreated, and plotted vengeance. Until Hanuvar arrived before the second war, all they had managed to accomplish was an occasional small raid, inevitably met with stern reprisal by the Dervan legions. With him at their head, Calenna was swiftly wrested from the Dervans and restored to the Isubre and Cemoni tribes, though in the end they could not hold it for very long.
                                                                                        —Silenus

before it gets too bad. Me, well, I brained one of their clansmen so I'm not welcome. And I think I'm bound for the ancestors soon anyway."

"What if that thing lures you?" Antires asked.

Acunix laughed. "Lures me to what? I'll take it to the high peak and do what the general said. I'll pack the damned thing in snow. There are deep rifts in the glacier on the west face; I'll drop it in one of those."

Antires looked doubtful. "Will you make it?"

"I'll make it." Acunix sounded certain.

Hanuvar offered his hand to his old companion.

The Isubre embraced him instead, and Hanuvar felt the man's ribs shift as he pressed close. Acunix stepped back, pressed his chest, and all three heard a disturbing crackle.

Acunix gave a ghastly smile to that. "It doesn't hurt," he assured them, then smacked Hanuvar's shoulder. He spoke to him in his tribal tongue. "Praise Darag, it was good to fight with you one last time, General."

"I couldn't have made it without you," he answered in the same language. "Thank you."

"Better to die in a clean fight than to live so foully." Acunix swept up his robe, thrust his cleaned axe through his belt, snatched the lantern, and started through the boulders and the dead men. After only a few steps, he stopped and turned. "General, what are you really doing here?"

"I'm going to free my people," he answered. "Derva razed my city and sold them into slavery."

"And you're going to get them back."

"Yes."

"Ah, Hanuvar, you should have been born an Isubre. Our gods love the mad and doomed. I'll pray they aid you before I breathe my last." He glanced upslope. "I should go, so I can do one last mad deed myself." He picked up the lantern and headed out. They watched him hike on toward the tree line. He paused just past the body of Calisia. In his accented Dervan he called back: "Make sure you put me in your play, Herrene!"

Antires replied, "I will!"

They heard his bark of laughter. He raised the stump of his arm and vanished into the trees.

Antires looked at Hanuvar. "You told him about that?"

"I did."

"I'm thinking it's going to be more of a historical chronicle, now."

"Good."

"I liked him," the playwright said, considering the trees where the Ceori had vanished. "I wish we could have saved him."

Hanuvar was full of such wishes, but he left this one unvoiced.

His friend turned to him. "Are you going to be all right?"

"It's possible. But we have to get moving. And we'd better get me downslope and seated in a saddle before the pain kicks in."

Hanuvar braced the wound with his hand as they led the horses away from the battle site.

Once they were back into the trees themselves, and he was mounted, he began to tell Antires what he would have to say to the Isubre scouts when they met them, should he himself no longer be conscious. In midexplanation the pain found him at last and left him breathless. But he forced himself forward, both in the saddle, and in his instructions. He looked back to the mountain height two more times, when they had a clear view. The first time, he saw only the trees, and the circling birds. Probably, he decided, Acunix had died of his injuries and lay beside the lantern under some snow heavy branch.

But later, when the pain was so great he saw spots, Hanuvar looked up a second time, and after he stared for a while, one of the spots resolved itself into a tiny figure fighting up the snowy slope above the trees, the light of the lovely ones shining in one hand.

※ ※ ※

Over the course of a single day, our roles were reversed. Hanuvar had cared for me while I struggled with the altitude and temperature and had risked his life to guide me to freedom. Then, as the pain from his wound set in, swiftly followed by fever, I found myself in the role of protector, and I felt myself ill-suited for it, for I knew our destination only through his words, and had no true experience caring for the injured.

While I had feared for Hanuvar in the past, as he faded in and out of consciousness I began to worry that he had taken his death wound. Only then did I realize how deeply I had internalized his goals, for I found myself wondering what would happen to his people were he to die. I even debated asking him for instruction on that account, but his periods of lucidity were infrequent, and I knew that I could not hope to replace him. For the sake of all those who'd been led into slavery, he had to live, and so I reviewed, again and again, what he had told me I must say to the Ceori when we found them. I only prayed that their healer was as gifted as Hanuvar believed.

I should also have been praying for divine intervention, for Evara's threat had materialized far to the south: Caiax had returned to the shores of Tyvol and was gathering an elite force to lead against us. Even had I known this, though, I could not have lent it any mental energy, for my cup brimmed over. Not the least of my fears was that the Ceori would see us as trespassers and attack before I explained our presence.

—Sosilos, Book Six

Chapter 14:
Thread From a Golden Loom

I

Leaving the other centurions to settle the men into the barracks, Marius followed orders and headed to the baths.

He passed through the tiled chambers where men from other units paddled in the cold pools and others propped themselves against the walls of the hot ones. He finally arrived in a room with a single hot tub. Its colorful red and yellow tiles depicted topless nymphs.

The air within was warm and soupy and thick, and reminded Marius of the lowlands of Icilia in the deep summer, which he remembered Caiax despising. He had been surprised that the general would extend an invitation to him for a meeting that was certain to lower the implied boundary between a patrician officer and a plebian centurion like himself. But then, he'd been surprised that the stiffly formal Caiax would be lounging in a tub in any case and wondered if the man had changed after his nearly mortal injury earlier in the year.

He should have guessed Caiax wouldn't be relaxing in a bath. As he stepped inside he saw the general sat on a regulation bench in front of a trestle table positioned right of the open doorway. No attendants stood behind him or waited to record what he said; he merely sat, passively, garbed in a red tunic and sandals, a lean man with graying hair, hunched shoulders, and a large nose.

The older man was never inviting, but what passed for a smile of satisfaction upticked one side of his face. "Ah, Marius. Good of you to come." He rose.

Marius saluted, then at Caiax's sharp wave, relaxed and took in the surroundings, trying not to let his surprise show. Caiax understood.

"I know," he said, almost as though he were amused by the change himself. "Ever since my injury, the moist air helps me breathe more easily. Maybe I'm going soft."

"I doubt anyone would think that, General. From what I hear, the surgeons thought you had a mortal wound, and think it the work of the gods you managed to heal."

"I have been blessed." Caiax sounded uncharacteristically earnest. He eyed Marius directly and almost sounded pleased as he continued. "You made it a day earlier even than I had hoped."

Marius waved the implied compliment away. "General Caiax sent for us, so the men marched as fast as they were able."

"I knew I could count on the Seventh's First Cohort." Caiax bent low to retrieve a lidded rectangular box of dark wood behind his chair. He presented it to Marius, who took it without comment. "Have this ground to powder and mixed in with the men's rations each morning."

"Yes, sir. How far are we marching?"

"To the foot of the mountains."

Marius hefted the small container. "This doesn't look like it will last eight hundred men more than one small dose."

"They need only a small amount. I will supply you with new content every day."

"As you command, sir. What is the stuff?"

"Those are special mushrooms that aided my own recovery. With them, I'm healthier than I've ever been in my life. I want the men of the Seventh to benefit as well."

"It's very kind of you, sir." Marius wasn't about to object, even though he guessed this was just one of those remedies older men sometimes became convinced would help them hold to their youth. "If you don't mind me asking, what are we after at the foot of the mountains?"

Caiax mouthed a one-word answer. "Hanuvar."

Caiax never joked, but Marius could not help staring to ascertain whether the general had discovered a strange sense of humor along with his health interests. "The actual man?"

The general's fist clenched, and his dark eyes burned with the familiar fire. "I saw him, Marius. One of his women gave me the wound."

"Is he crossing the Ardenines with an army?"

"No. And before you ask how I know, and how I will find him, I will simply say that you must trust me."

"Very well, sir. You know how to guide us to victory."

"Your faith is refreshing. I've spent too much time among my fellow senators, and physicians and priests. Unlike those faithless cowards, you know I have never failed."

"Indeed I do, sir."

"Good. Honor and glory await us all." Caiax returned to his chair and folded his hands on the table. "We leave at dawn. I will speak to the men, but I will not tell them of our objective until we're nearer our goal. Say nothing to them yourself."

"Of course, General."

"Dismissed."

Marius saluted but, before departing, added: "May I say, sir, that it is a pleasure to serve with you once again"

Caiax permitted this with a slight inclination of his head. "Thank you, Marius." As Marius turned to go, the general added: "Oh, make sure that you eat a little bit of those mushrooms as well."

He paused by the door. "Of course, sir."

Caiax lifted a finger in admonition. "A few days with them in your diet will change your entire perspective."

"Very good, sir." Box tucked under his arm, he left, patting it slightly and listening to the hollow echo from within. Mushrooms, eh? He planned to show them to the century's surgeon, but provided that they weren't poisonous he couldn't imagine they'd do any harm. Probably there wouldn't be much benefit, either, apart from humoring the general.

II

While they had left the snowfields of the high mountains, the chill clung to them as Antires led them down trail through the pines. He barely noted the temperature, though his lips were chapped and frost scored his cloaked shoulders. His attention was fully focused on the path and the ground to either side. While he had pretended to be a soldier in the past, he no longer had to imitate. Over the last months Hanuvar had taught him to scan not just for movement but the best points for ambush.

Every now and then he turned to check on the figure slumped in the saddle of the first of the horses behind him.

He had once imagined Hanuvar indomitable, but even the finest blade lost its edge when wielded too long. Racked by fever after a slice to his stomach, the great warrior had begun to fade in and out of consciousness. During a brief episode of clarity in the last hour he had ordered Antires to tie him to the saddle, and had Antires repeat what he'd been instructed to tell the Ceori. The nod of acceptance Hanuvar had given after Antires' faithful recitation had been almost imperceptible.

Antires knew his orders by heart, for he had an actor's retention for information.

Reassured that Hanuvar still breathed, Antires returned his attention to the trail. He suspected he had long since crossed into the territory of the powerful Ceori tribe known as the Isubre, though he had seen no settlements, nor sign of scouts. From time to time he had felt eyes upon him, but had spotted only the occasional bear, well distant, or a high-flying black eagle. Sometimes squirrels scolded him from the trees.

Hanuvar shifted in his creaking saddle. Antires glanced back at him, wondering if the man were trying to signal, then noticed the nearby birds had gone silent.

The Herrene halted and raised a hand, scanning the woods for the people he couldn't see. He addressed them slowly, in Dervan. "We have come in peace. My companion is guest-brother to Rudicia." He cleared his throat, discomfited by how dry it felt, and how much weaker it sounded than he would have liked.

He heard the crack of a stick behind them and turned, taking care to keep his hand from his sword hilt.

He saw nothing there, but when he looked to the front once more a trio of men had stepped onto the trail. They wore cloaks, and the checked, baggy pants typical of Ceori tribes. Thick torsos were clothed in long-sleeved shirts. Their faces were beardless, but heavy mustaches drooped from their upper lips. They at least were not a war party, for their hair wasn't limed into spikes; woolen caps covered their heads.

They had surely heard his words, though they hardly appeared welcoming. Their spears were leveled. Others emerged from either side of the trail, and a blue-eyed man in the center of the trio called to the others in the ringing, lyrical language of the Ceori. To Antires it sounded as though much of it rhymed.

Antires repeated that they had come in peace, and that Hanuvar was a guest friend.

"We heard you the first time," the blue-eyed man said in heavily accented Dervan. "But what is that to us? Who are you?"

"My friend is Rudicia's friend, from the great war against the Dervans." Antires indicated Hanuvar with a sweep of one hand. "His words, and his name, are only for her."

The pair from the left advanced to the side of the horse. They peered at Hanuvar and shook his leg; he swayed in the saddle. They called up to the leader, who listened, then spoke again to Antires: "It looks like your friend's words may soon be for the lord of the dark lands."

That's what Antires feared, but he put that comment to use. "If so, then you'd best get him to Rudicia fast. She will want to speak with him."

The Isubre scouts talked among themselves in their own language until the leader silenced them with sharp words. To Antires he said: "We shall see," and then relayed orders to his subordinates.

The escort closed in on either side and the leader commanded Antires to follow, starting forward without a backward glance.

He had expected a warmer welcome than this. He meant to exchange some level of communication with Hanuvar, but the general mumbled something Antires couldn't catch, then closed his eyes.

The rest of the journey was interminable, and Antires could scarce stomach the delay, knowing that each moment his friend might be growing closer to death. He then realized that this was what Hanuvar must have felt every moment of every day, multiplied by almost a thousand, and wondered how the man could possibly have coped with the pressure and remained sane.

They passed over hills and through vales and stopped to confer with another patrol before reaching a high valley populated with round thatched huts from which smoke rose. A few dozen of the homes were arranged behind a central wooden stockade. Others stood beside wooden pens and cultivated plots of land. Someone must have run ahead, because a welcoming committee waited just beyond the open gate, four men and a middle-aged woman. He wondered if she was the famed Rudicia, and was somewhat disappointed that she was not the knife-sharp beauty described by the poets. But, then, if this was her, she was at least fifteen years older than she had been at the time of those compositions.

The leader of their scouting party drew the group to a halt and bowed his head to those beyond the gate, speaking rapidly in Ceori. Isubre, Antires corrected himself. Many of the Ceori tribes had their own distinct languages.

The woman strode forward, flanked by mustached warriors. A twisted torc of gold wrapped her throat. Though age seamed her face, Antires revised his assessment, deciding a wild and regal beauty still graced her. Her light, curled hair, pulled back from her forehead, had gone almost completely gray.

She stopped before Antires. "I do not know you." Her accent was so thick it took him a moment to understand.

"You know him," Antires said. "And he needs your help."

Her bright blue eyes narrowed in a glare at him, and then she moved past, her bodyguard following. The woman's chin lifted as she inspected Hanuvar. The color drained from her face, and her nostrils flared.

Fury wasn't the sort of greeting Antires had expected, and he worried he had somehow delivered Hanuvar to the wrong place. But this was the territory of the Isubre, and Rudicia was the most powerful of the tribe's women chiefs.

Whoever she was, she turned and shouted orders. Hanuvar was cut from his roan and carefully lowered, then carried toward another of the huts. The woman turned to Antires and questioned him sharply. "What has happened to him?"

"He's been wounded in the stomach," Antires said. "He needs your help."

She gestured loosely at Antires as she gave more commands, then swept after Hanuvar.

The scout leader returned and beckoned to him. "Come, there will be food, and a fire."

"I should stay with my friend."

"The healer's going to look at your friend. And unless you're a fool, you'll take the offer of guest friendship from the Isubre, and enter to eat."

Antires reluctantly bowed his head, then followed the scout into another hut. Before long he was seated at a bench before a fire. Smoky lanterns hung low along the wall, well away from the thatched roof. He was grateful both for the warmth and the rabbit meat pie. They'd served him with a bowl and pitcher of the strong, infamously bitter Ceori beer. He'd heard the tribes had taken to Dervan wine, but none was offered him.

He finished the meat pie and wished there was another, but he forced some of the beer down. The door creaked behind him and he turned to find the assumed Rudicia, her expression grim. She was followed by another woman, and no bodyguard.

At first Antires thought the second lady younger, for she was slimmer and her skin smoother. But as both stopped before him he saw that her hair was entirely white, and guessed that they must be very close in age. So strong was the family resemblance that the two had to be sisters, although the second woman had finer, fairer features than the first, and had seen less sun. Antires could not help staring at an additional detail—the second woman's eyes were of different colors. The left was blue, the right green.

Both studied Antires intently, although the second woman did so without the other's scowl.

He climbed to his feet with a bow. "I thank you for this meal," he said. "Are you Rudicia, the great Chieftain of the Isubre?"

The woman confirmed her identity with grave formality. "I am Rudicia, Chieftain of the Isubre, though I claim no greatness. This is my sister, Bricta, my—" She followed with a word Antires didn't recognize or understand.

"I thank you for your hospitality," he said with a formal head bow. "Can you save my friend?"

"Your friend is far along," Rudicia said, "and may be done for. Where is his army?"

Antires hesitated only a moment. "He has no army."

Rudicia's wispy eyebrows climbed her forehead. "Why is he here then? My people cannot fight the Dervans alone. If that is what he wants—"

The door opened behind her and Rudicia fell silent. She half turned as a heavyset man entered the hut. Unlike the other men of the village, he had a short beard, all of gray. His receding hair, a mix of blond and silver, was pushed back from a high forehead. A swirling blue tattoo stood out on his left cheek and another spiraled along each of his powerful arms, bared to his shoulders. He bowed his head to Rudicia before speaking quickly in their own tongue.

They had a spirited exchange, several phrases passing back and forth between them. Bricta intruded calmly a time or two.

Finally Rudicia turned to Antires. The man waited grimly. She introduced him with a wave of her hand. "This is . . . what you would call a healer, though Velix is more than that. He feels the currents of the sky, and the beat of Mother Earth. He says Hanuvar is in a bad way. Only extraordinary measures can save him."

"Then make them," Antires said. "Or show me how."

"Are you a healer?" Rudicia demanded. "Who are you, and what are you to him?"

"I am Antires Sosilos of Cylene. I am his friend." He decided not to say that he was his chronicler, for he was not sure how that would translate. "I'm no healer, but I will aid him any way I can. Why do you hesitate?"

"Once, he came to my people." Rudicia bared her teeth. "He led them to such glories that our youth became drunk with high tales from their few surviving elders. But it was all for naught. He used us, and he would use us again."

Surely Hanuvar hadn't expected this kind of a welcome. Though off guard, Antires countered quickly, deciding blunt truth must be met with truth. "I think you used one another. You wanted the lands the Dervans took, and he wanted his own protected, as did the others who leagued with him—the old Herrenic colonies to the south, the other Ceori tribes, the great cavalry of the Ruminians—all of them. The Dervans were coming for us. He knew we could not defeat them unless we stood together."

"He was right," Velix said quietly. He spoke better Dervan than his chieftain.

"But he came too late," Rudicia continued bitterly. "If he had come in my grandfather's time, then, well, then the Dervans would have been destroyed."

"Men cannot choose the time of their birth," Bricta said.

Rudicia looked at her as though surprised by her sister's presence, then repeated her earlier statement. "He came too late. And now he is later still. What can he do, with no army? Why did his people not send him with one? He is the lord of a wealthy land."

Antires corrected her. "He's the lord of a shattered land. The Dervans destroyed Volanus."

At sight of their puzzlement he wondered if he had said too much, and if they would turn on Hanuvar because he had no strength behind him.

"We heard rumors, but did not believe them because Dervans lie," Velix said. "What is it he plans?"

"I don't know the full extent of his plan, but he crossed a continent to get this far, and he means to go further. Monsters and dark gods and Dervan soldiers and revenants and spirits could not stop him. The Dervans fear him like they fear no other. They burned his city and razed its fields and dragged its survivors off to slavery and *still* they fear him, even when they think he has nothing. They will fear him even after he dies, but they will fear him more if he lives. I don't understand why you delay."

"You want him to live, to win more glory," Rudicia said, triumphant, as though she understood Antires' motivation. "This is what he wants, and you want to see it."

"You think he wants glory?" Antires was stunned. "Either he's changed, or you never knew him."

Velix took a sharp breath, and Antires realized the challenge in his voice might be highly insulting to the honor-conscious Ceori. He explained: "There is no other general like him. He wants neither glory, nor land. He wanted to smash Dervan power only to save his people."

Rudicia opened her mouth to speak, but Bricta interrupted. "Something marches with a legion cohort that closes upon our mountains." Her voice was somber and quiet. "It is the seed of a terrible moment. And if Hanuvar does not wake to counter it, we will go down in death, and worse than death."

Rudicia spun on her sister, raising a finger to silence her, but Bricta continued, unperturbed. "Tell her, Antires Sosilos, of the frightful goddess who dwells in darkness. The one Hanuvar thought to drown in flame. It now has rooted in the Dervan general he thought was dead."

For a moment Antires fought confusion. And then he understood. "But he killed it!"

Bricta's eyes gleamed in the shadow. "It marches beneath a banner with a boar's head above the number of the legion."

The banner of Caiax. Hanuvar had said that Jerissa had thrown a spear through him.

Bricta faced her sister: "The Dervan general marches with a small number, but they grow mighty under the warped blessing of his goddess. If they win against us, her seed will take root in our people so that we are nothing more than food for her children. We must act now, or Hanuvar will die, and then we will follow."

Perhaps for the sake of guest politeness, Velix addressed his chieftain in Dervan. "Why don't you allow this, Rudicia? It's risky, but I can save him."

"You're like the others, you old fool. What my sister hasn't told you is that you'll die in the process. Are you so eager for death? Is my bed such a poor place for you?"

Though he looked momentarily startled, Velix absorbed this information with a pained smile. "Better to die for the success of my tribe then to live only for myself."

Antires had believed Rudicia angry before. Now her eyes positively burned. She switched to her native language, snapping at her sister before turning her ire upon her husband.

Bricta moved toward the door, gesturing for Antires. He followed her from the hut. The moment he shut the door the healer and the chieftain launched into a heated debate.

The seeress stopped only a few paces beyond the building, watching him. A chill wind pimpled Antires' flesh; he had forgotten to grab his cloak. Distantly a dog barked, and somewhere in the village an old man sang a quiet, mournful song.

He couldn't tell if it was the woman's different-colored eyes or merely the strength of her gaze that disturbed him.

Bricta did not address him, so he filled the silence. "The word your sister used to describe you—I didn't know it. But you're a magic worker, aren't you. A seer."

"A seer is close, I suppose."

"How much of the future can you see?"

Her smile was pretty. "Precious little. Looking at it is like glimpsing a tapestry through a crack in the door. Sometimes the room with the tapestry is dim, but sometimes it's brightly lit; always, when Hanuvar is near. It is that way when those with strong threads come close."

That was an interesting way to talk about the future, and one he'd never heard from the fortune tellers scattered through the countryside, many of whom he had long guessed to be charlatans. He found her mention of tapestries of particular interest. "A god spoke through a priestess to him recently. She said Hanuvar's thread had been removed from the loom of fate but hadn't yet been cut. Almost as though the gods had forgotten about him."

Bricta didn't appear surprised, and pushed a lock of hair back from her ear, suddenly seeming younger. "The gods are fickle and change their minds. Their attentions wander to other tapestries."

"Other tapestries?" Antires asked. She was proving most interesting.

She chuckled at him. "You think they're only working on one? They fashion countless at the same time, some with only minor differences. Perhaps in one you have blond hair or land rises differently or events happen in changed ways. A bad seer can stare at the wrong tapestry and foretell things that will never be."

"Are you sure of what you see? Do you know that you're looking at the right tapestry?"

She smiled gently. "I see possibilities. And I think so, yes."

"What have you seen?" He heard the desperation in his voice. "Can Hanuvar save his people? Will he live?"

"I know nothing of his people," she admitted. "But if my brother-in-law acts, Hanuvar will live, and then we have a chance against the dark mother."

"Will that kill Velix?"

She hesitated before her answer. "He will be in great danger. There are steps I may take to ward him. He must eat the black energy himself, and then fight it. If I aid him, he stands a chance. But he must act soon."

Antires looked meaningfully at the door, but neither the healer nor the chieftain emerged. He turned back to Bricta, realizing she was rich with more than one kind of knowledge. "You knew Hanuvar when he was younger, didn't you. What was he like?"

She smiled. "You are a myth maker, Antires Sosilos."

It impressed him she had perceived his nature, but perhaps it was obvious to the astute. "I don't want to make myths. I mean to be a truth teller."

"It is the same thing, with such a man. Do you see him with your own eyes?"

"I try."

"Can you see the truth of the sun?"

She was slipping into allegory, so he countered with something similar. "You can never gaze upon the sun, but you can glimpse it from the side."

"And am I a way to glimpse him from the side?" She laughed warmly. "You ask what he was like? He was bold and brilliant, weighted with concerns beyond ordinary, and given strength of will and great charm. I named him blessed by the gods. How is he, now, when the gods have turned their backs upon him?"

"Bold and brilliant," he repeated to her. "Bearing weights no man should carry, blessed still with strength of will. And charm."

"Then he is the same, but his duty is greater yet. I would guess his wisdom has grown with time. Be warned, Antires Sosilos, that the company of one so bright may see you burned."

In Hanuvar's company he had faced monsters and madmen and drowning and freezing. His response was solemn. "I've seen."

The door to the hut opened behind them and Rudicia emerged, shooting a dark look to her sister. The chieftain made room for Velix, who looked briefly at his wife, then strode for the large hut where Hanuvar had been carried.

Bricta, with a nod of farewell to Antires, walked after the healer.

"My husband goes to work the magics that well may kill him," Rudicia said to Antires.

"I should be there."

Her teeth shown. "And I should kill you, for bringing Hanuvar to us."

Antires met her eyes without fear. "If that is what it takes."

The chieftain said something in her language that sounded very much like a swear word. "He has worked his spell on you. All the young ones here will flock to him and follow where he points. Few will make it back. As before, so shall it be again."

"Better to have tried and failed," Antires began.

"Then not to have tried at all?" Rudicia finished quickly. "Do you think I will stay here, Herrene? No, I will march off with the rest of you fools, should he rise."

Only then did Antires fully understand. Rudicia had believed in him once too. She wanted to believe in him again, and she hated Hanuvar for that. Wordless, Rudicia moved toward the larger hut. Since he had not been told to wait, Antires followed.

Inside, Hanuvar lay on a cot that had been set upon a long wooden table. It resembled a funeral bier too much for Antires' comfort, so he was heartened to see the rise and fall of his friend's chest. The Volani general wore only a loin clout, and Antires was startled once more by the number of scars in the muscular flesh, and alarmed by the bruising around the diagonal wound sewn along his stomach. Pus oozed out from the threads, and the scent of it lingered with the distinctive stink of feverish sweat, with a stringent smell of vinegar and incense laying across all.

Oil lamps burned at the table's head and at Hanuvar's feet. Women in gray dresses stood to every side, and the powerful, heavyset healer wiped sweat from Hanuvar's brow with a dark cloth.

Velix thrust his hands into a bowl of liquid. Vinegar, from the sour reek that overwhelmed the incense burning in a nearby lantern. The healer thoroughly scrubbed his hands, then pressed them together and bowed his head, chanting solemnly in his own language to each of the cardinal directions.

Hanuvar's limbs shook, stilled. The strange-eyed seer stepped to Hanuvar's head, placed her hand to him and then spoke with urgency to Velix.

The chieftain listened and frowned, and turned her gaze upon Antires before addressing her husband venomously. "Yes, hurry, Velix," she said. "Rush down the road to death."

Velix ignored her, finishing his prayer before stepping to Hanuvar. At his upraised hand, the gray-clad women closed in, two at each side, one at Hanuvar's head, one at his feet. They swayed in time to the syllables they began to chant. Velix spread his arms and shouted at the sky.

Antires joined Bricta, watching just to the left of Hanuvar's head. While Velix continued to shout, the Herrene spoke softly to her ear. "What is he doing?"

He barely picked her words from the air. "He is challenging death for the man before him."

To Antires this seemed melodramatic.

Velix shouted once more at the sky and beat his chest before stepping to Hanuvar and placing a hand over his heart. He repeated the sounds the women had been chanting.

Bricta swayed in time with the others. Her right eye reflected the light more brightly than the left.

The firelight dimmed, and Antires wondered how, because no one stood beside it. The lanterns, too, dimmed, and the hut grew chill.

As his neck hairs stiffened, Antires searched the darkness for a moving spectral shape, or glowing eyes, so certain was he that death had entered the room.

Still chanting, the healer placed both hands upon Hanuvar's wound, rubbing a mixture of red and yellow paste over the bruised skin. Hanuvar shifted beneath his touch but did not open his eyes.

Velix's head tipped back and he sucked in his breath. His right hand rose trembling before closing into a fist, as though he strained to crush something in his fingers. The women continued their slow, solemn phrases.

Bricta swooned and crumpled at the head of the table.

Antires caught her under the arms before her head struck the floor. The ceremony continued; Rudicia hurried to check Bricta's breathing as Antires knelt with her. The chieftain put fingers to her neck.

"Her heart races," she told Antires.

"What should I do with her?" Antires asked.

"Do not open the door," Rudicia instructed. "Keep her head elevated."

Antires stood, lifting her into his arms. She was lighter than he had guessed, and her hair smelled of sage.

Velix returned both hands to Hanuvar's chest. While the women who ringed them continued to sway, their voices sank to a whisper. Finally Velix stepped away.

The women bowed their heads, turned three times in one coordinated movement, and took a single step back. On the instant, the lights brightened, and the fire blazed up.

Antires stared in surprise. Velix came to stand before his wife, bearing with him a green, medicinal scent. His chest and forehead were slick with sweat, and he breathed heavily. His hands dripped with red and yellow paste. As Rudicia barked a question in her language, Velix pressed the cleaner of his two hands to Bricta's throat and pulled back her right eyelid.

Antires wanted to know about Hanuvar, but it seemed rude not to ask about the woman in his arms. "What's happened to her?"

"She gave of herself, to help the spell. To help me," Velix said, with a look to Rudicia. "When I was sorely pressed."

"Is she going to be all right?" Antires asked.

"Maybe."

Rudicia snorted and said something sharp in her own language to Velix. It would have been polite to wait, but Antires had waited long enough. "And what about Hanuvar? Is he going to live?"

Velix made a fluctuating gesture with his hands, suggesting an object that might lean either direction. "We have pulled the sickness from him. But he was far down the path to the restful lands. He may not wish to return. He may not be able to return."

"He will return," Antires said.

"You say that," Velix said gently. "But you do not know how beguiling those lands are for those who have suffered."

"And my sister?" Rudicia asked, then added more in her own language. Velix replied in Dervan, addressing only Antires. "They will take your friend to a warm room, and let him rest. Bring Bricta with me."

Once again Antires was to be separated from Hanuvar. As he followed Velix, Rudicia saw him look over his shoulder.

"He will rise, or fall, on his own," she told him.

III

The ship rocked on the ocean swells. She was a swift vessel with a deep draw, designed for long ocean journeys, and Hanuvar stood at the rail, watching the lookout.

Eledeva flickered into existence on the port side, a glimmer of gold scales long as the ship, sinuously riding the air with tiny flicks of her flashing tail and great bright wings. Ancient she might be, but she sported in the waves like a youngster, racing the wind and the ship. She was eager for the sights of home and the company of her sister, whom she had not seen since she had flown off to found the colony with Hanuvar three years previous.

Finally she could stand it no longer, and soared out and away, promising a speedy return.

In some obscure way Hanuvar knew he dreamed, and searched the sky in dread, knowing what came next.

There was nothing playful in Eledeva's manner when she swooped back into sight, circling to call that the city was aflame and that Dervan ships surrounded her while great siege engines rose against her landward walls. Hanuvar ordered the ship to turn back for New Volanus and then asked Eledeva to carry him to the city.

In his dream that transpired in a blur. One moment the great serpent who had been his city's friend flew beside the ship, the next he was seated upon her neck, an honor almost never granted by any asalda, no matter how profound their trust of humans. Again he heard her keening despair for her sister, and for the people of the city she loved. The long flight faded to nothing and they were suddenly above Volanus. There was the Dervan trireme with the black-cloaked sorcerers, its mast and decks aflame from Eledeva's blazing golden breath. Burning figures staggered across the deck and threw themselves into the water, and as the orange flames engulfed the frantic mages he knew a brief moment of savage exaltation. Masses upon the walls of Volanus cheered, and he heard his name, as though he were the source of Eledeva's power.

Then the great asalda's body shook with the impact of the stone that struck her. In real life Hanuvar hadn't seen the launch or fall of the specific hunk of rock, though the Dervans had been desperately flinging them through the sky. But in his dream he saw it drop away as he was thrown clear and plunged toward the water so far below. He twisted into a dive, thinking that might soften the blow but certain he would be dead regardless. Eledeva's battered, bloody body fell beside him. She stirred. One of her great six-fingered claws snatched him and he knew dizziness as she twisted. He imagined seeing his daughter, her sea-gray eyes wide in horror as he plummeted with the ancient serpent.

Eledeva shielded him by striking the water with her back and then they were sinking, he still borne in her clutches. He lost all senses.

When he wakened at last he found himself once more astride the golden asalda, though she swam sinuously through the waves. Nothing but rolling whitecaps lay in every direction and when he asked where Volanus was, Eledeva gasped out that that it was nowhere but the grave. He demanded to return, and then she said she could not. He cursed at her.

"I'm badly wounded, Hanuvar," she said, and then he knew shame, and all his anger ebbed, vanishing with the all-encompassing urge to throw his life away in a final, suicidal onslaught against the Dervan legions. Volanus was beyond his help, but his friend needed aid. He would help her find it.

There were healers on their ship and he asked if she swam for it. She confessed then that they should already have come upon it. "I fear I have lost it. I do not know the seas as well as the skies. But we must be close to land by now."

In her pain and confusion she miscalculated, for Hanuvar later understood she had missed the Greater Lendine archipelago entirely. Eledeva swam through the night. Perhaps if clouds had not veiled the stars, they might have found their way, but they had to reckon without any navigational aids. Finally, in the predawn hours, she declared that she must rest. He thought she might die then, and he readied himself to die with her, but shortly before dawn she somehow found the strength to move, and with the sunrise they finally saw a distant spot of land. For a short while she swam with renewed vigor.

Then she breathed her last and helplessly he watched her vanish into the dark beneath him. It was already too terrible a blow to see his city fall, but to witness the passing of the winged serpent who had called Volanus home since time immemorial was one stroke too many upon the anvil of doom. Something deep within him broke. Weeping, he dove after her, screaming her name through the water.

The current shifted her once with a semblance of life and then she was gone, gone, and he knew he had to either sink with her or fight.

He kicked to the surface. He blinked salt water and tears from his eyes and finally found that shimmering blot upon the dark horizon. He snarled hatred at his weariness and began to swim.

In the dream he was on the island once more, fashioning the second raft, for the first had failed him, and somehow this time he reached Narata without that second impossible swim. This time it was Lalasa who met him at the shore, not soldiers, and she steered him to the clifftop and pointed out to sea.

"You have a battle to win," she said, and as she faded, he smelled the rancid grease that Gisco had used to weatherproof his cloak, and he was standing beside the signalman overlooking the great battle at the foot of the Ardenines. Briefly he thought he was in a shadowy hut, with Antires at his side, but then the Herrene transformed into the hirsute Gisco, pointing to a long line of Dervan soldiers advancing into the cold wind. Hanuvar had harassed them with his mounted scouts until the entire legion had risen in the early hours, rushing off without breakfast. Now they stumbled out of line as they crossed the countless little rivulets in this broken terrain.

Waiting for them were the well-fed, well-rested lines of Hanuvar's troops. The Dervans outnumbered but could not outflank them. The risky part was the two tribes of Ceori warriors he'd placed in the center—members of the Isubre and Cemoni tribes. They had set aside their ancient grudges for their deeper hatred of the Dervans, but they were uncertain allies. As the snowflakes swirled he saw that mass of spike-haired men and women, many shirtless, waving their weapons and shouting battle cries. Some were so eager for revenge they threw themselves across the Dervan line before he gave command.

But he had expected that, and watched the Dervans press against them a long moment before he told Gisco to sound the horn. From the ravine where they'd hidden overnight, his little brother Melgar emerged with a thousand foot soldiers and a thousand cavalry to hit the left rear flank of the enemy. At the same moment his skirmishers and main cavalry hit the right rear.

Though he knew he dreamed, he knew he had to win, and his hands were clenched. He ordered Gisco to signal the reserve to bolster the sagging center where the Ceori yielded to the press of the legion. He hadn't known at the time young Ciprion was there at the battle, or even who he was, but he searched for him now, spotting him in that small band who had cut their way free amidst the confusion. In his dream, Hanuvar wondered what would have happened to his own future, to his city's future, if a javelin had taken the young man down. Ciprion had grown to become the greatest Dervan general, and forced Hanuvar's retreat from Tyvol. If Ciprion hadn't won the second war, Volanus itself might yet stand.

But he could no more hate Ciprion than he could hate his brothers, and he wished the young man to safety.

"You've won."

Gisco stood grinning at him through his dark beard, then faded to nothing as a lovely dark-haired woman walked through him to stand close. She was mature, in the full flower of her beauty, with great dark eyes and curling ringlets of hair. A trio of necklaces hung about her graceful neck, each beaded with azure stones, and her wrists were heavy with jeweled bracelets. Her brief blouse was scarlet and sleeveless with a low neckline and she wore a flounced skirt favored by the women of Volanus. He was startled to note that there, above one slim sandaled foot, was the anklet he had presented his wife.

"You have won the battle, Hanuvar," she said, her voice smoky with approval and invitation. "And now you must choose."

This, Hanuvar knew, was no dream. All else had faded to insubstantiality, but the woman remained.

He bowed his head formally, mind racing with concerns. "Lady Neer."

She gestured to right and left, where the army had been replaced by an immense number of milling figures. Under the bright summer sun they were wispy and ghostlike, beautiful men and women, and not a one of them heeded him or his companion, for they were lost in their own conversations. But they looked askance at a woman of gray shining eyes who pushed through their midst and padded up to Hanuvar on pretty bare feet.

Lady Neer frowned at her and extended her hands to him. "I have always waited for you. You may rest in my arms, and close your eyes to the world."

He shook his head, backing away. "It's not time."

"You are very close. You have fought so hard, all of your life."

"I am not ready."

She smiled as though he were a child whose stubbornness amused her. "No one such as you ever is. Yet, come. You will find solace among your family, and your people. And Eledeva. They wait for you. I will lead you to them."

He looked at her extended hand. He had been lonely for so very long. What would it be like to speak with his father and his sister again? And what about his mother? He imagined the joy of seeing her face, long lost to his memory.

The possibilities warmed his heart. In the cool of the evenings might he sit under a flowering myrtle with Harnil and listen to musicians strum their lyres, or even learn to play, as both had longed to do? Would he see Melgar restored not only physically, but to his inborn joy? And what of Adruvar? What would it be like to hear that giant's laughter again?

Might he finally meet his lost sister, and his lost son? And what of Imilce, whom he had adored when young and come to adore again after long years absent? She had made space for him again in her own heart as well. And Ravella would be here—he supposed the two were likely friends by now. How he longed to see them both.

Lady Neer watched him, her eyes kind, and all knowing. All he had to do was reach forth.

He lifted his hands. He could see Eledeva and admire those shining scales and apologize again for cursing her, when she had saved his life three times over the course of a single, terrible day. Without her, he would have died on impact, or drowned. Without her, he would have perished in a useless welter of blood. Without her, he could never have reached that nameless island, and found his way to Narata.

He met the eyes of the goddess, and lowered his arms. Eledeva had preserved him so that he might live. So that he could find the remnants of their people, and bring them to the new home Eledeva had helped him found.

To surrender was to betray her. It was to betray his family, who had given their lives to protect his people. To surrender was to abandon the Volani now straining under the Dervan yoke. No one else was left to fight for them.

Lady Neer sensed his change in mood and addressed him once

more. "Come, Hanuvar. No one would think less of you if you rested at last."

"I would."

"For once, take the easy way."

He met those beguiling eyes. "You would have me turn my back on people who cannot help themselves, because it's easy?"

She lowered her hand, and her smile faded. "Choose me or not, in the end you will still be mine. And I am not so terrible. I am the end to suffering, not the beginning. And haven't you suffered enough?"

"It is my people's suffering that concerns me at the moment."

"And they too, in the end, will come to me. It shall not be so long a wait. It never is."

There was some truth in that, for the long years of his fight felt as though they had happened in a finger snap. Yet they had not seemed to transpire quickly while he was experiencing them. And for those in distress, days would stretch like anguished years.

Either she lied to him, or from her distant vantage it was impossible to understand how time passed differently for mortals depending on their circumstance.

The other woman drew closer. "That's right. Don't submit to the lady's charms. Come with me instead." Though her dark skin possessed odd gray undertones, she was voluptuous and compelling in an earthy way. She looked familiar, though Hanuvar could not place her. "I will lead you back to life, and give you many children. And I will bestow vengeance over your enemies."

Lady Neer favored him with a sympathetic smile. "Leave him be. He's tired of the fight. Can't you see?"

He spoke to the strange gray goddess. "What of my people? Can you help me free them?"

She smiled smugly. "They are lost already, and you know it. They will pass to Lady Neer, and their pain will ease. But your enemies will die in terror with the knowledge that you and I destroyed them!"

Hanuvar recognized her at last, even as she beckoned with her fingers. Her voice grew more strident. "Come—we will draw strength from the springs, where it is warm, and where our children will flourish. I have peered through Caiax's memories and witnessed how people of dozens of lands yearned to follow you. He will weaken soon, but you will be strong."

"I do not want your aid, or your children." He faced the Lady Neer. "Is this my only choice? Life in thrall, or death?"

"Working for another's purpose, or a well-earned rest." Lady Neer's dark eyes sparkled. "Lady Ariteen does not know you as well as I."

"I don't think you answered fully," Hanuvar said. "There is another choice."

She did not deny it.

Hanuvar bowed his head. "You're right, Lady. Eventually, we shall all come to you. I thank you for your offer. But I must refuse for now." He bypassed her and walked on toward the insubstantial figures.

"There is no other choice," Ariteen cried, indignant. "Don't look to them for help! They don't care. I care!"

She cared only for her own desires. The ghosts or gods parted before him without acknowledging his presence. Ariteen padded after.

"I will have you," she vowed. "You will come to love me!"

He ignored her, passing into a hazy twilight. Behind him, Lady Neer called, her voice heavy with amusement. "I will be waiting!"

"You must be patient, then," he replied.

"I am ever so patient."

He walked into a land and sky all of blue as Ariteen shouted indignantly and death laughed fondly at his foolishness. He moved on through the haze, and it lightened, showing him a winding path upon a flowered hillside. He climbed toward its summit. The scent of a warm broth struck his nostrils and a beam of sunlight resolved itself into a bright shaft shining into a dark room where he lay in furs. An older woman who reminded him of someone from his youth sat beside him. She squeezed his hand, whispering to him in a language he thought he knew, but couldn't place. He smiled at her.

IV

The men of the First Century had outdone themselves. No matter the rain that had pattered down all afternoon, they had marched seven more miles even than Marius had hoped. And rather than complaining about sore feet, the men were laughing over their evening rations and hoping they'd get to the fight soon. He was proud to be leading such exemplary soldiers.

They had set camp near a roadside fort in upper Calenna, where the garrison was so small there hadn't been room for the five double-strength centuries of the Seventh Legion's First Cohort, well over eight hundred men once their support staff was included in the count. The garrison commander, a centurion of recent vintage, was obviously curious about their mission, but had not dared inquire of Marius what their orders were and relinquished his quarters to Caiax.

Marius ducked under the low door arch and sidled past the general's body slave, leaving on some errand of his own, then came to attention before his commanding officer. A fire burned in the hearth; Caiax sat facing him at a small wooden desk, hunched in a shawl. A blank piece of paper sat before him and he looked up from it.

"Ah, Marius. At ease. Anything to report?"

"The men's spirits are high, sir. I don't think they minded the rain at all, even that last hour. By Jovren, I think they could have marched another ten."

"I think you're right," Caiax said with a proud smile. "I told you the mushrooms would work wonders."

"And you were right, sir."

If Caiax heard the hesitation in his voice, it didn't show in his own answer. "I'll have their next ration ready soon."

"Yes, sir. There's one small matter. Probably of minor concern, but I thought I should bring it to your attention."

"Yes?" Caiax asked impatiently.

"Some of the men have developed a minor infection. It's not interfering with their health, but the surgeon is worried because it's spreading and is resistant to treatment."

Caiax notoriously hated to be involved with minutiae, and his face took on color as he listened. Marius explained quickly. "I thought you should be informed, sir, because the coloration of the fungal growths, on the back of the men's knees and beneath their armpits, well, sir, they look like those from the mushroom supply."

The general's expression cleared, and he actually laughed, a sound Marius had only heard on a handful of occasions. "That's nothing to be worried about, Centurion. That's fine news. Ariteen has blessed the men."

"Sir?"

The general stood. "Ariteen has blessed me, and she has blessed this venture."

"I'm afraid I'm unfamiliar with this Ariteen," Marius explained, uncomfortable to admit so.

"Ah, don't worry. I'd never heard of her myself, but, then, she's a goddess of secrets, a harbinger of life and conquest. She blessed me when I lay dying." The general's eyes sought his own and burned with the peculiar fervor of the mad and the newly converted. "I healed, Marius, not because of surgeons, but in spite of them. They tried to remove her blessing, but it healed me."

Marius cleared his throat. "Your pardon, sir. Do you mean that the infection is a blessing?"

"Exactly! You talked about the health of the men. You didn't mention yourself, but look at you, still energized and ready to march even as the sun sets. That's the power of Ariteen. You shouldn't let a little thing like some mushrooms unsettle you. You're made of sterner stuff."

"Yes, sir," Marius agreed.

This time Caiax heard the doubt in his voice. "You still don't see. Ariteen has spared me so that I shall have the power to defeat all who stand in her way. She has made of me her chosen deliverer!"

After this astonishing declaration, Caiax tugged at his tunic. Marius could scarce believe what he sensed was about to happen—the general was lifting his clothing to expose his loincloth and lean thighs.

"Don't be squeamish, Marius. Look!" As the tunic rose past the general's undergarment, Marius' eyes fastened upon a long red scar, or tried to, for it was mostly obscured by the profusion of small, blue-gray mushrooms growing in and around it, and up his chest, toward the pits of his arms, and down toward his loincloth.

They were identical to the mushrooms the general had been presenting him each evening.

"You see?" Caiax said, then lowered the tunic. "They're all over me, and I'm in the peak of health."

Marius swallowed his bile. "Yes, sir."

"My slave has finished harvesting the ones from my back and will bring them to you just as soon as he's done washing them. There should be enough for a double ration tomorrow."

V

Antires watched the Ceori warriors queue up outside the hut that morning where Hanuvar waited. Most were grizzled middle-aged veterans, some with terrible scars. A few shepherded bright-eyed younger adults. Rudicia was speaking to them all, her expression somber, but her words could not dim the expectant eagerness on the faces of the warriors.

The Herrene sidled over to Bricta, watching with interest on the right. "What's she saying?" he asked.

"That Hanuvar can see them now. A lot of these men and women served under him. They've brought their children and grandchildren and nephews."

"None of them look angry."

Bricta turned to him in surprise. "Why would they?"

"Your sister is angry."

"Well, she sees further, doesn't she? All these remember is a daring man who led them to victories. They brought back gold, and stories. They want more. And the youngsters want it for themselves. Rudicia wanted security for the Isubre, at the least, and revenge, and the lands the Dervans stole."

"She got them, for a while."

"But a while doesn't count for much with someone like her, does it?"

"You don't seem upset, yourself."

"I know that if your happiness is dependent upon possession or achievement, your cup is always empty."

She continued to impress him, for this statement sounded less like the mummery one might hear from a fortune teller and more like the words of a well-schooled philosopher.

"I'm a little surprised that the Dervans don't have garrisons scattered through all these mountains."

She laughed at him. "They have their forts, on the flatter land, but they leave the rest to us. They know that if they press us, we can hide in the mountains and return a deadly toll. Those were the terms we agreed to when the last war ended. We have little they want here."

"And what do you want now?" he asked. "From Hanuvar, I mean."

"I want him to turn aside the coming danger he's attracted."

"Caiax," he said.

"The goddess behind him."

"And what about your lands?"

"If we march into lands the Dervans stole, we could not hold them. Not yet. Later, perhaps."

"Later, with Hanuvar?"

"Who knows what may transpire?" Bricta stepped away as Rudicia finished, and one of her bodyguards opened the hut.

The other Ceori were allowed in a few at a time. Rudicia and Bricta walked past them to stand at Hanuvar's side and Antires went with them.

The general had been able to sit upright for the last three days, though this morning had been the first time he had managed it without assistance. He spoke to the small groups as they presented themselves, greeting them in what sounded like fluent Isubre. The general sat behind a table carved with ornate animal images Antires had assumed to be lizards until Hanuvar had told him they were Ceori hunting hounds, twisted out of all proportion.

Hanuvar had allowed his beard to grow, in part to hide the gauntness from a week's sickness and little food, and in part because these men had known him with that beard and would better recognize him. His slate gray eyes were alight.

The visitors happily talked among themselves, gesturing to the general, and Antires could well guess they were pleased at how healthy he looked.

A huge man in early middle years walked up and Hanuvar stood, clasped his arm and laughed in pleasure. The Ceori was delighted.

"He remembers all their names," Bricta told Antires, both pleasure and pride in her voice.

This news astonished him. How could Hanuvar retain these names after so many years, when these warriors were only a small number of those who had marched with him? Could he truly have

kept tens of thousands of names at call from his memory? Or was it
that these were the most prominent of his veterans?

Though it seemed impossible, Antires strongly suspected the
former.

Hanuvar remained on his feet as a mass of younger men and a
number of women were introduced, and he addressed them in their
own language while gesturing to the older warriors and generating a
few belly laughs from them all. Antires watched, only learning later
what had been said, though he guessed its gist. Hanuvar told them he
was glad to be hosted among good friends and great warriors and
that he would give a select few of them instructions soon, if they
wished to follow to glory.

Afterward, the crowd dispersed, and Rudicia, Bricta, and a select
few warriors joined Hanuvar at the table in the chiefain's hut. Antires
sat at Bricta's side and liberally applied himself to the meat pies,
wetting his mouth with the bitter beer only when truly thirsty. The
seer translated for him without being prompted, for which Antires
was grateful.

Ceori scouts had watched the approach of a small force of
legionaries, not quite a thousand men. They marched under Caiax's
boar-head banner.

"They are coming for you," Bricta said. "But the goddess means to
have us all."

"Why does this goddess want us?" Rudicia asked. "Is this for
vengeance?"

"No," Bricta answered. "This is no Dervan god. She seeks
dominion for her children."

One of the warriors asked why the goddess was favoring the
Dervans, and Bricta answered.

"She is using them like a hunter uses dogs to drive game her way.
Were the greater gods interested in our fates, they would already have
stopped her." Bricta made a fluent gesture toward the mountains
beyond the chieftain's walls. "The mountain spirits are aware of her
and sense what she would do to them. They are with us, if only
because their own holdings will be destroyed should she take root
here. They warn me that these men are more than men, that they are
cold with the life of the goddess. They may not live long, but while
they do, they will be greater than men."

"How so?" Hanuvar asked.

"They are more resilient. Harder to kill."

"These are the forces of Ariteen," Hanuvar told them. "She likes warmth, and moisture, and darkness. There are hot vents in one of the nearby valleys, correct?"

Rudicia confirmed that there were. "But the Dervans will come for us here. Bricta foretold it."

"I can lure Caiax where we want him," Hanuvar promised.

Rudicia demanded an explanation curtly. "How?"

Hanuvar then shared his plans. Antires nodded in admiration as Bricta relayed the general's words to him.

"I will lose warriors with this," Rudicia said.

"Yes."

"We will win many arms," one of her advisors pointed out. "And strike a memorable blow against the Dervans."

Rudicia stared hard at Hanuvar, and Antires wondered what she was thinking. Perhaps she debated reminding him that none of this would have happened if he had not come to her.

But the Ceori were a fatalistic people and thought that all were born with certain dooms, so she might have been thinking something else entirely. Antires would have liked to have asked her but dared not. In the end Rudicia sat back. "We will follow Hanuvar's plan, and we will smash these Dervans who dare test us. Make ready."

VI

When Marius told the chief physician about the mushroom's source, he expected his fellow officer to be as disgusted as himself. But Rutilius was far more fascinated by their effect than their point of origin. He questioned closely about amounts, and times, and performance measures. And when Marius pressed about potential dangers, Rutilius posited that the benefits appeared to far outweigh the cosmetic drawback of a minor gray exudate that didn't even induce local inflammation. He enthusiastically speculated whether this small change in diet would double the effectiveness of Dervan legions, rescue those near death, and decrease the infirmity of age, likely imagining acclaim for introducing the mushrooms to the rest of their society, for he intimated he'd write a treatise about their healthful impact. Marius left feeling foolish and unresolved.

As a veteran of long standing, it went against all of Marius' instincts to discuss a superior officer's decisions with underlings, but finding no aid from the nominally independent physician, he turned to the cohort's lower-ranked centurions.

Here, too, any concerns fell on deaf ears. When Marius told his fellow officers about Caiax's condition and compared it to their own, they somehow saw the general's sacrifice as noble. They were impressed that their leader let himself go untreated for their betterment. Young Hortalus even said that he found the ground mushrooms a delicious addition to their normal fare, wishing he could get more, and his sentiment was echoed by others, who mocked Marius for being a worried old woman. Wasn't the legion otherwise healthy? Weren't the men in excellent spirits and fighting trim?

They would hear no more criticism of Caiax, and insinuated that Marius' questioning was dangerously close to treason. Marius realized with a depressing jolt that any later judgment tribunal would be drawn from these officers, since no others were stationed nearby. He had to reluctantly agree with his old friend Tertius, who pointed out the general's strategic decisions certainly didn't seem to be suffering.

None of them knew whether this foe they marched for actually existed, but Marius didn't mention that, and he pretended to find their arguments persuasive. He had served almost a quarter century in the legion, and reminded himself that this wouldn't be the first time a superior's orders had put him in a difficult spot. He had come out just fine before, and he resolved to do so again. In the end, all he could do was scrape the infection from himself each evening, and eat from his own emergency reserves.

Only two evenings after Caiax revealed his terrible secret they arrived in the foothills of the Ardenines. Scouts found numerous Ceori tracks. Even if Hanuvar was not involved, the tribes apparently were on the move.

In the hours before dawn, two of the camp sentries were struck by spears. The optio on watch shouted for alert as more spears showered out of the darkness and the legionaries scrambled to grab shields.

The assault ended as suddenly as it had begun, though the retreating Ceori shouted rude taunts.

Marius ran to the general's tent, astonished to find Caiax leaning over his map table. He had apparently ignored the call to arms.

"General?"

"Yes, Marius?" Caiax continued to study the map of the foothills spread before him, leaning on one mottled hand. "We've made contact with the enemy, have we?"

"Yes, sir. Skirmishers attacked us. They threw spears at our sentries." He wanted to say that they should have built a fortified camp, as was standard legion practice. He did not; Caiax had insisted upon marching them into the twilight, and there had not been time.

"It's almost disappointing that Hanuvar has proven so predictable."

"We must ready the men to counter the attack."

Caiax looked at him at last. Even in the dim lighting conditions it was obvious the whites of his eyes had taken on a gray pallor. "No, that's what Hanuvar wants us to do. That's how he's tricked us before. His men will be well rested. They'll lure us to wherever he wants us to go so he can spring a trap. Hanuvar thinks he can lead us into danger, but I know his tricks. Make sure the men are fed. I've sent Glabius out with their rations already."

"I'll see that the men are fed," Marius promised. He said nothing about the mushrooms.

Caiax remained beside his map table, his head nodding back and forth like a wind-blown bloom on the end of a long stalk. "Good. Report to me when they're ready. And silence those horns."

Repressing a shudder, Marius left. An optio ran up to report and Marius put his concerns for the future aside to care for the present.

Over the rest of the night the Ceori continued their harassment, but Dervan scouts reported the enemy always withdrew toward the same northeasterly direction. The maps showed that this led to a wide valley crowded with brush-covered hillocks up to the point where some plowed fields lay, and it took no great military scholar to judge it a fine battle site.

In the hour just before dawn, Marius was summoned to the headquarters tent, where Caiax still studied the map. Marius wondered if the general had actually moved since their last interaction. After a moment he spotted a still form lying in the shadowy tent corner. He recognized the plain beige tunic as that worn by Caiax's body slave. At first he thought the man's legs were wrapped in rags, then, under further scrutiny understood that they were coated in gray fungal threads.

He suppressed an oath and shifted his attention back to his commanding officer. "General?"

By the light of the two lanterns, subcutaneous bumps on the general's face were rendered starkly. Marius gulped to suppress his alarm at the thought that fungus might be growing beneath his own skin and repressed an urge to feel his face.

"Ah, Marius." Caiax's fingers fell to the map, one valley over. "There are springs here."

"Yes, sir." He wondered how Caiax knew that, because they weren't on the map. Probably the scouts had mentioned it to him.

"Hot springs are of tremendous use to us. It will enable our power to grow. We will send the skirmishers and one full century to follow the Ceori, as though we have fallen for Hanuvar's trap. They're to make a great deal of noise. I want Hanuvar to think they are a larger force. Our cavalrymen will follow at a distance, and disturb as much ground as they can, to raise dust."

He was certainly acting like the old Caiax. Seemingly of its own volition, Marius' gaze shifted to the slave's body. He forced his attention back to the general.

"Rather than taking the route Hanuvar wants, we will advance double time through this valley." He tapped the one with the hot springs. "Then we will cross into the one where Hanuvar has chosen for us to be at this pass, and hit him. At that point, our cavalry will advance and the enemy will be closed in from both sides."

The hand slipping across the map was gray and terrible, but the mind that guided it remained sharp.

"I like it, sir, although I do worry about separating such a small force."

"The scouts report we're fighting a small force. No more than a few hundred fighters."

"How will our men stay in contact if they're divided between the valleys?"

"Send scouts up on the foothills between the valleys to relay messages via flags. Come, Marius, you know how this sort of thing works."

"Yes, sir. But don't you think someone as astute as Hanuvar will see the flags, and have sentries placed at the cross points?"

"I'm sure he will have the latter, which is why we'll kill them. Now are there any other foolish questions, or do you mean to waste the early morning mist?"

"No, sir. It's all clear."

"Good. Then let's be on with it."

"Sir!"

Caiax's head bobbed as he shifted, then he pushed out through the tent with the same inflexible confidence to which Marius was accustomed.

He followed and almost bumped into Caiax when the general pivoted just beyond the tent flap.

The sentry waited only three steps beyond, his helmet brim outlined in the predawn gloom.

"A final order, Centurion. Hanuvar is to be captured alive."

Marius saluted. "We shall do our best, sir."

"It is not about best," Caiax said testily. "He is to be captured alive. At all costs. Is that clear?"

In the midst of battle any number of accidents might happen. If Hanuvar were fighting on the line, as he had been known to do, or if he happened to be near the troops during a javelin cast, or part of a mob running from a cavalry charge, there could be no guaranteeing his safety. Caiax was well aware of these dangers, for prior to breaching the walls of Volanus he had followed up his orders for capturing the city's seven councilors with an addendum, saying that while it was preferable to take them alive, their deaths might be unavoidable.

This morning Caiax had a different outlook. There was steel in his voice as he asked his next question. "Is that clear, First Spear[15]?"

"Yes, sir. I will pass the word."

"Very good. He is vital to our ongoing plans."

"Yes, sir."

Marius wanted to ask who the "our" referred to, because the only

---

[15] The senior centurion of a legion is known as the First Spear.   —*Silenus*

ongoing plan the empire would have for Hanuvar was a painful death before as many thousands as could be assembled to witness it.

But Marius passed along the commands, then organized the men into lines of march, ensuring that those who reacted to the next assault of the Ceori skirmishers would do so as if they were barely under control of their officers. Hanuvar's scouts would no doubt report that to him.

He then tried to report the men's readiness to Caiax. The general's tent sentry wasn't on duty, and when Marius pushed the flap open he discovered the sentry and Rutilius crouched in the dirt beside the body of the general's slave. A basket sat on the trestle table, half full of mushrooms plucked from Glabius' corpse. Neither the sentry nor the physician was harvesting now, though, for they were busily lifting fungus from the man's skin and popping it straight into their mouths, their faces contorted in ecstasy. They paused in their chewing as their heads swung to take in the cohort's senior centurion.

The sentry at least should immediately have shot to his feet and come to attention, and both should have reddened with shame, like men caught drinking on duty. But their looks were inscrutable, and Marius was overcome with the sense that he was the one who should apologize for intruding upon such a private matter.

He found his mouth starting to twist, to shape the curse words to get these men up and moving. But then he caught the scent rising from the fungus. At one level it was sickly; at another it beguiled like the most fragrant wine, or the aroma of warm, succulent roast pig. His mouth watered, and he took a single step forward.

He caught a look at the dead slave's face entirely distorted by the growth, then forced the air from his lungs, hoping the scent would be expelled with it. He retreated from the tent before he dared to breathe. Shuddering in disgust, he looked back at the canvas. His first thought was to call both men out. His second thought was to run both of them through. He was afraid if he faced them again the scent of the mushrooms would overrun his reason and he'd be unable to resist joining their feast. Shaken, he convinced himself he would decide what to do about discipline, and the terrible mushrooms, after the victory.

He found Caiax near the men readying their advance into the secondary valley, and decided to say nothing to him about the horrific scene he'd just witnessed, for fear of how the general might respond. Caiax quietly told him to initiate their plan the next time Hanuvar's skirmishers renewed their attack. More spears flew within the next quarter hour and Marius promptly ordered the century to give staggered chase. He then sent the rest of the cohort at double time into the parallel valley Caiax had pointed out.

If the men of the Seventh had always found Caiax cold, they had never found him cowardly, and today he marched with them rather than riding, rectangular shield in one hand, javelins at the ready. The sun had not yet risen, and the moon hung half hidden by a distant peak, painting the lands before them in shades of black and gray. No one looked tired. To the rear someone swore a personal battle cry, so eager was he for the fight. A centurion promised a week's latrine duty to the next soldier who made a sound.

Before long the horizon lightened, but Marius was not worried yet, for with the dawn came a mist, the better to conceal their movements. He scanned the heights for sign of their scouts. He saw none, which pleased him, for he'd told them to lay low until it became necessary to signal.

One of their own skirmishers sprinted back to report the first of the hot springs was close, and before long they were wending their way past the fissures from which steam rose over the rocky, cratered landscape. To right and left the valley narrowed, and word passed back that the advance party had killed a band of Ceori scouts and secured their line of march.

The sky lightened fully, but the valley floor remained in gloom because the sun had not risen over the shoulder of the mountains. Mist flowed about their knees. Energy coursed through Marius' system, and he saw excitement reflected in the expressions of those around him.

Caiax's bumpy face was spread with a wide smile. "These grounds will be perfect for us," he said. "It is a good growing place. For the children."

"Children, sir?" Marius asked.

"For the children of Ariteen. For my legacy. Soon, Hanuvar and I will spread her love through all the lands of the empire. Two great generals, marching beneath a single, victorious banner."

Marius looked to the legionaries striding to the right of them, hoping they hadn't heard. "Sir," he said quickly, "Hanuvar is our enemy."

"For now," Caiax said. "Soon he will work with us in service to the goddess. That is what she wishes."

From behind came a loud rumble of rock on rock. Some of their soldiers screamed in pain.

Marius whirled. A cascade of boulders rattled down the left hillside, pursued by a plume of dust. High on the right slope a bank of Ceori spearmen and slingers had risen from where there had been nothing but rocks moments before. The small band of Dervan skirmishers sent into the heights had utterly vanished.

Arrows, spears, sling stones, and rocks were hurled in profusion, and took deadly toll. Legionaries fell with bloody skulls and splintered legs. Soldiers dropped, impaled upon spears, dead or crying out for aid. Boulders ground scores of men into smears of blood and bone.

Caiax should have been shouting orders. He only turned, blinking in surprise at the slopes, as if he were coming upon a peculiar novelty. Marius shouted for his men to find their standards and form into testudos.[16] Progress would slow, but at least the men would be protected from the arrows, sling stones, and spears.

Unfortunately, those formations couldn't be held well while they moved over rough ground, for the pathway before them was cut by fissures and steam vents. Spears and stones rang off the shields, but more boulders smashed men flat, spraying their fellows with gore. Of what use was their greater strength and endurance against rock?

Finally, step by bloody step, a pitiful remnant climbed free of the mist and on toward a grassy summit. Here the Ceori waited en masse, and charged them.

They fought with the reckless abandon of their kind, men and women swirling into battle wearing little but checkered pants, their chests and faces painted in woad spirals. Their hair was limed to stand back in points. Their undisciplined charge would have broken against a proper legion line. But the soldiers had been scattered by

---

[16] The testudo, or turtle, is a close formation where the shields are carried by soldiers on the edge of the formation as a wall on every side, and soldiers deployed to the center raise shields overhead. It is extraordinarily effective for protecting a unit from spear and arrow fire.
—*Silenus*

the bombardments and were reluctant to form in large groups, when huge rocks might rain down upon them.

Marius' arm was not weary—the mushrooms, at least, had given him stamina. But it did not matter. No matter how many Ceori he cut down, more took their place, and man by man his legionaries were whittled down.

He punched his gladius through a Ceori's ribs. The weapon made a sucking sound as he pulled it clear. And then he breathed heavily and took in the view to right and left. At last, no more Ceori lay before him. But only a few dozen of his men were anywhere close.

The ground was littered with the dead and the grievously injured, a line of broken bodies stretching back to the deeper mist.

Somehow Caiax remained beside him. His helmet had an immense divot along the right side, but the wound had not felled the general, who appeared untroubled by the blue gray ooze that trickled down the side of his face from his nostril. His jaw was dislocated and twisted to one side, and he mouthed noises Marius could not understand.

A mass of Ceori spearmen waited on the slope above. A somber woman in helmet and corselet, bearing a bloodstained sword, stood at their head.

"Legionaries," she called in heavily accented Dervan. "Lay down your arms!"

His men fell silent. Caiax continued to gibber, and as he turned his head, gesticulating to Marius, the centurion saw that the eye on the flattened side of the general's head bulged from his skull. More gray fluid leaked from his mouth.

Marius could take no more horrors. He took his commander's head with a single slice. It proved simple, as though he had cut a flower stalk.

The head fell away, but there was no flow of blood. The brackish sludge leaking from the wound repulsed him, and the next thing Marius knew he was slicing and hacking until he rose, panting, from the still form that had once been the famed Dervan general. Inside the body he'd discovered bone, but no blood, and vast amounts of goo in various stages of solidity knit together with fungal threads.

The Ceori had watched it all. Marius threw his sword down

beside the ghastly body. Somewhere behind him he heard one of the optios trying to get the men to form up. Probably to arrest him.

"Optio," Marius called. "Stand down."

Confused, the optio barked for his men to hold their positions. Marius looked up at the Ceori woman, only then seeing the armored, bearded figure standing to her right. Hanuvar. It had to be. He bore Ceori arms, but held himself like a chieftain. A Herrene stood beside him.

"The general is dead," Marius shouted up. "My congratulations. You lured him, didn't you?"

Hanuvar's answer was a slight inclination of his head. It had always been the Volani's way to know the weaknesses of his enemy leaders.

"How many more follow you?" the woman called down, her accent thick. "Why did the emperor send you with your nightmare god?"

"I will tell you, lady warrior," Marius said. "We numbered only 856. The general planned to capture Hanuvar and march with him through all the lands, spreading the disease we carried. If I'd understood sooner, I would have stopped him sooner."

The woman laughed in derision. "You think you have earned our gratitude?"

He answered grimly. "No. You cannot let us live."

Behind him one of the men cried out, "No!"

"Silence!" Marius shouted. He then raised his voice higher, both so that the Ceori warrior woman might hear, and so that his own men understood the truth. "Caiax fed us the mushrooms. Many of us already show signs of infection, but all of us carry it. You can't just kill us. You have to burn us. You have to burn our clothes. You have to burn the lands where we walked, where the fungus might have taken root. You should be careful not to touch us, and to cover your faces with cloth so you don't breathe it in."

"Why do you tell us this?" the woman asked. "Is this another Dervan trick?"

Marius laughed without humor. It would be ironic if this moment of final truth were not trusted. He sought to explain it clearly, both for their sakes, and for the sake of Derva. "I care nothing for you. But what is in us cannot spread. Do you understand? If it lays hold of you, then you will take it to my people, and everyone you come into contact with. You must hunt down the cavalry and the century that advanced into your valley."

"They've already been dealt with," the woman said. "And as for your counsel, Dervan, I hear and believe you."

That, at least, was good to know. "Hanuvar," Marius said. "Why have you returned? Do you mean to march on Derva?"

"I honor your bravery," the great Volani called down to him. "But you ask for plans even my friends have never heard."

"I wish we could have met on a better battlefield," Marius called. "As true soldiers, not minions of a dark goddess."

"Had I my way, we would never have battled at all," Hanuvar said wearily. That sounded little like something the great trickster of war would say.

"Is there more you would tell us?" the warrior woman asked.

"Let us make ready for our gods," Marius said.

"Any warrior should always be ready for that," she said, but waved him to proceed.

He turned to the men behind him. "Throw down your shields, so they can make this quick. Do you understand? Throw—"

But he never finished the sentence. The Ceori had already launched their last attack. Spears, sling stones, and even arrows found their targets and the soldiers screamed in their dying agony. Marius was turning when something struck him in the face. It stung terribly until a sling stone smashed into his chest and hurt so much he almost didn't feel the spear. He staggered, clasping its haft with both hands, then fell. He struck his head upon a stone and knew nothing more.

VII

While Hanuvar had managed the strength to direct the battle's course, it sapped his energy, and Bricta insisted he rest for a full two weeks before he dared to travel. He did rest, though he exercised each day, slowly extending the sessions and the length of his walks.

Over the course of his stay, the Ceori took elaborate care of the lands where the Dervans had fallen. Their bodies had been burned along with all of their food supplies and their cloth; the very grass was razed wherever they fell. The best of their weapons were wiped thoroughly with vinegar and left under observation for a month; the land itself was to be carefully monitored for a generation. A misty valley had been transformed into a burned, rocky landscape, barren of life. That, Hanuvar thought, was the glory of war. He turned from his overlook and walked through the narrow pass where the Isubre village lay, then spotted Antires winding toward him.

"Well met, Hanuvar," his friend said as he neared. "Bricta tells me that you've been cleared for travel."

"Reluctantly."

The Herrene stopped before him. "She's worried about you. She told me that she thinks the gods have noticed you again."

"There's no point worrying about things you cannot change."

"She wants you to stay, doesn't she? There's a history there."

"We're old friends."

"Friends, eh?"

Hanuvar thought then of the first time he'd seen her, as she and Rudicia were introduced by their aged father. Rudicia was her father's chosen successor, and Bricta his seer. Hanuvar had nodded politely to both, finding them attractive in the way a man might admire a sunset, lovely but beyond his reach and not germane to his daily concerns. And then, over the banquet, he had been seated to Bricta's side. During a lull in conversation, she turned to speak to her father and one of her slim hands had brushed her tidy curls behind an ear. It was an unconscious, graceful, distinctly feminine gesture. Seeing it he felt as though a mule had kicked him in the chest.

The playwright's eyes had fastened on him, and Hanuvar gave him a gentle warning. "If you write your play or chronicle you can't have every woman I meet falling in love with me. No one will believe it."

"Even if you were in love?"

"Just because two people once found each other attractive—"

"—and still do—"

"—doesn't mean they slept together. Besides, Ceori women are private about such things."

"Really?" Antires sounded skeptical.

"Come. You want secrets, I will share one with you." He slapped him on the shoulder and guided him onto a trail through the hills between two valleys. His wound throbbed as they started up.

"Where are we going?" Antires asked.

"You'll see."

In a few moments more they arrived at a promontory where they could look out through a gap between larger peaks to the lowlands of the Tyvolian peninsula, green and lovely and sparkling with morning dew, as if diamonds awaited in abundance. Hanuvar gestured to it.

"When our army crossed, after struggling through the peaks, we reached a high plateau. The whole peninsula was below us, much like this, but we had an even better view."

"And that's when you gave a rousing speech," Antires guessed.

"Of course. You can probably write that kind of thing in your sleep."

"What did you say?"

He shrugged, a gesture of the Ceori. "I told the men that the worst was behind us, that the Dervans would never believe that we could have made that crossing, and that the enemy had no idea what was in store for them. There was more, too, but I didn't bring you up here to reminisce." He pointed through the gap. "Do you see there, where the river turns to the left?"

Antires answered in the affirmative.

"That's the Sarn, and it flows into a deep-watered bay. That's where we're going."

"There? Not Derva?"

"There. To a little northern town named Selanto."

❉ ❉ ❉

He explained that much of his objective, but it was not until we came down from the mountains and crossed the Sarn and followed it to a pretty bay fringed with pines and backed by snow-draped peaks and their tree-girt foothills that I thoroughly grasped the next phase of his plans.

Hanuvar straightaway rented a small building at the little harbor overlooking the docks and within a few hours laborers had arrived with desks and chairs and shelving. He returned in late afternoon as the movers departed, bearing with him a delightful feast of mussels and cod and fresh-baked bread and seared onions. He'd even splurged and located us two bottles of Fadurian, one of the most consistently sweet-flavored wines in all of Tyvol. With the door closed, he quietly raised a toast to the four corners of the world—which I gathered was part of a Volani tradition he had once alluded to—and then toasted me for my part in the venture.

We sat on stools, dining at the empty desk lighted from slatted shutters high in the wall. After so long with other fare, the seafood proved a delight, and I cannot tell you how wonderful it was to cross my lips with fine wine after subsisting on that wretched Ceori beer for long weeks. Some, it is said, grow so accustomed to its taste that they crave it, though I scarce believe this.

I knew Hanuvar had something in mind apart from recognition of our crossing, and hoped it would be a final explanation of his plans. Having waited so long, I found myself strangely reluctant to hear the truth, for I sensed a change in the air, and I could not guess where it would take us.

He raised his mug and encompassed the surrounding walls with a broad gesture. "I would like you to run this business."

"Me?" I couldn't have been more startled if Hanuvar had told me I was to grow a tail. "I'm no businessman."

He drank and set down the mug on the desktop with a conclusive thud. "I need someone I can trust. And they are in short supply."

"You wish me to, what, pretend to run a cover business?"

"No. We're to manage a shipbuilding firm. Over the next few days I'll buy the land south of here, and get to expanding, and then I'll see about finding you the help you need."

"I don't know anything about shipbuilding," I said. "And won't it take too long to build ships? Shouldn't we just buy them?"

"We need deep oceangoing vessels, not these coast huggers the Dervans use."

That immediately made sense, for I knew that New Volanus lay far across the ocean. But I was still confused about why he was wanting me to be in charge of the matter. "What are you going to be doing?"

"The Dervans have a list of all the slaves, and where they were sold. I'm going to procure that list. And I'm going to buy them, or free them. And then they're going to sail to New Volanus. On these ships."

It seemed to me that he had overlooked any number of potential challenges. "That sounds like a tall order," I said.

He chewed and swallowed another bit of cod, then replied. "Yes."

I gave voice to the most obvious of my worries. "Won't the Dervans *get suspicious if you keep buying up only Volani slaves? And you can't possibly have enough money to buy land, and build ships, and hire shipbuilders, and purchase everyone's freedom."*

"There are many challenges yet," Hanuvar agreed. "But my old intelligence network was still active as of four years ago, before I sailed out to found New Volanus. There's a chance that many of the agents are still alive. In which case not all of the slaves need to be purchased by the same person."

It had simply never occurred to me that he had an entire chain of allies already in place, and I suppose this is one of the crucial things he had meant to keep hidden from the Dervans. For all that, his plan still offered difficulties. Probably he had anticipated them, but I felt duty bound to point them out. Besides which, I was curious about how he planned to solve them. "Some of the Volani will be old, or infirm. Some owners will find their slaves too valuable to part with, or might even be fond of them. And some might not even want to leave."

"Problems abound," Hanuvar agreed. I would have liked him to have said more, but he did not, and I gathered he meant to solve each problem as it presented itself.

I pointed out another challenge. "There's the matter of you walking around the land of Tyvol. Won't you be recognized?"

"You've given me some practice with acting."

I chuckled. "Some. You could stand to vary your roles. And you could stand more practice."

"You have a few days to hone me before I leave," Hanuvar said.

While I had understood he would be leaving, it hadn't occurred to me until that moment that he meant to depart so soon, or that he might well be gone for long stretches of time. Perhaps it was apparent to you reading that he had meant this very thing from his first words, but I hadn't understood. I suppose I had been too startled by the idea of me managing anything apart from a theatrical enterprise. "Wait a moment. How am I supposed to record your travels if you're out wandering the countryside and I'm managing a shipyard?"

"You can ask the Volani all about their stories when they get sent to you. And I'm sure I'll need your special expertise from time to time."

That wouldn't do, and I told him so, vehemently.

"You wanted to help me, Antires," he reminded me. His gaze was searching. "This will help. More than any play. And I can't always be

seen in your company, can I? The revenants were already looking for an older man travelling with a Herrene."

That was very true, much as it pained me to admit.

"And there's one more thing you need to recall," Hanuvar added.

"What's that?"

His gray eyes leveled my own. "This story isn't about me. It's about my people. Without them, I'm nothing."

"I suppose there's some truth to that," I said glumly. "But their story is your story. If they didn't have you, they'd have no hope at all."

"One man's mad dream, a doomed quest, something like that?" Hanuvar smiled mordantly. "Try to keep the poetry out of it. I'm just a man too stubborn to quit. Besides, once I procure the list, the vast majority of the time middlemen should be able to manage the transfer of ownership. From here on out things should be a little simpler."

The future would prove this a vain hope, as you may be aware.

Though disappointed, I felt a measure of honor to be so valued by this man and tried to make light of my feelings. "And so he would not turn away," I said. "Though challenge lay at every hand, he raised his noble head and journeyed forth to walk the land where all his enemies had laired."

Hanuvar gave me a pained smile. "You can stop now."

But that only encouraged me. "He clenched his mighty hands with the sorrow he could never fully vent, and boldly eyed the road ahead."

"Mighty hands?" he repeated. "Boldly eyed? By the Gods, man, if you keep talking like that, they'll laugh you off the stage."

"How about striding on mighty thews?" I asked.

He groaned. "That's terrible. It occurs to me I've never actually read one of your plays. Maybe I ought to do that before I permit you to write anything down."

"Permit me?" I asked with mock outrage.

"Yes. I really ought to make sure that you're up to the task."

"You have no idea how many words I can rhyme with thews, do you?" I asked him.

He laughed long and well.

So we passed that meal in good fellowship. But while we dined, on and further on beyond that little harbor town, long days of travel distant, beyond the fields and the stores and the workplaces where the tiny remnant of Volani labored under the Dervan lash, behind the walls *of Derva and within his vast palace, the emperor rose from his marble throne and leaned over the ornate wooden table in his council room. He demanded again of his chamberlain, of his praetorian captain, of the dreaded legate of the revenants and the chief of his spies why Hanuvar had not yet been found, and when they would finally have him in their hands.*

Each promised with a single word. "Soon."   —Sosilos, Book Six

Afterword

Andronikos Sosilos

There is a certain charm to the way my ancestor speculates about the moments he or Hanuvar or other eyewitnesses he spoke with did not personally observe, but reading through these often lengthy and vacillating suppositions can, alas, be a challenge. The renowned historian Silenus, in recognition of these problematic scenes, sought to clarify the conjectures of Sosilos by diligently locating hundreds of additional eyewitnesses, but her weighty commentary, while fascinating and detailed, sometimes loses itself in minutia and in any case further disrupts *The Hanuvid's* narrative flow. The end result is that recent generations have found the work of my esteemed ancestor more and more challenging until many now regard reading it as drudgery. This struck me as so great a tragedy I resolved to find a more approachable means of presentation.

I removed my great-great-great uncle's first-person narrative, apart from several linking sections and the well-known preamble. Before his death he outlined how he could stage the work as a series of short plays, and I have divided his work accordingly, then removed the hesitant tone so often present in other portions of the narrative so that all sections of the account are stylistically similar. I admit to expanding freely upon some of the invented scenes and adding others of my own, though I leaned heavily upon my ancestor's work to do so, buttressed by the lengthy and detailed footnotes of Silenus.

I like to think Antires would be pleased with the result, for late in life he lamented that he had labored too hard to sound like a historian and wished that he had time to rework *The Hanuvid* as the plays he had once envisioned as a younger man. I flush at the thought of how Silenus might have reacted to my changes, however, for her commentary politely chides even the more mundane speculations of Antires, and I have expanded far further than he ever dared. That I based many of my own suppositions upon Silenus' outstanding research may have dismayed her even further.

This manuscript retains some of Silenus' footnotes, mostly in places where I was unable to easily incorporate her findings into the narrative, but only where I thought them either useful or interesting to the story. Those familiar with her commentaries will observe some of her most digressive passages absent entirely, notably the infamous three-page treatise upon the varieties of flowering trees most likely to have been encountered by Hanuvar and Antires during their journey through the provinces.

I can only hope that the resulting manuscript entertains and inspires, as the original *Hanuvid* did with its first readers. While I have taken liberties, I have constructed every scene depicting either Antires or Hanuvar, or others well known to either man, with almost entirely the same word choices used by Antires and been especially scrupulous about the preservation of the dialogue in my ancestor's final draft. If this adaption fails to capture your interest, or to approach the majesty of my ancestor's flawed but brilliant work, the fault must be laid entirely at my own feet.

Acknowledgments

This writer doesn't draft in a vacuum, and this book would never have come about if not for the advice and assistance of a whole host of people. Long years ago, John O'Neill read the first Hanuvar story in its embryonic form, and I will be forever grateful to him for his enthusiastic reception. I will likewise be eternally indebted to Joseph Goodman for giving Hanuvar a warm welcome, and then a home at *Tales From the Magician's Skull.*

I would be nowhere without the excellent guidance and editorial feedback of Bob Mecoy, and remain delighted by the way I've been welcomed at Baen, beginning with Sean Korsgaard's tireless championing of this work and moving on to Toni Weisskopf's glowing reception of the same. In the final preparatory stages, Joy Freeman and Scott Pearson provided insightful feedback and fresh eyes I needed more than I knew.

Many have assisted with encouragement and important feedback along the way, among them Simon Ellberger, Samuel Dillon, Ilana C. Myer, Jason Carney, Sydney Argenta, Chris Willrich, Greg Mele, C.S.E. Cooney, and probably others I've momentarily forgotten. Beth Shope and Kelly McCullough dug in deep and provided innumerable useful observations and suggestions. Loyal friend John Chris Hocking advised me on nearly every one of Hanuvar's adventures, even before some of them were put to paper. In the last few years my firstborn, Darian Jones, has been providing similarly gifted insight. The input of my brilliant muse, Shannon Jones, helped me hone the final versions of every section of this work, and I remain beholden to her for her painstaking efforts upon Hanuvar's behalf, as well as for many of the finest moments of our lives together.

The Following is an excerpt from:

THE CITY OF MARBLE AND BLOOD

The Chronicles of Hanuvar

✦

Howard Andrew Jones

Available from Baen Books
hardcover

Chapter 1:
A Theft of Years

The Tyvolian Autumn had not yet lost its battle to winter, but was hard beset. The browning oak leaves held a fiery red edge, and the leaves of poplar trees glowed a vibrant orange. Those already loosed from the branches decorated the trail ahead in patches like little carpets of flame. The air was rich with their musky sweetness, and the sharp, clean scent of pine needles.

Hanuvar and Antires worked to avoid the swish and crunch of the leaves they passed, even though they were deep enough into the woods they were unlikely to be overheard by humans. They were trespassers on this land.

His old knee wound was stiff in the chill, an intermittent, angry bite in Hanuvar's stride. He'd thrown a black cloak over his dark, long-sleeved tunic, pulled on leggings, and switched to boots, but his hood was down. His slate-colored eyes were narrowed in concentration. His gray-threaded, brown hair was worn short, cut straight across his forehead, and his face was clean shaven, accommodations to modern Dervan styles to better conceal his identity. If a little darker than the average Dervan citizen, his skin-tone was hardly uncommon, even among the ruling class, who spent far more time indoors than their social inferiors.

His companion continually fiddled with his own hood, indecisive about whether he wished to be shielded from the breeze, or to see along his periphery. Antires lowered it once more and scratched the side of his face. Hanuvar knew he was unused to the feel of the fringe beard and thin mustache he'd grown. Like the thick hair that topped Antires' head, it was dark and tightly coiled. He was younger than Hanuvar by nearly a quarter century, with fine features and smooth brown skin.

Antires addressed his friend quietly. "What's your backup plan if we can't get this land? Do you want to try for a different site?"

Hanuvar shook his head, no, and answered softly. "This little cove is ideal. Deep water. Well forested, which permits privacy as well as building materials, and it's just beyond the village's existing harbor." That would make the transportation of any additional supplies that much simpler, not to mention the movement of future passengers for the ships they would be launching.

"I thought you'd say that. But how are you going to get the old woman to sell?"

"First, we'll see the shrine. Then we'll see what we can do. It's not the owner who's the real problem. It's the priest." Alma herself had sounded amenable to selling the coastal portion of her land, but the priest, Eloren, had dissuaded her with an admonition that the gods would better bless the shrine if all the land around it was left inviolate.

The path beaten through the forest detritus by Alma's litter bearers extended in a mostly straight line from her villa, and was impeded only by intervening oak and pine. It ended in a tiny clearing. A small stack of firewood had been piled beside a blackened cookfire. Leaves to the other side were flattened as if some large rectangular object had rested there—her conveyance, almost certainly. A fallen tree bole nearby had been carved repeatedly with a knife, providing a canvas for crude, silly faces with staring eyes and broken noses. "One of Alma's slaves has a lot of idle time," Hanuvar said.

"And he's a latent master, judging by this portraiture." Antires' attention wandered with him as he stopped at a set of stone stairs vanishing through a dark square beneath the earth. A fresh coating of leaves dusted them in red and yellow, but they were curiously clean of dirt and sticks and weeds. "Looks like the old woman's had her slaves clean this place. Can you imagine being ordered to see to the maintenance of some haunted stairs in a dark forest?"

"I can imagine a lot of things." Hanuvar moved off, scanning the ground around the stairs. Antires followed.

"It's hard to believe she'd want to come here every week."

"Three times a week, lately," Hanuvar corrected.

"Do you think there's any chance she really is speaking to her dead son here?"

Antires smirked at Hanuvar's skeptical return look. The Herrene opened his hands, in an admission of his own uncertainty. His inflection, though, suggested he wasn't ready to outright dismiss the story. "I've seen some of the things you have."

"It took an immense expenditure of resources for my brothers to be reached from the dead lands," Hanuvar reminded him. "Once. And they barely spoke."

"That's not to say it couldn't happen."

"Anything's possible. But some things are more possible than others."

Having a poet's soul, Antires was always credulous about the fantastic, though he strove to adopt Hanuvar's more measured outlook, at least in his friend's presence. He watched as Hanuvar finished walking the area, then voiced his conclusion. "You suspect that the priest is up to something."

"That goes without saying."

"But Alma contacted him, not the priest her."

"The priest might have set up a situation then conveniently made himself available. It wouldn't be difficult for someone clever to get a sense of what Alma's son looked like, since his image is all over her villa. And if Eloren and his associates have designs on the lady's property, they might be poisoning her. Some poisons will tire a person out, and routine exposure will make them look older than they really are. As they're dying."

Antires' eyebrows climbed his forehead. "You think Eloren would poison an old woman?"

"I don't know that he would, but some people are capable of such a deed."

"I suppose you're right," Antires said, with a young man's subdued outrage over the callousness of humanity. "So what are you waiting for? Don't you want to take a look down these stairs?"

"In a moment." Hanuvar preferred to get a good sense of the ground before he advanced. He was shifting his attention back to the stairs when he heard someone treading across the leaves along the path from the villa.

He'd been informed the widowed landowner was scheduled to visit hours from now, so the intrusion was unexpected. He motioned his friend to retreat, then lay beside him, his belly against the cool forest floor. They watched from under a juniper across the clearing from the carved tree trunk.

Those nearing the shrine made no attempt at stealth. There were two, crushing dried foliage underfoot as they advanced. Glabius, the aging house slave who'd conducted Hanuvar into his fruitless meeting with the Lady Alma Dolorosa, bore an unlit lantern, and a second young slave shouldered a pack and carried a lantern of his own, as well as a pair of brooms.

Once they arrived at the stairs, the younger one dropped the brooms and set down his pack. He pulled his patchy cloak tight. He was a slim youth with close-set eyes.

"We'd best be quick about it." Glabius adjusted his own cloak on his brawny shoulders. "The mistress will be here soon."

"I am being quick about it." The younger man's voice twisted into a complaining whine. "Why did she want to come early?"

"The mistress is growing more and more... changeable as she ages."

"Changeable, or snippy?" the younger slave asked.

"Watch your tone."

The two men lit their lanterns, then descended the stairs. The younger one emerged very soon after, his hands empty and a warm glow of lantern light rising from the space below. He busied himself sweeping leaves from the upper stairs, then retreated. Glabius climbed into sight a little while after, his wrinkled face twisted into a frown.

"I needed help lighting the candles."

"You don't want to be down there any more than I do," the younger slave said stubbornly. "You just don't want to admit it."

More people were crunching up the path. Hanuvar shifted his attention from the bickering slaves to the priest Eloren, who arrived wrapped in an ankle-length blue cloak. The slope-shouldered dedicant to Lutar, lord of the dead, kept his hands in his sleeves and stepped to one side, a measure of pride in his manner that suggested a proprietary interest in his surroundings. He looked like an aristocrat walking the grounds he'd purchased for the construction of a new tenement. After Eloren came a similarly garbed younger priest bearing a basket of tinder. His face was smooth and rounded, his nose upturned at its tip.

Two muscular blond Ceori slaves brought up the rear, supporting a small curtained litter between them.

The younger priest knelt near the logs close to where Hanuvar and Antires lay, seemed to ponder adding some to the half-burned fuel in the dead camp fire, then arranged his tinder and pulled a stone from a pouch at his waist.

The litter slaves gently sat their burden down, and Eloren bent forward to open the litter's low door and offer his arm.

A veiny hand reached out to clasp it, and then Alma Dolorosa leveraged herself into sight, a small, pale, silver-haired woman in a black stola, wearing a black scarf under her black cloak. Her eyes, too, were black, as had been her expression when Hanuvar had met her this morning. Now, though, her face was bright with yearning. Locals claimed she was only in her fifth decade, though she looked and moved like an octogenarian.

Alma adjusted the heavy cloak on her spindly frame, and then the priest spoke with her in a low voice. They headed for the stairs, Alma walking swiftly, head thrust forward, face fixed in expectation. Together they descended into the earth.

The litter bearers stretched, greeted the two slaves who had tidied the place ahead of their arrival, then stepped over to the tree near the carvings. Hanuvar was momentarily puzzled by all their sideways and sometimes even backward movement until he realized that none wished to put their back to the stairs. They spoke in low voices, agreeing that Alma was looking worse. Her death was on their minds. One of the Ceori wondered aloud whether they would be manumitted in her will.

Closer by, the young priest sat on his knees, laboring a long while with his flint before he produced a spark to light his tinder. He'd just succeeded when Eloren returned from the shrine. The slaves barely glanced over. Apparently, they were accustomed to their mistress being left alone.

The younger priest made room for the older, and showed his palms to the flames as the fire spread. After a moment, he spoke quietly. "Did you suggest she spend less time there?"

Eloren's reply dripped scorn. "She's an old woman, Moneta. There's no changing her mind."

"Not if you don't try there isn't."

Eloren sniffed then spoke dismissively. "The gods set her on this path. And they've shown me what to do. If they wanted something different, they'd have spoken to you."

"So that's your decision?"

"You'll stay quiet," Eloren said.

The younger man pressed his lips together in disapproval.

Eloren pulled a wineskin from his belt and drank slowly, looking into the fire and disdainfully ignoring his companion. Hanuvar wished Moneta would object further, so that more might be learned, but the younger man remained silent.

A quarter hour later the old woman called to Eloren, her voice weak and raspy. He capped his wineskin then walked for the stairs and down them. He returned with Alma on his arm.

She looked utterly drained, although she smiled dazedly. Before long she was loaded into her litter and was being carried back to the villa, the priests following. Glabius and his assistant put out the fire, then descended once more, returning with lanterns and brooms and pack. The younger was complaining again. "I hate this place. I feel like those faces are watching me the entire time."

"Nothing's gotten you yet," his older companion responded. As they walked away, the younger could be heard grumbling about the underground chamber until his voice faded with distance.

Antires was ready to rise soon after, but Hanuvar held a hand for silence, then waited another long while before finally climbing to his feet.

Antires swore about being cold, then asked Hanuvar what he thought of what they'd heard.

"The young priest thinks the visits are bad for the old woman."

"That's it?" Antires sounded scandalized that Hanuvar had deduced nothing more.

And so he shared a few more observations. "The young one's a weak point that may give us leverage. Eloran is unmotivated to help her, likely because he's gotten her to leave this land to his order, or to himself personally, after her death. And we need to see what's down there."

"I didn't see that last part coming at all," Antires said.

Hanuvar unlimbered his shoulder pack and withdrew a small brass lantern. He discovered the Herrene eying him in admiration.

"How did you know we'd need a lantern?"

"It was a lucky guess."

"You don't guess, you plan," Antires said, which wasn't entirely accurate.

"I'd walked a lot of the land east of her home. I had seen no above-ground shrines or temples. The woods are thick enough that there might just have been one hiding here, but—"

"—but the odds were that it was below ground."

"Yes. But then even the inside of a temple would be dark."

"So, you're not quite as clever as I'd assumed."

"Or maybe I'm the one who packed the lantern." Hanuvar pointed back toward the villa. "Keep an eye out."

"Wait. You're going in alone?"

"Yes. Signal me if you hear anything. Can you mimic bird calls?"

"Oh, yes. Many confuse my dulcet tones with those of the heron, or an owl."

"Neither of which would be helpful."

"Neither of which I can actually imitate."

Hanuvar lit the lantern, shielding it with his body as he carried it in his left hand, and walked for the stairs. "Some time you'll have to remind me why I bring you along. Watch as well as listen. And not just for sounds—"

"—but the sudden lack of them. I know the routine. I'll just sit over there on the log and contemplate the local talent."

"No one likes a critic." Hanuvar started down. He took each step slowly, watching the edge of the lantern light as it fell upon each stair ahead. His gaze shifted to the ceiling, rounded above him. He saw then that he was advancing into a natural cave to which these steps had been added.

About halfway down he experienced the sensation that he was being observed. His skin prickled as hairs stood upright on his arms. He had anticipated the place would be disquieting from what Alma's younger slave said, but this was far more than that; the chamber toward which he descended radiated menace, and every one of his senses urged him to run.

He kept on.

A wide oval room lay at the bottom of the nine steps. The ceiling curved gently above to a high point of about three spear lengths. The chamber extended some sixty paces from side to side, and its ceiling dipped lower on the right edge before dropping raggedly to the floor, which was level apart from a rise on the left. Dirt and leaves had been swept into a neat pile to the right of the stairs.

The most interesting features faced the entryway. Just beyond a tall, squarish stone mass, a flat wall stretched the entire cave length, decorated by paintings of curiously unemotive faces with unnerving, pupilless eyes. He did not care to contemplate any of them at length; perhaps it was imagination, but it was from them that the spiritual malaise seemed to radiate.

The writing incised everywhere about the pictures was of a much more precise character, like that of an architect or professional scribe, though it too was curious, composed of a mix of Hadiran and Turian symbols.

He understood very little of the complex classical Hadiran language, with its bird-headed men and hundreds of symbols, but he had learned some Turian, and considered what the messages left here might mean. He then gave his attention to the life-sized image painted in the dead center of the wall just beyond the large stone altar, that of a sad-eyed, beardless youth in a sleeveless summer tunic, one hand offered to the viewer. The other held a bouquet of Turian wildflowers and thyme. By those plants, Hanuvar recognized the image for the god Kovos, whom the Turians believed guided the dead to their final resting place. His depiction would not have been out of place in some cave of the Turian hills, or in adjacent lands, for the Turians had been a power in the peninsula before Derva waxed large. They had survived long enough for some of their aristocracy to marry into that of the city-state before Derva expanded across the peninsula. But here, in the uttermost north of Tyvol, just south of the Ardenines, a Turian shrine to the opener of the ways had little precedence.

He turned his scrutiny upon the wide, chest high altar standing before the image. Once it had been copiously plastered in red, but much of that plaster had crumbled, exposing plain stones of the same sort composing the cave walls, shaped and fit closely together. Dripped yellow wax stained the altar's center, where some red plaster remained, along with the golden outline of a handprint. When standing directly in front of the altar, it appeared Kovos himself waited sympathetically to reach for the hand of whomever placed their own within the outline.

Hanuvar heard steps behind him and turned to find Antires descending with a pretense of stealth.

"This place is worse than a tomb," the playwright said.

"I told you to stay above."

"And I did. And now I'm here. Gods. This place is terrible. How can you stand it?"

Hanuvar started to chide him, but decided it might not be a terrible idea to have the younger man posted closer, especially because Hanuvar wasn't sure what might happen when he exposed himself to the sorcery.

"Stay on the stairs. Try to listen for activity above as well as here."

"The art's a better cut here, but hardly monument worthy. The god in the center has striking eyes, though."

Hanuvar set the lantern on the altar and fixed his attention on the unfamiliar symbols, trying to jar any additional information free of his memory.

"Can you read any of that?" Antires asked.

"A little."

"Prayers?" the Herrene suggested.

"I'm neither a magical scholar nor a Turian one, but I don't think these are prayers. There's a lack of formality and the emphasis isn't upon the god, or glory." Hanuvar pointed to one lengthy stretch of text. "Kovos isn't even mentioned at all."

"Kovos?"

"The Turian lord of the dead." Hanuvar contemplated the golden handprint and knew he would have to place his palm there.

Assuming that there was any possible chance that this worked, which of the countless he had known and lost might best advise him? His brothers? His father? His brother-in-law? His even longer lost elder sister?

He had loved and respected them all, and each might have guided him in different ways, but as he continued to study the Turian writing he realized there was only one whom he should try to reach.

Still he hesitated. He had never wished for a moment like this. Not with her. What might he say to Ravella now, except that he missed her? Would they resume their final argument, or were the dead beyond such troubles?

He reminded himself that Ravella was unlikely to appear before him. Probably this old shrine was simply the basis for an elaborate deception played by the priests.

He put his hand upon the imprint and whispered a prayer to the opener of the ways.

His expectations had been low, so when the eyes of Kovos took up an amber sheen Hanuvar's own eyes widened in astonishment. A moment later a humanoid shape formed of light drifted from the god.

Antires murmured in awe. Hanuvar's breath caught in his throat and his heart quickened. The shape drifted toward the altar, and him, blurry and uncertain at first, then broadening at the hips and narrowing at the waist. Long curling dark hair drifted down and past a graceful neck. Long black eyelashes blinked and full red lips opened before him even as the transparent figure floated but a sword's length out. She didn't wear the stola she'd been buried in, but the light green dress that had suited her so well.

"You have thought of me, and I have come." Ravella's voice was a whisper, with her remembered accent. They had spoken sometimes in Dervan and sometimes in Herrene and often, once they had become lovers, in her native Turian. Today she spoke in Dervan.

"Is that your wife?" Antires asked, breathless in wonder.

Hanuvar answered without looking at him. "No. Is this truly you?" he asked her.

"It is me, beloved." As Ravella spoke, her image sharpened. He saw the individual hairs upon her eyebrows, and the pupils of her dark eyes.

Feelings he'd thought long resolved constricted his throat. Sometimes she'd scolded him for avoiding the difficult in their talks, as he did now, shifting immediately to the present. The past was too painful. "I need your help. Do you understand the words on the wall behind you?"

She turned her head and shifted her body, drifting the while in an invisible wind, so that her dress and hair streamed languidly behind her.

"I can see so little of the living world." She turned back to him. "Only you are in clear focus."

He burned to ask if she had deliberately taken the poison, or if it had been the accident he'd told her brother. He thought he knew the answer to that, though, just as he understood why she hadn't wanted to leave her homeland, and why she could not have lived in Utria after his retreat. The Dervans would have taken their vengeance upon her.

"What do you wish to speak of?" Her smile was open and warm. He found himself hoping that any resentment she'd harbored had faded with her death, and that all that was left between them was the love they'd shared.

She sounded like Ravella, and she looked like her . . . But he had long ago been taught to see what was truly before him, not what he wished, and not what he hoped. After a moment of consideration, he decided how he might best test the veracity of what he was experiencing. "I want you to sing," he said. "That Turian folk song about the winding road. I can no longer recall the words, just snatches of the melody." And even that, now, had faded from his memory.

She blinked her long lashes and her voice rose in song. She began strongly, singing in her native tongue of a shepherd boy readying for his trip, but then she faltered. The melody died, and the words trailed away.

And sadly, then, he knew he witnessed a lie. "You're not real." He'd thought himself sad when he said it, but his lips twitched into a snarl.

"I am real, beloved." Her eyes rounded in sorrow. "You see me before you."

"You know only what I know of you. And nothing more. What are you, really?"

"I am your love, for now, and always."

He shook his head. "You lie. What are you?"

She extended her arms to him.

He lifted his hand from the altar. The moment he broke contact his breath left him; he felt as though he'd run miles in full armor. Ravella smiled sadly, then her image blurred, though she hung in the air for a while longer, like the afterimage of a snuffed candleflame. Finally she was gone.

Antires swore softly. "Who was that?"

"No one I know." Hanuvar labored to catch his breath.

"Are you well?"

"I'm fine." Oddly, the chamber itself no longer troubled him. He sensed the eyes upon his back as he turned to Antires, but their regard now was welcoming. The change in his perspective disturbed him more than the previous dread.

He shook his head, striving to shake off the lure of illusory serenity. He paced the area, lantern light pointed against the wall. On closer inspection, it looked entirely too flat to be natural.

"Who was that?" Antires asked. "I mean, who was it supposed to be? You never mentioned another woman."

"Her name was Ravella."

"She called you beloved. Did you have a mistress?"

"You sound shocked." Hanuvar ran his hands along the wall, over a pair of wide-eyed faces, feeling for an opening or seam.

"Well . . . I suppose I shouldn't be. I just thought . . ."

"I was in Tyvol for more than a dozen years. Did you think I'd be celibate that entire time?"

"I never gave it much thought," Antires admitted. "Couldn't you have sent for Imilce?"

Hanuvar stepped to the left edge, running his hand along the juncture where the two cave walls met. "We exchanged letters on the subject, but there was much to do in Volanus in support of the war, and Imilce didn't want to leave Narisia with relatives. And I'd vowed not to raise my child in an armed camp like I had been." He discovered a crack, but it appeared to be completely normal.

"What are you looking for?"

"Some kind of entrance. You could help. Feel along the right edge there."

"An entrance to what?"

"There's obviously something very strange about this shrine. I think there's more to it."

Hanuvar retreated from the wall. Antires ran his fingers along the right edge. "Did you love her?"

"You're getting rather personal, aren't you?"

Antires glanced back, then bent to rub fingertips along the floor seam. "I'm supposed to be your chronicler, aren't I? I should know these things. Did you love her?"

"Imilce, or Ravella?"

"Both. Were there others?

"Yes."

"Yes to the others?"

"Yes, I loved them both."

Antires sighed in frustration. "You're being deliberately obscure."

"My love life isn't germane at the moment." Maybe the wall had no more secrets. Hanuvar turned his attention to the altar.

"How could you love both? At once?"

With extreme care he inspected the altar's front with his hands, mulling the notion to tell the young man to be quiet. But then he remembered his own vow to be open with Antires, who had again and again proven his loyalty, and answered. "Imilce and I were young. She, younger than me. Not long after our marriage I had to assume control of the army, and only a few years after that, I was marching across the Ardenines. I expected to return to her, or be able to send for her, but the war dragged on."

"And you sought a mistress when you got lonely."

"Sought?" He'd been too busy to seek a paramour. "No. Ravella and I stumbled into one another. She was a widow and witty and irreverent and . . ." Thinking of her opened up a tide of memories he was in no mood to examine at present, or to share with Antires. He shifted his search to the altar's narrower left side and sought a swift way to explain. "It was a relationship of older people. A deeper one than I'd formed with Imilce. Not because I loved my wife less, but because I wasn't mature enough to love her more when I was with her. Does that make sense?"

"Yes. There's no opening in this wall." Antires joined him at the altar. "Any luck here?"

"Not so far."

The playwright watched his efforts. "What happened when you met Imilce again?"

"A long time had passed. Imilce and I were almost strangers. Our relationship was difficult for a while, because I was used to one woman and she was used to someone else as well."

"She had a lover?"

"Yes."

"And you weren't bothered by that?"

"Each of us consented to the arrangements. She was as human as I."

Antires tried to digest that information, then shook his head. "You Volani are strange."

"Eventually we grew close again, but it was . . . tricky for both of us." Hanuvar was starting to doubt there was anything to be found, but he slid his fingers along the altar's right side.

"How did Ravella die?

"She was poisoned."

"Gods. That's terrible. Did the Dervans kill her?"

"I suppose you could say she was out of good choices. Wait a moment. There are large seams in the floor here."

Antires bent to examine what Hanuvar had discovered. A fingernail's breadth of space lay between the altar and an irregularly shaped slab roughly two hand spans wide, cleverly worked into the floor beneath where he had stood before the altar. He tugged and found it unyielding.

"What do you think it is?" Antires had at last found something else to absorb his attention.

Hanuvar searched for leverage, finally finding a divot opposite the altar. He pulled harder, and lifted the covering piece away. Green light splashed up from inside the dark space. Hanuvar set the stone slab against the altar's side. He motioned for Antires to bring the lantern.

His friend focused the beam, revealing a cavity a gladius length deep and nearly as long. And it was plastered smooth and painted over with small, precise Turian characters of red and black. They ran in straight lines upon the space's walls, then circled the glittering emerald that lay in its center in a precisely carved hollow. Part of the gem's glow owed to the lantern's reflected light. But something deep inside changed slowly, now lighter, now darker, like the pulse of an ancient heart.

"That stone—how does it glow like that?"

There was much about sorcery Hanuvar didn't understand, but he could answer that question. "It's a focusing stone. Only the most powerful spell users can employ them to store magics." He looked up at Antires. "I saw one once before, when we overtook a cadre of magicians the Dervans were trying to use against us in the war." He gestured to some flakes of paper lying near the emerald. "I think our priest must have found this cache. Some papyrus was stored here, and removed. And there should have been built up debris or dirt hiding in the gap between the panel and the altar. He's opened it."

"Did he put the stone in here?"

"I think it's been in here for a long, long while. As long as this writing."

"What does the writing say?"

This was old style Turian, and some of the letters were slightly different from the ones Hanuvar had learned. Paired with Hanuvar's rusty and incomplete knowledge of the language and the odd angle he was forced to read at, it took him a while to understand enough to answer his friend's question.

"I think it's a spell, summoning some kind of spirit, or entity called a 'gatherer'—meant to protect the 'treasures' here. That might mean the vanished scrolls."

"Might it mean something else?"

It could at that. Hanuvar had already noted that there was another seam between the altar and the floor. He ran his fingers slowly along the lowest row of altar stones.

Antires had thought of another question. "If it's a guardian, why is it practically inviting interaction? Wouldn't a guardian try to scare people away?"

"The place is frightening," Hanuvar agreed. "Until you offer yourself. And then it becomes alluring. I no longer feel troubled here. I think it may be a honeyed trap. It drained some of my own life force when I tried to use it."

Antires swore in wonder. "You think if you were to keep coming here you'd age like Alma?"

"Yes. And I'd wager the more I used it, the more I'd want to come. I just don't know what the purpose is." Hanuvar had about to abandon his search when the stone under his fingers yielded to pressure. The sound of stone grating on stone startled him; the altar side shifted ever so slightly toward him.

He ran his fingers over the face of the altar's side nearest the god. It had never been plastered and on close examination some of the grooves suggesting separate stones had been carved to convey that appearance. A sturdy push sent a whole piece wider than his shoulders scraping inward as its upper third tilted out. It proved only a finger's length thick. With Antires' help he eased the heavy slab to the ground.

The altar itself was hollow, and opened into a narrow shaft of darkness.

"Well, that looks inviting." Antires shined the lantern into the cavity, revealing a decrepit wooden ladder covered in webs and dust. "Eloren might have found the first scrolls, but he hasn't found this. Or didn't want to drop into a spider infested hole. Yet you're going to want to look, aren't you?"

"I think I'll have to."

"You sound just as excited as I feel."

"You need to stay up there, on the stairs."

"You're going in there alone?" Antires' voice rose in consternation.

"Right now we're in a hole with only one exit. Pretty soon I'll be in a deeper hole. We're incredibly vulnerable. Anyone could sneak up on us."

Antires, who had just complained about venturing into the web-choked darkness, now sulked that he wouldn't be permitted to accompany him. Hanuvar walked him to the shrine's entry stairs, pausing on the threshold to listen but hearing only the natural noises of the woods. He exited to retrieve a sturdy branch, patted his friend on the shoulder, and returned to the altar.

He employed the stick against the webbing, then held the lantern further into the space. A rough floor lay only eight feet below. A passage opened to the ladder's rear.

Hanuvar tested the ladder's first rung, found that it held, dropped in the stick for further web-cleaning, and started down, lantern in hand.

When he reached the floor he found himself in a rough stone fissure just wide enough to accommodate a single traveler. Lantern light shining before him, he advanced through the twisting tunnel and then the passage sloped gently up, opening finally into a wide natural chamber that stretched before and behind him.

He stopped halfway into the area. The yellow light he bore spilled upon human teeth stretched in a mirthless grin. Two black eye sockets peered into eternity above. The man-high shelf-unit before him was crowded with human skulls, browned with age, each painted with Hadiran picture writing and cramped Turian letters. Hanuvar looked past the sightless decorations, seeing that another cavern opening lay beyond the wall their shelf rested against, then swung the light through the rest of the chamber.

More shelves stood in that cheerless place, crowded with sagging, spider-webbed scrolls. A great deal of the floor was inset with yet more pictograms and Turian writing, arranged in lines radiating from the blank wall that was the back of the surface Ravella's image had materialized from. Playing the light further, Hanuvar discovered another shelf holding different sized vials.

He advanced at last from his vantage point, keeping well clear of the lines and their writing, stopping in the threshold to the second cavern chamber.

Someone had labored to make this area more homey. It held a sagging bed, a table, three old wooden chests, and a shelf holding more amphora. Some of them likely contained lamp oil, for old-fashioned lanthorns stood upon both the table and the desk. He caught a flash of movement on his right and whirled, only to see a figure with a lantern, half obscured in a web covered doorway.

Hanuvar dropped hand to sword hilt, only to see the man he faced taking the same action. Hanuvar relaxed; the figure did the same.

He had found no adversary, only himself in a fine, body length bronze mirror fastened to the cave wall and caked with grime. Apparently the sorcerer who had kept his quarters liked to model his appearance. Judging from the dust and disrepair, however, it was easy to guess no one had walked this space for long years, possibly centuries.

"Relnus!"

That was the name Hanuvar had adopted for this province of Tyvol, and it echoed faintly to him. Antires was calling, and there was no missing the insistent quality of his voice. Hanuvar responded on the instant, hurrying to the main room and down the sloping rock and into the narrow passage.

"Someone's coming," Antires called, shouting in the hushed way of actors when they meant to suggest they were actually whispering.

Hanuvar reached the ladder and started up, only to have the first step break under his foot, slamming his heel against the floor. He started up again, keeping his foot to the part of the rung closest to the rails.

Antires loomed above him, waggling his fingers to urge speed. Now he did whisper. "There's a bunch of them, really close now!"

Hanuvar handed up the lantern and threw himself over the side, scrambling clear. Antires started for the entryway, his eyes large as he looked back. Hanuvar motioned him to help in lifting the concealing slab back in place.

That was a mistake. By the time Hanuvar stopped to replace the covering to the gem cavity he heard footsteps on the stairs, and a familiar voice. "I know you're in there," Eloren called.

Hanuvar left the void as it was and advanced to the bottom of the steps.

Three burly dock-side ruffians were ranged along the middle and upper stairs, with Eloren just behind them. He carried a lantern; two of the others bore nail studded cudgels and the other carried an axe.

"You two!" the priest said. "I should have known. You're not really land buyers, are you? You're magicians..." That thought trailed off, and then Eloren's voice grew more excited. "You found the gem!"

He had observed the glow from the altar's foot. Eloren reached up to touch his collar, raising a smaller emerald dangling here. "Little good it will do you without this."

Hanuvar wasn't sure what that meant, but he agreed. "You have me there."

"How did you know we were down here?" Antires asked.

"I've mastered this shrine's secrets," Eloren boasted. "I know when its energy levels rise and flow."

"You're more well informed than I would have guessed," Hanuvar said.

"Who sent you?" Eloren demanded.

Hanuvar turned up an empty hand. "This really doesn't seem like the way two practitioners ought to discuss such a matter, does it?" He indicated the hired muscle with a tilt of his chin. "There's no need for them. We can share secrets. I've just found a large one that might interest you."

"You're bluffing."

"Am I?"

Eloren studied him. "You're an old man with only an effete functionary at your back. Outnumbered. And we have the high ground."

Apparently the priest suffered the common delusion about high ground being a superior offensive position in singular combat. The rabble grinned at Hanuvar, by which he saw that they possessed the identical misconception.

He lifted his lantern while shrugging, fiddling with the shutter that spilled light against the wall to his left, as if nervous. "I admit, we'd heard of the emerald. But I hadn't fully assessed its powers before my associate called to me about your approach. I can show you where the hidden information is, and you can tell me more about its nature."

For a moment he thought Eloren would relent. Then the priest's full lips pursed. "No. I think not. If a bumbler like yourself could find it without even knowing what it is you're seeking, then I can surely locate it."

"So it's death you're after, then?" Hanuvar asked.

"For me, it's life. I'm through with them, boys," he said. "Take them."

"You heard him," the axe man said. "Take them down!"

Roaring, all three charged.

When the first reached the second stair from bottom, his nail studded cudgel lifted overhead, Hanuvar beamed lantern light into his face. The fur-draped attacker turned his head, squinting against the glare. At the same moment Hanuvar drew and sliced the thug's protruding abdomen. Blood sprayed. The thug screamed and Hanuvar shoved him to the right, tripping the cudgel bearer rushing for Antires. Off balance, that man stumbled down the final stairs.

That was all the advantage Hanuvar could give his friend, for the hirsute blond leapt at him with his axe raised. While still in mid-air the attacker discovered Hanuvar's lantern flying at his face. He warded himself with one arm and managed a fair landing, but his axe was out of line, with his arms exposed. Hanuvar's sword blow sheared straight through one forearm and halfway into the other. The axe dropped with the severed hand and the ruffian shrieked in agony.

A glowing, faceless humanoid shape streamed past Hanuvar and pressed to the axeman. Hanuvar's skin chilled even as the flow of blood from the terrible wound he'd delivered slackened and stilled.

Eloren called out in heavily accented Turian. "Attack him—the older one! Him!"

The faceless thing abandoned the pale axeman, who toppled limp and bloodless, then, swift as the winter wind, it swept forward. Not to Hanuvar, but to the man with the bloody belly wound, whose cries of pain rose to gasps of terror as it sank upon him.

That was apparently too much for Antires' club-wielding assailant, who gave up chasing the Herrene to dash for the stairs. His face was white in panic. He must have seen Hanuvar as an obstacle, for he came in with a wild swing. Hanuvar ducked and skewered him. He pulled out his blade as his opponent doubled over, then sliced again and kicked him clear. The attacker dropped, writhing in his death throes.

Hanuvar pulled his throwing knife.

"Not that one," Eloren was shouting. "Him. Him!" He pointed at Hanuvar. But the green spirit did not yet depart the paling man who moaned more and more feebly beneath its attentions.

Hanuvar took a single long stride and hurled his knife.

The cast was true, but the priest shifted, and the blade sank not into Eloren's throat, but his upper chest. He put hands to the blade, groaning in Turian: "Come back to me! Share the life—give me the life!" As Hanuvar charged, Eloren called out another phrase that sounded Hadiran.

The priest collapsed against the stair well, gasping as he yanked the knife free. He raised his emerald pendant like a shield. Hanuvar closed, grabbed the pendant and yanked it forward. The heavy chain didn't snap as he'd expected, but it did pull the priest toward him as he'd planned, so that Eloren seemed to dive onto the sword Hanuvar thrust through his midsection.

And then the glowing, man-sized entity was upon them. It spilled its emerald radiance, delivering warmth at the same moment, as though it were the personification of a gentle summer day.

Muscles throughout Hanuvar's body twitched, so that he could no longer finely control his actions. He retained hold of his sword but was unable to drive it on to Eloren's heart. His grip likewise froze upon the necklace. His quivering calves could not hold him upright, and he sank to his knees, fighting for balance with one leg resting on a higher step than the other.

And yet despite his anxiety at being unable to control his movements, the intensely tingling sensation passing over him was not unpleasant. He just managed to turn his head to observe the man-thing at his shoulder, seeing only the suggestion of hollows where eyes could be. It was otherwise featureless. The green light streaming forth blended with the being's extended digits.

Of a sudden, the creature's form diminished, its outlines fading until nothing was left but a glowing central core, which retained its full brightness for a moment longer until only the hands were left, shedding light.

And then that radiance too vanished and the thing was gone, its physical presence expended with its spell.

Hanuvar's muscles ceased their shaking. He released his hold on the necklace, discovering that the stone it had framed was cracked and blackened. He flexed his free hand and looked back to Eloren.

The priest's lantern sat beside Hanuvar's reddened knife and a shrunken body slumped in blood-soaked robes. It was only when Hanuvar leaned closer that he saw a pale boy with a young version of Eloren's features lying in the midst of the blood-soaked cloth. Fearful eyes in that smooth-skinned face looked up at him, and Eloren spoke with a voice pitched higher than before. "Don't kill me."

"I already have killed you," Hanuvar said. "But I can make your final moments less painful."

Boy Eloren coughed blood as he pressed his small white hands near the weeping wound in his stomach and the sword blade sticking upright from it, flaring golden in the lantern light.

Hanuvar looked down at the hilt of his sword and paused, seeing that the wrinkles around his knuckles had vanished; the skin was tighter across the back of his hand. A long scar on his lower arm had entirely disappeared. His graying wrist hairs had been restored to brown. Only then did he fully realize that the creature's strange magic had impacted him as well. His breath caught in his throat. "What has the spirit done?"

"What do you mean?" The scorn was strange from such a young voice. "Why do you play act?"

Hanuvar's voice was cool but it sounded somehow different to him. Less haggard. "I do not pretend. I don't know."

The boy's look was searching. "But you grasped the pendant so you would receive the energies!"

"I grasped the pendant so you could not ensorcel me."

The changed priest laughed fitfully, then coughed. Blood trickled from his mouth. He shook his head in disgust. "I've been undone by a fool. A lucky fool. You're young now. You stole my gift! My family has been searching for this shrine for generations, and you just stumbled into it."

Hanuvar was still wondering exactly how much of a transformation had been worked upon him. Antires stood at the base of the stairs, staring mutely. Certain that Eloren had little time, Hanuvar pressed for information.

"And what was the purpose of this shrine? To steal life force?"

"Mostly. There's supposed to be a hidden library as well—is that what you found?"

"I did. Rotted."

"And you really didn't know. Gods. Yes, the shrine was supposed to make casual visitors too uneasy, and then steal the life force of those who insisted upon investigating. The life was to power the magics, meant to repeatedly restore the wizard. But he died nonetheless; from what cause I do not know." The boy's voice grew weaker. He coughed again. "My ancestor . . . apprentice. Got the pendant. But it was no use without the shrine." He looked up at Hanuvar. "I . . . it would have healed me of the knife wound. But you . . . stabbed right as it filled me with life."

Having experienced the energy's debilitating effects himself, Hanuvar knew how impossible it would have been for Eloren to have worked some other spell, even if he hadn't been distracted by a mortal injury.

The priest struggled to level his weakening voice. "If you're not a mage, and you weren't after the shrine, why did you want this land so badly?"

"I'm just a man trying to help some people."

Eloren didn't look as though he believed him. "It doesn't matter now. You said you'd ease my crossing."

"I can. How long will this effect last on me?"

"How long?" the boy/man laughed. "As long as you live, you bastard!"

Hanuvar tore out his sword and brought it down across the little boy with the older man's eyes.